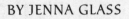

BY JENNA GLASS

The Women's War
Queen of the Unwanted
Mother of All

MOTHER OF ALL

THE
WOMEN'S
WAR

MOTHER of ALL

JENNA GLASS

NEW YORK

A Del Rey Trade Paperback Original

Copyright © 2021 by Jenna Glass
Map copyright © 2019, 2020 by David Lindroth Inc.

Published in the United States by Del Rey,
an imprint of Random House, a division of
Penguin Random House LLC, New York.

DEL REY is a registered trademark and the CIRCLE colophon
is a trademark of Penguin Random House LLC.

The map by David Lindroth was originally published
in slightly different form in *The Women's War* by Jenna Glass
published by Del Rey, an imprint of Random House, a division of
Penguin Random House LLC, in 2019. It appeared in its present form
in *Queen of the Unwanted* by Jenna Glass published by Del Rey,
an imprint of Random House, a division of
Penguin Random House LLC, in 2020.

LIBRARY OF CONGRESS CATALOGING-IN-PUBLICATION DATA
Names: Glass, Jenna, author.
Title: Mother of all / Jenna Glass.
Description: New York: Del Rey, [2021] | Series: The women's war; 3 |
"A Del Rey trade paperback original"—Title page verso.
Identifiers: LCCN 2020046531 (print) | LCCN 2020046532 (ebook) |
ISBN 9780525618423 (trade paperback) |
ISBN 9780525618416 (ebook)
Subjects: GSAFD: Fantasy fiction.
Classification: LCC PS3602.L288 M68 2021 (print) |
LCC PS3602.L288 (ebook) | DDC 813/.6—dc23
LC record available at https://lccn.loc.gov/2020046531
LC ebook record available at https://lccn.loc.gov/2020046532

Printed in the United States of America on acid-free paper

randomhousebooks.com

2 4 6 8 9 7 5 3 1

To the amazing women of the Baldwin School class of 1983. You took a lonely, bullied teen and showed her that people could be kind and that she was not alone after all. My life might have gone a very different direction if it were not for you.

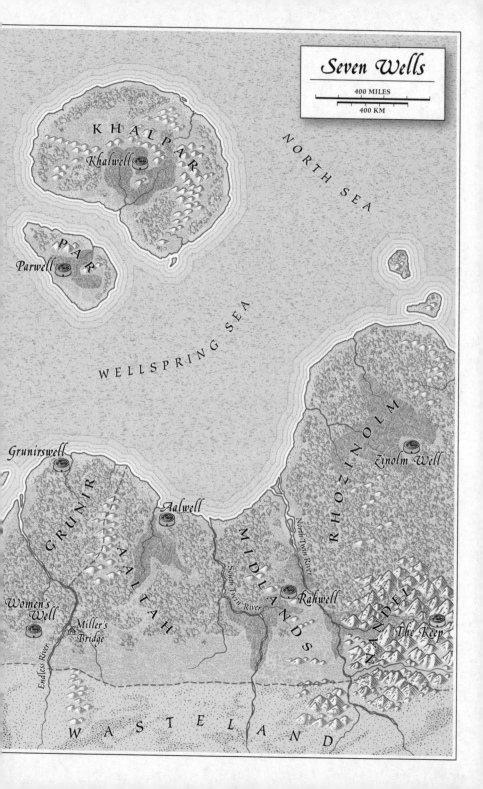

Part One

SCHEMES

CHAPTER ONE

The windows were open to let in whatever fresh breezes they could, but the air in the royal apartments was nonetheless stifling. Having spent more than a year living in the desert, Tynthanal had thought himself inured to heat, but the climate here in Aaltah seemed far more oppressive than that of Women's Well, where the air was bone-dry, and even in the worst heat of summer, the nights were cool. Here in Aaltah, the nearby sea added such a heavy dose of humidity that the air felt thick as porridge.

"Do sit down and eat," his wife, Kailee, urged, and he reluctantly moved away from the window to join her at the table where a small supper had been laid for them.

Kailee's face glowed with perspiration, and the few locks of hair that had escaped her headdress were plastered wetly to her neck, but she seemed to accept the discomfort with her customary serenity. A serenity Tynthanal envied as he tried futilely to push up the sleeves of his doublet.

"How I loathe civilian clothes," he muttered. Custom required he set aside the comfortable shirts and trousers he'd worn in the military and don the doublet and breeches of a gentleman—

with all the concomitant adornment—but he longed for the days when he could breathe inside his clothing.

Kailee smiled at him as she served herself a helping of stewed vegetables and ignored the beautifully roasted whole fish that took pride of place in the center of the table. Tynthanal frowned.

"I should have asked the cook to fillet it for you," he said, shaking his head at himself. Their marriage was in its infancy, and he was still getting used to dealing with his wife's unique challenges in life. It would be no easy feat to avoid fish bones when one could not see them.

Kailee shrugged. "I am used to making do. And I am not overly hungry."

"Well, you don't have to 'make do' anymore," he said as he portioned out a serving of fish, inspecting it carefully for bones before sliding it onto her plate. "I think I got them all, but be cautious anyway."

Her mouth quirked. Tynthanal was still learning how to read her expressions—he'd never realized before how much he'd relied on a person's eyes to give away what she was feeling—but he thought he saw mild reproach. "I have eaten fish before. I know to be careful. And I could have served myself if I'd actually wanted the fish."

Tynthanal winced and wished he were more at ease with his wife. It had been abundantly clear from the first moment that Kailee was far more self-sufficient than most people gave her credit for—and that she found it irritating, if not downright hurtful, when people offered unwanted help. He'd vowed not to be one of those people, yet it was astonishingly easy to fall into that trap. "My apologies," he said, serving himself while wrestling with the guilt that was becoming his constant companion of late. In Women's Well, Kailee had gained her freedom by marrying him, escaping the scrutiny of her father and stepmother—and Rhozinolm high society. And then he had abruptly snatched it back from her by accepting the regency and moving them to Aaltah, where her blindness would once again be treated as a source of shame. To make matters worse, he couldn't even be a proper husband to her, for his heart had remained in Women's Well with Chanlix and the child she carried. A pang of longing struck him, but he shoved it aside and tried to stay present with the woman he had married. Just because he did not—*could* not—love her didn't absolve him of his duties as a husband.

He shoved some fish into his mouth and promptly stabbed himself in the cheek with a fish bone. Kailee smirked when he extracted it from his mouth. Her worldly vision might not function, but with her Mindseye always open, she could see the aura of Rho that surrounded every living thing. Which allowed her to see many gestures—such as digging a fish bone out of one's mouth.

"You seem out of sorts," Kailee commented as she picked at her dinner. "Will you think me nosy if I ask why?"

"You're my wife," he said. "You're allowed to be nosy." He put a teasing lilt into his voice, although in truth her perspicacity often unnerved him. She shouldn't know him well enough yet to see that he was "out of sorts." He pulled at the neckline of his doublet, which was soaked with sweat and clinging unpleasantly. He should have asked for a *cold* supper but had been too distracted to think of it.

"I'm glad to hear it," Kailee said. "Are you planning to answer my question?"

He pinched the bridge of his nose and shook his head. "Let's just say my first council meeting as regent did not go especially smoothly."

She grinned. "And you *expected* it to?"

"Well, no," he admitted. "But it was far worse than I expected."

He'd known from the moment he'd committed to returning to Aaltah that his would be a difficult road. In the wake of the sabotage of Aaltah's Well and his half-brother's apparent death, he'd been appointed regent to his nephew, Delnamal's son, over the objections of nearly half the royal council. And if the infant king Tahrend had had any living male relative closer than a second cousin, Tynthanal would still be happily installed as Lord Chancellor of Women's Well.

He sighed silently at the attempt at self-delusion. Part of the reason he'd accepted the regency was that he'd hoped distance would ease some of the pain of not having been able to marry Chanlix. Seeing her every day had been misery—for both of them—and he imagined the pain would only grow sharper when the babe was born.

"How so?" Kailee tilted her head curiously, and he realized his original plan to spare her his turmoil had been misguided. Their marriage might be a sham, but she was wise beyond her years, and if he could only stop mooning hopelessly over Chanlix, he suspected they could become true friends. Surely he could give her that much.

"Let's just say that there is a palpable lack of enthusiasm about my regency. No one came right out and said it, but I was given the distinct impression that my continued service in that capacity is dependent on my ability to fix whatever is wrong with our Well."

"So have you been down to the Well?"

"Yes. The grand magus took me down right after the meeting. He's also offered to train me as a spell crafter in my 'spare time.'" He laughed grimly. "I understand why everyone hopes I can help, but it would take years for me to fully master the art of spell crafting, and I very much doubt I will be allowed years before people demand results."

No one knew exactly what had happened when King Delnamal took the Abbess of Khalpar to Aaltah's Well, but whatever it was had cost them more than their lives. Large portions of the cavern in which the Well resided had collapsed, leaving a substantial pile of rubble that would be weeks in the clearing. But worse than that . . .

"The Well is clearly damaged," he said with a shake of his head. "I've been to the Well many times in my life and know exactly how many elements should be spilling out of it. I'd estimate the flow is a little more than half what it used to be, and I have no idea why."

"You don't think the rubble explains it?"

He shook his head. "Certainly that's what the council would like to think, but . . . I'm not so sure. I guess we won't know until it's all cleared, though the grand magus tells me there's been no improvement that he can discern from what has already been cleared. I find that less than promising. If we can't restore it to its previous state, then it won't be long before we start running low on some of the rarer elements, and that may make it difficult for us to fulfill our trade agreements."

Kailee chewed her lip anxiously. "I would like to see it myself," she said, and though it was subtle, he saw how she tensed in anticipation of refusal.

It made him ashamed of his first impulse, which was not to refuse, but to try to talk her out of it. She'd made it clear that one of the reasons she'd come with him to Aaltah instead of staying in the comfort and security of Women's Well was that she hoped to clear Mairahsol's name. Everyone was sure the late Abbess of Khalpar was behind whatever evil had befallen the Well. Everyone except Kailee, that is.

"I'll take you down after supper," he promised, "though I'm not sure it will be very informative. At present, it's just a pile of rocks with elements leaking through the cracks."

Tynthanal had not mentioned the troublesome reality that, so far, no bodies had been recovered from that rubble. Witnesses had seen a veiled woman—whom everyone assumed was Mairahsol—descending the stairs to the Well, accompanied by

Delnamal, his secretary, and an obviously ailing common woman. They were all presumed dead—but if four people had died in the chamber, then why had no bodies been found?

"I'm sure you're right," Kailee agreed. "I don't expect I'll find the answers to all my questions that easily. But I'd like to look all the same."

She pushed back her plate. They had not done justice to the fine dinner the cook had provided, and Tynthanal made a mental note to stop by the kitchens and reassure the staff that they were not displeased with the meal.

"Are the kitchens by any chance along the route to the Well?" Kailee asked. "I know our cook back in Rhozinolm would have been beside herself to see so much of her meal come back un-eaten."

Tynthanal smiled and felt a little tug of friendly affection for his wife. He didn't imagine they were going to grow to love each other as a married couple ought—not when his heart still be-longed firmly to Chanlix—but he suspected in some ways they were kindred spirits.

"The kitchens are in the opposite direction, but I must admit to feeling restless after sitting in meetings all day long. I would appreciate the extra walk, if you don't mind."

"I don't mind one bit," she replied.

For the first nineteen years of her life, Kailee Rah-Kailindar had barely set foot outside her father's estate. She knew every twist and turn of the manor house, the location of every piece of furni-ture, the breadth of every doorway. She knew the trees and shrubs of the grounds, the walking paths and the copse of woods that led down to a tiny trickling stream. In that territory, she'd taken every opportunity to walk unaided—though servants and relatives alike insisted on guiding her whenever they saw her by herself.

Learning her way around the Aalwell palace was clearly going to be a much larger challenge, and she had no choice but to slip her hand through the elbow that Tynthanal offered. She was in no danger of walking into walls thanks to the element-filled luminants that were visible to her Mindsight, but things like steps and furniture and edges of rugs were another story.

"This palace was designed as a maze," she mumbled under her breath, her hand squeezing Tynthanal's elbow as she wrestled with dismay. She had not admitted it to *herself*, much less to her husband, but she was quietly terrified of the life she had committed herself to when she'd agreed to accompany him to Aalwell. No doubt her father—and likely also Queen Ellinsoltah—would have been insulted on her behalf if her husband had left her in Women's Well, but as long as the separation had not included a formal divorce, the treaties that were signed as a result of their marriage would have remained in place. She *could* have accepted his offer to let her stay—fully recognizing it as an offer rather than an insult of any kind—and that would have been the far easier path.

"I'm not sure it's fair to say the palace was *designed*," Tynthanal said with a thread of humor in his voice. "The oldest part of the palace—the part right above the Well chamber—is about the size of the royal palace in Women's Well, and it is laid out in neat rectangles with straight, if narrow, hallways. Everything else was added afterward by different kings in different ages, wings built on wherever it seemed convenient at the time. I freely admit its similarity to a maze, but I swear it was not done intentionally. Mind the stairs coming up."

He slowed his footsteps and allowed her to reach out with a probing foot to find the edge of the stairway.

"How many steps?" she inquired.

He cleared his throat. "Er, I don't know. I never counted them. But it's a fair number, and the stairway curves."

She nodded. It seemed that there was room for them to walk side by side, but she suspected that might be awkward on a long stairway. The luminants on the walls gave her a general feel for the shape and curve of the stairs, but her Mindsight couldn't show her the individual steps. "If you wouldn't mind just walking ahead of me, that will be easiest." The aura of Rho around him would serve as a moving beacon, showing her the way.

"All right," he agreed—for unlike so many others she had known in her life, he seemed to take it for granted that she knew best how to manage her blindness. She couldn't count the number of times well-meaning servants—and even on occasion her father—had insisted on putting their hands on her to help even when she'd tried to refuse.

Kailee smiled to herself as Tynthanal entered the stairway, putting one hand on each wall to show her the width. He walked at a comfortable pace, not taking exaggerated care, trusting her to let him know if she needed him to slow down. She imagined that if circumstances had been different—if she hadn't come into the marriage knowing full well that his heart already belonged to another—she might have fallen in love with him already.

After the promised brief stop by the kitchens to reassure the hardworking cook, they continued their journey downward to the palace's lowest level.

Kailee could tell they were getting closer to the Well by the increasing concentration of elements present in the air all around them. She had never been tested for magical talent—women never were in more traditional societies, and she hadn't yet gotten around to it in Women's Well—but she was nonetheless aware that she was well above average, based on the number of elements she could see. In Women's Well, where the vast majority of elements were feminine or neuter, the air near the Well was so thick with elements she sometimes had to strain to pick out the auras of Rho that indicated life. Here in Aaltah, where the Well produced at least as many masculine elements as feminine ones, the air seemed thinner, the elemental motes drifting far enough apart that Tynthanal's aura shone clearly.

Tynthanal turned toward her and held out his arm. "This is the Well's antechamber, and there are still some rocks and other debris on the floor."

She accepted the offered arm and allowed Tynthanal to guide her through the antechamber. Occasionally, he kicked aside small rocks on which she might have twisted her ankle, and she felt a glow of appreciation for his thoughtfulness.

Across the room, she saw the aura of a palace guard moving and heard a sound she recognized as the scrape of a key in a lock, then the lifting of a bar. Moments later, a door creaked open.

Kailee felt the characteristic hum of the Well under her feet as they crossed the threshold into the Well chamber itself. She had no concept of how much debris must be in the room, but the concentration of elements told her exactly where the Well was located.

Tynthanal came to a stop only a couple of steps into the room. "It's best we keep our distance," he said. "They've cleared some of the worst of it, but there are enough loose rocks and pebbles to make footing dangerous."

Kailee nodded her agreement as she scanned the room with her Mindseye. She had no need to proceed any farther.

"Why are you smiling?" Tynthanal asked.

She pointed toward an area off to the right of the Well, her pulse quickening with joy. Her desire to come to the Well—even knowing it was full of rubble—had been based on more than idle curiosity. "Because I can see a few motes of Nex over there, and unless I'm very much mistaken, Nex naturally occurs only in Women's Well."

She could feel Tynthanal's astonishment in the sudden jerk of his muscle. "I can see nothing but a pile of rubble. Even when I look with my Mindseye."

Kailee cautioned herself not to get too excited. Her Mindsight might have revealed what she had hoped to be the case—that Mairah had brought one or more magic items to the Well and that they were still there—but that didn't mean Kailee would be able to figure out exactly what they did or what had befallen the Well. And even if she *could* learn what had happened, there was no guarantee she would like the answer.

Kailee did not believe that Mairah was the wicked, evil woman everyone else believed her to be, but she did allow some room for the possibility that she was mistaken. Maybe Mairah had willfully damaged the Well out of nothing but sheer spite and malice. But she refused to accept that as the truth until she'd uncovered clear and certain evidence of it.

"There are a number of other feminine elements gathered close to the Nex. Do you see a cluster of Rai motes?"

"I do," Tynthanal said. He was the only man she'd ever known or even heard of who could see some feminine elements. "I assumed that was just a naturally occurring cluster."

Kailee shook her head. "Not based on the number of feminine elements I see around them. I suspect when your men clear that area, they'll find whatever spells Mairah may have brought with her to the Well. It seems likely that would help us figure out what went wrong."

Kailee had not known her husband very long, but even so she could not miss the slight tension that tightened the muscles of the arm she held.

"And don't worry," she added. "I am aware there is some chance I won't like the answer, but I'm willing to risk it."

He let out a soft sigh. "Very well. I'll have them start in the morning."

Kailee had not been raised in a tradition of great faith, but even so she said a silent prayer to the Creator and the Mother that she would find the evidence she needed to clear the name of the woman she had failed.

CHAPTER TWO

Alys was in her sitting room in the residential wing of her palace, eyes glazing over as she read through her treasurer's latest financial report, when one of the talkers on the mantelpiece behind her chirped.

Rubbing her bleary eyes, Alys glanced over her shoulder at the neat row of talkers, expecting the sound to have come from the blue-and-white one that was paired with Queen Ellinsoltah's. The Queen of Rhozinolm often reached out to her at odd hours, especially late at night. After all, as sovereigns, they had similarly grueling schedules that did not often leave them free for spontaneous conversations.

But the chirping flier was painted in black and gold: Tynthanal's colors. Alys bit her lip, embarrassed at the trepidation that spread through her as she approached the mantel and reached for the talker. She had received a brief letter from her brother when he had arrived in Aaltah to become the prince regent, but nothing since then. He had assured her when he'd left Women's Well that he was doing his best to forgive her for not allowing him to marry Chanlix, but it had been abundantly clear to both of them that he had not yet managed it. She was not anxious to face their newly chilly and formal relationship.

Placing the talker on the desk before her, Alys opened her Mindseye and fed a mote of Rho into it to complete the connection. When she closed her Mindseye once more, a miniature image of her brother hovered in the air before her.

He looked almost as tired as she felt, his eyes shadowed as he narrowly suppressed a yawn. Alys glanced down at the treasurer's report and wondered just how long she'd been staring at it without actually absorbing anything. Her eyes ached with weariness, and she should have gone to bed hours ago. However, if she didn't work herself to the very brink of exhaustion each night, she would lie abed with her mind churning and her heart aching until she sprang up once more. She had never felt so utterly alone before, and sometimes she wasn't sure how she could continue to endure it.

Tynthanal's eyes narrowed in what looked like concern. "I didn't truly expect to find you up at this hour," he said.

Had he perhaps *hoped* she wouldn't be up, so that he could tell himself he'd done his fraternal duty in reaching out to her and been thwarted through no fault of his own? "It's nice to hear from you," she said, and her throat instantly tightened. She missed her brother more than she could say, and that pain and longing was made ever so much worse by Corlin's absence and her continuing battle with her grief over Jinnell's death—a battle in which she could never triumph.

His eyes flicked briefly downward in what might have been guilt. "I'm sorry I've taken so long to reach out," he said. "I've been very busy, as you might well imagine."

"Yes," she responded. She was certain he was indeed kept very busy, but that was not the reason it had taken him so long to contact her. "How are things going? And how is Kailee settling in?"

He smiled faintly. "The court doesn't know quite what to do with her, but I've found she's more than capable of taking care of herself. I've become an expert at feigning obtuseness when people suggest, ever so subtly, that I ought to rein her in and make her behave like a proper lady."

Alys grimaced in sympathy. "In other words, they want you to hide her away somewhere so they don't have to be made uncomfortable by her open Mindseye . . . or by her free spirit."

He lifted one shoulder in a shrug. "I'm sure that's what they mean, but as I have no intention of doing any such thing, I don't much care. We went down to explore the Well chamber together, and Kailee saw a couple of motes of Nex under some of the rubble. I ordered that section of the chamber cleared, and I expect we'll know what's under there in a day or two. All thanks to Kailee."

Alys was gratified to see the spark of pride in his eyes, and she smiled, imagining Kailee's triumph at the discovery—although she hoped the girl would not be disappointed by what the searchers found. Kailee hoped to find evidence that Mairahsol had not intentionally damaged the Well, that she'd been acting out of some kind of selflessness—a difficult concept for anyone who'd known the late Abbess of Khalpar to swallow. Whatever was under the rubble was unlikely to clear Mairahsol's name, despite Kailee's optimism.

"But I did find something else that I wanted to tell you about," Tynthanal continued, holding up a small glass vial. He held it out to the talker, bringing the flaky red-brown substance inside it into clearer view. "There was a fair amount of what looks like dried blood in the Well's antechamber," he said, setting the vial back down again. "Everyone says there must have been some kind of a struggle between Melcor, Delnamal, and Mairahsol at the Well, but I have yet to hear a convincing explanation for why the blood was *outside* the Well chamber. If a struggle occurred,

I'd have expected it to be inside. And though there's a substantial amount of blood, it does not appear to be enough to indicate a fatal wound. Nor have any bodies been recovered."

Alys shivered in a sudden chill. "So you think Delnamal might still be alive?"

He examined her face with an unnerving intensity, and she could not blame him for being wary of her reaction. When she had received the news that Delnamal was dead, she'd been torn between jubilation and devastation. She wanted her half-brother dead, but she wanted him to suffer—as he had made her suffer—before his death.

"Let's just say I would not entirely rule out the possibility," Tynthanal responded. "Especially considering Xanvin is nowhere to be found. I would not have been shocked if she'd decided to return to Khalpar after his death, but I *am* shocked she left so fast and without telling anyone."

Alys had also been surprised when she'd heard that her stepmother had departed Aalwell so swiftly, but she had attributed it to the ravages of a mother's grief. No matter how much she herself might hate Delnamal, there was no question in her mind that his mother had loved him with all her heart, and expecting her to observe social niceties when she was in the depths of grief seemed unrealistic. But if Delnamal *hadn't* died that day—had in fact only been wounded—then Xanvin's disappearance took on a whole different meaning.

"I am trying to reassure Oona of my good intentions," Tynthanal continued, "and I hope that over time I might win some of her confidence. However, at the moment, she remains convinced I am the enemy. She flinches whenever I speak to her, and she claims to have no idea where Delnamal or Xanvin might be. And she would sooner cast herself from a tower window than let me get within arm's reach of our infant king."

He held up the vial of dried blood again. "I was wondering if perhaps the Women's Well Academy might research the possibility of developing a spell to identify a blood sample. If it is indeed Delnamal's blood outside the Well chamber, the royal council might permit me to question Oona more formally. I'm certain she knows more than she's telling."

Alys sat back and frowned, thinking about it. She was too newly come to the practice of magic to consider herself an expert—despite her considerable natural talent—but it seemed that such a spell ought to be within the realm of possibility. "Perhaps some alteration to a paternity test potion," she mused. The paternity test potion was much like the one used to analyze bloodlines for compatibility in marriage. Blood from both parties was combined with the potion, with the subsequent color change indicating the result. "I don't suppose you have a sample of our father's blood lying around?"

He smiled politely at the feeble jest. "I could ask the women of the new Abbey to work on a potion to compare the sample with my own blood, but . . ." He ended with a grimace and a shrug.

Alys had heard that Aaltah had rebuilt its Abbey after the late King Aaltyn had razed it, but the place was peopled with novice abigails who would not have the knowledge and experience to devise new potions. Not to mention that she—and, she was sure, her brother—was reluctant to make demands of women who were to all intents and purposes imprisoned.

"No," Alys said with a shake of her head. "We'll handle it here at the Academy. I'll contact you as soon as I know something, and then hopefully you can send the blood sample here via flier."

"Thank you." He reached up and rubbed his eyes. "I would rest easier if we could be sure he is dead. I keep hoping the workers will find a body under all that rubble. There were four people down there! How can we not have found a single body yet?"

"How are you faring otherwise?" she asked, for he looked

both tired and stressed, the lines of his face pinched with worry. As a former lieutenant commander in Aaltah's army, he had more experience with leadership than Alys ever had, but his ambitions had never included the throne. Being the regent—having all of the responsibility of a king with a great deal less of the power—was no doubt wearing on him as much as the crown of Women's Well was wearing on her.

"As well as can be expected," he said in a tone that made it clear that was all he had to say about it.

Alys swallowed the urge to press. This had been a civil and productive conversation—the easiest they'd had since she had first suggested the marriage with Kailee—and she was reluctant to strain it further. They would likely never return to the easy camaraderie they had once shared, so she would have to learn to be happy with what he could give her.

Mother Leethan reluctantly lit a fire in her hearth. Even in the height of summer, the nights were chilly high in the mountains, where Nandel's Abbey of the Unwanted clung to the side of a rocky peak. Ordinarily, Leethan would stockpile wood for the colder weather, warming herself by adding a woolen kirtle under her robes instead. But Prince Waldmir expected to see her living in comfort thanks to the generous contributions he had made to the Abbey since he'd divorced her, and it was a dangerous thing to disappoint his expectations.

A red-robed abigail knocked softly on the door of her office. "He has arrived, Mother," the girl said, and there could be no doubting to which "he" she referred.

Leethan glanced around the office one more time, hoping she hadn't forgotten anything. He always intended the gifts he'd brought over the years to be for her use exclusively, but she had a habit of sharing them. Whenever he paid a visit, she had to make sure she retrieved everything so that it would be on display when he arrived. She noticed that she'd forgotten to retrieve the snowy white ermine mantle she'd tucked around Sister Jaizal, her old friend who was currently suffering from an ague. It was against the law for an abigail to wear anything but the red robes and cloaks that were the uniform of the Abbey, but Waldmir had insisted he would never allow Leethan to be prosecuted for wearing his gift. Which was likely true, but she couldn't imagine wearing such a thing in the Abbey, so she always loaned it out as a bed covering for ailing abigails. She hoped he would not notice it wasn't here on display as it usually was.

"Show him up," she said, rubbing her palms nervously against her robes. These periodic visits were never truly comfortable for either one of them, but though she'd told him numerous times that he need not make them, still he kept coming. Perhaps it helped assuage the guilt that still haunted him despite his having remarried an unthinkable three times since he'd divorced her. And still, he was on the hunt for yet another new bride, his desperation to have a son growing greater as each year passed.

It had been several months since his last visit, which told her that his search for his next wife was not going well—and that he did not currently have a mistress. He'd been a lusty, vital man through his youth and most of his middle age, but more than a decade ago, he had confided in her that he sometimes had difficulty performing in the marital bed. And age had not improved his condition.

These days, his visits to the Abbey were as much the product of necessity as sentimentality. Although women's magic was legally forbidden even in the Abbey in Nandel, Leethan had learned how to make potency potions that she had provided for him on a regular basis. She wondered if his decision to visit now meant that he'd once more found a woman he wanted to bed, and she hated that even decades after their divorce, the thought of him bedding another produced a flare of jealousy.

That jealousy all but disappeared when Waldmir appeared in

her doorway, for the months since she'd last seen him had not been kind. He was even thinner than usual, his beard a starker shade of white, his eyes more shadowed. For the first time, he looked to her eyes like an old man. Leethan's heart fluttered with panic. How much time could she possibly have left to ensure that the visions she'd seen as a young bride did not come to pass?

Growing up in Grunir, Leethan had known that she would be a seer when she came of age. Although it was considered a "dirty" secret that no one talked about openly, both of Leethan's grand-mothers had been seers, and though Leethan's mother had re-jected the tradition, she had not stopped those old women from training Leethan once it had been clear that she had inherited the talent.

Many years ago, after the birth of her first daughter, Leethan had triggered a vision that changed the course of her life—a vi-sion she'd spent decades trying ever more desperately to prevent from coming true.

Most people scoffed at the idea that there were women who could see the future in visions. The Devotional made only an oblique reference to women who could receive visions sent by the Mother, and conventional wisdom held that such a thing was not literally possible. But the women in Leethan's family had been discreet worshippers of the Mother of All—the "heretical" religion that said the Mother was the first deity and gave birth to the Creator—and had taught Leethan that the Mother of All sent visions of futures the recipient was capable of affecting. Which meant Leethan *should* have been able to prevent her vision—one of Waldmir's youngest and least-favored nephews, Granzin, sit-ting on the throne of Nandel—from coming true.

Only in dire circumstances would someone so far down the line of succession take the throne. It would mean Waldmir had no sons to succeed him. But it also meant all his brothers and most if not all of his older nephews were dead, which Leethan surmised had to be the result of a war over the succession. She'd thought it clear that the Mother of All had been telling her it was her duty not to let Waldmir die without a son, and she'd done everything she could think of to fulfill her mission.

Leethan gave Waldmir as deep a curtsy as her arthritic knees would allow—she was younger than her ex-husband, but only by a handful of years—and hoped he could not read the distress in her eyes.

"You look well," he said when she rose from her curtsy.

"I am," she affirmed, relieved that he didn't seem to see anything amiss. "You, on the other hand . . ."

The young abigail who'd shown him in was halfway out the door and hunched her shoulders ever so slightly as she slid out into the hall. There was likely no one else in Nandel who would even *think* to address Sovereign Prince Waldmir in such an informal—some might say insolent—manner. But then Leethan was quite possibly the only person Waldmir had ever truly loved, and she could get away with a great deal. After all, what worse could he do after having divorced her and shut her up in this abbey?

The corner of his mouth twitched, and she wasn't entirely sure whether it was a smile or a frown he was suppressing. He nodded approvingly at the merry fire and removed the fur cloak from his shoulders, laying it carefully on the nearest chair.

"I know the Abbey is isolated," he said in the rumbling bass voice she'd always admired, "but you have surely heard tell of my recent misadventures."

The Abbey was not so isolated as all that, situated within sight of the walls of The Keep, Nandel's capital city. After all, what good was a whorehouse if it was not easily accessible to its customers?

"Yes," she said, allowing just a touch of acid into her voice. "I heard about the death of your latest intended. You have my condolences, Your Royal Highness."

Waldmir's eyes closed in apparent pain, which surprised her.

Thanks to his continued visits to the Abbey, she was well aware that he had formed no intimate connection with any of his wives after herself—having gone so far as to have one of them beheaded—and yet it looked for all the world like he grieved the death of Jinnell Rah-Sylnin.

With a heavy sigh, Waldmir opened his eyes and met her gaze squarely. "Will I ever have a son?" he asked.

Leethan's voice jammed in her throat, and she went still as stone. Each time she'd gotten pregnant, she'd prayed to the Mother of All that the child would be a boy, so that she could lay the specter of that vision to rest. And when she had borne daughter after daughter, she'd chosen to turn a blind eye any time Waldmir strayed from the marriage bed. An illegitimate heir was better than no heir at all. But as far as she knew, he had sired neither sons nor daughters outside of the bonds of matrimony.

On the terrible day when she nearly died in childbirth with their stillborn son, she had sunk into a despair so deep she had even considered taking her own life. None of her pregnancies had been easy, and the midwife had told her as gently as possible that she could not survive another one.

"Yes, I know you're a seer," Waldmir now said, misinterpreting the shock on her face. "I've known that for . . . quite some time."

She chewed on her lip as she considered what to say. The only person in Nandel she had ever told about her visions was Sister Jaizal, who had been her friend now for decades.

It was Sister Jaizal who—once Leethan confided in her—sat by her side and tended to her when she downed seer's poisons to trigger visions. Leethan could not believe Jaizal would ever have betrayed her confidence—even had she been inclined to do so, what contact would the old abigail have had with Prince Waldmir?—but she could not imagine how else he would know.

Waldmir sighed heavily and leaned against the chair on which he'd lain his cloak. "If there's one thing recent events have proven to me beyond all doubt, it's that to ignore women's magic is the height of folly. I have had enough of that folly, and I will not risk the health and happiness of another young woman if it is all to be in vain. So I ask again: will I ever have a son?"

Leethan's first instinct was to deny being a seer. Surely he could not really *know* the truth. He must only be guessing. Her grandmothers had told her that women with seer's blood in them had extraordinarily strong intuition, even if they never tried a seer's poison. That sometimes it was possible to guess at a woman's talent based on these preternaturally strong instincts. Perhaps Waldmir had heard that same story and that was why he suddenly thought her a seer.

The lie sat on the tip of her tongue, but somehow she could not force herself to give it voice, instead standing mute and indecisive before him. Even after the divorce, she'd still labored to prevent her vision from coming true. After she'd recovered from the first despair, she had redoubled her efforts to help him sire a son on another woman. When he visited her at the Abbey, she convinced him as often as possible to take one of the other abigails to his bed, hoping against hope that the woman would conceive. Because if Waldmir *didn't* have a son, then it would mean Leethan had failed to do the Mother of All's bidding.

The Mother of All did not give visions unless it was within the seer's power to affect the events, and if Waldmir died without an heir, then it was without question Leethan's fault. She could not put her finger on what exactly she could have done differently; however, she was sure that there must have been some piece of sage advice or some obvious precaution that she must have ignored during that final, fateful pregnancy. If she couldn't find a way to help Waldmir sire an heir, then the *only* way Leethan could have fulfilled the Mother's wishes was not to miscarry that baby. And that meant there must have been some way to prevent it.

"Please, Leethan," Waldmir urged more softly, his head bowed and his eyes lowered. He looked as vulnerable as she could ever remember seeing him. He was not a man who allowed others to see his vulnerabilities. Ever. And yet when he was around her, some of the walls that sealed off his heart weakened. "If there's still a chance I might have a son, then I must marry again as soon as possible for the good of Nandel. But I don't . . ."

His voice trailed off, and he rubbed his eyes, shaking his head.

"I don't want another loveless marriage. Please don't make me do it again if I don't have to."

Leethan had thought she'd hardened her heart to her ex-husband many years ago, and yet even so she felt a tug of sympathy. He had never been lighthearted or carefree, even in the earliest, happiest days of their marriage, but it was impossible to miss how the burdens of being sovereign prince—of always putting the needs of Nandel above his own—had chiseled away at all that was warm and happy within him. He had assured her many times—and she believed him—that if she could have borne him a son, they would still now be married.

She imagined he had felt some disappointment when she'd borne daughters instead of sons, though he had kept that disappointment hidden from her. But the birth of their stillborn son had been nearly as soul-destroying for him as it had been for her.

She was still lying abed, recovering from the birth that had almost killed her, when her husband, weeping openly for the only time in her knowledge, gave her the news that she was Abbey-bound. Even knowing the blow was coming had not fully resigned her to her fate, and she remembered begging shamefully for him not to send her away.

In fact, her pleas had moved him to the point that he offered to abdicate his throne to stay with her. He could not stay on the throne while married to a woman who could never provide him the male heir he needed, and he'd been willing to give it all up for her. She certainly had not *wanted* the divorce, but she'd known Waldmir's abdication would have been easily as problematic as his death without an heir. His brothers were dead by then, but he had way too many nephews, many of whom already hungrily eyed the throne. And thanks to her vision, she knew that if Waldmir did not have a son, almost all of those nephews and their sons would have to die for Granzin to end up on the throne.

Leethan did not want to be consigned to the Abbey, but she did not want Nandel to devolve into civil war, either, so she had refused his offer. But with each successive wife who failed to bear him an heir, Waldmir had grown more unhappy and more bitter.

"If you refuse to remarry," she reminded him gently, "then one or more of your nephews will likely seek to topple you from the throne. There will be war in Nandel."

He winced in what looked like pain. "If I'm never going to have a son, all I am doing is delaying the inevitable. I will die without an heir, and my nephews will tear Nandel apart in their eagerness to succeed me. So if I will have no son, there is no point in making some other woman miserable."

"Then perhaps you should try marrying a woman who actually *wants* to marry you," she responded, a little more sharply than she intended.

He snorted and shook that argument off. "I have already decided that I will not marry a woman against her will ever again." His eyes met hers with that familiar intensity. "I told you once that I will never love again, and nothing that has occurred since has changed my mind. I don't *want* another wife, and that makes it unlikely any future bride would be satisfied with me. So I ask you yet again: will I have a son?"

Leethan frantically racked her brain, desperately hoping the right answer would miraculously occur to her. Silently, urgently, she prayed for the Mother of All to tell her what to say, but there was no answer.

This time, she was on her own.

"I can't say that I know for sure," she hedged, staring at the floor to avoid seeing the look in his eyes. It was still theoretically possible that he could sire an heir, but between the vision, and common sense, and gut instincts, she felt certain he would not. "But based on what I have foreseen . . ." Scraping up her courage, she raised her head once more. "If you were going to have a son, you would have had one by now."

The look of anguish that appeared on Waldmir's face sent a stab of guilt through her heart. It was because of her failure that he'd married three other women, to each of their misfortunes, and because of her failure that Nandel was bound for a war of succession that would tear it apart.

Waldmir closed his eyes, and his hands clenched at his sides. "Then it has all been for nothing," he whispered hoarsely, and there was such grief and bitterness in his voice that Leethan flinched. "Everything I've done, everything I've sacrificed . . ."

"Maybe I'm wrong," Leethan said, willing to say just about anything to ease his pain.

"We both know you're not wrong. I have failed my people and my principality and dishonored my father's memory."

Leethan reached out a hand, wishing she could offer some comfort—and praying he would not ask her to tell him precisely what she'd seen. The look on his face was bleak enough already without seeing the evidence of how brutal the war that followed his death was destined to be. He would most definitely *not* want to know that it would be Granzin, of all people, who succeeded him. The only worse future she could paint would be Granzin's older brother—and Waldmir's least-favorite relative—Zarsha ascending the throne.

"Don't," he snapped, jerking out of her reach. His eyes flashed with fire and something that hinted at near panic. "Don't you dare pity me."

"I don't," she said, knowing full well that he would not understand the difference between pity and empathy. "But you're not the only one who failed. If only I hadn't lost our son—" Her voice suddenly hiccuped to a halt. All these years later, the loss still hurt, and the pain had nothing to do with the disappoint-ment of failure.

Some of the wildness faded from his eyes, and he let out a huge sigh. "I suppose the truth is it's neither your fault nor mine. We both tried our hardest. Thank you for sparing me from an-other marriage." He met her eyes briefly, then looked quickly away.

"I . . . may not be back for a while. There's just . . . no point."

Leethan tried not to flinch at that, then scolded herself. Surely she was long past pining for Waldmir's love. His visits had always been for practical purposes, not sentimentality. At least if he didn't visit the Abbey any more, she could comfort herself with the knowledge that he was not lying with other women.

"I will miss you," she could not help saying.

He took her hands and squeezed. "I will not abandon you," he promised. "I just need a little time to . . . come to terms with my fate."

Leethan gave him a tremulous smile and refrained from any further comment. But she couldn't help feeling somewhere deep down in her gut that he would not visit the Abbey again. And she hated the way her treacherous heart sank at the idea.

CHAPTER THREE

Corlin Rah-Sylnin had never felt less like the Crown Prince of Women's Well than he did right now, lying in a mud puddle with the blunted point of a sword pressing into his windpipe. His own sword had gone flying with his last, graceless attempt to parry, and his opponent had further immobilized him by stepping on his wrist. The pressure was just shy of snapping the bone, and it was sure to leave some impressive bruising and swelling in its wake.

Cadet Justal's eyes were alight with triumph, although Corlin couldn't see what made the older, larger cadet so proud of himself—it had been clear from the moment they'd been ordered to spar that Corlin was meant to lose and be humbled. If anything, Justal should be embarrassed that Corlin had lasted as long as he had.

Captain Norlix let the hulking third-year cadet enjoy his victory pose for far longer than necessary, and Corlin ground his teeth to keep any protest from escaping. During his time as a cadet in the Citadel of Women's Well, he had escaped the traditional hazing that ordinarily befell first-years because of his status as crown prince. Such was clearly *not* going to be the case in Aaltah. It did not come as a surprise, but that didn't make it any less unpleasant. What *did* come as a surprise was that instead of merely tolerating the hazing, Captain Norlix was openly encouraging it by forcing Corlin to fight a cadet two years older and substantially larger than he. If his instructor had it in for him already, Corlin wondered if he could survive his training.

Eventually, Norlix called off his dog and Corlin was allowed to rise, dripping, from the mud. Several of the cadets who'd been watching the match snickered and whispered to one another, and Corlin stifled a groan. He had, of course, landed on his backside, and he could only imagine what he looked like with mud coating the seat of his trousers.

Not so long ago, the laughter of his fellow cadets would have sparked his temper, and he would have said or done something that would have led to yet another painful and humiliating thrashing. Even now, his temper stirred, but all he had to do to quell it was remember the last time he'd given it free rein.

He remembered Cadet Smithson's cry of pain and surprise, remembered the bright splash of blood, remembered how the boy's face had gone ashen as his knees weakened and he fell to the barracks floor. All because Smithson had dared to try to calm him when Corlin was hacking up his bed in frustration at the news that his hated uncle Delnamal had died without being punished as he deserved. That Smithson had survived and fully recovered from the injury did nothing to assuage the guilt that Corlin suspected he would carry till the end of his days.

With what dignity he could scrape up, Corlin retrieved his sword from the far side of the sparring circle where it had landed, wondering if Norlix was going to punish him for losing by making him go another round. He was relieved to be commanded back to his place while Justal remained in the center, for though he didn't shy away from a fight, he was not especially eager to be trounced again.

Corlin's relief quickly gave way to a creeping discomfort when

Norlix ordered Cadet Rafetyn into the ring against Justal. Like Corlin, Rafetyn was a fourteen-year-old first-year cadet. However, the poor kid had yet to hit any kind of adolescent growth spurt. Standing at his tallest, the top of Rafetyn's head barely reached Justal's shoulder, and his chest was approximately the width of one of Justal's thighs.

Justal had no business sparring with first-years to start with— and of all the first-years, Rafetyn was by far the most overmatched. What was Captain Norlix thinking? Corlin looked on in horror as Rafetyn grimly entered the circle and took up a ready position without a hint of protest—although, with his build, he looked far more suited to a life of quiet scholarship than to life in the military.

"What's his story?" Corlin whispered from the side of his mouth to the cadet standing next to him, whose name he couldn't remember.

"Third son," the cadet whispered back without turning his head. "Runt of the litter. Only allowed into the Citadel because his father's a duke." There was an open contempt in his tone that grated on Corlin's nerves; it certainly wasn't Rafetyn's fault he'd been born small. Nor was it his fault his father was a duke. "There's a pool for how long he'll last before he'll go running back to his mama, if you want in."

Corlin decided he had no interest in learning the cadet's name. All bullies inherently reminded him of his uncle Delnamal and landed immediately on his enemies list. He wondered if there was a similar betting pool for him and decided it was likely. Although he had spent nearly his entire life in Aaltah, there was no question that the cadets considered him an outsider. His uncle Tynthanal might have become the Prince Regent of Aaltah, but everyone still saw Corlin as the son of a traitorous, uppity woman with delusions of grandeur, and the grandson of the witch who'd cast the Curse. It did not make for a comfortable and easy acceptance into their ranks, but he was resolved to tough it out.

Cadet Justal began the sparring session with an intimidating war cry and a vicious, sweeping swing of his sword. The swing showed no grace nor any particular skill, and a cadet of a similar size and strength would parry it easily and use the brute's momentum against him. Justal's reliance on his strength and size in place of skill was what had allowed Corlin to last a respectable amount of time in the ring against him. But when fighting someone as small and slight as Rafetyn, brute strength was too great an advantage.

Rafetyn met Justal's sword with a smooth parry, but the power behind the blow knocked him back and almost caused him to drop his weapon. He recovered more quickly than Corlin would have expected, once again getting his sword in place for a parry, but Justal was too strong for him. Their blades met and Rafetyn's arms gave way with the force, leaving Justal an opening to ram the pommel right between his eyes. There was a sickening crunch as the bone and cartilage of Rafetyn's nose collapsed and blood sprayed. Rafetyn's eyes rolled into the back of his head, and he went down.

Justal let out a whoop of victory, and Corlin saw more than one of the cadets in the circle look at the unconscious boy with sneering disgust instead of sympathy. Someone laughed, but a quick, sharp look from Captain Norlix silenced it.

Norlix gestured at Corlin. "You. Take him to the healer's office to get that nose fixed."

Corlin's temper made another attempt to flare into life, but he quelled it. He had a suspicion that Norlix had orchestrated this whole sparring session with the express purpose of scaring him, demonstrating just how rough and unpleasant life as a misfit cadet could be. If Norlix intended it as a message to show Corlin he was unwelcome, then the message had been received loud and clear. But if he thought he was going to frighten Corlin into quitting that quickly, he was in for a rude surprise.

Rafetyn was conscious and holding his bleeding nose when

Corlin reached him, but his eyes had a dull, glazed look in them, and he staggered when he tried to stand. Aware that the rest of the cadets were murmuring to one another—and that what they were saying was not complimentary—Corlin looped Rafetyn's arm around his own shoulders and helped him to his feet. The circle parted, and, with Corlin supporting the majority of Rafetyn's weight, they made their way out of the training fields and toward the healer's office.

On the eve of his official induction as a postulant in the Temple of the Creator, Prince Draios—younger son of King Khalvin of Khalpar—stalked the palace halls in search of his elder brother. He'd been in the midst of packing his belongings—well, supervising the servants who were packing his belongings—when he'd received the devastating message from his father, and it had taken every scrap of self-control he possessed to keep from killing the damn messenger.

The message had come from the king and been delivered in the form of an official decree, but Draios knew the idea had not sprung from King Khalvin's brain. The king admired his youngest son's devotion to the Creator and had been encouraging him for as long as he could remember to enter training for the priesthood as soon as he reached the age of majority. Today was his seventeenth birthday, and he had intended to be comfortably ensconced in the postulants' dormitory by the time the night was out.

Draios rounded the corner and stomped into the informal parlor in the residential wing of the palace. The room was empty, but the door to the veranda on the far side of the room was open. Knowing the veranda was Parlommir's favorite spot to take his repose between council sessions in the heat of a summer day, Draios stopped himself in mid stride and tried to settle his temper. There was no denying he was angry, but the Creator commanded him to show respect for his older brother. It would be preferable if he could *feel* respect, but lacking that, the best he could hope for was a convincing performance.

Draios forced himself to walk slowly, almost casually, out onto the veranda.

As expected, Crown Prince Parlommir was seated in a comfortable chair in the shade. A gentle breeze stirred the auburn locks he had left unbound around his shoulders, but there was nevertheless a thin sheen of sweat on his forehead. He'd been staring into the middle distance when Draios stepped through the doorway, but he abruptly sat up straight and gave his younger brother what could only be described as a wary look. If Draios needed any further evidence that Parlommir was behind this outrage, he now had it.

"You—" Draios started, but anger choked his voice off in his throat.

Parlommir held up his hands in a gesture of innocence, though the look in his eyes belied the charade. "I told Father you would blame me for this," he said with a shake of his head. He rose to his feet and moved to stand by the railing, peering at the gardens below. And not coincidentally putting a little more space between himself and his brother's anger.

Draios narrowed his eyes. "So you're going to sit there and claim it was *not* your idea to limit my ability to answer my calling?"

Parlommir gave him a look of supreme condescension. "You can answer your calling just fine! Father assumed—as did I—that you would report to the temple as planned. And surely he mentioned that he had made arrangements with the high priest to accommodate the unique needs of a king's son."

"The needs of a king's son," Draios sneered. "As if I am the only king's son ever to join the priesthood!"

"Of course you're not," Parlommir said in what he undoubtedly thought was a soothing tone. Instead, it sounded like he was talking to a small child or a simpleton. "But until I have a son of my own, you are second in line for the throne, and these are trying times. Father cannot afford for you to completely retreat from the world during your training. Surely you see that. Surely you see there is no *insult* in that."

Draios suffered a nearly unbearable urge to cross the distance between them and give Parlommir a mighty shove. If it weren't for the possibility that a fall from the veranda might not kill him, Draios wasn't sure he could have resisted. He stifled a groan, for he would now have to spend the night praying in penance for the sin of wishing his brother dead.

"How do you expect me to train as a priest while being forced to live apart from my fellow postulants and return to the palace every night?" he asked, and he hated the hint of whining he heard in his own tone. Parlommir had a unique ability to coax that particular sound from him, making him feel like a child when he was now officially a grown man.

Parlommir smiled at him—an expression that held an almost-believable warmth. It was smiles like those—full of convincingly feigned brotherly affection—that fooled their father into believing Parlommir had Draios's best interests at heart, when really he wanted to make certain that Draios never exceeded his own place in the king's heart. Their famously pious father had been nearly bursting with pride at Draios's decision to enter the priesthood, and so Parlommir had whispered in his ear and found a way to sabotage Draios's good works.

"I have faith that you will find a way, Little Brother," Parlommir said. "Surely piety like yours can withstand the challenge."

Draios gritted his teeth to stop himself from retorting. The image of shoving Parlommir over that railing once again flashed through his mind. Maybe if the push was delivered just right, the bastard would land on his head and he would break his neck.

Of course, their father would never, ever forgive Draios if something happened to Parlommir—even something that appeared to be accidental. The king had never looked at him quite the same way since the mysterious death of his fencing tutor when Draios was fourteen years old. Draios had taken great pains to avoid any untoward suspicion falling upon him and was nowhere in the vicinity when the man died. But the healers never were able to pinpoint the cause of death, and his father was very much aware that the tutor had humiliated Draios the day before by thrashing him.

If it hadn't been for the unexpected death of Draios's governess two years earlier—under similar circumstances—Draios thought he would probably have escaped the scrutiny. But though no one could prove he'd had anything to do with either of those unfortunate incidents, he knew both his father and his brother harbored . . . suspicions.

He was fairly certain neither of them had any idea that Draios had had anything to do with the recent death of Lord Jalzarnin. Jalzarnin, who had not long ago been the Lord High Priest of Khalpar, and who upon his disgrace had been removed from the position and given the title of High Priest of the Temple of the Creator—the second-highest-ranking member of the clergy! Draios had no interest in studying under a man who was as impious and incompetent as Jalzarnin had proven himself to be, and so he had made sure that a more suitable and holy man held the title when he was ready to become a postulant. But the other two suspicious deaths were more than enough to get him into trouble.

No. Tempting as the idea of Parlommir falling to his death might be, Draios knew he could not chance it.

Not trusting himself to speak, Draios turned and marched back into the palace without another word.

Ellin stood patiently as her ladies swarmed over her in a frenzy of plucking and pinning and smoothing. When they'd helped her into the carriage to take her from the royal palace to the Temple of the Creator, they'd barely allowed her to sit down for fear that a stray wrinkle might damage the splendor of the costliest garment that had ever touched her skin. A stunning—if miserably scratchy, heavy, and uncomfortable—bodice of cloth-of-gold was what most drew the eye, but the layers upon layers of embroidered and jewel-studded skirts were of the greatest concern to her ladies, who were most insistent that every flounce lie scrupulously flat and unwrinkled.

The only one of her ladies who was not obsessed with her dress was Star, who was blinking rapidly and looked as proud as if she were the mother of the bride.

To make sure her wedding day was as uncomfortable as possible, Star had laced her stays tighter than normal, and Ellin could barely draw in a deep breath, no matter how desperately she needed one. She couldn't tell if the racing of her heart was born more of excitement or of panic. This wedding was almost two years in the making, and she was having difficulty grasping that the time had finally come. Once, she had dreaded her wedding to Zarsha of Nandel. Then she had longed for it. Now . . . Well, now she wasn't entirely sure *what* she felt, thanks to Prince Waldmir's distressingly successful attempt to sow discord between them.

"Give Her Majesty room to breathe," Star said loudly with an aura of authority that instantly silenced the chattering ladies.

Ellin felt a couple more strokes and plucks, but the ladies reluctantly backed away.

"Thank you all," Ellin said, smiling warmly at the lot of them, though she made special eye contact with Star. Eyes still shining with unshed tears, Star nodded to acknowledge the thanks.

One of the temple's acolytes poked his head in the door, eyes downcast in deference—or possibly in concern that he might see something he ought not in the ladies' retiring room.

"If it please Your Majesty," he said, still looking at the floor, "all is ready for you."

"Thank you," she said, casting a reluctant glance at the crown she had put off wearing for as long as possible.

This was only the second wedding of a sovereign queen in Rhozinolm's history, and Ellin had hoped to wear the crown of her predecessor, Queen Shazinzal, for this ceremony. Unfortunately, although the crown had been well preserved and tended in its place of honor in the Royal Gallery, Shazinzal had apparently been of a more imposing stature than Ellin. The crown was so large that no amount of padding or creative hairdressing could hold it in its proper place. She could have had it cut down to fit, but that would have felt like a violation of Queen Shazinzal's memory, so Ellin had commissioned a new one to be made in its likeness.

A queen's crown was traditionally a dainty thing of filigree and delicate gems, but Shazinzal's wedding crown—and Ellin's modified reproduction—could as easily be meant for a king. The points and flourishes were fashioned of solid gold—not a hint of filigree wire in sight—with grape-sized sapphires forming a band around her brow. Star had to use two hands to hold the thing steady as she carefully laid it onto the headdress pinned into Ellin's hair. The headdress was equipped with clips to hold the crown firmly in place, but Ellin would have to keep her head steady and her chin raised to prevent the weight of it from tearing her hair out if the headdress shifted.

The Temple of the Creator in Zinolm Well was the second-largest building in all of Rhozinolm, second only to the royal palace. Today, Ellin knew, every seat on the ground floor and first balcony level would be spoken for, and the standing room on the highest level would be packed dangerously tight with those commoners lucky enough to earn a place. For all her roiling emotions, the moment Ellin stepped out of the dressing room door, she would cease to be an ordinary woman with ordinary emotions and would have to don the impenetrable mask of a queen. She closed her eyes, taking as deep a breath as the torturous stays would allow, settling that mask over herself. Then, her courage bolstered, she stepped out into the hallway, where her groom awaited her.

When she'd first met Zarsha of Nandel, Ellin had been completely immune to his charm and good looks. While every other woman in the court had all but drooled at the sight of him, Ellin had been so resistant to the marriage she was being forced into that she'd found even his good looks vaguely sinister. But now, nearly two years after their first meeting, seeing him in his wedding finery made her breath catch in her throat.

Although his itinerant life had made Zarsha's sensibilities very different from those of a typical Nandelite, his taste in clothing had always betrayed his origins. His entire wardrobe consisted of browns and grays and black, with only the most cursory ornamentation, as Nandelites considered ornamentation frivolous. But in marrying her and becoming her prince consort, he was formally leaving the court of Nandel, and he had fully adopted Rhozinolm marriage customs, which decreed that the bride and groom should be a matching set.

He wore a stunning doublet of cloth-of-gold over embroidered white silk breeches. Sapphires gleamed at cuffs and collar and shoe buckles—the first jewels Ellin had ever seen him wear. There being no custom in place for the headwear of a prince consort, she and Zarsha had decided on the narrow, understated crown of gold and sapphires that circled his brow. A smaller, more muted—and, she thought with a twinge of jealousy, lighter—version of her own. His still unfashionably short blond hair was slicked back from his face, leaving center stage to the shockingly blue eyes she had once found so cold and off-putting.

Zarsha grinned at her too-obvious appreciation, holding his hands out from his sides and turning a slow circle, to the amusement of their gathered attendants. Ellin gave a huff of exasperation, though the heat in her cheeks suggested she was blushing.

His grin was not as easy as it once had been—she had the distinct impression he was performing for their audience rather than for her—but even so the familiarity of the teasing eased the knot of tension in her belly.

"I tried to imagine you in something other than black, gray, or brown," she said, "but I found I couldn't do it. I might almost suspect you to be an imposter, did I not know better."

He bowed, and she was gratified to see the stiffness of the gesture. He might not be suffering with the weight of his crown, but at least he was feeling the constriction of the cloth-of-gold. Ellin understood the importance of ceremony, and there was no question that the royal wedding was an occasion requiring show-manship and ostentation, but she couldn't help wishing that the clothing did not have to be so terribly uncomfortable. Or at least that she did not have to wear it through the long ceremony, the even longer procession through the streets of Rhozinolm after-ward, or the nearly endless reception at the palace after that.

"I must admit, Your Majesty," Zarsha said as he straightened, "I suspected much the same when I saw my image in the mirror." His eyes took her in from head to toe, and though their relation-ship had been somewhat strained since their engagement, she could not miss the appreciation in his gaze. "You look . . . resplendent."

"I think you mean uncomfortable," she quipped, and he laughed. If he was feeling any of the nerves that grooms were supposed to feel on their wedding day, he was, as always, hiding it well. She, on the other hand, felt as if a school of minnows was swimming frantically around inside her stomach.

Zarsha stepped close to her, taking her hands and lowering his voice, although the echoing hall did not afford them much in the way of privacy. "We are in this together," he said urgently, squeez-ing her hands and staring intently into her eyes. "Now and al-ways."

"Does that mean you've forgiven me?" she asked softly, voice barely above a whisper. She had bowed to the pressure from Zarsha's uncle, Sovereign Prince Waldmir of Nandel, and signed the marriage agreement on the prince's terms without consulting Zarsha first. She'd done it knowing full well that Zarsha would object to the terms—terms that required him to enter into the marriage as a "bride," thereby forfeiting all his possessions as a "brideprice" to the Crown of Nandel. In the days and weeks that had followed, she had often recalled that fateful meeting with Waldmir, had gone over everything a million times, parsing every word and action. And every time she did, she came to the same conclusion: Waldmir had been in deadly earnest, and if she'd refused the terms or insisted on consulting Zarsha, then Rhozinolm's trade agreements with Nandel would never have been renewed.

"I love you," he said, "and with love comes forgiveness."

A lump formed in her throat, for Zarsha was so rarely evasive with her that it was impossible to miss the exceptions. If he had forgiven her, *truly* forgiven her, he would have come right out and said so. She swallowed past the lump, shoring up her emotional defenses. First and foremost, this was a marriage of state. Their ease and happiness as a couple—or lack thereof—was of little importance in the grand scheme of things.

"Then I suppose we'd better hurry up and get married," she said with false cheer and a smile that she suspected held a hint of panic.

CHAPTER FOUR

S ister Jaizal fluffed the nest of pillows she'd arranged on Leethan's bed while Leethan plucked a mote of Rho from the air to activate the seer's poison.

"*Must* you take one so strong?" Jaizal fretted when the poison was activated and ready. "I would think it wiser to start with a mild one and then try again later with something stronger only if necessary."

Leethan grimaced at the vial of poison in her hand, not relishing the prospect of the ordeal she was about to inflict upon herself. But she had not been able to sleep since she'd admitted to Waldmir that she did not believe he would ever have a son. The weight of that failure sat heavy on her shoulders. As if to make matters worse, she had—for the first time in five years—been awakened during her one good night's sleep by the strange recurring nightmare that had troubled her off and on for as long as she could remember. The dream always left Leethan shivering and filled with foreboding, and its echoes troubled her sleep for many nights afterward. Thank goodness it never occurred more than once every year or two! And she wasn't about to let it stop her from doing what she knew she must. She had failed the duty that the Mother of All had assigned her, but she hoped the goddess would give her a second chance to set things right.

"The Mother of All does not reward cowardice," Leethan said, feeling a brief twinge of pity for Sister Jaizal. In her younger days, Leethan had suffered the ravages of seer's poisons alone at night in her own bed, dampening the screams she knew the pain would draw from her throat by gagging herself with a woolen sock. There was something incalculably comforting about not having to go through the torment alone, but she knew from personal experience how wrenching it could be to watch a fellow sister's suffering.

Sister Jaizal snorted softly. "No one who's spent more than five minutes in your presence would accuse you of cowardice," she murmured, and Leethan couldn't help smiling. She'd had few true friends in the Abbey since she'd been named abbess more than a decade ago, but Jaizal had been steadfast throughout.

"Thank you for sitting with me. Again."

Sister Jaizal waved the thanks off. "You were a ninny to suffer in silence for so long. I'd have been happy to hold your hand *years* ago if only you'd told me what you were doing."

Leethan conceded that was probably true. But here in Nandel, women's magic was forbidden even in the Abbey, and until Waldmir had come to her and asked her to produce potency potions for him, she had feared the consequences of being found out. It was somewhat ironic to discover that, after all the pains she had taken to maintain her secret, Waldmir had known all along.

"Let us hope this is the *last* seer's poison I will have to take," Leethan said, though she suspected that was a little much to ask. The Mother of All discouraged her daughters from relying too heavily on visions by making the process of having one as grueling and unpleasant as possible, and Leethan hoped she hadn't put off doing this for too long. It had been years since she'd triggered a vision, as she'd been clinging to the hope that she might still help Waldmir father a son. It was past time she seek guidance again.

Climbing into the nest of pillows that would hopefully protect her from injury if she thrashed, Leethan settled in. Then, with a deep breath that she hoped would grant her strength and courage, she uncorked the vial of poison and gulped it quickly down.

The taste was indescribably vile, and her body instantly recognized the stuff as poison, doing everything possible to keep the liquid from going down. Her throat closed up, and her gorge rose, and if she weren't already well-versed in forcing the poison into herself, she might not have been able to stop herself from spitting it out.

Even once she swallowed, her stomach attempted to expel the poison, and though the burning agony in her mouth and throat made her want to scream, she clapped a hand over her mouth to keep everything—screams and poison and bile—trapped inside. She squinted her eyes shut, her body curling around itself. She was vaguely aware of Sister Jaizal gently prying the empty vial from fingers that had closed around it so tightly she was in danger of crushing it and cutting her hand.

"Let it out," the abigail's voice urged, but Leethan could only fight the pain by clamping down harder, muscles so tight it was a wonder her bones didn't shatter with the pressure.

There was nothing she could do now but endure and wait for the strange altered state of consciousness that allowed the vision to begin.

Leethan had first learned of her potential talent as a seer from her maternal grandmother during her girlhood in Grunir. Although women's magic was forbidden in Grunir to all but the women of the Abbey, Leethan had learned from her grandmother that there were more secret practitioners than conventional wisdom accounted for. Her first introduction to a seer's poison had occurred when Gram had taken one in her presence, warning her in advance that the experience would be upsetting and that there would be nothing Leethan could do to help.

The memory of watching her frail grandmother writhing in pain was burned into her brain, but for all the horror of the memory, she knew that the worst of the torment had lasted only a few minutes, just as she knew from questioning Jaizal in the aftermath of her previous visions that her own screams of agony lasted only five minutes or so. But with the level of pain caused by these poisons, five minutes was an excruciatingly long time, and it always *felt* more like an hour.

Finally, the pain began to ease and Leethan felt her struggles stilling, her consciousness drifting away from her room and re-emerging elsewhere. She felt only loosely connected to her body, the pain being one of the few reminders that her body even existed as she found herself in a sea of impenetrable blackness. When the blackness lifted, it was as if she were peering out of a window at a scene no window could possibly reveal.

Her greatest hope was that the Mother of All would reveal that Leethan's assumption that Waldmir would not have a son was mistaken; that there was still time for Leethan to accomplish the mission she'd been given. Her greatest fear was that the mission was now beyond her reach. But the sight that met her eyes when the vision began seemed entirely unrelated to what Leethan had always thought the Mother wanted of her.

Leethan saw herself, bundled in a heavy, fur-lined cloak that was too big for her. With one gloved hand, she held the hood tight to her face, burying her chin into the soft fur. The other hand held the lead of a furry, plump mountain pony, which followed her obediently and plodded easily through snow that reached her knees. Riding atop the pony was a small figure so deeply bundled in furs Leethan could make out nothing except that it was a child. Sister Jaizal, also draped in furs, rode a second shaggy pony and followed behind.

Leethan did not recognize the rocky mountain path over which the little caravan traveled, but it was obviously somewhere in Nandel, for theirs were the only mountains on the continent. The sky was a lowering, unpleasant shade of gray, and gusts of wind pulled at the cloaks and hoods of the three bundled figures. A gust pulled the hood from Leethan's hand and sent the edge of the cloak fluttering behind her, revealing that, underneath, she was dressed not in an abigail's robes but in warm, sturdy men's clothing. Her hair was pulled back into a club that sat tight to her head—a common style for the men of Nandel—and a casual observer watching from a distance would have thought her a man. Leethan noted that her face did not look much aged from the one she saw in the mirror every day, which meant the vision showed a not-too-distant future.

The same gust of wind that had revealed her clothing also gave her a better look at the small figure who rode atop the pony, and she discerned that the child was a little girl, no more than five years old. In the isolation of the Abbey, Leethan had grown unfamiliar with the sight of children—unless one counted the occasional teenage boy who was brought to the Abbey to be initiated into manhood by an abigail—so she could not guess who the child was. But the small, shivering figure had no business being out on the road in such conditions.

One thing was certain: the girl was a child of Nandel. Though her lips were blue with cold, and it was impossible to miss how she shivered, she showed no sign of complaining, instead readjusting her seat on the pony and burrowing deeper into her furs.

What in the Mother's name were Leethan and Jaizal doing out of their abbey, on the road in the snow with a small child and a winter storm looming on the horizon? Travel was never especially easy in Nandel, for there were passes that didn't fully thaw even in the summer, but Leethan would stake her reputation that the season was at the very least autumn, if not yet true winter—

a season in which no one would travel the most rugged passes unless in dire need. And no woman of Nandel would travel without a male escort, even in the best of weather.

The vision faded without imparting any further wisdom or explanation, and Leethan came back to her aching, sweat-soaked body with a groan.

"Shhh," Jaizal murmured, touching a cool cloth to Leethan's flaming face. "I am here, and all is well."

Leethan groaned again; she hadn't the energy to respond with anything coherent, like words.

She had worshipped the Mother of All ever since she'd been a small child, and her faith in the Mother's goodness and mercy had remained steadfast despite the hardships of her life. But it seemed that this night's vision would be yet another challenge to her faith.

What could the vision possibly mean? Surely traveling through the mountain passes in the winter with a small girl child in tow was not what Leethan needed to do to protect Nandel from the war she knew would follow if Waldmir died without a clear heir. And if the Mother of All did not intend for Leethan to prevent the war, then why had she given Leethan that long-ago vision of Waldmir's nephew on the throne? Did this mean it really *was* too late for Leethan to fix her failure?

Leethan had triggered the vision—put herself through hell—because she'd been seeking clarity. Instead, she was even more confused and helpless now than she'd been before she'd started.

Society expected Ellin, as a woman, to go all gooey and sentimental on the inside at *any* wedding—and at her own, she was expected to be bursting with joy and excitement. She had attended quite a number of weddings throughout the course of her life, and although she was far too well brought up and proper to let her true feelings show, she had never once felt the slightest urge to cry happy tears for the joyful couple. Truth be told, she had found weddings dull and tedious, for the ceremonies seemed to last forever, and the effort of feigning delight was exhausting.

She had hoped her own wedding would be something much different, but the ceremony was just as long, and she was about twenty times more uncomfortable in the stiff, sweltering cloth-of-gold with the incredibly heavy crown weighing down her head.

It didn't help that her anxious mind refused to settle down and concentrate on the priest's words. Thanks to her affair with Graesan, she did not have the virginal bride's fear of the wedding night, but it still held an enormous place in her thoughts. She had greatly enjoyed the few kisses she and Zarsha had shared, but those had all occurred before the engagement and the troubles that had come between them since. She couldn't imagine what it would feel like to kiss him now. Would she relax and abandon herself to his kisses—and all the rest of the wedding night—or would she stiffen and pull away?

Zarsha cleared his throat ever so softly, and Ellin realized she'd let her mind wander off. The priest was looking at her expectantly, and she had a moment of disorientation and panic as she tried to remember what was expected of her. She certainly hadn't heard whatever the priest had so obviously said.

She cleared her throat—the observers were going to think both she and her groom were coming down with an ague—and realized they were finally at the part where she and Zarsha would recite their vows. Thankfully, she had attended enough weddings that she could remember the start of the vows even though she hadn't heard the priest.

"I, Ellinsoltah Rah-Rhylban, in the eyes of the Creator and the Mother, pledge myself body and soul to you, Zarsha of Nandel," she began, and was surprised to feel the hint of stinging in her eyes. She'd never cried at a wedding before, and she had no intention of starting with her own!

Taking a deep breath, she continued with the modified vows she and Zarsha had worked out in conjunction with the priest. Traditional wedding vows—with their talk of female obedience—were not appropriate for a sovereign queen, and though she knew there would be some muttering and offense about this break from tradition, she had at least won the priest's grudging agreement that the vows needed to be altered.

The stinging, almost-in-tears feeling grew stronger as she listened to Zarsha reciting his vows, for it was impossible not to hear his love in his voice. She knew her eyes had to be suspiciously shiny, even as she kept the tears from falling. The nerves and anxiety and doubts had faded deep into the background, and she knew both of them meant every ceremonial word they said.

Finally, the ceremony was finished. Hand in hand, Zarsha and Ellin turned to face the cheering, joyous crowd. Ellin smiled her brightest court smile, her eyes scanning the faces in the rows closest to the altar. Some of those faces were lit with genuine happiness—Semsulin, her lord chancellor, and Kailindar, her uncle and lord chamberlain, both cared about her as a person in a way few others of the court did—but those courtiers whom she was sure had opposed the marriage were cheering just as enthusiastically, reminding her how much of court life resembled a stage play, where no one's words or expressions should be taken at face value.

The cheers continued as a company of royal guards took up their stations along both sides of the center aisle. The pews had already been infused with protection spells, and many of the jewels she and Zarsha wore contained even more active spells—including Kai shields. No spell or weapon yet invented could penetrate all the protections and harm them; the guards were merely a part of the pageantry.

As she waited for the guards to be in position, Ellin allowed her gaze to roam to the upper tier, where the commoners were packed in so tightly they could barely move. She was glad she'd put her foot down and insisted that Star be given an actual seat on the balcony, despite a few murmurs and sneers. It was nearly unbearably hot down here on the spacious ground floor. She couldn't imagine how hot it was up in the rafters with all those bodies pressed so close together.

Ellin blinked and drew in a startled breath when she thought she caught sight of a familiar face in one of the back rows—a face she could have sworn was Graesan's. She caught only the briefest glimpse before a tall man in the row in front bent to speak in the ear of the woman beside him, blocking her view of the back row. She kept her eyes riveted to the spot, but the tall man apparently had a lot to say—and Zarsha let her know with a gentle squeeze of her hand that it was time to go.

She tore her eyes away and nodded her acknowledgment, then the two of them began the long march down the aisle. She glanced back up quickly at the place where she'd seen Graesan— where she *thought* she'd seen Graesan—but though the tall man was no longer blocking her view, Graesan was nowhere in sight. Either he had left, or he had never been there in the first place.

CHAPTER FIVE

Delnamal sat on the balcony of the secluded manor house he and his mother inhabited on King Khalvin's sufferance. The heat of summer was in full force, and yet he shivered under a blanket, even with the sun beaming down on his face. His mother had suggested the fresh air and sunlight might do him good, and he'd felt too weak and miserable to argue with her. So weak, in fact, that he'd suffered the indignity of having a servant *carry* him out to the balcony and set him on the chair.

He closed his eyes, the lids too heavy to hold open, and waited for what he knew was going to happen. The mysterious illness that ravaged his body had sucked every drop of energy from him so that he could not be bothered to feel either dread or anticipation.

It felt like he was on the brink of death, with only one or two sluggish breaths left in his body. Although he'd experienced this bizarre cycle of illness many times before, he could not deny the irrational worry that this time—*this time*—his body would fail him for good.

He had been seen by three healers already—his mother would

have brought in every healer in the kingdom if Khalvin would have allowed—and each had declared himself mystified by Delnamal's illness. The first—who had been a friend of Xanvin's and unquestionably competent—had seen him in Aaltah, right after the accident. Delnamal had been unconscious at the time, and he heartily wished his mother had thought to bring the healer with them to Khalpar. Maybe as the illness developed, that worthy would have had the skill to diagnose and cure it. The two that Khalvin had grudgingly allowed Xanvin to hire had struck Delnamal as second-rate—and that was being generous. The last one had sat by Delnamal's side when the cycle reached its nadir, watching with his Mindseye in case it should reveal some heretofore unknown magic, but it had all been in vain. And Khalvin had declined to send any others.

With a groan, Delnamal did something he very rarely did, for he did not like to be reminded that he—a king's son!—had so little magical power: he opened his Mindseye.

Naturally, he expected to see what he always had in the past: his own aura of Rho shining brightly in the midst of a thin veil of other elements. Men more powerful than he were nearly blinded by the abundance of elements in the air, but his own middling talent meant his worldly vision was only somewhat impaired. But what he saw right now was like nothing he'd ever expected.

The aura of Rho that surrounded him looked thin and patchy, but that was not what caught his attention. The thing that nearly took his breath away was what *else* he saw in his own aura.

Interspersed with the motes of Rho were a dozen or so other, crystalline motes—motes that he recognized as Kai. Only magically talented men could see Kai—Delnamal was genuinely surprised that a man of his middling gifts had been able to see it in the first place—and that only when they were teetering on the brink of a violent death. And he had never even *heard* of anyone possessing more than one mote.

Swallowing hard, he closed his eyes and then opened them again—the effort requiring nearly all the strength he had left to him—but that did not make the impossible motes of Kai go away.

Clearly, his suspicion that the healers who'd seen him before were incompetent had been correct, for not one had mentioned seeing Kai in his aura. He vaguely remembered his mother saying the healer who'd first treated him had seen what he thought were shards of Kai in his vomit, but how he could have missed those Kai motes in Delnamal's aura was a mystery.

Delnamal looked downward and suffered another shock. A superstitious chill iced his spine as his gaze landed on his legs, which were propped on a footstool before him. Beneath the aura of mingled Rho and Kai, his legs were filled with branching streams of small, spherical, black motes. Streams that moved with every sluggish beat of his heart. As he stared at them, he saw that there were flashes of other colors in the depths of the black, and that rather than being perfectly round, they were faceted like crystals. A quick glance at the rest of his body showed that those streams moved through him from the tips of his toes to the tips of his fingers and everywhere in between.

Whatever those strange, unsettling motes were, they were *inside* his body. Their movement slowed as his pulse faltered, and he decided they weren't just in his body, they were in his *blood*. His stomach tried to turn over, objecting to the very thought of those black motes poisoning his blood, but he hadn't the strength even to gag. His eyes were starting to close of their own volition, and his lungs decided that taking in more air was just too much work.

Just as his eyes had almost closed, he caught sight of one of those strange black motes suddenly ballooning in size and rising into the air above him. And then it burst with a pop he could almost hear.

The outside of the mote crumbled like a pile of ash in a gust of wind, dissolving into nothingness and revealing a compressed inner core of Rho—way more motes than could possibly have fit inside the small black sphere it had once been. Those motes shot outward as if they'd been packed in under pressure, revealing yet another mote that had been hidden deep in their midst—a mote of crystalline teal and purple that was unmistakably Kai.

The black dust had dissipated as if it never existed, but the Rho and the Kai both sank downward and were absorbed into Delnamal's aura.

The moment those motes met his aura, Delnamal experienced the unmistakable surge he'd felt each time his strength had waned to its absolute nadir, when he was almost convinced he was dying. The sensation was like nothing he could describe in words. The best he could do was to say that, from the brink of nothingness, he suddenly felt as though every nerve in his body and mind came alive at once. Energy rushed through his blood, his back bowed with a strange combination of ecstasy and pain, and he felt like weeping, laughing, and screaming in anger all at once.

He knew from overhearing the servants' superstitious rumblings that he was quite a sight to behold when these "fits" overtook him, and he often recovered from them to find himself lying on the floor with his knees tucked up under his chin and his face wet with tears.

He was grateful when, this time, he came back to himself and found he was still in his chair, although his body was curled into a little ball and blood dripped from his mouth where he had bitten his lip. He had regained control of his body, but his emotions continued to riot, coming one after the other with little rhyme or reason. Fury then terror then deep bitterness. There were occasional bright flashes of joy, but these were always short-lived, overwhelmed by everything less pleasant.

The first few times it had happened, he had lost hours to gibbering incoherence, his mind fleeing helplessly from the onslaught. He imagined he might easily have gone mad if he hadn't eventually—and ever so slowly—found a way to shelter himself from the worst of the tumult. It wasn't something he did consciously, not some technique he could learn to control or call upon at will. It just happened over time that his mind fought for purchase in the overwhelming flood of emotions. At first, it could do nothing but cling helplessly, desperately, as the waters battered and bruised him. But now he seemed able to pull himself out of the flow once the worst of it had passed. These days, the tumult lasted only a few minutes before he was able to eagerly—and fully—withdraw.

He was aware that others would find his method of coping . . . unhealthy. He knew instinctively that the emotions that flooded him in these moments were not *his*—at least not *only* his. But when he withdrew from the flow, it was not just the foreign emotions he left behind. In his eyes, it was a fair trade, but of course he had no intention of explaining to anyone—least of all his mother—what he was giving up to maintain his sanity.

Shuddering, he forced himself to sit up straight, fighting his way free of the sweltering blanket he no longer needed. Sweat coated his skin, and he used the edge of the blanket to wipe it and the blood and the tears from his face.

Groaning with the effort, he pushed himself to his feet and stretched. He was a far cry from hale and hearty, but he felt so much stronger and more vigorous than he had mere moments ago that he felt almost capable of breaking into a sprint. His formerly sluggish pulse raced and he breathed deep.

Tentatively, he allowed himself to think about what he'd seen with his Mindseye, bracing in case the nausea that had tried to rise at the sight of that foreign substance in his blood should overtake him. But with his emotions comfortably distant, he experienced nothing more than curiosity when he put his mind to it.

He had no idea what those strange motes could be—he had never heard of anything remotely like them—but clearly they had something to do with the disaster at Aaltah's Well.

He remembered seeing something rising out of the Well after

Mairahsol threw herself in, and he'd seen the flash of Kai motes in that something. But his *first* impression had been of *darkness* rising from the Well, and he wondered now if what he'd seen hadn't been these impossible motes that now filled his blood— motes that *contained* Kai, but were clearly something altogether different.

Whatever had risen from the Well, it had slammed into his back when he tried to flee, lifting him bodily off the floor and smashing him into a wall as the chamber crumbled around him. By all rights, he should have died. When his mother and Oona had found him, he'd been unconscious, and he had remained so for days, even under the care of the healer.

He opened his Mindseye once more, looking at the strange motes that infused his blood. There were hundreds of them, if not thousands. And if what he had just witnessed was the same thing that happened every time he regained his strength, then it was obvious those motes were responsible for his continued life— and all those motes of Kai in his aura. Perhaps the healer in Aaltah had not seen any Kai in his aura because he had not yet begun this cycle of waxing and waning at that time.

The servants—having seen him through many of these epi- sodes over the weeks he'd been residing in Khalpar—had help- fully left his cane propped against the side of a neighboring chair. Delnamal gave the damn thing a sneer of distaste before grudg- ingly grabbing it with his gnarled, nearly useless hand. With this fresh burst of energy, he could walk unaided for the time being, but the rush would soon abandon him, and he preferred to lean on the cane rather than risk a humiliating fall.

Delnamal crossed the short distance between his chair and the edge of the balcony, setting his cane to the side and leaning his elbows on the railing as he surveyed his paltry domain.

King Khalvin no doubt expected Delnamal to feel grateful for the generous gift of this secluded manor house in the country- side. Considering the strain that had characterized their relationship since Delnamal had ascended to the throne of Aaltah, it was likely only his mother's persuasion that had won him even that much. But even with his emotions comfortably distant, he couldn't help recognizing the ignominy of his position, forced to live on his uncle's sufferance. He'd been all but exiled to this crumbling old manor house a day's travel from the closest city, with nothing but a skeleton staff of servants to see to his needs. This was not how a king ought to live. Even a king in exile.

He smiled faintly as he gently tucked that little pocket of bitterness away with all the rest of his emotions. In the old days, he would have been carried away on the wave of it and wallowed in misery for hours. Now, he could acknowledge that the bitterness existed and then shut it off as surely as he could shut off a luminant by plucking out the Rho that powered it.

A breeze rippled through the woods that surrounded the manor house—there was no town nearby, and their closest neighbor was an hour's ride away on horseback. He watched the trees sway, then felt the breeze catch at his doublet and breeches, which flapped around him. He looked down at himself in chagrin, realizing he needed to call for a tailor yet again. It had been more than a month since he'd stopped vomiting, and yet he still had little appetite, so the weight kept dropping off him. He had once been quite fat—at the time, he'd vainly thought of himself as *portly,* but when he looked at some of his unaltered clothing, the truth was undeniable. Now, he seemed to be growing thinner by the day.

A footstep sounded on the balcony behind him, and Delnamal let out a quiet sigh. It had been a long time since anyone had granted him more than a handful of minutes of privacy, and he'd been enjoying the moment of solitude.

He turned, keeping one ruined hand on the railing for support. The initial rush of his recovery was already fading, and he was unsure of his ability to stand unaided. He conjured a thin smile for his mother, who hovered anxiously in the doorway.

"I am quite all right now, Mama," he told her, preempting the question he knew was on her lips. "And I am not contemplating tossing myself off the balcony to my tragic death."

His mother bowed her head, but he saw the blush that heated her face anyway and knew he had correctly guessed the source of her anxiety. Everyone seemed to think he was wallowing in a pit of despair, but he knew they were only seeing in him what they thought they themselves might be feeling in his shoes.

He had lost . . . everything. He had been the king of one of the three great kingdoms of Seven Wells. He had had wealth, and stature, and power. He had had a beautiful wife and an infant son—both of whom had remained in Aaltah while his mother had spirited him away to safety. He had had health and strength and fully functioning hands, and he was now a frail, easily tired invalid who could barely bend his fingers enough to hold on to his cane—and that only when he wasn't on the brink of one of his strange fits. How could a man such as he not live in abject misery?

"Is there anything you need, my son?" Xanvin asked, her voice low and deferential and modest. She was, as always, the picture of demure Khalpari womanhood, and Delnamal had no doubt that she loved him still, no matter the changes in him, no matter the troubles his actions had caused them both. But there was also no doubting that she was now afraid of him, for reasons he had to admit puzzled him.

In the days before the accident, when his grip on his kingdom—and perhaps also on his sanity—had been slipping, he could see now that he'd been dangerously erratic, his temper only one incendiary word away from exploding. He'd roared and snapped and blustered and threatened, and even in the face of all that, his mother had been only cautious, not fearful, when in his presence. And yet *now* she feared him. Just because she didn't understand what was happening to him.

He wished he could tell her everything he had learned today, but she might think him delusional.

"You've already given me everything I need," he told her. He made a concerted effort to add some cadence and inflection to his voice, to sound as much like his old self as possible, and yet the slight tightening around the corners of her eyes told him he had failed. In the old days, it might have annoyed him that she found fault in the flatness of his voice, but now he merely noted and dismissed it. "You gave me life and freedom—such as it is—and a safe place to rest and gather myself. You have more than fulfilled your duties as a mother."

Xanvin bit her lip. Her hand strayed to the miniature Devotional that hung on a chain from her waist. Knowing her, there was a full-sized copy hidden somewhere in her voluminous skirts. She had always clung to the Devotional with the ferocity of a small child with a favored toy. He could almost picture her putting her thumb in her mouth while clutching the thing as if it were the answer to—and her shield from—everything that troubled her.

"I want more for you than that," she said, her voice so soft a gust of wind nearly obscured the words, if not the sentiment.

"I want more, too," he assured her, gazing out again at the dull woods that were all he could see from any window in the manor house. He wanted to look out his windows and see a teeming, busy, glorious city filled with people. People who served *him*, naturally.

"Mark my words, Mama," he said. "I will be king again."

Delnamal smiled at the look of shock in Xanvin's eyes. She had thought him caught in the throes of despair, in danger of doing himself an injury to end his pain. Now here he was declaring his intention to rule again.

"I imagine you're feeling no small amount of skepticism," he said, still smiling. He tried to take a step toward her in a moment of overconfidence. His knees threatened to buckle beneath him, and he hastily grabbed for the cane he had left leaning against the balustrade. He chuckled as he used the cane to regain his balance.

"I am well aware that I am not in any shape to reclaim my throne just yet. But my mind is clearer than it has ever been, and I believe my body will continue to get stronger."

That, he had to admit to himself, was a lie. He did not imagine there was much chance of any further recovery of his body, but it was certainly true that he was getting better at dealing with the aftereffects of his fits. He doubted his ability to retake his kingdom when he was prone to such unseemly public displays, but he believed that once he had that under control, he'd be in a stronger position. And surely he could make great use of all those Kai motes in his aura.

"I was rash and impetuous and so desperate for approval that I displayed no judgment whatsoever," he said. "But I see the error of my ways now, and I will not make the same mistakes."

"How can you possibly hope to retake Aaltah?" Xanvin asked with a shake of her head.

He was certain his mother was even now calculating exactly what she needed to say to talk him out of this ridiculous quest. Once upon a time, her lack of faith in his abilities would have sent him into a rage—or at least a pout—but now it solicited no more than a flicker of annoyance, easily shunted aside.

"You let me worry about that," he said. "It will naturally require a great deal of planning and preparation. But believe me when I tell you it will happen. I will take back my kingdom. I will take back my wife and my child. And my mother will once more be the Dowager Queen of Aaltah, with all the comforts and respect that goes with it."

That Xanvin thought he was delusional was clear from the look on her face, although she did not attempt to reason with him. Most likely, she hoped this was some passing whim that would go away before it had the chance to do any damage.

But it was not a whim. He did not fully understand what was happening to him or why, but he *did* know it made him far more powerful than anyone could ever have imagined. He did not know yet exactly what he was going to do with that power, but it would surely be something glorious.

One day, he would be the greatest king Seven Wells had ever seen. All he needed was time and patience. And those were two things he had in abundance.

Kailee was on the verge of retiring for the night when Tynthanal finally returned to the royal apartments after yet another long and grueling day. If theirs had been a traditional marriage, she imagined she might have felt very put out indeed at how little time her new husband spent with her, but his duties were such that he could have spent all the hours of the night working and still found more to do. Especially now that he was trying to cram a lifetime's study of spell crafting into whatever stolen hours he could find.

"You weren't waiting up for me, were you?" he asked when she rose from her chair to greet him.

"No," she lied easily. "I just wasn't sleepy yet." A yawn threatened to give her away, and she held it off by sheer force of will.

To make her lie entirely convincing, she knew she should engage in some pleasant small talk, but anxiousness and impatience got the best of her. "Did they find anything in the Well chamber today?"

It was taking longer than Kailee would have hoped for the workers to finish clearing the debris and reach whatever magic items she suspected lay beneath.

Tynthanal hesitated just a beat before answering, and although she could not see the expression on his face, she imagined he was giving her a look of gentle reproach. She wasn't even sure why she had lied and said she wasn't waiting, except that she knew he thought she was being childishly optimistic in her hopes that the evidence found in the rubble would clear Mairah's name.

"We did indeed," he told her. "Several things, in fact. We found a bag that was clearly Mairahsol's, and also a wineskin filled with some kind of potion. I have sent it to the grand magus to analyze, although I suspect he will not have great success. He is one of those stubborn individuals who is still convinced of the inferiority of women's magic, and I suspect the potion contains feminine elements, which he cannot see."

"Then why did you send it to him?" she asked, quite reasonably. "*I* would probably have more chance of figuring out what it is than he, and the Women's Well Academy would almost certainly be your best option."

"I know," Tynthanal agreed. "But I need the grand magus's full and enthusiastic cooperation if I hope to fix our Well, and he's the sort who would take offense at what he would see as a lack of confidence." He made a short sound of frustration. "Pandering to fragile egos has never been my favorite thing, but I know I must learn to do it if I'm to have any success as regent. When he's satisfied that he has had an adequate opportunity to examine it, then I will send it on to Alys."

Kailee was equally frustrated, though she wasn't sure why she was so anxious to get her hands on that potion. She had crammed in as much magical training as she possibly could during the short months that she had lived in Women's Well, but that hardly made her an expert. Mairah had been practicing magic for most of her life, and though Kailee's talent was comparable, her experience was not.

"I can bring it to you first," Tynthanal said, and she could hear the smile in his voice. "I know you will want to look at it."

She shook her head ruefully. "You read me too easily," she quipped, even as she cherished a spot of warmth in her belly. Her blindness—or, more accurately, the milky whiteness of her eyes that told all the world that her Mindseye was always shockingly open—had made her all but invisible to those around her for most of her life. Even her father, who unquestionably loved and cherished her, rarely *saw* her the way this virtual stranger did.

"I can read you even when you're not in the room," he teased, holding up one of his hands. "Which is why I brought the notes we found stashed in Mairahsol's bags back to the apartments with me."

Kailee let out a glad little cry and couldn't resist the temptation to give her husband a quick hug. Immediately on the heels of that burst of enthusiasm came the realization that it was already late in the night, and that one thing she was *not* capable of doing with her Mindsight was reading. She rocked back on her heels and bit her lip.

"I . . . I don't suppose you've read them already and can tell me what they say?" she asked tentatively.

Tynthanal sighed. "I've glanced at them," he told her, "but only long enough to tell that interpreting them will not be a quick and easy task. There are more than fifty pages, and they appear to be in no discernible order. I can say with certainty that Mairahsol had no intention for anyone but herself to read and make sense of them."

"Oh," was all Kailee could think of to say.

"I thought perhaps you and I might go over them together. I think reading them aloud—or at least *trying* to—might help us make sense of them."

"Really?" she asked, cocking her head at him and hardly daring to hope he was being sincere.

"Why do you sound so surprised?" he asked gently. "You know more of women's magic than I, and you certainly were closer to Mairahsol than anyone. Who would be better for this purpose than you?"

Kailee's throat threatened to close up, and her eyes stung. She rarely gave in to the temptation of tears, but her husband's surprising kindness and respect nearly undid her. She reached out and put a hand on his arm, admiring the feel of his firm muscles beneath her palm.

"Thank you," she whispered, embarrassed at how overcome she was by this small gesture that suggested he saw her as a valuable human being. She had not fully appreciated how much her family and even the household servants had treated her like a helpless child until Tynthanal had shown her what it was like to be respected as an intelligent adult. The urge to do more than touch his arm nearly moved her to incaution, but she forcibly stopped herself from throwing her arms around his neck. She had already hugged him once, and doing so a second time might be uncomfortable for both of them.

Tynthanal was her husband in name only, and destined to remain that way. He could barely speak Chanlix's name without his grief and longing leaking into his voice—a reminder that even if she *wanted* to come between them, she couldn't. There was no room in Tynthanal's heart for her.

She would continue to be his wife and his friend and his ally, but she must never allow herself even a moment's illusion that she might be anything more.

"Shall we sit down and make ourselves comfortable?" Tynthanal asked. "If you're half as tired as I am, we won't be able to get very far tonight, but we can at least get started."

Swallowing a lump that tried to form in her throat, Kailee forced a bright smile. "Yes, of course."

CHAPTER SIX

Star gave Ellin one last warm, encouraging smile before slipping out the bedroom door and closing it behind her. Ellin shook her head at that closed door, wishing she could somehow learn not to be so transparent to her lady's maid. Most people who looked at her saw nothing but calm self-assurance, but even with her court mask firmly in place, Star always knew when she was troubled. Or nervous.

"There is no reason to be nervous!" Ellin scolded herself. She was not a blushing virgin bride, and the activities of a wedding night were not altogether unfamiliar. She had never lain with *Zarsha*, it was true, and yet the sweating palms and racing heartbeat had taken her entirely by surprise. She closed her eyes and breathed deeply, trying to gain control of herself before the door to Zarsha's adjoining bedchamber opened. He was the only other person who saw through her as thoroughly as Star did, and she couldn't bear to have him see her like this.

Wiping her palms on the diaphanous white nightdress that revealed far too much even with the extra cover of the dressing gown, Ellin drew in one deep breath after another, hoping to find some semblance of calm. She winced when the hinges of the adjoining suite door squealed, then turned to face the man who was now her husband without having found any hint of the calm she sought.

Zarsha wore a heavy brocade dressing gown—brocade? He never wore anything so ornamental!—and a pair of velvet slippers. The dressing gown was cinched tightly around him so that she could not tell if he wore a nightshirt underneath.

With a grin that looked a little strained, Zarsha glanced at the hinges that had so loudly announced his entrance. "It seems the servants missed one detail when they were preparing the consort's suite for me," he said in a tone that was meant to convey dry humor. But Ellin could have sworn she heard a shadow of her own nerves in his voice.

"Perhaps they merely meant to ensure that you would not sneak up on me during the night," she quipped with forced levity.

He chuckled. "And perhaps we'd best both dispense with attempts at humor. We're neither one of us in the right frame of mind for it."

Ellin bit her lip and rubbed her hands on her nightdress again. Did Zarsha being nervous as well make her feel better, or worse? She honestly couldn't tell. Her body ached with exhaustion after the long and grueling day, and yet she suspected she would get no wink of sleep tonight. She could only imagine how she would have felt if she were a virgin on top of it all. She'd been nervous when she'd slept with Graesan the first time, but it had been nothing like this.

"We don't have to do this tonight," Zarsha said quietly, and she realized he was still standing in the doorway as if poised to retreat. "We've both had a very long day."

She dug up a scrap of her courage and looked him in the eye. "Do you not *want* to do this tonight?" she asked, though she knew the answer. Zarsha had made no secret that he desired her.

His eyes took a leisurely tour of her barely concealed body, and there was no missing the lust that flared in them, although he still hesitated in the doorway. "I want to," he said simply. "But I want *you* to want to, as well."

The corner of Ellin's mouth twitched, this time with genuine— if perhaps a little harsh—humor. "Somewhere in Nandel, your uncle is squirming with some unexplained discomfort." Men of Nandel were taught never to take a woman's wants and needs into consideration. And they certainly wouldn't dress in *brocade*.

Zarsha snorted softly. "I am no longer a Nandelite, but a man of Rhozinolm. And even when I owed my allegiance to Nandel, I never would have dreamed of taking a woman to bed by force. Even my wife."

She frowned and cocked her head. "So what would our wedding night have been like if all had gone according to plan long ago and you'd taken me back to Nandel to marry me?"

"You mean back when you hated me?"

Shame heated her cheeks, and she dropped her gaze briefly to the floor. She was not at all proud of how she had treated Zarsha back in those days, when she had been so stubbornly in love with Graesan that she'd preemptively declared Zarsha the enemy and disliked him on principle. She wanted to assure him she'd never hated him, but she wasn't sure that would be the truth.

"Back when I didn't know you," she said. "When I hated what you represented and didn't try to see who you really were."

"I would never have forced you to my bed," he assured her.

"Why not?" she asked with a curious cock of her head. "Nandel is hardly the only place where such practices exist. My own mother taught me that a wife is not free to refuse her husband's attentions, and that was long before our engagement was planned."

Zarsha looked away, fidgeting with the sash on his robe. "It's just . . . not my way."

If he hoped being evasive would dampen her curiosity, he was sorely mistaken. Especially when she could so clearly see the flush rising in his cheeks. "I know things aren't fully right between us," she said softly, "but surely you know you can confide in me."

"It's an ugly story," he warned, meeting her eyes only briefly.

She bit her lip. "You don't have to tell me if you don't want to."

He cleared his throat. "When I was twelve or thirteen, my father was stationed in the Midlands. I was working with a fencing tutor at the time, and he had a daughter who was only a couple of years older than I. She was . . ." His blush deepened. "Let's just say that boys my age tended to make asses of ourselves whenever we caught a glimpse of her."

Ellin crossed her arms, suddenly regretting having asked for the story, afraid it would lead somewhere her mind did not wish to go.

"Anyway," Zarsha continued, "my tutor overheard a conversation between me and some other boys. We were being callous brutes, and the conversation shames me to this day. Even then, I did not find the idea of taking a woman by force appealing, but I made as many lewd and boorish comments as they, trying to get a laugh. I was the only Nandelite in our little circle of friends, and I put a shameful amount of effort into trying to fit in."

He shook his head. "None of us had any idea my tutor overheard, and I could not understand why he seemed so harsh and angry with me during our next lesson. When I finally dared to ask him, he . . ." Zarsha shuddered. "I won't describe the details, but he put on a very convincing show of trying to rape me."

Ellin gasped and covered her mouth, eyes going wide in horror.

"He didn't actually do anything," Zarsha hurried to reassure her. "As soon as he knew I understood what he was threatening, he let go of me and asked me to imagine what it would be like to be a girl and live constantly with such a specter hanging over me." He shuddered, finally meeting her eyes once more. "I was too embarrassed to tell anyone what happened, though I stopped the fencing lessons until we moved once more. Once the initial shock wore off . . . Well, let's just say that I understand too well the horror and hopelessness of being overpowered like that and would never do it to someone else. It was a hard lesson, cruelly delivered, but it was certainly effective."

Ellin's heart ached for Zarsha's loss of innocence, but she couldn't help admiring him for using that trauma to make himself a better, kinder man. Not everyone would have taken the lesson so . . . constructively.

Zarsha forced a grin as he smoothed the dressing gown. "I am nothing if not a master of pillow talk, wouldn't you say?"

She took a couple of steps closer to him. "Thank you for trusting me enough to tell me about it," she said, hoping the confession signaled the beginning of true forgiveness. He reached out and took her hand, raising it to his lips.

"Do you want me to go?" he whispered as he brushed a kiss across her palm.

Ellin looked into those striking blue eyes of his. Eyes that had already shaken off the terrible memory and darkened with desire.

"I think . . ." she said, then bit her lip quickly before finding her courage once more. "I think that is not what I want. Not at all."

"I am delighted to hear that," he rasped, then pulled her into his arms.

Alys admired Chanlix's fortitude as the Lady Chancellor of Women's Well led her through the halls of the Academy and into the office she still maintained at the back of the building. She had given up her larger, grander office to the woman who had been named grand magus in her place—a former abigail by the name of Rusha, who had won the honor because of her impressive magical talents. It was Rusha who had invented the fearsome spell they called Vengeance—a spell that could only be triggered by women's Kai and that struck its male victims permanently impotent. Both Alys and Chanlix were somewhat leery of the appointment, for Rusha's judgment and ethics had proven questionable in the past, when she'd tested Vengeance on a man who was to all intents and purposes an innocent. Rusha seemed to have blossomed and changed since being freed from the Abbey, however, and both Alys and Chanlix had agreed she deserved a second chance.

In the late stages of Alys's two pregnancies, she'd found it cumbersome and exhausting even to balance the household books—something she could ordinarily do while practically asleep—yet so far Chanlix showed no sign of slowing down.

"Are you *sure* you shouldn't be taking it easy?" Alys asked, unable to stop herself. Chanlix had already spent the entire day fulfilling her duties as chancellor, and Alys felt guilty asking her to come to the Academy after hours. However, she required discretion, and there was no one she trusted more than Chanlix.

Chanlix gave her a look of exasperation as she gestured Alys into her office, leaving the honor guards who dogged her footsteps to wait in the hall. "*Really,* Your Royal Highness," Chanlix said, "you are worse than a husband. I'm pregnant, not ill."

Alys swallowed the urge to fuss more, despite an almost overwhelming need. As hale and hearty as Chanlix seemed, they were both well aware that a pregnancy for a woman of Chanlix's age was fraught with potential dangers. In private, Alys would admit to herself that she was terrified on her friend's behalf, although she tried her best not to let that terror show.

Chanlix closed the office door and waddled over to her seat behind the desk. She sat with an audible sigh of relief and rested her hands on her swollen belly. The woman fairly radiated contentment, though Alys was sure she was more than ready to have the ordeal of childbirth behind her.

"You can't expect me not to fuss," Alys said with a fond smile. "I've never been an auntie before."

Chanlix raised an eyebrow at her, and Alys grimaced.

"Delnamal's child doesn't count," Alys said, though it was uncharitable of her to hold the infant's parentage against him. "I may technically be his aunt, but I will never be his auntie."

"He's an innocent baby," Chanlix chided her. "And he is your blood. Don't you think—"

Alys waved her friend's words off. "I won't pretend it's fair," she said, "and maybe someday I'll be able to look at the child and not see Delnamal. But that day has not yet come."

Chanlix flashed her a sympathetic smile, and something inside Alys relaxed. She suffered from not a small amount of guilt for her feelings toward the infant king, and it was comforting to find that Chanlix—despite her gentle disapproval—did not condemn her.

"Well, let's have it, then," Chanlix said, reaching her hand across the desk.

Reluctantly, not sure she wanted to know the results of this test, Alys withdrew the vial of dried blood that had arrived via flier from Aalwell. The blood Tynthanal had found outside the Well chamber. The blood that her gut already insisted came from Delnamal.

She laid the vial in Chanlix's palm, then clasped her hands together in front of her to keep from fidgeting as Chanlix prepared the potion that held a modified version of the bloodline spell. Instead of testing whether the two individuals whose blood was combined could produce children, the spell would test whether the two individuals were related by blood.

Chanlix activated the potion, then scraped about half of the dried blood into an empty vial. She held the vial out to Alys.

"Do you need a pin?" Chanlix inquired as Alys took the vial.

"No," Alys said, removing a pin from her headdress. She quickly pricked her finger, then squeezed a drop of blood out and into the vial. Her stomach gave a little lurch as she watched that drop ooze down the side of the vial, making a visible path through the dry flakes that clung to the glass. She was not usually squeamish, but somehow the sight of her own blood mixing with what could be Delnamal's made something inside her recoil.

Handing the vial with the two samples to Chanlix, Alys replaced the pin in her headdress and stuck her finger in her mouth, though the bleeding had stopped already. She couldn't bear to watch as Chanlix poured the activated potion into the vial and swirled everything around. She wasn't even properly sure she could say what she wanted the test to reveal. She had been devastated to learn of Delnamal's death, heartbroken at the realization that she would never have her revenge, never be able to confront him and punish him for Jinnell's death. But there had also been an undeniable relief at knowing he was no longer out there, no longer threatening her life and the lives of everyone she still cared for. If he had survived the disaster at the Well . . .

A soft, dismayed groan drew Alys's eyes to the vial in Chanlix's hand. A vial that was now filled with milky white fluid, which signaled a match. She could feel Chanlix looking at her face, gauging her reaction, but she could not tear her eyes away from the vial.

"So," Alys said softly. "Now we know."

Chanlix put the vial down and shook her head. "We know this is his blood," she countered. "That is *all* we know."

"He is alive," Alys said with a certainty she could not explain. "Xanvin spirited him away somehow. I am *sure* of it."

While Chanlix didn't look as positive as Alys felt, there was a certain grim resignation to her voice when she said, "Perhaps Tynthanal can have another talk with Oona. If Delnamal survived, she would know. She would have to."

"You may be right," Alys said. "But though I was never especially close with my stepmother, I did grow up in her household, and I know how she thinks. I'm sure she was not happy that Delnamal married a woman she considered beneath him, and she was likely as scandalized as anyone at court that they did not wait until she was out of mourning to wed. I wouldn't be surprised if she'd failed to consult Oona before spiriting Delnamal away.

"Still, it can't hurt to ask," she concluded. "I will contact Tynthanal via talker as soon as I return to the palace. Do you . . . do you want to be there?"

Chanlix smiled and stroked her belly, though it was impossible to miss the flare of grief in her eyes. "I think not. For the time being, I think a little distance is good for both of us. He needs to focus on Kailee and making the marriage work, and he won't do that if he keeps mooning over me."

It was on the tip of Alys's tongue to argue. In her estimation, Tynthanal had no interest in trying to make his marriage to Kailee into anything real, and distance was not going to change that. But perhaps Chanlix needed the illusion to help herself move on.

"He will ask after you," Alys warned, because she would be shocked if he didn't.

"Then tell him the baby and I are both well, and leave it at that," Chanlix said firmly. "When the babe is born, I will be more accommodating, but until then . . ." She shrugged. "It's just better this way." Her voice cracked ever so slightly, belying the calm pragmatism of her words.

Alys's already broken heart broke a little more for her brother and her friend.

Living on her father's estate in Rhozinolm, Kailee had spent an inordinate portion of her life struggling with boredom. She had rarely been allowed to leave the estate, and when there were parties or dinners, she was forbidden to attend. Not that she would have wanted to, for it would have been impossible to ignore the discomfort the nobility of Rhozinolm showed around her. The only true social life she had known had been during her brief stay in Women's Well, and she had never realized how deeply she'd hungered for it. Until now, when it was denied her once again.

Oh, she'd known what she was giving up when she'd agreed to—nay, *insisted upon*—coming to Aaltah to support her husband. But it turned out that returning to the solitude of her old life was a great deal harder than she'd been prepared for.

The only saving grace was that Tynthanal refused to treat her like an embarrassing secret. She joined him for every dinner, every ball, every reception, and he forcibly included her in every conversation. But he couldn't force the nobility to accept her, and being tolerated was almost as bad as being shunned.

Her days were long and tedious and dull. Several times, she'd tried inviting ladies who had seemed marginally more accepting to join her for tea, but those invitations had been politely declined. She didn't dare tell Tynthanal she'd even made them, for she was sure that if he learned her invitations were being rejected, he'd intervene and somehow force the ladies to attend.

It was her lady's maid—a kind, matronly woman who had never shown any sign of being discomfited by her blindness— who had suggested she extend an invitation to Queen Oona, who was now considered the dowager queen with Queen Xanvin's whereabouts officially unknown.

Oona was nearly as much of a social pariah as Kailee, although for very different reasons. From what Kailee had heard, she'd been a respected and popular member of the minor nobility, but her reputation had taken some damage when she had married Delnamal without having completed a year of mourning for her previous husband. It had not helped that Delnamal had been a wildly unpopular king—and after the disaster at the Well, Oona had lost any social standing she might have had.

In her darkest moments, Kailee had believed Oona would also issue a polite rejection. Even after the dowager responded in the affirmative, Kailee had been sure she would cancel at the last moment. So when a footman appeared in the informal parlor of the royal apartments and informed her that her guest had arrived, she felt momentarily flummoxed.

"Shall I show her in?" the footman asked when Kailee's surprise stole her voice.

"Yes, of course," she hurried to say. "And bring the tea tray, if you please."

Kailee was not used to feeling shy, but she found herself fussing at her clothes, smoothing nonexistent creases and touching her hair to make sure it was all tidy. She heard footsteps in the hall, then saw the white glow surrounding two figures who were moving closer to her. One figure was smaller than the other, and Kailee knew that would be Oona, so she turned her smile in that direction.

"Your Majesty," she said, dipping into a respectful curtsy. "How good of you to come."

"It was good of you to invite me, Your Highness," Oona replied. Unlike many others at court, there was no sneering undertone in Oona's voice when she used the honorific. "There are those who believe that a woman in mourning should not receive any social invitations."

Kailee scoffed, although there was some truth to the dowager's words. The older generation considered it unseemly for a woman in mourning to be seen to enjoy her life in any way, but thankfully the custom of socially burying a grieving widow was falling out of practice.

"I'm afraid I'm shockingly uninterested in doing what is considered proper when I don't believe it's right," she said, displaying the candor that many found as distasteful as her blindness.

Oona chuckled softly. "I have heard that about you."

Kailee smiled. "No doubt. Won't you have a seat?"

She waved Oona to a comfortable sofa and took a seat herself on the opposite end, neatly stepping around the sharp corners of the coffee table. Oona said nothing, but Kailee could almost feel her curiosity.

"When one cannot see inanimate objects," she said, "one learns to make mental maps of where said inanimate objects reside."

In Rhozinolm, where she had been forced to pretend her Mindseye was demurely closed at all times, relying on those mental maps had been the only way she'd been able to navigate her father's estate. But here in Aaltah, Tynthanal had already begun making different accommodations for her in the royal apartments, and he had dismissed the fiction of her total blindness from day one.

Thinking a certain level of candor might help her create a bond with the dowager queen, Kailee decided to be more open with Oona than she might ordinarily have been.

"It helps that the table is made of Aalwood," she admitted. "There's enough Aal in it that I can see it clearly." The wood was so densely packed with Aal she could even make out the floral design carved into its trim.

In any other kingdom, using Aalwood for an inanimate piece of furniture would have been an extravagance. As prized as the wood was for its beauty, it was its potential for magic that made it Aaltah's most prized export. But here in Aaltah, it grew plentifully enough for Kailee not to feel impossibly self-indulgent furnishing the apartment with it.

Oona's aura shifted ever so slightly, showing just the tiniest hint of discomfort with the idea that Kailee's Mindseye was open. Kailee stifled a sigh of disappointment and suffered a pang of longing for the acceptance she had experienced in Women's Well. Certainly there were people living there who still scorned women's magic and felt uncomfortable with it being openly embraced, but they had been very much a minority.

The discomfort of the moment was broken when the footman

returned with the tea service. Both Kailee and Oona sat quietly while the service was laid out and a cup of fragrant tea poured for each of them.

"You were aware that my Mindseye is always open, were you not?" Kailee asked when the footman departed. Oona's teacup rattled in her saucer, betraying her surprise at Kailee's indelicate words.

"Yes," Oona murmured, taking a hasty sip of tea.

Kailee raised her own cup to her lips, felt the heat radiating from its contents, and decided she would save herself the scalding. She put the tea on the Aalwood table, giving Oona another moment to come to grips with her bold conversational style.

Oona sighed, then put her own cup down, as well. "Clearly, we are not mincing words today, so I suppose I'll come right out and ask you: am I here because Prince Tynthanal asked you to speak with me?"

Kailee felt the heat rising in her cheeks and mentally chided herself for not realizing how Oona might take the invitation. She was well aware that Tynthanal's first gentle attempt to ask Oona about Xanvin's mysterious departure had not gone especially well. It was no surprise Oona thought he had assigned his wife the task, and that the invitation to tea had been more of a summons than a social call.

"Not at all," she hastened to assure Oona. "I believe my husband will want to speak with you again, but I had no ulterior motives in inviting you." Now that Alysoon had confirmed that the blood they had found at the Well was Delnamal's, Tynthanal had every intention of questioning Oona once more about the night the Well had been damaged, but so far he had not had a chance.

Oona shifted in her seat, her skirts rustling with the restless movement. "Even women who were once my closest friends no longer make social calls or invite me to do so," she said with no small amount of suspicion in her voice. "I find it hard to credit that the wife of the prince regent would do so without reason."

Kailee considered her response for only a handful of heartbeats before she chose brutal honesty, as was her wont. "I didn't say it was without *reason,* just that it was without ulterior motive." She held up her hands in a helpless gesture. "I know no one here but my husband, and I have yet to meet anyone who will speak more than the barest minimum to me because my eyes make them uncomfortable. Every invitation I have sent out has been declined. Conventional wisdom suggested that you would not wish to socialize with me when you so distrust my husband, but I make a habit of ignoring conventional wisdom, so I invited you to join me for tea."

She did not mention her awareness that Oona was as much of a social outcast as she herself was, but she was sure Oona could make that inference on her own.

"There is nothing more sinister in my motives than loneliness," Kailee finished. Deeming the tea was finally cool enough to drink, she retrieved her cup and took a cautious sip.

Oona did the same, and Kailee had the suspicion they were both using that moment to gather themselves. Kailee wasn't sure what she'd expected of this visit, but she'd certainly been hoping for something less awkward and uncomfortable.

"I did not mean to be unkind," Oona said softly.

Kailee blinked. "You weren't. I should have realized how you would interpret the invitation and made it clear that it was purely social. I'm used to being a nobody, not the wife of a prince regent."

Oona scoffed. "I don't imagine you were ever a *nobody.*"

"I might as well have been," Kailee retorted. "For as long as I can remember, people said—within my hearing—that I belonged in the Abbey. That I was an embarrassment who should be kept out of sight. I'm sure there are a great many people in this court who feel the same, and I have no doubt that people are even now muttering that Tynthanal should divorce me."

Kailee knew for a fact that her father was terrified that such would happen. Kailindar never would have agreed to let her marry Tynthanal if he hadn't been under the impression that she would live in Women's Well, where divorced women were not forced into an abbey. Just as she knew that Tynthanal would never condemn her to the Abbey of Aaltah.

"Anyway," Kailee continued, "my point is that I am not used to guarding my words or my actions, and sometimes that makes me careless, for which I apologize."

"You've no need to apologize," Oona assured her. "I was not alarmed by your invitation."

Kailee grinned. "Merely suspicious."

Oona coughed delicately and took a sip of her tea.

"We are sisters-in-law," Kailee said. "I have a feeling we are both in need of allies at court, and that we can help each other."

"That may be," Oona agreed. "But though I refuse to hold with the old traditions and lock myself away for a year, I also don't want to make myself vulnerable to even more gossip. One visit for tea will be seen by many as obedience to a royal command, but I must be circumspect. I don't wish to be unkind, but . . ."

Kailee told herself to ignore the stab of disappointment at yet another rebuff. "But being seen socializing with me would be another black mark on your record."

Oona sighed. "The court can be a vicious place when you are in disfavor."

"You don't have to explain that to me," Kailee reminded her, and was unable to keep the edge out of her voice. She should *not* be allowing this to hurt her feelings. She'd known what she was getting into when she'd come to Aaltah, and had always counted herself as strong and resilient. But it seemed her stern mental talking-to did nothing to ease the ache of rejection.

CHAPTER SEVEN

Delnamal emerged from the bridle path that led through the woods and let out a quiet sigh of relief to see the manor house. His legs were groaning in protest at what had turned out to be—for his frail body, at least—an epic journey that had pushed him to his breaking point. Leaning heavily on his cane, he took a moment to breathe slowly and deeply, resting up for the final effort of making his way home.

He grimaced. The manor house was *not* home, would never be his home. It was merely a way station, a place to stay safely hidden while he recuperated. His home, his *true* home, was in Aaltah, and today's successful walk—however taxing it might have been—proved that he was ready to begin contemplating how he might restore himself to his former glory. He doubted he would ever come close to regaining the strength he had once taken for granted, but he had now gotten into the habit of forcing himself to exercise every time he had the strength to do so. Today's walk had been the longest he had yet managed, and the improvement was heartening. He could already feel his strength ebbing, knew that by this evening he would have another one of his fits. But he could clearly see that his exercise regime was strengthening him. Now, he didn't lose all his progress when the cycle of waxing and waning hit its nadir.

When the manor house was in sight, Delnamal found that he had pushed his body to its absolute limits by walking the looping bridle trail that was, all told, less than a mile long. His progress might be noticeable and heartening, but he had the stamina of a sickly old man.

He had to stop for rest three times before he reached the veranda, and at that point his legs gave out entirely. He collapsed into an uncomfortable metal garden chair and closed his eyes as his heart pounded and he drew in one labored breath after another. He was thankful his mother and the servants stayed inside. Perhaps he had *finally* trained them to stop asking if he was all right every five minutes. Their hovering was driving him mad, and though his temper no longer rose to the surface with the same ease and frequency it once had, he was still capable of calling it up at will—as the footman who had last tried to give him unwanted help had discovered. Delnamal suspected his mother had sold some of her jewelry to bribe the man into silence over the injuries Delnamal had given him; his cane, he found, could inflict a surprising amount of damage even wielded by frail hands.

Slowly, Delnamal's heart rate calmed and his breathing eased. A temperate breeze rustled the leaves around him, the soft susurrus accompanied by the occasional chirping of birds. Delnamal usually paid no heed to the sounds of country life, but with his limbs throbbing from exhaustion, they produced a pleasantly soothing backdrop that had his mind drifting toward sleep despite the torturous discomfort of the metal chair.

A much louder, closer sound jerked him awake, and he turned to glare at the tiny songbird in a cage that hung from a hook in the veranda's ceiling. The little blue puffball made an unholy racket for something so small, and his mother had brought it outside precisely because the sound of its song grated on Delnamal's nerves. He glared at the thing as it continued to caterwaul, but his body still felt too exhausted to contemplate moving inside to escape the noise. He glanced over his shoulder at the manor house door, for once hoping that his mother was hovering and would come remove the annoyance. But of course, when he *wanted* her to hover, she was nowhere to be seen.

Delnamal shook his head at the bird, unable to comprehend how anyone could find that constant chatter pleasant. He certainly wasn't going to fall asleep while the creature insisted on singing—though perhaps he should be grateful for that. He didn't imagine his body would appreciate even a short sleep on this damn chair.

Unable to sleep and unwilling to make his way back into the house, Delnamal opened his Mindseye to examine once more the mystery that filled him inside and out. He now kept a mental inventory of the Kai motes in his aura and had confirmed that their number increased by one each time he suffered a fit. The sight of all that Kai made his mind spin with possibilities, and he was now accustomed enough to the black motes moving through his blood that the sight of them no longer disturbed him.

He wanted to spend some quiet time contemplating his future, planning out how to use all that glorious Kai. However, the damn bird was still yodeling away, the constant noise making it hard for him to think. He turned to glare once more in its general direction—and that was when he experienced yet another shock.

At the center of the aura of Rho that surrounded the bird hovered a tiny, spherical mote that looked just like the ones pulsing through his blood.

As weak as he still felt, Delnamal scraped up enough strength to rise to his feet. Leaning heavily on his cane, he crossed the short distance between himself and the birdcage until his nose was practically touching the latched door so he could get a closer look.

There was no question that the mote in the bird's body and the motes in Delnamal's blood were the same. Both looked like spheres from a distance, their tiny facets only visible upon closer examination. And both occasionally flashed with color from somewhere deep inside.

On impulse, Delnamal reached up to unlatch the door to the birdcage. His hands were barely functional, the latch a severe challenge to his dexterity, but eventually he managed—more by luck than by skill—to open it.

The bird made a sound of alarm, and he heard the frantic flutter of its wings as it tried to fly away, the faceted mote moving with it.

He could not have said what compelled him to do such a thing, but he reached toward the mote, his finger hitting a feathered breast. The bird pecked at his hand, but the pain barely registered in his mind as his hand suddenly passed through the feathers and flesh and touched the mysterious mote.

Delnamal pinched the tiny mote between his thumb and forefinger. The bird went suddenly still and silent. He pulled the tiny crystal toward him, meaning to examine it more closely.

There was a last peep of protest, and then a soft thump. The mote crumbled in his fingers, the black outer shell fragmenting into a dustlike cloud that quickly dissipated. A puff of Rho—much smaller than the one that emerged from the motes Delnamal had seen burst within himself—spread out of the broken mote, revealing a miniature Kai crystal within. The Rho and the Kai both drifted into Delnamal's aura. He shuddered as emotion surged in his breast and his heart sped. His legs gained strength even as his eyes pricked with tears.

The effect was brief and less overwhelming than the bursting of one of the motes within his own blood, but based on the surge of energy and the slight brightening of the Rho in his aura, he guessed he'd gained another hour or two of vitality before he teetered on the brink of death once more. Disappointingly, the miniature Kai drifted downward after it hit Delnamal's aura, sinking slowly and inevitably into the earth. But considering how much Kai he had already gathered—and how much more he stood to gain as the motes in his blood continued to burst and fuel him—the disappointment was brief.

Rubbing his fingers together where the faceted mote had once been, Delnamal closed his Mindseye. He was not surprised to see the bird's lifeless body on the cage's floor. The pretty blue breast was entirely unmarked, and no one looking at it would have any idea that the bird had not died of natural causes.

Kailee's eyelids were getting heavy, and she shook her head to try to stave off sleep as she reached for the cup of tea on the side table. The only prolonged private time she and her husband had together was during the stolen moments before bed, and so Kailee waited up for him each night, no matter how tempting the lure of sleep. The need to finish deciphering Mairah's notes helped her stay awake.

Although the notes were jumbled and disorganized and, according to Tynthanal, scribbled in a hand that seemed almost deliberately hard to read, they had learned some shocking information so far, although Kailee could not say they were any closer to understanding what was wrong with Aaltah's Well.

When Mairah had fled Women's Well, she'd taken with her a potion that she claimed, when added to a seer's poison, would allow a seer to trigger a vision of a past event. The claim had been met with a good deal of skepticism—even Kailee, who knew and liked the woman so many others reviled, had thought the claim either an exaggeration or an outright lie. But if it was a lie, it was one Mairah had committed herself to heart and soul.

According to the notes, Delnamal had forced Mairah to take the potion herself with a powerful seer's poison she'd feared might kill her. Instead, the dangerous cocktail had allowed her to learn more about how the Blessing was cast.

Neither Tynthanal nor Kailee was sure whether to believe the fantastical story. Mairah claimed that there was a special kind of Kai that could only be formed by the willing sacrifice of a woman. The three women who had cast the Blessing had each taken her own life, forming a unique and especially powerful mote of this sacrificial Kai that had fueled the spell they'd used to change the nature of Rho and make it impossible for a woman to conceive or carry children against her will.

According to Mairah, a spell cast using sacrificial Kai could affect a Well, although the notes also stated that the introduction of men's Kai to a Well could have catastrophic results. Mairah claimed that in the course of developing her potion, she'd triggered a vision that showed her all of Aaltah reduced to a wasteland and that this would be the result of masculine Kai being introduced into the Well.

The notes included the formula for Mairah's seer's poison additive—which Tynthanal had already arranged to send to Women's Well for analysis—but that was the last portion of the notes Kailee and Tynthanal had been able to make sense of so far.

After the section about the Blessing, the notes devolved into what seemed to both of them like little more than gibberish. There were *suggestions* that the notes pertained to a spell designed to undo what Mairah called the Curse, and there was a hint that whatever spell she was crafting would be triggered with the sacrificial Kai, but that was about all they'd been able to make out. Kailee felt convinced that the sudden lack of clarity had been no accident—that Mairah had been using her notes to try to convince others that she was genuinely attempting to undo the Blessing, but that her purpose was something else entirely.

Unfortunately, Kailee had not yet come up with even a guess as to what that something else might be. She had suggested that tonight, when Tynthanal read through the notes aloud again, he recopy all the sections that felt vaguely coherent so that they could separate them from what she felt sure was the camouflage Mairah had used to hide her true purpose. But the task could not begin until Tynthanal returned from the formal ball Kailee had left hours ago.

Kailee jerked awake at the sound of an opening door. Her chin had come to rest against her chest, and she had sunk down into her chair in what she supposed was a most unladylike and unattractive position. Rubbing her eyes, she struggled upright.

"Sorry to wake you," Tynthanal said softly, his voice warm with gentle humor. "But I don't suppose you would have thanked me if I'd left you sleeping in that position."

Kailee yawned and stretched, her neck making an audible pop in the process. Her ribs ached where one of her stays had dug into them, and her foot had fallen asleep. She wiggled her toes as much as her shoes would allow and flashed her husband a rueful smile.

"I was not asleep," she said, making no attempt to sound convincing. "I was merely resting my eyes."

"Uh-huh," he agreed, coming to sit on the chair across from her. "I'm sorry I'm so late. It never ceases to amaze me how much self-important noblemen love to hear themselves talk. I was beginning to fear I'd still be trapped in the banquet hall at dawn."

She smiled sympathetically, knowing Tynthanal must have been fairly crawling out of his skin with the desire to get away. He was a far cry from a natural-born politician, and though he would have recognized it as his duty as prince regent to quell his impatience and maintain a good relationship with the rich and powerful nobles who'd attended the ball, she imagined he'd more than once entertained the fantasy of knocking some of their teeth out.

"You don't have to apologize," she told him. "I'm well aware of how many bridges you have to mend after the mess Delnamal made of this kingdom."

Kailee had no doubt that if it weren't for her shocking eyes, which made so many people so terribly uncomfortable, she, too, would have been trapped at the ball for many long hours, listening to and otherwise entertaining all the women of the court while their husbands discussed politics. She knew that more than one member of the court had suggested to Tynthanal that she resume her erstwhile habit—vigorously enforced by her stepmother—of wearing a veil over her eyes. It was not her blindness, per se, that made her into such a social liability. It was the shocking impropriety of seeing a woman with her Mindseye open in a land where women's magic was considered shameful and dirty.

Tynthanal held something up in the air. Something that she could see at once was a magic item, for it was packed full of elements. "Are you too tired to take a look at this tonight?" he inquired.

All hints of sleep fled from her mind when she realized exactly what he was holding. With a soft exclamation, she held out her hands and barely resisted the urge to snatch it.

"I'll take that as a no," Tynthanal said, laughing as he laid what felt like a wineskin on her outstretched hands. The liquid inside sloshed softly as she took it.

The grand magus had been stubbornly reluctant to hand over the mysterious potion that had been found with Mairah's things, which had frustrated Kailee no end. She'd been sure she was more likely to make sense of it than the male spell crafters of the Academy, but she'd begun to despair of ever getting hold of it.

"So your grand magus could make nothing of it?" she asked with an ironic arch of her eyebrow.

"Shockingly, no," he responded with a smile in his voice. "I will send it on to the Women's Well Academy tomorrow, but I know you wanted to take a look at it first."

Kailee studied the elements that had been bound into the potion. There were two she didn't recognize, and one that she had seen before, although she didn't know what it was. But the others were very familiar. Her pulse sped, and something fluttered in her belly. She couldn't have said whether it was excitement or dread.

"Except for the Sur, every element I recognize in here is also present in the potion Mairah gave me."

The potion that was designed to forcibly close Kailee's Mindseye. Others had tested the potion to ensure that it was harmless, and to determine that it would indeed force an open Mindseye closed temporarily. But so far, Kailee had not tried it herself. She had yet to sort out exactly how she felt about the potion. She was certain Mairah had meant no insult when giving it to her. The woman had certainly not been the soul of sensitivity, but she had given the potion to her in secret so that Kailee need never worry about being pressured into trying it. Subsequent events had forced Kailee to tell both Tynthanal and Alysoon about the potion's existence, and she'd been pleasantly surprised that neither seemed inclined to push her.

Tynthanal sat back in his chair, and though he said nothing, Kailee was certain his mind was traveling the same path as her own.

In all likelihood, this potion was some modified—possibly more powerful, and, with the addition of Sur, no longer temporary—version of the one Mairah had given Kailee. Mairah had, for some reason, brought that spell with her to Aaltah's Well.

"The emphasis on sacrificial Kai in these notes is no coincidence," Tynthanal said. "Mairahsol was planning to use her potion and some sacrificial Kai to forcibly close the Mindseye of everyone in Aaltah. That would explain why there was a second, unidentified woman who was seen heading toward the Well with her. Because Mairahsol had no intention of ending her own life to cast this spell, but had found a sick, desperate woman who would do it for her."

Kailee stifled her immediate urge to leap to Mairah's defense. She had to admit, the evidence seemed damning—especially considering the terrible damage that had been done to the Well chamber as well as to the Well itself.

"But she didn't use the potion," Kailee finally said, holding up the full wineskin.

"They did find the cap of a second skin in the rubble," Tynthanal countered. "It seems likely—"

"No," Kailee interrupted impatiently. "If she'd cast that spell, then everyone in Aaltah should be Rho-blind, and we're clearly not."

"Just because she cast it doesn't mean it worked according to plan. It was not something she could possibly have tested before the fact."

But Kailee shook her head, certain she was right. "If that's the case, then why would she have brought *two* wineskins with identical potions in them to the Well? I'm sure that whatever happened down there did not go according to anyone's plans, but Mairah did not sabotage the Well."

Tynthanal's silence was as eloquent as words.

Chewing on her lip and frowning, Kailee tried to remember some of the more jumbled and nonsensical sections of the notes Tynthanal had read to her. She seemed to remember there being some mention of the element Grae, which was often used to produce antidotes to potions.

And with that thought, suddenly a great many things made sense.

"She was trying to redeem herself," Kailee announced. She knew that she was talking too fast, making herself sound frantic, if not outright hysterical, but she couldn't seem to stop. "She wanted to win her way back to Women's Well, and she thought to do that by closing the Mindseye of everyone in Aaltah, to neutralize Aaltah's threat."

There was another eloquent silence.

"Don't you see?" Kailee asked, a hint of desperation in her voice. "There was some part of the notes that talked about using Grae. If we read that again with what we now know, I bet we'll find that she was also devising an antidote potion that could be used to undo the damage she planned to cause. She would close the Mindseye of everyone in Aaltah until Women's Well was safe, and then she would use her antidote to set things back to rights."

Tynthanal sighed. "I know you liked her, but—"

"No!" Kailee insisted. "I didn't just like her, I *understood* her, which was more than anyone else ever tried to do. I know she was more than capable of malice, and I won't pretend what she was planning to do was a *good* thing. The effects on Aaltah and on thousands upon thousands of innocent people would have been *devastating.* But she would not have planned it if she didn't believe it was for a good cause, even if her beliefs were misguided. And if she *had* done it, we would not have found this at the Well." She held up the wineskin. "And we also would have found bodies. I don't know what *actually* happened, but it was not what Mairah intended. And if we read the notes again with our new understanding, we may well learn a great deal more."

Tynthanal reached up and scrubbed a hand through his hair, which Kailee had come to recognize as his favorite nervous gesture. She fully expected him to make another attempt to convince her that Mairah had been an evil bitch who had nothing but spite in her heart, for him to dismiss her arguments as being nothing but feminine sentimentality. But it turned out she was not giving her husband enough credit.

"Very well," he said. "Let's go through the notes again. One way or another, we're going to figure this out."

CHAPTER EIGHT

Corlin stood in the mess hall and contemplated his options, none of which was appealing. The rest of the first-years had been relegated to a set of tables at the very rear of the hall. He'd arrived late to the midday meal, but doing so had been a conscious decision, as he'd hoped to avoid the inevitable jockeying for position that occurred when the cadets lined up to get their food. He'd arrived *so* late, in fact, that he found himself behind even Rafetyn, the two of them getting the dregs that their fellow cadets had already picked over.

Rafetyn was even now approaching the most sparsely populated table, his shoulders stiff with tension. Corlin shook his head. The rest of the first-years were a miserable lot. They *could* have left the table empty to start with—there was plenty of room for the four boys at the table to find places elsewhere—but instead they made the grand show of sitting at the empty table so they could all dramatically get up and move when Rafetyn sat down at the other end of it.

There were still two empty seats at the other tables as Corlin approached, but he found his feet taking him toward Rafetyn's table instead. For the last several weeks, Corlin had dutifully joined the more accomplished cadets and tried to make friends, but today he decided he was sick of it.

Rafetyn looked up at him with wide, startled eyes as Corlin stepped over the bench and took a seat directly across the table from him. In his peripheral vision, he could see the table of cadets to his right staring, then whispering to one another.

"Umm," Rafetyn said with a quick sideways glance at their comrades, "this might not be a good idea."

Corlin shrugged and tried to tear a hunk off the heel of bread on his tray. "Good ideas are overrated," he said, then gave up on trying to tear the bread with his hands and set his teeth to it. The crust refused to give way.

Rafetyn, who also had a heel of bread on his tray, picked it up and plucked some of the soft insides out. "Your teeth'll break before that crust will," he advised, and Corlin had to concede the point. "And if you stay at this table any longer, you're going to live to regret it."

Corlin had no doubt the boy was right. He could feel the scorn of his fellow first-years like a palpable force. If he got up and left the table now, he could probably salvage the situation, pretend he'd sat with Rafetyn just to get the kid's hopes up only to dash them. And yet he felt no pressing need to do so. If the other first-years were going to warm to him, they'd have done so by now. Not to mention that he had not warmed to any of them, either.

Following Rafetyn's lead and pulling out what little soft bread he could find, Corlin shrugged again. "I'm sick of playing their games."

"Believe it or not, their games can get worse," Rafetyn muttered darkly, digging into the mushy, overcooked soup that had been scraped from the bottom of the serving bowl.

After everything he'd been through since his uncle Delnamal had become King of Aaltah, Corlin couldn't dredge up even a hint of dread at the prospect of cementing his position as a social pariah. He had not come to the Citadel of Aaltah to make friends, nor had he come because he thought his life would be easy here. After all, if he'd wanted an easier life, he could have stayed with his uncle Tynthanal at the royal palace and applied himself to other studies. While it was not unusual for a crown prince to spend some of his youth at the Citadel, tradition favored more academic pursuits.

"I can handle it," he said. At least he would be in a better position to fight back than Rafetyn was. While he was not especially large for his age, he worked harder and more diligently at his drills than anyone else in the class, making him both stronger and quicker than he appeared.

Rafetyn gave him a doubtful look. "They'll come at you in numbers when they do," he said. "They've seen you spar and drill, so they won't underestimate you."

"So be it." If Rafetyn could take the abuse the others dished out to him, then surely Corlin could do the same.

As they ate, Corlin wondered what Rafetyn was doing at the Citadel in the first place. While it was certainly a popular choice for second and third sons, Rafetyn could not be more unsuited for it.

Rafetyn noticed his scrutiny and smiled crookedly. For everything he suffered, his spirits seemed surprisingly unscathed. "You're wondering why I haven't had the good sense to wash my hands of this place and run home."

"Well . . ." Corlin hedged, then cleared his throat. "If you don't mind my saying, it doesn't seem you're especially called to the military life."

Rafetyn gave him a look of mock amazement that made Corlin's cheeks heat with embarrassment. "You don't say?"

Corlin cleared his throat again, shifting uncomfortably.

Rafetyn waved his hand dismissively. "It's all right. I know I've got the body of a ten-year-old and the martial spirit of a gentlewoman. But my father wants a soldier, and what my father wants, my father gets."

Corlin's breath caught with a sudden stab of pain, which he tried to hide. His own father had been dead more than two years now. He couldn't count how many people had advised him that the grief would never completely go away, and yet the grief that occasionally snuck up on him never failed to inspire some self-loathing, as well. He was a grown man now, and there was no excuse for being moved nearly to tears at the very mention of the word "father."

"What about what *you* want?" Corlin asked, pushing his soup around his bowl with no appetite. He knew his late father would be disappointed to see him at the Citadel—he would have preferred a much safer and more mundane life for his son—but just as his mother had done, his father would have deferred to his wishes once he realized they were sincere.

Rafetyn snorted. "He's made it clear that his wishes are more important than anyone else's. So, here I am."

"What would happen if you quit?"

Another snort. "Not an option." He shoved his food aside and met Corlin's eyes with a piercing stare. "If you've already placed a bet for my exit date, you have lost your money. My body may be weak, but my mind is not. I will stay in the Citadel until I reach my majority, and I will prove every sneering bastard in this whole place wrong."

There was a hearty dose of determination in Rafetyn's voice, but Corlin also glimpsed something akin to desperation. It made him think the boy was more afraid of going home than staying in the Citadel, no matter what their classmates might put him through.

"I would not bet against you," Corlin said with more confidence than he felt. Unless Rafetyn put on a late growth spurt, it was hard to imagine how he could withstand the rigorous training of the Citadel while also dodging the malice of his peers.

"You probably already have," Rafetyn said coolly, perhaps sensing his lack of conviction. "But I won't hold it against you."

"I did not," Corlin said with some dignity. Then, on impulse, he added, "If I were going to place a bet, it would be *for* you, not against you."

Rafetyn snorted. "I'll believe it when I see it."

Without another word, Corlin rose from the table, having already spotted the cadet whom he knew was in charge of the bets. All eyes were on him as he crossed the distance between them, emptying his coin purse into his hand as he walked.

"Twenty crowns Cadet Rafetyn will go the distance," he said loudly. The entire mess went silent.

"Well, go on," he said when the cadet just stared at him, slack-jawed and disbelieving. "Put it in your book."

It was a princely sum, and he suspected if he were betting against Rafetyn, it would be rejected as too rich. However, under the circumstances, it no doubt seemed like easy money.

The cadet shrugged, raking in the coins. "Have it your way," he said with a greedy gleam in his eye. "But don't come crying to me when you lose."

Corlin rolled his eyes, then returned to Rafetyn's table to find his fellow cadet gaping at him. He wasn't entirely sure what had moved him to place the bet—logic still said Rafetyn could not possibly last—but he did not regret it. And his gut said the bet wasn't as crazy as it appeared.

Rafetyn grinned at him, then shook his head ruefully. "You have just made the target on your back ten times larger by siding with me."

"Let them come," Corlin responded, feeling a fierce sort of eagerness building in his gut. He had been on his best behavior since he'd arrived at the Citadel of Aaltah. He knew his uncle Tynthanal had given the lord commander a thorough recounting of his behavior problems in Women's Well, which had led to a chilling lecture and warning from the man himself before Corlin had been allowed to set foot on the grounds.

"You are here already on probation," Lord Aldnor had told

him, glaring at him from under bushy gray brows. The man had a thoroughly intimidating glare, and Corlin's pulse had raced at being on its receiving end. "There will be no warnings and no leniency. Step out of line even a little, and you will pay the price."

Corlin had believed the man implicitly, and since his entire purpose for entering the Citadel of Aaltah was to prove that he could learn to control his temper, he had vowed to turn himself into a model student. It was getting steadily harder to keep that vow as time passed and his only outlets for the rage that often threatened to consume him were drilling and sparring, which both required a great deal of control.

He would never have admitted it, but he might almost say he looked forward to the inevitable consequences of befriending someone who was even more of an outsider than he himself was. If the others ganged up on him, then he would be under no obligation to control his temper or measure his response. The beating he'd take would quite possibly be worth it if he could only vent his feelings.

"So," Zarsha asked when the sitting room door closed behind him, "what is this surprise you've been teasing me with all night?" He waggled his brows at her, and Ellin laughed.

"It's not *that* kind of surprise," she said, shaking her finger in a mock scold.

He stuck his lip out in an exaggerated pout. "How cruel of you to get my hopes up. I'd thought you'd come upon something scandalous and original in the library and wanted to test it out with me."

She snorted softly. "We've barely been married a week. Surely we aren't in need of anything exotic to spice up our relationship yet. Or are you trying to tell me you're bored already?" She made sure to keep her voice light and teasing so that he didn't worry for a moment that she meant it. It was impossible to miss Zarsha's enthusiasm in the marriage bed—or her own, for that matter. She didn't believe their marriage and their nightly festivities had completely healed the wound Waldmir had inflicted on their relationship, but it had gone a long way toward smoothing it over.

Zarsha stepped toward her, his eyes smoldering as he took her hands and lowered his voice to a heated murmur. "If I live to be a hundred, I'll never grow bored with you," he said, and kissed her so thoroughly she almost forgot what she'd been planning to show him.

Slowly, reluctantly—her pulse was speeding and her body suddenly aching with desire—Ellin pulled away from the kiss.

"I'd better give you your gift now or I'll never get around to it," she said as his eyes continued to burn into her.

"I'm all for gifts," he said suggestively, reaching for her.

"Be serious," she scolded, slapping his hand gently. "This will only take a moment."

He gave a dramatic sigh, but subsided. Ellin nodded her approval and moved to the locked cupboard in the corner. She began second-guessing herself as she unlocked the cupboard, wondering if bringing up the subject of what Zarsha had had to give up to marry her would sour the mood. However, it was too late to change her mind now.

"I had hoped to have this gift ready for you on our wedding day," she said, reaching into the cupboard and pulling out the small, heavy coffer she'd stored there, "but I opted for discretion over speed. I hope you will agree that I made the right choice."

Turning to Zarsha, she held out the coffer with both hands. He frowned at her thoughtfully and cocked his head, clearly curious.

"I do seem to remember having received a gift on our wedding day," he said. "Or has memory failed me?" He glanced down at the understated sapphire ring he wore on his thumb. Most people in Rhozinolm would consider it an almost insultingly plain gift for a prince consort, but knowing Zarsha's Nandelite disdain for ornamentation, she'd chosen a small stone in a simple setting. Her reward was seeing him actually *wear* her gift, which she suspected he would not have done had it been more elaborate.

Ellin let out a small sigh. "I suppose 'gift' isn't truly the most appropriate term. It's more of an apology. Open it."

She did not like the sudden hint of wariness she saw in Zarsha's eyes. He lifted the lid gingerly, as if afraid something might leap out at him. And when he saw the collection of coins within, he winced.

"You will have a respectable income as my prince consort," she said, her voice trembling at the utter lack of joy in his eyes, "but I know you will want to try to help your retainers despite Waldmir's prohibition, and I did not want you to have to wait . . ." Her voice trailed off, for it was obvious she'd miscalculated.

Zarsha took the coffer from her hands and set it aside.

"I've offended you," she whispered.

"No!" he responded with gratifying speed. "It's not that at all." He forced a strained grin. "I've no problem with being a kept man, at least not under the circumstances."

"Then what is it?" she asked. "I promise you I've been utterly discreet about collecting the money, and it is all my own. There will be no uncomfortable questions, if that's what you're worried about."

He rubbed his eyes, then looked away. "It's not that at all. It's just . . ."

"*What?*" she demanded, feeling a pulse of frustration.

He sighed. "It's just that I don't need the money. I've already sent money to all the retainers I could locate and have arranged to send more over time."

She blinked in confusion. "But how? Your uncle confiscated your entire estate!"

Zarsha nodded. "All my legal, aboveboard possessions, yes. But, er . . . I have some money and goods socked away in every kingdom and principality in which I've spent any significant amount of time. I'm not upset with you for trying to give me money—it was a kindhearted and generous gesture. I'm merely uncomfortable admitting that Waldmir's attempt to ruin me financially was . . . not as successful as he might have hoped."

Ellin moved over to a sofa and sat down heavily, feeling like a naïve little fool. Given everything she knew about Zarsha and his well-practiced habit of sniffing out secrets, she should have guessed he had money Waldmir didn't know about. He was a good and kind man, but he was not a perfect one. He'd originally come to Rhozinolm as something of a spy, after all, and he'd been blackmailing his uncle for years. If he would blackmail Waldmir to protect himself and those he cared about, it wasn't much of a stretch to imagine he might blackmail others for money.

"Tell me where the money comes from," she said. "I want to understand exactly what kind of man I married."

He flinched ever so slightly at the bite in her voice, then rallied. "I have never lied to you," he said. "I admitted I was a spy." He cleared his throat. "I just . . . didn't mention that Waldmir wasn't my only employer."

"Nor the only person you were blackmailing."

Zarsha's eyes flashed, and it looked like he would almost snap at her but held himself back. He rubbed his hands together. "I have never used people's secrets to extort money from them. The money I have stored away is payment for information only."

But Ellin was getting used to Zarsha's habit of telling the truth without telling *all* of the truth. "You haven't extorted money out of people," she mused, "but can you tell me you haven't extorted *information* for which you were paid money?"

He squirmed and looked away again. "No. I can't tell you that." He took a deep breath and then met her eyes again.

"You've already seen my information network at work, and you have benefited from it. I can't pretend everything I've done has been strictly ethical, but it has always been for the greater good. I wouldn't betray the secrets of someone who didn't deserve it."

Ellin folded her arms and narrowed her eyes at him. "You admitted you spied on me in the beginning. It's how you found out about my relationship with Graesan!"

He nodded. "And I told you I never shared that information with anyone. I know a great many secrets that will go with me to the grave, no matter who wants to know them or how much they are willing to pay."

She threw up her hands. "Then if you're so blameless, why haven't you told me about this before?"

Zarsha plopped heavily into an armchair across from her, shaking his head. "I have no good excuse," he admitted, "save perhaps long habit. As someone who has trafficked in other people's secrets, I suppose I'm reflexively protective of my own."

"And are there any other big secrets you're keeping that will cause strife between us if I ever learn of them?"

She hoped for a quick denial—she was fairly certain she would believe it—but instead Zarsha was silent for a long time, and her heart sank.

"Graesan tried to come see you," he finally admitted, looking at his clasped hands instead of at her.

"What?" she cried. So she *had* seen him up there in the rafters at the wedding!

"I intercepted him," Zarsha continued, still talking to his hands. "I told him I would secure him a place in the royal guard of the Midlands. No one there will quibble over him using the name Rah-Brondar or have any reason to suspect he'd ever been called anything else."

It was a sad reality that, in Rhozinolm, Graesan's prospects had been limited due not only to his illegitimacy, but because his mother had been his father's housemaid. It was a stain he had never succeeded in washing off, despite his father having granted him his name.

"In the Midlands," Zarsha continued, "with no one knowing the circumstances of his birth, he can start over as a proper gentleman, with the hope of being promoted according to his merits." He finally looked up. "My only condition was that he not see you before he left."

Ellin blinked at the sudden sting of tears in her eyes. She could honestly say her love for Graesan was a thing of the past, but she could see only one reason why Zarsha would inflict such a condition. "You didn't trust me not to fall into his arms if we saw each other again?" she asked acidly.

Zarsha's eyes widened. "Gods, no, that's not it at all!"

"Then why?"

"Because a lot has happened between us since last you saw him, and I was afraid . . ." His hands rubbed restlessly up and down his legs. "I was afraid you might remember what it was like to have an uncomplicated lover and that I might suffer by comparison."

Ellin surprised herself—and Zarsha—by laughing. And once she started, she found she couldn't stop.

"What did I say that's funny?" Zarsha asked earnestly, but his own lips started to twitch even as confusion swam in his eyes.

Ellin shook her head at her husband. "Zarsha, dearest," she said, barely keeping it together, "I wouldn't have the faintest idea what to *do* with 'uncomplicated' these days." Then the laughter faded and she sighed, feeling exhausted with emotion. "I have even less in common with Graesan now than I did when we were together. I would have liked to have seen him so that we could say goodbye properly as we didn't before, but that's all."

Zarsha nodded, staring at his hands once more. "I will arrange to send a talker to him so that you can confirm I didn't bury him in some secret grave."

Ellin rolled her eyes. "I might have suspected you of such a thing once, but not anymore."

He shrugged. "Then I'll do it so you can have your proper goodbye. Please forgive my moment of insecurity. And . . . my other sins."

She smiled softly at him. "As you pointed out, your other sins, as you call them, have been and will likely continue to be of great use to me. I cannot say I am entirely comfortable with the notion, but it would be hypocritical of me to criticize when I have every intention of taking advantage of your connections should the need arise. I object only to the fact that you kept it secret from me."

"For that, I apologize," he said. He rose from his chair and came to sit on the sofa beside her, taking her hands and rubbing his thumb over her knuckles. "Gathering and keeping secrets has given me power when I once felt I had none, and I'm afraid I've allowed it to become something of an addiction. I will do better. You have my word on it."

Ellin accepted his vow by leaning forward and planting a kiss on his lips.

CHAPTER NINE

Alys examined her companion out of the corner of her eye as the two of them walked back to the palace after visiting the Well. Duke Thanmir—youngest brother of the Sovereign Prince of Grunir—was by far the highest-ranking individual who had ever deigned to visit her fledgling principality, and though his visit had already lasted the better part of a week, she still wasn't entirely certain of its purpose. She was getting rather weary of playing hostess—especially when she did not understand his motives—though she would never be so foolish as to show him anything other than the utmost courtesy. She had hoped that with Delnamal off the throne of Aaltah, Grunir would become a more eager trade partner, but so far the sovereign prince had proven less accommodating than she would have hoped. Insulting his little brother would not be the way to win his support.

When they returned to the palace, Alys invited the duke to join her for tea, rather hoping that he would decline. Her hopes were dashed, and though she had many more pressing matters she should be dealing with, she found herself in the parlor of the royal residence chatting with a man who had as yet made no indication of how long he intended to stay.

Politics was a game of subtlety and deceit, and ordinarily Alys considered herself fairly skilled at it. But for reasons she could not entirely fathom, the subtlety was grating on her nerves, and she eventually lost her patience with the game entirely.

"Forgive me," she said, putting down her teacup and looking Duke Thanmir directly in the eye, "but I'm afraid my curiosity is getting the better of me, and I have to ask—"

"Why am I here?" he interrupted, his smile showing off the laugh lines at the corners of his eyes. He was not a traditionally handsome man, with his thinning hair, thick torso, and short legs, and yet there was something very warm and appealing about him. She suspected he was a man with whom many people shared confidences they shouldn't, and she was wary of stumbling into the same trap herself.

Returning his smile, she raised one shoulder in a shrug. "Well, yes. Women's Well doesn't tend to attract visitors as exalted as yourself, and I cannot imagine that you are here merely as a tourist."

"I'm not so exalted as all that," Thanmir demurred. "My father had to cobble together a dukedom for me, as it had been a long time since a sovereign prince of Grunir had managed *three* sons. I am comfortable and not without influence, but I have not the authority to speak for my brother and formally represent my principality."

Alys's eyebrows drew together in puzzlement, and she stifled a sigh of disappointment. So much for her hopes that Thanmir might help her establish a trade agreement with Grunir.

"I am here on a more . . . personal matter," he said, and a little of his self-assurance bled away. He glanced down at his tea, swirling it around in his cup while failing to take a sip. "I don't know how much you know about my . . . circumstances."

It was Alys's duty as sovereign princess to familiarize herself with all the royal families in Seven Wells, but the degree of her knowledge correlated closely to those family members' influence.

As a royal duke, Thanmir was, as he'd said, not without influence; however, he had never been what she would call a major player, so she knew only a little about him.

"I know that you're a widower," she said, then her throat tightened and she had to swallow hard before she could say the rest. "And I know that you lost a daughter."

It was a pain she knew all too well, and just saying the words was enough to cause her grief to rise up and try to strangle her. Technically, she should be putting aside her mourning wardrobe now that the one-year anniversary of Jinnell's death had passed, but she had not yet done so. The grief was still painfully near the surface, ready to strike the moment she let down her guard.

"Yes," Thanmir said, and though he remained composed, she could not fail to hear the matching grief in his voice. "I lost my eldest daughter just a few months before you lost yours," he said. "Are you aware of the circumstances?"

If Thanmir had been of more prominent standing, Alys was certain half of Seven Wells would know all the gory details, for there was certainly a sensational story behind the mundane facts. "I know that an inquest found that her husband habitually beat her and that she managed to fatally wound him the last time he did so, although her injuries were too severe to survive."

Thanmir closed his eyes, his hands visibly clenching so that she feared he might break the teacup. Then he let out a long, slow sigh and opened eyes that were now shiny with suppressed tears. "How I wish that son of a bitch had survived so that I might murder him with my bare hands. I will never, *ever* forgive myself for allowing Zallee to marry him. But she and I—and the rest of high society—were all fooled by the face he put on in public."

Alys understood what he was thinking, what he was feeling. She clasped her hands together in her lap to hide the trembling as she fought off the terrible memory of Jinnell's head hitting the ground at her feet. A memory that often jerked her out of sleep soaked in sweat and with a racing heart.

Thanmir sucked in a deep breath and blinked a few times. The pain was still visible in his eyes and etched into the lines of his face, but his voice was steady. "There are a great many details about what happened that are not publicly known. And that is why I am here."

Alys was far from eager to hear those details, but she could hardly say so.

"May I tell you something in strictest confidence?" he asked.

Alys cocked her head at him. "You would share a confidence with me on such short acquaintance?"

"There's a reason I did not mention the purpose of my visit until I'd had a chance to speak with you more than once and to get to know Women's Well. I had reason to believe that you could hear my daughter's story without putting the blame on her shoulders, but she is very dear to me, and I could not risk trusting the opinions of others. I had to see for myself."

Despite no fair amount of dread—clearly the confidence Thanmir planned to share was an unpleasant one—Alys could not deny she was curious. His daughter was dead, so why should it matter if Alys placed blame on the woman's shoulders or not?

"Unless sharing your confidence would be vital to the protection of my principality," Alys said, "you can rest assured that I would mention it to no one."

Thanmir smiled faintly at her equivocation, but she thought it only fair to be completely honest.

"I can live with those terms," he said, then fidgeted with his teacup. The nervous gesture once again piqued Alys's curiosity. He lifted the cup halfway to his mouth, then put it and the saucer down again without taking a sip.

Thanmir cleared his throat, then seemed to steady himself. "Zallee was killed because she caught her husband in the act of . . ." His face flushed with what Alys could immediately see was rage, rather than embarrassment, "of violating my youngest daughter." His eyes flashed, and his fists clenched in his lap.

Alys gasped in sympathy, covering her mouth. She knew that Thanmir had a son and heir, and she'd known about his murdered daughter, but she hadn't realized he had a younger one, as well. "H-how old is your youngest?" she asked, her insides clenching.

"Shalna was thirteen at the time. Word was only just then getting out about the existence of women's Kai, and only a select few of the nobility knew about it. I was one of them, and I had told both of my daughters—despite the sovereign prince's strict orders that I share what I knew with no one. I did not for a moment imagine that either of my daughters would ever need to use women's Kai, and yet I felt it my duty as their father to protect them with this knowledge."

Thanmir cleared his throat again and looked away. Alys chose not to push him. As terrible as the story of his daughter's murder already had been, clearly the situation was even worse than she'd imagined.

"My girls were very protective of each other," Thanmir continued. "I know that Zallee had endured a great deal of abuse from her husband with a stoicism that broke my heart. I offered to spirit her away from him under a false identity, so that she might start again elsewhere without fear of ending up in the Abbey, but she would not hear of it. She feared her disappearance would cause a scandal that might damage Shalna's marriage prospects." He rubbed at his eyes. "How I wish I'd ignored her objections. I should have taken her away by force if necessary."

"You couldn't have known," Alys said, her heart aching with sympathy as she thought about her own never-ending self-recrimination over leaving Jinnell in Aaltah while she'd studied in Women's Well. She knew that there was no comfort to be had in logic.

Thanmir offered her a thin smile. "Perhaps not everything," he conceded. "But I *did* know Solgriff was a danger to Zallee, and I did nothing to protect her. I will never forgive myself, have no *desire* to forgive myself.

"But I have yet to finish the sordid story. When Zallee caught her husband in the act, something inside her snapped. She'd endured so much abuse herself, but she'd done it for Shalna's sake, so that Shalna might have a better future."

Thanmir shook his head. "She attacked him with a fireplace poker, but he was a great deal bigger and stronger than she, and he wrestled it away from her. Then he beat her to death with it while Shalna screamed and screamed."

Thanmir's lips twisted into a fierce snarl. "But Solgriff had *not* learned the secret of women's Kai, and Shalna *had*. My fierce little girl used her Kai against the murderous son of a bitch. Dropped him dead, though less painfully than he deserved."

Alys wondered if getting revenge like that had done anything to heal the wounds the monster had formed on the poor child's soul. She could not imagine going through that at any age, much less at thirteen.

Thanmir unclenched his hands, and there were white crescents in his palms from where his nails had dug in. "I helped my girl cover up the full truth of what happened by beating the body enough so that it looked like he died from the battering. I know there were questions asked at the inquest, but because no one knew about women's Kai, they never truly suspected Shalna. However, there are a few people who know the whole truth. For the most part, I trust them, but . . ." He shrugged. "Well, it's a dangerous secret."

"Ah," Alys said, finally understanding his purpose in coming to Women's Well. To Alys's way of thinking, only a monster would blame Shalna for what happened to her. However, when the girl went on the marriage market, her lack of chastity could be a severe impediment. If Thanmir *didn't* reveal it, he ran the risk that his daughter would be repudiated on her wedding night and sent directly to the Abbey. But if he *did,* then high society would in all likelihood shun her, no matter how unfair. "You're hoping that when she comes of age, we might find a husband for her here in Women's Well."

"Well, yes," Thanmir said, twisting his ring again in a way that clearly said that was not the whole of it. "But she will not come of age for years yet, and for all that time, we will run the risk that someone might talk and ruin her—or even level an accusation of murder against her."

Alys sucked in a breath, for though social ruination in Grunir might not damage the girl's marriage prospects in Women's Well, an accusation of murder—and a possible prosecution for it— could lead to her imprisonment or even death.

"But then . . . I don't understand what you want from me," Alys said.

Thanmir sighed heavily. "When my wife died bearing Shalna, I had no interest in ever remarrying. She was the love of my life, and there is no room in my heart for another. My title and estates are secure, and I am not in need of any financial assistance, so there seemed no point. But now Shalna's future is very much in doubt, and . . ."

Alys's heart thudded against her breastbone, and she wondered at herself for being so terribly dense. She had been receiving marriage proposals off and on nearly the entire time she'd been sovereign princess. It had always been easy to politely decline those proposals, for she had most of the time been in mourning, first for her father, then for her daughter. And because of the tenuous place of Women's Well in society, not one of the proposals had been made by a man who was truly suitable to marry a sovereign. But a royal duke . . .

"Are you . . ." She cleared her throat as her voice caught, her whole body clenching with anxiety. "Are you asking me to marry you?"

He smiled at her, those laugh lines at the corners of his eyes making a return appearance, although his expression was still shadowed with sadness. "I am aware that it is possibly the least romantic marriage proposal in the history of Seven Wells, for I refuse to make it under false pretenses of any kind. I am not in truth looking for a wife, and from everything I've heard of you, I doubt very much that you are looking for a husband, either. Nonetheless, a match between us would have many advantages for both of us—and for both our principalities."

Alys wanted very much to reject the proposal out of hand, as she had rejected every other proposal that had come her way. She had told Tynthanal once that she was resolved to the idea that she would one day have to marry again, as was expected for a widowed sovereign. Her visceral reaction to Thanmir's proposal suggested she'd been lying to both her brother and herself.

"I—I'm still in mourning," she said, though technically that was no longer true.

Thanmir nodded. "I understand. I don't believe I will *ever* be out of my own mourning, no matter how much time passes. And I will not pressure you to answer me, nor will I put the proposal in writing unless and until you tell me you are willing to entertain it."

"What you really want is to bring your daughter to Women's Well, is it not? I would happily welcome both of you to our principality. There is no need for a marriage."

Thanmir reached for his neglected tea, taking a sip although it had surely gone cold and unpleasant by now. "I'm a royal duke," he said. "I cannot uproot my family and move to Women's Well without a reason. Not without causing irreparable harm to my son and heir, who is not yet wed. My brother would not openly condemn me as a traitor for abandoning my homeland, but he would certainly feel betrayed by it, and the rest of the court would follow his lead." He shook his head. "No, I would have to have a legitimate reason, and marriage to a sovereign princess is the only reason I can imagine my brother accepting."

Alys prided herself on her ability to make decisions based on what was good for her principality, her ability to set aside her personal interest in order to do her duty. Her mind knew that accepting the duke's proposal was the logical choice. If she had to remarry someday—which she had already determined she must—then why not someone like Thanmir? His lineage was impeccable, he would help her forge an alliance with Grunir, he would not come into the marriage expecting a loving and dutiful wife, and he was not in need of an heir. Not to mention that she actually *liked* him. There were far too many men in Seven Wells who would have already sent young Shalna to the Abbey in disgrace for the sin of being attacked.

"I'm so sorry," she found herself saying, in spite of all the arguments of reason, "but I'm . . ." She sighed and shook her head. Refusing him was foolish and selfish. She fell silent as her duty and her grief fought a vicious battle within her.

"But you're not ready to think about marriage yet," Thanmir finished for her, nodding.

The sympathy and understanding in his eyes made Alys feel even more of a fool for balking. She dried her suddenly sweaty palms on her skirts. She fixed her gaze on the unadorned, solid black expanse of silk, unable to bear that sympathy.

"On the day my mourning should officially have ended," she said, "my lady's maid thought to dress me in a gown of deep blue so dark it might almost be mistaken for black. She's been with me a long time and knows me very well, so she thought I should gently transition out of my mourning attire rather than casting it wholly aside. But when she approached me to attach the bodice, I . . ." She swallowed hard. "Well, let's just say I panicked." She looked up once more to meet his kind eyes. "If I cannot face a dark blue dress without panic, then I cannot entertain a marriage proposal. I'm very sorry."

He waved the apology off, finishing his cold tea and setting the cup aside. "That's quite all right," he said. "I meant it when

I said I had no intention of pressuring you or of demanding an answer. If and when you *are* ready to entertain marriage proposals, I hope you will keep me in mind. And I hope that you will allow me to visit again and perhaps even bring Shalna so that you might meet her."

Alys took a deep breath, hoping in vain that it would steady her. Thanmir might not be *overtly* pressuring her, but there was no question in her mind that he hoped meeting Shalna would help sway her to accept his proposal. However, there was no good reason to deny the request, and it was actually a relief that she could so gently refuse his proposal without slamming the door on future possibilities.

"You and your daughter may visit anytime you'd like," she said.

The mingled hope and desperation that momentarily flashed in Thanmir's eyes reminded her once more that there was more than her own life and happiness at stake, and she halfway hoped that somewhere down the road she would find the courage and strength she needed to put aside her mourning and fully rejoin her life.

Delnamal slipped quietly into the servants' quarters in the dead of night. Back in the royal palace in Aalwell, he'd been only vaguely aware of where the various servants' quarters lay, and he never would have deigned to set foot in them. Even now, he considered it unseemly—almost unclean—but he stuffed that discomfort and distaste into the same coffer within himself where he confined all of his other inconvenient and unwanted emotions.

Although he was the lord of this manor and had every right to treat even the servants' quarters as his own property, he had no desire to draw any attention to himself. Instead of bringing a bright luminant to light his way, he made do with a pathetically small candle.

If the manor house were fully staffed, as it ought to be, even the most senior staff would be sharing rooms, but it was convenient to the night's experiment that King Khalvin had insulted his sister and his nephew by granting them only the barest minimum of servants to run the house. The housekeeper and the most senior of the housemaids each had her own room. Delnamal, naturally, did not know who slept in which room, but luckily no one woke when he oh-so-quietly opened bedroom doors until he found the maid he sought.

He couldn't remember the woman's name—it was something like Hope or Faith or Charity or somesuch nonsense—but she was clearly near the end of her serviceable days. It was even possible that she'd been rousted out of peaceful retirement to serve him.

After his discovery of the mysterious and impossible element that filled his blood and resided in the breast of his mother's songbird, Delnamal had surreptitiously opened his Mindseye to examine some of his servants. His observations had shown him that each servant had one of those faceted spheres in his or her chest, as did birds and animals. He'd sneaked a chicken out of the henhouse to confirm to himself that what had happened with the songbird had not been a fluke. It hadn't, and Delnamal had helped himself to two more chickens since—the servants thought they were contending with an especially clever fox.

But as satisfying as those chickens were, he couldn't help wondering whether the experience would be more intense and long-lasting if he could pluck one of those motes from the breast of a human. He'd stifled his curiosity for a couple of days, but it kept eating at him. And then he realized that the household's most senior housemaid was just elderly enough that her mysterious death would not raise too many eyebrows.

When he'd examined the housemaid with his Mindseye, he'd seen that her sphere did not look like everyone else's, for a fragment of its outer shell seemed to have broken off and was hovering just above her shoulder.

There was no reason Delnamal should expect to be able to see feminine Kai; however, women's Kai was said to take the form of a solid black crystal, and that was clearly what he saw clinging to the housemaid.

He slipped into the room, carefully and quietly closing the door behind him and setting the candle down. He looked at the sleeping woman with a shake of his head. From what he knew of women's Kai, it was an entirely new element that had not existed before the casting of the Curse. Which meant only women who'd been raped since the Curse was cast possessed it. Delnamal couldn't imagine being desperate enough to take a shriveled old woman by force, but clearly someone had done so. And clearly, like men's Kai, women's Kai was not in fact *created* but was, at least in a manner of speaking, there all along.

Opening his Mindseye he looked once more at the chipped, faceted orb in the housemaid's chest, feeling a longing that combined the sensations of hunger and thirst and lust.

This isn't just stupid, an annoying, weak little voice mumbled in the back of his mind. *It's* wrong! *She's an innocent old woman who's done nothing to deserve this.*

Delnamal noted the voice—and the rush of guilt and horror that accompanied it—with a thread of mild interest. Intellectually, he knew the voice was right, that killing an old woman just to satisfy his unwholesome curiosity was an abhorrent sin. He had to admit that he had never been the most moral and righteous of men, but even when he had engaged in acts of cruelty, he had always felt—at least at the time—that his act was justified. This time, there was no question of that being the case. But it was strangely easy to shunt aside his natural human inhibitions, to lock them up with the rest of his emotions where they wouldn't bother him.

He took hold of the mysterious mote, his fingers lightly brushing the old woman's chest, and she gasped in what he assumed was pain and fear. Luckily, she was not as loud as the chickens, and he very much doubted anyone nearby would wake at the sound. Reverently, he pulled the mote from her chest, holding his breath in anticipation.

As with the motes he had stolen from the songbird and chickens, this one burst apart the moment it left the old woman's body. The black outer layer broke away to reveal the core of Rho motes along with a mote of Kai in shades of red fading to pink. He felt a moment's surprise that apparently masculine Kai was not present only in men. Then a rush of indescribable strength and pleasure and emotion flooded him—far stronger than anything he had felt from killing the birds—and his mind was swept away on a wave that left him incapable of thought.

Eventually, he regained control of himself, once again stuffing the excessive emotions away and merely reveling in the feeling of strength and power in his body. He felt better than he had since the accident at the Well, and it was all he could do not to let out a whoop of joy.

Before he closed his Mindseye and slunk out of the room, he noted that the aura of Kai motes that hovered around him now had a new addition—a mote of red fading to pink that looked exactly like the Kai that had resided within the old woman's chest. Instead of drifting away, as the birds' miniature Kai motes had, this mote of Kai had joined all the rest in Delnamal's aura. If taking the faceted mote from the breast of people meant he could add even more motes of free Kai to his own aura . . .

Delnamal stifled a laugh of pure delight, reminding himself to keep quiet and not wake anyone. It would not do for someone to find him hovering over the corpse. The servants already eyed him with superstitious dread. He felt as strong and vital as he did directly in the aftermath of one of his fits, and he had yet another mote of Kai at his disposal—without having to sacrifice one of the mysterious motes in his blood.

Nearly giddy with the rush of possibilities, Delnamal slipped quietly from the room.

CHAPTER TEN

T ynthanal was shown into the dowager queen's parlor and was surprised to find Oona holding the infant king in her arms when he entered. Over the last couple of months, Oona had lost some of the aura of fear and wariness that had emanated from her when he'd first arrived. However, he knew that she still feared his intentions and worried that he might harbor ill will toward his half-brother's son, and she had assiduously avoided allowing him to set eyes on the child.

Oona rose to her feet and approached, four-month-old King Tahrend fussing softly at the movement. She smiled down at her son while still giving the impression she was carefully watching Tynthanal's expression, searching for some sign that he was a danger.

"I thought it was time you meet your nephew," she said.

Tynthanal had come to the dowager's apartments with his emotional armor firmly in place, for he meant to question her once more about what had happened on the night of Delnamal's disappearance. Now that he had tangible evidence that his half-brother might have survived the disaster at the Well, he hoped Oona might be more forthcoming about what had truly happened that night. He did not for a moment believe she did not know at least *some* of it.

But he had not been prepared for the sight of the infant Prince Tahrend nestling in his mother's arms. The knowledge that, any day now, Chanlix might give birth to his own son struck him with such ferocity that it took an effort of will to suppress a gasp. It hurt more than he could have imagined to think of Chanlix going through that ordeal without him, and he longed with every fiber of his being to see the woman he loved holding their baby as Oona was holding the infant king just now.

Oona chuckled softly, misinterpreting the emotions that were no doubt written on his face. "I gather you've never been this close to an infant before? I promise he doesn't bite."

Tynthanal tried to pull himself together. If anyone in Aaltah was aware that he had a bastard child on the way back in Women's Well, they had not remarked upon it. He did not feel inclined to explain himself to his half-brother's wife, so it was best he put his emotions aside for the moment. "On the contrary," he said, forcing himself to see the child that was before him instead of the child he imagined soon being born. "I met and held both Jinnell and Corlin within days of their births."

Of course, thinking of the moment he'd first held little Jinnell in his arms while his sister beamed with pride did not help him keep his emotions at bay. A lump formed in his throat, and it no doubt showed in his voice.

"May I hold him?" he asked, unsure of the wisdom of the request when he was already feeling so . . . overcome.

Oona's arms briefly tightened, hugging the baby closer to her breast as if to protect him from some danger. Tynthanal doubted she did it consciously, and he tried not to feel insulted by the gesture, though he did not entirely succeed. He did not try to coax or reassure her—in part because he did not trust himself to speak.

Oona let out a quiet sigh and bit her lip. Then, as if steeling herself for some terrible ordeal, she shifted little King Tahrend into position to allow Tynthanal to take him.

It had been many years since Tynthanal had held a baby, but his body remembered how, and soon his youngest nephew was resting comfortably in his arms. Tahrend stared up at him with large hazel eyes, and Tynthanal felt sure the baby was about to let out a yowl of protest at being handed over to a complete stranger. But Tahrend must have liked what he saw in his uncle's eyes, for instead of crying, he let out a contented coo and smiled.

Tynthanal could have sworn he felt his heart melting right then and there, and he once again remembered the swell of love he'd felt when he'd held each of his sister's children for the first time. Perhaps some of the warmth he felt now was colored by those memories—or by the yearning to one day hold his own son like this—but for the first time since he'd received word of Tahrend's birth, he was entirely certain that no hint of the hatred he felt for his half-brother would taint his affection for his latest nephew.

Oona hovered anxiously and looked half-inclined to snatch the infant from Tynthanal's arms.

"He has your eyes," Tynthanal said, for it was true. He also had a round face that was uncomfortably reminiscent of Delnamal's, but that observation he would keep to himself. He smiled briefly at Oona before looking back down at the infant in his arms.

"Hello, Nephew," he said softly, to which the baby cooed again. "I'm very pleased to make your acquaintance." Tahrend looked delighted, and the innocent joy in those eyes smoothed over the rough edges of Tynthanal's mixed emotions. Tahrend reached out an inquisitive hand to pat Tynthanal's face, melting his heart just a little more.

"He seems to like you," Oona said almost reluctantly. "He's usually fussy with strangers."

"But I'm not a stranger, really," Tynthanal answered. "I'm family, and he can sense that. Just like he can sense that I love him already." He met Oona's gaze, holding her eyes firmly with his. "He knows that I would never allow harm to come to him if I can help it."

A little of the tension eased out of Oona's shoulders, and he hoped she heard the sincerity in his voice. He had never thought of himself as a lover of children—his sister's being the only children he'd spent any significant time around—and he had approached fatherhood with a great deal of ambivalence. But holding Tahrend now, he knew that he would love his son with every inch of his heart. And that he would do everything in his power to find a way to return to Women's Well long before Tahrend came of age to hold the throne in his own right.

Tahrend's eyes drifted closed, and Oona smiled indulgently. "It's past his nap time," she said.

"Thank you for letting me meet him," Tynthanal replied, handing the sleepy baby back to Oona with a surprising degree of reluctance.

Oona settled the little king in his curtain-draped crib, and Tynthanal wished he could leave on this note of pleasant accord. But while meeting his baby nephew had been a happy surprise, he'd come to Oona's apartments with a much grimmer purpose in mind.

When the baby was comfortably settled and Oona turned back to him, Tynthanal broached the purpose of his visit.

"I know that Delnamal is alive," he said, and watched the warmth leach out of Oona's face. He presented it as a certainty, although he was fully aware that Alys's test on the blood he had found outside the Well chamber only suggested the possibility.

"Y-you are mistaken," Oona stammered, but the alarm with which she had received his statement was almost as revealing as a confession.

"I'm afraid the evidence is on my side," he said, trying not to sound more accusatory than necessary. "And if he's alive, then you must know where he is."

Oona shook her head and looked on the verge of tears. "He isn't. I don't. I—"

"I will not ask you to betray him," Tynthanal reassured her, and it was true, at least for the moment. "I imagine Xanvin took him to Khalpar and they have taken refuge with King Khalvin. But I don't believe the two of them left Aaltah without confiding in you. And if you know anything about what happened down in the Well chamber, then I need you to tell me. The *kingdom* needs you to tell me."

Oona shook her head again, but there was no conviction to the gesture. She was well aware that her denials would not convince him.

"Please, Oona," he said more softly. "I have to find a way to repair the damage to the Well. And I'll have a better chance of doing that if I know what actually happened there."

Oona chewed her lip for an impossibly long time, and Tynthanal allowed her the freedom to think.

"I . . . I don't know much," she finally admitted, now staring at the floor. "I know that my husband thought the Abbess of Khalpar could reverse the Curse by casting some spell on the Well, but everyone knows that."

"He told you nothing about what happened, even once he knew it had gone horribly wrong?" Tynthanal asked with infinite skepticism. If nothing else, his half-brother would have been spewing justifications for what he'd done, throwing blame around to anyone he could think of except himself.

"He couldn't," Oona said simply. "He was unconscious, and did not wake up at all before we parted ways."

"Tell me what happened. Anything you know might be helpful."

Oona moved restlessly over to the crib, peeking through the curtain to ensure that Tahrend was sleeping peacefully. Or perhaps merely taking a moment to gather herself.

"Xanvin and I found him in the Well's antechamber," she said in a voice little above a whisper. Even with her back turned, he could see the chill that shivered through her. "He was unconscious, and his hands . . ." She hiccuped and sniffled, discreetly dabbing her eyes. "He was hurt very badly," she finished. "We had a healer see to him and repair his hands as much as possible, but it is unlikely he will ever regain full use of his fingers. The healer had no explanation for why he did not regain consciousness."

Oona finally found the courage to face him once more. The remembered horror in her eyes made Tynthanal regret forcing her to relive those terrible moments.

"Even though he was unconscious, he vomited periodically," she continued with a shudder. "The healer said . . . he said he saw what looked like tiny shards of Kai in the fluid that came up. He said he'd never seen anything like it and he didn't know what to do for it."

"I need to speak to this healer."

Oona bit her lip. "Xanvin sent him away. Me, she trusted to stay silent. Him, not so much."

"And Xanvin did not wait for Delnamal to wake up before traveling to Khalpar?" Tynthanal asked, struggling against frustration.

Oona shrugged. "She waited as long as she dared. She wrote to me once when they reached Khalpar and assured me that he was recovering. But I have not heard from her since."

It was not hard to see the hurt in Oona's expression, but it wasn't *Xanvin's* silence that hurt her. Tynthanal bit his tongue to keep in an acid comment about Delnamal's treatment of a woman who clearly—and against all reason—loved him. Perhaps with his maimed hands, he had not the dexterity to pen a letter himself, but he surely could have dictated one.

"Do you know how to reach him?" he asked gently. "If there's any way you can find out from him exactly what happened at the Well . . ."

Once upon a time, Delnamal had had a sense of duty, even if he had often resented that duty. Perhaps if he knew what was happening to his kingdom in his absence . . .

"I can try writing to King Khalvin," Oona said doubtfully. "I'm sure he knows where Delnamal is, though I don't suppose he thinks particularly highly of Aaltah right now."

Tynthanal could not help but agree. Thanks to Delnamal's erratic behavior, diplomatic ties between the two kingdoms had been strained even before the disaster. And now that Tynthanal had been chosen as prince regent, Khalvin had let his displeasure be known by recalling his own ambassador and expelling Aaltah's from Khalpar.

"You must reach out to him as a concerned wife, rather than as a representative of Aaltah," Tynthanal said. "Tell him nothing about our troubles, but ask only for him to tell you how you might go about reaching Delnamal." The magic of fliers—even those spelled to deliver messages specifically to a person rather than to a place—required the sender to have at least some idea of the recipient's location.

"I know you still aren't sure whether to trust me," he continued. "But I will not ask you to share anything with me about your husband's location. I only ask you to find him and ask him what happened at the Well."

Oona nodded. "I will try," she said, and Tynthanal let out a long sigh of relief.

Xanvin gave a cry of gladness when she stepped into the parlor and saw the caged bird that Delnamal had purchased. Well, that he'd had one of the servants purchase on his behalf. She hurried over to the cage and began to make small cooing noises, tapping at the bars ever so lightly. The bird—uncommonly bold—sat still on its perch and cocked its head first to one side, then the other, then fluttered its clipped wings restlessly.

Delnamal realized with a touch of chagrin that he had made a mistake. He had not told his mother that he was the cause of her last pet's demise, and she naturally thought he had bought this bird as a gift for her.

As far as he could tell, no one had any inkling that he was responsible for the death of the songbird, the handful of chickens, or the hapless serving woman who had "passed peacefully in her sleep." Everyone thought the decreasing number of "fits" he suffered—and his increasing strength in between them—was a sign that he was healing naturally. Which was convenient, to a point. But rusticating here in the wilderness, he'd had more than enough time to himself to think, and he'd quickly come to realize that his current circumstances were not sustainable. The secret could not last forever unless he never indulged again, and he had no intention of suffering a life of self-denial. So he had embarked on a plan to make of his secret a strength that might well gain him everything he wanted and more.

He wished now that he'd not been so impatient, that he'd put just a little more thought into his plan before implementing it. His mother would likely have been more open to his proposal if he'd chosen a chicken meant for tonight's dinner for this demonstration.

Ah, well. He could buy her another songbird easily enough. Though truth be told, he'd enjoyed the silence the death of the last bird had brought to the manor house.

"Don't get too attached, Mama," he said, closing the parlor door and snicking its lock shut. For the time being at least, this demonstration was to be just between himself and his mother.

Xanvin's smile dimmed, and she clutched the cage possessively as she turned to look at him. She could not help but notice that he'd locked the door, nor could she fail to hear the bird's death in his words.

"What do you mean, my son?" she asked, carefully placing herself between him and the cage.

"I brought you here to show you something. Something that I believe will change how King Khalvin thinks of me."

At the moment, Delnamal's uncle clearly thought of him as some kind of failure and embarrassment. A secret to be kept tucked in a hidden manor house in the middle of nowhere. Someone he helped even that much only out of a sense of family obligation. But once he understood how Delnamal had been changed, the king would come to realize that his scorned nephew wasn't so useless, after all.

"Delnamal . . ." his mother said, her voice filled with compassion, and lacking in anything resembling respect.

Once upon a time, that tone would have set his nerves on edge and sparked his temper. He was aware of the spark even now, just as he was aware of a spark of guilt. Not for hurting the bird—the death of a single songbird was of no consequence—but for the pain that death would cause his mother. A good son, a decent human being, would have seen the look on her face when she beheld that bird and instantly changed his plans. But as with all inconvenient emotions these days, he shunted this aside.

He smiled faintly at the singular sensation of being able to *choose* whether to snap at his mother or not. Her body language said she was waiting to absorb whatever verbal blow he was about to deliver, though his smile seemed to knock her off her stride.

"Please step aside, Mama," he said in a completely neutral tone of voice. "I promise I will buy you another bird." His smile broadened. "I will buy you an entire flock, if you'd like." And a new house in which those damned birds could sing to their hearts' content without his having to listen to the cacophony.

"What are you going to do?" she asked, and this time there was a faint quaver in her voice.

"Step aside, and you'll see."

Delnamal strode forward as if there was no question his mother would do as he asked. For all that she'd been raised to observe the Khalpari imperative that a woman be subservient to men at all times, she ordinarily had a fair amount of steel in her backbone. Certainly she had often stood up to him, even when he was in a rage, though he was aware she chose very carefully when to make a stand and when to step aside. He more than half-expected her to hold her ground, but when she met his eyes, something very like fear spread over her face, and she stepped out of his way.

Another stab of guilt, set aside effortlessly.

Xanvin wasn't the only one who was frightened. The caged bird's primal instincts warned it that danger approached, and it hopped to the far side of the cage, as far away from the door as possible. Its useless wings battered at the cage's bars, and it called out loudly and repeatedly as Delnamal opened his Mindseye.

With his Mindseye open, he couldn't make out the door's mechanism, so he had to open it by feel—tricky with his mangled fingers—his gaze fixed on the tantalizing mote that was trying so desperately to escape him.

After he'd killed the housemaid and her mote of Kai had come to join the rest of the Kai that surrounded him, he'd put a great deal of thought into exactly the nature of that faceted globe he saw inside of every living creature, and what it meant that the housemaid's mote had been chipped, with a shard of it hovering in her aura.

Conventional wisdom said that masculine Kai was formed by a man's violent death, and that women's Kai formed when a woman was raped. But it was his belief now that the Kai wasn't *formed* at all. Both the element known as masculine Kai and the one known as women's Kai were but fragments of a larger element—*whole* Kai, which in many ways resembled an egg. A black outer shell surrounding the white Rho and the precious yolk of Kai at the center. He had decided to call the egglike element that only he could see "Rhokai," for it contained both the element of life and the element of death.

Turning his attention back to the frantically shrieking bird, he reached his hand into the cage. Moments later, the room went quiet as the bird's wings stilled and its cries of distress ceased.

Delnamal shivered in blissful delight as his body absorbed the bird's life force.

Behind him, he heard Xanvin's harsh gasps of breath and knew his gentle mother mourned the stupid bird. Yes, a chicken already destined for the dinner table would have been the wiser choice, but he hadn't given the issue a moment's thought. Careless of him, for distraught people could be highly annoying.

Closing his Mindseye with a contented sigh, Delnamal turned to face his mother. Her eyes were wet and shiny with tears, and she held both her hands clasped in front of her mouth as if to try to contain her horror. A ring of white surrounded her pupils as she stared at her son. He had made a tactical error when he'd chosen the songbird for his demonstration, but at least he had realized in advance that he should not tell her about the aura of Kai that floated around his body. One terrifying fact at a time was enough for a woman with as gentle a soul as his dear mother.

"What have you done?" she whispered, shaking her head.

"It turns out not everything that happened to me at Aaltah's Well was bad," he said, disappointed to find that the hum of euphoria he'd experienced from absorbing the bird's Rhokai was fading already. He'd been spoiled by the long-lasting effects of the maid's death, and wished he could engineer another such opportunity.

He explained his theories about the nature of Kai, and of the new element he had dubbed Rhokai. He gestured at the pathetic bundle of feathers that lay still at the bottom of the cage.

"It also seems that removing that mote of Rhokai is fatal, at least to birds." Even when he admitted what he had learned about the nature of masculine Kai, he had no intention of allowing his mother to know just *how* he had learned it.

Xanvin was still shaking her head and staring at him, aghast. He had expected her to be unsettled by his demonstration, but he had underestimated the strength of her reaction.

She put her hand to her chest, rubbing fretfully. "It's in me, too?" she asked.

"Yes, Mama. It's in everyone." He smiled faintly. "It seems that the only true difference between magically gifted men, ordinary men, and women, is whether they can *see* the Kai. I shall be most curious to observe a natural death someday to see why no one has reported seeing Kai in those cases. My conjecture is that it is only violent death that breaks open the Rhokai to reveal what is beneath, but of course I am not certain."

The horror on his mother's face only strengthened, and he realized how callous he'd sounded in his curiosity—nay, *fascination*.

"Forgive me for upsetting you, Mama," he said. He tried to remember how to make his voice sound sympathetic—not that he'd ever been especially good at it—but his mother showed no sign of being soothed. "But I knew if I wrote to King Khalvin and claimed to have this power without confirmation from someone he knows and trusts, he would likely call me a liar."

"W-what?" Xanvin stammered, made stupid by fear.

"When Khalvin realizes the power I possess," he explained patiently, "he will understand that I must not be kept hidden away in some remote estate where I can contribute nothing to society. I am a weapon the likes of which the world has never seen." He gestured again at the dead bird. "I believe I was given this power by the Creator, and that He means for me to set the world back to rights for Him."

The line was delivered smoothly enough, although Delnamal believed no such thing. All his life, he had *tried* to believe in the Creator, to believe the teachings of the Devotional that meant so very much to his mother. But the truth was, he never truly had. What he *did* believe was that Khalvin was even more fanatically religious than his mother, and that convincing his uncle that this power was a gift from the Creator was the surest way to free himself from his exile.

"I have written a letter to the king," he continued, drawing a rolled sheet of parchment from his doublet. His hands were not capable of manipulating a quill, but he had purchased a scribes' spell that had made the task possible. He had had to sell some of his mother's jewelry in order to afford the expensive spell, and he could tell by the frown line between her brows that she'd thought he intended to use it so that he might write to his wife. She might have balked at selling her jewels if she'd known he intended to contact her brother instead.

He pointed at a small writing desk tucked in the corner of the parlor near the window. He had already laid out a fresh sheet of parchment, a quill, and a pot of ink. "In it, I explain what I can do and how the two of us together can become holy warriors to further the Creator's glory. With my power and the might of Khalpar's navy, we can take back Aaltah and march on the abomination that is Women's Well. I believe I can use my power to destroy that unholy Well, and that once I do, it will be as if the Curse never happened.

"All I need you to do is write to your brother and confirm that you have witnessed this power and that it is not some delusion born of desperation."

Xanvin continued to gape at him. For the first time ever, he saw not the faintest trace of a mother's love in her eyes, for there was nothing but horror and bone-deep fear. Perhaps Delnamal would have felt the same in the days before he'd been so indelibly changed. He wondered if a good, hard slap would break her out of that shock, but worried it might only make things worse. So instead, he merely waited patiently while she gathered herself.

Slowly, intelligence crept back into his mother's gaze, although the horror was still clearly visible. She dropped her hands away from her mouth, immediately grabbing for her Devotional and holding it clutched between both hands against her belly. He was doubly glad he had not chosen to tell her the full truth. As unsettling as this power was, his greatest strength lay in the aura of Kai that surrounded him. He hoped that King Khalvin would see Delnamal's power and his aura as an asset, rather than an abomination, but so far his mother's reaction was not promising.

Xanvin's color did not look good, and she was still breathing hard, but at least she was no longer frozen in terror. She swallowed, then licked her lips before she spoke, ever so tentatively.

"I'm not sure my brother would interpret your . . . power in quite the way you imagine," she said.

"Oh?" he asked with a raise of his eyebrows. "How else might he interpret it? Surely he will know that I would not have been changed like this unless it was by the express will of the Creator."

"Th-this power of yours . . ." She cleared her throat, then swallowed again in a way that suggested she was struggling to keep her gorge down. "It is very . . . dark."

"Ah!" Delnamal said, understanding immediately where she was going with this, thanks to her endless sermons and enforced readings of the Devotional. "You fear your brother will believe my powers have more to do with the Destroyer than the Creator. Is that it?"

According to the Devotional, the Destroyer had been the son of the Creator and the Mother. Aside from being death incarnate, the Destroyer had further desecrated His father's creations by seducing and sleeping with the Mother. In punishment, the Creator had cast His son from the heavens and imprisoned Him deep beneath the earth. It was said the Wasteland marked the place where the Destroyer fell to earth, His evil stripping all hints of life from the place. Delnamal did not believe a word of it. What had happened to him at the Well was a freak accident, brought about by the twin indignities of Melcor's unexpected death and Mairahsol's deadly scheming.

Eyes widening with fear again, Xanvin nodded silently. Delnamal most likely *should* have anticipated the direction of her thoughts, but he had failed to do so. His temper—and the self-loathing that he had never quite been consciously aware of when he was its helpless victim—attempted to derail his powers of reasoning, but it flickered and died away before it could cause him much grief.

He had never been a quick thinker or skilled liar, but it was clear to him now that it was his own feelings of guilt and anger and inadequacy that had held him back, for he easily embellished his explanation to assuage Xanvin's fears.

"Tell him that if my powers were granted by the Destroyer, then it could only have happened if the Creator had decided to temporarily release His son from His imprisonment. Perhaps it is only the power of the Destroyer that can counter the Curse. We must have faith that when the Curse is undone, the Destroyer will be returned to His prison and all will be well once more."

It did not take a keen observer of the human condition to see that his mother was far from convinced by his logic. But then, it was not his mother he needed to convince. She was nothing but a messenger, and she did not have to believe the message to write it.

"You will write to your brother on my behalf, will you not, Mama?" he inquired. His voice was calm and level, and he made not the slightest hint of a threat. And yet he knew full well that in her current state of mind, his mother would hear the threat all the same.

Xanvin was a proud, brave woman. But she was not a stupid one.

She bowed her head—whether as a token of respect or to avoid looking at him, he neither knew nor cared. "Of course, my son."

CHAPTER ELEVEN

I n an act that she suspected held just a whiff of desperation, Kailee scheduled a quartet of musicians who were all the rage among the noble houses to play for her one afternoon, inviting nearly every noblewoman who resided in Aalwell to join her. Most quickly sent terribly polite responses declining the invitation for reasons real and fictional. A handful were rude enough not to reply at all, but to her surprise, Kailee did receive two acceptances. One was from an elderly matron—a woman old enough to feel herself beyond the reach of the court gossips—and one was from the dowager queen.

By the time Oona arrived for the event, the elderly matron had taken a seat on a sofa in the corner and promptly fallen asleep, as evidenced by her delicate snores.

"Well," Kailee said brightly as she invited her only awake guest into the parlor where the musicians were set to play, "at least we will be able to hear the music without being interrupted by endless gossip and giggles."

Oona chuckled softly. "What a pleasant way of looking at things," she commented. In a different tone of voice, it might have sounded sarcastic or condescending, but Kailee detected nothing but warmth and gentle amusement.

The servants had, overly enthusiastically, set out two rows of straight-backed chairs before the small stage they had placed beside a pair of open doors that led onto a balcony. A gentle rain was falling, which was just enough to keep them all indoors despite the temperate weather. Kailee and Oona each took a seat in the front row.

"Is it terribly rude of me to say how pleasantly surprised I was that you accepted my invitation?" Kailee asked. It had certainly seemed clear to her that Oona had no inclination to further sully her already troubled reputation by associating with the prince regent's scandalous wife.

Oona seemed momentarily taken aback—as many people were by Kailee's unusual bluntness—but she quickly rallied. "I must ask your forgiveness for how I acted when last we spoke," she said. "After I left, it became clear to me that I was treating you in exactly the way I was complaining about others treating me. That is not the kind of woman I wish to be."

Kailee did not like to think of herself as a cynical person, but she couldn't help wondering if perhaps Oona had simply decided her own reputation was beyond repair and therefore not in need of such vigorous defense. She was glad for the company, however, as the musicians began to play, thankfully drowning out the snoring matron.

Kailee closed her eyes, not wanting even her Mindsight to distract from the startlingly sweet music. She had heard that the quartet was extraordinary, but she had assumed that most of the fanfare had been due more to fashion than to actual quality. The flute, especially, moved her, its pure and delicate notes soaring over the rest in counterpoint to the melody. Something about that ethereal, ringing sound as it flittered and floated on its own path and somehow magically complemented the melody made Kailee's throat ache with longing.

A soft hand touched her arm, and she heard the rustle of Oona's dress as the dowager leaned toward her. "Are you quite all right, dear?" Oona asked quietly, so as not to disturb the musicians.

Kailee opened her eyes and was startled to feel the wetness on her lashes. She smiled and dabbed at her eyes. "Yes," she breathed. "It's just so beautiful."

Oona patted her arm again and seemed to accept the explanation, but Kailee wondered if she would have been quite so affected by the beauty of the music if she weren't so terribly lonely. She swallowed the lump in her throat and took a deep breath, pulling herself back together. She had never been especially bothered by loneliness during her life in Rhozinolm. Surely with a little more time, she would get used to the social isolation once more and would stop dreaming of the warmth and acceptance of Women's Well.

Kailee and Oona thanked the musicians profusely when they finished playing, and Oona took care of waking—and seeing off—the matron, who had slept through the entire event and managed to speak no more than a sentence or two to her supposed hostess.

"Would you like to stay for tea?" Kailee asked, not eager to be left alone once more.

"That would be lovely," Oona said, yet again taking Kailee by surprise.

Once they were seated and each had a cup of tea, Oona revealed the true reason she had accepted the invitation.

"I wrote to King Khalvin, as your husband urged me," Oona said. "He promised that he would send my letter to Delnamal, and I have no reason to believe he did not do so."

Kailee hated that she felt a tiny pang of hurt to discover that Oona had not come in the spirit of friendship, after all. She had come because she was less uncomfortable speaking to Kailee than to Tynthanal.

"But you have no reason to believe he *did* do so, either," Kailee said. "In other words, you have not heard from Delnamal."

Oona sighed quietly. "No," she said. "But I can't say I'm surprised. I knew when I decided to stay in Aaltah that it was something he could never forgive." It sounded like she was on the
verge of tears.

"Then why did you stay?" Kailee asked, unable to tamp down
her curiosity.

Oona sniffled. "I have two children to think of," she said.
"Delnamal never quite warmed to his son, and he made little effort to disguise his disinterest in my eldest."

Kailee had almost forgotten that Oona had a child from a previous marriage.

"Both of my children will have a better future here in Aaltah
than they would have if we'd gone with Delnamal, even with the
difficulties of my social standing. And I myself wasn't eager to
face life as a fugitive."

"Surely any reasonable man should understand that decision,"
Kailee said, hoping the words did not sound sarcastic. Nothing
she'd heard about the former King of Aaltah had painted the
picture of a reasonable man.

Oona shook her head. "The man he once was would have
forgiven me." She sighed. "But the man he once was would never
have given himself cause to flee in the first place." The dowager
leaned forward, earnestness oozing from what Kailee could make
out of her body language. "I'm sure your husband painted as
unflattering a picture of my husband as mine did of yours," she
said, "but neither of them has an unbiased view. Delnamal was a
good man, once."

Kailee had heard a great deal about Delnamal from any number of people, and none of it painted the picture of a good man.
She attempted to maintain a neutral expression, but her skepticism must have shown.

"He was!" Oona insisted. "Not to his siblings, I have to admit that. But their father has to take some of the blame for making it so obvious that he preferred them to Delnamal. And lest you think that preference was all in Delnamal's mind, remember that I have known him since we were both children. His father could not have made it more clear that Delnamal was the least of his children, just as Alysoon and Tynthanal made it clear that they despised him. They were not as overtly cruel as many children can be, but they were not kind, either. Tynthanal especially."

Kailee was surprised by the rush of defensive anger that swelled in her breast. "I cannot believe Tynthanal was ever unkind!" she remonstrated, though she immediately heard her own words as nonsense. No one was *never* unkind.

"He was always supremely skilled with a sword, as Delnamal never was," Oona said. "He oftentimes offered to 'tutor' Delnamal in the guise of helping him improve. Delnamal's pride insisted he accept, even knowing he would be trounced. Those 'lessons' invariably left him humiliated and covered with welts and bruises." Oona's voice took on a brittle note. "Tynthanal was eight years his senior—basically a grown man beating up a child while presenting it as 'help.'"

Kailee squirmed, wanting to rush again to her husband's defense. She could not conceive of kindhearted Tynthanal acting that way toward anyone, much less his own brother, and yet . . . Almost everything she knew about Delnamal she had learned from his half-siblings, who made no secret how much they hated him.

"Added to all that was the burden of being heir to the throne," Oona continued. "From the moment he could talk, Delnamal was hammered from all sides by the need to do his duty above all else, to set aside his own wants and needs for the good of others. I'm ashamed to say that when his father refused to allow us to marry, I begged him to run away with me." Oona's voice broke. "I know he wanted to. Wanted to quite desperately. But he could not refuse what he saw as his duty, no matter how much it hurt, and no matter how much bitterness it stirred in him.

"He changed after that. The bitterness took root and grew, but he was still a decent man at heart. Do you know that in the aftermath of the Curse, he spent a great deal of his own money buying spelled kerchiefs to give out to the rescue workers in the Harbor District? He knew that they were almost all commoners who could not afford to protect themselves from the dangers and diseases that came with clearing the debris after the flooding. No one asked him to do that. And no one gave him any credit for it, either."

Kailee gritted her teeth in an effort to keep in the retort that wanted to burst from her mouth. Having lived in Women's Well surrounded by women who had once resided in the Abbey of Aaltah, Kailee knew what had been done to them on Delnamal's orders while he sat on his horse and watched. She very much doubted it was common knowledge outside of Women's Well, and certainly it wasn't something Delnamal would have shared with his wife.

Oona shook her head again, sighing with what sounded like regret. "That may very well have been the last genuinely kind thing he ever did," she admitted. "Losing his heir, losing his hope of ever *having* an heir by the woman he was forced to marry . . . That broke something inside him. He had . . . so much anger."

"But you married him anyway," Kailee pointed out. "Married him while you were still in mourning for your first husband." A husband whom Tynthanal suspected had died at Delnamal's order, though she refrained from saying that part.

"I still loved him," Oona admitted. "*Love* him. I cannot forget the man he once was, the man I fell in love with all those years ago. I was aware how much he had changed when I married him, but I was as foolish as any lovestruck maiden and somehow convinced myself my love could heal the wounds in his soul."

Impulsively, Kailee reached out and put her hand on Oona's shoulder. Whatever she herself might think of Delnamal, she could not help but be sympathetic to Oona's obvious pain.

"I will endeavor not to hold your husband against you," Kailee said, "if you will endeavor not to hold mine against me."

"It's a deal," Oona said, and although there was still a thread of caution, maybe even wariness in her voice, there was just a trace of warmth and humor, as well.

When Delnamal had built the current abbey on the ruins of the one his father had had razed, he'd decided that the place should no longer be run by an abbess. Instead, he had created the new position of administrator of the Abbey and assigned to it a commoner named Loveland. Tynthanal had met the administrator only once, but even that had been enough to inspire a comprehensive dislike of the man. If the royal council would have let him, Tynthanal would have dismissed Administrator Loveland immediately, for there was no missing his cruelty toward the women who were supposedly in his care.

When he received word that Loveland had come to the palace and was requesting a private audience, Tynthanal had half a mind to refuse. Despite how little real power the royal council had allowed him, he certainly had no trouble filling his days—and his nights—with the business of running a kingdom in crisis. So far, the diminished output of the Well was causing more inconvenience than anything—it sometimes took longer than usual for the Academy's spell crafters to find certain rare elements, so their production was slower—but that inconvenience created an outsized panic in those who depended on the elements to survive.

Instead of sending the man away, Tynthanal had had his secretary tell Loveland that he would try to squeeze him in sometime during the day, then waited to see if he would go away. If a long wait inspired him to return to the Abbey, then whatever he wanted to talk about couldn't be that important, Tynthanal reasoned.

Hours later, he'd forgotten about Loveland entirely, assuming the man had left. But when his secretary told him the administrator was still waiting, Tynthanal regretfully decided he'd better grant the audience, after all.

Loveland's bow when he was shown into the office was decidedly inelegant and awkward. Perhaps that could be the result of his very limited contact with royalty, or from his dislike of being in a subordinate position. Tynthanal had seen quite clearly when he'd visited the Abbey that Loveland enjoyed the frightened subservience of the abigails. One way or another, Tynthanal would get rid of him eventually, but it would likely be easier to manage if he could only make some progress toward healing the Well—thereby finally winning his council's wholehearted approval.

Ordinarily, Tynthanal would at least have made an effort to be polite, but the day had already been long and trying, with more political maneuvering than he could stomach.

"My time today is quite limited," he said brusquely as Loveland was rising from the bow. "Whatever it is, please make it quick."

The man's hands twitched ever so slightly—as if he had grown accustomed to hitting people who talked to him in that tone of voice. Tynthanal couldn't help noticing the fading bruises on the knuckles of his right hand.

"I beg your pardon, Your Highness," Loveland said, though he didn't sound particularly apologetic. "I fear this might not be a terribly quick conversation."

Tynthanal made an impatient hand gesture. "As quick as possible, then."

Loveland shifted in apparent discomfort and cleared his throat. "My abigails have noticed something . . . unusual of late. I assumed at first that it was nothing but a flight of fancy. Or perhaps merely a coincidence. But now . . ."

Tynthanal did not like the sound of that. Not one bit. And he had the sinking feeling that he understood the source of Loveland's discomfort. Whatever it was the abigails had noticed, he'd ignored it for who knew how long before finally, reluctantly, bringing it to Tynthanal's attention. And whatever it was, it was severe enough that he'd decided to bring it directly to the prince regent rather than working his way up through the trade minister, who was his immediate superior.

"Well, what is it?" Tynthanal prompted. "I assume that the damage to our Well has affected the supply of feminine elements as much as it has masculine and neuter ones." In point of fact, Tynthanal had personal knowledge that it had, but most people outside of Women's Well had no idea he could see feminine elements at all.

"Er, yes," Loveland agreed, "but that's not the issue." Loveland licked his lips. "Thanks to the Curse, the demand for midwives has been unusually low over the last couple of years. But it appears that since whatever events occurred at the Well when that Khalpari witch cast her spell on it, the demand has become . . . significantly lower still."

Tynthanal could not hide the chill of unease that shivered through him. "How low are we talking?"

Loveland shifted again. "Very low."

Tynthanal rose from his chair, pushing it back with more force than necessary. *"How low?"* he demanded, wishing Loveland would just spit it out already.

"You understand that the Abbey serves only the gentry, so that—"

"Answer the question immediately, or I'll have you removed from your post." He doubted the council would allow him to do that even now, but it made an effective threat, nonetheless. An expression of genuine alarm—almost panic—lit Loveland's eyes.

"There have been five calls for a midwife since the incident. And two of those turned out to be false alarms."

"So, a total of three new pregnancies," Tynthanal said faintly. He would have loved to think it a mistake, or an exaggeration. But even considering that the count would not include any woman who was not of noble birth—and any noblewoman who disdained to utilize the services of the Abbey or who lived far enough away from Aalwell to make using one of their midwives impractical—that was an appallingly low number.

Tynthanal shook his head in horror. "Three pregnancies in more than three months . . ." He let his voice trail off, and realized it was more urgent than ever that he and Kailee figure out what Mairahsol had done to the Well.

A part of him wanted to upbraid Loveland for waiting so long to report this terrible trend, for failing to listen to his abigails when they warned him that the birth rate was falling. But that would require him to spend more time in the man's presence, so instead, he dismissed him. And began pondering when and how he should share this news with his royal council.

CHAPTER TWELVE

Leethan groaned when she found herself standing alone on a windswept cliff overlooking a rocky beach. It had been only a month since she'd last suffered a recurrence of the nightmare that had plagued her since she was a teenager, and she'd hoped she'd have at least another year or so before another one came. Never before had she had two of them in such a short period of time. She closed her eyes tightly, willing herself to drift back into the depths of sleep—but it had never worked before, and it wasn't going to work this time, either.

When she opened her eyes once more, the horizon was filled with sails as a tremendous naval battle took place under a lowering sky. If this were happening in reality, the fighting would be too far away for her to hear anything, but the wind carried the sound of clashing swords and cries of agony to her ears. When she looked down at the beach, ghostly figures of armored men wavered into being, attacking one another with a ferocity she could hardly bear to witness.

Leethan groaned again as she suddenly found herself no longer standing on the cliff above it all, but perched on a rocky outcropping in the middle of the chaos. The figures that battled and died around her were all insubstantial, their faces and forms impossible to make out when she looked straight at them, although they seemed real enough in her peripheral vision. And the sounds . . . For those sounds alone, she would label this dream a nightmare! She covered her ears so she could at least muffle the screams and wondered how so many men could find the idea of battle exciting, even pleasurable.

The battle raged on for what seemed like forever, the bodies piling up—until suddenly all those bodies and soldiers were gone as if they had never existed. Sighing in relief, she let her hands fall from her ears and waited for the final phase of the dream to begin. The part that was the most strange and made no sense whatsoever.

Three men shimmered to life on the wet sand, just out of reach of the waves. She could tell they were men because of their physiques and because they wore men's battle armor, but they were all facing away from her.

The men stood lined up in a row, far enough apart that they could not touch one another with their outstretched arms. Leethan noted that one of the men wore a helm decorated with a jeweled crown, the likes of which would only be worn by a sovereign who was destined to "lead" his men into battle by giving them orders and hanging back himself. To that man's right was one who wore a cloak and hood over armor that, when the wind tugged his cloak out of the way, was revealed as a light coat of mail, hanging from a cadaverously gaunt figure. And the third man was dressed in the plain, utilitarian armor of a man of Nandel.

The three women appeared next, each taking her place facing one of the men. As with the soldiers who had fought and died on that same beach, the faces of the three women blurred whenever Leethan tried to focus on them. One had hair that was almost entirely gray under a simple, unadorned headdress; one wore a crown over salt-and-pepper hair and was dressed in mourning

black; and one of them wore a court gown that revealed the neck
and shoulders of a young woman, though her face was no more
visible than the others'.

Three women, facing three men. And with unnerving certainty, Leethan felt as though the fate of the world rested on
them.

First, the old woman stepped forward and slashed her wrists,
laying each one open. A tricolored mote formed in the air before
her, looking like three separate crystals had fused together—one
red, one white, and one black. It was unmistakably some form of
Kai, though Leethan had never heard of Kai looking like that or
being formed by suicide.

It was patently impossible for Leethan to see with both her
worldly vision and her Mindsight at the same time, but this dream
did not care about what was possible.

The woman seized the mote of Kai, pushing it toward the
man standing across from her. As soon as the mote touched him,
he collapsed and died at her feet.

One by one, the women slashed their wrists and created those
motes of red, white, and black Kai. One by one, they sent those
motes at the men who stood opposite them. And one by one, the
men sank lifeless to the ground.

But those three motes of Kai did not disappear upon the death
of the men; instead, the motes drifted toward one another and
merged. A bright, blinding light suddenly seared Leethan's eye-
balls.

And she awoke with a half-choked scream in her throat.

More than a fortnight passed, and Delnamal had yet to receive a
response from King Khalvin. He'd asked his mother if she had
received a reply to her own missive and had been surprised when
she'd lied and told him she had not. But he'd *seen* the butler hand

her a flier, and he had seen the furtive way she had looked around when she'd read it. He'd been lurking in the woods at the time, hidden from her view by distance and brambles.

The man he used to be would have been furious at the attempted subterfuge, but he'd done nothing more dire than give her a long, cold stare. Eventually, she'd broken down and admitted that yes, the king had replied to her letter, and no, it was not the reply Delnamal hoped to hear.

He considered demanding she tell him exactly what the letter contained, but quickly realized he did not in actuality care. Based on his mother's too-obvious fear, it was clear the tone of the letter had been less than conciliatory, and Delnamal didn't need the details.

It was a setback, to be sure, and Delnamal found himself momentarily paralyzed with fear that despite his terrible newfound power, he might be as helpless now as he had been when he'd first arrived in Khalpar. But fear had no more power over him now than did anger, and he let it flow through him and away, thinking what an easier, better life he would have led if he'd known how to do this all along.

There was nothing to do but write to the king again. And again. As many times as necessary to persuade the man to give him an audience, where he might demonstrate his power in person.

He did not like the whiff of desperation he sensed in this plan, nor the feeling that he was begging his exalted uncle for help. But pride was perhaps the most unhelpful emotion of all, and he would not allow it to stand in his way. He could not even begin to form a plan to take back his kingdom while exiled in the hinterlands, kept secluded like the embarrassing family secret his uncle thought him to be. He *needed* to gain an invitation to Khalwell so that he might have a private audience with the king.

In the meantime, Delnamal had no choice but to supplement

his strength with nothing more than the occasional purloined chicken or unlucky rabbit he discovered in a snare and not yet collected for the stewpot.

It was a paltry existence, and it meant he was back to the cycle of his strength waxing and waning that was tiresome in the extreme. But he had patience now the likes of which he had never known before. He could bide his time until eventually, inevitably, Khalvin answered him—or at least sent someone out to the manor house to speak to him in person.

All he had to do was be patient. And resist the sometimes nearly overwhelming urge to help himself to the fat, juicy motes of Rhokai that were so tantalizingly close to him at all hours of the day and night.

Kailee heard her husband groan softly and push his breakfast plate away, and she watched the aura of his hands as they patted a belly that was visibly more rounded and softer than it had once been.

"I have got to stop eating like this," he said, then laughed at himself. "Which is something I should have thought of *before* I cleaned my plate."

Kailee smiled. "You should endeavor to hire a less skillful cook," she teased.

"I spent most of my adult life in the military," he reminded her. "We made a habit of eating quickly and thoroughly, whether the food was good or not. It's a hard habit to break now that I spend most of my day sitting and have no time for exercise."

"You were the Lord Chancellor of Women's Well, which was hardly a military position."

"But I was a very *active* lord chancellor. My duties here keep me nearly tied to my chair. I haven't swung a sword for a month." He snorted. "No wonder Delnamal grew so enormous once he became king."

Kailee winced at the venom in his voice and couldn't help remembering Oona's story of the sword lessons he'd given his little brother. She had defended Tynthanal at the time, and she reminded herself that he had a great many reasons to hate Delnamal. Although no one had told Kailee straight out that Chanlix had been one of the abigails Delnamal's men had savaged under his orders, she had easily surmised the truth. So Tynthanal had already thoroughly hated him even before Delnamal had killed Alysoon's daughter.

"You know that I visited with Queen Oona the other day," she said, still working on the remains of her own breakfast.

"So I had heard," he replied. "You will let me know if she says anything that might help us locate Delnamal, will you not?"

Kailee frowned at him. She had hoped he'd be happy she was forming something resembling a friendship rather than seeing that friendship through the lens of what might be useful to him. "I will not spy on her, nor will I betray her confidence." There was a sharp edge in her tone that she had never used with him before. Her friendship with Mairah had begun with just that kind of betrayal, although at least in that instance Mairah had been fully aware of Kailee's ulterior motives. Kailee had never bothered to deny them, which had in a perverse way made it easier for them both to set them aside.

"I didn't mean to give offense," Tynthanal said, "but you have to know that it's vital we locate Delnamal."

"So that you can kill him, you mean?" She pushed aside her unfinished food, her appetite now gone.

"So I can find out what happened to our Well and fix it!" he countered.

"Do you mean to tell me that's the *only* reason you want to find him?" she asked with a little heat of her own. She had no doubt he wanted to fix the Well more than anything, but she was equally certain that even if Oona reached Delnamal and learned what had happened at the Well, Tynthanal would not be satisfied. His silence in response to her question confirmed her suspicion.

She tried to remind herself that Tynthanal was incapable of seeing straight where his half-brother was concerned. "It isn't enough that he's fled the kingdom in disgrace and can never come back? Is it vitally important for the good of all of Aaltah that you also hunt him down and kill him to punish him for everything he's done?"

Tynthanal sat back in his chair, and she felt sure he was gaping at her in shock.

"I know you've a kind heart," he said, "but can you really mean to tell me that he doesn't deserve to die?"

"Very likely he does," Kailee had to agree. "However, that does not mean it is of such vital importance that I betray the one and only friend I have at court so that you can hunt him."

Tynthanal sighed. "I didn't mean it like that," he said. "And if you are making friends with Oona, then I am glad for you both. She does not deserve to bear the blame for what her husband did."

"She told me about the sword lessons you gave Delnamal when you were growing up."

"What?"

"Did you try to 'tutor' Delnamal in swordplay?" she asked.

"Well, yes," he replied, sounding nonplussed. "He was pathetic at it. He came to me one day blubbering because Father had accused him of not practicing enough. I know our father found Delnamal's ineptitude embarrassing and was not always gentle about telling him so. Delnamal asked me to help him improve, and so I did."

"Hmm," Kailee said, for it all sounded quite reasonable. Except there was a touch of something in his voice that did not entirely ring true, some faint echo that might well have been guilt. It was possible she was reading things into it, but because she'd spent her life without the ability to see facial expressions, she liked to think she was especially good at reading voices. "And when you tried to teach him, you trounced him?"

He gave an impatient sigh. "Yes, of course. I did say he was terrible at it. He was clumsy and slow and had nothing resembling patience."

"Did your teaching help him improve?"

Tynthanal scoffed and shook his head. "No. He was hopeless."

"But you kept 'teaching' him anyway, didn't you?"

Tynthanal fell silent, his body going still.

It was a telling silence.

"Why keep teaching him if it wasn't doing any good?" she pressed, feeling more than a twinge of disappointment. She did not like to think of her husband as a bully, and she had rarely seen him be anything but kind, and yet it seemed clear to her that he had not treated his half-brother quite as well as he'd claimed.

Tynthanal remained silent for a good minute or two, and she gave him the space and time to think.

"He was a little shit even as a kid," Tynthanal finally said, the vulgarity surprising Kailee so much she gasped. "Forgive my language, but he was."

"Meaning it was okay for someone eight years his senior to beat him up under the guise of being helpful?" she retorted indignantly, and Tynthanal sighed.

"No," he admitted. "I told myself I was being helpful, but of course you're right. If I were truly being helpful, I would not have kept doing it once I recognized it was hopeless."

"So you found a socially acceptable excuse to beat up on a younger, weaker boy."

He bowed his head. "I never allowed myself to think of it that way, and yet when you say it . . . I suppose I must admit you have the right of it. But it doesn't forgive what he became."

"I never said it did. I'm merely suggesting that your desire to find and punish him has more to do with your personal feelings than with the good of Aaltah."

"Maybe," he conceded with obvious reluctance. "I'm sorry I

suggested you betray your friend's confidence. The request was insensitive, and I'll try to do better."

Moments ago, Kailee had been disappointed in her husband, but now she felt a glow of warmth she wished she could ignore. Her experience with men was perhaps somewhat limited, but she hadn't met a great many of them who were willing to apologize to the women in their lives with any degree of sincerity. Just her luck to be married to one of them while knowing beyond any doubt that his heart could never be hers.

Alys bade her honor guardsmen wait outside as Maidel opened the door to Grunamai's home. When Alys had first met Maidel, the young woman had been so ashamed of the birthmark on her face that her eyes were always downcast, her body always slightly canted so that the side with the birthmark was farthest from view. Maidel had come a long way since then, and though she performed the necessary respectful bow, she raised her head afterward with no hesitation.

"Thank you for coming, Your Royal Highness," she said. "Lady Grunamai is most anxious to speak with you."

"So I heard," Alys said with false cheer, for though she was relieved that Grunamai had finally regained consciousness, the messenger who had fetched her said the seer was still in dangerously poor condition.

When she'd first received the request from Tynthanal to have one of her seers try to re-create one of the potions he and Kailee had deciphered from Mairahsol's notes, her inclination had been to refuse. But she'd allowed Tynthanal and Kailee to convince her of the importance of testing it, and now she was regretting it.

Alys had known that taking a standard seer's poison was unpleasant, even for the most gifted seers. But if she'd had any true concept of what Grunamai would go through after downing the modified poison, she would have stuck to her first instinct to refuse.

The house felt unnaturally still and quiet as Maidel led the way up the stairs to the seer's bedroom, where she had lain unconscious for two days since she'd downed the poison. Alys was not surprised to find Chanlix sitting at her friend's side, though the straight-backed chair could not be comfortable with that formidable belly.

"You should be resting while you have the chance," Alys chided gently, for Chanlix was due any day now. And it didn't matter how many times Chanlix scolded her for hovering; she just couldn't help it.

"That's what I told her," said a voice from within the shadows of the bed curtains. Those curtains had been tucked aside—no doubt for Chanlix's sake—but the room was gloomy enough that Alys couldn't get a good look at Grunamai's face until the woman groaned and moved over into a patch of light.

It was all Alys could do not to gasp at what the light revealed, and though she tried to hide her horror, she was sure it showed in her face. Two days ago, Grunamai had been a plump and vivacious woman of middling years, with sparkling eyes and a contagious laugh. During her stint as an abigail in Aaltah, she'd apparently been nicknamed "Sister Dimples," and there had been no missing the why of it. But though Grunamai attempted one of her trademark smiles, her cheeks were so hollow that not a hint of a dimple appeared, and her eyes were frighteningly dull.

"Please picture me performing the requisite curtsy, Your Royal Highness," she said, her voice uncharacteristically thin and weak. "I'm afraid my body is not up to doing it for real."

Alys swallowed hard as guilt gnawed at her.

"Don't do it, Alysoon," Chanlix said, sounding rather cross, which was unlike her. Just as it was unlike her to address Alys so informally. "Don't take all the blame on your shoulders as if you were the only one responsible for the decision."

Grunamai started to speak, then broke down coughing. Chanlix reached over and squeezed the other woman's hand, her brow furrowed with concern. Still looking at Grunamai, she said, "We all knew that taking a seer's poison was dangerous, and that testing unknown potions was dangerous. And we all agreed it was worth the risk."

" 'Dangerous' is too weak a word to describe this," Alys said, approaching Grunamai's bedside and taking in her unhealthy pallor and the faint trembling of her hands.

"It was worse than expected," Grunamai admitted, her voice raspy from the cough. "I would have been wiser to mix the potion with a less potent seer's poison, as it seems to have exacerbated the effects, but there was no way anyone could have known. And I was fully aware of the risk when I agreed to test it."

Alys sat gingerly on the woman's bedside and knew that logic would do little to assuage her guilt. It was common practice at academies elsewhere in the world to test new magic on prisoners or impoverished volunteers who could not turn down the lure of "easy" money, but Alys had refused to allow the Women's Well Academy to do so. Magic was tested on animals or on *true* volunteers, even though that put limits on the kinds of magic they could produce.

"Still," Alys started, "I should have—"

"I still have family back in Aaltah," Grunamai interrupted, perhaps too ill to consider the breach in protocol. "They may have disowned me, but I still care about them. Whatever is wrong with Aaltah's Well, I want it fixed so that my sisters and their children are safe. I *wanted* to test this potion."

Alys remembered all too well how Grunamai had screamed in agony when the poison first began its assault. She was glad she herself did not have a seer's talent, for she didn't know if she'd have had the courage to take a poison if she knew what it would do to her.

Chanlix shifted on her chair, wincing in discomfort and letting go of Grunamai's hand so she could put both hands on her belly. "Could we perhaps discuss the results of the test? I think you're both right and I should get a little rest, but I'm not leaving until I know what Grunamai saw and how well it matches what you remember."

Mairahsol's notes had claimed her potion, when added to a seer's poison, would cause the seer to have a vision of something that had happened in the past. Something that the seer herself had never witnessed. The problem being that if the seer had not witnessed the events, then it was hard for her to know whether what she saw in her vision was accurate. To that end, Alys had asked Grunamai to trigger a vision of an event Alys herself had witnessed and never told anyone about. Something it was impossible for Grunamai to know, but that Alys could verify.

There was no point in *not* checking to find out whether the spell had worked, so Alys set aside her guilt for the time being—knowing full well she would revisit it later.

"Very well," she said. "Tell me, Lady Grunamai. What happened the very first time I peeked at a primer?"

Elsewhere in the world, it was strictly forbidden for a respectable woman to study magic, and yet Alys had been fascinated by magic long before her Mindseye had developed. She'd also had a thirst for knowledge—especially knowledge that was deemed unsuitable for girls—and had made a frequent habit of sneaking into the library in the residential wing of the palace. It was in that library that she had found the forbidden magic primer. It had included detailed paintings of the elements, along with descriptions of what those elements were capable of, and she'd been fascinated.

Even in her weakened state, Grunamai smiled. "It seems you were a precocious—and naughty—child. I saw a child of maybe seven or eight years sneaking into a darkened library in what looked like the middle of the night. You were carrying a candle instead of a luminant, and you were moving so furtively I was sure you had slipped out of bed under the nose of your governess."

Chanlix glanced quickly over at Alys, raising her eyebrows in inquiry. Alys nodded to acknowledge the veracity of what Grunamai had said so far. It was impossible for *anyone* to know about that forbidden night, for Alys had never spoken of it, not even to her late husband.

"I saw you find the primer," Grunamai continued, "and you were looking through it when you heard voices approaching. You quickly shoved the primer back on its shelf, then hid behind a brocade curtain."

Alys's face heated with remembered embarrassment. She'd been frightened at the time, knowing she'd be thrashed for her audacity if she was caught, and she'd pinched out the candle's flame moments before the library door opened.

"Come here, you," she heard her father's voice say, and at first she'd thought he'd been speaking to her, that he'd seen her sneak in and might take her over his knee.

Then there was a muffled feminine giggle, followed by footsteps and the swish of long skirts. The door slammed shut, and the sounds that followed were ones that a little girl had no place recognizing, although even at that age, Alys had had at least an inkling of what was going on. She *did* enjoy acquiring forbidden knowledge, after all.

Grunamai smiled, reaching over and patting her hand gently. "I imagine it was traumatic for a girl so small to hear that, even if you perhaps didn't fully understand what you were hearing."

Alys raised one shoulder in a faint shrug. "I had the gist of it. Enough to feel properly mortified and to fear that my parents would see my knowledge on my face the next time I saw them. I stuck my fingers in my ears as soon as I realized what was going on, but . . ."

She let her voice trail off in amusement, and only then noticed the slight widening of Grunamai's eyes. She frowned as Gruna-mai looked quickly away.

"What is it?" she asked, unable to fathom why the other woman suddenly looked so uncomfortable. It was impossible to spend much time in the Abbey of the Unwanted and remain a prude, so surely the sight of Alys's parents having sex could not have had this effect on her.

"Nothing," Grunamai said unconvincingly. "I'm only picturing your discomfort."

Alys's frown deepened. "That's not it."

Grunamai squirmed in the bed as if trying to escape Alys's scrutiny.

"Tell me what's bothering you," Alys commanded, but Grunamai started coughing and shook her head. Alys was half-convinced the cough was forced, but she was reluctant to press in case she was wrong.

"I suspect the woman in question was not your mother," Chanlix said, and it was clear from Grunamai's expression that she'd gotten it right.

"Of course it was!" Alys protested, an almost reflexive need to defend the memory of her parents' happy marriage. "My father would never . . ." She cleared her throat and tried again. "I was only eight when that happened. It was *before* the troubles started, when my parents were still very much in love."

Chanlix gave her a look that held a hint of pity. "It was before the troubles got bad enough for you to know about them," she said. "Mother Brynna told me there had been other women in the latter stages of the marriage. She did not tell me *much* about what happened between her and the king, but I do know it was more complicated than anyone supposes."

Alys shook her head. "It was *my mother*," she insisted, hearing once again that feminine giggle and trying to remember if she'd truly recognized it. It had sounded like her mother. Hadn't it? Or had her child's mind merely leapt to the expected conclusion?

"I'm sorry, Your Royal Highness," Grunamai said, sounding more weary now. "I did not realize . . ."

"No apologies necessary," Alys hastened to assure the other woman. "You have made a heroic sacrifice in testing the potion, and if I learned an uncomfortable truth, it's my own fault for choosing that memory to have you see."

Grunamai said something else, but Alys was unable to hear her over Chanlix's sudden cry of pain. The cry was quickly followed by a gasp as Chanlix clutched her belly. She met Alys's eyes, looking both frightened and excited.

"It's time!"

CHAPTER THIRTEEN

Ellin opened her eyes, stretching and yawning, to find herself, as always, alone in her bed. She sat up and rubbed the grit from her eyes, wondering if she would ever wake in time to find Zarsha still beside her. They'd been married a full month now, and he had shared her bed the entire time, leaving the bed in the consort's suite untouched. But in all that time, she'd never once awakened before him.

There was a rustling sound outside the bed curtains, and the air filled with the mouthwatering scent of freshly baked pastries and generously spiced tea. Dishes rattled on a tray, and soon the curtains parted to reveal Zarsha holding that tray.

Ellin smiled at him and sat up, fluffing some pillows behind herself. "Star," she said with a shake of her head, "you look nothing like yourself today. I hope all is well."

Zarsha grinned at her and set the tray down over her lap. "Star is enjoying a much-deserved sleep-in."

Ellin covered her mouth with the back of her hand to hide a yawn. With the curtains shut, she had little sense of the exact time of day, but it felt early. If the tray of food weren't teasing her senses, she might easily have turned over and gone back to sleep.

Her days always began with a breakfast tray from Star, though she usually consumed that breakfast in hurried nibbles while Star was dressing her for the day, for a queen had not the luxury of lying abed.

"I know that look on your face," Zarsha said as he reached for a steaming bun that dripped with honey. He tore off a corner of that bun—getting honey all over his fingers—and held it to her lips. "I've woken you early so that we might have a little time together before you begin your day. You have time to eat a proper breakfast."

The tantalizing scents of yeast and honey persuaded her not to scold her husband for depriving her of the extra sleep she probably needed, and she opened her mouth and allowed him to lay the morsel on her tongue.

"Mmm," she hummed in pleasure, savoring the burst of flavor. She enjoyed watching Zarsha lick the excess honey from his fingers, as well, but she knew he had not awakened her early in hopes of a morning romp. Which was a shame, for the troubles that still lay between them were so easily cast aside when they were in bed together and it was impossible to *think* through all the *feeling*.

There were two teacups resting on the tray, and Ellin filled each while Zarsha tore off another corner of the bun.

"You don't have to feed me," she scolded.

"I wasn't planning to," he responded, then popped the corner of bun into his own mouth. "This is delicious," he said with his mouth full, "and there's more than enough for two."

She grabbed for the tray to hold it steady while he climbed over her to position himself at her side on the bed, his left arm draping over her shoulders. Not the easiest position for eating, but Ellin found she could not object. She could not deny that she still felt . . . uncomfortable with Zarsha's long habit of seeking out—and keeping—secrets. But he'd promised he would keep no more from her, and when she was cuddled next to him like this, it was easy to believe him. It was only when he was not by her side that she sometimes wondered if she was being dangerously naïve about him.

They ate in companionable silence for a few minutes, elbows occasionally jostling, the tea occasionally threatening to escape the confines of its cups with their movements. Between them, they finished off every crumb of pastry on the tray until they were left with nothing but the tea, which had finally cooled to a less-painful drinking temperature.

Ellin had to admit she was enjoying this semblance of a lei-surely morning, but of course it couldn't last. Queens did not get leisurely mornings. Nor did prince consorts.

"If you have something you think we should talk about," she said regretfully, "we'd probably better get to it. I don't suppose we'll have much longer before we're interrupted."

Zarsha sighed. "No. I don't suppose we will." He took an-other sip of his tea, then set the cup aside and turned to face her. "I've been thinking lately about the succession."

Ellin blinked in surprise, for the subject seemed to come out of nowhere. "Oh? Why?"

He smiled wryly. "Because likely sometime in the not-too-distant future, we're going to have our first child. And if that child should happen to be a girl, I would hope that she can suc-ceed you to the throne."

Ellin's chest tightened with sudden panic, and she covered her discomfiture by refilling her teacup, giving the task more atten-tion than it deserved.

She'd lain with Zarsha practically every night since the wed-ding, and yet somehow, she had never put any thought into the possibility of children. At least not to the possibility of having children *soon*.

It was what was expected, of course. Producing children was supposed to be the primary purpose—if not the *only* purpose—of marriage, and newly married couples often had children within the first year or two. Surely everyone assumed Ellin would provide an heir to the throne as soon as possible, for that was one of her most urgent duties as a sovereign.

But just the *thought* of adding a baby to her already chaotic and often bewildering life was enough to make her heart race and her palms sweat. She'd been through *so* much change in the past two years, all of it so vast that she still struggled to cope with it. And what more dramatic change could there be than having a baby?

Beside her, she felt Zarsha grow tense, and realized that her fidgeting with the tea was doing nothing to hide her feelings.

"Of course," Zarsha said, his voice tight with some emotion she could not put a name to, "we'll only have children if you *want* to."

"I want to," Ellin reassured him hastily, turning to her husband in hopes that she could read his feelings as well as he could read hers. Unfortunately, Zarsha was much better at being inscrutable than she was. The tension in his body and the tightness in his voice told her he was feeling *something* with alarming intensity, but she couldn't tell from looking at his face whether it was anger or sadness or hurt or something else entirely.

Whatever it was Zarsha was feeling, Ellin wanted it to go away, so she tried forcing a tremulous smile. "I'm being a ninny," she said. "I want to have children. I just hadn't given it any thought, for some reason. And I certainly hadn't thought about what would happen if our firstborn is a daughter."

Every word she said was true, but there were many that went unspoken. As well as being her husband, Zarsha was in many ways the closest friend Ellin had ever had. It was possible that if she told him she wasn't ready to have children yet, he would understand. After all, he'd been understanding of her relationship with Graesan even while he'd been aggressively courting her. But it seemed to her more likely he would take her reluctance as a sign that she did not fully trust him after he'd revealed how he'd created his information network—and after he'd prevented Graesan from seeing her. She had declined his offer to arrange a meeting with her former lover via talker, but she couldn't help the residual stir of resentment she felt whenever she thought of what he'd done.

His always-piercing gaze seemed to take in too much. "Are you still angry with me for keeping secrets?"

"Are you still angry with me for agreeing to Waldmir's terms?" she countered.

Zarsha sighed. "Touché," he said, then gave her a wry grin. "I don't suppose our relationship will ever be completely uncomplicated."

"And yet I love you anyway," she said, meeting Zarsha's eyes and willing him to hear the sincerity of her words. For all that had come between them, for all her occasional doubts and worries, of that she had no doubt.

He reached out and stroked her cheek, and she closed her eyes with pleasure. What she had felt for Graesan was a candle flame compared to the roaring bonfire of her feelings for Zarsha.

"And I love you," he assured her. "We are neither of us uncomplicated people."

She laughed, for she suspected he was right.

"Now that we've established that," Zarsha continued, "do you mind if we talk a little more about the succession? Whether we have our first child soon, or years from now, I think it best we begin laying the groundwork as soon as possible. You know that as the law is currently written, a daughter would stand below any sons we might have—and below Kailindar and his sons—in the line of succession."

Ellin nodded. "She would only succeed to the throne under dire circumstances, as I did."

"Exactly. I don't want that for our daughter, if we have one. And I think it would be easier to convince the council to change the law *before* we have a daughter on the way."

Ellin bit her lip, momentarily letting go of her internal qualms and approaching the issue with logic. "Easier, perhaps," she agreed. "But still not easy. The council is now at least grudgingly accepting of my rule, but I hardly enjoy their wholehearted support. And they unquestionably see me as an exception to the general rule that females are not capable of handling such masculine responsibilities. Far easier for them to believe that I am a rare, exceptional woman than to admit the possibility that women in general may be capable of much more than they imagine."

Zarsha swigged some tea, frowning in thought. "Regrettably, you're probably right about that," he finally concluded. "But that's why we have to start trying to change their way of thinking as early as possible. Don't let them get too comfortable assuming that you will bear a son, and that son will succeed you and return things to 'normal.' We have to change their perception of 'normal.' Does that make sense?"

She nodded, though she was perhaps not as hopeful as he that such a thing was possible. "I suspect I can convince Semsulin and Kailindar that I am not the only woman capable of ruling," she said thoughtfully. "Semsulin has often referred to me as extraordinary, but I've never had the sense that he holds other women in contempt. Kailindar clearly adores his daughter, and I can tell just by talking to him that he respects her even while he's often exasperated by her. The trade minister will certainly support me." The trade minister and Kailindar were the only two members of the council she herself had chosen; the rest she'd inherited from her grandfather's reign.

"But the *rest* of my council members . . ." She sighed. "Nothing I do will ever win over my lord high treasurer or my lord commander." Those two men had been firmly in Tamzin's camp when her cousin had tried to yank the throne out from under her, and though they had ceased their active resistance, she was under no illusion that they would support her in any radical changes.

"Then perhaps you should look into the possibility of replacing one of them. The junior members of your council will be easily swayed by powerful voices like Semsulin's and Kailindar's as long as you can muzzle the strongest opposition."

Ellin shivered and hugged herself, unable to fight off the visceral memory of the last time she'd dismissed one of her council members. She would never forget the terrible day when he'd tried to assassinate her, when one of her guards had given his life to protect her. She could still feel the weight of the dying man's body on top of hers, feel the hot blood that covered her.

Zarsha put his arm back around her shoulders and squeezed. She suspected he would have pulled her into his arms if it wouldn't have upset the tray and risked soaking them both with hot tea.

"It needn't be anything as dramatic as Lord Creethan's dismissal," he said gently, his hand stroking up and down her arm. "It could be something as innocuous as giving your lord commander some gentle inducement to retire. He is getting on in years, after all, and he could easily have retired five years ago."

The suggestion startled a short laugh from her. "You mean bribe him?"

Zarsha grinned at her. "I would never use so crass a term. Sounds terribly disreputable, and clearly something beneath the dignity of a queen. No, 'persuade' sounds much more noble."

"Hmm," Ellin said, rolling the idea around in her head. "So far, I've had very little success persuading Lord Khelved of *anything*."

Zarsha's grin remained firmly in place. "I have every confidence you'll find a way." The grin faded, replaced by something a good deal more tentative. "And failing that . . ." He cleared his throat, and squirmed.

"Failing that, what?" she asked with no small hint of suspicion in her voice.

"Failing that, and with your permission, I could approach him about some financial improprieties I've discovered." The tentative look on Zarsha's face was replaced with something more like a challenge. "I did not go *looking* for secrets among your council members, but thanks to my contacts and my habits, I do occasionally stumble upon things I'm not actively looking for."

It was on the tip of Ellin's tongue to voice a quick and unequivocal refusal. What Zarsha was suggesting was flat-out wrong, and though she could justify using his sources to provide information about the workings of other kingdoms and principalities, it was much harder to justify using them against her own people.

"It may not be necessary," Zarsha reminded her. "You can be more persuasive than you give yourself credit for, and Khelved is obviously not entirely overjoyed to serve on your council. If you give him a graceful and dignified way out, he might jump on it."

Ellin turned to him, catching his gaze and not letting it go. "Do you swear to me that you will not make any attempt to interfere unless I specifically ask you to?"

Zarsha put his hand over his heart. "I swear."

She let out a long, tense sigh. "Then I'll see what I can do."

Tynthanal returned to the royal apartments almost an hour earlier than usual, and Kailee could not decide if she was relieved or distressed. She'd spent the entire evening battling a combination of nerves and indecision, and she felt as if telling Tynthanal of her conclusion would make it irreversible.

Her husband noticed her state of agitation immediately, taking her hand and giving it a supportive squeeze. "What's wrong?" he asked, and she knew he was already bristling with the suspicion that someone at court had been unkind to her.

As usual, she had spent the entire evening after the tediously long dinner banquet alone in her apartments, for though she should by rank be the most important lady of the court, she had ceased accepting even the pitifully few invitations that came her way. It was less unpleasant to decline than to attend an event at which she would be pointedly ignored. No one had as yet had the nerve to be openly rude to her—hence the continued insincere invitations and the ridiculously convenient, but technically plausible, excuses given when declining her own—but she was very much aware of the constant subtle snubs and the too-loud whispers whenever she entered a room. She could not claim those did not hurt—no matter how used to them she might be—but that was not at all what troubled her tonight.

"I've decided to try the potion Mairah made for me," she blurted out, impatient with herself for dithering. It was not like her to be indecisive, and she sternly ordered herself to stiffen her spine and find her bravery.

"Oh?" Tynthanal asked, giving her hand another squeeze. "What brought this on?" He guided them both to the sofa, and she saw his head turn toward the pair of vials she had set out on the coffee table. One held Mairah's potion; the other, an antidote that she could quickly quaff if she found she did not like the effects.

Kailee shrugged. "I just . . . thought it was time I made a decision."

"Yes, but why?" he asked again, and she could hear the frown in his voice.

Kailee blinked, for this was not at all the reaction she'd been expecting. Surely he was *eager* for her to try it. He had never treated her as though he felt she was a liability, but clearly she *was*, in her current state. She was a nonentity at court, when she could—no *should*—be his most dependable ally. And if she could only close her Mindseye, she could be . . . well, not accepted. Not really. It wasn't as if everyone would suddenly *forget* she'd been walking around with her Mindseye open all her life. But she could perhaps not be so steadfastly excluded, and might eventually come to have some small fraction of the influence the wife of the prince regent ought to.

"What do you mean?" she asked, flummoxed.

Tynthanal chuckled. "It's a simple question, Kailee. You seem to get along well enough without physical eyesight, and I have the impression you would be . . . bereft if you lost access to your Mindsight."

Kailee squirmed, for somehow she had not prepared herself adequately for this conversation, despite having mentally rehearsed it about a thousand times. "But I am . . . an embarrassment as I am."

Tynthanal scoffed. "That is your stepmother talking. It certainly isn't me. Have I shown any sign that I'm embarrassed by your eyes?"

Kailee clasped her hands together in her lap, for it was true that he never had. He'd been uncomfortable with her when they'd first met, but that had been because he was in love with Chanlix and was being coerced into marrying Kailee instead. But even then, what she had sensed had never been anything like distaste or embarrassment, and he had made it abundantly clear his resistance to the marriage had nothing to do with *her*. He would have been equally resistant to marrying *any* woman who was not Chanlix.

"You've been very kind to me," she said softly. "But surely you must want me to try the potion so that—"

He reached over and squeezed her hands again. "Please do not concern yourself with what you think I might want. The only thing that matters is what *you* want. So, do *you* want to close your Mindseye?"

She licked her lips, unwilling to voice the immediate "no" that came to her mind. Tynthanal let go of her hands, and she found herself unable to keep them still, picking at the rough edge of a fingernail in a way that would have earned her a sharp rebuke from her stepmother. Lady Vondelmai had always meant well and was not an unkind woman; however, Kailee could only imagine how she might have reacted had she heard Kailee had access to a potion that would close her Mindseye and had not yet even bothered to try it. Smelling salts would for certain have been necessary.

"I want to *see*," she said, but it might as well have been Lady Vondelmai speaking through her voice. "How can I *not* want to see? Without physical eyesight, I cannot read, I cannot see art, I cannot walk without danger of tripping over things . . ." She let her voice trail off. Vondelmai had always made those shortcomings seem appalling, and though Kailee had to admit to a certain curiosity as to what it would be like to have physical eyesight, there had never been any great yearning in her heart. No matter how much people told her there should be.

"There are ways to get around those inconveniences without stripping you of your Mindsight," Tynthanal said, then reached into his doublet and pulled out something that was packed full with the feminine element, Rai. "I wasn't going to show this to you just yet, because I have a long way to go before perfecting it, but it seems now is the time, after all."

"What is it?" she asked, taking the object when he handed it to her and finding it was a small glass vial filled with liquid.

"I'd been thinking it might be nice if you could read Mairahsol's notes for yourself," he said. "So I've been working on creating an ink into which I can bind elements. The vial you're holding is regular ink with powdered ruby mixed in. It's pretty dreadful to write with, and I was planning to meet with the grand magus to see if he has a better suggestion. I think we will have to mix the ink with some kind of metallic or crystalline powder so that it can hold enough motes to be legible, but I believe it is possible. When we have something that will write more smoothly, I'll write out a primer for you and teach you how to read."

Kailee clapped one hand over her mouth to try to contain a small sob as her eyes flooded with tears.

"What's wrong?" Tynthanal asked in alarm.

Her throat was too tight and achy to answer, but she threw her arms around his neck and squeezed to signal that the source of her tears was not unhappiness. He hugged her back a bit awkwardly, for though he had on occasion touched her arms or hands, he almost never actually *embraced* her. If ever she needed a reminder that he did not love her as a husband ought to love his wife, all it took was one of these awkward, uncomfortable hugs.

Kailee reluctantly let go of him and sat back, brushing the tears from her cheeks.

"I hope it wasn't presumptuous of me to work on this without asking you first," Tynthanal said, and Kailee tried hard to get a grip on her emotions so she could reassure him.

"That is the single kindest thing anyone has ever done for me," she whispered hoarsely, tears threatening to burst from her eyes again as her heart squeezed in her chest.

Oh, but his kindness was dangerous! She knew, beyond a shadow of a doubt, that his heart could never belong to her. He was a man of great loyalty, and having given his love to Chanlix, he would never have room in his heart for Kailee. She did not dare allow herself to feel anything more than friendship for him, or her heart was destined to be broken. And yet . . .

"It is the least I could do after dragging you here when you'd finally found acceptance in Women's Well," he said.

Kailee forced a tremulous smile. "You didn't drag me," she assured him. "And you needn't worry about me. I knew exactly what to expect when I chose to come with you to Aaltah." She wiped more wetness from her cheeks.

There was a moment of fraught silence, and Kailee hoped Tynthanal was not seeing too much of what she was feeling. The last thing she wanted was for him to know she was in danger of losing her heart to him, for she feared that would awaken even more guilt than he already felt. The situation was not at all of his making, and he did not deserve that burden.

"So, let me ask you again," he finally said, breaking the silence. "Do you actually want to try Mairah's potion?"

Taking a long, deep breath, Kailee admitted the truth. "No."

"Then don't."

CHAPTER FOURTEEN

Alys was torn between joy and grief and guilt as she activated the talker that was linked with Tynthanal's. Knowing he would never be available to talk during his busy daylight hours—and doubting that he carried the talker with him at all times—she'd waited until nighttime to contact him.

She tried to wipe all hints of grief from her face as her brother's image shimmered to life in the air above the talker. She did not want to frighten him even for a moment, and she knew he would instantly interpret any distress in her expression as meaning something had happened to Chanlix or their baby. Fearing her perceptive brother would see the shadow in her eyes no matter how hard she tried to hide it, she dispensed with any greetings and preliminaries and smiled broadly.

"Congratulations," she told him. "You are the father of a healthy baby girl. Mother and daughter are now resting comfortably, and the midwife assures us that Chanlix is exhausted, but otherwise well."

Tynthanal seemed at a loss for words, his mouth opening and closing a couple of times as his knees buckled and he sat heavily on a settee. The image suddenly went blurry and indistinct, and there was a soft thumping sound, followed by a curse.

"Sorry," Tynthanal said, the image of his face once again appearing. "I dropped the talker."

Somewhere behind him, Kailee laughed lightly. She soon appeared in the image, her face alight with joy.

"Congratulations, Papa!" she said. If she harbored any jealousy toward the woman who'd just borne her husband's baby, there was no hint of it in her face or voice. She turned her head in Alys's direction. "And to you, too, Auntie."

Alys laughed in delight, for that was a title she'd never thought would be hers. "I look forward to spoiling my niece atrociously," she said.

Tynthanal still looked like he was in shock, as if it was only now sinking in that he was a father.

"I know Chanlix and the babe must rest for a while after the birth," Kailee continued, "but I hope Tynthanal may meet his daughter via talker as soon as possible. Tomorrow, maybe?"

Tynthanal looked briefly terrified, but then a tentative smile appeared on his lips. His eyes were suspiciously shiny, and Alys thought that she had never seen her brother look so open or so vulnerable in all his life. It wasn't hard for Alys to guess what was going through his mind.

"Of course Chanlix wants to see you," she assured him. "I spoke with her briefly earlier this evening, and she specifically said that you and she needed to talk about the babe's name."

It was considered bad luck to decide upon a baby's name before the birth, though many parents did so, satisfying the superstition by assuring themselves they were merely "discussing" rather than "deciding."

"She did make it clear that the baby will be Rah-Tynthanal rather than Rai-Chanlix, unless you or Kailee objects," Alys said.

Alys was certain Tynthanal would have no objection himself save the worry that his wife might be offended. The name would be a source of gossip, of course, and there would be those who deemed it pretentious and inappropriate, but Tynthanal would never allow his child to be treated as a bastard.

"Of course the child is Rah-Tynthanal," Kailee said without a moment of hesitation. Her lower lip stuck out in an exaggerated pout. "I do wish everyone would stop treating me like a cuckold."

Tynthanal winced at Kailee's indelicate choice of words, but Alys laughed. Kailee had never been one to use polite euphemisms.

"We're just trying to protect your honor," Tynthanal said, but Kailee made an unladylike sound of frustration.

"My honor is my own to protect or not as I see fit," she said tartly. "I have spent all my life as my father's embarrassing, poorly kept secret, and his love for me never lessened the sting of it. I will not have this baby suffer the same fate for the sake of my vanity."

Alys smiled wryly. "You'd better abandon your argument, Little Brother," she advised. "Kailee is a force of nature, and it is as useful to argue with the rain as to argue with her."

"There!" Kailee said, without awaiting a response from her husband. "It is decided." She patted Tynthanal's shoulder. "The women in your life have spoken."

Tynthanal shook his head, but he was smiling now, too. "Far be it from me to offer my own opinion when the women have spoken." But despite the rueful words, it was clear he was relieved with the decision. He'd been perhaps a bit of a reluctant father when he'd first heard that Chanlix was pregnant, but he would throw himself into the role with his whole heart, and he would never wish to deny his daughter his name.

"And now," Kailee said, "it is time for you to tell us what *else* has happened. Clearly Chanlix and the baby are well, but there is something not quite right in your voice."

Alys grimaced. She'd been afraid of what Tynthanal might see in her face, but she'd never thought to fear what Kailee—perceptive, insightful Kailee—might hear in her voice.

Tynthanal, still distracted by the joy of being a new father, shook his head and looked momentarily confused. "Is she right? Is there something wrong?"

Alys sighed, hating to deliver the news.

"One of the seers at the Academy, Lady Grunamai, tested the potion you sent us. She used it with a seer's poison she told us was well within her tolerance."

"Oh!" Kailee exclaimed, her hand flying to her mouth, for she could no doubt tell from the grimness of Alys's tone what had happened.

"She recovered consciousness long enough to tell us of her vision," Alys said, "and there is no denying its accuracy. She saw something that happened to me as a child, something that I never told anyone about. However, she drifted away after telling us her vision, and she never woke again."

Chanlix would be devastated when she learned the news, for of course no one was going to tell her as she recovered from nearly twenty-four hours of labor. Kailee started crying quietly, and Tynthanal's eyes were shadowed with pain and guilt. Alys knew exactly how he felt.

"The potion worked exactly as Mairahsol claimed it would," she said. "And her notes did warn us it exacerbated the side effects of the seer's poison. I had the healers examine Grunamai after she'd passed to see if we could determine what happened, and they found she had some abnormalities in her heart. They believe that, without those abnormalities, she would have eventually recovered from the poison."

Tynthanal nodded, though the guilt was still obvious on his face. "We all agreed the potion had to be tested," he said. "And I'm certain that Lady Grunamai volunteered to perform the test."

"Of course," Alys confirmed, though Grunamai's acceptance of the risks did little to assuage her own guilt. "She was fully aware of the dangers of testing the potion, and she believed it was necessary. She said she still had family in Aaltah she cared about, and it was important to her to do anything she could to help you repair the Well."

Tynthanal closed his eyes for just a moment, and when he opened them again, his expression was grim. "She verified for us that the potion works as Mairahsol claimed it would. However, we will be no closer to repairing the Well until we find out what damaged it in the first place. Which means we need another seer to take a dose."

Alys clasped her hands together, dreading her brother's response to what she had to say. She had always assumed that the seer who tested the poison would take it a second time—if she was willing—once they'd confirmed the accuracy of the vision it granted. Even knowing that there was a risk, she'd never given serious consideration to the possibility that the seer might die.

"With Grunamai's death," she said, "we are left with only three seers in the Academy. Two of those are young mothers, and the last is only sixteen years old and almost completely untried. I'm afraid I can't ask any of them to take a potion that might kill them."

Tynthanal frowned. "I realize it is a terrible risk," he said, "but Grunamai wouldn't have been taking the risk in the first place if I had any seers available in the Abbey of Aaltah. This is too important for us to be overcautious. You said yourself that Grunamai had a heart defect, and—"

"No," Alys said simply, cutting off his argument. "I fully understand the importance of finding out what happened at the Well, but my duty as sovereign princess is to put my own principality's needs above others'. I can't—I *won't*—ask another seer to risk her life to help Aaltah."

Tynthanal gaped at her. "You can't mean that! Aaltah was once your home. We are close to defaulting on several trade agreements, and no one is eager to embark on new ones when they can't be certain we will deliver. I don't need to tell you how ugly it will get if our economy collapses. You've read the same history books as I."

Alys grimaced, for he was right—she had. Despite such grim stories having been considered inappropriate for her delicate feminine sensibilities. Her father had never once remonstrated when he'd caught her reading Tynthanal's books growing up. Financial troubles on the scale that seemed inevitable if the Well wasn't repaired had led to riots and revolutions and general atrocities in the past.

Alys let out a sigh, for she was very aware that she was putting people she cared about in harm's way by refusing. Almost the entire staff from her old manor house had remained in Aaltah— only her lady's maid, Honor, having come with her—as had her in-laws.

"I know, Tynthanal," she said. "But I'm not in a position to help you at the moment."

"There is more," Tynthanal said darkly, then told her the horrifying report that had come to him from the Abbey of Aaltah about the sudden dearth of pregnancies. "It is a closely guarded secret so far, but that cannot last, and when the citizens of Aaltah begin to figure it out . . ."

Alys's chest ached with sympathy—and not a little dread. It would be frighteningly easy for public sentiment to turn against Tynthanal if he wound up not being able to fix the Well, and she wondered if he might not have been better off if she'd refused to allow him to take the regency.

"That doesn't change anything," Kailee said, and Alys was absurdly grateful to her sister-in-law for not forcing her to say it herself. "Women's Well can't absorb another loss, and the women of the Academy have too much to lose. Even if she asked one of them to take the potion, they might well refuse after what happened to Grunamai. But perhaps you can ask Queen Ellinsoltah if one of the seers in *her* abbey would be willing to take the risk."

She turned her head toward Alys. "And perhaps you'd be willing to offer that seer a place at the Women's Well Academy in exchange for her service? Surely there is a seer in the Abbey of Rhozinolm who'd be willing to take the risk if it meant she could leave the Abbey for good."

Alys smiled at Kailee, though of course the younger woman could not see. "That sounds like an elegant solution, and I would be happy to offer that seer a place. I'd even be happy to compensate the Crown for the loss, if that would make it easier for Ellinsoltah to overcome any resistance she might face at the unusual request." She had little doubt that the trade minister and some other members of Ellin's council would become suddenly and perversely possessive of this so-called Unwanted Woman if she should be deemed of use to a foreign power.

"There," Kailee said with a nod of satisfaction, patting Tynthanal's hand, "that settles it. See how much easier it is to solve problems when you stop being reflexively prickly?"

Tynthanal scowled at her, although Alys thought she detected a hint of humor and respect lurking in his eyes. "I was not being prickly. I was doing my duty as prince regent."

"And Alys was doing her duty as sovereign princess. I suppose it's lucky for all that I am neither one."

Even with the shadow of guilt still haunting her, Alys couldn't help but laugh.

Corlin paced the confines of the cell he'd been peremptorily shoved into. There was little room for it, and he was making himself dizzy with the constant quick turns, but better that than sitting down on the bench with nothing to do but think. Pacing, he could at least try to escape himself, *try* to escape all the thoughts and feelings that demanded his immediate attention.

A solid punch had left him with an aching loose tooth and the taste of blood in his mouth, but the pain was an almost welcome distraction. He had promised everyone—including himself—that he would spend his time here in the Citadel of Aaltah as a model cadet, and for almost three months, he'd managed—with an effort of will—to keep that promise.

Now, here he was again, locked up in a military stockade awaiting discipline because of a humiliating inability to control his temper.

To be fair, he *had* been sorely provoked, and anyone seeing the start of the altercation would know that Cadet Justal had been the instigator. But of course, no one had seen the start of it, and by the time they'd been pulled apart, Justal's bloody nose had somehow made him into the victim. Never mind that he was a full head taller than Corlin and a known bully.

None of that would matter, Corlin was certain. Justal's reputation as a bully was nothing next to Corlin's, thanks to his history. Lord Aldnor had warned him when he'd first entered the Citadel that there would be no benefit of the doubt extended to him, and he knew that he was in for a beating more severe than any he had yet survived.

He should have been afraid, he knew. Any sensible person would be. And yet for all the emotions that roiled through him, fear was nowhere to be found. He would face his punishment like a man, accepting it as his due for once again failing everyone who cared about him. He only hoped no one would send word to his mother about it. He was well aware of how much pain he'd already caused her by his disciplinary issues in Women's Well, and he had no desire to cause her more.

Corlin growled in frustration as his thoughts—and the guilt—caught up with him despite the constant movement. He just barely stopped himself from punching the wall, knowing full well it would make him look even more like someone who was irretrievably out of control.

Panic shot through him finally as he wondered if Lord Aldnor's promise of no leniency meant he was on the verge of being expelled from the Citadel. Again.

Footsteps sounded in the hallway, and a sergeant Corlin didn't know entered the otherwise unoccupied cell block. Corlin took in a deep breath, tamping down the emotions as best he could as he stood at strict military attention and tried to look dignified. Hard to do when his uniform was caked with dirt and dried blood.

The sergeant looked at him contemptuously as he unlocked the cell door and stepped aside.

"Out!" the sergeant barked. "Lord Aldnor wants a word with you."

Corlin forced a grin he did not feel as he exited the cell. "Oh, is that what they call it here?"

It was flippant and insubordinate and wildly inappropriate, and the sergeant's scowl was not at all surprising. What *was* surprising was the fist that suddenly drove into Corlin's solar plexus, stealing every sip of air from his lungs and causing his legs to give out.

"Oops," the sergeant said. "My hand slipped. Now catch your breath and get back on your feet. Keep your mouth closed, or my hand might slip again, and you wouldn't like that."

Corlin gritted his teeth. He was pretty certain casual violence of the sort the sergeant had just offered was against regulations, but he was hardly in a position to complain about it.

Clutching his midsection, Corlin did as he was told. The sergeant grabbed his arm in a grip far more brutal than necessary when Corlin was complying, dragging him through the cell block and out into the hallway beyond.

Corlin's breath was still labored, and the sergeant was walking so fast that it was all he could do to keep his feet under him. He hoped the beating he was about to receive would not be a public one, but conceded to himself that it likely would be, just to add to the general humiliation of the whole ordeal.

This being his first experience with discipline at the Citadel of Aaltah, Corlin was not familiar with the stockade, so when the sergeant brought him to a stop in front of a closed door, Corlin did not know what was behind it. The sergeant let go of his arm, sneering at him.

"Straighten yourself up as best you can, Cadet. You look like you've been rolling around in the mud with the pigs."

Corlin bit his tongue to keep an unwise retort from escaping his mouth, then brushed ineffectively at the dirt on his uniform. Setting his shoulders and raising his chin, he presented as dignified a façade as he was able. The sergeant opened the door and gestured him inside.

Since the death of King Aaltyn, Corlin had faced an embarrassing number of beatings, first from the brutal tutor his uncle Delnamal had assigned to him, then from his superiors at the Citadel of Women's Well. It would be a lie to say he'd never been afraid, but he could at least claim that he'd never been so afraid he couldn't hide the fear beneath a heavy veneer of stoicism. But he'd allowed himself to forget that being locked up in the stockade was not the usual procedure for cadets, nor had he contemplated what it would mean to be in a place usually reserved for adult military prisoners.

The room the sergeant gestured him into made no attempt to disguise its purpose. Military justice was often administered in public, both as a means to humiliate the offender and as a cautionary tale to others, but "often" was not the same as "always," and this room had clearly been designed specifically for those punishments that were not being carried out in public.

The far wall featured an array of manacles that would allow several prisoners to be shackled at once, and though the room appeared scrupulously clean, Corlin could swear he scented blood and sweat on the air. A fine tremor passed through his whole body, his heart suddenly speeding with something very like terror. He had promised his mother that when he returned to Women's Well, he would take the flogging he rightfully deserved for what he had done to Smithson—a promise it was clear she intended to make him break—but she would have no say in this.

He swallowed hard and reminded himself that he'd more than earned it.

Behind him, the sergeant chuckled darkly, and Corlin stiffened his spine. Afraid he might be, but he had no intention of providing the sergeant with any more amusement than absolutely necessary.

The door across from him opened, and Lord Aldnor entered the room. Corlin stood at strictest attention, staring straight ahead while the lord commander looked him up and down and shook his head. Corlin was fairly certain that if the man was looking for fear, he wasn't finding it.

"I believe I made it clear that there would be no leniency for you, Cadet Corlin," Lord Aldnor said. His voice was deep and gravelly, and he sounded stern even talking about the weather. It was all Corlin could do not to shrink at the tone of his voice right now.

"You did, sir," Corlin said. He lowered his gaze to the floor in shame and submission. "I have no excuse. I'm sorry."

As he was looking at the floor instead of at Lord Aldnor's face, Corlin wasn't sure what to make of the silence that followed his declaration. Perhaps Lord Aldnor knew full well that Corlin *could* have offered an excuse for his behavior. It certainly wasn't unknown to the lord commander that Cadet Justal was a bully.

Corlin raised his head once more and met his commander's eyes. He could not read what he saw there, but he didn't think it looked like anger or even disappointment. There was something, though. Something grim and hard. Corlin tried to take heart from the fact that the lord commander was not carrying a whip, though of course a man of his stature was hardly likely to wield the thing himself.

"You are prepared to accept your punishment without complaint?" Lord Aldnor inquired.

Corlin refrained from pointing out that he was hardly in a position to do anything else. Complaining would certainly not save him. "I am, sir."

Aldnor nodded. "Yes. And that is a part of the problem, isn't it?"

"Sir?" Corlin blinked in surprise.

"The prince regent gave me a full accounting of your record in Women's Well and of the disciplinary actions that were taken against you. If you were not the crown prince, you would have been dismissed long before you were."

"I am aware of that, sir. And I—"

"What your record has shown me is that disciplinary actions have not made any lasting impression on you. I thought perhaps you had finally learned your lesson after almost killing a fellow cadet."

Blood rushed to Corlin's face, and he dropped his gaze to the floor once more as shame threatened to overwhelm him. He would never forget the sensation of his sword biting through Smithson's flesh, never forget the cry of pain and surprise that had finally broken through Corlin's blind fury. Even now, he swore he could smell the copper scent of blood and feel the rush of horror that filled him when Smithson fell. It was little more than good luck that had saved Smithson, for if Corlin hadn't found the healer as quickly as he had . . .

"It does seem that the incident had *some* effect on you," Lord Aldnor continued. "After all, you went nearly three months without losing your temper, which according to your uncle is a record for you. My conclusion from this fact is that being punished has no effect on you, but seeing someone else hurt because of your lack of self-control makes a much more lasting impression."

Corlin felt as if the floor had just fallen out from under him, and he raised his gaze to Lord Aldnor's face once more, hoping that he had somehow misunderstood. Surely the lord commander wasn't implying . . .

The back door opened once again, and Corlin saw Captain Norlix enter the room, tugging a wide-eyed, terrified-looking Rafetyn behind him. Corlin started shaking his head vigorously back and forth.

"No," he choked. "You can't!"

But Captain Norlix was dragging Rafetyn toward one of the sets of manacles along the wall. The cadet was so small and frail that even after Norlix lowered the chains as far as they could go, Rafetyn had to stand nearly on tiptoe for his hands to reach that high.

"Please!" Corlin cried, holding out both hands and taking a step toward his friend. He'd forgotten all about the sergeant who'd been standing silently behind him throughout. The man grabbed both his arms and yanked him back, holding him in an iron grip.

Tears filmed Corlin's vision, and he made no attempt to blink them back. Surely the lord commander wasn't cruel enough to do this!

"Please, Lord Aldnor," he begged as the tears spilled over. He could not *bear* this! "I will take whatever punishment you think I deserve, and I promise I'll never get into trouble again. Just please, don't do this."

Lord Aldnor shook his head. "There is no point to a punishment that teaches you nothing. Learn to control your temper—and show you are *willing* to control it when you know how—and Cadet Rafetyn need stand in for you only this once. But mark my words: break the rules again, and we will all end up right back in this room."

Corlin let out an incoherent cry of protest as Lord Aldnor turned to Captain Norlix and said, "Begin."

The beating was delivered with a leather strap, rather than with a whip, and for all his obvious fear, Rafetyn did not utter a sound. Corlin, on the other hand, humiliated himself by scream-ing and begging like a child, and he couldn't be bothered to care. Life had given him little reason to believe in fairness, but never in his wildest dreams could he have imagined this level of injustice from the Lord Commander of Aaltah. Tynthanal had assured Corlin that Lord Aldnor was a good man, despite the differences that had arisen between the two of them when Tynthanal had forsaken Aaltah for Women's Well. Clearly, Tynthanal had been wrong.

When it was over, and Corlin was allowed to return to the bar-racks while Rafetyn visited the healer, he seriously contemplated leaving the Citadel in protest. But that would leave Rafetyn en-tirely friendless and unprotected. Not that Rafetyn would *want* his friendship after what he'd suffered on Corlin's behalf. But even if they were estranged, Corlin could still look out for him in a way that no one else would.

Nothing Corlin could ever do would make up for his losses of control, and nothing could ever assuage his guilt over those who'd been hurt by it. However, he knew deep down inside that he would never risk letting Rafetyn take a beating for him again. If Justal and the others ganged up on him, then he would take whatever abuse they dished out and not fight back. As long as he could trust himself not to get Rafetyn punished again, it was his duty to stay at the Citadel and lend whatever help Rafetyn would allow him to offer.

No matter how guilt-ridden and miserable he felt, Corlin would do his duty.

CHAPTER FIFTEEN

Tynthanal couldn't remember the last time he'd felt *nervous*. Afraid, sure—as a lifelong soldier, he'd long ago learned how to cope with and function through fear. But what he felt now as he waited for Chanlix to answer the chirping of her talker was entirely different and outside of his experience, and he couldn't put a finger on why that should be. His heart was racing, and when Chanlix answered the call and an image materialized before his eyes, he suddenly found that he could not breathe.

Chanlix was in her bed, comfortably reclining in a generous nest of pillows, beaming as she held a small bundle in her arms. He could see nothing but the swaddling until Chanlix repositioned the bundle, showing him a scrunched up, tiny face with red cheeks and closed eyes.

"Meet your daughter, Papa," Chanlix whispered. If she was attempting not to wake the babe, she failed, and Tynthanal was struck dumb when he got his first glimpse of hazel eyes that looked like a miniature version of his own.

Tynthanal put a hand to his heart, his chest tight with emotion—not least of which was longing to take mother and child both into his arms and hold them close to him for hours on end. His eyes stung, making him blink, and he couldn't have spoken even if his mind were capable of coming up with words.

Chanlix's eyes, too, were shiny with suppressed tears. "I do wish I could let you hold her."

He forced himself to breathe and tried to shake loose the knot in his throat. "So do I," he rasped, drinking the babe in with his eyes. "She takes my breath away."

Chanlix stroked a finger over their daughter's cheek, her face alight with the same reverence Tynthanal was feeling. "Mine, too," she said.

He couldn't help reaching a hand toward the image, touching the baby's face and wishing he could feel what he was sure was deliciously soft skin against his fingertips. "We have a daughter," he said, shaking his head in wonder.

"So we do," Chanlix affirmed. "And we'd best go about naming her, as I'm already tired of calling her 'the baby.'"

Tynthanal managed a half-hearted chuckle, though it was hard to laugh when he was feeling so overwhelmed. "I presume Alys told you that Kailee and I are agreed she is Rah-Tynthanal."

Chanlix nodded. "She did, though I never had much doubt of that."

"Have you thought about what you would like to name her?"

"I've been toying with the idea of Tynel—naming her for you and for my late mother, with whom I was very close as a young girl."

"She's already Rah-Tynthanal," he reminded her. "You needn't name her for me twice. Perhaps you should consider *Chanel* instead."

Chanlix rolled the name around a couple of times, saying it with differing inflections, then shaking her head. "No. I want to be reminded of you when I say her name, and I will not be saying 'Rah-Tynthanal' very often."

Tynthanal managed a grin that felt a little more genuine than his previous laugh. "You never know. She may turn into a mischief-maker, and you may be one of those mothers who addresses her child by her full name when scolding."

Chanlix returned the grin even as she demurred. "Our daughter will be a perfect angel who never needs scolding. I still like Tynel."

Tynthanal wondered if perhaps he should defer to Chanlix's preference—after all, it was Chanlix who would have the raising of her—but he decided to make one last try. "It is lovely that our daughter should have a piece of my name and a piece of your mother's; however, you and I made her together. *You* deserve to be honored in her name, as well."

Chanlix frowned and said the name "Chanel" again, still looking dissatisfied with it.

"How about Chantynel?" Tynthanal suggested in the spirit of compromise.

He could tell at once from the flare of light in her eyes that Chanlix liked it. She looked down at the babe in her arms, who was already drifting back into sleep.

"What do you think, dearest?" Chanlix whispered. "Would you like to be called Chantynel?"

The babe opened her eyes for just the briefest moment, and Tynthanal laughed.

"There," he declared. "She already recognizes it as hers."

Chanlix dropped a gentle kiss on their daughter's head, then turned her attention back to him. Their eyes met, and Tynthanal was struck with such a pang of longing he could hardly bear it.

"How I wish I could be there with you," he said, his throat tight with emotion.

Chanlix blinked rapidly, her eyes shining with unshed tears. "Me, too," she rasped. "But you are needed in Aaltah." She dabbed at her eyes with a corner of the baby's blanket. "And you have a wife."

He closed his eyes in pain. "I have grown . . . very fond of Kailee," he said, "but it's time to give up the pretense that my feelings might ever rise to the level of love. You are and will always be the wife of my heart."

"Don't say that," Chanlix replied. "For all our sakes, you must try to love the woman you're married to. Pining does none of us any good."

He scrubbed a hand through his hair. "Feelings don't care whether they're doing us any good or not. But I will try to put the bitter ones aside for now," he said, fixing his gaze on the sleeping baby. "We have a daughter, and she is beautiful and perfect. Let us both focus on that joy."

Chanlix forced a brave smile, as did he. But as sweet as the joy of seeing little Chantynel nestled in her mother's arms was, the bitterness and pain remained a constant undertone long after they said their farewells.

Draios brushed a stray crumble of ash from the front of his doublet as he continued to peruse the charred remains of the letter one of his spies had retrieved from the hearth in his father's office. A great deal of it had been eaten away by the flames, but the parts that had been spared were tantalizing.

It was the third such letter he'd gotten his hands on in these last few weeks, and he was almost grateful for his brother's machinations, which had forced him to return to the palace every night instead of sleeping with his fellow postulants in the temple's dormitory. If he'd resided at the temple, he might never have known these letters existed, much less endeavored to get his hands on them. He shivered at the thought that perhaps the invisible hand of the Creator was at work, making a seeming setback into a triumph.

There had been almost nothing left of the first two letters, except for the surprising fragment of signature on the second. Draios had believed his cousin Delnamal was dead, and it both intrigued and infuriated him to find that such was not the case.

This third letter had been rescued from the flames far earlier, so that there were whole paragraphs intact in places, even if it was still frustratingly incomplete.

What he knew for certain was that Delnamal was alive, living in seclusion with his mother in the countryside, an "honored guest" of King Khalvin. He could also piece together his cousin's claim that he had gained some sort of extraordinary power that he believed would allow him to retake his kingdom—and perhaps even undo the effects of the Curse. Delnamal believed his power to be a gift from the Creator, although inconveniently, the section of the letter explaining the nature of this power had been eaten away.

It was an outlandish claim, to be sure. Especially when one considered Delnamal's reputation, which was hardly that of a man of faith. From what Draios had heard of his cousin, Delnamal was a gluttonous, intemperate buffoon of a man with the temperament of a spoiled toddler. But though Draios could not have said why, something about the fragments of the letter he could read resonated with him and struck him as sincere.

Draios put the scrap of paper down on his desk, brushing more ash from his clothes and hands. Then he sat and began painstakingly reconstructing every mark he could make out onto a fresh sheet of parchment so that he might read and study the contents without making quite so much of a mess. The exercise did not gain him any new insights into the message's content. Nor could he figure out why his father seemed to be *ignoring* what could potentially be information that was of vital importance both to Khalpar and to the rest of the world. But Delnamal wouldn't be writing so many letters if he were getting any satisfaction out of the king, nor would he still be hidden away in the countryside.

With a grunt of annoyance, Draios pushed away from his writing desk. His mentor at the temple had given him an assignment to write a treatise on filial duty as defined by the Devotional, meant to be delivered first thing in the morning—an attempt to ensure Draios lived the life of a devoted postulant even when away from the temple. He hadn't started it, yet he was too distracted by the intriguing promises of Delnamal's letter to set his mind to the task. He likely had a sleepless night ahead of him, but he was not unused to such, as he regularly performed voluntary fasts and overnight prayer vigils to demonstrate his devotion to the Creator.

It was possible, of course, that Delnamal was a lunatic. But even so, if there was the slightest possibility that he had the power to undo the Curse, surely it was worth hearing him out! Draios had first set his sights on becoming a priest mainly—he was ashamed to admit—because he'd hoped to impress his famously pious father. But if his father was ignoring Delnamal's letters, then it seemed to Draios that perhaps his own piety had now outstripped his father's.

How he wished he could simply *talk* to his father about the letters, but he knew only too well that he could not. If he admitted to having spies in the palace—and using them to gather intelligence from the king's private offices . . .

It was all Parlommir's doing, Draios was sure. The crown prince's piety was no more than skin deep, and yet their father respected him—and *listened* to him—as he never had Draios. There was no doubt in Draios's mind that Parlommir was well aware of Delnamal's presence in their kingdom, just as he was no doubt privy to the contents of the letters. And because Parlommir cared only for the venal world of politics, he would not feel the pull that Delnamal's claim had inspired in Draios.

Draios felt as if the Creator himself had reached out through the words in that letter, calling him to action. Touching the fragments of the burnt pages caused his heart to race with excitement and longing.

There was a reason this letter had come into his hands, and that the fire had not entirely consumed it. Draios felt in his heart that he was *meant* to find it, and that he was *meant* to rectify his father's error in ignoring it.

Obviously, the best way to gain a true understanding of what Delnamal could do would be to go visit the man in person—which would also allow Draios to get a feel for his cousin's sincerity and commitment to the cause. However, such a visit would be . . . difficult to engineer. He could not very well ask his father's permission when he wasn't even supposed to know Delnamal was alive. Nor could a first-year postulant be granted permission to put aside his duties for the two or three days he would need to make the round trip.

His mind still buzzing with thoughts and half-finished plans, Draios forced himself to pull out a parchment and an ink pot so that he might write his assigned treatise. But when he was finished, he vowed he would spend the rest of the night performing a prayer vigil. By the Creator's will, his night of prayer would lead him to the answers he needed.

Ellin had met Mother Zarend once before, when she'd dismissed both her trade minister and the woman he had appointed abbess before her. It had been a shocking breach of propriety that had caused some of her royal council to reach for their smelling salts at the inconceivable notion of a queen setting foot within the walls of the Abbey. However, she'd been unwilling to approve a replacement for the former abbess—who, with the trade minister, had found ways to coerce her abigails into working the pavilion without triggering the creation of women's Kai—without first meeting and speaking with the woman.

This second visit to the Abbey was certain to evince more hand-wringing and worries about her maidenly honor, but now at least she was a married woman. She had no doubt one or more of those fine gentlemen would take her aside to remind her that it was beneath her dignity as a queen to associate with the ruined women of the Abbey. And, as she had done before, she would ignore them.

Mother Zarend was a plump woman of perhaps sixty who had somehow, miraculously, held on to her spirit and her sense of optimism through more than two decades of Abbey life. Ellin had liked the woman enormously from the moment she'd met her, and she heartily approved of the changes she had instituted in the Abbey. As she was led through the hallways toward the abbess's office, Ellin heard the occasional echo of laughter, and even the air felt somehow less oppressive. She hoped that was reflective of reality rather than being a figment of her fanciful imagination.

The young abigail who'd been leading her through the maze of hallways to the abbess's office was clearly flustered and nervous, and Ellin realized—way too late—that she should have sent word she was coming and reassured everyone that she did not bear bad news. Surely every woman who'd caught sight of her—or heard murmurs of her presence—worried that some calamity might befall the Abbey, though Ellin hoped she'd established at least a modicum of trust by dismissing the former trade minister and the cruel and greedy woman who'd been abbess before.

Ellin's conviction that she should have sent word ahead was strengthened when she was shown into the office and saw the alarm in Mother Zarend's usually sparkling eyes. Ellin was now nearing the end of the second year of her reign, and she was still occasionally caught off guard by the fact that her power made her intimidating.

Ellin smiled warmly as the abbess greeted her with an elegant bow. "You are looking well, Mother Zarend," she said, hoping the warmth of her tone and smile would put the woman at ease in a way that mere words would not. "And I cannot tell you how pleased I am with how the mood of the Abbey has changed under your guidance."

Mother Zarend regarded her with what Ellin would term cautious optimism. "I have done very little," she said modestly. "I have merely followed the guidelines that you set for me."

Ellin clucked her tongue. "We both know the myriad—and often twisted—ways guidelines can be interpreted. After all, Lord Creethan was supposedly following my guidelines, too."

Mother Zarend's nose crinkled with distaste. She had been well past the age when she might be expected to work the pavilion when Creethan had been trade minister, but the woman had already been terribly protective of the younger abigails who had suffered under his cruel policies. Policies that the former abbess had tolerated and condoned without a hint of remorse.

"Every woman in this abbey is grateful to you for putting an end to it," Mother Zarend said. "Even those of us who were not coerced into working the pavilion suffered to see our sisters so abused."

Thinking about the policies Lord Creethan had instituted made Ellin's blood boil even now. The man—with the abbess's help and approval—had systematically tested the bounds of women's Kai, trying to find a way to force the abigails to work the pavilion without generating Kai. The two of them had discovered that offering "rewards" for women who worked the pavilion neatly sidestepped the issue. Those "rewards" consisted of such things as beds and adequate food and time to rest.

Mother Zarend started to speak, then hesitated.

"Go on," Ellin prodded. "You may speak freely with me."

The abbess licked her lips nervously. "I'm sure there are many in this abbey who are at least mildly alarmed by your visit. We are well aware that the Abbey's earnings have decreased now that fewer abigails work the pavilion, and—"

Ellin cut her off hastily. "That is not why I'm here," she assured the older woman. "I was well aware of the effect my orders would have on revenue." She had urged the new trade minister to raise the prices for the potions produced by the Abbey to try to offset some of the loss, but knew that it wasn't enough to make up the difference.

Mother Zarend sighed in relief.

"If you don't mind, we should probably sit down," Ellin said. "This is unlikely to be a short conversation."

Mother Zarend blushed, her golden complexion too light to hide it. "I beg your pardon, Your Majesty! Where are my manners?"

Of course Ellin had not meant her suggestion as anything like a rebuke of the abbess's manners, and she reminded herself for what felt like the twentieth time today to be more sensitive in her communications.

When they were comfortably seated before a modest fire that nonetheless dispelled the chill, Ellin decided to broach the subject of her visit without preamble.

"I've had an unusual request from the Prince Regent of Aaltah," she said. "He is in need of a seer, and the Abbey of Aaltah apparently has no seers in residence."

"In need of a seer?" Mother Zarend asked in evident confusion. "I've never heard of someone being *in need* of one." The abbess's eyes narrowed, and she demonstrated the quickness of her wits. "Surely if he was in need of the services of a seer, he would have first asked his sister to provide one. I can accept that Aaltah does not presently have any seers, for its Abbey is very young. But surely some of the abigails who are now in Women's Well have the necessary skill."

"They do," Ellin confirmed. "But the task he requires the seer for is dangerous, and Princess Alysoon is reluctant to risk any of the seers of the Women's Well Academy."

The abbess's air of suspicion strengthened. "But *you* are not so squeamish about risking the life of an Unwanted Woman?" she challenged.

"Of course I am," Ellin said, trying not to feel hurt by the accusation. "I'm certainly not *ordering* anyone to accept the risk, and Prince Tynthanal has no interest in doing so, either. He is looking for a volunteer. And if someone from our abbey were to volunteer, Princess Alysoon has agreed to grant her a place in the Women's Well Academy."

Mother Zarend's eyes widened, and she sucked in a quick, startled breath. No woman who entered the Abbey did so of her own free will, and no woman who entered the Abbey thought to escape it save through the ultimate escape of death. Princess Alysoon had chosen her lure wisely.

"So, just how dangerous is this task?" Mother Zarend asked when she regained her composure.

"It's hard to quantify," Ellin responded. "The seer will be required to take a potion that works in conjunction with a seer's poison. One of the Women's Well seers volunteered to test it, and though she proved it was effective, she became gravely ill from the effects and passed away. The healers say it might have been the result of a weak heart, but they cannot say for sure that a fully healthy woman would fare better. I would recommend that no woman who is not young and healthy volunteer for the mission. And I would make sure she fully understands the dangers involved."

Mother Zarend met her eyes. "Forgive me for saying so, but I'm not sure you fully understand what it is like to be imprisoned in the Abbey—even now when you have done away with the worst of the abuses. I suspect there are very few women here who would not happily risk death for the hope of freedom."

Ellin was struck speechless, the words exploding somewhere in her chest and taking her breath away. She had thought that by doing away with mandatory service in the pavilion, she had taken a large step toward making life in the Abbey tolerable.

Mother Zarend's voice gentled, although Ellin could not miss the steel that flashed in her eyes. "Before you became queen, you had some personal experience of what it feels like to have your freedom taken away by men. If you extrapolate from that, you might find my claim less . . . shocking."

Ellin swallowed hard, surprised to find that the abbess knew how she'd resisted the forced engagement to Zarsha. At the time, she'd been very careful to voice her objections only to her parents and her grandfather, projecting the image of the dutiful daughter and loyal subject of the king whenever she was out in public.

But of course, the abbess was right, and Ellin did have first-hand knowledge of what it felt like to lose her freedom. If not for the Blessing and the terrible effect it had had on the royal family, Ellin would have been shipped off to Nandel to live as Zarsha's property. No amount of begging had moved her father or the king, and as a noblewoman, her only choices were to obey or be sent to the Abbey herself.

She had lived under that terrible pall for only a handful of weeks, and yet she well remembered how many nights she had spent weeping into her pillow in despair. But even as horrible as it had been, she'd had more choices than the poor abigails of the Abbey of the Unwanted.

Taking a deep breath to steady herself, Ellin nodded. "You are right, and I must apologize for my failure in empathy. I have improved conditions at the Abbey, but I see now that isn't enough. I must work toward abolishing it altogether."

To her surprise, Mother Zarend shook her head. "I don't believe that should be the goal," she said hastily. "Keep in mind that the women who reside here have been disowned by their families. Many of them were mistreated long before they set foot behind Abbey walls. They may hate their prison and long for freedom, but there is nowhere safe for them to go."

Ellin frowned, puzzled. "What are you suggesting?"

"If I may be so bold, I might suggest that instead of abolishing the Abbey, you work to change it even more. Make it a *refuge* for unwanted women, rather than a prison. If the abigails were here of their own free will and could leave whenever they wanted to, the misery would be all but erased."

Ellin chewed that over, trying to imagine how she could possibly make it happen.

"You could not make the change all at once," Mother Zarend continued. "You would have to gradually chip away at our chains." She smiled suddenly and unexpectedly. "But then you've already shown a distinct talent for such things. I believe that if you want to change the Abbey from a prison to a refuge, you will find a way."

Ellin tried not to let the abbess's confidence overwhelm her, for it was all too easy to see ways in which such a crusade might fail. But then the world had transformed in almost unimaginable ways over the past two years, so perhaps it was not unreasonable to hope she could make a change of that magnitude if she set her mind to it and moved carefully.

"I will think on it," Ellin promised. "And I will call on you again to discuss any plans that come to mind to make sure I don't accidentally make things worse."

Mother Zarend rose from her chair and gave a deep curtsy. "Thank you, Your Majesty," she said. "And I will bring your proposal to my seers. I suspect you will have more than one volunteer to choose from."

Ellin smiled at her. "I will leave any choosing to you, if you don't mind. I trust your judgment in this more than I trust my own."

"Very well."

Draios stifled a yawn as he sat in the antechamber outside the office of Lord Eldlin, the High Priest of the Temple of the Creator—and Draios's mentor, at least in theory. As the son of the king, it was appropriate he accept mentorship from only the most exalted members of the clergy, but he couldn't say he'd been overly impressed with Lord Eldlin. The man was in his dotage, constantly fretting about some new ailment or another, his temper and his patience always short. Draios had no doubt the man was wise in the ways of the Creator, and he adhered to the teachings of the Devotional with more diligence than many priests of Draios's acquaintance. But he was otherwise most tiresome, with a droning, nasal voice that always made Draios feel sleepy and bored.

Draios shifted in his chair and crossed his legs. It wasn't Eldlin's voice that was making him sleepy at the moment. Since reading the letter that had been rescued from the flames, Draios had spent a great deal of time in contemplation, and last night had been his second nightlong vigil of the week as he prayed to the Creator for guidance. He was feeling the effects of those sleepless nights, and even his annoyance at Eldlin's insistence on keeping him waiting was not enough to keep his eyelids from drooping.

He was halfway to sleep when the door to Eldlin's office finally opened and an acolyte beckoned Draios to enter. Scowling at the lad who had caught him napping, Draios rose to his feet and stretched, his body stiff from having spent the night on his knees. The acolyte flushed and hurriedly looked away. Draios paid him no further heed as he entered his mentor's study to find Eldlin poring over an ancient, illuminated Devotional spread out over his desk.

It was all Draios could do not to roll his eyes. He believed that, like his father, Lord Eldlin was a genuinely devout man; however, Eldlin made his devotion into a kind of ongoing performance that was—in Draios's estimation—unseemly. Yes, as the high priest, it was certainly his duty to project an image of perfect piety at all times, but Eldlin took this duty to the extreme. Sometimes, Draios wondered if perhaps the excess signified an attempt to compensate for a faith that was not as flawless as it appeared, although he tried to stifle that uncharitable thought whenever it arose.

Draios stood in front of the high priest's desk, hands clasped behind his back as he waited patiently for attention. Well, perhaps not truly patiently—his hands were clasped together rather tightly, and he had to consciously relax his face to stop his teeth from grinding. All postulants were meant to be treated equally within the temple—regardless of worldly rank—and Draios had the feeling Eldlin took pleasure in the freedom to treat his king's son as if he were just an ordinary man.

Finally, Eldlin set the Devotional aside and turned his attention to Draios.

"What can I do for you, my son?" Eldlin asked in a tone of polite disinterest. "Should you not be preparing for morning services?"

"I am prepared," Draios said, reminding himself not to snap at the man from whom he intended to ask a favor. Postulants were meant to spend the hour before the morning service in solitary meditation, but Draios hardly felt such was necessary after he'd performed an all-night vigil.

It was during last night's vigil that the way had come clear to him. That the Creator had been behind the happenstance that had allowed him to retrieve the fragment of letter from Delnamal, he was certain. Else why would the flames not have finished their work? He had quickly deduced that he must visit Delnamal to bear witness to whatever strange new power the man claimed to have, but there were two major impediments that stood in his way: his duties to the temple, and his duties to his father. Draios was certain he could gain his father's permission to travel for a couple of days if he had already obtained permission from Lord Eldlin, so practically speaking, it was only Eldlin Draios had to convince.

He'd prayed long and hard on the problem last night, for postulants could only be excused from duty in the case of illness or death in the family. While Draios hadn't been able to stop himself from fantasizing about creating a particular death in his family, he had managed to shove those fantasies aside and focus

on a more practical solution. It unfortunately involved lying to
Lord Eldlin, but over the course of the long night, Draios had
found peace with that small sin. He had a much greater sin in
mind should Lord Eldlin refuse his most reasonable request, but
he had faith the Creator would not force him to sully himself in
such a manner.

Lord Eldlin gave him a look of such skepticism that Draios
could not help his hackles rising.

"I spent all of last night in prayer," he said tightly, "and
through that prayer, I have felt a calling."

"A calling, you say?" Eldlin said, his skepticism strengthening.
"I had assumed you had *already* felt a calling, else you would not
have become a postulant."

Eldlin massaged the fingers of one hand with the other, and
Draios hoped he was not about to hear a tale of woe about how
the old man's joints ached. He wasn't sure he'd be able to resist
picking up the heavy tome on the desk and smashing it down on
his mentor's fingers to give him a taste of *real* pain. The disrespect in the high priest's voice was enough to put Draios's temper
on edge, and some unworthy part of him wondered if it wouldn't
be best for all involved if Eldlin turned him down, after all. The
man ought to have retired from the priesthood—or at least from
the office of high priest—long ago.

"I felt a *special* calling," Draios grated through his teeth. He
forced himself to calm, knowing that his calling would hardly
sound genuine if he could not hide the anger his mentor had
spurred in him. If he'd been called by the Creator, he should feel
nothing but awe and longing. And, he reminded himself, he *had*
been called. Just not in the way he planned to explain to Eldlin.

"In the wee hours of the morning, a sudden . . ." He stopped,
as if at a loss for words. He had practiced in front of the mirror
before leaving the palace, calling up the feeling of wonder that
had filled him when he'd read Delnamal's letter and felt the hand
of the Creator at work. He let that wonder shine in his eyes, star-

ing at Eldlin with wide-eyed earnestness as he raised a hand to the middle of his chest. ". . . *yearning* in my heart. I have never felt the like," he said a little breathlessly, shaking his head.

He had hoped that his performance would banish the surliness and disbelief in Eldlin's face, but the old man frowned at him fiercely. "And what is it, precisely, you yearn for so desperately?"

Draios's hand slipped into the pocket of the unadorned brown tunic he and every other postulant wore. The pocket held the miniature Devotional every acolyte, postulant, and priest was required to carry with him at all times, but it also held a simple gold band with a raised dome of embedded diamond chips. The ring itself was naught but a trinket in appearance and value—Draios would never think to wear such a thing. However, its plain appearance was designed to hide its sinister purpose.

Hastily, he pulled his hand out of his pocket, reminding himself that the ring was meant to be a last resort. If Lord Eldlin insisted on standing in the way of Draios's calling, then whatever action Draios was forced to take against him was forgivable, even *necessary*. A few fasts and a night of penance would purge the sin from his soul, and he could continue doing the Creator's bidding with a clean conscience. The same could not be said if he allowed himself to strike out of anger, and considering how Eldlin was regarding him now, it was best to keep the temptation out of immediate reach.

"I have been called to pilgrimage," Draios said, aware that some hint of his temper had crept into his voice, spoiling the effect of his pronouncement. "I have never visited the Shrine of the Holy Penitents, and what I felt in my heart last night was that I must pay a visit there to formally shed my sins before continuing my education as a postulant."

It was a pilgrimage that most postulants undertook before beginning their time at the temple, although it was by no means required. Draios likely would have undertaken it himself had he not indulged in the sin of impatience. He had been anxious to get out from under his father's and his brother's watchful eyes the moment he reached his majority—hence his decision to enter the temple the day after his birthday. If he'd known he'd be forced to return to the palace every night, he'd have made a different decision.

Eldlin somehow managed to look down his nose at Draios despite being seated. "The time to undertake the pilgrimage was *before* you dedicated yourself to the temple. When you have finished your first year, you will be allowed more privileges, but you are already absent from the temple far too often." He held up a hand to forestall Draios's protest. "I am aware that it was not your decision to reside elsewhere during the training, but even so . . ." He shook his head, already reaching for the gigantic Devotional to pull it back into place in front of him.

"I'm afraid taking a leave from the temple this early in your training is out of the question," Lord Eldlin concluded, his eyes now on the page rather than on Draios.

Fury rose in Draios's breast. Not only had Eldlin denied his most reasonable request, he was treating Draios with a deplorable lack of respect!

"You cannot mean for me to ignore the Creator's calling," he protested, his hand slipping back into his pocket. This time, he felt no qualm whatsoever about slipping his smallest finger into the ring.

"I'm too old to confuse a young man's boredom with the Creator's calling," Eldlin said, not even bothering to look up from his Devotional. "You are dismissed, Postulant."

Draios's hand was shaking with rage as he withdrew it from his pocket, the ring on his finger with its dome of diamonds turned to face inward. If Eldlin hadn't been so dedicated to making his show of indifference, he might have seen the error of his ways and reversed his decision. However, his eyes remained glued to the page, and he did not see the ring that ought not be on a postulant's finger. Nor did he see Draios opening his Mindseye and activating the spell contained in the small reservoir of potion underneath the dome.

"Are you quite well, Lord Eldlin?" he asked suddenly, his Mindseye now closed as he leaned over the desk and brazenly put his hand on the old man's arm.

Lord Eldlin started and tried to jerk his arm away—not out of any alarm, but in outrage.

"What is the meaning of this?" Eldlin hissed. "Unhand me this instant."

"You are looking pale," Draios told his mentor with what he felt sure was a sinister smile. "Is it your heart again?"

Lord Eldlin gasped suddenly as Draios activated the mechanism within the ring, piercing Eldlin's skin and delivering the potion into his system.

For most men, the potion Draios had just administered would be harmless. It was nothing but a particularly strong version of a healer's stimulant, meant to rouse the unconscious. But for a man whose heart had already twice attempted to fail him . . .

Eldlin rocked back in his chair, his whole body going taut as his eyes widened and sweat bathed his face. He tried to cry out, but the sound that escaped his lips was far too faint to carry.

Draios slipped the ring off his finger and returned it to the pocket of his tunic, crossing to the other side of the desk and loosening the collar of the high priest's vestments.

"Are you having trouble breathing, Your Grace?" he asked. "Let me help you."

He used the edge of his tunic to wipe away the tiny spot of blood that was visible on Eldlin's arm where the needle had poked him, although he did not imagine that there would be any particular inquest into a death that could not look especially suspicious with Eldlin's history.

He waited a few moments longer, making sure Eldlin was close enough to death that a healer could not arrive in time to save him, before he began shouting frantically for help.

Part Two

VISIONS

CHAPTER SIXTEEN

Draios dozed off and on throughout the carriage ride from Khalwell to the manor house where Delnamal resided. He had left the temple and returned to the palace in the confusion surrounding the high priest's death. He'd hastily called for a coach and had his valet pack the bare minimum of necessities, then headed out immediately. He'd left a note for his father, claiming Lord Eldlin's dying wish had been that Draios make the pilgrimage to the Shrine of the Holy Penitents and that he was on his way to honor that wish. It was unlikely the king would believe the excuse—and Parlommir would be livid at what he'd undoubtedly consider active disobedience that required punishment—but if Draios should find what he believed he would in Delnamal's powers, then all would be forgiven.

And if he was wrong? Well, he could always continue on to the shrine and turn his lie into the truth. Even if his father didn't wholeheartedly believe the lie, he would hardly say so in public, and Lord Eldlin's successor would be in no position to disbelieve the king's son without the king's support.

Draios awoke from a light sleep when the coach bounced over an especially deep rut in the road. Rubbing the weariness from his eyes, he looked out the window. The coach lurched again, and he scowled at the rough and pitted road, which clearly did not see enough use to warrant regular maintenance. Forest loomed overhead, blocking out the light, while roots jutted from the ground and reached for the muddy track, seeking to engulf it and reclaim it for the wild.

Consulting a map he had tucked into his doublet, Draios saw that the road supposedly passed through a small town—a village, really—about an hour's ride from the manor house, but Draios must have been asleep for longer than he'd realized, for he saw no sign of civilization from the time he opened his eyes until the moment shortly after dark when the stately, aging manor house came into view.

The manor house itself was brightly lit, both inside and out, with a multitude of luminants that lent the place a glow that was visible from a long way away. Xanvin and Delnamal might be living far from the city, but there were enough lights in and around the house to give the impression of a small village.

Two rough-looking servants rushed from a coach house that squatted in a rare pool of shadow off to the side. Looking out the window of his coach, Draios saw that both were armed. Perhaps they were what served as Delnamal's honor guard these days, though it hardly seemed the former King of Aaltah needed such protections out here in the middle of nowhere. Both sets of eyes widened—and hands fell away from sword hilts—when they caught sight of the royal crest that adorned Draios's coach.

The coach pulled up to the front of the house, the two servants hurrying to catch up and meet it there. The chevals that had tirelessly pulled the coach from Khalwell came to a smooth stop, and Draios waited patiently for the driver to dismount and open the door for him.

Stepping down from the coach, Draios took a moment to stretch muscles stiff from the long ride while also assessing the manor house before him. A little bit of research into the place

had revealed it to have originally been the country estate of a
royal duke, who had used it almost exclusively to host epic hunt-
ing parties. He would have thought that with only Delnamal and
Xanvin and a minimal staff in residence, much of the house would
be shuttered and dark.

The two servants/honor guardsmen finally caught up to the
coach, both panting and out of sorts. One of them sketched an
inelegant bow, and the other followed suit with unseemly delay.
Draios's nose wrinkled as he detected the scent of alcohol wafting
from one or both of them. Clearly the servants assigned to care
for King Khalvin's esteemed guests were not the cream of the
Khalpar crop. In his haste to leave Khalwell before anyone
thought to stop him, Draios had failed to bring his valet with
him, thinking it easier to avail himself of one of Delnamal's
men—a decision he was already regretting.

"Forgive us, Your Highness," one of the men said, still looking wide-eyed and generally alarmed. "We did not know to expect you, or we would have prepared a grand welcome."

In the background, Draios could see hurried movement behind a number of the lighted windows, no doubt the frenzied
scurrying of the rest of the serving staff. He had not given a second thought to arriving at Delnamal's manor house without
warning, but now that it was too late he realized it was hardly the
height of good manners.

Then again, Draios was the king's son, and Delnamal and his
mother were living in this house at the king's expense. Surely the
pair did not require strict adherence to social customs under the
circumstances.

"I am here to visit my aunt Xanvin and my cousin Delnamal,"
he said, eschewing the polite apology that a lesser man would
have felt obligated to issue.

"Of course, sir," the first servant said with another bow. The
second man seemed to have swallowed his tongue, along with his
good sense, for he did nothing but stand beside his fellow and

stare. Draios guessed it was from this second servant that the scent of alcohol wafted.

The front door opened, and a man appeared silhouetted against the lights of a massive chandelier behind him. There were luminants glowing on both sides of the entryway, but the man stood just far enough back that the light failed to hit him. He loomed in that doorway for a long moment, a strangely menacing shadow that for some reason set the hairs on the back of Draios's neck to standing on end.

Then the man took a couple of steps forward into the light, leaning heavily on a cane as he did so.

Draios frowned in confusion. King Delnamal was reputed to be a man of considerable girth, and while he was hardly *young*, he was not old and feeble enough to need a cane. And yet even with no words spoken, the frail man who stepped into the light and leaned heavily on his cane carried with him an air of authority that left no question in Draios's mind as to his identity.

Draios stepped around the servants—who showed no signs of developing any intelligence—ignoring them as he approached the entryway and studied the man who had once been the King of Aaltah.

Draios knew the man was in his early thirties, but he would have guessed him to be at least sixty, probably older. Never of great stature to begin with, Delnamal's back was bent enough to make him look even shorter, and great wattles of skin hung loose and limp from what had no doubt once been a substantial double chin. His eyes and cheeks were as sunken as those of a man dying of wasting sickness, and yet when Draios met that gaze, he saw a depth of intensity that nearly took his breath away.

"Prince Draios, I presume," Delnamal said when Draios had climbed the short set of marble steps and stood directly before him. He spoke in easy, if heavily accented, Parian that he had likely learned from his mother.

Draios raised his eyebrows, surprised to be recognized by this man he had never met. "How do you know who I am?" he asked, glancing over his shoulder at the coach to confirm his suspicion that the royal crest was not visible from this angle and in the darkness.

"I made a deduction," Delnamal said with a shrug that looked painful and awkward. "You look too much like Mama not to be a relative, and a close one at that. But unless customs are very much different from those in Aaltah, Crown Prince Parlommir would not arrive without warning or fanfare. Therefore, you must be Draios."

Draios tensed ever so slightly at what he suspected was a sly insult, a suggestion that only Parlommir was an important enough figure to require any fanfare. "I am here to pay a social call," he said stiffly. "There was no need to bring a retinue." He frowned at the coach as the servants finally began to make themselves useful, unloading the scant baggage and leading the chevals toward what Draios presumed was a stable.

"You are, of course, most welcome here, Your Highness," Delnamal said with a smile that looked more predatory than welcoming. "Whether as an official representative of the Kingdom of Khalpar or as my dear cousin."

Draios shivered, telling himself it was naught but a reaction to the chill breeze, until he realized he was all but holding his breath. He forced what he hoped looked like a casual, relaxed smile, intrigued by his own reaction to a man who clearly posed no threat to him. He had never before encountered anyone who made him uneasy—was, in fact, used to having that effect on others instead—and he could not quite pinpoint what it was about his cousin that triggered this sense of wary alertness.

"As far as the court of Khalpar is concerned, you died in an accident by the Well of Aaltah," Draios said. "I only recently learned that you and my aunt survived and were living here, which is why I decided to pay a visit."

"Hmm," said Delnamal, and Draios wondered what had made

him speak so plainly. By his words, he'd just made it abundantly clear that his father did not confide in him, which was hardly the picture of authority he'd been planning to project.

Delnamal smiled, though the expression did not reach his eyes and carried no true sense of warmth. "Well then, Cousin, please do come in. I am very pleased to meet you, and I am sure my mother will be, as well. We have a great deal of catching up to do, don't we?"

Draios shivered again, and there was no pretending it was from the cold this time. Something about Delnamal was just . . . *wrong*. A man more faint of heart—and with less faith in the Creator—might well have turned away, fleeing that sense of wrongness in superstitious terror. But Draios saw in that wrongness hope. Hope that Delnamal truly did possess some secret power that he'd only hinted at in the sections of the letter Draios had rescued from the flames.

His father was a fool, Draios concluded, to dismiss Delnamal's claims without even investigating them. For the good of the kingdom—indeed, for the good of all of Seven Wells—Draios would learn just what it was Delnamal could do, and how his abilities might be used to restore the world to its natural order.

Delnamal assessed his princely cousin as they entered the manor house's formal parlor, which had not seen use once since Delnamal and his mother had taken up residence. The house was woefully understaffed, but having anticipated an august visitor eventually, Delnamal had insisted the parlor be kept spotless and ready.

Three impressive vases filled with flowers cut fresh from the garden showed that Xanvin, too, had been prepared for visitors, despite her stated opinion that Khalvin was not open to Delnamal's message. She was conspicuously absent, although she must have heard the commotion of Draios's arrival. She had not joined him for dinner, either, claiming—through her lady's maid—to have a headache. Of course, Delnamal knew that was a polite fiction—one his mother likely didn't expect him to believe. There was no missing the very different way she had regarded him since he'd demonstrated his newfound power, nor was it possible not to notice how often she found excuses to avoid being in his presence.

"Would you care for some brandy?" Delnamal asked, gesturing toward the decanter on the sideboard. "It is of most excellent vintage." Or so he had been told. Just a handful of months ago, he'd been unable to go more than an hour or two without numbing himself with alcohol, but he'd found since the incident at the Well that neither food nor drink brought him any pleasure. He ate and drank only because of the need to sustain himself, and the fine brandy did not tempt him.

"A brandy would be lovely after the journey," Draios agreed, and Delnamal rang for a servant to pour.

Draios looked at him askance, and Delnamal realized the prince expected him to pour the drink himself as an act of hospitality. He gave the boy a rueful smile, indicating his cane before making his way to the nearest chair and all but collapsing into it. He saw Draios take in the state of his hands, which had previously been well hidden by the drape of his sleeves.

"Forgive my shortcomings as a host," Delnamal said, "but I'm as likely to pour the brandy on the floor as into a glass." He had supped from the Rhokai of an injured squirrel he had happened upon in the woods this afternoon, but the burst of strength the tiny animal had lent him was long gone. By tomorrow morning, he would likely not have the strength to get out of bed, and had he been a religious man, he would have thanked the Creator for sending Draios *now*, before the weakness was any more advanced.

A footman answered Delnamal's summons and quickly poured the requisite drink, handing it to Draios before once again hurrying out. Delnamal was certain his mother had told no one about the power he had revealed, and yet he had the feeling that the servants were growing increasingly wary around him, the whispers and mumbles growing more urgent. It was possible that, soon, staff would begin to quit—and that could make his situation even more awkward. Tonight, he would have to put on a convincing show so that he might win Draios over to his side.

"I had heard tell you were injured," Draios said, "but I had not realized the extent."

Delnamal shrugged, a part of him still surprised by how little the infirmities of his body bothered him. To be sure, they were inconvenient, but whenever he started to feel sorry for himself or thought to indulge in a good pout, he found he could not be bothered.

"I am well enough," Delnamal said, then fell silent a moment as he once again examined the puzzle of Prince Draios. His mother had told him everything she knew about her two nephews, and he was well aware that the boy was in training for the priesthood. She had never even mentioned the possibility of Draios putting in an appearance, for as a postulant, he should have been bound to remain in the temple he served.

"To what do I owe the pleasure of this visit?" Delnamal asked, cocking his head and paying as much attention to Draios's body language as to the actual words of his reply.

Draios's eyes narrowed ever so slightly—perhaps he was not used to being questioned quite so boldly. Delnamal remembered what it was like to be an insecure prince, and even in this brief encounter, he'd recognized the signs. It was not uncommon for a second son to feel somehow lesser, and Delnamal could almost see the chip that sat heavily on Draios's shoulder.

"Why, I came to meet the cousin and the aunt that I had never met before," Draios claimed, repeating the patent falsehood. King Khalvin had made it clear that he intended Delnamal and Xanvin to live in obscurity as a state secret, and there was no reason to believe he would permit anyone—much less one of his sons—to pay a social call.

If Delnamal were playing politics, he would at least pretend to believe the lie for the sake of politeness. But he'd never been much good at the game of politics, and he was not much interested in playing it now. "Lies bore me," he said, watching the young prince's face closely, gauging his reaction, measuring his temper.

Prince Draios was far better at hiding his anger than Delnamal had ever been—back in the days when he had allowed himself to be swallowed whole by that anger. There was almost no discernible change in his expression or body language, and yet somehow Delnamal *knew* he had angered him. Just as he knew—without being able to define exactly *how*—that Draios was uncomfortable, if not actively intimidated, by him. Delnamal was not yet sure if that was good or bad.

"Your diplomacy could use a little work," Draios said with a fair imitation of a wry smile. "I don't know about Aaltah customs, but in Khalpar it is considered impolite to accuse one's guest of lying." Crossing his legs, Draios leaned back more comfortably in his chair, projecting an image of ease that failed to convince.

"Diplomacy has never been my strong suit, or so I have been told. Nor has patience. I had been led to believe that you were in training to become a priest, which as I understand it, should leave you without the leisure to make casual visits to the countryside. And you did not arrive with an entourage, which makes your visit even more curious."

Draios raised an eyebrow. "And I myself had been led to believe that you were living in careful obscurity, cut off from the outside world. How did you know I was in training to enter the priesthood?"

Delnamal had to give the young man credit. He was hard to rile, at least outwardly. If he were merely paying a social call as he claimed, it seemed unlikely he would have tolerated Delnamal's rudeness as well as he had so far, which helped confirm what Delnamal had suspected from the start: Draios wanted something from him.

Delnamal was well aware that many people considered him . . . well, if not precisely *stupid,* then at the very least not very bright. In point of fact, he had—though he would never have admitted it out loud—bought into the idea himself, which had made him constantly defensive about his intellect. But with the Rhokai that now inhabited his blood and gave him control of his emotions, he could clearly see that what had held him back was *not* a lack of intellect, merely a lack of focus and clarity. It was hard to think when your emotions were running rampant, when you were always trying to defend yourself from the judgment of others. He'd seen the world through a haze of anger and hurt and resentment and bitterness.

He offered Draios a conspiratorial smile. "Your father may choose to hide me in the countryside like the family embarrassment, but that does not mean I am completely cut off. I may be in exile, of a sort, but I am still a king, and I am not without resources."

Delnamal was overstating his position, naturally, for he had access to none of the riches that ought to be his, and his mother's knowledge of her Khalpari family was outdated at best. But despite his reduced circumstances and his limited resources, it was relatively easy to get such basic information as the prince's entry into the Temple of the Creator. Putting that information together with his own mother's piousness and her descriptions of her brother's even stronger adherence to the Devotional, Delnamal gathered that the surest way to win the young man's support—and through him, his father's—was to appeal to his religious beliefs.

"Since you seem to be reluctant to come right out and tell me why you are here, I will make an educated guess," Delnamal said.

"I recently sent a letter to your father, explaining that what happened to me at Aaltah's Well has altered me in ways I did not comprehend when my mother and I first arrived in Khalpar. He has not seen fit to respond to my letter, nor has he sent Prince Parlommir or anyone else to discuss how I might be useful in the efforts to undo the Curse and restore the world to its natural order.

"You have interrupted your studies and come to me out here in the wilderness because you disagree with your father's decision to ignore my letter. You are hoping to learn more about what I have to offer so that you might persuade your father to reconsider should you find me convincing."

Again, he watched Draios's face carefully. The prince was clearly an expert at subterfuge, at hiding his reactions and presenting a nearly unreadable visage to the public. Delnamal himself could hardly claim to be an expert at reading people, but even so he picked up on some subtle hint of discomfort that most ordinary people would have missed. Something that told him his guess, while close, had not precisely hit the mark.

"You are here without your father's knowledge or consent," Delnamal continued, and saw by the slight tightening of Draios's eyes that he had sniffed out the source of the prince's discomfort. "Your father is a cautious man. One who would like to see the world restored to order, but who has little inclination to take an active role in that restoration. I saw evidence aplenty of his reluctance to take action when I tried to secure his support for my own efforts."

This time, Draios went so far as to shift in his chair, which was well-nigh a temper tantrum from one who seemed to take pride in masking his thoughts and feelings. Something cold and hard flashed in his eyes and was quickly suppressed. "My father and I are both men of faith," he said, "but we differ in our interpretations of the Devotional's teachings. My father's faith leads him to believe that the Creator Himself will correct the imbalance in our world if we but trust Him. I, on the other hand, feel that we as His children have an obligation to help right the wrong that was done to all of Seven Wells."

Delnamal nodded approvingly. It would have been much easier to take back his kingdom and destroy Women's Well if King Khalvin were a man of action, but it was clear Draios could become a powerful ally if Delnamal cultivated him correctly.

"Indeed, that is how I interpret His will as well," he said, thankful for the first time that his mother had repeatedly tried to ram her religious beliefs down his throat. He had found her teachings and her piety a sore trial, but now that he needed the help of a pair of religious fanatics, he was pleased to find he had the tools required.

Khalvin's piety was well known, and whether he was willing to lead his troops to war or not, there was no question he believed that the Curse was an abomination. Nor was there any question that he agreed Women's Well had no right to exist. All Delnamal had to do was convince the man that it was the Creator's will that he take action, and it seemed Draios would be an admirable proponent for his message.

"I believe what happened to me at the Well of Aaltah happened for a reason," Delnamal said. "It was the Creator's will that I be changed as I am, that I become a weapon the righteous can use to prove their worthiness and devotion to Him."

Draios absorbed that for a moment, then seemed to come to some internal decision. "I will be entirely honest with you if you will but do me the same courtesy."

Delnamal smiled and nodded. "Of course," he said, though he very much doubted Draios intended true honesty. The Devotional might demand honesty, but even the most pious often found ways to justify straying from the path.

"You are right," Draios said. "I am here without my father's consent or knowledge. In fact, he did not tell me that you and my aunt were living in Khalpar at all. I only learned you had survived the disaster at the Well because I rescued a letter from the flames."

"That is . . . disappointing to hear," Delnamal said with admirable calm despite a momentary spike of temper. "My mother cautioned me that he might not take my claims seriously even with the sworn confirmation she provided, but I had hoped she was wrong."

"I'm afraid your letter was badly damaged by the flames by the time I rescued it," Draios confided. "I couldn't make out much other than that you and your mother had survived and were living in the country. And that something had happened to you at the Well that you believed could be used in our battle to reverse the Curse."

"Ah," Delnamal said, finally understanding all the shifts in currents he'd sensed throughout the conversation. "You have not been made privy to the details about what happened to me."

"No," Draios agreed with too-obvious chagrin.

"I think this is perhaps something I should show you, rather than trying to explain," he said, ringing for a servant as his pulse thrummed with eagerness. With the prince staying the night, it would not do for Delnamal to allow his strength to wane as it inevitably would by morning. Demonstrating his power was a risk—especially considering his own mother's horrified reaction. But every instinct in his body told him that Draios would respond very differently. He was almost certain that was a genuine insight and not a rationalization to justify doing what he wanted to do anyway.

A footman came to his call, and Delnamal ordered the man to bring Bandar to the formal parlor—Bandar being one of the embarrassingly drunken honor guardsmen who'd greeted the prince's coach.

"While we wait," Delnamal said, "I would ask you to open your Mindseye and take a look at me."

• • •

Tynthanal's heart started sinking even before his trade minister began to speak, for the moment he had entered the chamber for this morning's council meeting, the man had been looking at him strangely. Unfortunately, he knew deep down in his bones why that would be—Administrator Loveland reported directly to the trade minister, and there was only so long Tynthanal could have expected the man to keep silent. Especially as the most alarming aspect of the Well's damage became more obvious.

"It has come to my attention," the trade minister said when the lord chancellor gave him leave to address the council, "that our Well may be even more seriously damaged than we originally realized."

Tynthanal clenched his fists under the table as the trade minister delivered the news and the rest of his council gasped and gaped in dismay. In the month since Tynthanal had spoken with Loveland, there had apparently been only two new pregnancies recorded, making a grand total of five since the Well was damaged. The data only encompassed the city of Aalwell and the women who used the abigails as midwives, but it was nonetheless stunning.

"You don't look surprised," the lord chancellor said, turning to glare at Tynthanal.

He grimaced, fully aware that he had made a stupid mistake. All well and good to keep the news to himself as long as possible, but he had known better than to expect it to stay a secret forever. Perhaps the truth would be no more palatable if he'd informed his council immediately, but at least they would not all be looking at him with such shock and ire.

"My apologies," Tynthanal said, knowing the words inadequate. "Administrator Loveland did in fact inform me of this problem earlier. It seemed to me at the time best not to cause a panic until we were certain it was not some kind of fluke." He did not say so out loud, but there had also been some part of him that had hoped he would find a cure for whatever ailed the Well before ever having to bring this deficit to anyone else's attention.

"Cause a panic?" the chancellor said with no small amount of acid in his voice. "Is that what you think of your royal council?"

Tynthanal pinched the bridge of his nose and wished he would develop better political instincts. He had not meant to be insulting in the least, but now that it was too late, he could clearly see his mistake. Explaining that it was the panic the general public would feel when his council members proved unequal to the task of keeping the secret themselves would not improve the situation.

"Has there been any progress in discovering what ails our Well?" Lord Aldnor asked, ignoring the testy exchange.

Tynthanal knew his former commander had been one of the council members who'd voted against appointing him regent, but Lord Aldnor had shown no sign of holding a grudge. Tynthanal would have been more grateful for the change of subject if he could have provided a more enlightening update.

"I will speak with the seer in Rhozinolm tomorrow—or as soon as she is sufficiently recovered to speak. She is due to take the seer's poison today, and I have high hopes that she will be able to tell us exactly what happened to the Well."

"Is that all we're doing to try to address the issue?" Lord Zauthan, the lord chamberlain, asked with a sneer. "I hardly think it's wise to put such faith in superstitious nonsense. We must take a more *active* role in fixing the damage."

Tynthanal let out a grunt of frustration, for this was a frequent refrain from both his lord chamberlain and his lord chancellor—the two highest-ranking members of his council, both of whom had entertained hopes of being named regent over Tynthanal. In fact, if either one of them had been willing to set aside his own ambitions and name the other to the position, Tynthanal would still be in Women's Well.

"Lord Draimel and I will continue our work together," Tynthanal said, nodding in the direction of his grand magus. "We are doing everything we can to diagnose the problem, but it is like nothing anyone has ever seen before. And until we know precisely what is wrong, it's hard to craft a plan to fix it."

Tynthanal had presented some version of that argument so many times he felt almost like he was reading from a script. It generally worked to silence his critics, but the mood in the council chamber felt different today—more fractious.

"I've heard it whispered that the *problem*," Lord Zauthan said with narrowed eyes, "is that we have appointed as regent the son of the witch who cursed the Wellspring."

Lord Aldnor scoffed loudly. "Remind your whisperers that the Well was broken *before* Tynthanal became our prince regent."

Tynthanal was thankful for the swift and reasonable defense, but the lord chamberlain's words nonetheless chilled him. He'd known since he'd accepted the regency that there was danger to undertaking a task he did not know if he could accomplish. Because he was his mother's son, there was a certain segment of the population who would always regard him as suspect. There was already some low-level unrest among the masses as the treasury continued to dwindle and the Crown was forced to reduce some services that not everyone agreed were nonessential. And because of Aaltah's failure to keep up its side of certain trade agreements, shortages were beginning to be felt. Shortages that would only get worse as time went on.

"Yes, yes," Zauthan responded, "we all know that. I'm not saying that *I* believe as much. But as our belts get tighter with no solution in sight, those whispers will get louder, whether the accusation is logical or not."

Tynthanal did not think he was imagining the hint of eagerness he detected in the lord chamberlain's eyes, and he doubted the man had ever wholly abandoned his ambitions. He didn't see any calculating looks on the faces of the rest of his council members, but that was likely to change if the Well remained impaired for much longer.

Although he was not a religious man, Tynthanal sent a fervent prayer to the Mother to help Rhozinolm's seer find a solution.

CHAPTER SEVENTEEN

Alys could hardly believe how much Shelvon had changed in the last few months. When she'd been married to Delnamal, Shelvon had always appeared pale and wan, and her smiles had been rare and fleeting. She'd been reluctant to look anyone straight in the eye, and she rarely spoke unless spoken to first. In short, she'd been the epitome of Nandel womanhood, having been raised to believe women were inherently inferior to men.

Even after defying Delnamal by spiriting Corlin away with her to Women's Well, she'd still been noticeably meek and shy. But everything had changed on the night Delnamal had sent a man to Women's Well to kidnap Shelvon and she'd used the sword lessons Lord Falcor had given her to fight the brute off until help arrived.

In the immediate aftermath, Shelvon had been coaxed into giving introductory sword lessons to a handful of women, and that had been just the start. Now, her classes were always full, and she was growing in confidence every day. Time spent in the sun had bronzed her skin—though not enough to hide her Nandel ancestry—and she practically gleamed with good spirits.

Shelvon entered Alys's office and performed an elegant curtsy.

"Thank you for agreeing to see me," Shelvon said when she rose.

"As if there were any chance I'd refuse!" Alys responded. "I'm always delighted to spend time with you, whether it's on official business or as family."

Shelvon blushed. Her self-confidence might have grown a great deal, but there was still room for improvement. Alys had told her many times that she still considered Shelvon her sister-in-law, despite Delnamal having divorced her in absentia. But Shelvon never quite seemed to believe it, which was a shame.

"Let's sit," Alys said, motioning to the informal—and unusual—seating area she'd insisted on installing in her office. It was almost scandalous for there to be anything "informal" in the royal palace outside the residential wing, but defying conventions was one of Alys's favorite things.

They both took a seat on the sofa and engaged in friendly small talk for a little while before Shelvon got around to explaining the purpose of her visit.

"I have a proposal that you may find totally outrageous," she said.

"Oh?" Alys said, raising her eyebrows. Shelvon was not someone from whom she'd expect to receive "outrageous" proposals. "I think I like it already. Do go on."

Shelvon ducked her chin just the tiniest amount, but the hint of meekness vanished almost as soon as it appeared. "I'd like to propose that the Citadel of Women's Well accept and train women."

Alys's jaw dropped. The idea of women handling swords at all was unthought of anywhere else but in Women's Well, but to have them in the Citadel? Alys could only imagine how horrified some men would be at this intrusion into the staunchest bastion of masculinity. But that wasn't the only reason Alys found the proposal so surprising.

"It was my impression that when Lord Falcor offered to teach women in his spare time, he had very few takers. And those who *did* come quickly lost interest."

Shelvon nodded. "That's true. But I believe things have changed since I began teaching my own classes. There is clearly interest."

"Interest in learning how to swing practice swords perhaps," Alys conceded. "But that doesn't necessarily mean there's interest in becoming soldiers."

"Not necessarily, no. However, I do know that I have several students who seem to have a natural talent and who definitely would be interested. I'm not advanced enough myself to teach more than the basics, and now that I'm kept busy with teaching, I don't have time to further my own lessons. It seems to me that in a principality in which women outnumber men by at least two to one, training women to fight might be advantageous."

Alys had to admit there was a certain logic to Shelvon's argument. The population of Women's Well continued to grow, but it was naturally women who were most drawn to it. And their tiny army was not adequate to protect the territory they now held. But the thought of women joining the Citadel, training to be soldiers . . .

"Your suggestion is certainly unconventional," Alys hedged, trying to imagine how the citizenry of Women's Well—and the rest of Seven Wells—would react. People had adapted to Alysoon serving as sovereign princess—a title that had never existed before she'd claimed it—and they had also adapted to having Chanlix serve as a lady chancellor. There was certainly some grumbling about it, and there were those who had looked askance at an unmarried, pregnant woman—now mother—who had once been an abigail serving on the royal council, but the resistance had been less than she'd expected.

Shelvon smiled at her with a hint of mischief glinting in her eyes. "What about Women's Well *is* conventional?"

Once again, Alys was struck by how much Shelvon had changed, how much lighter and happier the young woman had become. And how very much more self-confident.

"Give me a little time to think about it," Alys said. "And to talk it over with Lord Jailom." She imagined her lord commander would be best suited to determining whether his men could tolerate the idea of sharing the Citadel with women.

Shelvon bowed her head respectfully. "Of course, Your Royal Highness," she responded. But the smile and the light in her eyes said she believed she had already won.

Tynthanal fed Rho into the chirping talker that stood on his desk. The talker was linked to one of Queen Ellinsoltah's. He hoped she was reaching out because her seer had tried and survived Mairahsol's seer's poison.

He expected to see Ellinsoltah shimmer to life in front of the talker, but what he saw instead was a frail, middle-aged woman reclining in a bed with her eyes closed. Ellinsoltah then entered the picture, coming to sit on the bed beside the woman, who was obviously ill.

Tynthanal experienced a pang of sympathy, for he knew without having to be told that this woman was the seer who'd agreed to use Mairahsol's potion, and it had clearly laid her low.

"This is Shabrynel," Ellinsoltah said as she laid a gentle hand on the woman's shoulder. Shabrynel opened her eyes and sat up a little straighter, though the effort cost her. "As you no doubt have guessed already, she volunteered to try the seer's poison."

"It's a pleasure to meet you, Lady Shabrynel," Tynthanal said, and saw the woman start ever so slightly, then chuckle.

"And you, Your Highness," she said in a husky voice that suggested a raw and painful throat. "I have been Sister Shabrynel for so long I almost thought you were speaking to someone else."

"Well, you are Sister Shabrynel no more," Ellin said firmly. "As soon as you are strong enough, I will arrange for transport to take you to your new home in Women's Well."

Shabrynel's eyes lit at the idea, and Tynthanal tried to soothe his aching conscience with the knowledge that Shabrynel would gain her freedom in return for her ordeal. Assuming she recovered. Alys's seer never had.

"The Kingdom of Aaltah—and I personally—thank you for the efforts you have put forth on our behalf," Tynthanal said, though in truth he felt strangely pretentious in speaking for the kingdom. Prince regent he might be, but he had yet to grow accustomed to the title. And if he couldn't find a way to fix the Well, he might never have a *chance* to grow accustomed to it. He could not stop hearing his lord chamberlain's voice as he almost gleefully mentioned the whispers he'd heard. Or made up.

Shabrynel smiled, the corners of her eyes crinkling in a way that suggested she smiled often, despite her circumstances. "I'd take that poison ten times over if it meant getting to leave the Abbey for good." She shuddered. "Although once was really more than enough."

"I heartily agree," Ellinsoltah said, giving the woman's shoulder a comforting squeeze. "I would not ask anyone to go through that a second time." She looked up and met Tynthanal's gaze. "That poison is horrific." Her eyes shone as if she might be on the verge of tears. "I've seen some terrible things in my life, but . . . I'm embarrassed to say I had to leave the room for a while during the worst of it."

Shabrynel reached over and patted the back of the queen's hand. It was an inappropriately familiar gesture, but Ellinsoltah showed no sign of being offended.

"You've no cause to be embarrassed, Your Majesty," Shabrynel said. "It is not pleasant to watch a seer take even a mild poison. I certainly had no expectation that you would be present in the first place."

Ellinsoltah shrugged. "If someone is going to suffer in my service, then I think it is beholden on me to bear witness."

Tynthanal smiled. "I see why you and my sister get along so well."

Alys was old enough to be Ellinsoltah's mother, and yet the two of them had clearly bonded very early in their relationship. If anyone else had sat on the throne of Rhozinolm as the world changed so drastically, the alliance between Rhozinolm and Women's Well would never have happened, and Women's Well would have been destroyed by now.

"Yes, I suppose you do," Ellinsoltah replied. "Now perhaps it is time for Shabrynel to tell us what her vision revealed. I wanted you to be present for this so that we can both hear the firsthand account." She turned to Shabrynel and asked gently, "What did you see?"

"I saw two men and two women in what I presume was Aaltah's Well chamber. One of the women wore a veil."

"That would be Mairahsol," Tynthanal murmured.

"The other looked . . . very ill. I believe one of the men was King Delnamal, as he was described to me, but I don't know who the second was."

"At a guess," Tynthanal said, "it was likely Lord Melcor. He was Delnamal's secretary and was seen going down to the Well on that night. He hasn't been seen or heard from since."

Shabrynel nodded. "Yes, that makes sense. I don't understand exactly what was happening, but the man—Melcor—gave the sickly woman a knife. She held that knife to one of her wrists as if to slash it, but then she attacked Melcor instead. She wounded him, and while they struggled over the knife, they fell into the Well."

Ellinsoltah gasped, and Tynthanal felt a pit forming in his stomach. He had not shared the information about the possible existence of sacrificial Kai, nor about the effects that Mairahsol claimed Kai—sacrificial or otherwise—could have when introduced into a Well. The information had seemed both too unreliable and too dangerous to spread. But if Mairahsol was right about what could happen . . .

"Moments after they fell in," Shabrynel continued, "the Well started to make rumbling noises."

Tynthanal remembered the section of Mairahsol's notes that suggested there would be catastrophic results if men's Kai entered the Well, and he shivered at the realization that yet another outlandish claim he and Kailee had found in those notes appeared to be true.

"King Delnamal began hurrying to the exit," the seer said, "but Mairahsol instead grabbed a potion out of a bag. Then she slit her wrists and threw herself into the Well."

The pit in Tynthanal's stomach grew larger and harder.

"Wait," Ellinsoltah said, "are you saying that Mairahsol *killed herself*?"

"Yes," Shabrynel confirmed.

"That does not seem in keeping with what I've heard about the woman up until now."

"Maybe not, but that's what I saw. Up until the moment she went into the Well, I was watching with my physical vision, but it looked to me as if she activated the potion she'd pulled from the bag with Kai before she jumped."

Ellinsoltah frowned. "But she wouldn't have to *die* to use women's Kai."

"That's because it *wasn't* women's Kai," Tynthanal said, for suddenly Mairahsol's notes seemed much more trustworthy. "At least not the kind we're familiar with."

He told the others what he and Kailee had learned about sacrificial Kai. "We believe her plan was to use the sick woman's sacrifice to close the Mindseye of everyone in Aaltah," he finished. "Obviously, the woman did not cooperate, and I don't know what Mairahsol was trying to accomplish by performing the sacrifice herself. Or why it didn't work as planned."

Shabrynel frowned. "I don't believe she was trying to cast the same spell," she said. "Whatever the potion was she used, she had to retrieve it from her bag, so clearly it wasn't the one the other woman was supposed to trigger with her sacrifice. Also, she could rather easily have fled the Well chamber when the rumbling started. She and Delnamal were alone, and I feel certain she could have outrun him. Perhaps she had little chance of escaping in the end, but it appeared to me that she had a chance to run. She certainly looked like she *wanted* to. But instead she turned back and grabbed that potion."

Tynthanal shook his head, unable to imagine the little bundle of scorn and spite that was Mairahsol choosing to sacrifice her life. For anything. But it turned out Shabrynel's story wasn't finished yet.

"When Mairahsol jumped into the Well, my vision shifted to Mindsight." The woman shivered suddenly, and beside her, Ellinsoltah reached for another blanket to wrap around her.

Shabrynel smiled up at her. "Thank you, Your Majesty." The smile quickly faded as she huddled in the warmth of the blanket.

"After Mairahsol entered the Well," she continued, "something . . . unimaginable rose out of it. It looked like a thick black gout of smoke, only it didn't move like smoke, and it looked strangely . . . solid." The color was slowly leaching from her face, and her eyes looked distant and frightened.

Both Ellinsoltah and Tynthanal gasped at her.

"Whatever it was, it shot out of the Well with impossible speed. It hit King Delnamal in the back as he was fleeing. It bodily picked him up and slammed him into the wall of the Well's antechamber. The smoke disappeared into his body as bits and pieces of the chamber rained down, but the rumbling had stopped. When it was done, Delnamal lay senseless—but breathing—in the rubble. I could not see the smoke anymore, but . . . I *sensed* it when I looked at him. Something about him made the hairs on the back of my neck stand up. I was heartily glad when the vision ended."

She shivered again, her eyes sliding closed as if she'd used the last of her strength recounting what she'd seen.

"Rest now," Ellinsoltah said softly, tucking the covers up under Shabrynel's chin. "You have given us a great deal to think about."

That was an understatement.

Ellinsoltah leaned closer to the talker, and Tynthanal gathered by the movement that she had picked it up and carried it out of the bedchamber, leaving Shabrynel to her well-earned rest.

"What do you think?" she asked when she'd settled in a chair in what looked to be a sitting room.

Tynthanal blew out a deep breath. "To be honest, I'm not sure *what* to think."

"Nor I," Ellinsoltah agreed. "I can't even decide whether Mairahsol jumping into the Well was meant to be malicious or heroic."

Tynthanal's first instinct was as always to assume the worst where Mairahsol was concerned. He had spent very little time in her company when she'd visited Women's Well, but she was exceedingly skilled at making a bad impression. Kailee was the only person he knew who hadn't instantly disliked the woman, and she had insisted Mairahsol had not been acting out of malice. Clearly whatever Mairahsol had been planning was *not* what had actually happened, and he had to admit that the events as described made it unlikely the woman had been trying to close everyone's Mindseye when she threw herself in the Well.

"Kailee and I will examine the notes again," Tynthanal promised. "Maybe with what we know now of events, we will be able to piece together exactly what happened and how to fix it." He groaned and pinched the bridge of his nose, for he wanted easy answers and none seemed to be forthcoming. He did not imagine his royal council would be terribly impressed with the intelligence he had just gained—some of them would go so far as to actively disbelieve it—and he imagined the grumbles would be louder than they had been before.

He thanked Ellinsoltah again and tried to convince himself to regard this new information as a step in the right direction rather than a bitter disappointment.

Zarsha and Ellin were just polishing off the remains of a lovely private dinner in the royal apartments—a delicious luxury and indulgence, when ordinarily their dinners turned into tedious and lengthy affairs of state in a formal banquet hall—when a page entered the cozy parlor and bowed. He bit his lip nervously, his eyes taking in the dinner dishes. It was a rare page who relished the prospect of interrupting a royal dinner.

"I beg your pardon, Your Majesty, Your Highness," the boy said, "but a flier has arrived marked urgent. Your secretary said I should bring it to you right away."

Ellin was glad they'd finished eating, for a flier marked as urgent might well be just the sort of thing to ruin a good meal. With a silent sigh, she began to reach for the message, then realized the page was addressing Zarsha, not her. She and her husband shared a quick, anxious look before Zarsha turned to the boy and offered an easygoing smile that effectively hid any turmoil.

"Thank you, lad," he said, his expression and tone so warm Ellin could see the boy practically basking in it, forgetting his earlier concerns about the interruption. Even in her concern, Ellin felt a warm glow in her chest to see him thoughtful enough to put the page at ease when he must be as filled with foreboding as she.

When the page had been dismissed—sent off with a selection of sweets that neither Zarsha nor Ellin felt inclined to eat—Zarsha grimly broke the seal on the message.

"It's from Waldmir, isn't it?" Ellin asked, though she needn't have, for she recognized the seal.

"It is," Zarsha confirmed, his whole body radiating tension. "And the only reason I can imagine him sending me a flier is if he believed he had news to deliver that would cause me pain."

Ellin suspected he was probably right about that. It was clear that Waldmir had no intention of ever forgiving or trusting Zarsha, and that he would never stop striking out at his nephew in any way he could.

"Do you want me to stay while you read it?" she asked softly. "Or would you prefer privacy?" Like most men of her acquaintance, Zarsha was not fond of letting others see his vulnerability, and she fully expected him to retreat to his own rooms to face Waldmir's message. Which only went to show how much she still had to learn about her husband, despite feeling as if she'd known him half her life.

Zarsha took a deep, bracing breath and met her eyes. "Stay with me," he said. "I . . . I have a feeling I'm going to need you. When my uncle strikes at someone's heart, he rarely misses."

Ellin rose from her chair and went to stand behind Zarsha as he broke the seal on the letter. She put both her hands on his shoulders and gave them a firm squeeze of support, biting her lip anxiously. She was quickly disabused of the notion that she might read the letter over Zarsha's shoulder, for Waldmir had written in Mountain Tongue, the native language of Nandel. Zarsha had taught her a few words of his language, but nowhere near enough to allow her to read the letter. Instead, she read the increasing tightness of Zarsha's shoulders, the shallowing of his breaths, the tremor that ran through all his muscles.

"What is it?" she asked, her own hands squeezing tighter on his shoulders in anticipation.

Zarsha crumpled the letter and threw it halfway across the room with a roar of rage and anguish that brought palace guards running. Ellin hastily dismissed them, then gathered Zarsha into her arms as her own heart pounded in sympathetic pain. Zarsha hugged her back so tightly she could barely breathe, and she waited in dread for him to gather himself enough to speak.

"He knows about the money I've been sending," Zarsha whispered harshly before his voice died once more.

Ellin closed her eyes, knowing that she bore much of the blame for whatever horror Zarsha was now suffering.

"What has he done?" Ellin asked, dreading the answer.

Zarsha shuddered and gently extracted himself from her arms, turning away from her and rubbing his face with both hands.

"He's taken the money, naturally, saying it was rightfully part of my 'brideprice.' But of course that's not near cruel enough for him," Zarsha continued, his breath coming harsh and loud. "No, he had to remind me of just how much power he has over me, of how easily he can make it worse."

He turned back toward her, and his eyes were shiny and rimmed with red.

"He's sent her to the Abbey," he rasped, shaking his head. "A helpless five-year-old girl who may just as well be his daughter as mine."

"No!" Ellin cried, the horror piercing her heart. "You said he would not hurt a child!" The accusation came out before she had a chance to censor herself, and she wished she could take it back as she saw her words cause her husband even more pain.

"Oh, but she's not being hurt," Zarsha said, the bitterness dripping from his words like noxious poison. "She's merely 'visiting' with the abbess, who was Waldmir's first wife. Keeping an old woman company." He swallowed hard. "It's just a threat, really. She's too young to understand what the Abbey is or to know what it means to be sent there. It's *me* he wants to hurt, and he's reminding me what I have to lose if I try to go around him again."

Yet again, Waldmir was making Zarsha choose between the well-being of a helpless little girl who might be his daughter and the well-being of servants he had tried so hard to protect.

There was no question whom Zarsha would choose, though the choice itself would fill him with guilt. It was an uncomfortable admission to say that one child's life was more important than the lives of over twenty servants. Then again, it was clear that the "help" he'd tried to send had not, in fact, been helpful at all.

Grinding her teeth—and hating that she had no choice but to treat Waldmir as an ally and trade partner despite his loathsomeness—Ellin determined that somehow, they *must* find a way to get little Princess Elwynne away from Waldmir and Nandel.

CHAPTER EIGHTEEN

Draios did not like the uncomfortable feeling that he was somehow following Delnamal's command; however, he was far too curious not to do as his cousin suggested and open his Mindseye. He had no inkling what to expect, but there was no earthly way he could have prepared himself for what his Mindsight revealed.

Having witnessed a few violent deaths over the course of his life, Draios had seen masculine Kai in person before. He knew exactly what it looked like, and that there was nothing else that in any way resembled it. So there was no mistaking the myriad colorful crystals that surrounded Delnamal for anything but Kai, and yet . . .

"Impossible, I know," Delnamal said. "But you cannot doubt the evidence of your own eyes."

Trying very hard not to show how unnerved the sight of all that Kai made him, Draios shut his Mindseye and suppressed a shudder. No *wonder* his cousin had felt so very wrong to him from the moment they'd met.

"That is . . ." Draios started to say, but found he could not put into words everything he was feeling.

Delnamal smiled, the expression almost warm, although the sight of that skeletal face left Draios chilled. "I know," he said gently. "Believe me, I know. But when you look at it as a gift, given to me by the Creator, perhaps you will see what an asset I can be. And what you saw with your Mindseye is not all of it. When Bandar arrives, I will show you what else the Creator has allowed me to do. I must warn you in advance that this demonstration will be . . . disturbing. Mine is a power that should not exist, but it is because of that very fact that I believe it was granted to me by the Creator."

Despite what he'd just seen with his Mindseye, Draios wondered if his cousin might not actually be mad. After all, it was not uncommon for madmen to have such grandiose illusions about their own importance. But something inside of him, some animal instinct, kept shouting that the man was dangerous. That had to mean something, and Draios found his pulse racing as one of the disreputable honor guardsmen who'd greeted his carriage entered the room.

The guardsman bowed to Draios as was proper, but even as he did, his gaze seemed to remain warily on Delnamal. As if he, too, sensed a creeping dread in his master's presence.

"You asked to see me, Your Majesty?" the guardsman inquired of Delnamal, his words ever so slightly slurred.

Draios raised an eyebrow at the address, surprised to find that Delnamal still styled himself a king.

"Yes, Bandar," Delnamal said, rising from his chair with some help from his cane, then gesturing to the guardsman. "Please come closer, there's a good man."

That Bandar was reluctant to follow the order was written all over his face, but he approached nonetheless, his gaze fixed on the carpet below his feet. The timid, submissive approach was unseemly for an honor guardsman, and Draios frowned at the man. Clearly the king had not deigned to send a high caliber of staff to his nephew's secret manor, but this Bandar character hardly seemed fit for guarding chickens, much less a king in exile.

"Good, good," Delnamal said, sounding rather like he was praising an obedient dog. "Now close your eyes for me and keep them closed."

Draios cocked his head to the side, finding this whole display perplexing even as the hairs on the back of his neck rose. Bandar visibly swallowed hard, and for a moment Draios thought the man might turn tail and flee. Had he perhaps seen demonstrations of Delnamal's mysterious power before? Or was he fearing being on the receiving end of a madman's rage when the "power" failed to manifest?

Delnamal gave the man what was no doubt meant to be a soothing smile, but though his facial muscles mimicked the expression effortlessly, there was not a speck of warmth to be seen in his sunken eyes. "There is nothing to worry about," he told his honor guardsman. "I just want to show His Highness something that is not fit for any but royal eyes."

That Bandar was not convinced by the attempt at reassurance was clear from his expression, and Draios couldn't help noticing the nervous look the man shot in his direction. The look begged Draios to intervene on his behalf, and yet Draios saw no reason why he should do so. The man was obviously a disgrace to his uniform, and if Delnamal's demonstration should cause him pain, then it was his due for cowardice and drunkenness while on duty.

Seeing no path to escape, Bandar did as he was ordered and closed his eyes. His entire body was tight with tension, and there was a visible sheen of sweat on his brow.

As soon as the guardsman's eyes were closed, Delnamal opened his Mindseye. Leaning heavily on the cane in his left hand, he reached out into the air in front of him until his fingertips made contact with Bandar's chest.

Bandar jumped in surprise, his eyes popping open, a startled bleat escaping his lips. He took one hasty step backward, then froze in his tracks.

Delnamal's reaching hand closed on something. Something Draios could not see, so it had to be an element. Draios debated opening his own Mindseye, but decided quickly that he did not want to see Delnamal's unholy aura again.

Bandar cried out in what sounded like pain, although Delnamal was no longer touching him. His body jerked backward, and if Draios could not see with his own eyes that the man was not bound, he would have thought him tied in place. Bandar struggled against those invisible bonds, the cry of pain turning into a full-throated wail.

Delnamal's hand jerked suddenly, and the wail was abruptly silenced.

Bandar's body fell to the floor in a heap. Delnamal laughed softly, pressing his clasped hand against his own breast as his shoulders straightened and he tossed the cane aside.

Kailee pushed the remains of her lunch to the side and reached for the primer she'd already been poring over for hours. The elemental ink Tynthanal had invented—and that the grand magus had perfected—curved and swooped over the pages, and Kailee suspected her interest in learning this once-impossible skill was becoming something of an obsession.

It had taken several lessons before she'd made sense of how the various symbols represented sounds, but Tynthanal was a benevolent and patient teacher—even though their lessons stretched late into the night and left him with precious little sleep. Still, she knew there were better ways for a prince regent to spend his time, and she had now gained enough skill to carry on learning without him. By the time he returned to the royal apartments tonight, she would have amassed a wealth of questions to ask him, but he assured her she was learning at an impressive pace.

With a quill and a bottle of elemental ink, she began painstakingly copying the next lesson in the primer, for there was no point, in her mind, of learning to read without learning to write at the same time.

She was cleaning up an inelegant blot of ink when the door to the queen's parlor opened, startling her enough to nearly overturn the whole ink pot. Blushing, she steadied the ink pot and pushed back her chair.

Her Mindsight did not allow her to distinguish individual auras; however, she was so thoroughly familiar with the magic items Tynthanal habitually wore and carried that she recognized him.

"Tynthanal!" she cried in surprise and perhaps just a little alarm. This was the first time since he'd taken office as regent that he'd shown up to the apartments while the sun was still up. "What are you doing here at this hour?" Her voice sounded a little shrill to her own ears.

"Nothing bad has happened," he assured her. "It's just that I learned some information that I thought you would like to know immediately. Do you have a moment?"

She appreciated the politeness of assuming she had a busy schedule in which she might have trouble finding time, although the evidence to the contrary was laid out on the table before her. She thought guiltily that it was untidy of her not to have rung for a maid to remove the remains of her luncheon.

But by the time Tynthanal had finished telling her about the vision that had been related to him by the seer from Rhozinolm, the luncheon dishes were the least of her concerns. She sat in silence for a long moment as she suffered a pang of grief over Mairah's death. How she wished she'd succeeded in persuading Mairah to stay in Women's Well before it had been too late!

"I'm sorry about Mairahsol," Tynthanal said with his customary gentleness.

Kailee waved that off. "I was under no illusion that she had somehow survived."

"I know. But you didn't know she'd died like that."

Kailee had him explain the vision one more time, then nodded. She was unquestionably saddened by Mairah's death, but she believed now that her faith in her friend had been at least partially vindicated. It seemed that while Mairah had gone to the Well with the purpose of triggering her spell to close the Mindseye of everyone in Aaltah, what she had ended up doing instead was saving the kingdom from what she believed would be a terrible disaster.

"You realize this means Mairah gave her life to stop Melcor's Kai from damaging Aaltah's Well, don't you?" she asked, all but daring Tynthanal to contradict her. "We at least know that much from having read her notes."

"Assuming those notes are accurate," he reminded her. "She was, after all, writing them in such a way as to convince Delnamal that she was genuinely trying to undo the Blessing, and neither one of us believes that was the truth."

She huffed impatiently. "You are *determined* to paint her as the villain, no matter what the evidence tells you."

"I'm merely determined not to make up my mind prematurely," he countered. "Do you have a theory as to what exactly Mairahsol was trying to accomplish by sacrificing herself?"

Kailee thought back to everything they had learned from the notes, frowning in concentration. There had been so much in there that she was certain were patent falsehoods, and also much that seemed to be entirely irrelevent. But there was that one section of the notes that had mentioned using the element Grae, although it hadn't been clear in the context just what that Grae was for.

"I'm sure Mairah had designed an antidote to undo the Mindseye spell she was planning to cast on the Well," she mused out loud. "And from what I learned at the Women's Well Academy, I gather many antidotes to potions are delivered in the form of a purgative of some sort."

She heard the sharp hiss of a quickly intaken breath, and knew that Tynthanal was finally thinking along the same lines as she.

"If the spell to close the Mindseye needed to be triggered by sacrificial Kai," he said, "then it stands to reason that the antidote would need to be triggered the same way."

Kailee nodded, sure they now had the answer. "Mairah meant to cast the Mindseye spell, and the other woman who was in the Well chamber with her was meant to be the sacrifice. However, she didn't follow her script."

"Melcor was fatally wounded instead, and he and the woman fell into the Well," Tynthanal continued.

"Mairah then used her purgative potion—triggered by her own sacrifice—to try to purge Melcor's Kai before it could damage the Well."

"And yet," Tynthanal said, "the Well is still damaged in ways it is hard to comprehend. And I'm not sure anything we've learned tells us how to fix it."

"I'd venture a guess that the Well is damaged because of some unintended consequence of the spell Mairah cast," Kailee said. "Perhaps it purged more than it was supposed to? Or perhaps the damage already caused by Melcor's Kai was irreversible, and Mairah's spell merely kept it from getting worse."

"Perhaps," Tynthanal said, though he didn't sound especially convinced.

Kailee's enthusiasm dimmed. "Can you at least concede the possibility that she gave her life to try to save Aaltah's Well, even in the face of a great deal of mistreatment that must have made her hate this place?"

"I will," he assured her. "Just as I will concede that whatever damage befell our Well must be laid squarely at Delnamal's feet, for he is the one who first recklessly endangered it and then fled the scene when it was clear things were going wrong.

"I still don't see the good in her that you saw," he concluded.

"But she was clearly more complicated than I gave her credit for, and she very likely saved us all from a much greater disaster."

It was not quite the utter exoneration Kailee had been hoping for, but it was a long way from the calumny with which things had started. In all likelihood, Mairah would still be remembered by many as a villain, but perhaps when people learned of her final selfless sacrifice, they would at least allow that she had redeemed herself in the end.

CHAPTER NINETEEN

D raios stared at the dead man who lay on the carpet before him, unable to comprehend what he had just seen, and entirely unable to pinpoint how he felt about it. On the one hand, he was no stranger to killing. He was aware that it was wrong, and had performed a penance each time he'd done it, but it had never really *felt* wrong to him, and it had certainly never upset him in any significant way. So seeing a stranger—one who'd shown himself unworthy of his position, no less—killed before his eyes should not have moved him one way or another.

Oh, he knew an *ordinary* man would be moved. But he was not—and had never been—an ordinary man. What was the death of some nobody honor guardsman to him?

But of course it wasn't the *fact* of the death that was so unnerving: it was the *method*.

"Wh-what did you do to him?" he found himself stammering. *Stammering!* Even as a small child he had never exhibited such signs of weakness.

Delnamal still did not look particularly well—his eyes and cheeks were still sunken, his hands gnarled and all but useless—but there was far more life and strength in his expression, and he stepped to the dead man's side with no hint of a wobble, the cane lying neglected where it had fallen.

"I believe that the Creator has gifted me with a very special ability," Delnamal said, then proceeded to explain to Draios a fantastical, borderline heretical theory on the nature of Kai, and about a new element, which he called Rhokai.

"Alone among men, I can see that mote of Rhokai," Delnamal concluded, showing no sign of shame at the hubris of his claim. A slight and sinister smile played along the edges of his mouth. "I can see it in everyone. I can see it in *you*."

Draios had to suppress a shiver, as well as the superstitious instinct to take a step backward. Away from the threat.

"And because I can see it," Delnamal continued, "I can *take* it." He nudged the body at his feet, watching it flop limply. "When I remove the Rhokai, it shatters, revealing a mote of Kai at its core. And if you were to open your Mindseye again, you would see yet another new mote of Kai hovering about me."

Delnamal looked up at him, and Draios could only imagine what the other man saw in his face. Certainly it was more than Draios had any intention of allowing him to see.

"Oh, don't worry," Delnamal said with a careless wave of his hand. "I didn't obtain the other Kai in my aura by killing people. Thanks to the events at Aaltah's Well, my blood has been infused with a great deal of Rhokai. These Rhokai motes periodically shatter and fuel me—leaving me with all this lovely Kai at my disposal."

"It is . . . unholy," Draios replied, nearly choking on the response. And immediately wondering if he should have kept it to himself. He had told no one where he was really going, and only his father and a few close advisers even knew Delnamal was alive. If Draios failed to return from this visit, no one would have a hint where to look for him.

Delnamal nodded sagely. "I thought so, too, at first. No man should possess this kind of power, and I spent many a long night at prayer, begging the Creator to save me from what I thought of as a horror.

"And in prayer, I realized that my power is meant to be used for good. Something rose out of Aaltah's Well, something dark and dangerous and impossible. It could have killed me. It *should* have killed me. So why didn't it?"

He looked at Draios inquiringly, for a moment reminding him of a far less benevolent version of his late and unlamented mentor.

"Because the Creator *meant* for me to have this power," Delnamal finished. "He knew it would take more than the ordinary powers of men to undo the abomination the witch unleashed on our world.

"I believe He has given me some of the powers of the Destroyer. Had I been wiser and stronger and more devout when these powers entered me, I could have ended the Curse right then. But I did not understand what He wanted of me, and my body was too weak from an excess of self-indulgence. I allowed my mother to spirit me out of Aaltah, and that will be a source of shame for the rest of my days.

"But the power still resides in me, and I now know exactly what I must do. I must return to Aaltah. Return to the Well that was the source of the original Curse. I, and I alone, have the power to undo what was done. But I cannot return to the Well unless and until I retake my rightful throne. And that is where Khalpar comes in."

Draios had listened to the entirety of Delnamal's speech in a state of perplexity and disbelief. His rational mind decried the explanation as the ravings of a madman. But when his mind tried to balk at the absurdity of it, his eyes returned to the dead man lying on the floor. A man who had died for no discernible reason.

Distantly, Draios was aware that he should be appalled at having witnessed a cold-blooded murder. Instead of listening to anything else the man had to say, he should be finding an excuse to hurry away, to return to the capital and send soldiers to storm the manor and arrest this dangerous creature. Almost more disturbing than his own lack of righteous horror was the realization that Delnamal had somehow read him well enough to know he would not be arrested for this horrific demonstration.

Delnamal bent and half-lifted the dead man, propping his back against a chair and resting his folded hands on his chest in a dignified pose. Delnamal's frame looked as frail as ever, and Bandar was not a small man. The wizened, hobbled figure who had met Draios at the door would never have been able to bend down so far, much less manipulate a substantially heavier man into a sitting position.

"You see that absorbing his Rhokai has made me stronger," Delnamal said triumphantly. "Just imagine how much stronger I could become as I worked my way through a battlefield. Imagine how many Kai motes I would have at my disposal, and how easily I could replenish my supply. I have as yet had no means to test my theory, but I'd wager my life that no shield spell could keep me from plucking the Rhokai from anyone who dared resist. Our foes would soon flee in terror once they understood what I can do."

Fleeing in terror seemed to Draios a most rational option, and yet he found himself rooted to the floor, imagining the scene just as Delnamal described it. Who in his right mind would stand his ground in the face of Delnamal's powers?

"I've given you a lot to ponder," Delnamal said. "Take some time to think and pray on it. If you come to believe that I am indeed the Creator's instrument, as I believe I am, then perhaps we can discuss how best to approach your father and convince him that we must go to war and return me to the Well of Aaltah."

Draios nodded, feeling so overwhelmed he could hardly string two coherent thoughts together. He had never truly believed Delnamal had any great power, he realized now. He had come out of some combination of curiosity and rebellion, telling himself he was on a mission from the Creator while simultaneously braced for what he suspected would be a crushing disappointment. He wasn't sure what to do in the face of this surprising reality.

"Yes," he murmured weakly, licking his lips. "I believe I must spend the rest of the night in fasting and prayer. I have faith that the Creator will let me know what He wants me to do."

The words were said with what he hoped sounded like genuine conviction. But in reality, his faith had never felt so shaken as it did right now in the face of what logic told him was an outright abomination.

From the moment Leethan had read Prince Waldmir's letter saying his youngest daughter, Princess Elwynne, would be paying a visit to the Abbey, she'd known what it meant. Even in Nandel, it was rare for children to be sent to the Abbey. A father possessed of an unwanted girl child typically waited until she shed her first woman's blood to send her away, but Leethan was aware of more than one occasion when some nobleman's rebellious daughter was sent to the Abbey for a "visit" to be taught a lesson.

It was a terrible lesson—the fact that the girl had set foot in the Abbey even temporarily devalued her as a potential bride and increased the chances she would become a spinster, at which point she would be sent back to the Abbey for good. Elwynne was unlikely to face such consequences for being sent to the Abbey—not when she was the sovereign prince's daughter and so very young—but still Leethan could not fathom what Waldmir was thinking. He had always had a vindictive streak, but she'd never seen it directed at a helpless child before. Had the realization that he would never have a son turned his bitterness into outright cruelty? Or was his malice perhaps directed elsewhere? That seemed the more likely explanation, though Leethan wondered exactly whom it was meant to hurt. There were those in the Abbey who whispered—unwisely, and no longer in Leethan's hearing after she'd issued a warning designed to terrify them into silence—that Elwynne might not be Waldmir's daughter after all. For the first time, Leethan wondered if Waldmir might not have the same suspicion.

Leethan watched from her tower window as a single carriage with the royal crest on its door entered the gates of the Abbey below. She had, of course, never met Waldmir's youngest. Even so, she knew exactly what the girl would look like. It could not be a coincidence that the Mother of All had sent her a vision of herself and Jaizal struggling through the mountains with a small girl child and that Waldmir would then send his five-year-old daughter to the Abbey. Clearly *this* was the girl the Mother of All meant for her to spirit away.

Leethan dragged herself away from the window, trying not to worry about the desultory smattering of snow that drifted on the wind. The vision had shown the three of them on the road in the snow, but Leethan had judged that it was not the snows of the heart of winter. Waldmir had said the girl would be staying at the Abbey for no more than a month.

That did not leave a lot of time for planning, and Leethan cursed herself for not having put more effort into working out an escape. Somehow, it had seemed that she would have plenty of time to make plans once the child arrived, having never thought the child would be Waldmir's daughter and therefore bound to leave in short order.

Leethan descended the three flights of stairs from her tower office to the Abbey's main entrance and opened the heavy wooden door, letting in a gust of frigid wind and a swirl of snow. The royal carriage stood unattended in the courtyard, the cheval that had drawn it inert with the removal of its Rho. A short woman in a serviceable but well-worn cloak stood at the carriage's door, one hand grasping the hood the wind kept wanting to whip away, the other reaching imploringly toward the carriage's interior. As Leethan approached, she could hear the brusque sounds of an impatient male voice from within, and moments later a little girl appeared in the doorway. She was crying miserably, a man—presumably the coachman—practically shoving her out the door.

The short woman—Elwynne's governess, obviously—let out a cry of dismay and tried to gentle the child's fall. Elwynne tumbled to her knees anyway, and the coachman glowered down at her.

"If you'd just stop carrying on," he complained, "you'd be inside and warmed up already." He jumped down from the carriage—his boot barely missing one of Elwynne's gloved hands—and slammed the carriage door shut as the governess gathered the girl in her arms.

Looking up, the coachman caught sight of Leethan approaching and offered her a sneer in lieu of a greeting. Without a word, he clomped to the back of the carriage and unlashed a small trunk and a satchel, letting both fall to the courtyard floor with a thump. Leethan bit her tongue to stop herself from issuing a scathing reprimand at this behavior that was so inappropriate for a servant. But if the brute had no respect for his sovereign prince's daughter, then he certainly would have none for an Unwanted Woman. The faster he was gone, the better.

The governess, having helped her charge to her feet, turned and saw Leethan approaching. The wind caught at her hood once more, this time succeeding in ripping it from her fingers and revealing a round, cheerful face framed by snowy white hair.

Leethan gasped with recognition. "Laurel!" she nearly shrieked, forgetting all semblance of dignity as she crossed the short distance between them and hugged the woman who had been governess for all three of her own daughters, many years ago.

The old woman returned the hug with a strength that belied her years—she had to be nearly eighty by now. By all rights she should be enjoying a comfortable retirement, and yet here she was not only acting as governess for a five-year-old, but also accompanying that five-year-old to the Abbey.

"It's so good to see you," Leethan said, her voice choking with emotion. In all her years in the Abbey, Leethan had seen no one from her former life save Waldmir and the occasional noblewoman who found herself repudiated and discarded. It would not have entirely surprised her if even warm and kindly Laurel had disdained to hug her now that she was an Unwanted Woman, and the embrace felt far better than it had any right to.

"And you," Laurel said, her voice quavering with a combination of age and emotion. And possibly cold. The wind was slicing through Leethan's robes, and the snow was falling with more vigor.

"Let's get you both inside," Leethan said. She noted that after having unceremoniously dumped the baggage onto the flagstones, the coachman was climbing back onto the driver's seat. Clearly, he had no intention of sullying himself by carrying the baggage into the Abbey. Leethan had half a mind to remonstrate, but figured that would only delay getting everyone out of the cold.

Unperturbed by the coachman's rudeness, Laurel stepped up to the baggage and perched the satchel on top of the chest. Then she took hold of the leather handle on one side of the trunk.

"If you'll take the other side," Laurel said, "we can carry it in ourselves. It isn't especially heavy."

Once again, it was on the tip of Leethan's tongue to protest. Laurel was far too old to be carrying her own baggage around, and Leethan was not exactly in the prime of youth, either. But little Elwynne—who had yet to say a word and had made no eye contact with Leethan—was shivering violently, and her lips were tinted blue. There was no point in wasting time with an argument.

As Laurel had promised, the trunk was not terribly heavy, but it was unwieldy, especially with the satchel on top. The snow made the flagstones of the courtyard slippery, and Leethan couldn't help watching the elderly governess with concern. Luckily, the carriage's arrival had not gone unremarked, and before they'd made it halfway to the door, several younger, more able-bodied abigails emerged and took the trunk from them.

There were no bedrooms suitable for visiting princesses in the Abbey, only dormitories and lurid playrooms. The playrooms were far more comfortable—meant to appeal to the noble clientele of the Abbey—and therefore Leethan had appropriated one of them for Elwynne and her governess. She'd had all the erotic art and toys removed, but there was no disguising the red-draped canopy bed. Elwynne—far too young to understand exactly what the Abbey was or what the red fabric signified, was delighted with the unexpected color—but Laurel blushed and looked down at her feet.

"Forgive me," Leethan murmured. "The dormitories are far less comfortable, so I thought . . ." She let her voice trail off, embarrassed at putting a five-year-old in a bed that had never been intended for sleeping.

"I understand," Laurel said, still blushing, "and there's no need to apologize. I must admit that I was rather . . . concerned about the accommodations we might find." She glanced at her charge with obvious affection as Elwynne explored the room in wide-eyed wonder, fingering the soft red linens. She climbed onto the massive bed and flopped into the nest of pillows at its head, smiling.

"Here now," Laurel scolded gently, "let's get that headdress off you first."

Elwynne lifted her head so that Laurel might remove the pins holding her headdress in place. Leethan noticed that the poor child had a scar marring her forehead just above her right eye.

Anywhere but in Nandel, the wound that caused that scar would have been treated with women's magic so that the child might not be disfigured.

When Laurel laid the headdress aside, Elwynne lay back down, clutching a silken pillow to her chest and closing her eyes. Her small body still shivered with cold, and Leethan hastily threw another log on the fire, knowing she would have to be frugal herself to compensate. Waldmir had made no mention of providing any additional funding to cover the expenses of housing his daughter and her governess, and the Abbey barely scraped by on the pittance that was left to them after they'd turned over most of their profits to the Crown.

Laurel removed her hooded cloak and laid it over the already-sleeping child. "I should have dressed her more warmly," she fretted. "I hope she doesn't come down with an ague." Elwynne huddled into the cloak, soaking in the residual body heat, and stuck her thumb in her mouth without appearing to wake.

Leethan grimaced at the sight, remembering Waldmir's adamance that his daughters must not suck their thumbs. When snapping and snarling at them hadn't been enough to stop them, he'd had them fitted with locked metal gauntlets that had chafed their skin raw. It was not an uncommon practice in Nandel, Leethan had been dismayed to find, and her insistence that elsewhere in the world, children grew out of the habit naturally had fallen on deaf ears.

Laurel read her thoughts easily and flashed her a sharp-edged grin. "One thing Elwynne does not lack is spirit. After one day wearing Prince Waldmir's gauntlets, she learned that the way to avoid wearing them was *not* to stop sucking her thumb, but merely to not let anyone who might report it to her father catch her in the act."

Leethan shook her head. "No child of that age can be cautious all the time."

Laurel stroked Elwynne's hair gently. "*This* child can. She is very possibly the most stubborn creature I've ever met." It was said fondly and with a smile, but Leethan could hear the worry behind the words. Stubbornness was a dangerous trait for a girl of Nandel.

"Is that why Waldmir sent her to us?" Leethan asked.

"I don't know what happened," Laurel said, tears filming her eyes. "As far as I know, the prince has not laid eyes on her for weeks. Neither I nor anyone else who is charged with her care has had any cause to complain of her behavior." She wrinkled her nose. "Well, no *special* cause. Certainly nothing that would move us to lodge a complaint with His Royal Highness."

Leethan frowned as the unpleasant rumor about Elwynne's parentage took on a new air of plausibility. "But there must have been *something*!" she protested. "He would not send her here for no reason."

"Not for no reason, no," Laurel agreed. "But the reason may have little or nothing to do with Elwynne." She gave Leethan a speculative look. "Do you know why he divorced his last wife?"

Leethan blinked, surprised by the question. "I assumed it was because she did not give him a son and he was growing desperate."

She had made that assumption because Brontyn had somehow never arrived at the Abbey after her divorce. There were only two ways she could imagine a divorced woman being sent to the Abbey and never arriving. Either she had experienced an "accident" along the way, or she had left Nandel altogether, which she could not do without Waldmir's approval. He'd already put one of his wives to death, so Leethan had no reason to think he'd have tried to hide Brontyn's death. Therefore, she deduced that Brontyn had been quietly and mercifully sent away. It was the same reason she'd discredited the rumors that Elwynne might not be Waldmir's daughter. She couldn't imagine Waldmir meekly accepting the insult of one of his wives cuckolding him.

"Maybe," Laurel said with a shrug.

"But you have your doubts."

"I do. I don't have to tell you that Prince Waldmir has never doted on his daughters. However, I couldn't help noticing that after the divorce, he stopped coming by the nursery to see El-wynne. He occasionally showed flashes of paternal affection for Princess Shelvon when she was a little girl, even after he'd had her mother beheaded. And yet Elwynne he has cut off almost completely."

Leethan gasped softly as she realized the rumor—or at least the suspicion—was not confined to the Abbey, after all. "You think she is not his."

Laurel shrugged again. "I think it is a possibility, though of course I would never say such a thing to anyone but you. One can only imagine how terrible it would be if word of such a suspicion should ever reach the prince's ears."

Leethan shuddered, having no desire to imagine it at all. No man of Nandel could easily withstand the shame of being cuckolded, but the sovereign prince least of all. Oh, how his nephews would salivate at such a show of weakness! There was a reason Leethan had silenced the rumors in the Abbey so harshly.

Elwynne made a sleepy murmur and turned over onto her side, snuggling deeper into Laurel's cloak. There had never been any question in Leethan's mind that she would do the Mother of All's bidding and spirit the child away from the Abbey. But with what she knew now, perhaps she would have wanted to do so even without the aid of the vision. Whether he had sent Elwynne to the Abbey out of bitterness because he was destined not to have a son, or whether because he believed the child was not his, her future in Nandel looked bleak indeed.

Glancing out the window at the snow that was falling more steadily by the minute, Leethan knew that it was past time she start planning her daring escape from the Abbey of Nandel.

• • •

Draios had eschewed sleep for yet another night of prayer and reflection. The challenge of making sense out of everything Delnamal had told him was more than a mere mortal could face, and more than ever, Draios hungered for the guidance of the Creator.

On its face, Delnamal's claim to be carrying a part of the Destroyer within him seemed like nothing but boastful arrogance, and if Draios had not seen with his own eyes what the former king of Aaltah was capable of, he would have dismissed it as the ravings of a lunatic. Certainly that was what his father had done, why Draios had only learned of Delnamal's residence in Khalpar because his spy had rescued that letter from the flames. Draios could hardly blame his father for the assumption, and yet . . .

Draios had read the same letter his father had—the parts of it he could make out, at least—and he had been intrigued enough by what he'd read to investigate. So why *hadn't* his father tried to learn more? It was his job as king to be a defender of the faith. Even if he thought Delnamal was mad, he should have investigated what was clearly a heresy if it was not the truth.

One thing was certain: Delnamal was in possession of a unique and terrifying power. Draios would never forget the sight of the honor guardsman's terrified face as Delnamal stole his Rhokai and his life, and it was hard to deny that such a power did not belong in the hands of a mortal man.

If the power was divine in origin, then how had it come to be housed within the weak mortal flesh of an impious and venal man, as the former King of Aaltah was reputed to be? Why would the Creator choose *Delnamal*, of all people, upon whom to bestow this gift? Should it not rather have been given to a man of piety and devotion who could be counted on to use it wisely?

It was nearly dawn when the answer to his litany of questions suddenly became clear, eliciting a startled and excited "Huh!" from his throat.

The power *had* been granted to a man of piety and devotion: himself! Delnamal was merely the fleshly housing of that power, a vessel that would eventually be used up and destroyed. Had not Delnamal said that the Rhokai he had absorbed needed to be returned to the Well of Aaltah? And how could that cadaverous wreck of a body be expected to survive the loss of that Rhokai? The man could already easily be mistaken for a days-old corpse if he lay still too long.

It was through the Creator's will that the letters King Khalvin had tried to destroy had been saved from the flames and delivered into Draios's hands. And it was through the Creator's will that the words he'd been able to make out had stirred Draios's soul enough to drag him out here to investigate. He was ashamed of himself for allowing any hint of doubt to creep in.

As the first morning light began to seep in around the edges of the curtains, Draios stretched his sore and weary limbs. His bed called to him, and his body urged him to answer that call. But his soul was soaring with wonder and joy and awe.

The Creator had infused Delnamal with unholy power and then led Draios to him. There was no reason He would have done so except that He wished Draios to make use of that power to set the world back to rights. His father was the King of Khalpar and renowned the world over for his piety, and yet it was *Draios* who'd had the wisdom and insight and instincts to hear the Creator's call!

"I will not fail you," he whispered to the empty room, sure the Creator heard his every thought and word and approved.

CHAPTER TWENTY

Jaizal plucked nervously at her robes as a soft tap sounded on the door. Leethan smiled at her fondly. Jaizal was capable of displaying a bland, unconcerned face to the world, but her restless hands always gave her away when she was distressed. She had taken Leethan's pronouncement that the two of them needed to flee the Abbey of Nandel with Princess Elwynne in tow with her customary calm and trust—until she'd met Elwynne the first time and recognized the difficulty Leethan had failed to consider.

It had not taken long for either of them to realize that even at five years old, little Elwynne possessed a steel backbone and a sharp mind. Quiet and generally soft-spoken as befitted a Nandel-born girl, Elwynne was frightfully observant, and though she might not understand why the women of the Abbey were disgraced and why there was a steady stream of men flowing in and out of the Abbey's front door, she had clearly formed the impression that Unwanted Women were not to be trusted.

She was not discourteous in the least, but she spoke almost exclusively to her governess and had regarded Leethan's attempts to befriend her with something very like suspicion. It had quickly become apparent that the child would not simply come away from the Abbey with two virtual strangers, and Leethan would not have abducted the poor girl by force even if she thought it possible to do so quietly and discreetly. Which left only one possibility that Leethan could imagine.

"Are you ready for this?" Leethan asked Jaizal as she moved to open the door.

"Are you?" Jaizal countered, and Leethan sighed.

"I don't suppose it matters," she murmured under her breath.

Leethan opened the door and invited Laurel into her sitting room. The room was drafty and cold—then again, what room in the Abbey of Nandel wasn't?—and Leethan had long ago learned to be miserly with her firewood. A single log smoldered in the grate, barely enough to keep the chill at bay, and both she and Jaizal were wearing cloaks intended for outdoor wear. The abigails' winter robes were of wool, but the Crown cut corners on expenses by providing only coarse, scratchy, and woefully thin material out of which to make them.

It was a sign of just where they stood in the eyes of society that Laurel—a lowborn servant—wore a brown woolen dress of much finer and heavier weave than that of the abigails' robes. But even she in her warmer clothes habitually wore a weighty shawl over her shoulders. She greeted Leethan with a smile and a quick hug, and Leethan's throat tightened with gratitude. It was one thing for Laurel to hug her after not having seen her for over twenty years; it was another to be willing to do so after the initial joy of reunion had worn off. Even the lowliest servant would usually treat an abigail—even the abbess—as an unclean creature beneath her notice.

"Come in, come in," Leethan beckoned, leading Laurel to the sofa near the fire. "You've met Sister Jaizal, have you not?" she asked, indicating her friend—and co-conspirator—with a sweeping gesture of her arm.

"I have," Laurel confirmed, gracing Jaizal with another of her warm smiles. Jaizal returned the smile with no sign of strain—except for the fidgeting hands, which only Leethan understood.

The three women sat by the fire, and Leethan served real tea—a rare luxury here at the Abbey. Usually "tea" at the Abbey was a thin, grassy-tasting drink made from steeping the dried leaves of a hearty mountain bush known as teaweed. It *smelled* like tea, but the taste was far less appealing.

Leethan endeavored to make small talk while they sipped their tea, though she was aware of the curiosity that was building behind Laurel's eyes. Clearly the governess knew that she had not been invited to the abbess's private rooms for a social call.

Eventually, Laurel put her teacup aside and gave Leethan a stern look that she had no doubt bestowed on many of her young charges over the years. "I think we'll all be happier and more comfortable if you'd just go ahead and say whatever it is you called me here to say," she prompted, not unkindly.

Jaizal looked for a moment as if she was about to intervene, her hands continuing their worried dance, this time fidgeting with the teacup instead of her robes. But she held her peace. Leethan appreciated the show of trust and hoped she was worthy of it. After all, her relationship with Laurel had always been unequal—she'd been a princess at the time, and Laurel merely her daughters' governess—and it was perhaps foolhardy to think she actually *knew* the woman.

"I have something important I want to talk to you about," she said, picking her words with great care. "What I want to share with you is . . . dangerous information. In many ways, we would all be better off if this conversation did not happen at all."

"Dangerous to whom, exactly?" Laurel asked with a tilt of her head and no hint of judgment in her voice.

"Everyone," Leethan said. "But I suppose you especially, for it will put you in an uncomfortable position. Which is why I wanted to warn you before I started talking. If you'd rather not know, then tell me now."

Laurel smiled faintly, though the shadow in her eyes said she was taking Leethan at her word. "Sounds like I won't know whether I want to know or not until after I already know."

Leethan chuckled nervously and slanted a look at Jaizal, whose fingertips were tapping against the teacup. Jaizal looked down at her hand and her fingers froze. She blushed and put the teacup down. At least when she started fidgeting again—which Leethan had no doubt she would—she might make less noise about it.

"Are you in some kind of trouble, dear?" Laurel asked gently.

Jaizal couldn't contain herself. "She's been locked up in the Abbey for decades. If that doesn't qualify as trouble, I don't know what does."

Leethan reached over and put her hand gently on Jaizal's arm, which was enough to quiet her friend's protests. Then, she told Laurel about the vision she had had and watched the governess's face pale and her eyes widen with every word.

When Leethan had finished, Laurel looked back and forth between her and Jaizal, as if hoping one of them would start laughing and admit this was all a prank. Leethan bit down on the urge to explain or cajole, letting Laurel absorb it all in peace.

"I had heard rumors about the existence of seers," Laurel murmured, her voice so soft Leethan had to lean forward to hear her. "Of course I'd heard them. Everyone has. But . . ."

"But you assumed it was superstitious nonsense," Jaizal interjected, and there was no missing the note of hostility in her voice.

For the first time, Leethan wondered if some of Jaizal's resistance to confiding in Laurel sprang from jealousy. She had been Leethan's closest friend and confidante for so many years that perhaps she was reluctant to share.

Laurel seemed not to notice the hostility. "I would not have put it in those terms. But I'd never seen any evidence to suggest it might be true."

"That's because you've had no contact with Unwanted Women before now," Leethan said, giving Jaizal her most quelling look. "It is no secret in the Abbey that genuine seers exist. It is more widely known outside of Nandel, where Unwanted Women practice magic. Growing up in Grunir, I knew from very early on that seers existed, but I imagine that is not the case here."

Even outside of Nandel, much of society viewed seers as charlatans. But the talent for visions ran in families, and only women who'd inherited the trait from both sides of their families could trigger visions. What that meant was that despite the skepticism of the general public, there were certain families—like Leethan's—wherein the existence and validity of seers was not questioned.

Laurel shifted in her seat, her expression filled with unease. "And you believe these . . . visions are sent to you by the Mother?"

Leethan had chosen to conceal her belief in the Mother of All; there were only so many shocks she was prepared to inflict on the governess. "Yes, I do. And I believe that the Mother wishes for Jaizal and me to take Princess Elwynne away from the Abbey."

Laurel chewed her lip, the wrinkle between her brows so deep it looked painful.

"Why?" she finally asked. "And where to?"

"I can't claim to know the answer to either question," Leethan admitted. "Not with any certainty, at least. It may well be that Elwynne is in some kind of danger here. I find it uncomfortable and ominous that Waldmir sent her to the Abbey at such a tender age."

"It's also possible the Mother has plans for her elsewhere," Jaizal added. "The reason need not be ominous, although the fact that Leethan saw us traveling through the snow does add a sense of urgency."

Laurel sighed deeply, nodding. "I can't help but agree," she said. "It is already frightfully late in the season to travel. I hope we will be leaving soon."

Jaizal and Leethan shared a look.

"There is no 'we,'" Jaizal said firmly. "Leethan's vision did not include you." Leethan made a sound of exasperation, and Jaizal hurried on to soften her words. "It will be difficult and dangerous enough for Leethan and me at *our* ages . . ."

Jaizal's voice trailed off as she realized there was no truly kind and polite way to end the sentence she had started, and Leethan swallowed a laugh.

Laurel was less restrained, her face breaking into a grin that showed off every one of her wrinkles. "Are you trying to figure out a delicate way to remind me that I'm old?"

Jaizal's face was a lovely shade of red that matched her robes. She had been rude enough that Leethan felt no urge to come to her rescue, and she planned to tease her friend about the faux pas mercilessly.

Jaizal cleared her throat. "Wherever we choose to go, it is a trip that would be hard on us if we were all twenty," she said, embarrassment giving way for the moment to trepidation. "And the consequences if we are caught . . ."

Laurel waved that off. "I'm old, not senile. I know a terrible risk when it looks me in the face. But if you think Elwynne will happily flee the Abbey with two women she barely knows, then you are very much mistaken."

"That's why we're confiding in you," Leethan said. "We're hoping you will convince her to come with us."

But Laurel was shaking her head. "The poor dear does not trust easily. Even with my help, it would take time to win her over, and by the time I convinced her to go with you, the snows would be upon us. No," she concluded, "if you want Elwynne to leave the Abbey—and not try to run away from you at the first opportunity—then I must come, as well."

"I fear what it means that I did not see you in the vision," Leethan said. "If you don't come with us, then that would explain it. If you *do* . . ."

Laurel nodded. "It likely means I won't survive the journey. I understand. But *you* must understand . . ." Her eyes teared up, and she blinked rapidly. "Elwynne has no one in the world but me. Her mother is gone, her father barely acknowledges her existence, and the rest of the household takes their cues from him. I cannot send her off into danger and stay here in safety myself—assuming I *would* be safe, which is no sure thing if Elwynne disappears while in my care." She dabbed at a stray tear. "I would risk a great deal to see Elwynne safe and happy, and I see neither safety nor happiness in her future if she stays in Nandel. This vision of yours is the first truly hopeful sign I've seen for her in a long time. I will convince her we are embarking on an adventure, and she will come along with no fuss whatsoever."

Leethan's reservations were not eased. However, it was clear that Laurel could not be dissuaded, and she had been thoroughly warned of the risks she was running.

"I am working to procure transportation for us, as well as some men's clothing that might make us attract less attention," Leethan said. "As soon as we have everything we need—and the weather is as friendly as it's likely to get—we will leave."

Laurel nodded briskly. "Very well. I will make sure I have a bag for myself, and that Elwynne is packed and ready so that we can leave on a moment's notice."

"You've been avoiding me," Corlin said.

Rafetyn, who'd been so loudly sloshing his mop in a bucket of water he hadn't heard Corlin approach, stiffened. He gave the mop a couple more desultory dunks.

"Aren't you supposed to be washing dishes at the mess?" he asked without turning around.

"It turns out I'm the fastest dishwasher in the Citadel," Corlin said, congratulating himself on the cleverness of his ambush.

For more than three weeks, Rafetyn had been skillfully—and creatively—avoiding Corlin's company. No matter how late Corlin arrived to meals, Rafetyn always managed to be later, so that, although they still shared the same table, there was never time to talk while Rafetyn was hastily shoving in what food he could manage. The highly regimented schedule of first-year cadets meant that there was almost no true leisure time in which Corlin might catch Rafetyn alone, and he dared not break any rules to try to engineer a meeting. Hurrying through his chore so he could catch Rafetyn trapped by his own chore was the only solution he'd come up with.

The mop made a wet flopping sound, splashing water on both of their trousers as Rafetyn lifted it from the bucket and slapped it on the barracks floor. From the looks of it, he was at most a third of the way through with the task, which was one of the most despised among cadets. Corlin imagined it was especially difficult for Rafetyn, with his slender build and questionable endurance.

Rafetyn gave Corlin a brief glance over his shoulder, his mouth set in a frown before he returned his gaze to the muddy floor and began scrubbing. "I haven't been avoiding you," he mumbled, but even the most skilled of liars could not have sold that particular fiction.

"I don't blame you," Corlin hastened to assure him. "I'd avoid me, too, if I were you. After I've said my piece, I promise I'll leave you alone."

Rafetyn grunted, but did not otherwise respond. As with everything he did, he was performing the job of mopping the barracks floor with intense dedication, as if the fate of nations rested in his ability to remove every fleck of dirt. There was no question he was a terrible cadet, but no one could deny his level of effort.

Corlin cleared his throat, finding that now that he finally had a chance to apologize, he felt remarkably tongue-tied and awkward. He was sorely tempted to prise the mop from Rafetyn's hands and finish the job himself, just to have something to do. However, the only thing keeping Rafetyn in the room was the need to finish his duty, and if he was as determined as Corlin suspected, he might just walk out if Corlin took the mop.

"First of all, I hope you know that I had no idea Lord Aldnor was going to—" He choked off the words, feeling once again the horror that had washed over him when he'd realized Rafetyn would suffer the punishment that was rightfully his. He cleared his throat again. "I'm so, so sorry," he said miserably, wishing that words could somehow undo the terrible damage he had done to his friend, however unwittingly. "I would happily have taken twice as many lashes if it would have spared you."

Rafetyn let out a heavy sigh and leaned his forehead against the mop's handle. Then he shook his head and turned around. He looked as miserable as Corlin felt.

"This is why I was avoiding you," Rafetyn said. "I knew you'd get all apologetic and I'd feel guilty."

"What?" Corlin cried, his eyebrows climbing nearly to his hairline. "Why the hell would *you* feel guilty? I'm the one who got you in trouble through no fault of your own!"

"I'm supposed to lie to you," Rafetyn said. "By omission if nothing else." He made a face. "I've been *ordered* to lie about it."

"What are you talking about?"

Rafetyn rubbed his eyes. "Lord Aldnor will have my head if he finds out I talked," he muttered, almost to himself.

Corlin shook his head. "You are making no sense at all."

Rafetyn started pushing the mop around again, staring at the floor. "You might not have known that I would take the punishment for you, but *I* did," he said.

Corlin blinked. "I don't get it."

"Once he knew you and I had become friends, he offered me a deal. Captain Norlix has more than once recommended my dismissal, and we all know I am not built to be a soldier. Lord Aldnor promised me that he would not accept the recommendation as long as I agreed to take your punishments."

Corlin could do nothing but gape, unable to comprehend what he had just heard.

Rafetyn heaved the mop into the bucket once more, dunking it furiously and sloshing water all over the floor. "He said you were far more likely to control your temper to protect someone else than to protect yourself, and that you were headed for a bad end if you *didn't* learn."

Corlin put his hand to his sternum, rubbing at the strange ache that had begun there. Their fellow cadets—and even Captain Norlix—considered Rafetyn a pathetic weakling because of his small size. That just proved what idiots they all were.

"You *agreed* to that?" Corlin asked, dumbfounded.

Rafetyn shrugged. "I'd agree to just about anything if it meant I didn't get dismissed."

"But why?"

Rafetyn met his eyes, and there was a hint of fire in his expression. "Because a few lashes with a strap are nothing compared to what my father would have done to me had I been expelled from the Citadel. I know Lord Aldnor knows that, or he'd have expelled me the first time Captain Norlix recommended it. Justal and the rest of them can do their worst; it is nothing next to what my father can and will do. My brothers eventually grew big and strong enough to fight back, but it's not looking like I ever will."

Corlin sat heavily on the edge of one of the bunks. Of course, he'd known almost from the start that Rafetyn was far from his father's favorite, but he had not grasped the extent of it.

"It was no big deal," Rafetyn said, once again turning to his work and shoving the mop across the floor. "Only a dozen lashes, and they gave me something for the pain before it even started."

"Still," Corlin said hoarsely, "they should have been mine."

Rafetyn grinned incongruously. "If you'd like to finish mudwrestling this mop in penance, I won't stop you."

Corlin leapt to his feet and all but snatched the mop from

Rafetyn's hands, though guilt still sat heavily on his shoulders. "It doesn't come close to making us even."

Rafetyn rolled his eyes. "Don't be so dramatic. Because of you, I've earned my place at the Citadel even if I don't belong here. I'll be out of my father's reach until I'm old enough to be free of him anyway. It's an easy trade." He tried for a fierce frown, though "fierce" wasn't an expression that sat naturally on his face. "I would prefer it if you *don't* get into any more trouble, though, if you can help it. Lord Aldnor ordered me not to tell you the truth because he was worried it would blunt the effect. If he guesses you know, then the next beating might not be so easy."

Corlin put his back into scrubbing the floor, making much quicker work of it than Rafetyn had. He met his friend's eyes briefly before looking away again. Knowing the truth lessened the fury he felt toward the lord commander and reduced the sense of injustice to some extent. Eventually, it might even help put a bit of the guilt to sleep, but he could never live with himself if he knowingly allowed Rafetyn to be hurt once more because he lost his stupid temper.

"It won't happen again," he swore.

It was not unusual when soldiers were sparring for clusters of people to gather around the low wall that separated the Citadel of Women's Well from the rest of the town. Those onlookers were almost always women and girls, admiring the beauty and danger of the male form as the fighters danced in the blazing desert sun. But today, the crowd was far larger and denser than usual, with a great many more men in attendance and a strange, tense undercurrent in the air.

Inside the wall, Lord Jailom had set up a small, temporary pavilion with chairs for Alys and her guests, so that they could observe the proceedings in comfort. Beside Alys, Duke Thanmir frowned at the throng of civilians gathered along the wall.

"Far be it from me to question your lord commander," he said quietly, "but I can't imagine that having so large an audience is going to improve the candidates' performances."

"They'll have to get used to it one way or another," his daughter Shalna said before Alys could speak. "He might as well know from the start how they'll respond to gawkers."

Alys smothered a smile, for Jailom had said something very similar when she had questioned his intention to have the potential female recruits for the Citadel "audition" in public. Perhaps Alys should not have been surprised by how open he'd been to the idea of allowing women to enter the Citadel. After all, it was he who'd first offered to teach women the basics of self-defense. He'd had few takers at the time, and it wasn't until Falcor had started training Shelvon that the idea first got some traction. Even so, she'd expected at least a little shock or discomfort from him when she'd brought him Shelvon's proposal. Instead, he'd immediately agreed that those of Shelvon's students who were interested should be given the chance.

Duke Thanmir made a noncommittal sound and frowned at the handful of women and girls who stood gathered outside the sparring circle, waiting for their trials to begin. Alys quirked an eyebrow at him.

"Have we finally found a way to shock you with our unconventional customs?" she asked.

When she had invited him to visit again and to bring his daughter with him, she had not expected him to take her up on the offer so very quickly. And yet here he was, back in Women's Well less than a month after his previous visit had ended. Alys had not consciously tried to shock him by inviting him and his daughter to watch the trials with her, but she wondered now if there wasn't some tiny part of her that was trying to discourage him.

"Shock is perhaps too strong a word for it," he said uncomfortably. "However, I must say, I find the thought just a little unsettling."

Alys caught the brief narrowing of Shalna's eyes and hunch of her shoulders. "Why should it be unsettling for a woman to know how to defend herself?" Shalna asked—and though she was obviously attempting to keep her voice level, there was no missing the tension in it.

Thanmir reached over and patted his daughter's hand. "I was referring to the idea of women as professional soldiers. How could I possibly object to them knowing how to defend themselves?"

Shalna looked unappeased. "Just about everyone back home would. As we both know."

Alys winced in sympathy, then quickly tried to banish the expression. She hadn't known what to expect from Shalna after her father had described the terrible attack she'd experienced. Alys supposed a part of her had expected the girl to have been broken by it, to be timid and frightened as Shelvon had once been. From the moment she'd first met Shalna, however, she'd known her expectations had been dead wrong.

Shalna had been brutalized and had seen her sister beaten to death, but there was unquestionably a fire in her spirit that showed in the sharpness of her eyes. And of her tongue.

Alys could not help liking her—something she suspected Thanmir was counting on.

Alys could not blame the duke for wanting to protect his daughter, to find a better and happier life for her. It spoke well of his character, as did the fact that he did not openly disapprove of the notion of women joining the Citadel, despite his discomfort with the idea. Alys supposed asking him to join her for the day's activities had been a test of sorts, and so far he had more than passed.

Lord Jailom himself put the female recruits through their paces, leading them in some of the basic drills that were taught to first-year cadets. In a traditional Citadel, the cadets would all be boys of noble birth, and they would have studied the drills with private tutors for years before becoming cadets. Women's Well had already broken with that tradition by admitting commoners to the Citadel, which meant Jailom and the instructors were used to teaching people who were completely new to swordplay. Shelvon's students were therefore at least as skilled as the average novice recruit, and more so than many.

Some of them were markedly more advanced than others, though all showed an enthusiasm for the exercise that Alys found surprising. She herself could not imagine how these women and girls could find it enjoyable to put themselves through such grueling physical effort under the hot Women's Well sun. Shelvon had designed a simple, single-layered shift dress—reminiscent of the plain, unadorned dresses favored by the women of Nandel—that could be worn over the lightest stays that were considered decent, but even so, the women were soon soaked in sweat.

The crowd of civilian observers shouted out encouragement, with only the occasional jeer. Alys noticed with satisfaction that those few who vocally disdained the fighters were faced with so much censure from the rest that they eventually slunk away. She also noticed that Shalna watched the action with a gleam in her eyes, leaning forward in her chair and catching her breath at some of the more dramatic movements.

Lowering her voice to a murmur, Alys leaned closer to Thanmir. "I'm sure I can arrange some private lessons with Lady Shelvon while you're visiting," she said.

Thanmir started, then darted a quick look at his daughter, who was too engrossed in the proceedings to notice. His eyes widened in what looked like alarm, for he could not possibly miss the enthusiasm that radiated from the girl's being.

"I'm not sure that would be the best idea," he responded in a voice equally low. "Not if she will have to return to Grunir society."

Alys frowned at him. "I think it would be a *particularly* good idea in that case. Who is more in need of self-defense than a woman whose reputation may be at risk?"

But Thanmir shook his head. "If word of what happened gets out, no sword skills are going to protect her." He met her eyes. "There is no hopeful future for her in Grunir," he said with certainty. "I cannot imagine trusting her to a man who might divorce her and force her into the Abbey, and the alternative is that she live as a spinster on my estate for the rest of her days. Even if no one ever learns what Solgriff did to her—and what she did to *him* in return—she will be shunned by society if she does not marry, for everyone would naturally assume that she was unchaste or somehow unsuitable."

Alys wished she could argue his assessment, but of course she could not. Only in Women's Well could a woman not be held to blame for the "sin" of having been raped. If Shalna were only a little bit older, Alys suspected she might have been able to find a suitable husband for her here in Women's Well, but the girl had only recently turned fifteen. It was not too soon to begin *discussing* potential future marriage arrangements, but there could be no contractual agreements for at least another two years.

Alys shook her head. "I'm not going to marry you out of pity for your daughter," she said, feeling once again the frisson of something near panic. It was somewhat embarrassing that her heart sped with fear and she wanted to run away at the very *thought* of marrying again, but that was exactly how she felt.

"Of course not," Thanmir answered smoothly. "I have already laid out my arguments for why marrying me would be to both of our advantages. I promised not to put pressure on you, and I mean to keep to my promise."

Alys scoffed quietly, although she did not argue. He might not be demanding an immediate answer to his proposal, but that was hardly the same as not pressuring her. Shalna gave an excited gasp as one of the women executed a particularly clever parry, and Alys returned her attention to the trials.

When all was said and done, Lord Jailom had offered a place in the Citadel to a half dozen of Shelvon's students. They would join on a trial basis with no contractual obligation on either side. And if after a trial period the arrangement seemed to be working well for all involved, then Jailom would hold another round of trials and perhaps enlist more recruits from the ranks of Shelvon's students. Shelvon beamed with all the joy of a proud mama, and Alys was truly happy for her.

CHAPTER TWENTY-ONE

Prince Draios had spent little more than a day at Delnamal's manor house, but that time had already wrought a conspicuous difference in him, and Delnamal congratulated himself on his deft handling of the young zealot. In some ways, he had his mother to thank for that. Her horror when he had demonstrated his power had helped him hone his pitch, had shown him that he needed to find a way to soothe those who saw its darkness as something that could not possibly come from so benevolent a source as the Creator. Far better to construct a narrative that acknowledged the power as coming from the Destroyer while still crediting the Creator as having gifted it to him than to allow others to imagine some story of the Destroyer working through him to wreak havoc.

Even with what he considered his deft handling of the story, Delnamal had not been entirely certain he'd convinced the young prince of the holiness of his mission. Surely a man with genuine faith and a modicum of common sense would reject all of Delnamal's self-serving explanations of his power. In the moment, Draios had agreed that it was best for everyone to explain Bandar's sudden death as a heart attack—Delnamal could only imagine the whispers in the servants' hall now that a second member of his staff had died unexpectedly—but he'd half-expected Draios to come to his senses by morning. However, after a night of prayer and introspection, Draios had declared that there was no other explanation for Delnamal's very existence save that the Creator had willed it.

Despite all of Delnamal's careful planning, he still found himself mildly surprised at how malleable faith could be, how easily a man could twist the teachings of the Devotional to his own desires and purposes. Delnamal could see the light of fanaticism in Draios's eyes, and he had no doubt the boy genuinely believed himself a true and faithful servant of the Creator. But, thanks to his mother, Delnamal had a clear image of what true devotion looked like, and he saw little sign of it in the young prince. True faith required one to bend one's desires to the teachings of the Devotional; Draios instead found ways to bend the Devotional to justify his own desires.

Knowing that the battle for Draios's soul was already won, Delnamal put his mind to getting the most he could out of his conquest.

Draios by himself was of little use to Delnamal's plans. Having decided at a young age to enter the priesthood, the prince had acquired little in the way of money or power that could be used to Delnamal's advantage. The support of a seventeen-year-old princeling would not help Delnamal raise an army, and that was what he needed to conquer Aaltah. Which meant that Draios was nothing more than a stepping stone, a way to finally make contact with the king and present his case. King Khalvin had ignored Delnamal's letters and dismissed Xanvin's, but surely he would be more inclined to listen to his priestly son.

When Draios rose for his second morning at the manor house, Delnamal was ready to set a trap into which the prince would happily throw himself headfirst.

"I must return to Khalwell today," Draios said reluctantly as the two of them enjoyed a hearty breakfast.

Xanvin had once again requested that a breakfast tray be brought to her bedroom, claiming continued illness. She had emerged from that room only briefly to say hello to the nephew she had never met. She'd looked convincingly pale, but Delnamal felt sure what ailed her was no physical illness.

She was his mother, and as many times as she'd annoyed him over the course of his life, he had always loved her. He remembered exactly what it had felt like to love her and to care about her feelings, and he was very much aware that only a callous and cruel man would care so little about the burdens he'd put upon her when he'd revealed his powers. He remembered not wanting to be callous and cruel—even while his treacherous emotions caused him to be so—but it was so easy now to sweep the guilt aside. Only in the mornings, when he was in that twilight land between sleep and waking, did he suffer the pangs of conscience and self-loathing that had once tormented him, and he often woke to a sense of horror and guilt that convinced him he must throw himself at her feet and apologize profusely for the pain he had caused her. Luckily, those feelings faded into obscurity by the time he rose from his bed.

"I have duties I must return to," Draios said with self-importance that might have made Delnamal laugh if he didn't need to retain the prince's good opinion.

"I understand," Delnamal said, then was unable to resist needling him just a little. "I don't imagine it was easy to win permission to take a leave from the temple when you are still a relatively new postulant."

Irritation glinted in Draios's eyes at the suggestion that a man such as he needed *permission* to do anything. But remonstrating would have made him seem impious, for of course all postulants were meant to be equal. Yes, Delnamal had well and truly taken the boy's measure.

"I will make time to speak with my father the moment I arrive home," Draios said. "I will confirm that I have seen your power with my own two eyes and that it is as fearsome as you say."

Delnamal made a noncommittal sound and took a sip of tea, wrinkling his brow as if deep in thought. "Are you sure your father doesn't already believe that my power exists?" he asked. "After all, he has not only my own word to go on, but his sister's, as well. Might it not be that he *fears* my power, rather than that he doesn't believe in it?"

A muscle twitched in Draios's jaw, and the table began vibrating ever so slightly as his knee bounced. Delnamal made as if to say something, then fell silent and looked away. It was a pretense, of course, a way to manipulate Draios into "persuading" him to talk.

The young prince helpfully jumped into the opening. "Please, Cousin, do not hesitate to speak freely with me. We have too little time together to waste it on delicacy."

Delnamal looked Draios straight in the eyes—an assessing gaze that made the young man sit up a little straighter and raise his chin. Oh, how he wanted to be an integral part in the revolution that was to come, in the war that would restore the old order to their world!

Delnamal held Draios's eyes for as long as the prince could stand it, smiling to himself when Draios finally looked away. Even then, Delnamal waited for the space of several breaths before he spoke again, as if choosing his words very carefully.

"I have a plan for destroying the Curse and restoring the world to its proper order," he said. "When I was the King of Aaltah, I bade your former abbess drink a seer's poison she had invented on my behalf. A poison that allowed her to see how the Curse was originally cast."

Draios looked appropriately stunned by the admission, his eyes widening almost comically before a frown took over. "But it was our former abbess who damaged your Well, was it not? It doesn't sound like we should put much store in what she had to say."

Delnamal had anticipated the objection. "I believe she was guided by the hand of the Creator, though she knew it not. It was through her actions at the Well that I gained my powers. And it was through her vision of the casting of the Curse that I learned how we can undo it."

Draios wavered for a moment, some part of him rational enough to suspect he was being lied to. But the part of him that wanted to be a hero was far stronger, and eventually he nodded his acceptance.

"How can we undo it?" the prince finally asked.

"It was cast using a form of Kai that was heretofore unknown, called sacrificial Kai. The Abbess of Aaltah, her daughter, and her granddaughter, willingly sacrificed their lives to create this special mote of Kai, which is the only thing capable of affecting the Wellspring itself."

Draios nodded again, for the explanation made sense with what was already known about the events of the terrible night the Curse was cast. The Abbess of Aaltah had sent a flurry of fliers to all the kingdoms and principalities, alerting them to what she had done, although she had not specifically mentioned the use of Kai. *That* he had learned from Mairahsol. He had reason to distrust much of what she had told him, but by her own actions she had proven the value of sacrificial Kai.

"I believe that to undo the Curse, another willing sacrifice will have to be made," Delnamal continued. "And I believe that *I* am the one who is meant to perform it."

Draios looked appropriately stunned, and Delnamal helpfully provided some pseudo-doctrinal support for his claim. "I believe the Creator means for me to return the Rhokai with which I have been gifted to the Well from which it originated. That is something that can only be achieved by my death, and I believe that my willing sacrifice will reverse the Curse and return all of Seven Wells to its natural state of holiness."

It was, Delnamal had decided, the perfect story to quell the last of Draios's doubts. No matter how deluded Draios might be, he was unlikely to wholeheartedly support Delnamal if he thought doing so would unleash his unholy power on the world. He must believe that the power was useful to his own ambitions, but that once the great quest was done, it—and Delnamal himself—would pose no threat to him.

Of course, Delnamal had no intention of casting himself into the Well. Once Prince Draios helped him win the support of King Khalvin, he would have no further use for the boy. And once Khalvin had helped him retake the throne of Aaltah, he, too, would become expendable. All of Khalpar was to him nothing more than a means to an end.

"You would do that?" Draios asked, his voice tinged with suspicion.

Delnamal met the young zealot's eyes. "If the Creator asked you to sacrifice your life for His glory, would you obey?"

"Of course," Draios said without hesitation.

Delnamal suspected the fool actually meant it. Just as he suspected that if Draios truly *did* receive such a command, he would twist himself in knots until he found a way to interpret it to mean something very different.

"Well then, you can understand my position."

But Draios still looked at him askance. "But you are not a priest, nor have I ever heard tell that you were a particularly holy man. I find it surprising that you would have the devotion necessary to sacrifice your own life."

Delnamal lifted one shoulder in a shrug. "My mother raised me to abide by the Devotional. I must admit that for most of my life, I failed her miserably. But the power that the Creator has granted me has changed me. How can I not obey His wishes when He has touched me so personally? Were it not for His grace, I would have died that day at the Well. I must repay my debt, and atone for my sins."

Delnamal was pretty sure Draios's instincts—perhaps even his common sense—were screaming at him that he should not listen to all this nonsense. Just as he was sure his desire for glory caused him to hang on every word.

"To undo the Curse," Delnamal said, swooping in for the kill, "I must retake my kingdom so that I might have access to Aaltah's Well. That is not something I can do by myself, no matter how much the Creator has blessed me. I need more than just Khalpar's support. I need its army and navy."

Draios scoffed, his lips twisting into a bitter grimace. "Even if I can persuade my father of your power and your mission, I cannot see him going to war with Aaltah. He is not what I would call a man of action."

For the first time, Delnamal acknowledged a twinge of doubt. His own emotional outbursts had unquestionably made his negotiations with his uncle more problematic than they had needed to be while he was King of Aaltah, but it was just as unquestionably true that Draios's assessment of his father was accurate: King Khalvin valued prayer and thought above action, and it was possible a man such as he could never be persuaded to launch an attack.

"That is why you need *me* to explain my power and my mission to him," Delnamal said, letting none of his own doubts color his voice even as his mind began rethinking the problem once again. Maybe Draios could be useful to him as something *other* than a mere conduit to his father.

Draios stiffened, his jaw jutting out. "My father may not value me as much as he ought, but he is still more likely to listen to his own son than to a disgraced nephew," he growled.

Draios no doubt intended his words to be insulting, but Delnamal was no longer vulnerable to the pain that mere words used to cause him.

"You misunderstand me," he said, making a calming motion at the young prince who was now visibly seething. The boy's relationship with his father was clearly a sore spot, and Delnamal realized at once that it made for a vulnerability he knew exactly how to exploit. "I did not mean to imply that your father would be more open to my words than yours. It is only that if he is *not* persuaded—or if he is persuaded and yet refuses to go to war— I have . . . tools at my disposal that you do not. Tools to help us ensure that the Creator's will is done."

Draios went pale with shock. "What do you mean?" he asked, although the look on his face said he knew exactly what Delnamal was suggesting.

"When we arrive in Khalwell," Delnamal said, "you must arrange a meeting with your father and your brother. I will present my case to them both. The Curse must be undone, and the world returned to its natural order. I will, of course, do everything in my power to persuade your father to help us fulfill the Creator's mission without any unpleasantness. But should he be blind to the truth, or should he prove reluctant to act upon it, then perhaps I can demonstrate just what my power can do."

Draios would have looked convincingly appalled, if not for the strange, greedy glint in his eye. "You mean to kill Parlommir." His voice showed the appropriate level of horror at the prospect, but that was not at all what Delnamal saw in his eyes. He suspected it was the same look that had come into his own eyes every time he'd spoken Tynthanal's name. It was a potent, toxic mix of hatred and jealousy and resentment, and Delnamal had no doubt that Draios had more than once wished his brother dead.

"I mean to do no such thing," Delnamal said stoutly. "My intention is to persuade your father to accept the Creator's will. I have perhaps not been as persuasive as I'd hoped when I wrote to him, but when he sees me in person—and when he has you there to help him understand how the Creator is working through me—I have every confidence that he will answer the Creator's call. It is only if he fails the test of faith that other, more unpleasant persuasions might be necessary. If such happens, then we must believe that it is part of the Creator's will that a man of genuine, wholehearted piety—such as yourself—succeed your father to the throne."

Draios, his face still pale despite the almost lustful expression in his eyes, made a great show of thinking it over with furrowed brow. But his conclusion had been inevitable from the moment Delnamal started speaking.

"Very well," Draios said with feigned reluctance. "I shall do as you suggest."

Delnamal suppressed a smile of triumph. No one but the king's own son would be able to smuggle an uninvited guest into a royal audience, but no palace guards would gainsay Prince Draios when he showed up with Delnamal in tow. Then one way or another, Delnamal would gain the men and weapons he needed to take back the kingdom that had been stolen from him.

Leethan shivered in mingled cold and dread as she and Jaizal made their way across the Abbey's courtyard under the light of a full moon. The heavy breeches and doublet she wore under her even heavier cloak felt awkward and oddly restrictive after decades of wearing nothing but her official robes, but she knew she would be thankful for them when they plunged out into the snow they were sure to encounter on their journey.

It was a bitterly cold night, the wind biting relentlessly at any patch of revealed skin, but at least it wasn't snowing, and the clear light of the moon would make traversing the narrow pass that led to the Abbey easier. She had waited longer than was strictly wise to stage this daring escape, but it had taken time to gather the supplies they would need without attracting attention, and a snowstorm—unusually vicious for this early in the season— had delayed them even further.

It was late enough at night that the stable was empty except for the two sturdy mountain ponies that had carried a load of food supplies to the Abbey earlier in the day. They were due to begin their short journey back to The Keep in the morning, and the Abbey would not receive another shipment of supplies for a fortnight. Leethan had drugged the wine she had left in the caravan driver's room, so he would wake in the morning far too ill to set out. She hoped that meant it would take a little longer before anyone noticed that she and the others were missing.

The stable was only warmer than the courtyard because of the lack of wind. The temperature would have had to dip much lower for Leethan to use the Abbey's meager supply of wood to warm the place, for the ponies were bred for Nandel winters. It was also pitch dark inside once the door was closed. Leethan drew a small luminant from within the folds of her cloak and lit it. The ponies regarded her curiously.

Laurel, leading a sleepy Princess Elwynne, emerged from the shadows at the back of the stable, where she had been waiting for them. Unlike Leethan and Jaizal, both Elwynne and Laurel were dressed in their own warmest clothing. Leethan would have had no way to obtain boy's clothing to fit Elwynne, and a little girl traveling with three men would have drawn attention they could not afford. But a little girl traveling with her governess and two men would be far less noticeable—as long as no one got a close enough look at Leethan and Jaizal to penetrate the disguise.

"Are you *sure* you want to do this?" Leethan asked Laurel anxiously, her every instinct screaming at her that the old woman could not possibly survive the hard journey ahead.

"Want to?" Laurel said. "Well, no, of course not." She laid a hand protectively on Elwynne's head. The girl leaned against her, silent and trusting. "But where my lady goes, there go I."

Elwynne smiled ever so slightly at being called a lady. Although it was well past her bedtime, she looked more excited than sleepy. Laurel had painted their nighttime departure as part of a playful prank, designed to surprise and flummox the rest of the abigails when they woke in the morning to find her gone.

"I reminded Miss Laurel to pack an extra cloak so that she would not be cold," Elwynne confided in a whisper, taking hold of her governess's hand and squeezing as if to give comfort. Leethan knew Laurel had tried to downplay the difficulty of the journey on which they were about to embark, but it seemed the child had sensed her disquiet.

"That was most thoughtful of you," Leethan said with what she hoped was a warm smile, even as she dreaded the ordeal that was to come.

Working quietly and as quickly as possible, Leethan and Jaizal dug through the straw to find the packs they had prepared. One held their own supplies, and one held feed for the ponies. The supply was far from adequate—the Abbey did not keep much feed, for the ponies only came every two weeks and stayed for only one night—but it was better than nothing.

"How much of a head start do you think we'll have?" Jaizal asked under her breath as she cinched the straps on the last saddle bag.

"Hard to say," Leethan answered just as quietly, for though she'd asked herself that question many times, she had yet to come up with a satisfactory answer. Their absence would be noticed by their sisters first thing in the morning, when none of them made an appearance in the dining hall. But the abigails had no means to pursue, even if they'd had the desire to do so. The ponies would be gone, and the Abbey did not possess any horses or chevals. "I don't believe any of our sisters will betray us by pointing out our absence to the caravan driver . . ."

Jaizal nodded. "But they will be frightened of what might happen to them if they stay silent, and that fear might overpower their loyalty."

"Exactly," Leethan said with a sigh. "If we're very lucky and our braver sisters keep the silence, then we may have a day or two before the pursuit begins."

Leethan had taken the sole flier in the Abbey's possession, so the only means to get word to The Keep was for the caravan driver to return on foot to sound the alarm. As long as he didn't realize anything was amiss, he might take the entire day to recuperate from his illness. Then, once he discovered the ponies gone, it would take him much of the next day to walk back to The Keep.

"But we should assume we will not be lucky at all," Laurel said after lifting her small charge onto the pony's back. "Let us walk and talk at the same time."

Leethan felt no inclination to argue.

CHAPTER TWENTY-TWO

Draios waited in the king's antechamber and fumed silently, unable to resist the urge to pace in an effort to work off his anger. The moment he'd returned to the palace, he'd sent an urgent request for an audience with both the king and Parlommir. He'd done it to preempt the summons he'd known would come—his father would be furious with him for having left Khalwell without permission, and he was unlikely to have been persuaded by the hastily concocted excuse Draios had left behind. However, the king's response had *not* mentioned that Parlommir had only this morning boarded the navy's flagship to oversee a training exercise that would keep him from Khalwell for a good three or four days. *That* Draios had only learned when he'd entered the antechamber.

"There's no need to worry," said Delnamal, who sat cloaked and hooded like a monk. His hunched back and the skeletal hand that clutched his cane made him seem like a frail, harmless old man. Draios knew they likely could have done away with the disguise—no palace guard was going to refuse entry to the king's son, even if that son had an uninvited guest trailing along in his wake. But the king's secretary would almost certainly have told the king Delnamal was here, and Draios and Delnamal both agreed it had better be a surprise.

"I'm not worried," Draios snapped. He could not see Delnamal's face under the hood, but he had the instant impression that the man was smirking at him.

Of course, Draios *was* worried. He had spent the previous night fasting and praying yet again, and he had come to the inevitable conclusion that he knew how this conversation was going to end. The king would consider every word out of Delnamal's mouth a heresy, immediately shutting his mind to the message the rightful King of Aaltah delivered. If Parlommir were here, as he was supposed to be, Delnamal could demonstrate his power on the crown prince, and there was every likelihood that the demonstration and the death of his heir would break Khalvin's will. Draios was prepared to accept whatever fate the Creator willed for him, but he had to admit to a certain degree of enmity toward his older brother that would make his regrettable death perhaps not as regrettable to Draios as it ought to be. But with Parlommir not here, Draios would have to rely on Delnamal's powers of persuasion, and of those he was not as confident. His father was undoubtedly pious, but he was far from a man of action. How likely was it that he would actually *listen* when Delnamal's message called for launching a holy war?

"Trust me," Delnamal said in a voice that sent a shiver down Draios's spine. "I will convince your father to see things our way. And we don't need your brother here for that."

Draios would have offered a cutting comeback, but the anteroom door opened and the king's secretary stepped out.

"His Majesty will see you now," he said, then looked down his nose at Delnamal's hunched figure. "Shall I have some refreshments brought for your guest while he waits?"

Draios gave the man a withering glare but didn't deign to answer as Delnamal laboriously climbed to his feet. Draios could see in the secretary's face that he wanted to bar the way. But the man was little better than a servant, and something he saw in Draios's face made him flinch and step aside.

Draios swept into his father's private audience chamber, which he used only when speaking with close friends and family, Delnamal trailing behind at a much slower and more laborious pace.

King Khalvin looked older than his years with his saggy jowls and the plethora of frown lines around his mouth and eyes. He was sitting at his desk, a Devotional resting in front of him and a cup of tea steaming at his side.

This private audience chamber was far more intimate than the huge public hall the king used for more formal audiences, but there was no mistaking that his father thought of this as a business meeting rather than a casual conversation with his son. Two palace guards flanked the open door, and two more were stationed behind the king's chair. Draios had long ago given up being insulted by his father's strict adherence to protocol. The king would send the guards away if asked, but it never occurred to him that their very presence was an affront. Draios was certain that his brother could request a private audience with the king and arrive to find the king's guards stationed *outside* the room.

Draios bowed—that, even the crown prince did in the king's presence—but he saw out of the corner of his eye that Delnamal did not. The disrespect made his teeth clench even while he simmered in his own resentment.

Then again, Delnamal still considered himself the King of Aaltah, so no doubt he felt himself King Khalvin's equal. Despite having to sneak into the audience in Draios's wake, and despite coming as a supplicant.

Draios rose from his bow to see his father scowling, which was the old man's most practiced expression. Especially around Draios. The scowl rested a long moment on Delnamal, who was still hidden behind his cloak and hood, before turning its full force on Draios.

"I was not aware you were bringing a guest," Khalvin said, his voice dripping with disapproval. But it was more than disapproval that Draios read in his father's expression; there was a certain wariness there, as well. Did he perhaps suspect that Lord Eldlin's death and Draios's subsequent—and hasty—departure from Khalwell were related? There would have been no evidence left behind to indicate that Eldlin's death was anything but natural, but still . . .

Khalvin dismissed Draios from his consideration before Draios had mustered an answer to what was almost a challenge.

"You needn't continue with the subterfuge, nephew," he said to Delnamal. "I know where my son has been these last several days, and it has not been at the Shrine of the Holy Penitents."

Delnamal tossed his head, causing the hood to slide down to his shoulders and reveal his hideous face. One of Khalvin's guards flinched ever so slightly. Draios had to admit the first glimpse was shocking, though a palace guard should have shown no such reaction.

"It is good to see you again, Uncle," Delnamal said, then took a seat without waiting for an invitation.

Draios smiled to see the way his father stiffened at the affront. Perhaps he still didn't understand that Delnamal considered himself a king and equal.

Khalvin's scowl deepened. "I wish I could say the same," he growled. "I thought our agreement was clear."

Delnamal nodded. "Yes, yes," he said dismissively. "You wanted me to stay in the country and never be seen or heard from again."

Khalvin leaned forward, planting both fists on his desk as his scowl turned into a glare. "I gave you shelter and money out of loyalty to my sister, but I can easily take both away. I can ship you back to Aaltah and let their regent and your erstwhile royal council decide what to do with you."

Delnamal raised an eyebrow. "Even knowing what I can do?" he inquired. "I *know* you received my letters."

Khalvin's gaze slid to Draios, and Draios could see his father's quick mind putting everything together.

Draios couldn't help another little smile, one that carried no small amount of malice. "I gather you understand now why I made that trip out to the manor house," he said. "If you're going to burn your correspondence, you should make sure the flames have finished their job before you walk away."

Khalvin rose to his feet, rage practically oozing from his pores. He was not one to shout—shouting was undignified, especially in a sovereign—but his furious voice carried all the weight of a roar.

"I will not tolerate disrespect! Not even from you, my son. Have a care with your words, or this audience will end right now."

All four guards in the room came to full attention, ready to leap to their king's command. Draios wondered if his father would actually go so far as to have him bodily thrown out of the room. Their relationship had always been prickly, although before it had been overtly cordial.

"Prince Draios did not know it at the time," Delnamal said, "but he was merely acting upon the wishes of the Creator."

Draios crossed his arms over his chest. "I do not need you to defend my honor, Cousin," he grumbled, though in truth it was something of a relief to have Khalvin's fearsome glare directed elsewhere.

"Do not speak blasphemy in my presence, Delnamal," Khalvin said. "That I will not tolerate from anyone."

Delnamal's eyes narrowed. In other circumstances, the use of his name might be considered unremarkable and perfectly proper between an uncle and his nephew, but there was no doubting that in this instance it was meant to be belittling.

While Draios had not expected this audience to go smoothly, he had never intended it to be so overtly hostile from the very beginning. What chance had they of convincing his father of the importance of their mission if he was incandescent with anger from the start?

Draios had to acknowledge that he bore most of the responsibility for the tone, and he vowed to find some way to de-escalate. Unfortunately, Delnamal did not seem especially interested in de-escalating.

"It is not blasphemy," Delnamal replied calmly. "It is nothing but the truth. The Creator has made me into His instrument, and it is His will that you make use of me. When you showed yourself unwilling to heed His call, He ensured my letter survived the flames to find its way into Draios's hands."

One of the guards behind the king was looking at Delnamal with open shock and horror, forgetting all semblance of detached professionalism. Draios cleared his throat ever so softly—just enough to draw the man's attention—then glared at him in a way that convinced him to school his expression.

The king was not so easily quelled, and his face was turning an alarming shade of red. Draios had warned Delnamal that he should ease into the topic gently, but the man had clearly only pretended to accept his advice. Draios supposed it was up to him to gain control of the situation.

"I have seen his power, Father," he said, "and it is fearsome to behold."

He would have preferred to make this admission without a quartet of guards overhearing, but it was clear to him that the king had no intention of dismissing them.

Khalvin's eyes fixed on Draios in a way that would have unnerved him if he didn't feel assured of the righteousness of his cause.

"I cannot believe you, of all people, would be swayed by this heresy," the king growled, his lips twisted into a sneer of distaste. "You are in training to be a *priest*! It will one day be your job to root out heretics and bring them to purity in the flames. And yet you *dare*—"

Draios took a step closer, a fire he had thought he'd long ago quenched burning in his breast. He had *never* enjoyed the luxury of a father's love and approval. Surely it shouldn't hurt so much to see that contempt so blatantly displayed for all to see. But he could practically *feel* the guards staring at him, absorbing every detail of the conversation and the tone. It was one thing for *Draios* to know his father did not love or respect him, but quite another for that fact to be revealed to a bunch of nobodies.

"I am a faithful servant of the Creator," Draios interrupted, no doubt giving the guards even more gossip to spread. It was a horrendous breach of protocol to interrupt the king. "He has shown me the path we must take to reverse the Curse and set the world back to rights. I am destined for greater things than mere priesthood. Would you have me ignore His call simply because you have been too wrapped up in your worldly duties to hear it?"

Khalvin looked like he might have an apoplexy any moment, his eyes practically bugging out of his head. "Don't think that because you are my son you are immune to the consequences of your words and deeds!"

Draios was shocked when he felt a pair of rock-hard hands fasten on his shoulders. He'd been so focused on his father's face that he had not noticed the guard approaching, nor had he seen whatever signal his father must have given the man.

Draios tried to jerk out of the man's grip, but the guard held on with the ease of long practice and superior size.

With a groan, Delnamal rose from his own seat. Draios noticed that Khalvin had not bothered to have a guard put hands on *him*—probably because he looked too frail to be of any danger.

"Forgive me, Uncle," Delnamal said, reaching up to rub his eyes as if they hurt him and taking a couple of placating steps closer to where the king still stood frozen behind his desk. "I clearly have done an imperfect job of explaining the situation. Please do not be angry with Draios. He has seen and heard things that you have not."

"This audience is over," Khalvin said, not bothering to acknowledge Delnamal with even the briefest glance, his entire focus on Draios. "I advise you both to leave quietly. And, Draios, since you seem to *admire* your cousin so greatly, perhaps you would care to spend some time as his guest out in the countryside. Clearly, you are not fit to return to the Temple of the Creator at the moment."

In his wildest fantasies, Draios had not imagined that his father would go so far as to *exile* him, even for bringing him news he did not want to hear. Once again, he tried to jerk away from the guard who held him, and once again, he failed. He turned his attention to Delnamal, who was still rubbing his eyes and was now directly across the desk from the king.

Draios's heart was slamming against his breastbone, his breath coming short. He would *not* allow himself to be dismissed like this.

"I think it's time we show the king what you can do, Cousin," he said to Delnamal. "If you would be so kind as to get this lout off me . . ."

Draios allowed himself only the briefest moment of regret that the guard would die simply because he had followed his king's orders. Palace guards, too, were required by the Devotional to put the Creator above all else, and the fool should have heard the righteousness of Draios's cause and disobeyed.

Delnamal chuckled and let his hand fall from his eyes, revealing that they were milky white. He hadn't been rubbing them at all—he'd merely been hiding the opening of his Mindseye.

Draios's stomach gave a sickening lurch, and the fight went out of him as he stared at his cousin and realized his own foolish error. He'd assumed the guard who held him would be the target of Delnamal's demonstration, and though he hadn't thought things through that far, it seemed to him possible that the demonstration would change the king's mind. But his cousin was no longer *interested* in changing the king's mind. If he ever had been.

"Delnamal, wait!" Draios cried, renewing his frantic efforts to shake off his guard, but Delnamal was already holding his hand out toward the king's chest.

Delnamal nearly moaned in ecstasy as the king's Rhokai flowed into him. Although he'd come to this audience hunched and feeble-looking, he'd still had a lingering store of strength from having killed Bandar two days ago, and when he added Khalvin's Rhokai to the mix, he felt stronger and more powerful than he'd ever felt in his life.

The king's lifeless body fell to the floor, everyone in the room staring in undisguised horror.

Things had never been destined to go according to Draios's plan, but Delnamal was disappointed that they hadn't gone according to his own, either. If Crown Prince Parlommir had attended the audience as he should, then both the king and his heir would now be dead, with Draios ready to take the throne uncontested. And the room would likely not be full of guards.

Delnamal did not like his odds against four well-trained men, especially when Draios seemed unlikely to be any use to him. But the intemperate young prince had been about to get them kicked out, and Delnamal had known he'd never get another chance. Now, he would simply have to make the best of a bad situation.

He plucked the Rhokai from one of the guards before anyone had regained enough sense to stop him.

Even through the haze of elements revealed by his Mindseye, Delnamal had no trouble seeing the other guard swinging a sword at him—one of the few advantages of his indifferent magical talent was that his worldly vision was not overly hindered by the opening of his Mindseye. Strangely, he felt no fear. He had become so skilled at shunting aside his emotions that he could now do so with nary a conscious thought. Instinctively, he raised one arm to shield himself, hoping that arm would stave off the death blow for just a few more moments.

He felt the sword make contact with his arm, knocking him back a couple of steps, but there was only the slightest hint of pain. The sensation distracted him momentarily, and when he glanced at the wound, he saw several motes of Rhokai flow from it like blood. Then those motes burst, giving him the familiar rush of energy and strength. The guard was swinging his sword again, and Delnamal stretched out his hand toward the man's Rhokai.

It should have been well out of reach. After all, the guard was more than an arm's-length away. But the man's aura suddenly went still, his sword arm frozen in mid-swing. The mote of Rhokai wavered in his chest, straining toward Delnamal's outstretched hand.

Behind him, Delnamal was aware of shouting voices—Draios and the other two palace guards yelling over one another so that no words were discernible—but he maintained his focus on the man who had wounded him, and suddenly that mote of Rhokai came free and burst with a silent pop.

The remains of the mote came obediently to Delnamal's hand, the Rho sinking into him as the bright Kai took its place in his aura. Delnamal didn't have time to think about how he had withstood the blow from the guard's sword—nor about the Rhokai that had flowed with his blood and then burst. Not when there were other guards bent on killing him.

The man who'd grabbed Draios had let go, and both he and his fellow had drawn swords. As far as Delnamal could tell, Draios was standing still, neither helping nor hindering the hesitating guards.

"Put down your swords," Delnamal said calmly, "and I swear you will live." He reached out one hand toward each of them, and though they were far enough back that even their swords couldn't reach him, he could practically *feel* those tantalizing motes of Rhokai quivering in their chests.

Neither guard moved—whether because of fear or because Delnamal had a virtual grip on their Rhokai, he didn't know.

Confident that he could rip out those two motes before the guards could reach him, he turned his attention to Draios. The haze of elements was enough to hide the young man's expression, but Delnamal could well imagine it was one of shock and grief.

"I'm sorry about your father," Delnamal said, lying easily, well and truly rid of the guilt that had once made his falsehoods halting and obvious, "but the Creator's will must not be thwarted. Khalpar must be made ready for the war that is to come, and Khalvin was not worthy of leading the holy army. I hope you see that."

Draios said nothing, but his very silence spoke volumes.

"Tell the guards to lower their swords," Delnamal continued. "I believe that until Parlommir returns to Khalwell to claim the throne, you will be regent in his stead. Am I wrong?"

He heard Draios stifle a gasp, but he didn't for a moment believe the thought had not already entered the young man's head. Bitter and ambitious and deluded he might be, but Draios was not stupid. As soon as his father had fallen dead, he had no doubt realized exactly what Delnamal had planned. And if Delnamal had him pegged correctly, he would quickly convince himself that all was going according to the Creator's will.

"You are not wrong," Draios replied, making a good show of being reluctant.

"This filthy beast killed the king!" one of the guards protested, and Delnamal felt him struggling against the virtual grip on his Rhokai.

It was most satisfactory—and persuasive—that Delnamal could hold the two trained palace guards at a standstill from a distance. He wasn't even using a spell that might wear off or be fought with a counterspell or shield spell. It was even more satisfactory that the guard had given Delnamal an excuse to further expand his understanding of the nature of Rhokai.

"You disrespect His Highness by daring to offer an opinion," he said. Keeping his grip on those two Rhokai motes, he bent and grabbed the sword that had sliced his arm, pulling it easily from the dead guard's grip. Then, his Mindseye still open, he slashed the sword across the protesting guard's throat.

The Rhokai mote in the guard's chest seemed to waver a moment as the man gurgled and gasped and fell to his knees. Seconds later, the mote burst open, the Rho flying free while the Kai hovered at the guard's shoulder. For a moment, Delnamal feared he had miscalculated, for when the Rhokai had burst, he'd lost his grip on the guard and could no longer hold him still. But either the shock of having his throat slit was too great, or the guard hadn't the magical talent to see the Kai, for he made no attempt to use that free Kai mote to strike out at his killer. Instead, he just keeled over and died, his Kai fading from view until it was no more.

Delnamal smiled in satisfaction. He had just confirmed his guess that violent deaths did indeed cause the Rhokai to shatter, and that was how the element known as battlefield Kai was "created."

"Stand down," Draios ordered the final guard. "There is no reason for you to get yourself killed, too."

Delnamal loosened his grip on the man's Rhokai, allowing him to move. Instead of charging toward Delnamal, the man took two hasty steps backward, putting Draios between him and Delnamal. Delnamal would have called the man a coward, except it was hard to maintain he had made the wrong choice under the circumstances.

Delnamal blinked his Mindseye closed and surveyed the scene.

Draios was deathly pale, his eyes wide and frightened-looking as he stared at something behind Delnamal's back. Delnamal could only presume the boy was staring in horror at his father's dead body; he did not look behind him to confirm his suspicion. Instead, he looked at his arm, expecting to see a terrible wound despite the complete lack of pain.

There was a visible slice in the sleeve of his doublet, and its edges were stained red with blood. But there was no wound to speak of. It was clear to Delnamal that the Rhokai he'd absorbed from Aaltah's Well had healed him.

"He opened you to the bone," Draios said, his voice hoarse. "I couldn't even understand why the blow didn't sever your arm, and now . . ."

Delnamal nodded with satisfaction. He could tell by looking at his hand and arm that whatever magic had fueled him when he consumed the Rhokai had not in reality restored his body to its former glory. The hand was still shriveled and misshapen, the flesh still gaunt; but what did appearances matter? He was standing easily on his own two feet, the cane lying on the floor by one of the dead guards. There was enough Rhokai in his blood that he could not readily tell if the healing had appreciably diminished it. But convinced as he was that it was only the Rhokai keeping his wasted body alive, he had no wish to use any more of it for healing purposes.

"I am protected by the Creator," Delnamal declared, though he did not for a moment believe an imaginary deity had anything to do with it.

Rhokai—not Rho—was the *true* element of life, present in every living being. But so far, he had seen no sign of it floating around loose in the air like other elements. He had a strong suspicion that if he were to peer down into Khalpar's Well, however, he would see motes of life-giving Rhokai in its depths.

The most basic way to use a mote of Kai was to touch it to an enemy—a very effective form of revenge for someone who did not have a battlefield Kai spell handy. Delnamal would have to perform another test to confirm it, but he suspected that when Kai was used in this manner, it killed by breaking the Rhokai mote in the victim's chest. He imagined that when Melcor's Kai had fallen into Aaltah's Well, it had met with and broken a mote of Rhokai within, starting a chain reaction. Mairahsol had clearly had some inkling what was happening and had tried to stop it.

Perhaps she had been trying to purge the Kai from the Well and had ended up purging the Rhokai, as well.

What was clear to him was that all of these events had been caused by *people*, not gods. Thankfully, Draios was too eager to believe to notice any lack of conviction in Delnamal's voice.

Delnamal held up the once-wounded arm. "This is a clear and obvious sign that I serve a holy cause. Wouldn't you agree, Prince Draios?"

Draios still looked shaken, his face so pale Delnamal wondered for a moment if the boy might faint. But Delnamal was offering him things he could not possibly turn down: the chance to style himself a holy warrior, and the chance to claim the throne of Khalpar for his own. The Devotional condemned patricide as one of the deadliest of sins, but Draios's agile mind would grasp at this doctrine-based excuse for accepting his father's murder.

Draios nodded, letting out a slow and steady breath. "My father was a good man," he said, "but he was set in his ways. He could not see the truth when it stood right before his face." He raised his chin. "The Curse must be undone, and the Creator has sent you to do the job. It is the duty of all of us here in Seven Wells to make sure you succeed. I will send a message to King Parlommir at once and request that he return to the capital immediately to assume his duties. And in the meantime, I will fill in for him as necessary."

Delnamal rubbed his face to hide his smile. He could only imagine the missive Draios would send his brother. Unless Delnamal was very much mistaken, Parlommir and whatever ships were involved in his naval exercise would not return to Khalwell at all, leaving Draios free to occupy the throne.

And if Parlommir was stupid enough to come back? Well, Delnamal had already shown himself more than capable of getting around troublesome kings.

CHAPTER TWENTY-THREE

Leethan had never known cold like this before. She'd thought that spending most of her adult life living in Nandel had prepared her for the hardships of this long and arduous journey, but she'd been gravely mistaken.

The sky had been ominously dark all morning, and Leethan groaned softly under her breath when the first few flakes of snow drifted down. Up until now, they'd been lucky with the weather, for though they'd seen precious little sunshine, the snow had held off. But these were the mountains of Nandel on the cusp of winter.

Leethan looked over her shoulder to see how the rest of their tiny caravan was reacting to the prospect of snow. She was leading the way, the pack pony in tow. Behind her, Laurel led the second pony, with little Elwynne huddled on its back. The child was almost invisible beneath her cloak and hood, her chin down and her hands tucked under, keeping herself as warm as possible. Laurel's face was grim with effort, and Leethan could only imagine how exhausted the old woman must be. They'd been traveling as hard and relentlessly as they could, pushing themselves to the brink.

The three of them had briefly debated just where their destination should be, but it had been hard to argue that they should go anywhere but to Rhozinolm. Elwynne had relatives on her mother's side somewhere in Grunir and maybe elsewhere, but neither Leethan nor Elwynne nor Laurel knew how to locate them or even what their names might be. The only person Leethan could imagine wanting to help the child was Elwynne's cousin, Prince Zarsha, who was said to be fond of her—and who might even be her father, if some of the whispers in the Abbey had been true, after all.

They had decided to take the short and brutal mountain route directly to Rhozinolm, theorizing that their pursuers would expect them to take the longer, easier route that would bring them to the Midlands first. Laurel continued to plod along stoically without a hint of complaint, but Leethan worried about her.

Jaizal took up the rear. Being younger than both Laurel and Leethan, she was less likely to fall behind or suffer some silent, unnoticed collapse. The conditions were highly unpleasant at the moment, but not yet brutal. When the snow started to pile up, the danger of succumbing to the cold would be much higher—and the visibility much lower. Leethan vowed to herself that she would look over her shoulder frequently to make sure the others were still with her.

As Leethan had known it would, the storm came on fast and hard. Within only a few minutes of the first flakes falling, there was already a substantial carpet of snow forming beneath their feet, making the footing treacherous. The path was narrow, and a fall could be deadly. Leethan had never been especially afraid of heights, but she found that she could not look over the edge without imagining what it would feel like to fall into the mists below. She hugged the side of the mountain as closely as she could.

Mountain storms being what they were, there were shelters carved into the rock at regular intervals on all the most frequently traveled trade routes. Unfortunately, the need for secrecy meant that Leethan had decided against using a trade route. The path they followed instead was too narrow for wagons or carriages, and it was generally presumed that no sensible person traveling by foot or horse would be out in dangerous weather. There were occasional shelters, but only when the path meandered by the mouth of a cave or other naturally occurring alcove. As the snow continued to fall, piling up thickly and making every step more laborious, Leethan prayed to the Mother of All that they would soon happen upon one of those shelters.

The Mother of All, apparently, wasn't listening. The snow piled up thickly around their feet as they trudged along the exposed path. Gusts of wind made the footing even more precarious than it had been, and with the heavy veil of falling and accumulating snow, it was sometimes hard to see where the path ended and the sheer cliff at its edge began.

Looking over her shoulder, Leethan could barely see the shadowed figures behind her, and anxiety gnawed at her nerves. She had not yet lived the vision the Mother of All had shown her, and logic told her that she and Elwynne and Jaizal were destined to survive the storm. But Laurel was another story.

"Are you all right, Laurel?" Leethan called over her shoulder. The wind tried to snatch the words away, but Laurel heard her. The old woman had wrapped a shawl around her head and face beneath her hood, so all Leethan could see was her narrowed eyes, barely visible in the storm-driven darkness.

"I'll manage," Laurel shouted back bravely, but her voice sounded alarmingly weak to Leethan's ears.

"And you, Princess?" Leethan called to Elwynne.

The child's chin was tucked to her chest, her hood pulled all the way down so that she looked like she might be halfway smothering in it. She raised her head ever so slightly. "Cold," she said, but it was more of a statement of fact than an actual complaint. She was a stoic little creature for one so young. She was also distressingly smart, and the fiction that they were embarking on an exciting adventure hadn't lasted long. Laurel explained that they were running from some bad men who wanted to hurt her, and though the news had frightened Elwynne, it hadn't terrified her. The child was not lacking in courage, that was for sure.

"I'm sure we'll find shelter soon," Leethan responded, wishing she actually *were* sure. The best she could manage was mildly hopeful.

Elwynne tucked her chin back down again.

They soldiered on.

Ellin shared a nervous look with Zarsha as Lord Khelved was shown into her office. She had come up with what she believed was the best possible inducement to convince Lord Khelved that it was time to retire as lord commander, but she had distressingly little confidence that the ploy would work. Zarsha gave her a faint nod of encouragement, and she searched deep inside herself to find a semblance of optimism to show her visitor.

Lord Khelved had once been a handsome man—or so Ellin had heard—but the years had not been kind to him. His skin bore the signs of a man who'd spent much of his life in the military, drilling in the hot sun, and his love of drink was advertised by his deeply ruddy complexion and bulbous nose. He had never committed the insult of arriving at a council meeting drunk, but Ellin had often surmised some of his more acid comments came when he was feeling the aftereffects of overindulgence.

Khelved performed the requisite bow, but his narrowed eyes and pinched lips said he was expecting unpleasantness.

"Please have a seat, Lord Khelved," Ellin invited, still smiling despite her pessimism.

The lord commander darted a quick, calculating look at Zarsha, who had pulled up a chair next to Ellin behind her desk.

Khelved made no comment about the prince consort's . . . unusual presence for this private audience, although she was sure he was already making assumptions. She had dismissed her honor guardsmen for this interview, fearing their presence would be counterproductive, but having almost been killed by one of her previous royal council members, she'd found herself unwilling to meet Lord Khelved entirely on her own. Especially if she should find herself in the unfortunate position of having to blackmail him into resigning.

"What's this about, then?" he inquired brusquely as he took his seat. He crossed his arms belligerently over his chest, scowling at her. He was never exactly a pleasant character, but this was unusually rude even for him. She wondered what he expected her to say, for she was certain his guess was nowhere close to the reality.

Ellin swallowed her instinctive desire to remind him of his place, but Zarsha was not quite so circumspect.

"Have a care how you speak to your queen, Lord Khelved," he warned in a conversational tone that belied the spark in his blue eyes.

"What's this about, then, *Your Majesty?*" Khelved shot back, and Ellin sighed. Such sniping hardly boded well for her hopes of a civil and satisfactory conversation.

She put her hand lightly on Zarsha's arm to discourage him from needling the man further, but kept her eyes on Lord Khelved. Her intention had been to try to ease into the subject, but she decided on the spur of the moment to take the direct approach instead. After all, Khelved was no fool: he would know a bribe attempt when it was presented, and she would only make herself look foolish by trying to pretend.

"As I'm sure you know," she said, "my father's dukedom reverted to the Crown when he died with no heir." Her throat tightened for just a moment as she remembered the terrible night when she had lost her grandfather, her uncle, and both her parents all at once. "For all your valiant years of service to the Crown of Rhozinolm, I would like to bestow that dukedom upon you."

She hoped her words had come out smoothly, though she spoke them with an effort. When the dukedom had first reverted, she had thought to reclaim it for herself—after all, if she was legally allowed to inherit the throne, then it stood to reason she could legally inherit the dukedom, as well. But her reign had been so tense and fraught that she had not bothered to expend the energy to lay claim to lands and a title she no longer needed. In truth she had felt very little emotional connection to the lands that had been her father's duchy, for she had visited their country estate only rarely, having spent most of her life in Zinolm Well. Even so, the thought of passing her father's legacy on to a man she disliked as roundly as she disliked Lord Khelved was not in any way pleasant.

"You don't have to be so nice and honorable about this," Zarsha had said to her when she'd presented her solution to the problem of Lord Khelved. "We can skip directly to the threat that we may need to use anyway."

But however much she disliked Lord Khelved, he had served honorably on her grandfather's royal council for decades. His "financial indiscretions," as Zarsha called them, were not grave enough in her opinion to excuse the practice of blackmail—unless there was no other way.

Lord Khelved sat still in his chair, blinking at her in confusion as if he wasn't quite sure he'd heard her right. He was already a wealthy and influential man, but adding a dukedom to his holdings would elevate him to an elite level that would otherwise have been beyond his reach—and would leave an enduring legacy for his son and his descendants.

Khelved thought about it for a moment, his eyes narrowing. "You mean to make *me* a royal duke?" he said incredulously.

"Not a *royal* duke," she clarified, a smile twitching the corner of her mouth. "I would have to adopt you into the royal family for that, and I think you're a little old to call me 'Mama.' You will not be in the line of succession, but you will still have all the lands and monies that come with the dukedom."

His eyes narrowed even farther. "How exceedingly gracious of Your Majesty to offer such a lofty title to one such as I! And with no strings attached!"

She lifted her shoulders in a hint of a shrug. "Well, yes, of course there are strings. Well, *one* string: the estate has fallen into some disrepair since it has become the property of the Crown, and it is hardly functioning at maximum efficiency. Restoring it to its former glory and making the most of its profits will require a great deal of work and commitment. I'm afraid it is more than you will have time for while you serve as lord commander."

His already florid face flushed a deeper, angrier shade of red as he grasped her meaning.

"Think about it before you answer," Zarsha said, interrupting what she suspected would have been a heated response before Khelved did more than open his mouth. "Your position on the council grants you a certain level of influence, but that influence is yours alone, and it dies—or retires—when you do. The dukedom is something you can pass on to your son, so that he might have influence as well, whereas I believe it's safe to say that he is not someone our queen would be inclined to select to a position on the council."

Ellin couldn't help wrinkling her nose at the prospect, for Lord Khelved's son was cut from much the same cloth as his father. She would not even give passing consideration to having him become one of her closest advisers.

Judging by the harsh lines of his jaw, Khelved was grinding his teeth, staring at Zarsha with a fulminating rage that seemed to Ellin too intense for the situation. She looked at Zarsha sidelong, but he maintained an expression of complete innocence, as if there were nothing hidden behind his words.

Ellin's heart gave an especially violent thump as she wondered if while Zarsha hadn't *lied* to her about anything, he had nonetheless concealed one salient detail: Lord Khelved was aware—or at least suspected—that Zarsha knew his secrets. If that was the case, then Zarsha was in a roundabout way reminding Khelved that his son would suffer social and financial consequences should Khelved be brought to trial.

"When you look at it in that context," Zarsha continued, "surely you can see that it is best for everyone involved if you accept this great honor that Her Majesty wishes to bestow on you."

Khelved closed his eyes as if in pain—or as if to hide his rage—and Ellin took that opportunity to give Zarsha a furious look of her own. She had meant to present her proposal without any hint of blackmail, and Zarsha had understood that intent. If she'd known Khelved suspected he was vulnerable, she wouldn't have agreed to have Zarsha present for the conversation.

Eventually—and grudgingly—Lord Khelved accepted the gift of a dukedom in return for his retirement, but the moment he left the office, she turned on Zarsha, too angry to form words.

He held up his hands in a gesture of innocence. "I know what you think just happened," he said, "but I can assure you I didn't mean what I said as a threat."

Ellin gripped the arms of her chair as she stared at him. "So you had no idea he knew you knew about his crimes?"

He met her eyes squarely. "No idea?" He shrugged and looked away. "I don't suppose I can claim I had *no* idea, but I honestly didn't think he knew. But his guilty conscience and his concern about what I might know clearly made him see a threat where none was intended."

"You should have mentioned that there was a chance," she snapped, not sure if she entirely believed him.

Zarsha bowed his head. "You're right. I should have." When he looked at her again, it was with an expression of chagrin. "You know I have been long in the habit of keeping secrets. I did not intend to in this instance, but I did not think it through."

Ellin took in a shaky breath as she realized this was the peril of marrying a spy. It was hard to see how he manipulated and deceived others without worrying that he might do the same to her. She believed he was sincere, but the doubt would be hard to shake entirely.

"I will do better," Zarsha promised. "I have a lifetime's habits and instincts to overcome, and it might take some time." He reached out and stroked one finger down her cheek. "You are the first person I've ever fully, wholeheartedly trusted," he said softly. "I'm finding that trust takes some practice—for both of us. But I love you, and I hope you love me, and we will get there. Together."

She shook her head even as she mustered a smile. "If you're fishing for reassurance that I love you, well . . ." The smile widened, almost against her will. "Yes, of course I love you. Idiot. But next time—if there *is* a next time—try for full disclosure, will you?"

Zarsha put a hand to his heart and bowed his head. "You have my word."

Lord Lyslee, Marshal of Aaltah and one of Tynthanal's most steadfast supporters on the royal council, looked uncommonly grim as he handed Tynthanal a small sheet of parchment, torn and stained by rain and muck. With a sinking feeling in the pit of his stomach, Tynthanal accepted the paper. He winced when he saw the unflattering image drawn upon it—that of a savage-looking man with fangs and claws, wearing a caricature of Tynthanal's own face.

"The night guardsmen interrupted the man who was putting these broadsheets up," Lord Lyslee said, "but he managed to outrun them. They took down all they could find, but . . ."

Tynthanal nodded as he read the broadsheet's painful message. "But he's sure to find other ways to distribute them."

According to the broadsheet, Aaltah's faltering Well and its plummeting birthrate were a punishment to its people for allowing the son of the witch who cursed the Wellspring to serve as regent. It stopped just short of openly claiming that only his death would heal the Well, but its implications were nonetheless clear.

Tynthanal set the broadsheet down and pinched the bridge of his nose. He'd known since he'd accepted the regency that there was a risk of becoming the scapegoat if he failed to heal the Well, but he'd thought he would have a little more time. Of course, when he'd accepted the regency, he hadn't known about the low birthrate, which was clearly becoming common knowledge despite all efforts to keep it quiet.

"One of my men got a good look at him," Lord Lyslee said. "I will make it a priority to hunt him down."

Tynthanal sighed and took his seat. "Maybe you can catch him, and maybe you can't," he said. "But either way, he's unlikely to be the last to entertain such thoughts."

Lyslee conceded the point with a shrug. "Perhaps not. However, most people do understand that the problem began before you were named regent. They will place the blame squarely where it belongs: on Delnamal."

Tynthanal made a noncommittal sound. He could see from Lyslee's face that the man was not wholly convinced by his own argument.

"You might want your men to take a careful look at anyone who is closely associated with our esteemed lord chamberlain," Tynthanal suggested, remembering the relish with which that dignitary had presented exactly the same rumor that appeared in the broadsheet. "Discreetly, of course. I would never suggest that he had anything to do with it."

Lyslee grimaced. "Already taken care of. I explained it was

merely because Lord Zauthan had caught wind of the rumor previously."

Tynthanal nodded, glad to have a man of good sense and
sound judgment serving as marshal. He more than anyone else
on the council would have a good feel for the mood of the people.

"How well will this message be received, do you think?" Tynthanal asked, lifting the broadsheet. "Is the idea likely to catch
fire immediately?"

The marshal's brow furrowed in thought, and he shook his
head, almost reluctantly. "Not immediately, I shouldn't think.
People are worried, but not quite panicked yet."

"*Yet* being the operative word," Tynthanal grumbled.

Lord Lyslee sighed. "I wish I could argue, but . . ."

Tynthanal stifled a yawn as he contemplated yet another night
studying magic with Lord Draimel, trying desperately to find a
cure for the Well's ailment. He did not believe the answer lay in
his studies there—he'd much rather have spent more time directly in the Well chamber—but Draimel insisted that poring
through the archives and learning the skills of a master spell
crafter were necessary to have any chance of repairing the Well.
Much as he might want to do so, Tynthanal knew it would be a
strategic mistake to argue. As grand magus, Draimel was the foremost expert in magic and spell crafting in all of Aaltah—in theory,
at least—and if Tynthanal refused to accept the man's instruc-
tion, it wasn't just Draimel who'd be angered by it. Those who
secretly—or, as in the case of Lord Zauthan, not-so-secretly—
wanted him to fail would see it as a sign that he wasn't even trying.

Lyslee leaned over the desk and picked up the broadsheet.
"For the time being, at least," he said, moving over to the fireplace, "I think it best we not discuss this unfortunate incident
with the rest of the council. It will only . . . distract from our most
important duties. Do you agree?"

Tynthanal shifted in his seat with no small amount of discomfort. He did not like the idea of keeping secrets from his royal council. There was a whiff of desperation—even cowardice—to the idea that sat poorly with him.

But Lyslee was right in that such an issue would perforce waste some of the council's time. With so many trade agreements faltering—and with the Crown beginning to default on several loans that would only make their situation more dire—the last thing they needed was to spend an hour arguing over what to do about a single man distributing broadsheets.

Tynthanal nodded. "For now, I think you have the right of it."

Lord Lyslee dropped the broadsheet into the fire, where the flames made quick work of it.

Leethan had hoped that when the road sloped downward and took them into a narrow valley, they might find the snow less heavy and the cold less fierce. But the storm they'd been struggling through for hours had no intention of letting them off that easy. The snow was knee high, and Leethan's legs trembled with fatigue—and quite possibly, frostbite.

It was dawn when they made their descent, and Leethan worried that they might be spotted by someone in the cluster of houses in the valley—barely enough to be called a village—that would be waking with the new day. The men's clothes that she and Jaizal wore would fool anyone seeing them from a distance, but if someone in the village got too close . . .

Leethan glanced behind her and winced to see how heavily Laurel leaned on the pony for support. The old woman desperately needed to rest in front of a hot fire. And the services of a healer might come in handy, as well.

The only good news was that once they reached the valley floor, they finally came upon a small shelter carved into the mountain wall. She nearly wept with relief, although she did not like the idea of camping so close to the village. She didn't know what they'd do if someone approached them. There was no telling how far behind the pursuit was. It depended on how long it had taken for word of their escape to reach The Keep, and on how desperate Waldmir was to recapture them. If he sent men on chevals after them . . .

But Leethan very much doubted that he would have. Chevals could travel faster and more easily on these mountain roads, but they were considered unmanly. Waldmir's soldiers would balk at riding them, and Waldmir would be too uncomfortable with the idea himself to force them to.

Leethan prayed to the Mother of All that she was making the right decision when she led the way into the shelter. There was barely enough room inside to fit all of them, and the ponies' hind ends stuck out. Luckily, their thick winter coats had already fully come in, so they would be fine.

Even if they'd had wood to light a fire, they were too close to the village to do so. Instead, they all huddled together for warmth and comfort, covering themselves with the rolled blankets the pack pony carried.

Their food stores and their water were all frozen, so they refreshed themselves with snow and put the food under the blankets with them in hope their body heat would eventually thaw it enough to eat.

Within minutes of lying down halfway across Laurel's lap, Elwynne was fast asleep. Leethan envied the child the ability to sleep in such discomfort. Exhausted as she herself was, she didn't see how she could fall asleep. Even with the blankets, she shivered with cold, and her whole body ached with fatigue.

Jaizal had no such trouble, her eyes fluttering shut only a few minutes after Elwynne's, but like Leethan, Laurel remained wide awake. The old woman was almost as pale as the snow, and her lips had a blue tinge that Leethan didn't like at all.

"I can't make it," Laurel said softly.

Leethan cursed herself for letting the governess come along. She'd known full well Laurel wasn't up to this long and arduous journey, and yet she'd allowed herself to be persuaded.

"To be honest," Laurel continued, "I never thought I could."

"What?" Leethan exclaimed.

Elwynne made a sleepy sound and snuggled closer to Laurel. Laurel smiled down at the child and rested a hand softly on the side of her head.

"The journey is too long, and the conditions too harsh. I can't feel my toes or the tips of my fingers, and the numbness is spreading." She shook her head. "No, your vision was right when it showed only you and Jaizal and Elwynne. I am not destined to make it all the way to Rhozinolm."

"Visions don't show destinies!" Leethan protested. "What I saw is not the inevitable future. The whole point of visions is to show me what lies ahead so that I may change it." Panic began to flutter in her breast as she remembered how badly she'd failed at changing things in the past. Perhaps she was destined to fail again. Perhaps by bringing Laurel along, she had ruined everything!

"Even so, you have to see the truth of my words," Laurel said, her voice calm and even. "Keeping me with you any longer will only slow you down, and that's something you cannot afford."

Leethan squirmed, wanting very badly to deny it. However, Laurel had fallen behind on multiple occasions today, and logic said even sleep and food were unlikely to be enough to fuel her through the rest of the journey.

"If Jaizal and I carry some of the supplies," Leethan said, "you can ride the second pony."

But Laurel shook her head. "It's hard enough just to walk in this snow. You can't also carry a heavy pack. Besides, riding on a pony won't make me any warmer." She looked down at the sleeping child on her lap and smiled fondly. "Getting Elwynne to safety is the most important thing. My life is almost over anyway, and hers has just begun."

Again, Leethan wanted to protest, but she couldn't.

"There's nothing you can do for me now," Laurel said. "But there is still something I can do for you."

Gently, she shifted Elwynne off her lap, her touch so soft the child didn't even stir.

"At the far side of this valley, the road diverges," she said. "Either route leads to Rhozinolm."

Of course, Leethan knew that from studying the maps. The two routes were almost identical in difficulty, the biggest difference between them being which town in Rhozinolm they came closest to. She had decided on the more northerly route because it would pass near fewer of these small mountain settlements.

"I will rest a little while," Laurel said. "Then, when I feel I am able, I will take the westerly route. I'll take some of Elwynne's things and make sure to 'drop' a couple of them along the way. If anyone catches up with me, the evidence will make them think we went west instead of north. I'll go as far as I can, give you as much time as I can."

"That is not an option," Leethan said firmly. "We will figure something out, and you will come with us."

"No, I will not," Laurel said just as firmly. "You'll either let me go on my own terms, or you'll have to tie me to the pony and haul me like cargo. This was my plan all along, even if it wasn't yours. I came to make sure Elwynne cooperated. And I tucked away an old cloak that was torn beyond mending simply so that I could tear it more and drop swatches along the way when I left you."

Leethan's eyes burned with tears, and when she tried to speak, the lump in her throat refused to let sound escape.

"When she wakes, tell Elwynne that I was too tired to continue and went into the village to find another pony to take me back home. I don't want her worrying about me."

"You would leave her without a goodbye?" Leethan asked through tears that would doubtless freeze on her cheeks if she didn't wipe them away.

Now it was Laurel's eyes that shone with tears. "I have no choice. She mustn't see that I'm continuing on instead of going to the village."

Leethan's heart hurt, and she dreaded facing Elwynne's distress when she woke to find her governess gone. Leethan hoped she could deliver a convincing lie. It would be harder now that Elwynne had already caught her out in one lie, but that meant she would have to be all the more convincing. "Will she want us to turn back, too?"

Laurel shrugged. "Maybe. But although she doesn't understand exactly what's going on, she does understand that she's in danger. If she gets too upset, tell her that you are taking her back to The Keep on a different, quicker route. I think she trusts you enough now to believe it."

Leethan's conscience writhed in discomfort. Not only was she thinking of abandoning an old woman to the elements, she was planning to lie to a child.

"You could go to the village," she suggested. "Seek shelter there."

Laurel's answer was a reproving glance, for of course she could do no such thing. Being captured after absconding with the sovereign prince's daughter was the absolute worst thing that could happen to any of them.

"It will be best for everyone this way," Laurel said gently. "If we continue on together, then either we will eventually be caught, or I'll eventually succumb to the elements. Or both. I *have* to leave."

If Leethan could have thought of another argument, she would happily have employed it. Heart aching, throat too tight for words, she nodded.

• • •

Alys's hands gripped the arms of her chair with such ferocity she wouldn't have been surprised if the wood had splintered. She would very much have liked to hide her emotions, but even the mention of Delnamal's name was enough to drive away her self-control.

The image of Ellinsoltah that the talker projected into the air before her shimmered, and for a moment Alys was afraid she might faint. She put her hand to her stomach, to the stays that constricted her ribs and made it hard to draw a full breath.

"You're sure?" she choked out.

Of course she'd already suspected Delnamal had survived the disaster at the Well, but she'd naïvely assumed he would spend the rest of his life cowering in obscurity until she finally had the means to hunt him down and bring him to justice.

"I'm sure," Ellin said grimly. "My sources tell me that Crown Prince Parlommir has set sail for the Midlands and that Prince Draios has taken the throne for himself."

Alys shook her head in denial. "But it's not possible," she said. According to Ellin's source, Delnamal had used magic to kill the king and some palace guards. "Delnamal never had any special aptitude for magic, and I've never heard of a spell that does what you describe. Surely your sources were mistaken." Up until now, the spell Alys herself had invented—which caused undigested seeds in its victim's stomach to sprout and grow at enormous speed—was the most lethal and terrifying non-Kai-fueled spell she'd ever heard of.

Ellin sighed and gave her a look that was almost maternal, although she was easily young enough to be Alys's daughter. "I would never have brought you this information without thoroughly investigating it first. Draios has taken the throne, and Delnamal helped him do it with some kind of magic that I would think was a Kai spell if I didn't know he'd cast it more than once."

"And that he's still alive," Alys continued faintly.

"Exactly. And we both know that if he has secured the support of Khalpar, he will have that of Par, as well. We must assume that he will want to take back the throne of Aaltah."

Alys groaned. Not so long ago, she'd lamented the fact that Delnamal had died without any help from her. But better she miss out on her revenge than to have him raise an army.

"He'll be coming for Tynthanal and me and Corlin," she said.

"That is my conclusion, as well," Ellin agreed. "I assume his first priority will be to take back Aaltah, but once he does that . . ."

"We can't let him take Aaltah," Alys said.

"Rhozinolm will do what it can to help. I have already spoken with Tynthanal and offered our support. Delnamal didn't make many friends during his brief reign, and I don't think I'll have any trouble convincing my royal council that he must be stopped."

Alys smiled faintly. Ellin's royal council had once been unwilling to agree that the sky was blue, but Delnamal's mismanagement of their trade agreements—and his utter lack of diplomacy—was coming back to bite him. And the retirement of Ellinsoltah's former lord commander—whose loyalty had been questionable, at best—had clearly improved her position.

The smile was short lived. Aaltah's military had been depleted when Tynthanal's company had defected to Women's Well, and had been reduced even further in Delnamal's ill-fated attempt to destroy Women's Well. And with the difficulties they were experiencing with the Well, their treasury was similarly depleted. They were vulnerable in ways they had never been before.

"Yes, he must be stopped," Alys said. "Thank you for sharing your intelligence. You have an impressive spy network."

Ellin nodded her acknowledgment. "A fact for which we should both be grateful. We will need all the intelligence we can gather in the days to come. I will endeavor to have someone meet with Prince Parlommir—or I suppose I should call him King Parlommir—as soon as he arrives in the Midlands. He should have ample motivation to see his throne restored, and thus might eschew his kingdom's prickly relationship with female sovereigns. I'm sure we can obtain even better intelligence from him."

The fact that Parlommir had fled to the Midlands rather than confront the man who'd usurped his throne gave Alys pause. How could Khalvin's youngest son—a young man only seventeen years old and in training to be a priest—have gained enough power to cause the rightful king to flee? Delnamal seemed the most obvious answer to the riddle, and yet she could hardly credit it.

Delnamal was a weak man, so ruled by his emotions and his petty jealousies that he was incapable of being effective at *anything*. He was an indifferent swordsman, a mediocre spell crafter, and a dismal negotiator. How had he become close to Prince Draios? And how could he possibly have the kind of magic that Ellin had described?

A sick sense of dread descended on Alys's shoulders. When Delnamal had "died" in the accident at the Well and Tynthanal had accepted the title of prince regent of Aaltah, it had seemed as if the war she had long feared had been averted. She had finally allowed herself . . . not to *relax,* exactly, but to anticipate the future with something approaching a sense of hope. Her own life might be in shambles—her daughter dead, her son estranged, her heart locked inside an impenetrable fortress—but at least she'd secured the safety of her burgeoning principality.

Now even that comfort was snatched from her, and Alys knew that if she was not very, very careful, she could all too easily lose herself in a tide of despair.

CHAPTER TWENTY-FOUR

"I want to talk to you about something," Tynthanal said one night when he returned to the royal apartments to find Kailee, as always, waiting up for him. He looked exhausted, with bags darkening under his eyes, and she wished he had the luxury to sleep late into the mornings as she did. She'd tried gently suggesting that he cut his days a little shorter so that he needn't attack all the kingdom's ills while battling chronic fatigue, but she hadn't been the least surprised when he'd demurred.

"Uh-oh," she said with a teasing lilt in her voice, although her insides clenched in dread, for she had never enjoyed any conversation that started with those words. "What have I done now?"

He snorted softly. "I am not Lady Vondelmai. I am not here to deliver a scolding."

"Oh, my stepmother was far from the only person to take me to task for my improper behavior," she said with a laugh, relaxing only slightly. In truth, she couldn't think of anything she'd done lately that should especially warrant attention, and Tynthanal was not one to scold. However, she was certain she hadn't misinterpreted the tone of his voice or the slightly ominous tenor of those words.

"Let's sit down," he suggested, shoring up her conviction that she was not going to like this conversation.

Kailee reluctantly took a seat on the sofa beside the fire, and he sat next to her. "What is it?" she asked, clasping her hands together nervously in her lap.

"There's nothing wrong," he assured her, then sighed. "Or at least, nothing new," he corrected, since he'd told her about the murder of King Khalvin and the role Delnamal had played.

"Then what is it I hear in your voice?" she asked.

Tynthanal rubbed his hands together, and she could tell from his aura that he was not looking directly at her. "War is coming," he said. "I don't see any chance that it can be avoided if even half the stories that are coming out of Khalpar are true. And Aaltah will be on the front line of that war."

The thought filled Kailee with dread, for though she had known no war during her lifetime, she had heard too much of the horrors of wars past. And yet even so, it was hardly a surprise.

"I believe we all assumed that was the case after what happened in Khalpar," she said, still not understanding where Tynthanal was going with this.

"Yes, but . . ." He shook his head and took a deep breath, his head turning toward her. "I know you came with me to Aaltah in large part because you wanted to clear Mairahsol's name. You have helped us to discover that she did not cause our Well to be damaged—that she in fact gave her life to protect it. That may not exactly clear her name, but you've done a great deal to help redeem her."

"Your point being?" she asked.

"My point being that you were *happy* in Women's Well, and you gave all that up to come to Aaltah with me. But now that you've done what you could for Mairahsol . . ." He shrugged. "I see no reason why you should have to stay here in Aaltah. Especially when war is looming. You will be both safer and happier in Women's Well."

Kailee's hands clenched in her lap, her lungs going tight so that she could barely catch her breath. "You're sending me away?" she asked, tears prickling her eyes, her voice trembling no matter how hard she tried to keep it steady.

"I'm not *sending* you anywhere," he assured her, putting his hand over both of hers and giving them a warm squeeze. "I'm just pointing out that the reasons you came with me to Aaltah no longer exist, so there's no need for you to stay. Especially when we know danger is coming."

Kailee closed her eyes and swallowed hard, willing herself not to cry, not to let him see how very much his kind offer hurt.

And he *was* being kind, she knew that. He saw how she was shunned by the court, saw how lonely she was, despite the friendship she and Oona were forming. He knew how much she had enjoyed learning magic, which she had been free to do in Women's Well but not here.

In point of fact, she would go back to Women's Well with gladness in her heart—if Tynthanal were coming with her.

What a ninny you're being, she thought. Tynthanal could not have made it more clear that he did not and could not love her. And if for some reason he went back to Women's Well with her, he'd be reunited with Chanlix and his infant daughter. She had *promised* herself not to do this, not to let her heart want something it could not have. And yet here she was nearly crying because he offered her a return to the place where only a few short months ago she had longed to go.

"Please don't cry, sweetheart," he said, giving her hands another squeeze. "I only want you to be happy."

She clenched her eyes more tightly shut, but felt the wetness on her lashes anyway. There was far too much sympathy—pity?—in his voice. She had told herself that although she had failed to guard her heart, she had at least kept her heartache secret. Yet another way she had lied to herself. Tynthanal was far too observant to have missed the signs.

She sucked in a deep, shaking breath, trying for all she was worth to get ahold of her emotions. What he was offering was the clear and practical solution to everything that ailed her. She could go back to Women's Well and bury herself in learning at the Women's Well Academy. The pain would be sharp and fierce at first, but time and distance would ease some of the ache in her heart. It was even possible—though she could barely encompass the thought—that she might fall in love with another. She knew Tynthanal well enough to believe he would not object. He would probably even be happy for her.

These were the things that her logical mind told her, and she willed herself to be sensible.

Instead, she found herself saying, "Please don't send me away. I understand why you want me to go, but—" A hiccup cut off her words, and she couldn't force herself to finish.

Tynthanal sighed and patted her hands, then let go. "I told you I wasn't *sending* you anywhere, and I meant it. Your father has written to me and all but *demanded* I do it, but I'll tell you what I told him: only you get to decide where you will live."

She swiped at the tears on her cheeks. "Am I a liability to you?" she asked. "I had thought once that it would cause you political discomfort if we lived separately, but clearly I am not exactly an asset as your wife."

"Nonsense," he said. "If anyone is a liability in our relationship, it is I. The people of Aaltah were willing to at least pretend to forgive me a great many things as long as I might be the savior of the Well. But my inability to fulfill that role is already beginning to turn public opinion against me. Which is all the more reason for you to return to Women's Well. If public opinion swings too wildly or quickly, you could be in danger simply because you are married to me."

"It's not as bad as all that," she said, though perhaps with her limited contact with the rest of the court, she wasn't in the position to know.

"Not yet, perhaps," he said, although there was just the slightest edge in his voice that suggested things might be worse than he'd let on. "But the risk remains."

Leaving was clearly the sensible thing to do. By staying, she would potentially put herself in danger for the privilege of battering her own heart to pieces day after day. What kind of life was that?

Kailee had always thought of herself as a sensible person, a *smart* person. The kind of person who accepted reality and just got on with it. But apparently, she'd been mistaken.

"I'm staying," she declared.

Tynthanal nodded, and she had the instant impression he was unsurprised by her decision. "Let me know if you change your mind," he said in a tone of weary resignation.

Ellin's stomach growled as she and Zarsha entered the royal apartments after a banquet that had stretched nearly to midnight. She put her hand on her belly as if that would stop the unladylike sounds from escaping and was glad that her husband was the only one to hear.

Zarsha smiled at her and leaned down to press a kiss on her cheek. "I'll have a light supper sent up, shall I?" he asked, but he was already stepping back out the door without awaiting her answer. She suspected he ate as little at these formal banquets as she did, each of them constantly being interrupted as people took the "leisure" of the banquet to approach them "informally." Which generally meant that they had some personal grievance or pet project they knew was not significant enough to earn them a formal audience.

It was tiresome in the extreme, and though Zarsha counseled her to set firmer boundaries, his inability to take his own advice proved it was harder than it sounded.

Zarsha reentered the sitting room, followed closely by Star, who hovered in the doorway. "I've sent word to the kitchens to send up a tray, Your Majesty," she said with a curtsy. "Would you prefer to undress now, or after you've eaten?"

Zarsha gave her a significant look, and she sighed silently. She knew that look. He'd learned something over the course of the banquet that he needed to speak with her about. She was eager to get out of the stays and her heavy brocade gown, and as always, her scalp itched and burned from the tightly pinned hair that was required to keep her formal headdress in place. But the gown and the headdress were in some ways her armor against the stresses of affairs of state, and she didn't feel prepared to discuss anything upsetting in her nightdress—and when Zarsha had that look in his eyes, it was always a sign of an upsetting conversation on the horizon.

"After, I think," she said. "Thank you, Star."

Star bowed her head and retreated, closing the sitting room door with a firm thunk. Ellin arched an eyebrow in Zarsha's direction, and he gestured her toward a pair of chairs before the merrily crackling fire.

"Uh-oh," she murmured softly. "I always seem to get distressing news when I'm sitting in that chair."

Zarsha laughed. "Don't blame the chair, love. It is but an innocent bystander."

Ellin sniffed, but felt oddly reassured. Zarsha was certainly prone to making jokes at inappropriate moments, but whatever news he bore couldn't be *too* bad even so. She sat and took a moment to close her eyes and enjoy the warmth of the fire after having traversed the chilly hallways from the banquet hall to the royal apartments. Then, she met her husband's gaze.

"What has happened?" she asked, bracing herself despite her own reassurances.

"I can't for the life of me decide whether this is good news or bad," he answered, "but it appears the Abbess of Nandel has fled the Abbey—and has taken Princess Elwynne with her."

Ellin's mouth dropped open in shock. Whatever she'd been expecting, it wasn't *this*. She shivered again in a phantom chill, glancing toward the window at the far end of the room, where a lacing of frost caught the flickering light of the fire. If it was cold in Rhozinolm today, she couldn't imagine what it must be like in the mountains of Nandel.

"It's being kept *very* quiet," Zarsha continued, "for obvious reasons."

Ellin snorted. "Most sovereigns would *not* keep quiet about it if a child of theirs was kidnapped. They'd be recruiting rescuers from every corner of their kingdom."

"Not in Nandel, they wouldn't," Zarsha argued. "Even if Waldmir had no doubts about her paternity, her abduction is an insult to his pride. *Especially* when it was perpetrated by his first ex-wife. He will want Elwynne *quietly* returned."

Ellin shivered again as she imagined the Nandel weather. Traveling in Nandel during the winter was always a perilous proposition. "Are you sure about that?" she asked, biting her lip with worry. "Might this not be some ploy to rid himself of a child he does not want?"

Zarsha's immediate dismissal of the possibility was comforting. "My uncle is not a good man, but he is not a murderer of children." His lips twisted into a bitter grin. "And if he *were* to decide to do something so heinous, you can be sure it would be an 'accident,' and not something that would cause him personal embarrassment like this."

The conversation was momentarily interrupted when Star delivered a tray from the kitchens, setting it on the small table between the chairs. By now, Star knew both of them too well to bother asking if they'd prefer to have the tray laid out in their private dining room.

Anxiety had chased away her appetite, but a waft of fragrant steam from the tray soon coaxed it from hiding. She glanced up at Star and smiled, realizing that the food had arrived far faster than expected for a hot meal.

Star returned the smile with a twinkle in her eyes. "You are always hungry after a formal banquet," she said simply. "Everything was already set aside and needed only warming to be ready."

"You are a national treasure," Ellin said.

"I couldn't agree more," Zarsha added.

Star gave him a haughty sniff, and Ellin stifled a laugh. Star's opinion of Zarsha careened wildly from near adoration to disdain, depending on how she felt he was treating Ellin at the moment. Her sniff suggested she was annoyed with Zarsha for keeping her obviously tired lady from going to bed immediately.

Star retreated, and Ellin's stomach gave another grumble, her appetite now fully restored by the enticing aromas.

"Eat first," Zarsha advised as he plucked a savory stuffed pastry puff from the basket that produced the most mouthwatering aromas. The pastry glistened with spiced oil that left an inelegant sheen on Zarsha's fingertips.

Ellin sighed with feigned exasperation. "Nandelites and their table manners," she lamented with a click of her tongue, spearing her own pastry with a fork and spreading a napkin on her lap to catch any errant crumbs.

"Barbarians," Zarsha agreed with his mouth full. Then he waggled his brows at her and licked the oil from his fingers. The gesture would have been seductive were it not for the worry in his eyes.

Ellin downed the pastry to still the complaints of her stomach as she tried to understand what the Abbess of Nandel had meant by abducting Princess Elwynne. Ellin knew nothing about the woman. She wouldn't even have known Mother Leethan had been Waldmir's first wife if Zarsha hadn't reminded her.

"Do you have any idea what the abbess is up to?" she asked. "Has she . . . made any demands?"

Zarsha waved that concern off. "I can't say I know Mother Leethan well—I was a child and living away from court when Waldmir divorced her—but I cannot imagine she means Elwynne harm."

"Do you suppose Leethan knows the child is not Waldmir's?" Ellin asked. Then, "*May* not be Waldmir's," she amended before Zarsha could correct her. He loved and protected little Elwynne as if he were certain she was his daughter, but Waldmir had never had a paternity test performed, both because it would require the use of women's magic—which was forbidden in Nandel—and because he considered the child tainted no matter who her father might be.

"She may have guessed it, or suspect it. Perhaps she saw danger for Elwynne when Waldmir sent her to 'visit' the Abbey and decided to spirit her away."

Ellin frowned skeptically. "So she decided to abscond with the child when the snows have already started? Seems an odd sort of protection."

Zarsha drummed his fingers against his leg, his face looking even paler than usual. No doubt he knew better than she the dangers of traveling through the mountains of Nandel at this time of year.

"Where could she have gone?" Ellin mused. "Where could she reasonably get to that she might hope to be safe?"

"Nowhere in Nandel," Zarsha answered immediately. "She apparently left the Abbey with Elwynne, Elwynne's governess, and another senior abigail. They took two ponies, and left in the middle of the night. Three old women and a girl child traveling without male escort would be conspicuous anywhere in Nandel. Even if they had friends or family who were willing to help them—and that is not the case—they would be far too noticeable entering any settlement."

"But it would be an impossibly long way from the Abbey to the Nandel border at this time of year," Ellin protested. "Would any of these women be accustomed to traveling through the mountains unaccompanied?"

She already knew the answer to her own question. The women of Nandel were the property of the men in their lives, and thus were hardly taught to be self-sufficient.

"It seems impossible and reckless in the extreme," Zarsha agreed. "How could three women over the age of sixty and one five-year-old girl hope to traverse the mountains—while being hunted, no less?" He ran a hand through his hair, his blue eyes pinched with worry and perplexity. "And *why* would they do it? Why *now*?"

Ellin shook her head. She could only imagine one or more of those women had felt they were under imminent threat such that the journey seemed the lesser of two evils.

"Do you hold out any hope that they'll make it?" she asked as gently as she could. It was clear from his expression that any hopes he might have were fragile.

Zarsha swallowed hard, then sucked in a deep breath. "I have to believe there's hope." He met her eyes. "And I cannot imagine they would have any destination in mind but Rhozinolm. I presume Mother Leethan still has family living in Grunir, which is where she was born, but they almost certainly would have disowned her when she was divorced, and it is a very long way to go."

Ellin agreed. "I would have to think the most likely scenario is that they have some reason to believe you might be Elwynne's father—and that the child is for some reason in danger. Perhaps someone in the Abbey has figured it out and threatened to tell?"

"I don't know," Zarsha said. "But what I *do* know is that Waldmir will assume they are coming here."

Ellin groaned as she easily followed that thought to its unpleasant conclusion. "And that you—or *we*—had something to do with her abduction."

He nodded. "It isn't as if we haven't spoken wistfully before about spiriting her away. When he gives up on keeping the whole thing secret, you can bet he will be contacting us demanding we extradite the women he will call traitors."

Ellin sat back in her chair and folded her arms across her chest. "He can 'demand' all he wants. Do you honestly think I would send that child back to him after everything you've told me?"

He looked at his hands. "I don't think you'd *want* to. But the diplomatic incident would be . . . damaging."

Ellin knew he was right. She also knew that her royal council—which was a great deal more loyal now than it had been throughout her short reign so far—would balk at insulting such a powerful trade partner. However . . .

"Waldmir can no longer hold our trade agreements over us," she said. "Our alliance is signed and sealed, and he has a great deal less leverage than he once enjoyed." Leverage he had used with ruthless efficiency in his personal vendetta against Zarsha. "If we have Elwynne here safe in Rhozinolm, there would be nothing stopping us from revealing the truth about her parentage and his need to use potency potions. Save a very practical desire not to see the principality that provides the majority of our gems and iron devolve into a civil war."

"So you would give her shelter here?" he asked with a fragile thread of hope in his voice.

"Of course I would," she said, fighting off a stab of hurt. She understood why he doubted her. When she had initially learned of his dalliance with Brontyn and the possibility that Elwynne was his child, she had taken it quite poorly indeed, and she had harbored that grievance for far longer than was logically justified. But she could honestly say that she now genuinely cared for the child, if only because *Zarsha* cared so much.

"We should send word to the towns nearest the Nandel border and have them on the lookout. If Mother Leethan and the rest should arrive, we can have them brought immediately to Zinolm Well."

Zarsha closed his eyes in relief. "Thank you."

She reached over and put a hand over his. "I'll also make sure to dispatch healers, in case their services are needed. If it is humanly possible to do so, we will bring her here safely, and she need never fear Waldmir again."

CHAPTER TWENTY-FIVE

Leethan had forgotten what it felt like to be comfortably warm as the days and nights passed in a welter of shivering misery and struggle. The three of them rested whenever they happened upon shelter, huddled together for some semblance of warmth. Elwynne had barely spoken a word since Laurel had "turned back," and Leethan was certain the child knew she was being lied to. Guilt ate at her, and she wished she had worked harder to convince Laurel to stay behind in the safety of the Abbey, even while she admitted to herself that it had not been possible.

If not for the sturdy ponies, Leethan doubted any of them would have made it out of Nandel alive. Their shaggy coats protected them in even the coldest weather, and as the rations and supplies dwindled, Leethan and Jaizal took turns riding on the baggage pony. The animal occasionally gave them baleful looks and threatened to balk, but it was apparently as eager to have the journey over with as they, for it bore its burdens and continued forward.

Leethan had lost all track of time, days and nights blurring together as they toiled through the snow and cold. Probably the only thing that saved them was that the weather gentled after that first snowstorm. The skies remained gloomy and gray, but no further snow fell, and the winds were chilling but relatively mild.

Leethan began to believe their impossible journey might actually succeed when she felt the occasional popping in her ears, which told her that they were finally beginning their descent. Slowly but surely, the air became warmer, the bite of the wind less sharp. The clouds parted, and on one glorious night when the temperature was almost comfortable, they spotted the lights of a settlement in the distance.

"That will be Falcon's Ridge," Leethan said, her heart leaping with hope.

"So we've made it," Jaizal said, her shoulders stooped with exhaustion and her voice weak. For the last two days of travel, she had spent most of her time riding, her joints stiff and swollen and aching. Leethan was the older of the two by three years, but Jaizal's years had been harder on her body. More than once during the journey, Leethan had feared her oldest friend would not pull through.

"Almost," Leethan said, studying her friend's face in the fading twilight. The town was likely farther away than it appeared, but her soul cried out for them to keep going through the night and reach it as quickly as possible. The deep hollows in Jaizal's cheeks and the squint of pain in her eyes persuaded her otherwise. "One more night of camping," she said in her most cheerful voice, "and tomorrow night we will sleep on real beds with a fire to warm our bones and food to fill our bellies."

"Is that Rhozinolm?" Elwynne asked, startling Leethan. She could not remember the child speaking when not spoken to first, at least not since Laurel had left them.

"Yes, child," Leethan told her, trying to read Elwynne's strangely inscrutable face. In all her years, she had never before met a child so young who was so skilled at hiding her feelings, and she had the unsettling certainty that Waldmir was to blame.

Waldmir had never been an especially warm and loving father to any of his daughters, but Leethan had always felt there was genuine affection behind his seeming indifference. She had no such sense with poor Elwynne, and she hoped the child would blossom now that she'd escaped the shadow of his thinly veiled disapproval.

Elwynne frowned pensively at the lights in the distance. "Papa says the people of Rhozinolm raise their children like wild animals. I don't want to be a wild animal."

Leethan wondered how *that* topic had come up. Up until now, Elwynne had ventured no opinion one way or another about the prospect of visiting a foreign land, but Leethan saw a flash of worry in the child's eyes in a rare, unguarded moment. Laurel had told Elwynne they were going to Rhozinolm to visit her cousin Zarsha, and the child had accepted the explanation with no questions.

"Your father has never been to Rhozinolm," Leethan said. "I have." Only once, and only when she was traveling from Grunir to Nandel for her wedding, but it was more than Waldmir had ever done. "Some of the children there are well behaved, and some aren't. Just like in Nandel. You will not become a wild animal."

Elwynne nodded and chewed her lip, still visibly anxious. Leethan didn't know how to reassure her, so instead she helped the child dismount from the pony and prepared their meager camp, hopefully for the last time.

Despite careful rationing, they were almost out of food. The ponies eyed their supper of dried meat hungrily, for their feed had run out the night before.

"You'll have some grass to munch on in the morning," Leethan told the creatures, laughing at herself a little for feeling guilty about eating in front of them.

Elwynne soon fell asleep, but Jaizal remained wide awake, though weariness showed plainly in her face.

"You should sleep, too," Leethan chided. She herself was too busy imagining the pleasures of a comfortable bed and a hot meal to consign herself to the misery of the bedroll yet.

"We haven't talked about how we're going to present ourselves in Rhozinolm tomorrow," Jaizal said.

Leethan realized with a start that Jaizal was right. Perhaps a part of her had never quite expected them to make it so far.

"Surely we will not admit our true identities," Jaizal continued. "We might find ourselves arrested for kidnapping."

And sent back to Nandel to be executed for their crimes, she did not say, but both of them knew full well what would happen if Rhozinolm chose not to give them shelter.

"No," Leethan agreed, thinking furiously. The three of them hardly looked like dangerous or suspicious characters, and yet their arrival from Nandel at this time of year—unaccompanied by any male escorts and dressed in men's clothing—was bound to raise questions.

They were an odd little party, to be sure. Leethan's dark skin and the strands of auburn hair that had not yet succumbed to gray were enough to mark her as not a native Nandelite, while both Jaizal and Elwynne obviously were. Elwynne bore no resemblance to either of them, and while Jaizal spoke a smattering of Continental, Elwynne was too young to have started language lessons and spoke only Mountain Tongue.

"I think I must claim Elwynne as my granddaughter," Leethan said. "That would probably be believed despite our lack of resemblance. And you can be her governess."

"And why are we traveling at this time of year—without a male escort and dressed as men?"

Leethan groaned softly. "I'll try to come up with a good story in the morning," she promised. "Right now, I'm too exhausted to be creative. And besides, it's possible we won't be asked much of anything at all. Anyone we meet might assume we are women fleeing the oppression of life in Nandel and refrain from asking us any questions. Especially when we have a small girl with us. The prospect of raising a girl child in Nandel is not a comfortable one to those who live elsewhere in Seven Wells."

Jaizal's doubt was clear in her eyes. She had lived all her life in Nandel and could not comprehend how differently women were treated elsewhere in Seven Wells. Indeed, even Leethan could hardly remember what it was like to have rights and freedom.

"And what will we do if you are right? How will we get to Zinolm Well? How will we—?"

"Jaizal, please," Leethan said, pinching the bridge of her nose. "One problem at a time. When we are safely in Falcon's Ridge, I'll send a flier to Prince Zarsha. I have to believe the Mother of All sent us here for a reason and that Zarsha will help us."

"Even though doing so will risk Rhozinolm's trade agreements with Nandel?" Jaizal asked.

Leethan let out a long, slow sigh. "Even so."

The last time Delnamal had set foot in a dungeon had been more than two years ago, long before his enlightenment. Then, he had found the dungeons of Aalwell depressing and oppressive, and he remembered quite clearly how badly he had wanted to turn around and flee. He marveled now at how weak and easily swayed he had once been. Even knowing that the prisoners had been locked up in the dungeon because they had deserved it, he had felt pity for them and preferred not to be faced with their suffering.

How different was the experience now, as he descended into the dungeons of Khalwell, flanked by two of Draios's loyal soldiers who would ensure that his visit encountered no protests. He breathed deep the wretched smell of pain and despair, and searched his soul for a reaction, *any* reaction. But he entered the lair of human misery with neither pleasure nor dismay. Truth be told, he didn't *care* about the dungeon one way or another. What he cared about was the reward that awaited him in the dungeon's darkest corner.

Delnamal leaned on his cane as he made his way down the narrow flight of stairs into the dungeon's lowest level, where those who had been condemned to death awaited their fates. He could have managed the stairs without the cane in a pinch, but the strength that had infused him when he had killed King Khalvin and his guards was finally beginning to ebb. Draios had agreed that it was crucial to their plans that he maintain—and even grow—his strength, and the boy had invited him to partake of the condemned without ever realizing he had not come up with the idea himself.

Delnamal smiled faintly as he reached the lowest level, pleased with the usefulness of the tool that fate had put into his hands. Draios was half-drunk on his own power already, planning the coming war with giddy excitement. His elder brother was still nominally king, and Draios a traitor, but with Parlommir and his small crew of loyalists having fled across the sea to the Midlands, there had been little to no resistance as Draios took his seat on his late father's throne.

Draios, Delnamal had found, was not a particularly rousing or persuasive speaker, for he had a tendency to resort too quickly to threats and intimidation. However, the man he'd appointed to the position of lord high priest was a different story. Having the young prince to thank for his unexpected elevation, the lord high priest had set to his mission of convincing first the priesthood and then the general population of the righteousness of the cause with great dedication and skill.

Soon, Draios would declare *Parlommir* the traitor and name himself king outright. And because he now had a stranglehold on the clergy, no one would dare gainsay him. Already, the priests were darkly hinting at the need to provide the populace with forceful demonstrations that belief in the holy war to take back the throne of Aaltah was not optional or subject to debate. Delnamal expected there would soon be a wave of arrests of those declared heretics for opposing the war.

Delnamal stopped by the first cell and looked at the miserable creature who resided within. A cadaverously skinny, pale man with his hair and beard matted with filth and his feet scabbed and broken with torture, stared at Delnamal with dull, suffering eyes. Eyes of a man who should welcome death. Even so, the prisoner took one look at Delnamal, then retreated to the farthest corner of the tiny cell, pressing himself hard against the cold stone walls and shaking.

A guard made to open the cell door, but Delnamal waved him off. At first, he had always touched his victims when stealing their Rhokai, but in the king's audience chamber, he had found he could reach the Rhokai from some distance. Now, he was inclined to test just how close he had to be.

Licking his lips in anticipation, as if the Rhokai would actually *taste* good, he opened his Mindseye. The prisoner's Rhokai shone with flashes of purple in the darkness even as the black outer shell seemed to disappear in the gloom. Delnamal reached his hand through the bars toward that Rhokai mote, beckoning it to him.

The prisoner made a choked sound of pain, and Delnamal smiled contentedly. He backed away one step at a time, trying to see how far he could go before he lost his virtual grip on that mote. There was so much he didn't yet understand about the nature and function of Rhokai, and he was very much looking forward to exploring its myriad mysteries. What happened to a person's Rhokai when he or she died a natural death? Or an accidental one? And what happened when a mote of Kai made contact with a mote of Rhokai? Was Delnamal's theory that the contact would break the Rhokai correct? Draios was just as interested in the results as he himself, and thus would allow him a shocking amount of latitude to experiment with the wretches in the dungeon.

He made it almost all the way to the far wall of the cell block—

which, granted, wasn't terribly large—before his grip finally slipped. The prisoner gave a sob of relief, but Delnamal did not allow him that reprieve for long. Two quick strides brought him firmly back into range, and he reached for the mote again.

With a gentle exertion of will, he urged the Rhokai to come to him. For a moment, it resisted, quivering in the man's chest as if loath to leave him. The prisoner moaned, and behind him, Delnamal heard the uncomfortable shifting of the guards who had accompanied him. But it was important that people see his power, that people know it was a power not of this world and therefore must have been granted to him by the Creator. *This* series of executions would be carried out in private, but there would be more to come, and Delnamal was determined that the next set become a public spectacle. Oh, how zealots loved to smite those they declared the enemy! The people of Khalpar would soon fall to their knees and worship him!

The prisoner gave a last sharp cry—one that set the rest of the prisoners shouting and weeping in terror—and then his Rhokai popped free and shattered. Delnamal had to bite his tongue to suppress a moan of near sexual ecstasy as the power filled him and the released mote of Kai joined the rest in his aura.

He savored that first glorious new mote, reveling in the strength that filled his limbs, at the renewed vigorous thumping of his heart.

Then, he moved on to the next cell.

Alys activated first the talker that connected to Tynthanal, and then the one that connected to Ellinsoltah, watching as the images of the other two rulers shimmered to life. She had never tried using two talkers at once before, but she'd seen no reason why it *wouldn't* work, and her assumption proved accurate.

Ellinsoltah looked at Alys with a smile that was half amazement, half amusement, then looked to her left. Alys could only assume she was looking at an image of Tynthanal, although thanks to the placement of Alys's talkers, it looked like she was staring at nothing. Alys quickly rearranged her talkers just to save herself the confusion.

"Three sovereigns meeting in one room," Ellin said. "Who would have thought of such a thing only a year or two ago?"

Alys and Tynthanal shared a smile, for they had invented the talkers working together, and they were by far the most sought-after magical export from Women's Well. They received orders even from Nandel, despite that principality's vaunted disgust at the very concept of women's magic.

It did not take long for Tynthanal's smile to be replaced by a deeply troubled expression that made Alys's hands clench in her lap. Of course he would not have requested this meeting to share *good* news, and Ellinsoltah was as aware of that reality as Alys.

"I have been hearing . . ." Ellin frowned and hesitated. "Let's just say *worrisome* reports from Khalpar. None of which I have yet been able to verify to my satisfaction."

Tynthanal grimaced and held up a scrolled letter for them to see. "I don't know what you've heard," he said, "but however worrisome you might have found it, the truth is almost certainly worse."

Alys cocked her head to the side, trying to decipher the few lines of writing that were visible on the letter. The handwriting looked vaguely familiar, although she could not immediately place it, and the image was too small for her to make out words.

"I did not think Aaltah would have much of a spy network left in Khalpar," she said, for Delnamal had so enraged what had once been Aaltah's staunchest ally that King Khalvin had expelled the vast majority of Aaltah's diplomats.

"We don't," Tynthanal confirmed. He unfurled the letter and held it close to the talker so that Alys could see the precise and elegant signature at its close.

"Xanvin!" she gasped, half exclamation and half question.

Lowering the letter, Tynthanal nodded grimly. "Indeed. As we assumed, she and Delnamal took refuge in Khalpar and had, until recently, been living in quiet obscurity in the countryside."

"Is she . . . is she all right?" Alys asked hesitantly. Her relationship with her stepmother had never been close, having started during her childhood with active hostility and then softened over time to grudging acceptance and respect. Alys found the woman's blind devotion to Delnamal—and her ardent religious fervor, which she felt compelled to try to impose on everyone around her—annoying to say the least, but she would not want any harm to come to her.

"She is," Tynthanal assured her. "Delnamal left her in the countryside when he and Draios went to court, and she is well enough."

"And how does she feel about Delnamal murdering her brother?" Alys asked. The fact that Xanvin had written to Tynthanal at all suggested that finally—*finally*—Delnamal had committed an atrocity even a mother's devotion could not allow her to ignore.

Tynthanal looked down at the letter in his hand and shook his head. "She apparently began this letter *before* she learned of Khalvin's death, but the assassination is what finally caused her to send it." His face lost a little of its color as his eyes scanned the text. Text Alys suspected he had already memorized. "What she has to say . . ." He sighed and scrubbed a hand through his hair. "Well, it sounds pretty crazy."

"Even after what we've heard about the circumstances of King Khalvin's death?" Ellin inquired, and Tynthanal conceded the point.

What followed, however, was more frightening than anything Alys could have anticipated, and she listened in rapt horror as Tynthanal read sections of Xanvin's letter describing the change that had come over Delnamal since the accident at the Well.

If Alys had not already heard the story of Khalvin's death, she would have dismissed out of hand Xanvin's description of how Delnamal had killed first a bird, then a hapless servant by removing what she called the "Rhokai" mote that lay at the center of every living being. But worse even than the terrifying and impossible power that Delnamal now possessed was the story he had woven around that power and somehow convinced the zealous Prince Draios to accept.

"'My son claims that he has been chosen by the Creator to set the world back to rights after the casting of the Curse,'" Tynthanal read from Xanvin's letter. "'He and Prince Draios intend to embark on what they are terming a holy war, and there is no question in my mind that they intend to reconquer Aaltah and attempt some form of magic against its Well.

"'I know you and my son have never been friends, but I hope you will acknowledge that the Delnamal you grew up with did in fact care about the well-being of Aaltah and took his responsibility as crown prince with great seriousness.'" Tynthanal's lip curled in distaste as he read this part, and he looked up from the letter to meet Alys's eyes.

"The Delnamal I grew up with whined incessantly about how burdensome his duties were and how terrible it was to always have to live up to so many expectations." He sighed. "But I suppose he wouldn't have found the duties and expectations so onerous if he didn't take them seriously, and he was certainly never anything close to a religious fanatic. He tolerated Xanvin's attempt to teach us all piety with the same mostly polite disinterest that you and I did."

Alys shrugged. "So what is Xanvin's point?"

Tynthanal scanned down the letter a little farther, then began to read again. "'I know your lack of faith will cause you to regard my own claims with as much skepticism as you regard Delnamal's, but I believe he could not have the power he has demonstrated if he were not being guided by a divine hand. However, I do not for a moment believe that the hand guiding him is that of the Creator.

" 'The Delnamal I raised, the son I loved and cherished, is gone. In his place is a hollow husk that has been filled with darkness. I do not understand how or why it has happened, but I believe my son's body is now inhabited by the spirit of the Destroyer. And that spirit will not stop at the conquest of Aaltah, nor even Women's Well. All of Seven Wells is in danger, and the Destroyer *must* be stopped.' "

Tynthanal shook his head and lowered the letter, looking back and forth between Alys and Ellin. A long, uncomfortable silence descended, and Alys had no idea what to do with it. A part of her wanted to laugh at the absurdity of it all, for in her heart of hearts, she had to admit to deep doubts as to the very existence of either the Creator or the Destroyer.

Eventually, Ellin broke the silence. "Unfortunately, some of the disturbing—and not yet fully verified—rumors I've heard lend some credence to Queen Xanvin's letter, although I am loath to ascribe any of what I've heard to the will of the gods."

"What have you heard?" Tynthanal asked, and Ellin told him of a rumor her spies had encountered, which claimed that Delnamal was somehow "feeding" himself—with Draios's cooperation—on unfortunate prisoners awaiting execution.

"As hard as it all is to believe," Ellin concluded, "I think we must act on the assumption that he does indeed have the powers Queen Xanvin claims. And if he and Prince Draios can truly convince the people of Khalpar that theirs is some kind of holy mission . . ." She shook her head, looking haunted. "I have heard that Khalpar is mustering troops, and it appears Par is doing so, as well. Perhaps a little more reluctantly—I'm told they are more inclined to ask questions about the circumstances of Khalvin's death and Parlommir's hasty departure—but they are in no position to make an enemy of Draios and Khalpar."

Alys groaned quietly, for the small island of Par had always marched in lockstep with its larger and far more powerful neighbor. When Delnamal had "died" and Tynthanal had become the Prince Regent of Aaltah, she'd allowed herself to hope that war no longer loomed on the horizon. Now, it seemed war was inevitable.

"Is there any chance we can reach a diplomatic arrangement with Prince Draios?" Alys asked, although if Delnamal had truly convinced the young prince that he was obeying the will of the Creator, it seemed unlikely.

Tynthanal shook his head. "I sent him formal condolences on behalf of Aaltah on the death of his father. He sent the flier back in pieces."

Alys winced, for Draios's father had responded in a similar manner when Alys had tried to contact him on behalf of Women's Well last year.

"There is to be no pretense of alliance or even tolerance anymore, it seems," Tynthanal finished. He scowled. "Certain members of the royal council have, of course, suggested that Draios's quarrel is with *me* rather than with Aaltah, and that if I'd just step down and let someone else be prince regent . . ." He sighed and shook his head. "You have no idea how tempting that might be."

Ellin snorted as she made eye contact with Alys. "You think not?"

Alys smiled briefly. How many times had she herself yearned for the halcyon days when she'd been an ordinary wife and mother, with no greater responsibilities than raising her children and managing her household?

But it was no laughing matter. The council had chosen to appoint Tynthanal to the position because he was the infant king's closest living male relative, and because they had believed Tynthanal, with his magical talents and his close ties to Women's Well, would find a way to repair the Well. If they began to see him as the reason for Khalpar's aggression, however . . . Thanks to the spell their mother had cast and the upheavals it had created, it would be frighteningly easy for him to transform in their eyes from a savior to a scapegoat.

"Perhaps you *should* offer to step down," she suggested. "Before things get any uglier than they already are."

But Tynthanal shook his head. "You know as well as I do that Delnamal would still want to wage war on Aaltah. He will want his throne and his power back, and he won't care if he has to raze Aalwell to the ground to get it."

Alys gave him a reproving look. "You know perfectly well that wasn't why I suggested you step down." Certainly she didn't need him to tell her about the mingled rage and entitlement that brewed in their half-brother's breast. He had been a terrible king, and she doubted even the power he had wielded had given him much in the way of joy or pleasure. But it *belonged* to him, and he was not one to give up his belongings without a fight.

"I'm not unaware of the danger," Tynthanal assured her. "Since I've shown no demonstrable progress in fixing the Well, I'm certain I would already have been ousted if my detractors could choose a single candidate to rally around." He laughed darkly. "In some ways, the threat from Khalpar and Delnamal may actually *strengthen* my position, redirecting the anger to where it belongs."

Alys shook her head, wishing she felt as certain as he seemed to. But she knew her brother well, and he was not the kind of man who would abandon Aaltah for his own safety. "You aren't the only one who could be in danger," she reminded him, though she was sure he was already aware of that.

Tynthanal nodded and turned to Ellin. "Might you be willing to host Prince Corlin for an extended visit should the atmosphere here in Aaltah prove inhospitable?"

Alys experienced a flood of relief at the suggestion, even as she regarded Ellin curiously. As often as they had spoken, and as warm as their relationship might be, Alys had not confided in her about Corlin's exile. She had, in fact, kept the situation as quiet as possible while still assuring Smithson and his parents that Corlin was being appropriately punished for almost killing his fellow cadet in a fit of rage.

Ellinsoltah showed no sign of surprise or puzzlement about why Tynthanal wouldn't merely send his nephew home if the environment in Aaltah soured. Rhozinolm was Women's Well's closest ally, but that didn't mean its spy network wasn't keeping tabs.

"We would be happy to have him. It is never too early to begin getting to know the young man who will one day be Sovereign Prince of Women's Well." She smiled, and though the expression was slightly practiced—a court smile, rather than a heartfelt one—Alys detected a hint of warmth in it.

"Let us hope it will never be necessary and that he may one day visit simply for the pleasure of making your acquaintance," Tynthanal said.

But Alys didn't think any of the three of them was in a particularly hopeful or optimistic state of mind.

CHAPTER TWENTY-SIX

Leethan stared anxiously out the window as the cheval-drawn carriage clattered through the sleepy streets of Zinolm Well. Elwynne lay on the seat across from her, wrapped in her fur cloak and sleeping the sound sleep of the exhausted.

The full moon shone bright and clear in the cloudless sky, its light strong enough to cast shadows. Leethan did not know exactly how late it was, but she was sure it was easily late enough to proclaim it early morning. She, too, should be sleeping—her body certainly kept sending her signals that she was in dire need of rest—but anxiety would not allow her to shut her eyes.

After all the time and effort she and Jaizal had put into concocting a cover story to explain their presence in Rhozinolm, it turned out they needn't have bothered. Rhozinolm's spies had already known they were coming, and there had been men in Falcon's Ridge waiting for them. Briefly, she'd feared they would be immediately sent back to Nandel, but it quickly became clear that wasn't the case. They were whisked into what appeared to be a private home and found that there was a healer waiting to see them, as well.

Leethan was thankful for Queen Ellinsoltah's care, for though

Princess Elwynne suffered from nothing worse than dehydration and bone-deep exhaustion, both Leethan and Jaizal had sustained some frostbite. Without the immediate treatment, Leethan might well have lost a couple of toes, and Jaizal was in considerably worse condition despite her lack of complaints. So much so that their escorts had insisted Jaizal remain behind under the healer's care for a few days while Leethan and Elwynne continued on to Zinolm Well.

Leethan would have demurred and stayed with her stricken friend, but though the men sent to escort them were dressed in civilian clothes and phrased their demands as "recommenda-tions," she was well aware that they were soldiers following or-ders. If they said she must continue on immediately to Zinolm Well, then she would be continuing on whether she wanted to or not.

The distance between Falcon's Ridge and Zinolm Well was far greater than the distance between Falcon's Ridge and The Keep, and yet with the aid of the cheval-drawn carriage and well-kept direct roads, they crossed through the walls of Zinolm Well the day after they'd first set foot in Rhozinolm.

Well, Leethan mentally corrected, it was technically *two* days later considering the hour, but it felt like an unbearably swift journey after the brutal labor of crossing the mountains on foot.

Her escorts had been painstakingly polite, yet frustratingly uninformative. She did not know exactly where she was being taken, or what her reception would be when she arrived. Obvi-ously, if Queen Ellinsoltah had known to expect her, Prince Waldmir had guessed she would head for Rhozinolm as well, and there was not a doubt in Leethan's mind that he had forcefully demanded she and Elwynne be returned to Nandel immediately. She took hope from the fact that they had been summoned to Zinolm Well, but still she feared this great kingdom might feel too dependent on the iron and gems from Nandel to defy Prince Waldmir—even if Zarsha did his best to help them.

The carriage arrived at its destination, which appeared to be yet another private home—one that just like the home in Falcon's Ridge she assumed was property of the Crown. But when Leethan made to step out of the carriage, the soldier who'd opened the door put out a hand to stop her.

"We will put Princess Elwynne to bed here," he said at a whisper, though truth be told the child would probably sleep through a full-throated shout in her condition. "You will have to wait a little longer to take your rest, I'm afraid."

Leethan swayed from a combination of exhaustion and alarm. "I am serving as the princess's guardian," she protested. "I can't just *leave* her."

The soldier made a soothing, patting motion with his hand—one which failed to soothe her in the least. "She is safe here. Queen Ellinsoltah has guaranteed both her safety and yours. You need not fear."

"I think that's for me to decide, not you," she said, too tired and anxious to bother being diplomatic.

To the soldier's credit, he took her quip in stride. "We can bring her with us if that would put your mind at ease. But she will be more comfortable in a bed, and she is clearly badly in need of sleep."

Behind the soldier, a sturdy, cheerful-looking woman emerged from the house. In the bright light of the moon, Leethan could clearly see from the pallor of the woman's skin and the wisps of blond hair that peeked through her headdress that the woman was of Nandelite ancestry. A fact that was confirmed when the woman smiled at her and spoke to her in fluent Mountain Tongue.

"You must be Lady Leethan," she said. "My name is Jewel, and I have been hired to look after Princess Elwynne, as we understand her governess did not arrive with her."

Leethan's eyes suddenly stung with tears. Tears she might easily have fought off if not for the exhaustion and the anxiety. At some point, Elwynne was going to learn the truth about what *really* happened to her governess, and she was going to hate both Leethan and Jaizal for the deception.

Embarrassed at her show of frailty, Leethan dabbed at the corners of her eyes and took a steadying breath. The circumstances of her life had not inclined her to trust easily, but they *had* taught her the importance of accepting reality. If Ellinsoltah's soldiers meant to rip Princess Elwynne from her and send the poor child back to Nandel, there was absolutely nothing she could do to stop them.

Leethan nodded at Jewel, her throat too tight to manage a polite greeting, and returned to her seat.

"Poor lamb," Jewel said softly as she climbed into the carriage, glancing at Leethan in a way that suggested she was not merely speaking of Elwynne.

Jewel slipped her arms under Elwynne and easily picked the girl up, her touch so gentle Elwynne barely stirred. Leethan envied the younger woman her strength, for she herself felt so weak she wasn't sure she could have lifted the fur cloak, much less the child.

"I will take good care of her until you return," Jewel promised.

"She is not good with strangers," Leethan fretted, hating the thought of Elwynne waking up in a strange room with no one familiar nearby to reassure her.

Jewel smiled down at Elwynne's face. "I suspect she will sleep for some hours still now that she is warm and comfortable. You will likely be back before she wakes, and if not . . ." She shrugged, as much as such a thing was possible with a sleeping child in her arms. "I've experience with shy children and will do my best to ease her fears."

Leethan nodded—she had already accepted the necessity of the separation, however much she disliked it. "Thank you."

With another friendly smile, Jewel let the soldier help her

down from the carriage and carried the still soundly sleeping El-wynne into the house.

"Only a little bit longer before you, too, can get some rest," the soldier assured her.

Leethan tried to take comfort from the fact that both Jewel and the soldier acted as though her return to this house was a foregone conclusion, but it was achingly hard to let go of her fears. She had no doubt that Prince Waldmir had loved her deeply throughout their marriage, and even their divorce. But she was under no illusion that that love would save her if Rhozinolm sent her back to Nandel as a traitor. It might grant her the mercy of a quick death, but then again, it might not. Waldmir's heart had grown harder and harder with the passing of each year, and his treatment of Elwynne suggested the revelation that he would not have a son had embittered him even more.

Against all odds, she must have dozed off for a little while, for she suddenly jerked awake when the carriage came to a stop. She blinked in confusion, glancing out the window and seeing a dark and nearly abandoned courtyard, bounded by an ornate iron fence. Opposite the fence was the towering façade of what could only be the royal palace. Leethan's head felt thick and slow. She hadn't known where she was being taken, but she certainly hadn't expected it to be *here*.

A royal palace was never entirely dark, for there were always people awake within, but it was still well before dawn. She doubted anyone with real authority was awake at this hour, but perhaps she was to be held here until someone was available to question her. Why she could not have been allowed to stay with Elwynne and sleep until then, she didn't know.

She stumbled with weariness when exiting the carriage and would have fallen flat on her face if the soldier hadn't caught her.

"Steady now," he said as he set her on her feet. "We're almost there. Follow me."

Stifling a yawn, she nodded and followed the soldier into the palace. They entered through what was obviously a servants' entrance, then followed a long and twisting corridor until they came to something that looked more like an opening in the wall than an actual doorway. The opening was flanked by two liveried men, who nodded to her escort.

Leethan followed him into the darkened hallway beyond, more puzzled now than ever. The servants' corridors had screamed their utilitarian purpose while still displaying a certain understated elegance. No one would mistake even the servants' wing as belonging to some ordinary manor house. But this darkened hallway was different, completely unadorned, and not fitted with luminants. Her escort lit the way with a handheld luminant that barely seemed to push back the darkness. She swallowed hard, wondering if this strange corridor led to hidden dungeons under the palace.

They reached what appeared to be a dead end, but the soldier opened his Mindseye and activated some spell, which caused a doorway to appear in what had looked for all the world like a blank wall. Leethan raised her eyebrows at him, and he offered her the tiniest hint of a smile.

Eventually, they reached a stairway and climbed until they entered yet another barren hallway, which led to a heavy door. The soldier knocked on that door and waited.

There was a sound of rustling clothing, and then the firm metallic thunk of sliding bolts. The door opened, and Leethan found herself face-to-face with an elegant young woman, wearing a jewel-encrusted bodice over voluminous skirts of heavy silk. Her headdress featured a filigreed golden diadem that sparkled with diamonds.

"You must be Lady Leethan," the young woman said with a welcoming smile.

Leethan, still feeling stupid with exhaustion, did not at first know what to make of the woman. Her mind was still dozing in the carriage, and it wasn't until she saw Prince Zarsha standing just behind the woman that she comprehended what was happening.

"Your Majesty!" she said with a gasp, then struggled to perform an elegant curtsy without allowing her weakened knees to collapse beneath her.

Leethan was mildly shocked when Queen Ellinsoltah reached out and put a hand on her arm as if to support her.

"Please come in and sit," the queen invited, drawing Leethan into the room. "I must apologize for dragging you here when I'm sure you are badly in need of sleep, but both Prince Zarsha and I felt it was imperative we speak with you as soon as you arrived in Zinolm Well. I have had tea and biscuits sent up, in case you are hungry, and I promise we will not keep you any longer than necessary."

Leethan, numb and wondering if she might not still be fast asleep in the carriage and dreaming, entered what appeared to be a bedroom. Swallowing hard, she looked around and blinked, but the magnificent canopied bed that dominated the room did not go away. It wasn't just *a* bedroom, it was *the queen's* bedroom. The queen and her prince consort led her through the bedroom into an adjoining sitting room. She glanced over her shoulder and saw that the door through which she had entered was now concealed by a tapestry.

The scent of tea teased her nostrils, and though her stomach was tight with tension, she happily helped herself to a cup when invited.

"Forgive the rather scandalous entrance into the queen's bedroom," Zarsha said as he settled himself on the arm of Ellinsoltah's chair, drawing a not-very-convincing stern look from his wife. "But until we've heard what you have to say, we thought it best to keep your arrival in Rhozinolm in general—and Zinolm Well in particular—a secret."

Thinking furiously, Leethan took a sip of tea. The need for secrecy might also explain why she'd been brought to the palace at this unholy hour. She'd thought it a coincidence that the ride from Falcon's Ridge had delivered her to the capital at such a late hour, but now she saw that it was by design. And the fact that Queen Ellinsoltah was at least for the time being keeping this secret seemed likely to be a good omen. If she were planning to hand Leethan back to Waldmir, there'd be no need for secrecy.

"I must thank you for your discretion," she said carefully, taking another sip of tea and willing it to do its magic. Both Ellinsoltah and Zarsha were perfectly dressed and coiffed, and they looked as fresh as if the sun were high in the sky. Leethan felt grubby by comparison.

Ellinsoltah smiled gently at her. "As you might well imagine, Prince Waldmir has demanded the return of Princess Elwynne and her 'kidnappers' should they make an appearance in Rhozinolm. We thought it best to dissemble, at least until we learned the reason for your precipitous—and perilous—flight."

"Yes," said Zarsha, his blue eyes suddenly focused on her with an unsettling intensity and his voice taking on crisp edges. "It is fortuitous for all involved that the healers have declared my little cousin to be in good health, considering the reckless risk you took with her life."

Leethan shivered slightly in the chill of Zarsha's gaze. He was well-known for being affable and full of good humor, but in that frosty stare she could clearly see the resemblance between him and his uncle. She formed the instant impression that he would make almost as bad an enemy as Prince Waldmir.

"I assure you," she said, "I would not have—"

"The princess could as easily have died as arrived in Rhozinolm," Zarsha interrupted. "You had best hope I find your explanation for dragging her through the mountains of Nandel during the winter satisfactory. And convincing."

Ellinsoltah put a gentle hand on her husband's leg as if to calm him, but Leethan had the instant impression that there was something slightly rehearsed to both his words and her gesture. Even so, she quickly abandoned any idea of embellishing her story to make it more convincing. If anything she said struck a false note, she might find herself in the hands of the royal inquisitor.

Instead, she settled for the truth, even if she feared it would not be believed. She told Zarsha and Ellinsoltah about her vision, but she also told them how disturbed she had been by Elwynne's banishment to the Abbey and how that made her fear for the child's welfare. She could not tell from their faces what Zarsha and Ellinsoltah thought of her reasoning.

"And why do you think Prince Waldmir has treated Elwynne so poorly?" Ellinsoltah inquired. "Surely even in Nandel there are allowances made for childish misbehavior, especially in one so young."

Leethan nodded. "Of course. But there are rumors . . ." She let her voice trail off, suddenly frightened of putting the rumors into words under Zarsha's knowing gaze.

"What rumors?" he asked, a dangerous edge in his voice.

Leethan cleared her throat and tried to look away, but found that she couldn't. "I doubt these rumors exist outside the Abbey," she hedged, "but within its walls . . . Well, there is some speculation that Elwynne may not be Waldmir's child. After all, Waldmir divorced her mother, yet Princess Brontyn never did arrive in the Abbey. Some think Waldmir had her quietly killed to punish her for her infidelity without having to admit it publicly."

"And are there any guesses as to whose child Elwynne might be if she is not Waldmir's?" he asked, still in that same menacing tone.

Perhaps, Leethan speculated, she might have handled this interview with more tact and foresight if she had not been so achingly tired. But it seemed it was too late to be careful and tactful now.

"I don't know what anyone else thinks," she said. "But it seems fairly likely that if she is not Waldmir's, she may well be . . . yours."

• • •

When Alys had first approached her grand magus, Rusha, about the contents of Xanvin's letter to Tynthanal, she'd done so with a touch of reluctance. She would have preferred confiding only in Chanlix, but Chanlix had quickly persuaded her that she needed Rusha's help.

"Among the spell crafters at the Academy," Chanlix argued, "Rusha is the most knowledgeable about Kai, both in its feminine and masculine forms."

Alys had to concede that such was the truth, for it was Rusha who'd gained illicit knowledge about Kai when she was an abigail of Aaltah, and it was Rusha who had used that knowledge to invent the spell known as Vengeance. If Alys wanted to understand the impossible power that Delnamal seemed to have gained—and learn how to counter it—Rusha was the best person to consult. Even if Alys *still* harbored some doubts about the woman's character.

For a full week after she'd given Rusha a copy of the letter Xanvin had sent, she had heard nothing, but she'd woken up this morning to find Rusha had requested an audience. She tried not to get her hopes up—logic told her there could be no easy fix to the situation—but she had to admit that she did not fully succeed. She granted Rusha the audience first thing, postponing the morning council meeting. Someday soon, she would have to discuss the situation with her full council, but for the moment, only she and Rusha and Chanlix were aware of the details of Delnamal's condition.

Rusha arrived bearing an ancient-looking battered scroll tucked under her arm along with a much fresher one that looked brand new.

"What have you found?" Alys asked, sitting on the edge of her chair as Rusha took a seat in front of her desk.

Rusha held up the battered scroll, then put it on the desk. "I obtained this from an old . . . acquaintance in Aaltah," she said.

Alys reached for the scroll, which seemed liable to fall apart at her touch. The parchment was yellow in places, brown in others, and there were tears and water stains obscuring some of the small, cramped handwriting.

"I took the liberty of copying it in a more legible form," Rusha said, laying the second scroll on Alys's desk. "You can read it at your leisure, but I can summarize it for you much more quickly."

"Please do," Alys said eagerly, for the scroll was quite long, and she could see from the first couple of paragraphs that it had been written in a florid, ponderous manner that would make it slow reading indeed.

"It's thought to be at least three hundred years old, and was written by an Adept spell crafter who was burned as a heretic," Rusha said. "As far as my contact knows, this is the only copy that survived its author's death. It was the scroll itself—which he distributed widely at the time—that was the cause of his execution.

"His heretical premise is that Kai and Rho are two equal parts of the same element. He calls this element the 'Seed of Life,' but by his description, it sounds very much like Delnamal's Rhokai. He claims he began seeing the Seed as soon as his Mindseye developed, but that he was urged by his family to keep quiet—for in Aaltah at that time, heresy was often punished by torture and death, just as it is in Khalpar these days.

"For years, he kept his knowledge to himself while surreptitiously studying the Seed—Rhokai. He saw it in every living creature, and he also saw flashes of it deep within the Well. He came to the conclusion that it was Rhokai that gave us life, and that the Wells supplied that Rhokai. In his opinion, the Wasteland isn't devoid of life because the Father imprisoned the Destroyer there—it's because it's too far away from the influence of any Well for Rhokai to reach it and spawn life."

Alys grimaced. "Hence being declared a heretic when he made the claim publicly."

"Exactly."

Alys absorbed all that, comparing it with Xanvin's account of Delnamal's power. "So it really does exist," she said. "It's not just a figment of Delnamal's imagination, or some wild story meant to camouflage the truth."

Rusha shrugged. "I can't say for sure, but it seems unlikely Delnamal and this Adept would come up with the same story three hundred years apart."

"Is it possible that Delnamal somehow got hold of another copy of this scroll?" Alys asked. "I don't want to put too much of our faith in it if there's a chance that Delnamal is making it all up and there's some other explanation for what he can do."

"As I said, this is thought to be the only surviving copy of the scroll, smuggled out of his home by his son just before the father was arrested. It doesn't mean there *can't* be another copy, but . . ." She shrugged again. "Perhaps it's superstitious, but to me, the scroll has the *feel* of truth about it. We see Rho around living beings, but we also see it floating around in the air and flowing freely from the Well. It is not *unique* to the living. Surely it makes sense that there is something inside us that gives us life— and that that something comes from the Well."

"Even if that gives us reason to believe Rhokai really does exist, it doesn't explain how *Delnamal,* of all people, sees it when no one else does. Or what happened at the Well to change him, for he certainly didn't see it before the accident." She shuddered, for thinking of Delnamal with magical powers and a whole king- dom at his back was enough to give her nightmares.

"I can only venture a theory," Rusha said, and Alys made a hand gesture to keep her talking.

"From Mairahsol's writings, we know that she believed mas- culine Kai was poisonous to the Well, and we have guessed that she performed her own sacrifice in an attempt to purge the Kai before it did too much damage."

Alys nodded.

"Based on the Adept's writings, I believe that the Rhokai mote inside us shatters when we die by violence."

Alys cocked her head. "Us? You mean *all* of us, not just powerful men?"

"Yes. The Adept said he saw it in every living being, and Delnamal said something similar. I think only powerful men are able to *see* their Kai when their Rhokai breaks, but I think it's present in all of us. I think that Mairahsol's attempt to purge it worked *too* well. She purged not only the Kai, but also the Rhokai—that's why Aaltah's fertility rate has gone down."

Once again, Alys shuddered, remembering Shabrynel's vision. "And somehow Delnamal absorbed it."

Rusha nodded. "It seems that way. The Adept said he never saw a Seed that was not contained either in a living being or in a Well. Maybe it can't exist without a vessel, so when it was purged from the Well, it went into the closest living being it could find."

Alys groaned softly. "And it's somehow keeping him alive."

"And because the Rhokai is part of him, the Kai motes released when it shatters belong to him and stay with him. Again, this is all just theory . . ."

"But it makes more sense than anything else I've been able to come up with. Even if it doesn't explain how he can steal other people's Rhokai."

"Like calling to like, maybe?"

Alys fingered the two scrolls absently and tried to stave off her sense of dread long enough to apply herself to the problem at hand. "So in order to kill him, we have to get that Rhokai out of him."

"That's what I believe as well," Rusha confirmed. "And if we can purge it from him while he's near Aaltah's Well, perhaps it will return to where it belongs."

Alys did not care to consider the other obvious likelihood— that the Rhokai would just move on to the next closest living being and the nightmare would begin all over again.

"I suppose we'd better begin researching purgatives, then," she said, and imagined she and Rusha—and probably Chanlix as well, for her wealth of experience—would have many a long night at the Academy ahead of them.

In the weeks that Draios had been serving as regent in his brother's stead, certain members of the royal council had been . . . half-hearted (to put it kindly) in their support of his rule. Thanks to the efforts of the lord high priest and the rest of the clergy, Draios had yet to encounter any true resistance to the war plans he was putting into effect, but he was well aware that certain members of his council were merely humoring him while they secretly longed for Parlommir to return to his abandoned throne.

The lord high commander had been seduced as much by the promise of a glorious war as by the desire to do the Creator's bidding, and the lord high treasurer was too weak-willed to offer any substantive resistance, though an occasional disapproving frown marked his discomfort with the situation. As long as he released the requested funds, Draios did not much concern himself with the little weasel's disapproval.

The lord chancellor and the lord chamberlain—the two highest-ranking members of the council—were a different story, and Draios could almost *feel* the resistance building within them. The lord chamberlain especially was a problem, for he had loved King Khalvin—his great-nephew—with something akin to a lover's passion, and it was not possible to look in his eyes and not sense the fulminating hatred he felt for the king's "murderer."

Draios had taken the old man aside and assured him he'd had no idea that Delnamal would kill the king, but the lord chamberlain blamed him for the death anyway.

"You must unite your council behind you," Delnamal had advised when Draios spoke of the resistance, as if dispensing a pearl of wisdom that Draios himself never would have considered.

Draios had been so irritated at the "advice" that he had put off what needed to be done for two whole weeks. He needed Delnamal to be clear that he was a weapon the Creator had delivered into Draios's hands, for Draios to use—or *not* use—at his discretion. It was *Draios* who would make all the important decisions, and Delnamal would do as he was told.

In this particular instance, doing what he was told involved accompanying Draios to the day's royal council meeting and standing over his shoulder, a cloud of menace shrouded in his habitual black cloak and hood. Although a steady diet of Rhokai had made Delnamal strong and able-bodied once more, he was still hideous to look at. Hideous enough that he could prove a distraction, so Draios had ordered him to remain cloaked and hooded when in public. His presence then became ominous and unsettling while not so . . . disruptive.

Draios took his place at the head of the table, well aware of the nervous glances his council members were casting toward the looming shadow behind him. Even his staunchest supporters found Delnamal's presence disturbing, and if Draios was being perfectly honest, he had to admit it made the space between his shoulder blades twitch to have the man standing behind him. There was something so very *unnatural* to the former King of Aaltah, something that chewed at Draios's nerves, leaving them raw and tender. But he was growing used to the sensation, and he was certainly better at hiding it than most of his council members.

Draios laid a sheet of parchment on the table, smoothing out its edges. There was some small part of him that balked at what he was about to do, that insisted it was *wrong,* but he had prayed on the matter night after night, and he was currently performing a voluntary fast that left him light-headed and weak. The Creator, in His great wisdom, was well aware that sometimes it was necessary to do wrong things for the right reason, and He had made His wishes clear. The fast would help salve Draios's conscience and strengthen his bond with the Creator, and he felt secure in the righteousness of his decision.

Certain members of his council, he was certain, would not be.

"I have here a writ of attainder," he announced to the council, "against my brother, Parlommir Rah-Khalvin."

The room filled with the sounds of gasps and cries of dismay. Even the lord commander paled just a little bit, although he and the lord high priest both recovered their composure quickly.

"His refusal to return to the capital and assume his duties at this crucial moment is a sign that he is unworthy of the title of king," Draios continued. "It is an act of treason to abandon his throne and his kingdom, and it is an act of heresy to refuse to do the Creator's will."

The gasps turned into a low murmur, its volume slowly rising as some members of the council nearly shook with outrage while their fellows tried to calm them.

"I have refrained from adding a charge of heresy or treason against Parlommir out of brotherly affection," Draios said, though those words stuck a little in his throat. He held his elder brother in some grudging respect—or at least had done so until the coward had fled his duties—but there was nothing resembling affection in his heart. He hoped, however, that the threat of even worse charges being filed might still some of the dissent. "But I will be forced to eschew such considerations should he ever attempt to set foot in Khalpar again."

The warning in his voice was, he thought, quite clear, but that did not stop the lord chancellor from slowly rising to his feet, his fists clenched and his eyes flashing fire.

"Let me get this straight," the man snarled, and he shook off the calming hand the grand magus tried to lay on his arm. "You are basically declaring yourself the King of Khalpar after murdering your father and accusing your brother of being a traitor. Do I have the right of it?"

There was another audible gasp in the council room, and several members of the council—including the grand magus, who abandoned his attempt to calm his fellow—recoiled at the virulence of the lord chancellor's words. Draios was not entirely surprised at the sentiment, though he had thought such an experienced courtier might at least *try* to be careful and diplomatic before so openly declaring himself the enemy.

"Your king is on a holy mission," Delnamal said before Draios could respond, and the very sound of his voice sent a shiver down Draios's spine such that he did not even *think* to scold his friend for speaking out of turn. "He is carrying out the will of the Creator, and anyone who fails to aid this righteous cause is a traitor to the Kingdom of Khalpar."

The lord chancellor sneered at him. "You have no voice in this council chamber! You are not even a citizen of Khalpar!" He turned to the other council members, gesticulating at Delnamal as he said, "I'm not sure this *thing* even counts as *human* anymore."

Most of the council members looked between Delnamal and the lord chancellor with expressions ranging from disgust to terror, and even his closest ally, the lord chamberlain, had as yet failed to stand with him.

Delnamal started to say something, but Draios silenced him with an upraised hand. "Enough," he said with what he believed was quiet dignity. "We are at a crossroads, and we must decide now if we are to be faithful followers of the Creator or whether we are to show ourselves no more holy than the heretics my father consigned to the flames." He pointed at the lord chancellor. "*You* have already shown your true colors and proven yourself incorrigible. Faced with all the evidence Delnamal and I have provided, you still refuse to bow to the Creator's will, and that is not something I can tolerate."

He made a small gesture, and two palace guards stepped forward to seize the lord chancellor's arms. Having guessed that at least one or two of his council members would balk at officially handing the crown over to him, Draios had fully prepared the guardsmen who had accompanied him. The lord chancellor shrieked in fury as he was clapped in irons, then seemed to belatedly realize how very deep was the hole he had dug for himself. The outrage turned to terror, and he began to stammer out excuses.

"You are a traitor to the realm," Draios said, speaking loudly enough to be heard over the man's shouts and protests. "You will be tried for your crimes, and when you are found guilty, you will aid our holy mission by giving your Rhokai to my cousin and fellow holy man, King Delnamal of Aaltah." He swept the rest of the room with a regal gaze. "And all you who would spit on the Creator by gainsaying your king's orders will meet a similar fate. One way or another, you *will* help us set the world to rights."

With a howl that sounded more animal than human, the lord chamberlain suddenly bolted from his chair, which was two seats to Draios's right. The howl was so unexpected and shocking that Draios was momentarily paralyzed and unable to think. A small part of his brain registered the flash of metal in the old man's hand, but the part of his mind that saw the danger couldn't seem to communicate it to his limbs. He stood there frozen with his mouth hanging open as the blade winked in the light, heading straight for his heart.

A sun-devouring shadow suddenly stepped between Draios and the lunging lord chamberlain, heedless of the danger. The blade sank to the hilt in Delnamal's chest. Draios would not have believed the frail old man could have had the strength for such a brutal thrust, but it was amazing what rage could do.

Delnamal let out a soft grunt that sounded more like annoyance than pain. Then he grabbed the old man's wrist in a grip far stronger than someone who looked like a walking skeleton should have been capable of.

The guardsmen who weren't currently in the middle of dragging the lord chancellor to the dungeons now converged on the lord chamberlain, wrestling him to the ground with such force that Draios heard the distinctive snap of breaking bones. The lord chamberlain went still, and when the guardsmen grabbed him to drag him out of the room, his head lolled limply on his neck.

The remaining members of the royal council had all pushed back their chairs and jumped to their feet, yelling and exclaiming and waving their hands about ineffectively.

Delnamal's hood had slid down, revealing his cadaverous face. Seeing that face—and the unholy calm with which the former King of Aaltah frowned, reached down, and plucked the knife from his chest—Draios couldn't help hearing the lord chancellor's words echoing through his mind: *I'm not sure this* thing *even counts as* human *anymore.*

The knife Delnamal removed had been buried to the hilt and was easily long enough to have pierced the heart. By all rights the man should be dead by now; instead, he stood there frowning at the bloody knife, as if being stabbed through the heart were nothing but an annoying inconvenience. There was a blood-rimmed tear in his doublet where the blade had pierced it, but it was about as much blood as one might expect to see if he'd been dealt a grazing wound rather than a death blow.

"I have been chosen by the Creator to fulfill His holy mission," Delnamal said as he tossed the knife onto the council table. "Until I have completed that mission and reversed the abominable Curse that weighs so heavily on us all, He will not allow me to die."

Draios shivered and swallowed hard. Half of him was terrified by the power Delnamal had just demonstrated; the other half wasn't sure *what* to feel, for Delnamal had also just saved his life by taking a knife strike meant for him. He stood rooted to the floor still, his tongue stuck to the roof of his mouth and his throat trying to close up with panic. Delnamal put a solicitous hand on his shoulder, and it was all Draios could do not to cringe away from the touch.

"Are you well, Your Majesty?" Delnamal asked.

You are the King of Khalpar, Draios scolded himself. *You are on a mission to restore the world to rights in the name of the Creator. You must rise above your superstitious fears.*

Draios took a deep breath through his nose, subtly throwing back his shoulders and raising his head, assuming a posture of full command. "I am well, thanks to your noble actions," he said, and Delnamal waved the praise away.

"I knew the thrust would not kill me," he demurred. "What is a little bit of pain in service to my king and my god?"

"You are too modest," Draios said, looking around the room. Not a man on the council had yet resumed his seat, and all stood staring at the two of them in fraught silence. Draios wondered how many of them wished the lord chamberlain's blade had struck true.

"My council is now down two very important men," Draios said. "It seems to me only fitting that I name *you* to the position of lord chancellor, at least until our mission is accomplished. Your counsel will be most appreciated as we plan our conquest of Aaltah and Women's Well."

More than one member of the council looked scandalized by the very suggestion, and yet there was no protest whatsoever.

"It is only fitting," said the lord high priest, and though moments ago he had looked as frightened as anyone else in the room, there was now a very different light in his eyes. The eyes, Draios knew, of an emerging fanatic. "If any of us doubted before that we are being guided by the Creator's hand, today's events must chase that doubt away." He looked sternly around at the other councilors. "You must believe either that Delnamal is a tool of the Creator, or that the Creator has allowed an abomination to walk freely upon the land of Seven Wells. As men of faith, there is only one conclusion you should draw."

"B-but," stammered the trade minister, who paused to clear his throat and collect himself. He stared at the lord high priest with an expression Draios could only describe as beseeching. A man who had lost his way and was desperate for someone to take his hand and lead him to safety. "But then how must we look upon the casting of the Curse? Might we not be forced to believe that that, too—"

"The Creator is testing us," the lord high priest interrupted. "He allowed the Curse to be cast knowing that He would also send us the tools we needed to reverse it. The Curse has been the cause of much suffering, but as an iron must be heated and hammered before it can become a sword, so must we men suffer the blows of the Creator's hammer to become worthy of Him."

Draios nodded his approval, some of the pent-up anxiety leaving him. Draios had chosen the right man to fill the vacant position of lord high priest. A wise and holy man who could see clearly when others were inclined to panic. Even Draios himself had felt his faith waver for just an instant, and he would have to add another fast day as penance for his weakness. He inclined his head toward the lord high priest, reminding everyone in the room that although he himself held the greatest power in the worldly realm, even the king must take guidance from the Creator's worldly instrument.

"Is there anyone who wishes to dispute the naming of King Delnamal to the temporary position of lord chancellor?" Draios asked.

Silence descended on the room. Draios smiled.

"Then so be it."

CHAPTER TWENTY-SEVEN

Leethan cursed when she opened her eyes to find herself standing alone on a windswept cliff overlooking a rocky beach.

"Not this again," she groaned, then shook her fist at the heavily overcast sky. "I need to sleep!" she shouted at it, but the sky was unmoved.

Usually she went *years* between dreams, and yet this was now the third time in less than six months. She did not like the uncomfortable suspicion that this felt portentous, and she knew from far too much experience that when she woke from it, her head would be throbbing and she would feel as if she hadn't slept for a week.

"Not now," she whined, rubbing at her eyes as if that would somehow make the dream go away. "Please!"

After all the suffering and terror she had faced while fleeing Nandel—and after her clandestine meeting with Queen Ellinsoltah and Prince Zarsha in the wee hours—her body ached for rest, and her mind felt strangely fuzzy around the edges. Gritting her teeth and screwing her eyes shut as tight as possible, she tried to *will* herself awake, hoping that she could then drift back into a blissfully dreamless sleep. She knew it wouldn't work—it never *had*—yet nonetheless she couldn't stop herself from trying every time the dream descended upon her.

Not caring a jot for Leethan's passionate wish for more sleep, the dream continued its unrelenting course until Leethan's ears were full with the screams of the dying men who fought in the phantom armies. The screams horrified her every time she heard them, carrying as they did untold depths of pain and terror. Ostensibly, they were the most upsetting component, and yet as usual, Leethan's nerves grew more taut, rather than less so, when they ended.

The armies faded from view, replaced by the trio of men with their indistinct faces. Leethan had long ago grown accustomed to the sight of them, to the point that she could conjure their images easily in her mind.

As always, Leethan's eyes were first drawn to the Nandelite man, for there was something about him she had always found compelling. Even before she'd known she was to marry a man of Nandel.

Leethan let out a soft gasp when she noticed the hilt of the Nandelite's blade, which bore a distinctive hematite cabochon on the pommel.

Leethan shook her head in denial and confusion. How had she never noticed that pommel before? She had memorized every aspect of this dream, could have described each character to the smallest detail—or so she had thought. It wasn't possible she had not noticed the hilt before, not given how many times she had had this dream!

She *knew* that sword, had seen its hilt poking up from the scabbard at Prince Waldmir's side more times than she could count. Her heart gave an uneasy thump. There was no denying that the Nandelite man was Prince Waldmir.

But now that she had realized the Nandelite was Waldmir, she couldn't help noticing the wrinkled hands of the woman who stood facing him. Hands that looked very much like her own—including the slightly crooked pinky finger she had broken in a childhood fall. She'd been afraid of the cantankerous healer her family habitually employed, so she'd kept the injury to herself. By the time anyone noticed, the bone had already started to heal.

Leethan's heart raced with panic as the rest of the dream unfolded just as it always had, fifty times more terrifying now that she realized the first woman to slash her wrists was *herself*.

"Nooo," she moaned, shaking her head in frantic denial as one by one each woman performed her gruesome sacrifice and the men fell.

Moments later, Leethan bolted upright in her bed, her heart pounding, her breaths coming in short pants, and her bedclothes soaked in sweat. Shivering violently, she hugged her knees to her chest, trying desperately to convince herself that she had somehow made a mistake, that she wasn't the old woman in the dream.

Teeth chattering with nerves, Leethan slipped out of bed and changed into dry nightclothes, stoking the fire and sitting directly in front of it as if its warmth could somehow dispel the chill that had settled deep into her bones.

"Rusha is doing excellent work," Chanlix assured her as Alys pored over the results of her grand magus's latest research. She hardly ever set foot in the Academy these days, and yet Rusha had continued Chanlix's practice of leaving a worktable open and available to her at all times. A fact for which she was now grateful, as she sat at that table well after the Academy's working hours were done, reading Rusha's notes by the light of a luminant.

"I'm sure she is," Alys murmured absently as she perused the list of formulae Rusha was considering for the Kai-fueled purgative spell they hoped would return Delnamal's Rhokai to the Well. The grand magus had come up with a half-dozen promising possibilities, but it was hard to know which version to choose when they could not perform relevant tests.

Chanlix snorted softly. "Yes, that's why you are here at this hour looking over Rusha's notes when she already gave us a full accounting of her research after our council meeting this morning."

Sighing, Alys sat back and pushed the notes to the side, meeting her lady chancellor's mildly disapproving face. It was true that the two of them and Rusha had already met privately to discuss the research in greater detail than Alys deemed necessary for the rest of the council to hear.

"The fate of all of Seven Wells may rest on this spell," she said. "My interest in studying the details of Rusha's notes has nothing to do with not trusting her and everything to do with me wanting to make the best, most informed decision I can."

"Uh-huh," Chanlix said with undisguised skepticism.

Alys huffed. "Look, I wouldn't have appointed her to the post of grand magus if I didn't trust her, and I have no cause to quibble with any of the work she's done since. She's been thorough and discreet, and I believe her to be on the right track."

"Then why are we here checking up on her notes?" Chanlix asked quite reasonably.

"*We* aren't," Alys responded with an ironic twist of her lips. "Sometimes I think you must keep watch at your window to see if I set foot anywhere near the Academy."

Chanlix clucked her tongue. "I can't help it that Chantynel's nursery window faces the front entrance. Nor could I help noticing the lights going on and your honor guardsmen standing sentinel."

Alys hadn't expected her visit to the Academy to go unnoticed—it was impossible for a sovereign to go *anywhere* unnoticed—but she hadn't considered that Chanlix would come to join her. Which was probably a sign of just how distracted she was, for this was not the first time her lady chancellor had noticed the lights in the Academy going on after hours and come to investigate.

"You should be spending this time with Chantynel," Alys said, then instantly regretted what had come out sounding like scolding.

Luckily, Chanlix did not seem offended. "I was watching her sleep when I saw the lights." She shook her head and looked down at her hands. "I know better than to do that," she said softly. "In the quiet of the nursery, with nothing to do but look at her, I have a bad habit of falling into melancholy." There was just the faintest hint of a rasp in her voice, but she forced a smile and met Alys's eyes once again. "Checking up on you is a pleasant distraction. And Chantynel's nurse has a talker so she can let me know if she wakes while I'm gone."

Alys wished she could say something to console her friend. Chanlix had seemed to be flourishing in her role as lady chancellor while she'd been pregnant, and although it was impossible not to notice that she missed Tynthanal, Alys had convinced herself that Chanlix's heart was on the mend. That had changed since Chantynel's birth, and though Chanlix still admirably executed her duties to the Crown and was clearly a doting mother, completely besotted with her daughter, her sadness was plain to see. Especially on days when she had spoken with Tynthanal.

"I wish . . ." Alys started, but found she couldn't put into words all the many things she wished could be different for her dearest friend. And her brother.

Chanlix smiled again, this time more genuinely. "Yes, don't we all. But come now, tell me why you're visiting the Academy in the middle of the night to study Rusha's notes if it's not because you distrust her work."

Alys shifted ever so slightly in her seat and instantly knew she should have fought off the urge, for the look in Chanlix's eyes sharpened. Chanlix knew her too well not to recognize the sign of disquiet. Which meant she was unlikely to accept an attempt to deflect her interest, but that wouldn't stop Alys from trying.

"You know that if I hadn't become sovereign princess, I would happily have spent the rest of my life at the Academy studying magic," she said. "I wanted to delve into the spell in more detail than it's sensible to ask for when everyone has so much important work to do."

"I'm glad to hear that," Chanlix said. "I was worried you might be here looking for evidence that the purgative will need to be triggered with sacrificial Kai." There was no missing the suspicion in her voice, and she was watching Alys's face with far too much attention.

Alys tried to keep her expression entirely neutral, but the narrowing of Chanlix's eyes showed her she'd failed. Her pulse fluttered a moment in something like panic at being caught out, though she shrugged in a way that she hoped looked casual despite everything. "Well, you have to know that is an important question to find an answer to."

Chanlix folded her arms over her chest and gave Alys a sternly maternal look, although Chanlix was a year younger. "Yes, but that doesn't explain why you're here perusing Rusha's notes in the middle of the night. If she concludes the spell will need—or even *might* need—sacrificial Kai, I'm sure she'll tell us."

Alys's hands had clenched into fists in her lap without her even noticing, which made continuing to try to deflect pointless. "Very well, then. I'm looking at her notes because deep down in here"—she thumped her chest—"I believe that to get that Rhokai out of Delnamal and back into the Well will require a sacrifice."

"And you believe *you* are that sacrifice," Chanlix finished for her, somehow managing to look both angry and frightened at the same time. "Because you hate Delnamal so much that you would like to be personally responsible for defeating him."

Alys gave a self-deprecating sigh as she looked down at her hands. Her stomach felt sour, her hatred for the man who had killed her daughter sitting inside her like a poison. Rotting her from the inside out. She thought fleetingly of Duke Thanmir and his gentle not-quite-proposal, and of her continued inability to see a future in which she might genuinely consider it. Delnamal had stabbed her through the heart, and she felt like the knife remained within her, burrowing deeper. One day, it would pierce what was left of her soul, and she had little hope that Delnamal's death—as gratifying as it might be—would heal the damage.

She blinked away incipient tears and raised her head to meet Chanlix's eyes. "It is not a comfortable thing to live with hatred," she said quietly. "I keep worrying that it will have a corrupting influence on me, that it might turn me into someone bitter and vindictive and I might not even notice it happening."

Chanlix patted her hand, and Alys was pathetically grateful for the simple touch.

"You are no more bitter and vindictive than anyone would be in your position," Chanlix assured her, "and a good deal less so than many."

Alys smiled. "Says the woman who wants him dead almost as much as I do."

Chanlix shrugged. "There are few who would mourn his death, and I am not among them. But I *would* mourn yours. More than you know."

"I sincerely hope it won't come to that," Alys said, willing her friend to believe her—even though she didn't believe herself. "But you're right to think that I fear it might, and if it does, I have to be ready."

Chanlix's expression was no longer one of sympathy, but one of stern warning. "Tell me you're not looking for an excuse to escape your grief," she said with a knowing look at Alys's black gown.

Alys let out a shaky breath. "I swear I'm not," she said with all the conviction she could muster. "I believe the purgative will most likely work with either masculine or feminine Kai, but it is my duty to plan for the worst. And if it *does* come to the worst, then I know it is my duty as a sovereign to find a volunteer rather than perform the sacrifice myself."

That it wasn't enough to convince Chanlix was clear from her lady chancellor's expression. But she must also have heard the implacability in Alys's voice, for she refrained from continuing the discussion.

"Very well, then," Chanlix said briskly, the corners of her eyes tight. "We will speak no more of it."

Somehow, Alys doubted that was true.

"You look terrible," Jaizal said with characteristic Nandelite bluntness as soon as she and Leethan had a moment alone in the Zinolm Well safe house that was—for the time being, at least—their new prison. Jaizal had spent an additional three days in Falcon's Ridge before being escorted to the city to join Leethan in their necessary but galling isolation. The hardships of their journey were still written in her frail frame and her hollow cheeks, and Leethan was thankful her oldest friend had made what was deemed a full recovery, with no fingers or toes lost to the frostbite. Someone had provided her with a modest, though nicely made, dress to replace the men's clothes she'd worn from Nandel. Leethan, too, had a new wardrobe, provided for her by the Crown.

"Have you looked at yourself in the mirror lately?" Leethan asked her friend with a small smile.

A maid entered the cozy parlor in which they had retreated to talk, and Leethan was delighted to see the steaming pot of tea she had not thought to order. She was so many years removed from being waited on by others that it never would have occurred to her to ask, and she had to stifle her instinctive need to reach for the tray before the maid set it down.

The maid smiled at her and at Jaizal, as if unaware that they were lowly Unwanted Women who expected no interaction whatsoever with polite society. Of course, since they were no longer *dressed* like abigails, it was likely easier to ignore their history.

"Cook thought you might like a nice cup of tea after your long journey," the maid said to Jaizal before turning to Leethan with a hint of anxiety. "I hope you do not find this . . . presumptuous."

"Of course not," Leethan responded, feeling a nearly hysterical urge to laugh. She wondered if the small handful of servants assigned to this house even knew her true identity. Perhaps they had no idea that she was the former Abbess of Nandel and thought she was some visiting dignitary. Which would certainly explain why no one seemed to look down their noses at her. "Please thank Cook for her thoughtfulness."

"We have a maid? And a cook?" Jaizal marveled when the young woman had retreated.

"Footmen, even," Leethan confirmed, "although I suspect they are guardsmen in disguise."

Jaizal chewed her lip as she took a seat before the merry fire and poured herself a cup of tea. "I did think the fellow who greeted my carriage had a rather . . . military bearing for a household servant."

Leethan swallowed a yawn and decided she needed the cup of tea as badly as Jaizal. She had not slept peacefully since arriving in Zinolm Well, the old dream sneaking up on her each time she drifted off. Never before had she had it more than once in a year, and now she was having it every night! Her head ached constantly, and though she was technically getting a full night's sleep, she awakened each morning feeling worse than she had when she'd gone to bed.

"You had the dream again," Jaizal said, and she did not phrase it as a question.

Leethan rubbed her eyes and sipped the tea, hoping it might wake her up. "It's that obvious?"

"To someone who's known you as long as I have? Yes. Although frankly, I've never seen you look *this* peaked afterward. Are you still unwell from the journey?"

Leethan put the tea down and tried to assess her own physical well-being. Was the hardship still telling on her body? It was hard to know when she felt this wretched.

"I don't think the journey has anything to do with it," she said. "It's just . . ." She let out a soft groan. "I've had the dream every night since I've been here."

Jaizal's eyes widened. "Every night?" she cried in evident dismay.

Leethan nodded. "But there's more," she said almost reluctantly. She'd known from the first recurrence of the dream that she would tell Jaizal all, that no one would be able to understand her creeping sense of dread like Jaizal would. And yet she felt an almost superstitious fear of speaking about it. As if speaking of it would make it real.

"Well, what is it?" Jaizal prompted when Leethan's voice faltered.

Leethan let out a shuddering sigh. "I noticed a detail I'd never noticed before," she said, wincing gingerly as if the words hurt. "I noticed that one of the three men at the end is carrying Waldmir's sword." Jaizal gasped. "And that the woman facing him has a bent little finger." She raised her own hand with its crooked finger.

Jaizal shook her head in denial. "That cannot be!" she protested. "You would have recognized Waldmir's sword long ago if that were true. And you certainly would have recognized yourself!"

That was what Leethan had told herself when she'd awakened from the first dream, but now she was not so sure. "I don't suppose it matters," she said, rather unconvincingly. "It doesn't change the substance of the dream."

Jaizal snorted. "You told me you first had that dream when

you were fifteen years old. Well before your marriage arrangement was even an inkling in your father's mind."

Leethan shivered and said nothing, for she had in truth suffered the dream twice before laying eyes on Waldmir for the first time. If the man in the dream had *always* been Waldmir, and the woman standing across from him had *always* been her, then . . .

Jaizal's shoulders slumped as she sat back in her chair, her already pale face now ghostly white. "You think the dream may be prophetic," she said in a bare whisper.

Leethan rubbed at her eyes as if she could scrub the thought out of her own brain. "There are no such things as prophetic dreams," she mumbled. Three days ago, she would have said so with much more conviction. "The Mother of All communicates with her seers through visions, not dreams. And no vision I have triggered has shown me anything like that terrible battle or the strange encounter between those three men and those three women."

Jaizal frowned fiercely. "Every man—and most women—in Nandel would tell you that *visions* don't exist, that they are merely hallucinations produced by women with troubled minds or outsized ambitions. Does that make it true?"

Leethan squirmed in her chair, then poured herself another cup of tea. Not because she wanted it, but because she wanted so badly not to think about Jaizal's words or their implications. Unfortunately, her friend wasn't content to allow her the silence to gather her thoughts—or hide from the truth.

"Just because we've never heard of a verifiably prophetic dream," Jaizal said with a touch of gentleness in her voice, "doesn't mean they don't exist. And I cannot but think that it is significant that you are suddenly having the dream again and that it is with you every night."

Leethan put down her teacup without having taken a sip. Her throat felt too tight with dread for swallowing, and the rapid pat-

ter of her heart said she was moments away from a full-out panic.
Even with only her oldest and closest friend to witness it, it was
mortifying to show such weakness, and Leethan wished she could
crawl into a deep, dark hole and hide until it passed.

Jaizal's hand closed over hers, squeezing tightly. "I know you
are afraid," she said quietly. "I don't blame you. But I don't think
ignoring the dream and what it might signify is going to make
you feel any better."

Leethan shook her head, hating the tears that burned her eyes
and dampened her lashes. "If the dream is prophetic," she said,
her voice rasping harshly, "then it means the Mother of All ex-
pects me to kill myself. I don't want to die. Especially not like
that." She had knowingly risked her life in leaving Nandel, but
though that had frightened her, the hope of survival—and of
freedom—had carried her through all her worst moments of
doubt.

"If it were a normal vision rather than a dream," Jaizal said,
"you would interpret it to mean it was possible that in the future
you could sacrifice your own life to kill Waldmir, I suppose. But
according to everything you've told me about how visions work,
it would mean that the Mother of All was presenting you with
that option and expecting you to work toward it or away from it
based on your own wishes. So unless you actually *want* to sacrifice your life to kill Prince Waldmir, you are seeing a future you
can avoid. Am I wrong?"

Drawing in a deep, shuddering breath, Leethan raised her
head once more and met Jaizal's eyes. Jaizal knew perfectly well
she was not wrong. As a woman of Nandel, she had been raised
to believe that seers did not exist, and thus everything she had
learned about seers had come from Leethan. But the two of them
had talked about visions enough—and Jaizal had seen her through
enough of them—that she knew full well that she wasn't wrong.

Leethan tried to cling to the words, to the hope they offered, but the sense of dread only lessened, rather than going away. "If it were an ordinary vision, then yes, that is how it would work."

"And *do* you want to sacrifice your life to kill Prince Waldmir?"

Leethan sighed deeply. "You know I do not."

Jaizal nodded. "I know there is a part of you that loves him still. Or at least loves the memory of the man he was when first you married him."

Leethan allowed the tiniest of self-deprecating smiles to tug at her lips. "He was never the man I thought he was, or at least that I forced myself to see because it made the marriage easier."

Her friend dismissed that with a wave of her hand. "You are quibbling over semantics. A man needn't be anywhere near perfect for a woman to love him, whether he deserves her love or not. Whatever Waldmir's faults, you were happy with him for many years. You'd be more willing to give your life to *save* his than to take it."

The words made Leethan wince, for she heard a disturbing level of truth in them. It made no sense that some corner of her heart still clung to the memory of their love. The man had *divorced* her and sent her to the Abbey of the Unwanted. And he'd divorced two other women since and had a third beheaded. How could even a small part of her still love him?

"A moment ago, you were trying to convince me that it *is* prophetic," she griped. "Now you're trying to convince me it isn't?"

Jaizal huffed. "I'm just saying it doesn't seem like a normal vision, if there is such a thing. Normal visions show you a future you can change based on your will, and they basically allow you to see real, literal events that haven't happened yet and may never happen."

Leethan had to acknowledge that was true. "It starts out seeming like a real vision, at least to some extent. There's nothing particularly strange about standing on a cliff and seeing warships on the horizon."

Jaizal cocked her head to the side. "Isn't there? You said you were alone on that cliffside and saw no one waiting on the beach below, unless the dreams you've had lately are different."

"No," she admitted. "They're not different. And it's true that with that fleet bearing down, there should have been people—an army—waiting for them."

Jaizal nodded. "And fortifications, barricades, trenches . . ."

"Yes."

"And the rest of the dream . . . ?"

She sighed. "I've never had a vision wherein I see faceless people. What I saw was the suggestion of a battle, rather than a real battle, no matter how convincing the sounds. And the confrontation between the men and the women . . . There was nothing remotely realistic about that."

"So," Jaizal concluded with satisfaction, "whatever the dream might signify, it is not a literal vision of the future. Which means you cannot assume that you are expected to commit suicide or even kill Prince Waldmir."

Leethan nodded an agreement, but her gut still roiled with worry. Perhaps what she'd seen was both prophetic and not literal. But no matter what, it hinted at a very dark future. A future she feared was much closer on the horizon than she wished to know.

CHAPTER TWENTY-EIGHT

Kailee set aside the last page of the epic poem Tynthanal had had copied out for her in elemental ink, feeling a rush of giddy excitement. Across from her, Oona applauded.

"Very well done!" Oona said, her voice showing her delight. "I hardly think you need my help anymore."

Smiling, Kailee ran her hand over the stack of papers that sat on the coffee table, scarcely believing she had made it through the entire thing without once having to ask Oona's help.

Tynthanal had begun the task of teaching her to read, but thanks to the constraints of his duties, he was never able to spend as much time on the task as Kailee would have liked. Once she'd struck up a friendship with Oona, she'd inadvertently found herself a new tutor. One who had nearly as much time on her hands as Kailee, thanks to her alienation from court.

"I could not have done it without you," Kailee assured her unlikely friend.

Oona gave a self-deprecating laugh. "Oh, I think you could have. You are far too clever—and too stubborn—to fail at anything you put your mind to."

Kailee felt the heat in her cheeks and knew she was blushing. She was not overly used to accepting compliments. "It would have taken a lot longer. And my penmanship could certainly use more work."

"That's simply a matter of practice," Oona replied. "But I'm happy to give you whatever help and encouragement you still want. We outcasts must stick together."

It was said with good humor and with not even a modicum of malice, but Kailee winced anyway.

Oona sighed. "We might as well embrace it, no?"

Kailee shook off her chagrin as best she could and forced a bright smile. "Yes, of course. Although I do wish I didn't feel so . . . useless."

"You're not useless!" Oona remonstrated quickly and with admirable conviction.

"I can perform none of the social functions ordinarily required of the wife of a prince regent. I am invited to the barest minimum of social functions, and then ignored when I attend. No one but you accepts my own invitations. I have no influence that can in any way help my husband, nor do I see petitioners, because the council—despite Tynthanal's attempts to persuade them otherwise—have deemed that it would be a waste of time because no one would show up."

"They aren't entirely wrong," Oona said. "There is very little use for a dowager queen at court, either, except to see petitioners. But I can tell you from personal experience that one's social standing greatly affects how many petitioners wish to visit. I am hardly kept occupied."

"At least you get to have the audiences in the first place," Kailee said. "Besides, you have two children to care for. I'm sure you do not spend your time in forced idleness as I do."

"Well, perhaps you will have children of your own soon. I must admit, they have a magical way of making me feel both vitally necessary and completely inadequate at the same time."

Kailee couldn't help a little grimace, for she would be having no children, at least in the foreseeable future.

"You do want to have children, don't you?" Oona asked, for thanks to the Blessing, it was no longer possible for a woman to conceive a child if she didn't wish to.

"I do," Kailee confirmed, although she had known since she was old enough to understand such things that she was not fated to be a mother. She had spent most of her life expecting never to marry and to eventually end up shut behind the walls of the Abbey of Rhozinolm. Tynthanal had never made any secret about his lack of desire for her, and even if he wanted her, she could not bed him without feeling she was betraying Chanlix.

Oona was silent for a long moment. "Are you and your husband . . . not intimate?"

Heat flooded Kailee's face, for she had never meant to reveal so much, not even to a friend. She urged herself to lie—she had to admit, rather guiltily, that she was good at it and well-practiced—but the words refused to leave her mouth. Which was likely just as well, for her blush had revealed the truth.

Oona laid a hand softly on Kailee's shoulder, but though her touch was gentle, her voice had sharp edges to it. "I have tried to give Tynthanal the benefit of the doubt despite how he treated Delnamal, but for him to scorn you because—"

"It's not that," Kailee said hastily. "He has never been anything but kind to me, and he is as thoughtful and considerate a husband as I could ever hope to find." She could almost see how Oona frowned at her.

"But then why . . . ? Unless I am very much mistaken, you love him."

Kailee's breath hissed in through her teeth, and pain stabbed through her chest as those words burrowed into her flesh. "Is it that obvious?" she asked with an unbecoming quaver in her voice. She prayed to the Mother that Oona was especially observant and that Tynthanal himself did not know how her stubborn feelings insisted on running away with her.

"It is no shame to love your husband," Oona said soothingly.

"And for those of us who do not get to choose our marriage, it is a rare and wonderful blessing."

Kailee nodded her agreement even as her heart sank a little lower. "Not when your husband loves another."

Kailee was certain that many of the women of the court already knew that Tynthanal had had a child with Chanlix. He refused to make a secret of the child's parentage, and his dalliance with a former abigail could not but raise a few eyebrows—and give ladies another reason to pity Kailee. But figuring Oona's isolation meant she had not heard the rumors, Kailee told her about Chanlix and little Chantynel Rah-Tynthanal. The two people Tynthanal loved above all others, and with whom Kailee could never hope to compete.

"I knew all of this before I married him," Kailee said. "I encouraged him to maintain his relationship with Lady Chanlix, because I did not want to come between them. She was very kind to me while I lived in Women's Well, even though she had so many reasons why she might hate me." She sniffled, then wiped at her eyes, surprised to find she was crying again. It was unlike her.

Oona squeezed her shoulder once more. "I'm very sorry," she said, and there was no missing the sympathetic pain in her voice. "I know all too well what it feels like to love a man you cannot have."

"But at least you knew that Delnamal loved you back," Kailee countered. And of course Oona *had* married him, eventually. Not that the marriage seemed to have brought her much in the way of joy.

"I don't think that was necessarily a good thing," Oona said. "Perhaps if I didn't know he loved me back, I could finally have given up on him and tried harder to love the man I was married to. I think I *could* have loved him, had I not already closed my heart to him when we wed."

"I'm sorry," Kailee said, ashamed of her selfish assumption. "I hadn't thought of it that way."

Oona waved off her apology. "Do you think it's possible Tynthanal might allow you to live apart from him in Women's Well? The arrangement is not unheard of, and it would give you the freedom to live your own life. Though I must say I would miss you very much."

"He's offered," Kailee admitted. "And all logic tells me I should accept. I just . . . I just can't."

Oona nodded. "You're not ready. But I hope with a little time you'll come to see that you deserve a life of your own and a chance to be happy. If Tynthanal can't give you that, then you should take advantage of the fact that the Blessing and the existence of Women's Well allows you to separate from him without the repercussions our predecessors had to face."

Everything Oona said was true and right. And yet Kailee didn't know if she would ever find the will to take advantage of the freedoms of this new world order.

When Chanlix rose from her obligatory curtsy, Alys couldn't resist the urge to give her friend a hug. Chanlix laughed and patted her back.

"One would think you hadn't seen me for months," Chanlix quipped, although she returned the hug with enthusiasm.

Alys squeezed a little tighter, then reluctantly let go. "I've seen my lady chancellor every day, and my niece's mother nearly as often, but I can't remember the last time I've had a cozy dinner with my *friend*."

The admission made Alys suddenly feel weepy, and she quickly turned to the table for two that had been set in her favorite parlor. A cheery fire burned in the fireplace, fighting off the evening chill, and a bottle of most excellent wine was waiting for them. Alys swallowed the lump in her throat as she poured two glasses without asking Chanlix if she wanted any. And she prayed Chan-

lix would not notice—or would at least *pretend* not to notice—
her fragile state of mind.

Composing her face, Alys turned to her friend with what she
hoped was a bright smile and held out the glass of wine. Chanlix's
face wore an expression of gentle concern, but thankfully she refrained from asking Alys what was wrong.

Mentally rolling her eyes at herself, Alys took a deep swallow
of her wine. There was nothing wrong, not really. Not beyond
the usual stresses and strains of being a sovereign princess in a
fledgling principality that some parts of the world would love
nothing better than to wipe from the map. And yet still, Alys was
struggling as of late, feeling the isolation of a sovereign's role
with more bitterness than ever.

"I'm sure we can arrange to do this more often," Chanlix said.
She smiled. "If you don't mind waiting until Chantynel is down
for the night to have your dinner."

Alys forced an answering smile and felt like the worst auntie in
the history of Seven Wells. Not that she didn't adore Chanlix's
infant daughter—of *course* she did!—but it was impossible not to
notice how thin Chanlix was stretched by the competing duties
of motherhood and statesmanship. Nor could Alys fail to see that
Chanlix often suffered from a melancholy that rivaled her own.
Even as Chantynel absorbed so much of Chanlix's energy, she
constantly reminded her mother of what she had lost. It hurt
Alys's heart that her friend was hurting and that she herself bore
a great deal of the blame for it.

"I don't mind in the least," Alys assured her. "But I do remember how precious was my sleep when I was a new mother, so
promise me you won't let me keep you too long."

Chanlix grinned at her. "Have your footmen ready a litter so
that they may carry me home when I start snoring at the table."
She took a sip of her wine. "And don't you dare pour a second
glass for me unless you wish to see me facedown in my soup."

Alys laughed—though not without another pang of guilt—and they spent the rest of the meal chatting amiably. But the moment the last of the remains had been cleared away, Alys sensed a change in Chanlix's demeanor. Instead of being contentedly sleepy as she should have been after a decadent meal and the second glass of wine she'd been unable to resist, something about her became sharper, more alert.

Alys's heart sank as she realized that Chanlix had *not* in fact suggested this casual dinner together as a pure act of friendship. It stung, although Alys felt instantly guilty for being selfish. When she had accepted the title of sovereign princess, she had accepted the reality that she could never again have a completely uncomplicated relationship. Not with friends, not with family.

"You have something you want to talk about?" Alys asked, keeping her voice as light as she knew how.

Chanlix smiled at her, but there was a hint of wariness—or maybe just concern—in her eyes. She hesitated a moment, then blew out a quick breath.

"I suppose I should just blurt it out instead of trying to find some subtle, tactful way to ask," she said ruefully, then met Alys's gaze with something of a challenge. "I wanted to ask you if you were planning to put aside your mourning wardrobe anytime soon. It has, after all, been over a year."

Alys could not prevent herself from flinching, looking down at the dour black brocade that draped her. Every morning, Honor offered her the choice of a black gown or a gown of some other dark, muted color, and every morning, Alys chose the black. Honor had finally stopped giving her reproving looks, and Alys wondered if she would someday stop offering the colored gowns.

Alys cleared her throat. "Yes, I know. It's past time. But . . ." She tried to articulate the horror she felt at the thought of putting aside the mourning, but she doubted her ability to put it into words. How could she explain the choking panic that assailed her, the roiling in her gut, the irrational—she *knew* it was irrational—feeling that to put aside the mourning was to dishonor Jinnell's memory?

"I never met your Jinnell," Chanlix said gently, "but from what others have told me about her, I don't think she would have wanted . . ."

"Don't!" Alys interrupted sharply, her eyes burning with tears she refused to shed. Never mind that she sometimes woke from a deep sleep to find her face and her pillow soaked with them.

Chanlix held up her hands in surrender. "All right. But as your friend, I'm beginning to worry about you."

Alys smoothed her skirts and stared at her hands. "I am not ready to be out of mourning," she said, her voice leaving no room for argument.

Chanlix hesitated a beat. "And is that what you've told Duke Thanmir?"

Alys couldn't hold back a startled gasp, her head suddenly whipping upward of its own accord as she met Chanlix's now challenging gaze. "What?"

Chanlix gave her a look of reproach. "Come now, Alys. Surely you don't think people haven't made the natural assumption about why a royal duke of Grunir is suddenly showing such an interest in Women's Well. Everyone knew what he wanted the first time he visited, and if they had any doubts, those were erased when he brought his daughter to meet you."

Alys was sure her face was turning an unappealing shade of red. She had been so taken aback when Thanmir had first suggested the possibility of marriage! And yet now that Chanlix mentioned it, of course it had been obvious. To everyone but her—and that only because she had somehow managed to keep herself willfully ignorant.

Alys coughed, then cleared her throat, squirming in her chair like a small child caught in a lie.

"He seems like a good man," Chanlix said gently. "Do you know that I was holding Chantynel the first time I met him, and he immediately charmed her and asked if he could hold her." She smiled in remembrance. "Most noblemen of my acquaintance would blanch in horror at the idea of holding an infant not their own, but Duke Thanmir seemed genuinely eager."

Alys was intrigued despite herself. "And did he know at the time that you are my lady chancellor?"

"He did," Chanlix confirmed. "And if he found it at all distasteful to have an unwed mother serving on the royal council, he did an excellent job of hiding it."

It was not hard to see that Chanlix had already formed a decided opinion as to how Alys should respond to Duke Thanmir's proposal.

The truth was, if Alys could only relieve herself of all her inconvenient emotions, she would readily admit that Chanlix was right. Thanmir was about as close as it was possible to get to the perfect husband in her current situation.

"He would be a wonderful addition to Women's Well," Chanlix enthused, in case Alys had not already gotten the point. "And young Shalna seemed very much like the kind of young woman who would fit in well here. Lady Shelvon says the girl asked her extensive questions about her sword school and might very well want to join up."

Alys nodded absently, for she could hardly argue any of Chanlix's points. As Thanmir had clearly intended when he'd introduced them, Alys had immediately liked Shalna and her fiery spirit.

Externally, there was very little resemblance between Shalna and the daughter Alys had lost. Jinnell had certainly been the possessor of a fiery spirit, but she had disguised that spirit under a veneer of primness and properness, to the extent that even *Alys* hadn't recognized it until Delnamal had begun his systematic campaign to destroy them. Shalna's spirit was much more overt, her eyes often flashing with challenge instead of demurely lowered. And she bore little physical resemblance to Jinnell, either.

Jinnell had been beautiful, with a willowy figure and raven-black hair reminiscent of her grandmother's. Shalna might at best be termed attractive, her face somewhat square in shape and her figure unfashionably thick, though her green-flecked hazel eyes and her rosebud lips softened her look, and her curly auburn hair gleamed a lustrous, rich red in the desert sun.

Despite this near-total lack of resemblance, Alys could not look at Shalna without seeing a shadow of her own daughter. And no matter how much she liked and admired the girl, she could not think about bringing Shalna into her household, making herself the girl's stepmother, without her soul recoiling in a toxic swirl of horror and terror. Horror that she might somehow be *replacing* Jinnell, and terror that she might once again fail in her duties as a protector.

Alys started when Chanlix reached across the table and laid a hand on her arm. She met her friend's sympathetic eyes, and it was all she could do to hold herself together and not burst into undignified tears.

"I can't pretend I know what you're going through," Chanlix said gently. "I have not the courage to put myself in your shoes and imagine something happening to Chantynel." Here her voice choked off, and she had to pause to take a quick breath. She shook her head. "No, I will *not* even allow myself to think of such a thing." She sighed. "But you cannot stay in mourning forever." She grimaced. "Not in *official* mourning, at least."

"I know that," Alys said tightly, still fighting against tears. "It is my duty to put my mourning aside and to do what must be done for the good of Women's Well."

She shuddered and swallowed hard, for though she was more than capable of putting that thought into words, it was a great deal harder to put those words into action.

Chanlix nodded. "And you know that Duke Thanmir would make an excellent match, especially as the two of you seem to get on well enough."

"The irony of my position is not lost on me," Alys said hoarsely, for she was well aware how selfish it was to speak to *Chanlix*, of all people, about her reluctance to enter into a marriage of diplomatic advantage.

Chanlix patted her hand. "Don't do that to yourself," she chided. "You know I *always* understood why it was necessary that Tynthanal marry Kailee and not me. And as reluctant as he might have been to do his duty, his situation was not at all the same as yours."

Alys forced a tremulous smile, for Chanlix was a better friend than she deserved. "I do not think I would be quite as understanding if our positions were reversed."

"I am not thinking only of the good of Women's Well," Chanlix said, ignoring Alys's statement. "I'm thinking of *your* well-being, too. I do not think you are doing yourself any favors by clinging to your grief."

Alys gently extracted her hand from under Chanlix's. "I'm sure you're right," she said, averting her eyes so that she might not see the sympathy and kindness in her friend's eyes. "However, I am not ready to let go of it yet. And though I appreciate that you are coming from a place of friendship and caring—as well as from perfect rationality—I must beg you to let this subject drop. I must focus my energies on the likelihood of war, and until we have dealt with the problem of Delnamal, there is little point in dwelling on the diplomatic implications of my possible future marriage."

It was a paltry and nonsensical excuse, and they both knew it. The war would come whether Alys put aside her mourning or not, whether she married or not. But though she hated herself for her weakness, the fact remained that she could not face setting aside her mourning attire without her soul screaming in pain, and until she could manage at least that much, there was no question of her accepting a marriage proposal.

Alys steadied herself with an iron will, forcing herself to look up once more and meet Chanlix's eyes with a stare she was certain conveyed how deadly serious she was. It was impossible to miss how badly Chanlix wanted to continue pressing, just as it was impossible to miss how worried her friend was. Although Chanlix had outwardly accepted Alys's assurance that she did not find the thought of triggering the purgative spell with her own sacrificial Kai appealing, Alys knew she was not convinced.

But as much as she clearly wanted to coax and cajole some more, Chanlix must have seen how futile it would be. She sighed sadly and bowed her head. "Very well, Your Royal Highness," she said, shifting immediately from friend to lady chancellor.

Alys's heart ached all the more for the distance that suddenly yawned between them. And yet she could not find the courage to reach across that gap.

CHAPTER TWENTY-NINE

Lord Darjal, Grand Magus of Khalpar, bowed deeply when he entered the king's study, although even when the man's head was down, Delnamal sensed his tension and vigilance. His face shadowed by the hood he now wore at all times, Delnamal smiled. There were occasions when the fear he triggered in Draios's court could be inconvenient, making otherwise intelligent men act like simpletons, but more often than not, it served as an effective incentive. Knowing what Delnamal could do—something that had become common knowledge since he'd performed the public executions of the former lord chancellor and lord chamberlain—no one wanted to risk defying him. Oh, there were still those who whispered amongst themselves and did not fully share the king's opinion that he was sent by the Creator for a holy purpose, but those whispers were oh-so-quiet and oh-so-careful.

Draios sat in the chair that used to be his father's. In an attempt to make himself look less like an untried boy and more like a sovereign, he had started growing out his beard. Unfortunately for Draios, there was a reason he'd chosen to remain clean-shaven previously. The beard—what there was of it—was thin and scrag-

gly and served only to make him look more like a boy desperately
pretending to be a man. However, as long as he had Delnamal
looming over his shoulder, no one was likely to inform him of his
shortcomings.

"You wished to see me, Your Majesty?" Darjal inquired when
he rose from his bow.

"Indeed," Draios confirmed. "I have a very important mission
I need you to undertake under the strictest secrecy."

Darjal's face revealed a touch of surprise and more than a
touch of wariness, but he let none of that show in his voice.
"How may I be of service?"

"I am aware that in these modern times, it is no longer considered appropriate or customary for kings to personally lead
their troops into battle. We are meant to direct the proceedings
from a safe remove, to send our men to their deaths without taking on any of the risks ourselves."

Darjal frowned thoughtfully. "There is no such thing as a safe
remove from a battle of the magnitude we are planning," he cautioned.

Draios waved that argument away. "My point is that although
it is considered customary for a king to keep his distance, I find
the thought of it . . . cowardly. Certainly beneath the dignity of a
true king."

Once again, Delnamal had to smile. A sharp glance from Darjal suggested he had caught a glimpse of the expression despite
the hood, but of course he dared not say anything.

Delnamal wished that he'd had even a fraction of his current
wisdom in the days before he had absorbed the Rhokai from Aaltah's Well. Back then, he had tried to get his way by brute force.
If an attempt at persuasion had met with even a hint of resistance,
his temper had reared its ugly head and taken over. How much
easier it was to manipulate people and get what he wanted without his erstwhile welter of emotions reducing him to sputtering
incoherence and threats!

As Draios continued to amass his troops, Delnamal had put some thought into what he needed to accomplish in the war that was to come. As terrifying as his ability to steal Rhokai was, his most devastating strength was the aura of Kai motes that surrounded him. He had every intention of adding more Kai to his aura by wading into the battle for Aalwell himself. He'd come to know Draios well enough by now to realize that the boy would never allow the man who was his greatest weapon to leave his side. Therefore, if Delnamal wanted to gorge himself on the battlefield, he needed Draios not to hang back safely as a king traditionally would do. If he even set foot on the battlefield in the first place.

And so Delnamal had, with a carefully chosen word here and there, planted the idea in Draios's mind that he would make a more kingly, heroic appearance if he marched into battle himself, and he could see at once that Draios very much liked the image of himself as a warrior king, leading his holy army to victory. Then all he'd had to do was suggest a way Draios might do so *safely,* to ensure that the boy would make it happen.

"It is true that kings of yore were expected to take to the battlefields themselves," Darjal said, with just a touch of condescension, "but the danger—"

"Is why I have conceived of a mission I would like you to undertake," Draios interrupted. Delnamal could not see the young king's eyes, but all he had to do was look at Darjal's face to know that he was on the receiving end of one of Draios's freezing glares.

Darjal inclined his head. "Of course, Your Majesty. Forgive my foolishness."

Delnamal rolled his eyes. He'd once thought his own grand magus one of the most obsequious men he'd ever met, but Darjal was every bit his equal. A fact of which he'd been aware when he suggested—in such a way that Draios believed it his own idea, naturally—this private meeting with Darjal.

Without turning, Draios made a slight hand gesture, which Delnamal interpreted as a command to explain "their" idea. An idea that was, naturally, entirely of Delnamal's devising.

"His Majesty would like you to invent two new Kai spells, made specially for him," Delnamal explained. "Naturally, when he steps onto the battlefield, he will be fully armed with every Kai spell he can carry. I will march beside him and provide him with all the Kai he needs to trigger those spells when necessary. But he must have a special shield spell that is fueled by Kai. I believe that with Kai as a triggering agent, a man of your talents can create a shield that will remain functional for as long as the battle may take."

Delnamal had no personal experience with battle, of course. Aaltah had been at peace for the entirety of his life, and he had never been the martial sort anyway. But he knew enough about magic and battles to know the fatal flaw of most shield spells: they wore off over time, and a man fighting for his life could not afford to open his Mindseye to replenish a failing shield.

The grand magus's brow furrowed in thought for a moment, then smoothed as he nodded. "I cannot promise that it will work, but I have an idea how I might approach such a spell."

"I intend to fight," Draios said. "I understand you are a man of caution who prefers to make no promises, but you *will* do this for me. Is that understood?"

Darjal blinked, and a muscle in his jaw twitched, but he made no other sign that the order had frightened or offended him. Delnamal was certain it had done both.

"Of course, Your Majesty," the grand magus said. "And what is the second spell you wish me to develop?"

"Because we can never be too careful," Draios said, "I would like you to create an illusion spell for me."

Delnamal nodded indulgently while Draios described the illusion he wanted the grand magus to create. It would be another Kai-fueled spell, and it would create two dozen images of Draios that would surround both him and Delnamal. This idea had been almost entirely of Draios's own devising, and Delnamal found it rather silly. As long as the king was under the protection of a Kai-fueled shield spell, hiding himself amidst a sea of doppelgängers was entirely unnecessary. However, Draios was in love with the image of himself as the invincible warrior, and while the shield spell would protect his life, it would not be visible and would not inspire the kind of fear that Delnamal's presence would. Draios thought of Delnamal as a large, snarling hound on a leash—he wanted the enemy to be as fearful of the handler as they were of the hound.

Darjal paled ever so slightly as he listened to the description. Delnamal wasn't sure whether the pallor was due to the idea of the spell—Delnamal had to admit that seeing more than two dozen men who looked exactly like Draios would be more than a little unnerving for the enemy. Especially when the illusions were impervious to wounds. Darjal *might* be picturing that fearsome vision. Or he might just be frightened that it was a request he could not fulfill.

The grand magus swallowed hard. "I . . ." He cleared his throat, his eyes turning inward as he thought.

"Surely there are illusion spells that might serve as a starting point," Delnamal said. "I know there are decoy spells that exist."

"Yes," Darjal replied slowly, "but those spells are not very sophisticated. They can create an illusion of movement, of a human figure seen through the corner of the eye for a momentary distraction. There is nothing that would withstand more than a passing glance."

"That is why I'm tasking you with inventing a new one," Draios said, with the tone of a man who was losing patience. "You may use a decoy spell to inspire your Kai-fueled version, or you may start from scratch. I don't care which. Just be sure to have it ready when the winter breaks, so that we may begin our glorious conquest and rid the world of the Curse as soon as possible."

That Darjal doubted his ability to carry out his orders was clear in both his face and voice. Nevertheless, he bowed deeply and gave the king his word that he would see it done.

Ellin had by now had so many private audiences with Nandel's ambassador that Zarsha had teased her with the threat that he might get jealous, but despite the ambassador's many requests for updates, she remained resolute in her claims that there had been no sign of Elwynne or the women who had "abducted" her from the Abbey of Nandel. It was an imperfect solution, at best, and she knew she could hardly keep her clandestine visitors shut up in their safe house indefinitely. But to admit she had them would bring far more strife and diplomatic headaches than she wished to face. She had enough troubles already!

It seemed like every day some new and unsettling report reached her from Khalpar. There was no longer any question that Delnamal had developed a terrifying new power—too many people had now witnessed his ability to use his magic to steal the life from a person without so much as a touch—and King Draios was preparing his kingdom for what he believed was a "holy war." His intended target, based on the reports, was Aaltah—so as to retake the throne on Delnamal's behalf—but there was little doubt he also intended to destroy Women's Well. And, based on his belief that the Devotional demanded women be subservient to men, there was just as little doubt in Ellin's mind that he meant to topple *her* from her throne, as well. So she did not need additional complications from her most vital trade partner.

The ambassador had only recently left her office after what had become an almost daily meeting when one of her talkers chirped. She glanced over her shoulder at the neat row of hand-carved birds that sat on the shelf behind her desk, then groaned softly to herself when she saw which one was chirping.

Waldmir's.

She did not want to answer—especially not after the tension of her latest conversation with the ambassador—but he did not strike her as the kind of man who would give up easily. With a heavy sigh, she picked up the talker and put it on the desk in front of her, then looked back and forth between the two honor guardsmen who were tasked with protecting her at all times, even within the safety of her palace.

"I require privacy for this conversation," she told them firmly. She trusted these men with her life, and with a great many state secrets, but she knew Waldmir would insist on total privacy. All well and good for *her* to trust her men, he would say, but that didn't mean *he* should be expected to do so.

As her honor guardsmen were leaving—with the expected looks of mild reproach—she opened her Mindseye so that she could activate the talker's spell. By the time she closed her Mindseye so that her worldly vision might return, a miniature image of Waldmir was hovering above her desk.

"Prince Waldmir," she said with a respectful nod, "how nice to hear from you."

Waldmir snorted. "Save the diplomatic small talk for my ambassador. He's been well versed in all that frippery, but I have no patience with it."

Coming from anyone else, this utterance would have been shockingly rude and might have caused her to end the conversation before it began. It was *still* shockingly rude coming from Waldmir, but Ellin was by now familiar with his disdain for diplomacy and his avowed preference for bluntness.

"Fine," she said. "What do you want?"

She had the momentary satisfaction of seeing Waldmir taken aback. Ordinarily, she tried to maintain some semblance of politeness even when her every word had a sharp edge to it, but after having beaten her head against the ambassador's thinly veiled hostility already, she had as little patience for it as Waldmir.

Waldmir recovered from his surprise quickly, though she had the impression he remained annoyed. He was used to the women of Nandel, who were taught from their earliest childhood to be quiet and defer to the men who legally owned them. What an effort it must be for him to deal with a woman who was not just his equal, but his superior! Although to his credit, he rarely treated her like the lesser creature he no doubt still believed she was.

"I want my daughter back," he said. "I know you have her."

Ellin let out a soft groan and pinched the bridge of her nose. "I *just* had this conversation with your ambassador," she griped.

"Yes, I know. He informed me."

"Then you know we have no further news," she said, then softened both her voice and her expression to convey sympathy. "I fear it is time to prepare yourself for the worst. If the princess were going to make it to Rhozinolm safely, she would be here by now."

"Which she is," Waldmir responded with an impatient wave of his hand. "We found her governess's body under the snows, but no sign of the abigails or my daughter. If they had died on the journey, we would have found them by now. Let's not waste time arguing over a falsehood."

"It is *not* a falsehood," Ellin responded with some heat, and very little guilt. In the early days of her reign, she had felt twinges of conscience whenever political necessity had forced her to lie, but she had come to terms with that discomfort long ago. "It is past time that you accept reality. There are numerous routes the others might have taken, and it might not be possible to find their bodies until the snows melt. If then!"

Waldmir crossed his arms, his cold eyes glinting in the afternoon light. If he were physically present, she might have found the stare intimidating. "I know Leethan is a seer," he said. "And I know she puts a great deal of faith in her visions."

Ellin started at that, for it was rare for a man of Nandel to acknowledge even the existence of women's magic, and she would have expected Waldmir to dismiss the possibility of seers as nothing but feminine superstition.

"I can think of no reason why she would have fled the Abbey with Elwynne except that she did so at the prompting of one of those visions," Waldmir continued. "I won't claim to understand these visions or how they work, but I know enough about them—and about Leethan—to very much doubt she would have attempted such a dangerous journey only to die in the crossing."

"But even if that's the case, there's no reason to be so certain she intended to come *here*," Ellin argued. "She was born in Grunir, wasn't she? Perhaps she has gone home to her family." A family that would very likely refuse to acknowledge her after her banishment to the Abbey, but it still seemed to Ellin like a perfectly reasonable assumption.

The cold glint in Waldmir's eyes was now matched by the sneer that twisted his lips. "You have a woman's skill for lying, I'll grant you that, but I am tired of playing this game. My men interviewed the women of the Abbey in hopes of gaining more information about Leethan's plans. It's clear she confided in no one, but in the course of these interviews, my men encountered some speculation that the child may not be mine. I expect Leethan was well aware of this speculation and that she thinks she is taking Elwynne to Rhozinolm to deliver her to her 'true' father."

"Why do you care so much?" Ellin asked in exasperation. "Isn't it better for you if Elwynne is gone? You need never again fear that she will be proven not to be your child, and therefore you need never fear the humiliation of having your people know you were cuckolded by your own nephew. Unless it's just that you hate the idea that you have lost your leverage over Zarsha now that you no longer have his daughter as a hostage."

"She's not Zarsha's daughter," Waldmir said. "She's mine."

Ellin blinked, for there was no hint of doubt in Waldmir's voice. "You can't know that," she said faintly. "Unless . . ."

Waldmir nodded. "Unless I lowered myself to using women's magic to test her paternity," he finished. "You already know that I have on occasion resorted to using women's magic when I felt it necessary."

Ellin did indeed know that. In fact, Waldmir's reliance on potency potions to fulfill his marital obligations was one of the secrets Zarsha held over his uncle's head. According to Zarsha, if the people of Nandel believed he needed a potency potion to perform, their hatred of women might cause them to deem him functionally a woman and therefore unfit for the throne. Which seemed ludicrous to Ellin, but obviously Zarsha understood the ways of Nandel better than she.

"Elwynne is my daughter," Waldmir finished. "I will make no claims to a great and abiding paternal love for the girl, but she is *mine*." Ellin could not see anything but Waldmir's upper body, but there was a sound that could only be the pounding of a fist on wood. "Give. Her. Back."

This was a new and unpleasant wrinkle in an already complicated game. Waldmir already thought that Princess Alysoon had "stolen" one of his other daughters—Shelvon, the erstwhile Queen of Aaltah, who had fled to Women's Well and been divorced in absentia by her husband. Ellin knew he had demanded the woman's return, although it was no secret that if she returned to Nandel she would be instantly locked up in the Abbey. He did not value his daughters as people, but he *did* value his possessions.

"We. Don't. Have. Her," Ellin responded, leaning forward in her chair and returning his challenging glare with one of her own.

"You had best reconsider your position," he growled. "You

will soon need to decide whether to send your army to the aid of Aaltah and Women's Well. I imagine you might find it difficult to win over your royal council to such a war if I was to renege on our trade agreements."

He was not wrong about that, and there was no doubt that if he was telling the truth about Elwynne's true paternity, she had very little cause to keep the girl in Rhozinolm, even if there weren't so much at stake.

However, although she suspected Waldmir was telling the truth, there was no reason to accept him at his word. And also, if Leethan's vision had led her to bring Elwynne to Rhozinolm, surely there was a *reason* for it. Ellin wasn't sure how much faith to put in Leethan's vision, but she most certainly needed time to think and present the new facts to Zarsha before she made any decision.

"If Elwynne somehow manages to arrive here despite all the odds," she said, "then I will be willing to consider sending her back home in the spring, when it is safe to travel once more. But I will tell you one more time: as of now, she is not in our custody. Rest assured I will contact you the moment that changes."

Without waiting for Waldmir to issue more threats, Ellin opened her Mindseye and plucked the mote of Rho out of the talker, ending the conversation.

CHAPTER THIRTY

I t was well past bedtime, but Leethan refused to surrender to sleep until she had absolutely no choice. Her whole body ached with exhaustion, and she knew without having to look that her eyes were bloodshot and her cheeks gaunt. But though she longed to crawl into bed and sleep, she knew the effort would be futile. The dream that had only occasionally troubled her throughout the course of her long life had now prevented her from getting anything resembling rest for the last seven nights. In desperation, she had tried napping during the day, but the dream insisted on visiting her then, too.

She sat in a chair by the fire in the safe house's cozy parlor, while the rest of the household—save for a few of the queen's men who guarded them—lay snug and snoring in their beds. She had tried distracting herself with needlework, but had found wielding a needle while sleep-deprived led to bloody fingers. Then she'd tried reading a book, but her sluggish mind refused to focus on the page, wandering off at the slightest provocation. Now she found herself doing nothing but staring at the flames and brooding. Eventually, she would likely fall asleep in this chair and relive the cursed dream yet again, and there was nothing she could do to stop it.

Her chin was just dipping toward her chest when she heard a soft knock on the front door. The sound jerked her awake, and she heard the door opening, followed by voices conversing quietly. She frowned in the direction of the hallway, wondering who could possibly have come calling at this time of night.

Not that anyone came calling at any time of day. Neither Leethan, nor Jaizal, nor Elwynne had set foot outside the house since they'd arrived, and Leethan knew she was not the only one chafing at the confinement, however well she might understand the need for secrecy.

She sat up straighter as footsteps approached. She expected to see one of the house's faux-footmen come through the door to announce the unexpected visitor, but sucked in a breath of surprise when she saw that it was Prince Zarsha himself.

Feeling clumsy and slightly stupid, Leethan rose to her feet and curtsied. She wasn't entirely sure what the official protocol for meeting with the prince consort was—only a small handful of men in all of the history of Seven Wells had ever borne that title, and it was ordinarily one that lasted only for the few days between the man's marriage to a sovereign and his own investiture as the new sovereign—but she assumed he should be granted exactly the respect she would grant any other sovereign's spouse.

"Forgive me, Your Majesty," she said, fighting off a chill of foreboding that said he was not here to deliver good news. "I was not expecting . . . That is . . ." She cleared her throat and shook her head, wishing she could fight off the fog that kept her thoughts so indistinct.

"No need to apologize," he answered swiftly, frowning at her ever so slightly. "I should perhaps have sent word that I was coming, especially at this hour. And, er, I am properly addressed as Your Highness, though far be it from me to be a stickler over such a triviality." He looked ever so slightly uncomfortable with the honorific, which she supposed reflected his Nandel sensibilities. He was the most cosmopolitan Nandelite she had ever known, but it was clear from his unfashionably plain dress that he retained some of the Nandelite disdain for ostentation and ceremony.

Leethan fought a yawn as it occurred to her that Zarsha should by all rights have discovered the entire household asleep at this late hour. "Is something wrong?" she asked, although she was too tired to muster the level of alarm his unexpected presence might reasonably have caused.

"No, no," he hastened to assure her. "Please forgive the late hour, but it is not easy for me to slip away from the palace unobserved, and I did not want to risk arousing curiosity about this house or its occupants."

"Would you like some tea?" she asked, belatedly realizing that although she did not own the house, it was nevertheless her duty to serve as hostess. She frowned as soon as the offer was made, sure that the kitchen staff were already long in their beds.

Zarsha waved off the offer. "No need to trouble yourself or anyone else. And please do sit down. You look . . ." He frowned. "Are you unwell?"

Leethan grimaced and accepted his suggestion that she should sit. Weariness dragged at both her limbs and her mind, and she longed for sleep—*true* sleep, *restful* sleep—with a passion that bordered on desperation.

"I'm fine," she lied, forcing a half-hearted smile. "I just haven't been sleeping well," she added when she saw that his frown had not abated.

"It's more than that," he responded. "You're not still worrying we might send you back, are you?"

"No." She hadn't even thought about the possibility in the last week. But that dream . . .

Well, she was still doing her best to convince herself the dream was *not* prophetic, but apparently some part of her had already

decided that it was, for that was the only way she could explain
her lack of worry about being sent back to Nandel. As diplo-
matically wise as it might be for Queen Ellinsoltah to give in to
Prince Waldmir's demands for her return and that of little Elwynne, the dream suggested that she and Waldmir would meet
and confront each other on the shores of a sea.

Zarsha raised an eyebrow at her. "Then what is it?"

"It's nothing," she insisted, but even she could hear the lack
of conviction in her voice. Ordinarily, she was a very private person, one who had long ago learned to keep her thoughts and her
fears to herself. She shared a great deal with Jaizal, but even with
Jaizal she always kept a hint of reserve. Even so, right now she felt
as if the truth were hammering at her breastbone, demanding an
escape. "I've been having some disturbing dreams. I've had them
before, so it's nothing to be concerned about."

"You are in Rhozinolm now," Zarsha reminded her. "There
are a wealth of potions available at the Abbey that are specifically
designed to help with troubled sleep. You need but to ask, and
your servants will acquire some for you. They are not especially
expensive, and well within the budget we have set aside for your
comfort."

"Thank you, Your Highness," she said with a bow of her head.
If she truly were trying to keep her troubles to herself, she could
easily have stopped there. A quick change of subject might not
fully reassure Zarsha that all was well, but surely he would be
satisfied with having suggested she procure some sleep potions.

Indeed, she had every intention of changing the subject by
asking him why he was visiting—it certainly wasn't to present
polite inquiries into the status of her health and welfare—but
somehow her tongue was reluctant to obey her. Instead of changing the subject, she found herself adding, "It is a perfectly reasonable suggestion, but I doubt it will help."

Zarsha cocked his head at her, his curiosity fully piqued.

What had come over her? It seemed exhaustion had chipped

away at her self-control and all but erased her habitual reticence. Either that or she simply felt so desperate for a solution that she couldn't stop herself from seeking aid even from someone who was little better than a stranger to her.

"What is it you wished to see me about?" she belatedly asked, knowing full well she had told him far too much to expect him to let it go. Not when he was looking at her like that.

"Tell me what is troubling you first," he insisted. "When a known seer seems so troubled, it is more than a little worrisome to those of us who believe in the validity of visions."

"It's not a vision," she said. "I haven't triggered one of those since I left the Abbey." She was in no condition to withstand the torments of a seer's poison even if circumstances had made her think drinking one was a good idea. "It's just a dream."

Zarsha shifted in his chair. "I've never known a dream to leave anyone looking quite as haunted as you now look."

"It's *not* just a dream," said a voice from the doorway, and both Leethan and Zarsha jumped. Jaizal smiled at their startled expressions as she entered the room. She was wrapped in a dressing gown, her hair tucked up under a nightcap. If she hadn't spent most of her youth whoring at the Abbey, she would not have let *any* man—much less the Prince Consort of Rhozinolm—see her in such a state of undress, but any semblance of modesty had long ago been beaten out of her.

"Forgive me for interrupting, Your Highness," she said to Zarsha, giving him a quick curtsy. "I am Sister Jaizal, though I presume you don't need me to tell you that."

Leethan noted that Jaizal had used the correct form of address for him, and she wondered how long Jaizal had been listening in the hallway.

"Pleased to make your acquaintance," Zarsha said with a dry little smile on his lips. "Why do you say it is not just a dream?"

"Jaizal, please," Leethan begged, her eyes suddenly burning with tears. It was bad enough that she'd burdened her friend with the knowledge of these dreams; she did not want to tell yet another person about them.

Jaizal gave her a quick, pitying look before she turned her attention back to Zarsha. "She's had a recurring dream off and on for most of her life, but she's never before had it more than once or twice in a year, and it's usually several years between occurrences. She's had it every night since she arrived in Zinolm Well. I cannot help thinking that the dream is prophetic, and Leethan believes so as well, no matter how desperately she denies it."

Leethan tried her best to glare at her friend, but she just didn't have the energy. Besides, it had probably been too late to keep her own counsel even before Jaizal had entered the room.

Zarsha groaned and rubbed his eyes. "I cannot imagine the prophecy is an encouraging one, or it would not leave you looking so wasted," he said to Leethan.

"I know of no documented incident of a truly prophetic dream," Leethan insisted. "This is . . . this is . . ." Her voice trailed off as she failed to find a more palatable explanation to serve up.

"Tell me about the dream," Zarsha said, and it was not a request.

Leethan bowed her head in defeat, her eyes once again filling with tears. The *last* thing she wanted to do just now was speak about the dream, and yet it seemed she had little choice.

Jaizal came to sit on the arm of Leethan's chair and put a comforting arm around her shoulders. Leethan was grateful for the gesture and felt a childish urge to curl into the warmth of her friend's body and hide her face. But if she was to tell Prince Zarsha about her dream, it was best to get that ordeal over with as quickly as possible.

Leethan looked at her hands rather than at Zarsha's face as she recalled the details of the dream. She had gained no new revelations since she'd recognized Waldmir's sword and her own hand, and the whole story sounded vaguely ridiculous to her own ears.

She was more grateful than she could say for Jaizal's warm and comforting presence at her side, even as a part of her was cursing her friend for forcing her hand.

When at last she'd finished her story, she risked a glance at Zarsha's face, expecting to see skepticism, if not outright disbelief. He would find the dream ridiculous, and her worries that it might be prophetic were just foolish flights of fancy. She was so sure of it that it took her a moment to comprehend his true expression, which was one of downright shock.

Zarsha closed his eyes for a moment—whether in an attempt to school his expression or just in thought, Leethan could not guess. When he opened them again, the intensity of them was so fierce and chilling that she nearly jerked back in her chair. His demeanor was so different from Prince Waldmir's that one rarely reminded her of the other, but she unquestionably saw the family resemblance in those eyes.

"Are you aware of what has been happening in Khalpar recently?" he asked.

Leethan shook her head. "Even when I was in the Abbey, my knowledge of world affairs was always terribly outdated, and I've heard nothing of the goings-on in the world since I left it." Not only was the world meant to forget about the abigails who were condemned to live behind the Abbey walls, but the abigails themselves were discouraged from displaying too much curiosity about the world of which they were no longer considered a part.

"So you have not heard of the murder of King Khalvin? Or of Prince Draios's seizure of the throne and the man who helped him accomplish it?"

She gasped, sharing an astonished look with Jaizal. "I assure you, I know nothing of any of this. I cannot even fathom—"

"You had better not be lying to me," he interrupted, those eyes still locked on hers, keeping her pinned in her seat when she wanted to jump to her feet and pace in agitation. "There will be consequences if you are."

Leethan held up her hands in a gesture of innocence and sur-render. "If any of this happened before we fled the Abbey, word had not yet reached us. And who do you imagine we might have encountered since then who would think to tell us about any upheaval in Khalpar? And what does any of that have to do with my dream?"

Jaizal's arm tightened protectively around her. "And why have you gone from inquiring politely after her dream to accusing her of lying and threatening her with punishment?"

Leethan would have smiled at the ferocity in Jaizal's voice if she weren't so disturbed by Zarsha's reaction to her dream. Even her sleep-deprived mind could work out that something in her dream struck him as being connected to the upheaval in Khalpar.

Zarsha let out a long, hissing breath. "Forgive my discourtesy," he said, but his voice was still tight and his expression still forbidding. "But if you truly have heard nothing about Draios and his rise to power in Khalpar, then I very much fear Lady Jaizal may be right when she suggests the dream is prophetic."

Leethan might have thought he'd called her friend "Lady" Jaizal instead of "Sister" Jaizal by mistake if he and his queen hadn't done the same with Leethan when she'd first met them. Whatever their fate was to be, it seemed unlikely they would find themselves confined to the Abbey of Rhozinolm. She was much more eager to think about the deep meanings of his chosen address rather than the implications of his words. Jaizal, however, was braver and bolder.

"Why do you say that?" Jaizal asked.

Leethan and Jaizal listened in horror as Zarsha described the murder of King Khalvin and the role former King Delnamal of Aaltah had played in it.

"Delnamal is now very much the power behind the throne in Khalpar," he said. "He has convinced Draios that he is an instrument of the Creator, sent to wage a holy war in an effort to undo what he and his supporters call the Curse. And according to the reports we have received, Delnamal's face and body were ravaged by the accident at the Well, and he therefore wears a dark cloak and hood whenever he is seen in public."

Leethan felt as if all the blood had drained from her body, her head suddenly swimming so that she had to grab the arm of her chair lest she fall out of it. "That cannot be," she whispered harshly, shaking her head. She closed her eyes as if somehow that would allow her to escape the truth.

"If you've had dreams of a skinny man wearing a dark cloak and hood over mail facing off against a woman in a crown, and you've been having them for many years, then . . ."

"It cannot be," she tried again, shaking her head harder.

Jaizal patted her shoulder comfortingly, although her voice had a touch of bite in it when she said, "Yes, I'm sure it's just a coincidence that you've dreamt of a man like that and one should happen to be rising to power right now."

Leethan opened her eyes and gave Jaizal a gently scolding look even as she tried to absorb the enormity of the revelation.

"I will have to tell the queen about this," Zarsha mused, a haunted look in his eyes. "I can't claim I know what to do about it, but we will have to act upon the assumption that it is not just an ordinary dream." He rubbed his eyes as if this new information had suddenly made him tired. Then again, it was late at night, when sensible people would already be in their beds.

"I must return to the palace now," he said, rising. "We will have to talk about this some more, of course, but first I must inform the queen."

It looked for all the world as if he was planning to turn around and immediately hurry off. Leethan stood, perhaps a little too suddenly as her head swam again.

"Your Highness," she called, reaching out to him although he was well out of her reach. He turned back to her, his impatience to be on the move painted across his face. "You came here for some reason other than to hear about my dream."

A hint of color warmed his cheeks, and he looked quickly down at his feet and shook his head. "My apologies," he murmured. "I came to ask if you would obtain for me a small sample of Princess Elwynne's blood, such that we might determine for certain whose daughter she might be. Prince Waldmir claims he has tested her and she is his, but . . ." He shrugged. "He cannot use women's magic himself, and since *you* consider Elwynne's paternity to be in doubt, it seems he did not engage you or one of your abigails to perform the test."

Leethan sighed, happy to think about *anything* other than the potentially prophetic ramifications of her dream. "He would most likely have engaged a foreign source to perform the test. While we do perform some magic in the Abbey of Nandel despite the law, we don't have the breadth of experience that might be found outside of Nandel. Also, he likely would have sent the samples anonymously so that whoever tested them would not understand the ramifications of their verdict."

"So you think he's likely telling the truth?" Zarsha looked crestfallen, and Leethan realized for the first time that he'd truly *hoped* the girl was his own.

"I wouldn't go that far," she hedged. "I imagine under the circumstances he is claiming certain paternity in order to pressure your queen for Elwynne's return. He would most certainly lie if he felt it expedient. I will obtain a sample for you."

She could see by the look in his eyes that Zarsha was inclined to believe his uncle's claim, and that he was saddened by it. "Will you send her back to Nandel if Waldmir is her father?" she asked.

Zarsha huffed out a breath. "Not if I have any say in the matter. He's already made it more than clear that he considers her tainted by her mother's infidelity. I will protect her to the best of my ability, one way or another."

He left unspoken the reality that the decision was not his to make.

Alys plucked the mote of Rho out of the talker, and Queen Ellinsoltah's image dissolved before her eyes. She had every intention of doing the same with the talker linked to Tynthanal's, but
he had other ideas.

"Alys, please don't read too much into all of this," he implored her, and she cursed him for his powers of perception.
When Ellinsoltah had told them of the recurring dream that had
plagued the sleep of Nandel's former abbess, she had done her
best to treat the news with an air of polite skepticism. She did not
claim to disbelieve Leethan of Nandel, but she had—she'd
thought—kept her expression neutral.

"What do you mean?" she asked, hoping her face revealed
nothing but perplexity.

Tynthanal's eyes narrowed, and the tone of his voice turned
nearly accusatory. "I saw the look on your face when Ellinsoltah
described that final confrontation."

It took every ounce of Alys's courage not to avert her gaze like
a guilty child. Ever since she and Chanlix and Rusha had begun
working on the purgative spell that would hopefully remove the
stolen Rhokai from Delnamal's body, Alys had been trying to
fight off the idea that the spell would need to be triggered by
sacrificial Kai. More specifically, *her own* sacrificial Kai. But she
had sworn to Chanlix that she did not believe a sacrifice was necessary, and her rational mind had accepted that as the truth. Right
up until the moment Ellinsoltah had recounted Leethan of Nandel's dream.

"What look are you talking about, Brother?" she inquired.
"You cannot deny that if the dream is indeed prophetic, it shows
a distinctively frightening future."

"I saw you make the same connection that I did—and that
likely Ellinsoltah did, as well. If Leethan has recognized herself

facing off against Waldmir and has also seen a figure that we all recognize as being Delnamal, there is only one logical conclusion as to the identity of the crowned woman who faced him."

Alys leaned back in her chair and sighed. Yes, it was fairly obvious that if the cloaked and hooded figure was Delnamal, then the crowned woman must be Alys. Just as there was no missing the similarities between what had happened in the dream and what had apparently happened on the night their mother had led the casting of the Blessing. Three women had—apparently of their own free will—slashed their wrists and given their lives to enact the Blessing. And now Leethan dreamed of three women—including herself and Alys—slashing their wrists and thereby defeating Waldmir and Delnamal and an unknown third man. A man who, based on circumstances, was likely Draios.

"Yes," she admitted reluctantly. "I can see that I must be the crowned woman." And it seemed very much like a confirmation that she would be required to use her own sacrificial Kai to trigger the purgative spell, although she knew better than to say that to her brother. "But I have learned enough about visions in the past couple of years to know that this dream is not at all the same as a vision. Visions show a tangible reality, and this . . ." She shook her head. "Well, I'm quite certain the scene Leethan described is *not* something that will happen literally."

Her reassurance did nothing to calm the worry that Tynthanal made no attempt to hide from her. "So you are not now taking the dream to mean you must kill yourself for the greater good."

"Of course not," Alys lied, although considering the way her brother was looking at her, it seemed unlikely she would convince him. "I take it to mean that I will have an important role to play in the war that will come, and that it will be up to me to stop Delnamal. But I was already assuming that anyway, so this dream tells me nothing new."

"Uh-huh," Tynthanal said with a heavy dose of skepticism. "So Chanlix is wrong to be worried about you?"

Alys blinked in surprise, though of course she was aware that Chanlix and Tynthanal had been talking more frequently since the birth of their daughter. She'd known Chanlix was worried about her, but she hadn't thought she was so worried that she'd mention it to Tynthanal. She wondered if Chanlix had also mentioned the courtship of Duke Thanmir, but it was a topic she herself had no intention of bringing up.

"Chanlix is a dear friend," Alys said, "and I know she is concerned. She thinks my reluctance to shed my mourning attire is unhealthy, and she is most likely right. But just because I am not yet ready to come out of mourning does not mean I'm looking to throw my life away." She rolled her eyes as if the very thought were ridiculous, as if the image of ending her own suffering for a heroic cause weren't disturbingly seductive.

"I'm glad to hear that," her brother said with a sigh of relief, although she did not think she had entirely quelled his worry. "I hope you remember that you have people who love you, people who will always be there for you when you need them."

Alys's eyes suddenly stung with tears, and her breath seemed to stick in her throat. She could not respond one way or another, or she felt she might shatter into a million pieces.

The expression on Tynthanal's face softened. "I can't remember the last time I put it into words, but *I* love you, Alys. None of the troubles that came between us ever changed that."

The ache in her heart was more than she could bear. When she had allowed both Tynthanal and Corlin to leave for Aaltah, she had known it would hurt, and that it would continue to hurt for a long time. But she had not fully appreciated how deep that ache would run, how much damage it would do to her psyche. How deeply, terribly alone she would feel.

She drew in a steadying breath through her nose, closing her eyes and focusing on forcing that air past the tightness in her throat. How she hated these feelings that plagued her, that distracted her from her duties and kept her awake at night. She was a sovereign princess, with a whole principality counting on her to keep a cool head and make the right decisions at all times. She had not the luxury of giving in to despair or wallowing in her own maudlin grief and loneliness.

"I love you, too," she managed to force out, opening her eyes and proud of herself for not crying, though she suspected she would lose the battle with herself the moment she cut the connection. "Please don't worry about me. I promise I'm not reading too much into Leethan's dream. My guess is that the three women will play a crucial role, and that our role will likely involve a sacrifice of some sort. But I will not leap from that to the idea that we must all slash our wrists on the battlefield. There is more at work here than we yet know."

She did not think Tynthanal was entirely reassured—and she suspected Chanlix might be even less so, when she learned of the dream—but after another long, searching look, he finally let the subject drop.

CHAPTER THIRTY-ONE

Ellin embraced her husband, knowing even her love wouldn't be enough to ease his pain. "I'm so sorry, dearest," she murmured against his shoulder. A part of her marveled at her tightened throat and stinging eyes, for when Zarsha had first told her Princess Elwynne might actually be his daughter, she'd been so jealous and angry she'd contemplated changing her mind about marrying him. Now, when they had the test results that confirmed that Waldmir had told them the truth when he'd claimed Elwynne as his own, she was on the verge of tears.

Zarsha gave a shuddering sigh as he held on to her. "I always said she *might* be my daughter," he said hoarsely, "but I think on some level, I always believed she truly was. Certainly I *loved* her as if she were my own." Another sigh. "And I still do, no matter what the test says."

Ellin patted his back. "Of course you do," she murmured, for that had been obvious to her from the moment he'd first told her about his affair with Elwynne's mother. Zarsha had loved the child and done everything he could to protect her, even not knowing if he was the father, and even though he'd spent very little time in Nandel since her birth. Princess Elwynne was a virtual stranger to him, and yet he still felt responsible for her.

"I told you before that it didn't really matter to Waldmir which of us was her father," Zarsha continued. "The results of the test don't change that."

Ellin might have argued—after all, Waldmir *had* tested the girl's paternity, which suggested it mattered at least a bit—but the argument seemed to have little bearing, so she kept her silence.

"He will never forgive her for her mother's infidelity," Zarsha continued, his voice full of anguish. "If we send her back to him . . ."

His voice choked off, but Ellin didn't need to hear the end of the thought. Waldmir had firmly established that Zarsha would do anything to protect Elwynne, regardless of the girl's true paternity. If Ellin sent her back to her father, Elwynne would be held hostage against Zarsha for as long as Waldmir lived.

"We won't send her back," Ellin said, the words rising from her throat before she had a chance to put much thought into them.

She felt Zarsha's whole body start, and he pulled away from her to look down into her eyes. She read in his expression grief and hope and fear.

"If we send her away at all, it will be to her mother. You said she was living in Grunir, didn't you?"

Zarsha shook his head. "That would be sending her back to Waldmir. There is no question that he knows exactly where Brontyn is living and will be keeping watch. Our choices are to hide her or to send her to Waldmir."

"Well, that decides it," she said firmly.

"You are the Queen of Rhozinolm. It can be of no possible benefit to your kingdom to keep Elwynne here now that we know I'm not her father. And we have no legal standing to keep her."

She reached up and cupped his face with one hand. "I've done a great many things I didn't want to do for the sake of my kingdom," she told him. "But I will not send a helpless little girl back to Nandel and a father who cares so little for her that he sent her to 'visit' the Abbey at the age of five."

"But—"

"And I could argue that sending her back to Nandel is not in the best interests of Rhozinolm, since her father can use her as a hostage against us."

It was a weak argument, and the look on Zarsha's face said he knew it. He was right, and her duty was to put the needs of her kingdom above all else. But Zarsha had already lost so much when she'd bargained with Waldmir for their marriage agreement. So many people he'd cared for had already suffered, and no matter how much she tried to convince him he was blameless, he carried that responsibility on his shoulders all the time. She could not send the girl he loved as a daughter back into Waldmir's clutches.

Zarsha turned his head and kissed her palm, his eyes closing. "I love you," he whispered, causing her to smile fondly at him. "And I'm more grateful than you know that—"

"Zarsha, I'm not sending her back," she said firmly. "We can continue insisting that they never arrived."

"Your council—"

"Has already actively supported the lie, even if not all of them believe it. As long as they have no concrete proof that Elwynne is here, they will not contradict me."

He shook his head. "That cannot last. It's a miracle we've kept it secret as long as we have."

"Not a miracle," she corrected. "We've just chosen the right people to trust."

He pinched the bridge of his nose. "Have you considered that Leethan's dream seemed to suggest that Waldmir might be involved in the battle she spied? And that he clearly stood in opposition to her and to Alysoon? He is nominally our ally at the moment, but it would hardly be surprising if our kidnapping his daughter was the reason he chose to ally with our enemies instead."

"Yes," she said softly. "I *have* considered that. But I've also considered the fact that Leethan brought Elwynne here because of a vision. She believes the Mother guided her into bringing Elwynne to us. Perhaps Waldmir is *supposed* to ally with our enemies instead. Maybe he needs to be defeated so that the people of Nandel might finally embrace the new world order instead of clinging to the past."

Zarsha let out a bitter snort of laughter. "I don't suggest you present that line of reasoning to your council."

She smiled ever so slightly, trying to imagine the horrified faces of her councilors if she suggested such a thing. "I will keep them in the dark for as long as I can," she said. "If we are lucky, this whole thing will be over before any of them dares to suggest I'm not telling the full truth."

In reality, she very much doubted such would be the case, and she knew from his expression that Zarsha did, as well. If Waldmir kept insisting that Elwynne was in their custody, and if he should get any more forceful or threatening in his demands for her return . . .

Well, the council would support her to a point, but they would not allow her to make an enemy of Waldmir at a time like this. Her council had already agreed that they would need to help defend Aaltah and Women's Well against the forces of Par and Khalpar, the tales of Delnamal's new power so terrifying that there had been little in the way of argument. The last thing any of them would want was to make an enemy of their most dangerous neighbor.

Draios could not see Delnamal's expression thanks to the shadow of the hood, but he felt certain the man was scowling fiercely at the grand magus. From the pinched and nervous look on Lord Darjal's face, it seemed he made the same assumption.

"I do hope you're not going to disappoint His Majesty once again," Delnamal said in that whispery rasp of his, and Draios had to suppress a shudder as Darjal lost just a little bit more color. A nagging voice in the back of Draios's mind muttered that a man who'd been chosen as the Creator's champion should not feel so very . . . unwholesome. But Draios dismissed that voice as ever. The Destroyer's power and influence were corrupting Delnamal's worldly body, but Draios *had* to believe the Creator had full control of the weapon He had unleashed on Seven Wells.

"I cannot make any promises," Lord Darjal said, and though his voice came out sounding strong, the fear in his eyes and his tight, clenched body language spoke volumes. "This is magic such as the world has never seen, and there's no telling . . ." His voice trailed off, and he gave Draios an imploring look.

If the man were any more frightened, he might piss himself, and though Draios found the previous failures annoying, he did not think it particularly useful to threaten the grand magus. Fear was sometimes a good motivator, but spell crafting required a degree of creativity that might be hard for a terrified man to muster.

"I understand the difficulty of this task," Draios said soothingly, "and I believe that you will succeed, whether it is with this try or another. We still have at least a month before the winter eases enough for our invasion of Aaltah to begin."

He was eager to set sail as soon as possible, but even with his very limited training in military strategy, he knew that a winter attack was inadvisable, with storms both on land and at sea causing delays and costing lives. The navies of Par and Khalpar were the most feared in all of Seven Wells, but even *their* great battleships were vulnerable to those storms and would likely enter Aaltah's waters scattered and damaged.

"Yes," Delnamal agreed in a croon designed to send shivers up the spine. "We have time. But if I begin to feel I am expending my Kai for nothing, I might find myself tempted to replenish it on the spot."

"Enough," Draios said as he made a slashing motion with his hand. He wanted to reassure Darjal that he would not allow Delnamal to steal his Rhokai—it would be imbecilic to kill his most powerful spell crafter when the mission was not yet accomplished— but he did not want to show any sign of dissension. "Let us just try the spell and see how it works, shall we?"

He held out his hand to Darjal, who dragged his eyes away from the looming threat of Delnamal with an obvious effort.

"Of course, Your Majesty," Darjal said, bowing his head as he held out his hand.

Draios took the large, loose diamond that held the grand magus's spell, cupping it in the palm of his hand. Once the spell was perfected, he would have the diamond set into a brooch that he would use to fasten his cloak over his armor when he marched into battle. He held the diamond out to Delnamal, who plucked an invisible mote of Kai from the air near his chest. Draios wondered briefly whose life would be fueling this test, but shoved that thought aside. The lives that Delnamal took were of criminals and heretics and traitors, and they were serving their kingdom far better in death than they had in life.

The air seemed to shimmy and swirl when the mote of Kai activated the diamond's spell, and Draios felt a quick stab of pain in his eyes. Pain that he could tell by Darjal's gasp was not limited to his own eyes.

The pain faded quickly, though his vision still felt blurry and indistinct, and he had to blink repeatedly before it returned to normal.

When it did, Draios found himself surrounded by a veritable sea of men who looked exactly like him. Some of those doppelgängers were more perfect than others, he noted. The ones closest to him looked real and solid enough to touch, while the ones farther away were semi-transparent. One of those more distant copies had materialized right on top of Darjal, who made an undignified squeaking noise as he hastily backed away, brushing at his skin and clothes as if he'd walked into a spiderweb.

Draios surveyed his miniature army as he took a step forward. He grinned with pleasure when he saw that although they stayed with him, they did not move in lockstep. Some mirrored his smile, while some of their faces remained impassive. When he took a couple more steps, he found himself no longer in the very center of the group, although as he continued to move left and right, forward and back, he found that there were always several doppelgängers surrounding him.

Darjal cleared his throat, but when he spoke it was still impossible to miss his disquiet. "I did not want you to always be the very center of the grouping," he said. "I thought someone might guess that would be the case and therefore figure out which one was the real you."

Draios nodded approvingly, while some of his doppelgängers nodded along and some frowned. He noticed that while Darjal had appeared to be addressing him directly, the man's eyes darted back and forth between him and the two closest doppelgängers. He remembered those first few moments, when his eyes had stung and his vision had gone blurry and he'd been forced to close his eyes and then blink. Had Darjal in that moment of confusion lost track of which one of these images was real?

"And do you know which one is me?" Draios asked.

Darjal winced, and Delnamal let out a little snort.

"Well, he does now," Delnamal growled, and Draios realized that his doppelgängers had remained silent when he spoke. Delnamal turned to the grand magus.

"You still have several kinks to work out," he said, but he sounded less threatening than he had previously. "The visual illusion does less good if the enemy can identify His Majesty the moment he makes a sound."

Sweating now with nerves, Darjal nodded. "I'm certain I can fix that," he said. "Just as I can make the ones around the edges more solid."

"And make it so they don't appear right on top of someone or something so that it's obvious they're not solid," Draios added dryly.

"Yes, Your Majesty."

Draios smiled broadly as he looked once again at his little personal army. Darjal had put a great deal of careful thought into the spell, making the figures move and shift about constantly to add to the confusion. Flawed they might be, but he could only imagine the terror they would strike into the heart of the enemy. Especially when the looming specter of Delnamal and his devastating power marched beside him.

"You have done well, Lord Darjal," he said, and the grand magus bowed with an audible sigh of relief.

Tynthanal could see by the thinly veiled alarm in Lord Zauthan's eyes that the lord chamberlain had some idea why he had been summoned. If Tynthanal had had any doubt of the man's guilt, that look of alarm would have vanquished it. Zauthan glanced longingly at the chairs before Tynthanal's desk—perhaps his knees were feeling a little weak—but Tynthanal had no intention of inviting him to sit.

Without a word, Tynthanal pushed a piece of parchment across the desk. The parchment was covered with the untidy script of a man not much used to writing and detailed the confession of a commoner named Hunter. Hunter had twice previously eluded the night watch, who had caught him in the act of posting broadsheets calling for Tynthanal's removal. Lord Lyslee's men had quietly arrested Hunter and brought him to the marshal for questioning, and the whole sordid story had come out.

Zauthan nervously read the first few sentences of the confession—which Hunter had defiantly signed "Hunter Rah-Zauthan"—and his face turned an unhealthy shade of gray.

"Would you truly have acknowledged paternity if he'd helped you remove me from the regency?" Tynthanal asked in a conversational tone that belied the fury within him. He'd never had much patience with men who refused to acknowledge their illegitimate offspring, and he had even less for men who took advantage of household servants. Hunter's mother had apparently been his wife's lady's maid. When she'd gotten pregnant, Zauthan had quietly transferred her to another household, where she claimed to be a widow. He had discreetly provided for his illegitimate son, but had denied the boy his name. Then, when he'd needed a rabble-rouser, he'd promised Hunter an official acknowledgment of paternity—and the right to use his name—if Hunter would post the broadsheets.

Zauthan looked down at his feet and did not respond. According to Lyslee, Hunter was nearly thirty years old, and it seemed likely that if Zauthan were ever going to acknowledge paternity, he would have done so long before now. Tynthanal felt no small amount of pity for Hunter, although that could not excuse his decision to post seditious broadsheets—especially not when the kingdom was on the brink of war.

"What is to become of me?" the lord chamberlain asked, and there was a slight quaver in his voice.

Tynthanal grunted in disgust. "You're not even going to ask about your son?"

Zauthan's eyes flashed. "He knew what he was doing, and he knew the risks. I told him he should stop after the first time he almost got caught, but he chose not to take my advice." Anger made him bold, and he lost the submissive hunch in his shoulders. "Besides, my relationship—or lack thereof—with my son is not your concern."

Tynthanal had to acknowledge that was true, although the lord chamberlain's lack of concern only deepened Tynthanal's dislike of the man. He had agonized for a long time over what to do about Lord Zauthan's crime, for though in ordinary times, the laws of the land called for Zauthan to be arrested, tried, and appropriately punished, these were not ordinary times.

"If I have you arrested and you go to trial," Tynthanal said, "you will be attainted for sure. All your lands and titles will be forfeit to the Crown."

Zauthan raised his chin. "I know what the punishment for sedition is."

"And what do you have to say for yourself?"

Anger sparked again in his eyes, but Zauthan quickly lowered his gaze. When he spoke, his voice came out softly. "I did what I thought was best for Aaltah, though I don't expect you to understand."

Tynthanal snorted. "No, I don't understand how trying to sow discord when we're on the brink of war is best for Aaltah."

Zauthan made a sound of frustration. "No, of course not. I told Hunter to distribute the broadsheets before we knew what was happening in Khalpar. Once I knew war was coming, I tried to stop him." He met Tynthanal's gaze, his expression one of challenge. "I never liked the precedent of giving the regency to a traitor, but I allowed myself to be persuaded because I hoped you might have the skills and knowledge to fix the Well. But it turns out you haven't. Even so, I would not endanger Aaltah's stability and unity by striking out at you *now*. I hope you will give me at least that much credit."

Tynthanal made a noncommittal sound as he studied Zauthan's face. He believed there was some truth in what the lord chancellor was telling him—in Hunter's confession, he'd mentioned that his father had asked him to stop distributing the broadsheets, but he'd been so desperate to be acknowledged that he'd kept at it anyway. Always before, Zauthan had served Aaltah admirably, and he had stopped challenging Tynthanal during council meetings as soon as they'd discovered that Draios had declared himself king and was preparing Khalpar for a holy war.

Even so, Tynthanal did not believe that Zauthan's motives had been as pure and innocent as he claimed. He might have convinced himself unseating Tynthanal was for the good of Aaltah, but there was no question that ambition had played a role in his decision making, as well.

"So, *are* you going to arrest me?" Zauthan inquired.

Tynthanal realized he'd already hinted at the answer when he'd framed the arrest as a hypothetical. Clearly, if he were planning to arrest the lord chamberlain, they would not now be having this fairly civil conversation. Even if such a high-profile arrest would not cause a great deal of strife and division, Tynthanal had other reasons for not wanting to do it, for the attainder would leave Zauthan out of the running for the regency. Tynthanal didn't think the other members of the royal council were foolish enough to try to unseat him at a time like this, but he didn't like to present the temptation by narrowing the field of possible replacements.

"If you're willing to meet my conditions, then I will let you off with a warning," he said. "It's a better fate than you deserve, but Aaltah is more important than either one of us."

"What are your conditions?" Zauthan asked with a hint of suspicion in his voice. "I will not become your lackey."

Tynthanal rolled his eyes. "I've no use for one of those anyway. I will always value your honest opinion during council meetings. But if I catch even the faintest whiff of sedition wafting from your direction . . ."

Zauthan shook his head. "That ship sailed long ago. If we lose this war, the regency will not exist. And if we win this war, you will be the hero who saved Aaltah, and no one would dare question your right to continue serving as regent."

Not an enthusiastic declaration of support, but it was the best he could hope to get from a man like Zauthan. It was hard to think beyond the war that loomed on the horizon, but Tynthanal imagined if it somehow happened that they won the war without fixing the Well, his regency would come under fire again after the glow of victory wore off. But he would think about protecting his position later, after the dust cleared. For now, he would accept Zauthan at his word.

"Very well, then. I will file this confession away, and it need never again see the light of day."

Zauthan raised an eyebrow. "File it away, eh?"

Tynthanal shrugged. "I'm not an idiot."

"And what of Hunter? Will you ask Lord Lyslee to release him?"

Tynthanal couldn't tell if there was genuine concern in Zauthan's voice, or if he was just pretending to care because he could tell Tynthanal expected him to. He gave the lord chamberlain a sharp-edged grin.

"On the condition that he join the conscripts who will defend our walls. And that he does so under the name Hunter Rah-Zauthan."

Zauthan's jaw dropped open in shock. "You would *reward* him for spreading broadsheets? At a time like this?"

Tynthanal's grin widened as he enjoyed Zauthan's shock. "No. I would punish *you*. You are clearly not eager to acknowledge your bastard, but if you fail to do so, this confession may well pop up again when you least expect it."

Zauthan sputtered, but he was hardly in a position to argue. That he was escaping with his lands and titles intact was far better than he deserved, and he knew it. Lord Lyslee—who as Aaltah's ultimate authority on law and its enforcement was naturally a stickler—had argued quite fiercely that both Zauthan and Hunter be punished to the fullest extent of the law, even if that punishment was to be deferred until after the war. But Tynthanal still believed that keeping his royal council intact and defending against internal division was for the best, and his marshal had grudgingly allowed himself to be convinced. Only time would tell if Tynthanal had made the right decision.

CHAPTER THIRTY-TWO

Corlin tried to hide the flutter of apprehension in his gut as he was shown into Lord Aldnor's office. He had been a model cadet for months now, suppressing his temper with a skill that surprised even him. He'd half-expected Captain Norlix—who showed no sign of warming to him even after all this time—to hold him back from joining the ranks of the second-years when he turned fifteen, but he'd advanced without incident, Rafetyn following only a month behind. He anxiously reviewed his every recent action, searching for some incident that might have gotten him in trouble, but he could think of nothing. He wasn't *perfect*, of course, but he had kept his word and not done anything to warrant another beating, no matter how sorely Cadet Justal and the rest of the bullies tried him.

Corlin studied the lord commander's face for clues as he stood at attention before his desk, but he could see no hint of Lord Aldnor's agenda in his expression. At least he didn't look angry, though he did not immediately turn his attention away from the paper he'd been perusing.

"Have a seat," the lord commander said, still not raising his eyes from the paper.

Corlin let out a silent sigh of relief. If he were in some kind of trouble, he would never have been invited to sit.

Lord Aldnor nodded briskly and set the paper aside, folding his hands on the desk and fixing Corlin with his familiar steely gaze. "I'll get straight to the point. Your uncle has . . ." He paused, frowning. "Well, he hasn't exactly *ordered* me, but his polite request has some teeth behind it. We'll say he has *asked* me to release you from the Citadel and send you to Rhozinolm."

"What?" Corlin cried in outrage, forgetting himself and leaping to his feet.

"Sit down!" Lord Aldnor snapped, and Corlin immediately obeyed despite the pounding of his pulse.

"Forgive me, sir," he grated from between his clenched teeth as he wrestled with the temper he had been arrogant enough to think he'd mastered. "I did not mean to speak out of turn."

Lord Aldnor scowled at him, but issued no further reprimand. "No one needs to tell you that war is coming."

That was obvious to anyone with a functioning brain. The entire second-year curriculum had been overturned, lessons in history and tactics and strategy giving way to relentless sparring drills and stints helping to build and enhance the fortifications around the city's walls. The physical labor was exhausting, but Corlin was very aware of how his chest and shoulders were filling out, and his swordsmanship had improved to the point that he could hold his own—and sometimes even win—against third- and fourth-years. Even Justal was becoming wary of entering the sparring ring against him.

"No, sir," Corlin responded. "And that is why I find the idea of leaving the Citadel so . . . distressing."

Lord Aldnor nodded, and Corlin thought he caught a brief expression of sympathy in the older man's eyes. "I understand. But though we always try to protect our cadets, and we send them into battle only as a last resort, there is no question of holding them back during an outright war."

Corlin nodded. "Of course not. We will need every warm body. We all understand that we will be going into battle, sir. Just as we all understand that at least some of us are unlikely to come back." The thought of battle made Corlin's stomach knot, although he knew some of the other cadets—idiots all, in his opinion—actually looked *forward* to it. Corlin had never participated in a battle himself, but he had witnessed the terrible aftermath when Delnamal had sent a small band of soldiers to attack Women's Well. He'd seen the death and the injuries and the suffering, and there was no question in his mind that battle was worthy of dread, not excitement. But that did not mean he would shy away from it.

"I became a soldier the moment I joined the Citadel," Corlin continued. "A soldier's duty is to fight."

"But you are not just any cadet; you are the Crown Prince of Women's Well."

Corlin shrugged. "In the Citadel, we are all equal. Isn't that what we get taught day after day?"

Lord Aldnor sighed. "That is a lovely fantasy, which we do our best to make a reality. However, in the case of a crown prince—especially one who has no younger brothers who might step up and take his place—there are other considerations."

Corlin gave that argument only a moment's thought before rejecting it. "Women's Well will find an heir, if it's necessary. I do have a baby cousin there, and it's not like my mother will be fighting and at risk of dying. If Aaltah falls, then the question of who might occupy the throne of Women's Well becomes irrelevant."

Lord Aldnor gave him a crooked smile. "And you will make the difference between victory and defeat?" he asked. "You have a high opinion of yourself."

Corlin's temper tried to stir again, but he hushed it easily, for of course Lord Aldnor had a point. Corlin was just one man, and his presence or absence would hardly sway the course of the battle. He did not *want* to fight, did not *want* to experience first-hand the horrors of battle. And yet the thought of fleeing to relative safety in Rhozinolm was . . . abhorrent.

"I didn't mean it that way, sir," he said, as he envisioned his fellow cadets fighting and dying on the battlefield. Rafetyn was still his only actual friend, but there were several others he at least didn't dislike. And even those he despised, he still felt some loyalty to. His heart stuttered at the thought of Rafetyn forced onto the battlefield. He would look like a child fighting among grown men, and though Corlin was sure most if not all of his fellow cadets felt a similar grudging loyalty and would look out for Rafetyn despite their scorn for him, none would defend him as Corlin would, if he had a chance.

"All I mean is that the succession is not of immediate concern," Corlin said. "Not immediate enough to warrant abandoning my duties as a cadet and a soldier."

"I feel certain your mother would disagree."

Remorse stirred in Corlin's gut. He could well imagine what his mother was feeling right now, the dread that was likely keeping her up at night. He wouldn't be surprised if she was the reason Tynthanal had approached Lord Aldnor in the first place.

"As would the mother of every cadet in the Citadel," he responded. "As would the wives and mothers and children of every soldier. I am not better or more important than any of the other cadets who will fight. If I didn't intend to fight when necessary, I would not have joined the Citadel in the first place. I knew from the beginning that war was likely."

Lord Aldnor leaned back in his chair, and Corlin could see that the lord commander was thinking furiously, even if he couldn't guess *what* the man was thinking. Corlin sat up straight and proud, hoping that Aldnor would not see the faintest whisper of the fear and dread that plagued him. He was terrified of going into battle, and yet the thought of running away was even worse. His sister had *died* because he had run away from danger, and although logically he knew it had not been his fault, it would forever *feel* like his fault.

Finally, Lord Aldnor came to a decision and sat up straight once more.

"As I mentioned, Prince Tynthanal has not gone so far as to order me to send you away." He smiled ever so slightly, though the expression was so brief Corlin might have missed it if he'd blinked. "He is a soldier at heart himself, and I know it is eating at him that he must fight this war from the sidelines. He will understand how you feel. If you are certain this is what you want, then I will present your argument to him, and we can hope he will not elevate the request to an order."

Corlin's first response was that he himself should present the argument, but then he realized how much more dispassionately and convincingly Lord Aldnor could present it. Surely Tynthanal was more likely to listen to his calm and collected lord commander than to his frantic fifteen-year-old nephew.

"Thank you, sir," he said, praying that he was right and Tynthanal would let him stay despite his mother's pleas to the contrary.

The members of Ellin's royal council filed out of the room one by one, heading to the formal luncheon that was scheduled to break up the day whenever an especially long session was anticipated. These days, *every* session was long and grueling as they prepared for the war even the most optimistic of them knew was coming. Oh, there were a couple who grumbled about the danger and expense of a war and who would likely have preferred to let Aaltah fight on its own, but every story about Delnamal and Draios that trickled in made the necessity of defeating them more and more obvious.

Ellin was dismayed—if not entirely surprised—when instead of following the others to the banquet hall, Lord Semsulin remained behind.

"If I might have a word in private, Your Majesty?" he asked.

She sighed, for it wasn't hard to guess what he wanted to talk about. "Of course," she agreed, nodding to the honor guardsmen who'd been waiting to escort her to lunch.

The guardsmen both bowed and stepped out of the room, allowing Semsulin to close the door behind them. Ellin did not feel like sitting—she'd been sitting in her chair all morning and would likely do so for much of the rest of the afternoon, so she remained on her feet, trying to stretch surreptitiously as Semsulin approached. He regarded her with that too-knowing gaze, and it was all she could do not to look away in shame.

"I think it's time you tell the full truth," he said. "I can see Sovereign Prince Waldmir using the accusation that we have illegally detained his daughter to work some advantage for Nandel, but I don't see how 'accidentally' losing a caravan of iron and gems is in any way to Nandel's advantage."

Ellin pinched the bridge of her nose as a headache tried to form there. She and Zarsha were both reasonably certain that they had successfully kept the secret of Elwynne's presence in Zinolm Well. If Waldmir had discovered the truth beyond doubt, he would have presented his evidence when he demanded Elwynne's and Leethan's return. But it was also clear that lack of evidence was not going to prevent him from holding Rhozinolm responsible for their disappearance. He claimed—through his ambassador—that the caravan had been lost to a brutal mountain storm, and the story was very plausible. It was a rare caravan that traveled through Nandel at this time of year, and Rhozinolm had paid a hefty premium for the swift delivery. But the loss was too convenient to be believed under the circumstances.

"We need him to 'recover' that shipment as soon as possible," Semsulin continued when Ellin didn't say anything. "The last thing we need is a shortage of iron and gems when we're on the brink of war."

She narrowed her eyes at him, for of course she knew that. And he *knew* she knew that.

She would have loved nothing better than to keep disavowing any knowledge as to Princess Elwynne's whereabouts, just as she continued to do with Waldmir. But as Zarsha had pointed out, there was only so long she could keep the secret from her council. If Semsulin had already decided she was lying about it, it seemed likely others would soon follow suit.

"I cannot send her back to him," she said. "I *will* not." Semsulin opened his mouth to protest, but she cut him off with a sharp hand gesture. "It's not open to negotiation. I am through capitulating to Waldmir's demands."

Semsulin was well aware of the concessions she'd made to secure Zarsha's hand in marriage—and the vital trade agreements that came with it—although he was unlikely to agree that protecting her husband from yet another heartbreak was worth the risk of antagonizing Waldmir at a time like this.

Semsulin's lips pinched together tightly, and she imagined he was suppressing his first, natural response to her obstinacy. He was capable of an impressively chilling glare, but Ellin had no intention of allowing herself to be intimidated.

"I didn't tell you about it because I knew you and I would not agree about what needed to be done."

He nodded, still glaring at her. "And because you thought it would be best if the members of your senior council believed they were telling the truth when they assured the Nandel ambassador that the princess is not in our custody."

She shrugged. "Yes, that, too."

Realizing that by keeping Elwynne she had already passed the point of no return as far as her relationship with Waldmir went, she finally told Semsulin the great secret she and Zarsha had been keeping about Elwynne's parentage. He listened in impassive silence. Semsulin was a master of self-control and could mask his thoughts better than anyone Ellin had ever met.

When she was finished, he thought it all over some more, his face still revealing nothing. Ellin held her tongue and waited.

"So," he finally mused, his eyes distant with thought, "you are reluctant to send Princess Elwynne back to her father because Zarsha is attached to her?"

Ellin could detect no particular emotion or opinion in the lord chancellor's tone, but she bristled anyway as she prepared herself for a fight. She didn't expect Semsulin to agree with her decision to keep Elwynne hidden, but he was certain to take it better than the rest of her councilors. In the earliest days of her reign, Semsulin had occasionally treated her like a flighty young girl with no training for her position, but he had quickly learned to respect her. He was the *only* member of her council who she was sure would never refer to her as "just" a woman. If she could not persuade him to support her, she might eventually find herself forced to send Elwynne back to Waldmir, for though the authority of a sovereign was considerable, it was not absolute.

"Waldmir has been using that poor child as a hostage since she was born," Ellin said stiffly. "Just because we now know she is not Zarsha's daughter doesn't mean he will suddenly stop caring about her—or that Waldmir will stop using her to hurt him. And through him, *me*. It is not as strategically advantageous as you might think to deliver her back into that man's hands."

Her argument was weak, and she knew it. Zarsha was her husband and the Prince Consort of Rhozinolm, and he had proven more than once that his first loyalty was to her. He was not of a disposition—or in a position—to damage the interests of Rhozinolm because of any threats Waldmir might make toward Elwynne if she returned to Nandel. Her desire not to send Elwynne back had nothing to do with the strategic interests of Rhozinolm, and Semsulin knew it.

The lord chancellor gave her a stern, almost paternal glare.

"Please, Your Majesty. Don't insult me. It's bad enough that you've lied to me for as long as you have."

She stiffened even more. "I am your sovereign queen," she snapped, mustering a glare of her own. "I don't appreciate being scolded like a misbehaving child."

Semsulin shrugged. "Well, I don't appreciate being treated like a potential enemy instead of as a trusted adviser. Have I given you any reason to believe I might betray your trust or your confidence if you confided in me?"

It took some effort for Ellin not to look guiltily away. It was true that Semsulin had steadfastly stood by her, even when she'd made decisions with which he did not agree.

Semsulin must have seen the guilt on her face despite her effort to hide it. He gave her a half-smile that held a hint of sadness. "I am on your side. I am *always* on your side."

She shook her head. "Not on this," she said. "You're on *Rhozinolm's* side—as well you should be—and I admit I am aware that keeping Princess Elwynne from her father is not in Rhozinolm's best interests."

The expression in Semsulin's eyes sharpened. "Refusing to return Prince Waldmir's rightful daughter to her home when we have no legitimate cause to hold her here is definitely not in Rhozinolm's best interests. However, if Princess Elwynne is in fact *Zarsha's* daughter, then he can assert his paternal rights and you would have just cause not to comply with Waldmir's demands."

Ellin frowned at him. "But we've confirmed she *isn't* Zarsha's daughter."

He nodded. "But I will presume you did so anonymously, in such a way as to hide for whom the paternity test was being performed?"

"Yes, of course."

"Then no one knows you have performed the test. You have already established a friendly relationship with Mother Zarend.

Don't you think it might be possible to persuade her it would be best if a test of Zarsha's paternity came up positive?"

Ellin gasped softly. For all that she considered herself to be a skilled courtier, for some reason it had never occurred to her to lie outright about the results of the test. "But Waldmir has already had the test performed on his behalf," she protested.

"Do you suppose he has made that test public knowledge? He availed himself of women's magic! And in doing so, he made it clear that he himself questioned the girl's parentage. If we were to publicly declare that Elwynne has been tested and confirmed as Zarsha's daughter, what do you suppose Waldmir could do about it? *Especially* when one takes into account that he doesn't truly want her?"

She gaped at her lord chancellor, hardly believing what she was hearing. "You would support this tactic? You believe it would be in the best interests of Rhozinolm?"

He scoffed. "No, it's clearly not. The kingdom would be best served if you were to send Elwynne back. There is no question of that. But I can clearly see that isn't happening, so I must consider how best to keep her here without destroying our alliance with Nandel. If Zarsha claims paternity—and we create the 'proof'—then, while Waldmir might be personally furious at being outmaneuvered, he would have no legal grounds for demanding Elwynne's return. Even the Sovereign Prince of Nandel needs the cooperation of his royal council to take action, and he will not have their cooperation if the child is not his."

Ellin slowly lowered herself into her chair, her knees feeling suddenly weak. Why hadn't she thought of that? Why hadn't Zarsha?

Semsulin offered her a surprisingly sympathetic smile for someone with so dour a nature. "This is why sometimes you need to seek advice, even when you fear you will not like it," he chided gently. "Both you and Zarsha are too close to the issue, too emotionally invested in its outcome, to think straight." He smiled that little half-smile of his again. "Which is why you need someone cold and unfeeling like me to help you through it."

She let out a heavy sigh that turned into a hint of a laugh. "Thank you."

Semsulin's reputation throughout the court was indeed of being cold and unfeeling, which was why he was roundly disliked despite the high respect in which nearly everyone held him. But underneath the steely exterior, Ellin was beginning to think he had a much softer and more sentimental side than anyone had guessed.

Not that she would ever insult him by saying such a thing out loud.

There was no question that his suggestion was dangerous. She could only imagine Waldmir's fury, not just at the lie, but at the very public accusation that he'd been cuckolded by Zarsha. His fear of that revelation was the reason that Waldmir had not used Brontyn's infidelity to level a treason charge against her and Zarsha both. It was possible that the news might be shocking enough to cause one of Waldmir's nephews to attempt to take the throne.

"Let me talk this over with Zarsha first," she said, for though Zarsha had little left to lose in Nandel, he did have a brother who lived there and might be in the line of fire if the succession came into question. But it would certainly be nice to let go of the secret. She could bring Elwynne and Leethan and Jaizal to stay at the palace as her guests, rather than hiding them away.

"Of course, Your Majesty," Semsulin said, bowing.

Ellin was surprised to find a hint of a smile on her face as she envisioned bringing Elwynne to the palace. She did not think of herself as a particularly motherly sort, and she was certain she was not yet ready to have children of her own. Just the thought was enough to cause a flutter of apprehension, and she was continually thankful that the Blessing meant she would not have one until she was ready. But the idea of becoming Elwynne's make-believe stepmother was not unappealing—especially when she thought of how happy it would make Zarsha.

Leethan locked her bedroom door with a stab of guilt. Jaizal had seen her through so many visions over the time they'd known each other, and Leethan had always taken comfort in her friend's presence as the seer's poison ravaged her body. But this time, she knew, Jaizal would ask too many questions that Leethan was not prepared to answer. It was best for all involved if Leethan suffered in private.

Jaizal insisted that Leethan should not read too much into the fact that the very night she told Prince Zarsha about her dream, it had stopped coming to her.

"It just means that you have fulfilled the Mother of All's wishes," Jaizal insisted. "She *wanted* you to report the dream to the queen, and through her to others. You did your duty, and now it is over."

But Leethan didn't think even Jaizal was convinced that was the case. If the dream was indeed sent by the Mother of All—as both Leethan and Jaizal believed—then there had to be a reason that it showed her facing off against Waldmir and sacrificing her life.

Although the dream made it clear to her that she had a vital role in the war to come, and that she was required to perform a sacrifice—whether literally or only figuratively—she still could not fathom exactly what it was the Mother of All wanted her to do. How could her sacrifice stop Waldmir?

The only chance she had of figuring out her mission from the Mother of All was to trigger another vision and hope for a clearer message. And so she had quietly arranged for one of the house-maids to take a trip to the Abbey and purchase a seer's poison for her.

Making herself as comfortable as possible in her bed, propping pillows all around herself to protect her if she thrashed about, Leethan opened her Mindseye and activated the poison with a mote of Rho. Then, pinching her nose, she bolted it down, shuddering at the taste that was both bitter and cloyingly sweet at the same time. She stuffed a handkerchief in her mouth in hopes it would muffle any screams she could not prevent from escaping.

The pain was no easier to bear for all her familiarity with it, and she was dimly aware of her body writhing on the bed as her back arched and her heels drummed on the mattress and her teeth clenched convulsively on the handkerchief. She heard a thin keening sound sneaking out from around the cloth, but for the most part it worked to keep her screams contained, and there was no sign that she had roused the household. She wept freely as she waited to be borne away by her vision. Eventually, she was rewarded.

Out of the blackness that had blinded her when the poison first seeped into her blood, a small light began to glow, growing brighter and larger as she waited patiently. The pain of the poison ebbed, though it did not go away entirely. She had to pause to suck in a few deep breaths to fill her tight lungs before the vision sprang into sharp focus and she recognized her surroundings.

She was in the throne room of the royal palace in Nandel, a great, cavernous hall that was literally built into the side of a mountain. The austerity of Nandel meant that instead of being sumptuous and elegant, the room was—in the eyes of someone foreign-born such as she—barren and cold and forbidding. Dim luminants shone from unadorned iron chandeliers and iron sconces set into the stone walls and pillars. A narrow rug of silk, woven in shades of gray and black, ran from the entrance of the hall to the dais upon which the throne sat, but it was the only softness visible anywhere. There were no tapestries to warm or brighten the walls, no upholstered chairs or settees. Just the oc-

casional stone bench or hard wooden chair for those visitors too
infirm to stand.

The throne at the top of the dais was as unassuming as the rest
of the room, carved of stone with simple lines and only the barest
adornment. At the moment, the throne was empty, although the
hall itself was packed with the nobility of Nandel, with a row of
palace guards in their gray livery standing at attention on each
side of the long rug. People were murmuring softly to one another, their clothing rustling with their subdued movements.
Coughs and sneezes were stifled hastily, and yet the hall was filled
with a loud din, thanks to the echoing nature of the space.

Leethan shivered, for this vision bore a striking resemblance
to the long-ago vision of Waldmir's nephew, Granzin, ascending
to the throne, which had dominated her life with Waldmir for so
long. That, too, had begun in this room with an empty throne,
but the people in attendance had been dressed in summer-weight
clothes, with nary a hood or cloak in sight. This version of the
vision took place in what looked likely to be the heart of winter,
based on the array of fur-lined mantles and cloaks on display.

Those echoing murmurs suddenly went silent, and Leethan—
whose viewpoint was from somewhere above, as though she were
floating in the air near the chandeliers—turned to see that a
young woman had appeared in the doorway. She looked to be in
her mid to late twenties, with pale skin bronzed by the sun. Thick
blond hair draped loosely over surprisingly broad shoulders, and
the muscles of her neck were corded like a man's. But it was not
her appearance that nearly sucked the breath out of Leethan's
lungs. It was the heavy silver crown, adorned with simple hematite cabochons, that made her feel suddenly dizzy, for she knew
that crown well, having seen it many times upon Waldmir's brow
on ceremonial occasions.

It can't be, a shrill voice in her mind protested.

There was currently a sovereign queen on the throne of
Rhozinolm, and a sovereign princess on the throne of Women's

Well, but surely, *surely* such a thing was not possible in *Nandel* of all places! Women in Nandel didn't even have the right to own property, for they *were* property. Property of their fathers or husbands or, in the case of those confined to the Abbey, of the Crown.

If Leethan had been present in body, she would have rubbed her eyes to try to make them see more clearly. As it was, all she could do was stare in amazement as the young woman progressed down the length of the long rug. And as she passed, everyone in the audience bowed or curtsied. The woman walked with her head held high, every once in a while catching the eye of someone in the audience and nodding or smiling as she approached.

Eventually, she climbed the dais and took a seat upon the throne, and Leethan's disembodied view suddenly swooped down from the rafters, bringing her close enough to get a proper look at the woman's face.

It was impossible not to see the resemblance to Waldmir in the woman's high, sharp cheekbones and hawklike gray eyes. And then Leethan noticed the small scar above her right eyebrow.

"Impossible," Leethan muttered to herself, but the scar was too distinctive to deny. Elsewhere in Seven Wells, a child who split her head open so severely that it would scar would be treated with women's magic to preserve the purity of her skin, but in Nandel, where women's magic was forbidden, even the sovereign prince's daughter was forced to live with the disfigurement.

After having recognized the scar, it became impossible for Leethan to continue denying what her vision was showing her: little Princess Elwynne, now fully grown, wearing the crown of Nandel.

When Leethan had seen Granzin on the throne, he had been a man of about twenty-five or thirty years—approximately the age he was right now—so this vision clearly took place in a future that was more distant. Did it mean Granzin, too, was destined to die without an heir? But even if he did, it seemed far more likely some distant male relative would succeed rather than Waldmir's youngest and least-favored daughter!

The vision faded without giving Leethan any hint of an answer.

She had triggered the vision in a search for clarity, hoping the Mother of All would show her something that would make sense of the dream and tell her what she was expected to do. And yet she now felt more muddled than ever.

If she chose to accept Jaizal's assertion that she had already fulfilled the Mother of All's wishes where the dream was concerned, then she could determine two things from this vision. One was that somehow, impossibly, there was a future in which Elwynne could become the Sovereign Princess of Nandel; and the second was that—just as impossibly—it was in Leethan's power to make that future happen.

Weeping with a combination of frustration and exhaustion, Leethan pulled the makeshift gag from her mouth and curled up in the covers of her bed, pulling a pillow over her head as if she could hide from the world.

Part Three

SACRIFICES

CHAPTER THIRTY-THREE

Delnamal leaned against the ramparts, gazing down at the palace courtyard far below. He had this high vantage point all to himself, the guards who were usually stationed here having fled obediently when he dismissed them. Technically, he had no authority to dismiss palace guards from their duties, but he had not been surprised when the men had beaten a hasty retreat without even a token protest. Draios had already made it clear he had no interest in protecting his people from Delnamal's wrath should they invoke it.

His heavy cloak flapped in the wind, and although none of the soldiers standing at attention below as their king addressed them looked up, he'd bet his life that every last one of them was aware of his looming presence high above.

Draios had invited Delnamal to stand by his side when he addressed the scores of officers who had come to hear him preach his vision of the glorious war in which they were soon to engage, but Delnamal had gracefully declined. They were likely to set sail for war in two to three weeks, four at the most. All was now in readiness, and though Draios had shown himself madly deluded in his fanatical quest for glory, Delnamal remained worried that the young man might suddenly be struck by good sense. Keeping his distance as much as possible seemed the wisest course of action, lest he unwisely say something that pierced the illusions Draios spun for himself.

Delnamal let his gaze drift away from the scene below, looking off into the east, from whence the fleet would eventually set sail. The sea was not visible from Khalwell, but Delnamal imagined he could see it in the mists of the distance. And across that sea was Aaltah. His kingdom. His home.

The thought aroused nothing resembling sentiment in his breast, and as a gust of wind dragged his hood off his head and bared his hollow cheeks, he turned away from the view.

There was no question he was looking forward to the endeavor. In the height of battle, he would devour more Rhokai than he had ever dreamed of, and power would buzz in his veins with an intensity he could scarcely imagine. But his thoughts were turning increasingly to what would happen *after* the battle, and he had as yet found no answer that felt satisfying.

Draios would have to go, naturally. When Delnamal refused to throw himself into the Well and reverse the Curse as he'd promised, he would lose Draios's allegiance once and for all. He was persuasive, and Draios was gullible, but there were limits.

Killing Draios would not be difficult, not when Delnamal was glutted with extra Kai from the battle. But what would he do after that?

"What do you want?" he asked himself softly, the wind snatching the words away before they reached even his own ears.

Such a simple question. One that he had never before had trouble answering. Always what he wanted was that which he could not have, and most of his life had been spent cursing the injustice of it all. But now, with this incomprehensible power of his, he could have whatever he wanted . . .

And he had yet to find an answer to his own question.

Did he want to sit on the throne of Aaltah once more? Certainly that was within his reach, or would be soon. He could do away with the royal council altogether, so that he need not saddle himself with a roomful of hand-wringing, complaining old men who would try to thwart his every move. Once the people of Aaltah saw what he was, what he could do, they would be as frightened of him as the people of Khalpar, and no one would dare oppose him.

But what was the point of being King of Aaltah? He had not enjoyed the power when he had had it, for it came with so many responsibilities and duties that it had subsumed his very life. And really, why would he want to rule a kingdom if he cared nothing about the land or the people? As weak and pathetic as he had once been, the duties of the throne had worn on him. In fact, his failures might not have wounded him so if he hadn't cared so much about doing right by Aaltah. If he took the throne now, he would have no such cares to fuel him.

No, Delnamal decided, shaking his head. He had no interest in sitting on the throne of Aaltah. But conquering it without keeping it seemed so . . . pointless. He would enjoy killing his half-siblings, gouging the Rhokai out of their chests and using their deaths to help fuel his continued life, but even that victory seemed small and mundane.

"What do I want?" he asked again, an edge of frustration creeping into his voice, for he still could not find an answer that truly resonated.

He sighed heavily.

"I don't want Aaltah," he decided aloud, and that felt right. Although the thought of putting all that effort into conquering it and then letting whoever was left put it back together when he was gone . . .

Well, that wasn't satisfying at all.

"Ha!" Delnamal said, the sound startling a crow that had had the nerve to settle on the ramparts nearby. Almost absently, he opened his Mindseye, reaching out and grabbing the bird's tiny mote of Rhokai and tugging it toward him. It was of paltry satisfaction when he was now used to consuming the larger motes that resided inside human beings, but he appreciated the flicker of pleasure anyway.

He was tying himself up in knots trying to map out the entire future of what was sure to be a very long life, but in reality there was no need to see so far into the future. He would start by conquering Aaltah, and there would be satisfaction in that. But if he wanted to conquer Aaltah and didn't want to rule it and didn't want to leave it for someone else to rule . . . well, then he would have to destroy it.

For one moment, the shocking thought seemed to nearly stop his heart, and a helpless cry of horror tried to rise in his throat. The man he once was—the man who had *loved* Aaltah despite all the faults of its disloyal, ungrateful people, who had taken his duties as caretaker seriously despite his bitter resentment of the responsibility—wanted very much to scratch and claw his way up out of the deep, dark oubliette in which Delnamal had buried him. What he was considering was an atrocity of unfathomable proportions. One that could be of no possible benefit to himself.

Delnamal shoved those childish thoughts back down into the depths of himself. It was not true that destroying Aaltah's Well was of no benefit. He might not be eager to be saddled with the responsibilities of a throne once more, but he did want to assure himself of a long and comfortable life.

As long as there were no witnesses to Draios's murder, the credulous fools who so slavishly followed their deluded king could be convinced that the death—and the devastation that followed—had been a tragic accident. Even a great act of self-sacrifice on Draios's part. And then Delnamal could lead them—and whatever desperate remnants of Aaltah's army were willing to join them—to march on Women's Well. Delnamal was sure he could find a way to induce his dear sister to help him re-create whatever it was Mairahsol had done to Aaltah's Well in the first place, and he could stock his body with another huge dose of Rhokai.

He could live to be a hundred or more, with a legend so fearsome that no one would dare deny him anything he wanted. He could conquer all of Seven Wells, stripping those Wells of their Rhokai one at a time until he returned in triumph to Khalpar to live like a king, with all the wealth and trappings and none of the responsibilities.

The wail of protest that had tried to break out of its confinement subsided until he could feel nothing whatsoever besides the *rightness* of this new, more focused plan.

For three days, Alys had been pondering the various ways she might present her decision to her loved ones and her royal council, and none of those imaginary conversations had gone well. In the end, she had decided to start off by talking to the two people from whom she expected to receive the most spirited—and personal—resistance: Chanlix and Tynthanal.

Wanting to keep that first conversation as private as possible, she arranged for Chanlix to come visit the royal apartments after hours, while simultaneously arranging for Tynthanal to join them via talker. Of course, they'd both asked her for some hint of what she wanted to talk about, but she'd told them only that it was personal and very important.

Chanlix arrived first, and Alys tried to put her lady chancellor at ease by offering her a late-night aperitif. Chanlix crossed her arms over her chest and gave Alys a hard look.

"While I have a suspicion alcohol might make this conversation easier to bear," Chanlix said, "I have the distinct feeling I may need my wits about me."

Alys laughed nervously. "Come now. There's no reason to be dramatic about this."

Chanlix snorted. "Of course there is! You are never secretive, so when you summon me to your apartments to talk while refusing to tell me what about, I know damn well it's not going to be a pleasant conversation."

Alys pinched the bridge of her nose, as if that would somehow erase the stress that had pulled her brows together. Her pulse was already racing, and her palms were sweating. But as much as she dreaded the conversation—nay, *argument*—they were about to have, she did not dare put it off any longer.

The talker on the coffee table chirped, saving Alys from having to respond.

"Please have a seat," she invited with a wave of her hand toward the sofa as she opened her Mindseye and plucked some Rho to complete the talker's connection. Even with her Mindseye open and her back turned, she swore she felt Chanlix's scowl on the back of her neck.

When she closed her Mindseye and took in the image of Tynthanal that now hovered over the table, it was all she could do not to flinch, for the way he was looking at her made it clear he had reached a conclusion similar to Chanlix's.

Tynthanal nodded briefly at Chanlix, then fixed his attention on Alys with a chilling stare while foregoing any traditional, polite greeting.

"If the purpose of this meeting is to tell us that you've now decided your purgative must be cast with sacrificial Kai that only you can produce," he said with icy precision, "then we might as well end it now."

Belatedly, Alys realized that he and Chanlix had already spoken to each other to prepare for this meeting. She knew each of them had already harbored some suspicion that Alys was contemplating such a thing, so it was only natural that they conclude that was the reason behind her request.

Alys forced a bright smile that she knew neither of them would believe. "Well, you'll be happy to know that isn't what I wanted to talk to you both about."

Tynthanal looked almost comically surprised, and Chanlix looked downright suspicious.

"Oh?" Chanlix said with a tilt of her head and a narrowing of her eyes. "I can't tell you how relieved I am to hear that, although I don't know why else you would be so evasive about this meeting."

Alys was too agitated to sit down, but she was not helping her cause by standing there hovering, so she forced herself to take a seat on the other end of the sofa and fold her hands in her lap. There would be no easing into this conversation, and both Chanlix and Tynthanal were more than ready to jump down her throat. She might as well just lay the truth out on the table.

"I still believe that my purgative can be cast with ordinary Kai," she assured them. "That is why I am sending four of our new female cadets from the Citadel along with our men to help defend Aaltah." While Women's Well had by far the smallest military force in all of Seven Wells, she had had no trouble convincing her royal council that they must send every man they could spare to Aaltah, for if Draios and Delnamal got a foothold there, then Women's Well could never stand against them. "Each of them is in possession of a mote of women's Kai, and if they can get close enough to Delnamal, they will use that Kai to cast the purgative spell."

"Much appreciated," Tynthanal said, but his body language said he was still braced for a fight. "We have recruited a couple of women from the Abbey here for the same purpose, but the more motes of Kai we have available, the greater our chances of success."

Alys nodded. "Yes, of course. Just as I am sure you will equip your most powerful men with the spell in case they should have the misfortune to have Kai available to them during the battle."

She fought against an almost irresistible urge to leap to her feet and pace, but she knew she would be much better off projecting an aura of composure and resolve. "My concern is: what if I'm wrong?"

"Alys . . ." Tynthanal said warningly.

She held up her hands. "It's a legitimate question, and one that deserves attention however much we might not like it."

"Don't go there!" Tynthanal snapped, glaring at her.

"I have to," she said simply. "*You* have to."

"There's no reason to think—" Chanlix started, leaning forward in her earnestness, but Alys cut her off.

"Not talking about it doesn't make the possibility go away. If there is *any* chance that Leethan's vision is genuinely prophetic—"

Tynthanal growled impatiently. "It's *not*. At least not literally. You said so yourself!"

"Probably not," she responded. "But I don't think it's too far-fetched to think it's *possible* that I am the only one who can stop Delnamal. And if I am to stop him, I must do it in Aaltah, which means I cannot sit safely here in Women's Well when the Khalpari invasion begins."

"No," Tynthanal said with stubborn finality. "You are a sovereign princess, and you belong in your own principality."

"Exactly!" Chanlix agreed, her eyes flashing.

Although their reactions were exactly what she'd been expecting, Alys wished it could be otherwise. "My duty is to protect Women's Well," she said. "If Aaltah falls, then my being here will be of absolutely no use to my people. The only way to protect Women's Well is to make sure Aaltah holds off the invaders. It would be irresponsible of me not to prepare for any eventuality—including the possibility that my purgative spell will not work unless used with sacrificial Kai."

Tynthanal scoffed. "Even if that's the case, there's no reason it must be *yours*. We can find—"

"Someone less important than me to sacrifice her life?" Alys asked, letting an edge enter her voice.

"You are a sovereign!" Tynthanal snapped back. "I am a career soldier who was once the Lieutenant Commander of the Citadel of Aaltah, but although my heart cries out for me to fight alongside my men on the battlefield, I understand that my duty as the prince regent is *not* to fight but to lead."

"There is too much at stake to leave anything to chance or to leave any possibility not accounted for," Alys argued. "I know you two are worried I have some kind of death wish, but that is not what this is about, I promise you."

Chanlix and Tynthanal shared a look, and Alys could see quite clearly that that was indeed what they both feared. And she couldn't blame them. She could admit to herself that the sacrifice held a certain appeal, that the thought of shrugging off all her burdens and all her grief was not as unattractive as it should have been. But even so, she had searched her soul to make sure she was not striving toward that selfish escape, and she was convinced that her motivations were sane and rational.

"My argument is simply that if there is *any* chance that Leethan's dream means I am the only person who can defeat Delnamal, then I must be in Aaltah to meet him. We can all hope and assume that such is not necessary, but to ignore the possibility . . ." She shook her head firmly. "No. That would be irresponsible, and that is a sin of which I cannot be accused."

Chanlix and Tynthanal shared yet another look, and Alys guessed each was hoping the other would come up with an effective counterargument.

"I know neither of you likes this idea," Alys said. "I know that when I bring it before the royal council, there will be those who insist my place is here and will not listen to my reasoning." She turned to Chanlix. "I am very much hoping you will not be among them. I will need an ally, who can speak for me as a council member, rather than as a concerned friend." Hence, the reason she had decided to brace the two people whom she feared would object the most strenuously in advance and in private.

"Even if you can persuade your council to agree with you," Tynthanal grated, "you are a foreign sovereign, and therefore not free to enter Aaltah without the express permission of myself and my royal council."

"A fact of which I am well aware," she said, then smiled thinly. "Just as I am aware that your council will perhaps not feel terribly welcoming toward me."

He snorted. "That's putting it mildly."

"And yet, given the circumstances, I'm certain you can persuade them to allow me entrance."

Yes, she was sure he *could* persuade them; it was just a question of whether he *would*.

Alys turned her attention to Chanlix, and her heart gave an unpleasant squeeze when she saw the tears standing in her friend's eyes.

"I know you are frightened," she said, "and I know you want me to be safe. But we will none of us be safe unless Draios and Delnamal are defeated. I hope you understand that I must do all I can to make that come about." Her own throat tightened, and she sternly commanded herself to stay strong and resolute.

She looked at Tynthanal once more. "I know this is hard on you," she said, her voice turning raspy. "I know full well what it's like to have someone you love throw themselves into danger. If I am forced to accept my only remaining child marching into battle, then you must accept having me come to Aaltah in case I am needed." She gave Chanlix a look that she hoped conveyed both apology and authority. "And you must accept letting me go. I trust I can count on you to serve as my regent until I get back?"

Chanlix sniffled and blinked, and though it was clear she very much wished to remonstrate some more, she managed a jerky nod.

Tynthanal's eyes were darkly shadowed, his shoulders slumped in defeat. "I will talk to the council," he said, not meeting her eyes. Then without another word or glance, he cut the connection.

Draios dismissed the page with a peremptory wave, not thinking until the door had closed behind the boy that he should have at least uttered a thank-you before doing so. But he'd been too impatient when he'd seen the iron-gray flier that the page had been carrying, knowing the fate of the war he was about to wage might well lie in the message the flier carried.

For half a heartbeat, Draios found himself thinking it a shame that he did not have access to the amazing talking fliers that were produced in the heretical principality of Women's Well, for his negotiations with Sovereign Prince Waldmir could have been completed in a single day if such a convenience had been available. The moment the thought flickered to life, Draios dismissed it with a grunt of disgust and vowed penance in the form of a fast and a sleepless night spent in prayer. The magic of Women's Well was a blasphemy, an insult against the Creator, and no man of faith should entertain even a moment's longing for its use!

Hand trembling ever so slightly in anticipation, Draios coaxed the rolled paper out of the flier's clawed feet, then broke the wax seal. He smiled with both relief and excitement when he read the short letter from Waldmir that accompanied a longer, signed agreement.

Between them, Par and Khalpar had by far the largest navy anywhere in Seven Wells, but the sovereign princes of both Grunir and the Midlands had already stated their intentions to help defend Aaltah against any attack. Powerful as Par and Khalpar were together, they would have been massively outmanned if they'd had to face the full combined forces of two kingdoms and two principalities when they made landfall.

Draios saw the hand of the Creator at work in the peculiar set of circumstances that had allowed him to court an ally who historically refused to lend significant military support to foreign powers. If Waldmir's child had not been kidnapped and taken to Rhozinolm—or if Rhozinolm had at least had the good sense to send the brat back instead of claiming Prince Zarsha was her true father—the Sovereign Prince of Nandel would likely have sat back quietly and observed as his larger neighbors went to war. Moreover, he would have continued supplying Rhozinolm with all the iron and gems they needed to prepare for war.

Draios rolled up the scrolled papers with a nod of satisfaction. Waldmir had not only agreed to hold up any future shipments to Rhozinolm, but had also agreed to lead his own army into battle against Rhozinolm, his supposed ally. The massing of his troops would send a clear signal to that kingdom's weak and illegitimate sovereign that she could not afford to send any but a token force to help defend Aaltah, effectively clipping her wings and keeping her out of the fight until such time as Draios could afford to deal with her.

Agreeing to take Waldmir's brat off his hands with a generous brideprice to be paid when she reached her majority and was ripe for marriage was a small price to pay for the glorious victory that would be Draios's once Aaltah fell and the Curse was eliminated. Draios could only assume that Waldmir was telling the truth about the child's parentage—surely he would not be so determined to retrieve her if she truly were the child of the Prince Consort of Rhozinolm. If it should turn out the child truly *was* Zarsha's, then the agreement would be null and void, and Draios had won Waldmir's aid at no cost to himself. And if she *was* Waldmir's daughter and Draios later decided he did not wish to marry her . . .

Well, once Aaltah had fallen to his forces and he had put a king of his own choosing on its throne, one who would be forever beholden to him . . .

Draios smiled. He would marry whomever he wanted, and Waldmir would have no way to enforce a contract that in reality could not be legally binding until the child was of age anyway.

Yes, this was a clear sign of the Creator's continued approval of Draios's choices. He could hardly wait until the weather cleared enough for the fleet to launch. He almost wished his father were still alive, for it would have been sweet to rub the old man's face in the glory that could have been his. He hoped that Parlommir could be captured alive, for he would certainly be fighting on the side of the heretics. Even knowing full well that it was impious of him, Draios very much looked forward to seeing his superior and sanctimonious brother quivering in pathetic terror as the heretic's pyre was prepared for him. It would be a fitting end to the era of the Curse, and it would herald the dawn of a golden age of piety into which Draios would lead not just his own kingdom, but all of Seven Wells.

CHAPTER THIRTY-FOUR

Delnamal awakened with a jerk, a choked scream rising from his throat. His breath seized in his lungs, not allowing the sound to escape as the nightmare sank its claws deep into his soul. His cheeks and his pillow were wet with tears, and he frantically tried to throw himself out of the bed, his legs tangling in the covers.

There was no time!

He finally tumbled to the floor, his knee making solid contact with the frame of the bed on his way down, sending a sharp crack of pain through his leg. He tried to rise, but his knee objected and sent him to the floor once more.

Already, he could feel the emotion ebbing.

"No," he moaned, looking all around, searching for something, *anything* that would allow him to stop this.

There was no weapon nearby, but if he could somehow make it to the window across the room . . . It would be a very long way down to the flagstones below.

Gritting his teeth against the pain, he began to crawl, though he feared he was too late.

You owe Aaltah nothing, an insidious voice whispered in his

mind, a voice that sounded so much like his but that *wasn't,
couldn't* be. He *loved* his kingdom, would never want any harm
to befall it. And that was true whether he sat on its throne or not.
He had made many a regrettable decision, but he was not a monster.

But then, was it really so terrible to be a monster?

He paused mid-crawl as the thought struck him. Greed and
selfishness were seen as sins in polite society, and the Devotional
taught that taking care of others was the height of virtue.

Well, Delnamal had *tried* that. He'd sacrificed his wants and
needs time and time again for the good of his kingdom. And
what had it gotten him?

Nothing.

No love. No respect. No loyalty.

Trying to take care of others was a certain path to disappointment and despair. Far easier to take care of *himself.* He did not
have to take *guesses* as to what he wanted, did not have to face
shame and calumny when he guessed wrong or when his wishes
conflicted with those of others.

Taking a deep breath, he sat back on his heels halfway between the bed and the window he'd been planning to toss himself out of.

From now on, he would have to take special care every night
when he went to bed to make sure there was no weapon within
easy reach. And he would have to seal the window. Even without
the tumble from the bed, he did not think he could have crossed
the distance and made it out the window before sanity returned,
but there was no reason to take chances.

Someday, he would find a way to rid himself of the last ves-
tiges of his earlier self. It was decidedly inconvenient to wake up
in this kind of panic every day and to be forced to take measures
to protect himself from a hysterical suicide attempt. But he was
secure in the knowledge that he could weather the storm for as
long as need be.

Delnamal waited until his pulse had calmed and the sweat had dried on his brow before rising to his feet.

Alys was going to miss the glorious desert sunsets, she decided, as she inelegantly hiked up her skirts and dipped her bare feet into the very edges of the spring that surrounded the Well. The sky was painted with reds and yellows and oranges, with occasional wisps of clouds streaking through the colors like the broad strokes of an artist's brush.

When she had first ventured out to the Well on this, her final evening in the home she had created for herself, her mood had been melancholy almost to the point of being maudlin. It was her own decision to leave Women's Well and travel to Aaltah, and she knew it was the *right* decision. But it was hard, too. Especially when in her heart of hearts, she did not believe she would ever be coming back—no matter how many times she'd reassured Chanlix and Tynthanal and her royal council.

There was something about the Well that was immeasurably soothing, and as soon as Alys had slipped off her shoes and felt the gentle hum of the Well's power in the soles of her feet, the clenched fist inside her chest had relaxed, and it had become easier to breathe. She dug her toes into the wet, sandy earth at the edges of the spring and breathed in deep the scent of greenery and budding flowers. The trees that grew around this remarkable, impossible Well had no business growing at all in the harsh desert sun, even though there were sporadic rain showers that quenched the land within the Well's influence and then quickly burned themselves out when the winds carried them away.

Her peaceful reflection was interrupted by the sound of men's voices from behind her. With a small sigh, she glanced over her shoulder. Her honor guard had fanned out to block the path that led to this secluded spot by the spring's shore, keeping as far back as possible to allow her some illusion of privacy. She saw now that

Duke Thanmir stood on the other side of the guardsmen, his hands raised in a gesture of surrender. He had stopped a respectful distance back, getting only close enough to the guardsmen that he could speak to them without shouting. Alys shook her head slightly, and was surprised to feel the hint of a smile playing about the corners of her mouth.

By all rights, Thanmir should have had no idea that she was planning to leave Women's Well for Aaltah, but it could be no coincidence that he had chosen yesterday, of all days, to pay yet another visit, this one unannounced and unexpected. She had been too busy with her travel preparations to play the part of a proper hostess, but she supposed since she was standing idly by the Well, she was rather short on excuses to avoid him at the moment. She gestured for her honor guardsmen to let him pass and walked gingerly out of the water so that she need no longer hold up her skirts. She did not, however, feel inclined to put her shoes back on just yet, even if there was an uncomfortable feeling of intimacy in being barefoot in his presence.

Thanmir bowed elegantly. "I don't mean to intrude on you, Your Royal Highness," he said. "I am here entirely on a social call, and if you would prefer to be left undisturbed, I will leave without insult."

She smiled at him, for she believed him. Although it was impossible to miss his continued desire to convince her to marry him, he did a remarkable job of making it obvious without resorting to anything that felt like overt or uncomfortable pressure. Whenever she allowed herself to forget the prospect of marriage— and everything that went with it—she enjoyed his company immensely, and she was always aware of how well the two of them understood each other. Even the most empathetic and well-meaning of her friends and family couldn't *truly* understand the pain and the guilt that burdened her, but Thanmir knew all too well what that felt like. With him, there was no need to hide or deny the pain of her loss.

"Please stay," she said. "I regret that you've traveled all this way only to have me vacate the premises so soon after your arrival."

Thanmir shrugged. "As you've no doubt already guessed, I had an inkling you would be going to Aaltah soon."

She glanced at him out of the corner of her eye, wondering just how much he knew. And how he knew it. By his own accounts—and by everything she'd learned about him through discreet inquiry—he was not an especially influential or well-connected member of the court of Grunir, despite being the king's brother. He did not sit on the royal council, and she did not think he would be kept apprised of any but the most critical details of politics. Certainly the war coming to Aaltah was critical, but only a tiny handful had any idea that Alys might have some part to play before it was all over.

"What made you think that?" she asked, trying not to sound actively suspicious.

Thanmir walked to the water's edge, gazing into the crystal clear spring instead of looking at her. He was silent for a long time, and Alys began to doubt he would answer her.

"Grunir will be sending what support we can to Aaltah," he said quietly, "but the forces my brother is sending are all volunteers and men who belong to the Citadel, so my son will not be among them. However, I can say for certain that if he were marching into battle, then I would be right on his heels. The thought of losing another child is . . ." His voice choked off, and Alys saw that his eyes were shining. He blinked and cleared his throat, then shook his head.

Turning to her and meeting her eyes, he said, "I don't suppose I have to put into words how unbearable such a thought is."

Something dark and enormous and hungry rose from the depths of Alys's soul, and for a moment she feared she would be entirely subsumed by the grief and guilt that would never leave her. It was very likely that, even if she didn't believe herself necessary to the effort to stop Delnamal, she would have found some different reason why she absolutely had to go to Aaltah. She could not march into battle by Corlin's side to protect him, but she yearned to be close, to show him how much she loved him and to be there if he needed her.

Was that the true source of her conviction that she alone could take down Delnamal? Was her belief in Leethan's vision nothing but a thin excuse manufactured to convince others she had a purpose for going?

She turned hastily away from Thanmir, unable to face him, and unable to speak as she battled her demons. She heard his footsteps approaching and tensed, fearing he would attempt to touch her and she would shatter. But of course he had too much sense to do something so foolish.

"I was never an especially religious man," Thanmir said softly, "and what faith I had was shattered after what happened to Zallee. But for you, I will pray once more. I will pray for the safety of your son, and for your own safe return to Women's Well."

Swallowing hard, Alys turned back toward him, though it took all the courage she could muster. Even though he did not know about Leethan's dream and the end it might or might not have foretold for Alys, he had to know that there was a reasonable chance she would not survive. Aaltah's navy—even with the support of Rhozinolm—was no match for Khalpar's, and though the ground forces should give Aaltah an advantage in numbers, it was hard to calculate how much Delnamal's dark magic would affect the battle.

"If I do return," she said, "and if I have not been given some reason why I must mourn again . . ." Her voice failed for a moment as some panicked little girl inside her screamed not to put such a thing into words, even words so vague—but she fought that terror down and finished with something approaching calm.

"I will put aside my mourning," she promised him. "And if you care to make a formal proposal, then I will give it my earnest and sincere consideration." She gave him the smallest of smiles. "I would like to promise I will accept, but . . ."

He returned the smile, and it was impossible to miss the spark of hope in his eyes. "But it is hard to think clearly about the future when war looms so close on the horizon."

She blew out a breath. "Yes. Just so."

Alys wondered if even this half-hearted promise was made possible in part by her conviction that she would not be coming back. But it was useless to speculate, and she knew that if she *did* come back, the world would be a very different place. Maybe she would even be ready to fully rejoin the living in that new and different world. And if not . . . Well, Thanmir was a most understanding man.

Kailee had not thought it possible, but as the preparations for war intensified in Aalwell, she saw even less of her husband than she had before. She tried to tell herself this was a good thing—the last thing she needed was to give herself even more opportunities to pine after the man whose heart could never be hers. Unfortunately, it seemed she was perfectly capable of pining without having to be in his presence, and she hated herself for it just a little bit. Hated herself for being foolish and sentimental enough to lose her heart even when she'd gone into the marriage fully prepared to defend herself against that possibility. She had always thought of herself—and heard herself labeled—as strong-willed, but apparently her will was not as strong as all that.

So it was that her heart gave a treacherous little lurch of happiness when one cold and snowy night, when the weather was particularly atrocious, Tynthanal returned to the royal apartments as the sun was just beginning to set.

"Most of the court is snuggled up safely in their own houses tonight," he told her cheerfully, "so I thought we'd forgo the formal banquet and have a quiet dinner here, just the two of us."

Kailee turned away from him and held her hands out to warm them by the fire. Not because she was cold, but because she feared her face might tell him too much about how welcome the prospect of a quiet dinner for two was. She wished she could have discerned some hint of romance in his voice, then cursed herself for being a lovesick idiot. And she reminded herself of Lady Chanlix and Tynthanal's infant daughter. She had no right to long for romance.

"That would be lovely," she said, hoping her voice showed nothing of her burst of melancholy.

The dinner table discussion quickly chased away even a shadow of the romance Kailee wished she'd stop longing for, dominated as it was by talk of the war that was coming. Tynthanal was far more open and honest with her than she suspected most men of Aaltah were with their wives, and though the news seemed universally grim, she could not help appreciating his candor.

"I suppose we must be grateful for the snow," she said. "I always used to look forward to the spring, but now I am dreading it."

"As are we all," Tynthanal agreed. "Even those who usually seem eager for war and its so-called glory feel the dread of this one. If the information weren't coming from so many reliable sources, I'd suspect Delnamal of starting these rumors of his powers for the express purpose of sowing fear in his enemies."

Kailee clicked her tongue and gave him a teasing smile. "And if you respected his intelligence enough to give him that much credit."

She could not see his answering smile, but she heard it in his voice. "Well, yes, that too."

The moment of levity passed, although Kailee could not have

said what it was that caused her to suddenly go on alert. She could not consciously see any change in her husband's body language, nor discern a change in his breathing, but something told her he had gone tense. She bit her lip in anxiety and hoped she was imagining things. But she was not.

After a brief, fraught silence, Tynthanal said, "I think we should revisit the idea of you going back to Women's Well."

Kailee crossed her arms over her chest and tried not to flinch. Here she was trying to manufacture some hint of romance out of their cozy dinner for two, and he was once again talking about sending her away. "I thought we settled that months ago," she said.

He nodded. "Yes. When we did not know that Aalwell would face an invasion in the spring. Circumstances are different now. Many people are—"

"No," she said through gritted teeth. "Ours may not be a marriage of love, but I will not be cast off like some inconvenient—" Her voice cut off on a hiccup, and she battled to regain control of herself. She was letting him see far too much.

He reached across the table and covered her hand. "There is no question of me casting you off," he said. "I merely want you to be safe and comfortable, and you will be neither if you remain in a city that will soon be under attack and might even be subject to a long and grueling siege. You can't have failed to notice how many wives and children are leaving the city whenever the weather cooperates."

Kailee urged herself to slow down and think before she spoke. Having Tynthanal realize how she felt about him would add yet another layer of humiliation, and she had already been far too unguarded.

On first blush, fleeing to Women's Well before the attack was an eminently practical suggestion. As Tynthanal said, the wives and children of those who could afford it and had someplace to go were leaving the city at a steady pace. Not to mention that she had spent the happiest days of her life in Women's Well and a part of her longed to return.

So why *wouldn't* she? She had the uncomfortable suspicion that her true motivations were far from logical, but her reaction to the very idea of fleeing was surprisingly visceral even so.

With a little shake of her head, Kailee decided she would examine her true motivations later. What she needed now was a way to explain herself to Tynthanal. A way that would not make her sound like some lovesick female—and that would make enough sense that he would not take the decision out of her hands.

"Do you honestly believe I would be any safer in Women's Well?" she asked. "If Aaltah falls, then you can be certain Women's Well will fall swiftly afterward. Fleeing might buy me another few weeks or even months, but the fact remains that my entire future rests on whether Aaltah can stand against Delnamal's attack."

Although she was extemporizing, the words had the feel of truth to them. And that truth led to another.

"I have spent all of my life being made to feel that I am useless," she said, remembering having this same conversation with Oona. Only this time she had an actual solution in mind. "I cannot stand to be useless now when there is so much at stake, and I have an idea of how I can help the war effort."

Tynthanal sat back in his chair, and she imagined he was gaping at her in surprise. "What is it you have in mind?" he asked, and the fact that he didn't dismiss the very idea that she might be helpful—and that his voice showed nothing resembling disdain or condescension—made her heart squeeze softly.

"I'm going to suggest something shocking," she warned him, and Tynthanal laughed.

"I would almost be disappointed if you didn't."

She smiled despite herself. "From everything you've told me, the Abbey of Aaltah is currently barely functional as a source of magic."

"That is true," he agreed with a thread of caution in his voice. "All the more experienced abigails who used to reside there are now in Women's Well, so they have no experienced guidance."

She nodded. "I am not an especially experienced spell crafter," she said, for she had studied only briefly at the Women's Well Academy before her marriage to Tynthanal had brought her to Aaltah, "but I do know how to make a good many different varieties of healing potions. I can teach the abigails how to make them, and we can stockpile them for when they are needed."

Kailee was surprised to find her pulse speeding with excitement at the idea. Her words tumbled out a little faster as she tried to forestall the most obvious objection she could see coming.

"I know women's healing potions are generally not as potent as the kinds of healing spells the Academy of Aaltah is no doubt producing even now, but surely in times of war it's best to have as many healing options as possible. And to be perfectly honest, I don't think my presence at the Abbey will do any further damage to my nearly nonexistent social standing."

Even with her perfectly logical arguments—and after his easy acceptance of her presence in the Women's Well Academy—she expected him to be discomfited by her suggestion and to offer some form of protest. Even his silence in the immediate aftermath of her hurried rationalizations felt ominous, and his heavy sigh afterward had her shoulders drooping in anticipation.

"I feel that it is my duty as your husband to see to your safety above all else," he said, "and I expect your father will heatedly remind me of that fact if I *don't* send you to safety."

Kailee bit down on her lip to stop it from quivering, for though his words sounded like the precursor to a refusal, there was something in his voice that made her hold her breath.

"But it would seem hypocritical to accept my fifteen-year-old nephew's decision to risk staying in Aaltah—and risk a great deal more than that as a cadet of the Citadel—and then reject my

adult wife's decision to stay. So if you are truly dead set on staying, then I will not forcibly send you away."

"And will you let me train the abigails?"

"As long as you understand that there might be unpleasant
consequences. The court may snub you now, but they will likely
be less subtle and polite about it if they feel you tainted by asso-
ciation."

Kailee snorted. "Most of those who'd be rude to me will be
fleeing to their country estates anyway. And if I can teach the
abigails how to produce potions and those potions save lives,
then it is worth any additional slights I may have to endure."

Tynthanal leaned forward, and she could feel the intensity of
the stare she could not see. "You do know that you could teach
the abigails, then leave for Women's Well afterward. Right?"

"I know," she said. "But I honestly don't see much point in it.
My fate and Aaltah's are irretrievably intertwined. I will stay until
my fate is decided, one way or the other."

CHAPTER THIRTY-FIVE

Alys arrived at the royal palace in Aalwell late in the night, having spent far more time than necessary seeing to the delivery of all the magic items and potions she had brought with her from Women's Well for the war effort. She knew herself well enough to recognize that her excessive fussing was an attempt to keep so busy with mundane details that she would not have to think about, nor even truly *feel*, the emotions her return to the land of her birth had engendered.

But eventually, everything had been sorted out to the point that she couldn't even pretend to have reason to linger, and she'd reluctantly accepted the need to go . . . home.

It had been a long time since the royal palace of Aaltah had been her home. Most of her time in Aaltah had been spent in her late husband's manor house, which Delnamal had long ago "confiscated" and no doubt sold to some other noble family. But she'd been born and spent all of her childhood in the palace, and there was some small part of her that would forever label it home, whatever her other feelings about it might be.

Once upon a time, Alys had had her own suite of rooms in the palace—rooms that had been kept ready for her throughout her marriage. Delnamal had, of course, had those rooms stripped bare, their contents burned or sold. Alys knew Kailee had been tasked with refurnishing and redecorating the suite for her, and though she would never have said so out loud, she experienced some trepidation as to what she would find. Kailee's lack of eyesight didn't concern her—Kailee had a lifetime's experience compensating—but her bold, impish, *youthful* spirit led Alys to worry the suite might be too garish and modern for her own more staid tastes. But from the moment she first stepped into the anteroom, she saw she needn't have worried.

Honor—having entered the room close on Alys's heels so that she could immediately begin directing footmen where to put Alys's cases—clucked her tongue. Alys grimaced to realize her relief was written so clearly on her face, and she and her lady's maid shared a rueful smile.

Alys walked from room to room as the footmen continued to carry in her baggage and was pleasantly surprised to see that Kailee had somehow managed to retrieve some of her old things from wherever Delnamal had sent them off to. There was an overstuffed armchair in the parlor by the fireplace that Alys had loved to curl up in to read, and a dainty escritoire inlaid with golden roses, and even a beautifully detailed silken rug that her stepmother had always heartily disapproved of for having far too much red in it to be strictly proper in a princess's bedroom. The new furniture and decorations Kailee had chosen matched the style of the pieces she had miraculously retrieved, and though the room no longer looked as she remembered it, it still instantly felt like *hers*. The thoughtfulness made her eyes tear up for a moment.

Alys tried to stretch some of the kinks out of her neck and back as soon as the footmen retreated, but there was only so much stretching her stays would allow, and she yearned to get out of them.

"We can leave the bulk of the unpacking for tomorrow," she told Honor. "For now, let's just find my nightdress and dressing gown." Both her body and her mind yearned for sleep, although she felt certain the welter of emotions within her would keep sleep at bay for a long time if she didn't avail herself of one of the sleeping potions she'd brought with her.

Honor frowned at her. "Surely you plan to pay your respects to your brother before taking to your bed?"

Alys frowned back, her stomach giving a nervous flutter. She had spoken to Tynthanal many times since he'd come to Aaltah to serve as regent, but that wasn't the same as coming face-to-face with him. Talking with him via flier, it had been easy to forget—or at least *pretend* to forget—the troubles that had come between them when she'd refused to let him marry Chanlix. She did not imagine that pretense would be possible in person.

"Surely it's too late at night to trouble him now," Alys said, although she knew that her own duties in Women's Well generally kept her up a good deal later than this.

Honor clucked her tongue again, sounding very much like a disapproving mother. "Is *that* why you spent so much time seeing to the disposition of the caravan?" she asked. "So that you could put off facing your brother for one more day?"

The guilty flush that heated Alys's face made a denial pointless. There were so many scars eating away at her soul, and sometimes she lacked the will to pick at them. She lowered her gaze to the rug and chose not to answer.

It was possible Honor would have scolded her—she had known Alys far too long to hold her tongue despite the difference in their stations—but whatever she was about to say was forestalled by a knock on the anteroom door.

Honor gave her a droll look as Alys's heart suddenly tripped over itself in panic, for they both knew there was only one person likely to come looking for her at this time of night.

"Seems the decision is being taken out of your hands," Honor said as she went to open the door.

Alys had to bite her tongue to stop herself from calling Honor back. But surely she was not such a coward as to run from her own brother, no matter what difficulties lay between them.

After gracing Tynthanal with a curtsy, Honor slipped from the room without a backward glance, and Alys was left alone with the brother who had been her best friend for most of her life.

The months Tynthanal had spent as Prince Regent of Aaltah had aged him. There were strands of gray in his dark hair, and the crinkles at the corners of his eyes—crinkles she would previously have termed laugh lines—were deeper and more plentiful. It was also abundantly clear that his duties inside the palace had curtailed or even eliminated altogether his daily training regimen. His usually nut-brown skin had faded to the color of tea with too much milk in it, and he had grown . . . well, not *fat*, but at the very least *stout*.

Somehow, when they'd been speaking via talker, either the subject matter of their conversations or the small size of his projected image had caused her to miss all these signs, and she found herself surprised to be faced with a little brother who for the first time in his life looked his age.

Tynthanal's regard was as measured and assessing as her own. She saw his eyes sweep over her from head to foot as the corners of his mouth tugged downward in a hint of a frown. She raised her chin defiantly, sure he was going to tell her what he thought of her continued mourning blacks. She had seen that frown more than once when they'd spoken via talker, and she braced herself for the disapproval she was sure was coming.

But instead, Tynthanal spread his arms. "We are not so estranged that we cannot greet each other with hugs, are we?" he asked.

Tears suddenly stinging her eyes, Alys hurried into his arms. "I've missed you so," she croaked, the admission escaping her lips before she had a chance to think better of it. And threatening to let everything else she was thinking and feeling bubble up out of control.

"And I you," he said, and it didn't even sound forced. He broke the hug and smiled down at her tiredly. "I'm sorry for all the turmoil I put you through," he said, his hands squeezing her shoulders. "I acted like a spoiled child, and I took out my anger at the situation on you when I knew full well you were doing the only thing you could."

Alys's throat closed up, and she found herself incapable of speaking. He had apologized to her before he had left Women's Well, assuring her that he understood that it had been her duty to arrange his marriage to Kailee. But he had also made it clear that understanding it and accepting it were two different things. She hardly dared allow herself to hope that maybe now he had finally come to forgive her.

Alys cleared her throat, although her voice came out hoarse all the same. "I'm sorry, too."

"You have nothing to be sorry about," he said with a dismissive wave of his hand. "You were in the right, I was in the wrong. Now, how fares your lady chancellor? She tells me she's doing well, but then she would likely say so whether she was or not."

Alys let some of her tension out on a long sigh before answering with a fond smile. "She is doing an extraordinary job of juggling her duties as a mother with her duties as a member of the royal council. There is some grumbling occasionally," she admitted, for Tynthanal would never believe that even Women's Well would adapt with great ease to having a single mother serve as the second-highest-ranking person in the whole principality. "But overall, everyone is adapting well. When I told my council she would be regent while I was gone, they all seemed to take it as a given." Which, of course, it would be if Chanlix were a man.

"And your daughter . . ." She smiled faintly at the image of her little niece. "She has charmed the members of the royal council one by one. I do hope we can arrange for you to meet her in person when this is all over."

Tynthanal closed his eyes and nodded, but they both faced the future with a healthy dose of doubt. There was still far too much strife on the horizon, far too much death and destruction and uncertainty . . .

"Let us hope so," Tynthanal said, then swiftly changed the subject. "I've arranged for Corlin to have leave tomorrow so that he may come and spend some time with you before . . ." He shrugged. "Just before."

Alys took a shaky breath, trying hard not to think about the possibility that it might be the last time she and her son saw each other. Corlin would be going into battle, and she . . . Well, even if no one else believed it, she was still convinced it was her fate to die defeating Delnamal.

"Thank you," she said. Her voice came out tight with anxiety and dread. "How much . . . How much does he know?"

His eyes narrowed. "You mean have I told him you've come to Aaltah 'just in case' you need to slash your own wrists to defeat Delnamal?"

She fought the urge to look guiltily away. He had already made his disapproval and disagreement abundantly clear. And yet he had not forbidden her to come, which told her that he did not think her interpretation of Leethan's dream quite as ridiculous as he claimed. She met his flashing eyes with an unblinking stare. Tynthanal grunted and backed down, looking away and scrubbing a hand through his hair.

"Of course not," he said. "There are only a select few who've been told about Leethan's dream, and Corlin is most definitely not one of them. I don't like keeping that particular secret from him, but he hardly needs that worry when he's likely to get his first taste of battle." He held up his hands to forestall anything she might say. "He and the rest of the youngest cadets will be kept well away from the fighting if at all possible, but we have to be realistic in our expectations."

She nodded her reluctant acceptance, though she still wished heartily that Corlin were just a little less brave and honorable and had left Aaltah when he had the chance.

Tynthanal reached out and put his hands on her shoulders, his fingers squeezing so hard it almost hurt. "Promise me you aren't planning to throw your life away," he urged. "If not for my sake, then at least for Corlin's. He's suffered enough loss already."

She winced slightly, for in all her planning for the battle that was to come, she had not once allowed herself to think of the aftermath, of how Corlin would feel if he survived and learned she had given her own life, that she had *known* she would die and had not told him. But as much as her actions might hurt him, she could not allow his pain to stay her hand.

Raising her chin, she once more met her brother's eyes. "I promise you I will not throw my life away. If I sacrifice myself, it will be because all other hope is lost."

Tynthanal closed his eyes and lowered his head in a gesture that signified both acceptance and dread.

Despite a distinct lack of leisure time—and privacy—Corlin had spoken to his mother several times via talker since he had arrived in Aaltah, but somehow the prospect of seeing her in person did not compare. He had spent all of the previous night tossing and turning in his bed, trying to anticipate what the reunion would feel like, and rehearsing what he would say.

When Corlin had left Women's Well, he'd been very angry with his mother. Not for exiling him—that decision he well understood after he'd almost killed Smithson—but for the role she had played in Jinnell's death. His anger with his mother had been no more logical than his anger with himself—neither one of them could possibly have anticipated what would happen, nor could they have prevented it—but knowing that had failed to quench the flame of his ire.

During the long and sleepless night, he had searched the depths of his soul, examining what remained of the anger. Once, it had been a living, breathing being residing just under his skin, ready to spring into action at the slightest provocation. He still sensed it lurking there, but it was much more deeply buried and harder to provoke. Even Cadet Justal had not goaded it to the surface in the months since Rafetyn had taken Corlin's punishment, and it was not for lack of trying. Surely if he could let go of his anger enough to tolerate Justal's abuses, he could find it in his heart to forgive his mother.

It was mildly irritating that Tynthanal had sent a pair of honor guards to the Citadel to escort Corlin to the palace. It felt rather ridiculous to be flanked by honor guardsmen while he wore the uniform of the Citadel, but arguing would not do him any good. Outside the walls of the Citadel, he was Crown Prince Corlin, not Cadet Corlin, and protocol required he have an escort.

The trip through the Harbor District, up the cliffs on the risers, and through the royal palace passed in near total silence as Corlin brooded and mentally rehearsed. He could not say with any certainty that he knew what to expect. Would he be facing Sovereign Princess Alysoon, who hid behind a mask of court-trained composure? Would he face the terrified, weeping mother who had resisted letting him set foot in the Citadel in the first place? That prospect was nearly unbearable, and even thinking about it made guilt stir. He was convinced that staying to fight was the right thing to do, that it was his duty as a man and as a soldier. Even so, he could easily imagine how frantic with worry his mother must be. The grief of losing Jinnell had almost broken her, and he did not like to think of how tortured she must feel at the moment.

The first thing he noticed when he was admitted into his mother's sitting room was that she was still dressed in deepest mourning in a gown of unadorned black. He'd seen when they'd spoken via talker last that she was still wearing black, but somehow he had hoped she would have put it aside by now, half a year after her official mourning should have ended. He quickly executed a formal bow, as required by protocol; however, protocol had less to do with it than a desire to hide his disapproving thoughts.

He lifted his head when he was sure he had his expression under control, and saw that his mother's eyes were shining with suppressed tears, her hands clasped tightly together in front of her. Corlin had made no secret of how much he despised maternal hugs, and he could see the supreme effort she was making to restrain her natural instinct to sweep him into her arms.

Smiling tremulously, she shook her head. "I can't believe how much you've grown!"

Shame stirred in his breast as he heard the anguish in her voice—anguish she was clearly trying hard to suppress. He had once thought it childish and below his dignity to allow his mother to hug him now that he was a grown man, but he suddenly realized that it was his refusal that had been childish. He crossed the distance between them and put his arms around his mother's waist.

"Oh!" his mother gasped in surprise, and her answering hug was so fierce he could hardly breathe. He felt the fine tremors in her body and knew she was crying. It was all he could do not to cry himself, in large part because of all the pain he knew he'd caused her.

"I'm sorry, Mama," he said as she pressed her head into his shoulder and wept openly. When had he become tall enough that his mother's head was at the level of his shoulder? Maybe her surprise at his growth was not a mother's exaggeration after all. "Sorry I've been such a terrible son."

Still sniffling, his mother shook her head and pushed away from him, looking into his eyes. "Nothing could be further from the truth!" She forced a smile, though her eyes were still swimming. "You are far and away the best son I've ever had."

She surprised a short laugh out of him, and something inside him unclenched. He had dreaded an emotional reunion, but it was not as unpleasant as he had imagined.

"I'm happy to hear that," he answered, mirroring her smile momentarily.

Still smiling, she dabbed at her eyes and looked him up and down in wonderment. "Your father fretted that you would take after him in height and build," she said, "but clearly he needn't have worried. You are the spitting image of my father in his younger years."

Corlin's father had looked every bit of the scholar he was, and Corlin had to admit that before his latest growth spurt, he'd worried that his fellow cadets—except, naturally, Rafetyn—would quickly become too large and too strong for him to keep up.

"Life in the Citadel agrees with me," he said, flexing his biceps so she could see how strong he'd grown from all the drilling.

Her smile remained in place, but he couldn't miss the distress that shone in her eyes, and he cursed himself for bringing up his military service so soon. He braced for her onslaught of pleas to change his mind and leave for Rhozinolm and was pleasantly surprised when they didn't come.

"I can see that," she said. "And I hope you know that I'm proud of you."

Corlin did a double take, for that was about the last thing he'd expected to hear. "You are?"

"Of course I am! Tynthanal has kept me updated on your progress." Her smiled turned into an ironic grin. "I found his reports far more informative than yours."

He looked down at his feet, ashamed of his reticence. He knew his mother, knew she'd have let their talker conversations carry on for hours on end if he'd only opened up to her. But he'd always been so aware of how unhappy she was with his decision to join the Citadel, and he'd told himself she would not be interested in the details of his service. He realized now that had been his own discomfort talking, for it was *he* who didn't want to face the distress he imagined seeing in her face. Funny how facing the possibility of death in battle was changing his perspective.

"I guess I must beg your forgiveness again," he said. "I had convinced myself you didn't really want to hear about my life in the Citadel."

She sighed and patted his shoulder. "I won't lie and pretend I am pleased with the life you've chosen," she said. "Especially when we are on the brink of war." Her voice tightened, and he feared for a moment she would start crying again, but she quickly regained her composure. "But I can respect it. And I can be proud of you even while I'm terrified for you."

Something deep inside him relaxed as he realized he would not have to argue his case to his weeping mother. He was confident his need to fight with his comrades was strong enough that he could have held firm, but the burden of guilt that already sat heavily on his shoulders would have become ever so much heavier.

"Thank you, Mama," he said. "That . . . means a lot to me. And now I must ask: why are you here? I've asked Uncle Tynthanal, but his answers have not been very satisfying."

It made no sense for the sovereign princess of another principality to place herself on the front lines of a war, even if the fate of her principality was heavily dependent on the outcome of that war. "You wanted me to go to Rhozinolm and sit the war out because I am the crown prince," he continued, "and yet here you are arriving in Aaltah when we all know the attack is imminent. I don't understand."

His mother would not meet his eyes as she asked, "What has your uncle told you?"

He crossed his arms over his chest. "Why? So that you can coordinate your lies with his?" He asked the question without the heat or venom that once would have colored his tone, but his mother flinched anyway. That flinch told him his guess was correct and there was more to her visit than Tynthanal had admitted.

"Please, Mama," he said, as gently as he knew how. "I'm not angry. I just want to know what's going on."

She reached up and cupped his cheek in her hand in a way that he ordinarily would have objected to. "I understand. And I know that my coming here is irregular." She let her hand drop and shook her head. "But the two people I love most in the world are here, and if Aaltah falls . . ." Her shoulders hunched and her breath caught. "If Aaltah falls, I cannot bear to go on. So I will be here with my son and my brother, and I will lend whatever magical support I can."

There was some truth in her answer, Corlin knew. Just as he knew it wasn't the *whole* truth. "Don't you think that as the Crown Prince of Women's Well, I have a right to know?"

His mother sighed and gave up the pretense. "You know all of the truth I'm willing to share," she said. "For the time being, you have declared yourself a soldier of Aaltah first and Crown Prince of Women's Well second. Therefore, you will be privy to what a soldier should know, rather than what a crown prince should know. When the dust settles, and if we both survive, then you may ask me again for the full truth and I will give it to you."

He burned to ask more questions, for her very unwillingness to talk told him the answers were important. But he knew that implacable look in her eyes, knew he had no chance of changing her mind.

Only when his visit was over and he was traveling down the cliffs on the risers did it occur to him to wonder what his mother had meant by "if we both survive." Maybe he was overthinking it, but in retrospect it seemed to suggest some possibility that he might survive and she might not. He tried to convince himself that she had merely shied away from saying "if *you* survive." But his efforts were unsuccessful, and he feared her presence in Aaltah had a much grimmer and more dangerous purpose than she'd let on.

● ● ●

From the moment Tynthanal laid eyes on Parlommir, the man had put his teeth on edge, and though Tynthanal knew his reaction had nothing to do with Parlommir himself, it was embarrassingly hard to set it aside. It was just that Parlommir looked so much like Delnamal! They had the same round face, the same short stature, and very similar nasal voices, although Parlommir was far thinner than Delnamal. Tynthanal made the mistake of commenting on the resemblance, and it was immediately clear that he'd delivered an insult when none was meant.

"Forgive me," Tynthanal said, reminding himself that Parlommir would hopefully be back on the throne of Khalpar where he belonged when this war was over and that it was never too soon to start building a stronger alliance. "I have heard that Delnamal now looks nothing like he did when I last saw him."

Parlommir's lip curled in distaste. "He is a wasted corpse of a man who has no business walking this earth. I saw him when he first arrived in Khalpar, and it was all I could do not to order a funeral pyre built on the spot." He shook his head. "I do not claim him as family, and I shudder to think that my aunt gave birth to that abomination."

Tynthanal decided that he was better off not trying to explain away the comparison any more than he had, and reminded himself to choose his words like a politician. Parlommir had come to Aalwell with his men to help defend Aaltah not because he cared intrinsically about Aaltah's fate, but because he knew his chances of regaining his throne if Draios conquered Aaltah were near nonexistent. It was Tynthanal's job to try to forge an alliance that would survive beyond the moment.

"Xanvin did her best with him," he said, for he knew it was true. "She is a good woman and is in no way to blame for what Delnamal became. I know she tried her hardest to shape him into a good king, but it was not meant to be."

Parlommir huffed and took a seat before the unlit fireplace without awaiting an invitation. The two of them had had their formal introductions earlier, during a public audience, but Tynthanal had thought it best they meet privately as well, so he had invited Parlommir to join him in the Rose Room in the residential section of the palace for an after-dinner drink. Based on the tension he felt in the room so far, he wondered if he had made a tactical error.

"It sounds as if you are fond of my aunt Xanvin," Parlommir said, giving him a challenging stare.

Tynthanal poured them each a brandy, then took a seat across from Parlommir before answering. "I was only six years old when my father married her. She was more of a mother to me than my own mother ever was. So yes, I am fond of her."

"But not of Delnamal?" There was a spark of challenge in Parlommir's eyes, as if he were somehow certain that Tynthanal and his half-brother were close despite all the obvious evidence to the contrary.

"No!" Tynthanal said emphatically. "Never him. And what of Draios? Were you two close before he murdered your father?"

The spark in Parlommir's eyes was brighter this time. "It was *Delnamal* who murdered my father!"

"And Draios who stood by and watched and then helped himself to the throne afterward. Shall we stipulate that neither of our brothers is a good man and leave it at that?"

The edge in his voice was sharp enough to slice through steel, but to his surprise, Parlommir sighed and relaxed back into his chair, staring into his brandy as he swirled it around without drinking. He was quiet for a long moment, and Tynthanal chose not to break the silence.

"There was always something not quite right about him," Parlommir said eventually. He held up his glass, and then took a sip. "I have a long habit of checking for poison before I take a drink, and even though Draios is now across the sea from me, I'm finding it hard to shake."

Tynthanal's eyebrows rose, for somehow he hadn't imagined

it was that bad. "But he was supposedly in training to be a priest!" he protested. "Surely . . ."

Parlommir waved that off. "His 'faith' isn't even skin deep. He's always hoped his priestly ambitions would help hide his true nature. Father held out some hope that faith would eventually mold him into a decent man, but I never did." Some of the color drained from his face, his eyes growing haunted. "I should have tried harder to make Father see what Draios really was, but I thought as long as I took precautions to protect myself, all would be well. It never occurred to me that he might . . ."

Grief sat heavily on Parlommir's shoulders, and though Tynthanal could hardly say he had warmed to the man, he did feel a great deal of sympathy.

"Just as I never would have guessed Delnamal would execute our niece," Tynthanal said, feeling a fresh stab of grief of his own over poor Jinnell's death. There was some doubt now—planted in Alys's head by Waldmir—that Delnamal had truly killed Jinnell, but he was responsible for her death whether he'd ordered it or not.

For a while, the two of them sat in silence, each privately dealing with his own grief and the guilt that accompanied it.

"They must be stopped," Parlommir finally said. "Both of them."

Tynthanal raised his glass. "On that, we can agree."

Parlommir nodded, and they both drank.

Thinking the ice between them had thawed as much as it was likely to, Tynthanal decided to prod just a little. "And after we have defeated our brothers and you are back on the throne of Khalpar? Will you decide that my sister and I are tainted by our mother's actions—as your father did—and refuse to establish diplomatic relations with us? Or with Queen Ellinsoltah, for that matter? I know you don't believe that a woman has any right to be a sovereign."

Parlommir licked his lips. "I will not insult you by pretending

I am comfortable with the idea." He sat up straighter in his chair, as if preparing himself for a fight. "I am in full agreement with my father that the world was better off before the Curse was cast, and if I should find it in my power to reverse it, I would do so without hesitation."

Tynthanal shook his head. "There, I cannot agree. There's a reason much of the world now calls it the Blessing."

"*Women* call it that!"

Tynthanal scoffed. "Can you blame them? But they are far from the only ones. I have a wife and I have an infant daughter, and I am thrilled that they will have choices in life that their predecessors never did. *I* call it the Blessing, and I truly mean it."

Parlommir heaved a sigh. "Then I suppose we will have to agree to disagree. I am not as religious as my father was—or as my brother pretends to be—but I believe in the teachings of the Devotional. Women are *meant* to submit to men, and the Curse has subverted the true natural order."

Tynthanal felt the angry flush heating his face and neck and could do nothing to suppress it. He leaned forward and opened his mouth for a sharp response, but Parlommir cut him off before he could speak.

"*However,*" Parlommir said, "unlike them, I believe it's necessary to live in the world that *is,* rather than in the world as I should like it to be. Your sister is the sovereign princess of a powerful principality, and Ellinsoltah is queen of one of the three great kingdoms. I cannot guarantee we will be allies in the aftermath, for I cannot see the future. But I will treat with them—or not—based on what is best for my kingdom rather than on my own personal preferences. Will that satisfy your concerns?"

In all honesty, it didn't really matter whether Tynthanal was satisfied or not. He was hardly going to refuse the help that Parlommir and his men could offer, for Aaltah's forces would be spread thin enough already. A fact of which Parlommir was certainly aware.

"Fair enough," he said with a nod. "I look forward to a renewed and mutually beneficial relationship between our two kingdoms when the war is won."

"That, I will drink to," Parlommir responded, raising his glass. But both Tynthanal's assertion and Parlommir's response revealed far more uncertainty and anxiety than either would be comfortable voicing out loud.

CHAPTER THIRTY-SIX

Only a few scant hours ago, the city of Tidewater had been overrun with soldiers waiting their turn to board their transport ships. Draios, Delnamal, and the small force of elite warriors who were assigned to protect them during the battles to come had waited until the streets had emptied before leaving the comfort of the inn Draios had commandeered for their use. Although the worst of the winter weather had cleared, the day before had been dreary and rainy, leaving the streets awash with mud and standing water. The passing of so many men, wagons, siege engines, chevals, and horses had only worsened the conditions of the roads, and Draios chided himself for not thoroughly thinking through his decision to board their party last. The throngs would have cleared effortlessly for him if he'd chosen to board first, and he'd not have arrived at the docks splattered with stinking mud.

He took a moment to admire the view from the dock before climbing aboard the boat that would take him to his ship. To his knowledge, this was the largest fleet ever assembled in the history of Seven Wells, and it was glorious. He had ordered every seaworthy vessel in all of Khalpar to join the invasion, and so there were cargo ships and fishing boats and any number of smaller craft interspersed with the massive warships. All of Aaltah would quail like frightened children when they saw the forces that were arrayed against them.

Draios chose to see it as an auspicious portent that the rain and gloom of the day before had parted, and the sun was shining brightly on this long-awaited day of the fleet's departure.

"The Creator is smiling on us," Delnamal commented with a satisfied nod.

"So He is," Draios agreed as he shook off a sailor who tried to help him into the boat. He glared at the man, who ducked his head but remained hovering close at hand. The boat rocked ferociously when Draios first set foot in it, and he feared for a moment he might need that helping hand after all, but he caught his balance before such was necessary.

He had to suck in his cheeks to stop himself from smiling when he saw that Delnamal was clearly waiting for a similar offer of aid from the sailor—and not getting it. It was possible the man had taken Draios's refusal to encompass his whole party, but more likely that he was reluctant to touch the walking cadaver that hid behind the robes and hood. The fact that even his own men drew back when Delnamal walked in their midst suggested that he would easily scythe through a battlefield.

Realizing no help was forthcoming—and perhaps too vain to stoop to asking for it—Delnamal climbed in. Luckily for all aboard—especially Draios, who had not yet taken his seat—Delnamal was so emaciated that his unbalanced weight caused only a mild rocking motion.

Draios sat at the bow, breathing in the fresh, salty sea air as his men took up their oars and rowed toward the flagship. He would have cut a more impressive figure standing, but thanks to his decision at an early age to enter the priesthood, he had little experience riding around in boats and had nothing resembling sea-legs.

He had made sure his rooms on the flagship were fully stocked with potions against seasickness.

Men cheered from the decks of their ships as Draios's boat passed, and he waved graciously as he soaked up their enthusiasm. To think that his father had been loath to launch his kingdom into war! These men—from career soldiers to recent conscripts—were alight with martial spirit and excitement, fueled by the sure and certain knowledge that they were doing the Creator's bidding. There had been rumblings of doubt when Draios had first taken the throne, but between his swift and unequivocal punishment of those who fomented it and the sermons and teachings of the priesthood, the kingdom was now firmly behind him. He wished that Parlommir could see him now. The last he'd heard, his big brother and his band of traitors had gone with the forces from the Midlands to help in the defense of Aaltah. Draios had commanded his men to take their would-be king alive if at all possible, but one way or another, he was destined to die soon.

Once he had boarded the flagship, Draios took a moment to lead the men in prayer, calling on the Creator to bless their journey, and remind all involved that those who were lost in the battles to come would be amply rewarded in the afterlife.

Then, he gave the order, and the fleet set sail.

Ellin held herself together through sheer force of will until the moment Star reluctantly left the dressing room after preparing her for bed. Her maid had only once asked her what was the matter, but it was not through lack of concern. Star had noticed her disquiet immediately, and Ellin had feared her maid's kindness and consideration would shatter her. She'd put Star off with the warning that what was troubling her was an affair of state that she could not talk about, and though it was clear that Star wanted to ask questions—or at least find some way to make her feel better—

she had respected Ellin's wishes and kept those questions to herself.

But when the dressing room door shut behind her, Ellin's shoulders drooped, her eyes stung, and the tears finally burst free.

That was how Zarsha found her moments later—having been alerted by Star about her fragile state of mind. Instead of immediately deluging her with questions, Zarsha took her into his arms and held her while she let loose the control that had been holding her together since the morning's council meeting.

Zarsha scooped her into his arms and carried her into the bedroom, laying her down in the shadowed privacy of the curtained bed and climbing in after her, never once losing contact. She snuggled against him, burying her head in his shoulder and feeling his chin rubbing against the top of her head. And still he did not demand she explain her tears. She sniffled and wondered if that was because he had learned when she needed silent support, or because he already knew what had caused the outburst. Perhaps a combination of the two.

Eventually, the tears began to subside, leaving her head and chest aching and her body weak. She took a deep, shuddering breath and reveled in the luxury of loving her husband and being loved by him in return. She couldn't imagine having to face the hardships she'd already survived—and the horrors that were on their way—without him by her side. And to think that she'd tried for so long and so hard to avoid marrying him!

"You already know why I'm crying, don't you?" she asked in a hoarse whisper. The fact that Zarsha had no official place in the government of Rhozinolm never seemed to keep him in the dark for long. Most people outside of Nandel held Nandelites in contempt, thinking of them as little more than uncouth barbarians. But Zarsha had spent most of his life away from his homeland, and fit in with polite society far better than any other Nandelite she'd ever met. And he was such an inveterate charmer that he had won over the court of Rhozinolm in ways she never would have guessed possible when he'd first visited.

Zarsha's arms tightened around her. "I know Waldmir has begun to amass troops on our border and that we have not received a single shipment of gems or iron we were promised. And I can't tell you how sorry I am for the role I played in getting us into this mess."

Ellin shook her head. "It was *my* decision not to return Elwynne to Nandel," she said. "I knew we risked making an enemy of him when I decided."

"Yes, but it's a decision you never would have made if it weren't for me."

Ellin sighed. "The fact is, Waldmir has only ever been a reluctant ally, and he has always been on the hunt for a better deal. It's why he made our betrothal so difficult, and it's why he was courting Delnamal's support while doing so. You said yourself that he has always hungered for more prestige for Nandel." She settled more comfortably against Zarsha's shoulder.

"He's already guaranteed that the next sovereign of Rhozinolm will be half Nandelite!" Zarsha protested. "What more could he want?"

Ellin ran a soothing hand down his chest, wrinkling her nose at the wetness of her tears on his nightshirt. She felt him start when he realized the answer to his own question.

"He's doing it again!" he exclaimed. "Using one of his daughters to try to *buy* a kingdom."

"We don't know that for sure," Ellin cautioned, "but given his history, I think it's likely. He has never been happy to have his legacy run through you, and if Draios painted a convincing picture of Waldmir's grandson sitting on the throne of Khalpar, in a world where the Blessing has been eliminated . . ."

Zarsha made a sound of disgust. "Yes. I see how such a future would tempt him."

"And likely would have even if Elwynne had never left Nandel," Ellin reminded him gently, though she doubted she could persuade Zarsha—or even herself—that the two of them were entirely blameless.

She swallowed hard as a lump tried to form in her throat once more. In the end, it didn't matter *why* Waldmir had chosen to ally with Khalpar. What mattered was that the army massing along the border between Rhozinolm and Nandel was a threat that could not be ignored. Which meant Ellin was no longer free to send the bulk of her forces to Aaltah's aid.

Zarsha's arms tightened around her. "What did you and the council decide?" he asked.

Ellin had faced a dizzying array of difficult decisions since she had taken the throne, but today's had been the most agonizing of all. "We will send our ships in support of Aaltah," she said, "but no ground forces. The bulk of our army will march west to defend the Nandel border. Which is *exactly* what Waldmir intended."

Zarsha cupped her face in his hand, lifting her chin so that she was looking into his eyes. "Naval support is what we do best," he reminded her. "If our ships can win the naval battle, then Aaltah won't need our ground forces."

She kissed his hand. "I appreciate that you're trying to make me feel better," she said, "but we both know we won't win the naval battle. Not with both Par and Khalpar sailing against us at full force."

From all reports, their enemies were throwing every ship at their disposal against them, including conscripted merchant and fishing vessels. For this "holy war," Draios had stripped the fields and harbors of his kingdom bare, amassing a force that any other king would have found hopelessly reckless. With their naturally occurring iron and gems, and with the elements produced by the Wells of Par and Khalpar—which were extremely well-suited for water-based magic—the enemy fleet was likely to cut through the continental forces with few enough losses that the outcome of the war would depend on the defenders on land. And the threat from Waldmir meant that Ellin could not help.

Zarsha kissed her softly. "You have done what you can to help our allies," he said. "Aaltah is not without support, and they've been planning their defense for as long as Draios has been planning the attack."

She nodded noncommittally, for it seemed to her that Draios, in his fanaticism, had prepared with a wild abandon that might well leave his people impoverished and starving in the aftermath, but that would overwhelm more responsibly formed forces. And no matter that she truly had no choice but to defend her own borders, she could not help feeling that her refusal to send her army to Aaltah's aid was a betrayal of the first order.

Zarsha sighed. "Nothing I say is going to make you feel any better, is it?" he asked, and there was a hint of anguish in his voice.

Ellin looked into his dear face and felt a not unpleasant flutter in her chest. "You make me feel better just by being you," she told him with a wan smile. "But perhaps you could also . . . take my mind off things." She waggled her brows suggestively, and though the proposition was forced and perhaps even a bit awkward, she felt an instant stirring of desire. And from the way Zarsha's eyes darkened, she knew that he felt that stirring, as well.

"It is the least I can do," he agreed as his hand slid down her hip toward the hem of her nightdress.

CHAPTER THIRTY-SEVEN

Alys felt a moment of shock when the door to the king's study opened and she saw Tynthanal sitting behind the massive desk. She had not set foot in the room since before the death of her father, and although she had, of course, been expecting to find Tynthanal, there was still something vaguely disorienting about it. In some ways, she realized, she had never really had the time she'd needed to mourn her father properly. For a moment, she thought the grief of all her losses was about to swamp her and drag her down into despair, but she shook her head and fought it off.

Tynthanal waited in sympathetic silence while she gathered herself, then gestured her to one of the chairs in front of his desk. Stiffening her spine, she took her seat and gave her brother an inquiring look, for his summons had not given her any hint as to why he wanted to see her.

"Queen Ellinsoltah contacted me a short time ago," he said. "Her spy network is . . . impressive. She says the Khalpari fleet has set sail."

Alys gasped. "So soon?"

Tynthanal shrugged. "It's no surprise," he told her gently.

"They were always going to set sail as soon as the weather was favorable."

Alys knew that, of course. She had timed her own travel to Aaltah accordingly, so that she need not be absent from Women's Well any longer than necessary. And from the moment the caravan she'd traveled with had arrived at the walls, she had seen evidence of how busily the city of Aalwell was preparing for the attack that was to come.

The Harbor District—which had never fully recovered from the massive flood that had destroyed it upon the casting of the Blessing—had been forcibly evacuated, its residents installed in a rough encampment above the cliffs. To appease the rich nobles and merchants, the "riffraff" was encamped outside the city walls, although even the most haughty had to admit the commoners should come inside when the Khalpari forces arrived.

For now, the Harbor District was the sole property of the Citadel of Aaltah, its buildings harboring much of the army that Tynthanal had gathered. Those who could afford to do so—and who were not among the fighting men who'd stayed behind—were packing up their households and moving farther inland, desperately hoping that when the smoke cleared and the dust settled, they would have homes and estates to return to in the capital.

"Ellinsoltah says that she has information about the Khalpari battle plans," Tynthanal continued. "Information she thought it would be best to share with both of us at once. I have also, on her suggestion, invited the lord commander to join us so that we might plan our strategy."

Belatedly, Alys saw the talker perched on Tynthanal's desk. Her heart began thumping hard as she realized just how imminent the war really was. Even as she'd toured the city and seen the preparations, some part of her had still thought of it as a distant event, rather than an immediate threat. A fleet the size of Khalpar's would take longer to reach Aalwell than any trade vessels, but that still gave them less than a week to make final preparations for the attack.

As she was absorbing the reality that war would be upon them so soon, one of the palace pages showed Lord Aldnor into the room. Although it was not strictly necessary for her to do so—as Sovereign Princess of Women's Well, she certainly outranked him—Alys stood to greet him with a respectful nod.

"Lord Aldnor," she said, searching his face for any sign of dislike or contempt. Tynthanal had told her his old commander thought of both her and her brother as traitors to Aaltah and that Aldnor had not been one of the council members who'd voted to appoint Tynthanal as regent.

But if Lord Aldnor harbored any ill feelings toward her, he did an effective job of hiding them. He gave her a shallow bow, then gave her brother a deeper one.

"Your Royal Highness, Your Highness," he said, fixing his gaze on Tynthanal. "Your message said you had received intelligence?"

"Not quite yet," Tynthanal said, gesturing at the two chairs.

Lord Aldnor waited for Alys to retake her seat before he took his own. She saw his glance dart to the talker sitting on the desk, and his eyebrows rose.

"It is Queen Ellinsoltah who has received the intelligence," Tynthanal explained as he opened his Mindseye and plucked some Rho from the air to power the talker. "She will tell us what she has learned."

It only took a minute or so for Ellin to respond to her talker—obviously she and Tynthanal had coordinated this meeting and she had been awaiting his call. It was all Alys could do not to chew her lip in anxiety as Tynthanal introduced Lord Aldnor to the Queen of Rhozinolm.

"Prince Tynthanal says you have received intelligence about the Khalpari plans?" Aldnor prompted almost immediately, apparently as anxious as Alys to hear the report.

"Yes," Ellin confirmed. "We have a high-ranking informant

serving at the Citadel of Khalpar. He has sent word that he is to be a part of a small force that will accompany both Draios and Delnamal into battle."

Alys gasped, her eyes widening. "Delnamal is going to fight?" she asked incredulously, sharing a startled look with Tynthanal. She shook her head. "The Delnamal I knew was a coward and a bully and never would have put himself personally at risk."

"But the Delnamal you knew didn't have the power to kill his enemies with some unholy magic no one has any idea how to counter," Ellin said. "From what I hear, he considers himself all but invulnerable."

"I won't disagree that Delnamal was a bully," Lord Aldnor interjected, "but I don't think he was as much of a coward as you think. He made spectacularly poor decisions—often for reasons that spoke more to personal animus than good sense—but his actions at the Well were those of a deluded fool, not a coward. I am not surprised to hear his pride has spurred him into fighting. I find the thought of *Draios* marching into battle far more surprising."

"I agree," Tynthanal said. "From everything I've learned about him, he has had no military training whatsoever."

Ellin nodded. "My sources are in agreement about that. He decided to join the priesthood at an early age and therefore never had anything more than the most basic nobleman's training. And it has been over a century since any king or sovereign prince felt the need to march into battle unless it was as a last resort, when all else was lost."

"Then why?" Alys asked, shaking her head.

"We don't fully know," Ellin said. "At least, we don't know why Draios is planning on fighting and accompanying Delnamal. What my source *was* able to learn is exactly what they are planning to do."

Tynthanal leaned forward in his chair. "We're listening!"

"I'm sure you've heard by now that Draios has convinced his

people that they are embarking on a holy war, and that Delnamal is somehow a weapon sent to them by the Creator."

Alys wasn't the only one who shook her head at the very idea. The Khalpari were a much more religiously inclined people, but it was still hard to accept that they would see anything holy in what Delnamal had become. But then perhaps their faith insisted that something so evil as Delnamal could not exist outside the will of the Creator, and that therefore he and Draios had concocted an explanation that was destined to fall on receptive ears.

"Apparently," Ellin continued, "Delnamal has convinced everyone that he can undo the Blessing by sacrificing himself at the Well of Aaltah."

"What?" Alys cried in shock. She didn't know what she'd expected to hear, but it certainly wasn't *that*.

"There has to be some mistake," Tynthanal said, looking as disbelieving as Alys felt. "Delnamal would never . . ." He let the words trail off.

"This is madness," Alys whispered as she tried to imagine her half-brother sacrificing himself for *anything*.

Ellin's shoulders lifted in a half-hearted shrug. "I'm just reporting what my contact has learned. If the fleet breaks through our blockade, they will sail straight into the harbor to make landfall. Delnamal is to be part of a small force that plans to scythe its way through the resistance and head straight to the Well."

"That's suicide!" Lord Aldnor protested. "No one with any sense would attack Aalwell from the harbor. It's far too easy to keep an invading army bottled up down there. Delnamal can't expect to get all the way up the cliffs, into the palace, and down to the Well from there against our resistance."

Alys could do nothing but agree. The risers—magic-powered platforms that provided easy, if expensive, transport from the Harbor and Terrance Districts below the cliffs—would be frozen at the top of the cliffs as soon as the first enemy ship was spotted, and the only other way to get to the city proper, where the palace was located, was to travel up one of two narrow, zigzagging roads at each end of the harbor. These roads would be blocked and booby-trapped and heavily defended. The attackers would be forced to ascend in a narrow column of no more than three men abreast and would be vulnerable to attacks from the ramparts above. They would travel in a hail of arrows, crossbow bolts, rocks, and magic.

"It seems Delnamal feels his powers will render him invulnerable," Ellin said, though there was no small amount of skepticism in her voice.

"And what about Draios?" Tynthanal demanded. "You said he and Delnamal would be making for the Well together. How can Draios possibly hope to survive, even if Delnamal is right and he can withstand all our defenses?"

"I don't know," Ellin answered. "Our contact believes Draios is in possession of some kind of extraordinary Kai spell that will protect him, but he has not been able to learn anything about what it does. He just knows that there have been multiple private meetings between Delnamal, Draios, and the grand magus."

Lord Aldnor was frowning fiercely. "With all due respect, Your Majesty," he said, "I believe you are being lied to. What you are describing is impossible. I believe the lie is designed to weaken and divide our defenses. Neither Delnamal nor Draios has anything resembling military experience, but they do have military advisers. It makes no sense to attack Aalwell by coming at us through the Harbor District and trying to climb those roads. The ships are far more likely to make landfall at Wellshead Beach, and then come at the city from behind. They want us to divert our forces to the harbor and leave our walls vulnerable."

That certainly seemed the more logical way to go about things, Alys thought. Wellshead Beach offered a conveniently long and hard-to-defend stretch of sandy beach less than half a day's travel from Aalwell. An army landing there would be forced to deal with Aalwell's heavily defended walls, but the walls would be easier to breach than the cliffs.

"I can guarantee that I am not being lied to," Ellin said with an edge in her voice. "I would not even bother sharing this intelligence if I thought that were a possibility." The corners of her mouth tugged downward. "Although I must admit there's always the possibility that my *informant* has been lied to. He agrees with your assessment of the plan, Lord Aldnor, and has told me he believes he and the others are being sent on a suicide mission. However, he also believes Draios and Delnamal can pull this off, even if all the lesser mortals—he used that specific term—perish in the effort. There is magic in play here that is like nothing the world has ever known, and that makes me reluctant to dismiss any possibility, however outlandish it might sound."

Tynthanal shook his head. "We need more men," he said bluntly. "If we must guard against the possibility of attack from either side, and must also man our fleet in hopes of stopping them before they make landfall . . ." He sighed in frustration.

"I am sorry," Ellinsoltah said, but there was steel in both her voice and face. "I have committed as many troops as I can when my own kingdom is also under threat. You have a substantial force ready to fight for you, and it may be that our navies can defeat them before a land war even begins."

Alys's gut told her that although Aaltah would have naval support from Rhozinolm, Grunir, and the Midlands, they would be outnumbered and outclassed by the full force of the navies of Par and Khalpar.

"Whichever direction they come from," Ellin concluded, "I feel certain that Delnamal and Draios will be attempting to make their way to your Well."

"But not because Delnamal plans to sacrifice himself," Alys said—for if there was one thing she was certain of, it was that. "The power he gained might have changed him, but not that much. He wants to undo the Blessing, but he would never, ever give his life for any cause."

"I agree," Tynthanal said. "I suspect he has some other nefarious plan to damage the Well out of pure spite, and he has secured Draios's aid by making a promise that boy would find appealing."

The lord commander looked skeptical. "In my experience, Delnamal is not what I would call a skilled liar, nor did he ever show much talent for manipulation. We of his council were willing to give him our loyalty and the benefit of the doubt, and yet he still managed to alienate practically every one of us during his short reign."

"I think you all need to stop thinking about him as the man you once knew," Ellin interjected. "Whatever changes he's undergone have turned him into someone who could persuade a young priest in training to murder his own father, exile his own brother, seize the throne of Khalpar, and launch what he has billed as a holy war. Either his power is so frightening as to be persuasive all on its own, or he has somehow gained other skills of persuasion. It doesn't matter which."

Tynthanal groaned and leaned back in his chair, his face lined with stress and strain. "We have to plan for the worst, which means assuming his navy will be able to fight its way past ours. And I fear that if we divide our forces, we will not have enough men to defend *either* approach fully."

A heavy silence descended on the room, lasting for the balance of a minute as dark thoughts swirled. Then Lord Aldnor sat up straighter in his chair and leaned forward, peering at Ellin's image with intensity.

"Did your informant say the *invasion* was going to come from the harbor, or that *Draios and Delnamal* would?"

Ellinsoltah frowned. "Well, he said the attack would come from the harbor." Her frown deepened. "But he was speaking specifically about his own orders."

Lord Aldnor nodded. "And likely *assuming* his party would be trying to break away from the rest of the army to climb the cliffs. But I cannot see any way that it makes sense for an army to attack us from the harbor when the only way up the cliffs is on narrow roads we can defend with so few men."

"Not *that* few," Tynthanal protested. "Not when there are two of them on opposite sides of the harbor."

Aldnor made a placating gesture with his hands. "But few in comparison to the whole of our ground forces. It's hard to believe that even their unusual magic would allow them to bring an army up those roads successfully."

Alys started as she realized exactly what Aldnor was suggesting. "You think their ground forces will come overland to the walls, but that Delnamal's party will head for the harbor, hoping it will be lightly enough defended that they can use their magic to fight their way through."

Aldnor nodded. "It's the only thing that makes sense. Getting a small force up one of those roads seems much more plausible than trying to get an army up it."

Aldnor and Tynthanal began discussing plans to defend the roads with as few men as possible, and Alys let her mind drift away. The defenders would, of course, be armed with the purgative spell she had created, so that should they be so unfortunate as to have access to Kai, they might trigger it and hopefully remove Delnamal's stolen Rhokai. Alys would make sure that the female cadets she had brought from Women's Well—with their women's Kai readily available—were stationed along whichever route was deemed most likely for Delnamal to travel.

But for reasons she couldn't fully explain, hearing this report only strengthened her conviction that it would be up to her to stop Delnamal. She would hold her tongue for the time being, but when the meeting was over and she could snatch a moment of Tynthanal's time, she would suggest what seemed to her the obvious fail-safe.

If Delnamal was truly headed to Aaltah's Well, then if he somehow managed to get through all the myriad defenders who would try to stop him, Alys would need to be in the Well chamber waiting for him. Ready to perform her sacrifice in a situation that everyone would agree left her with no other choice.

Tynthanal would argue, of course, but the argument would be more reflexive than anything.

Although she did not believe it would last, something very like peace descended on Alys, releasing some of the tension that had kept her whole body clenched for so long. She was not eager for the war to begin, and she would still have many horrors and terrors to confront. But there was an end in sight, and she was ready to face it.

Ellin paced the length of her private study, wishing she could run and scream and tear the crown off her head so that she would not have to face yet another horrifying decision. Standing by the fireplace, Zarsha watched her pace, his arms crossed over his chest, his face ashen as they both tried to absorb the terrible proposal that Lady Leethan had laid at their feet.

Still pacing, Ellin pressed her hands to her stomach, where a hard knot of dread had formed and refused to let go. She shook her head.

"I can't possibly approve this," she said, her voice shaking. She did not meet Zarsha's eyes, instead fixing her gaze on the carpet at her feet.

Zarsha did not respond. Right now, she desperately needed his love and support and advice, and yet she knew full well that it was impossibly selfish of her to lay any of this at his feet. The only member of his family he had ever shown any fondness for was his brother, but family was still family.

"It's horrendous!" she nearly shouted, as if Zarsha had argued with her. She risked a glance at him and saw that there was a rim of red around his eyes, and his teeth were clenched in an effort to hold in his emotions.

She didn't make a conscious decision to cross the room and throw her arms around him, but soon she was holding his taut body against her and laying her head on his chest, desperately seeking a comfort that was nowhere to be found.

He held her tightly against him, and she could hear the speeding of his heart as her ear pressed against his chest.

"It's war," she heard him say hoarsely, his voice so soft she almost thought she'd imagined it.

She shook her head, still pressing close to him. "I won't do it," she said. "I can't. It's too . . . It's too . . ."

She couldn't finish the sentence.

"Even if we discount her dream," Zarsha continued, his voice a little stronger, "you have to admit that her plan would be . . . effective."

"But there are limits to what can honorably be done. Even in war."

"I don't think Delnamal and Draios care much about those limits. And if Leethan's plans could free up our troops so that they might march to Aaltah's aid . . ."

Ellin pushed away from him and looked up into his face. His eyes shone with suppressed tears, and everything about his expression screamed of anguish, telling her how badly he wished to deny his own words.

"That doesn't make it right," she protested.

Zarsha stroked a thumb over her cheek. It was only then that she realized she was crying. "Is it better to deny her permission and let Waldmir's army hold us back until Aaltah falls?" he asked, then grimaced and shook his head. "Waldmir has chosen to side with monsters, and those who march with him have done the same."

"So what you're saying is that we should agree." Ellin shuddered, her mind supplying helpful images of Lord Creethan's assassination attempt against her, then twisting the dagger into her heart by reminding her of Tamzin's screams of agony as he had died. As she had *killed* him. That she was even *considering* Leethan's proposal was a sure sign that she was a monster herself.

Zarsha pulled her back into his arms, and she didn't know if he meant it to comfort himself or her. Or maybe he just couldn't bear meeting her eyes at the moment.

"I'm saying there are some times when the best you can do is pick the lesser of two evils. And this is one of those times."

Ellin closed her eyes, for she knew as horrible as Leethan's plan might be, it stood a reasonable chance of working. And it was hard to quantify how many lives it might save.

"I will procure the spell she needs," Zarsha said, as if Ellin had already given permission. And maybe her failure to argue meant that she had.

"We will tell no one else of this," he continued. "There must be no chance that Waldmir could receive a warning. Besides, there is no reason to burden anyone else's conscience with the weight we will be carrying."

Ellin sucked in a deep breath. It did not make her feel calm, exactly, but she at least felt a core of steadiness somewhere deep inside. Once more she looked up and met Zarsha's eyes, nodding.

"We will bear this burden together," she said softly.

Zarsha managed a sad smile while the anguish still shone from his eyes. "Together," he agreed.

"You can't be serious!" Jaizal protested, her voice going shrill with a combination of incredulity and alarm.

Leethan winced in the face of her friend's distress, although she had been well aware of exactly how Jaizal would take her declaration. "I'm afraid I am," she said as gently as she knew how and watched Jaizal's eyes fill with tears. Guilt stabbed through her, for although she had told Jaizal that she planned to travel with Rhozinolm's army to the Nandel border, she had not been honest about exactly why.

Ever since the vision she had triggered in secret, Leethan had been putting her mind to the puzzle of how Elwynne could possibly end up on the throne. The idea that Nandel could change its attitude toward women enough to allow such a thing seemed impossible, at least in such a time frame. Maybe several generations down the line, but during Elwynne's youth?

Her mind could barely encompass the possibility, and yet she had too much faith in the Mother of All to dismiss it. Somehow, it was possible for Elwynne to take the throne of Nandel one day, and some action of Leethan's could lead to that future.

"I-I don't understand," Jaizal said miserably, shaking her head. "After all these years, you are finally, *finally* safe! And you would march with an army going to war because of some stupid dream? One that any fool would know not to take literally, even if she actually believes it to be prophetic?"

"It's more than just the dream," Leethan said, although she had no intention of telling Jaizal about the vision. Jaizal's mind would likely follow the same path as her own had once she knew what the future might hold. If she knew for certain that Leethan intended to sacrifice herself . . .

Leethan let that thought trail off, for in reality there was nothing Jaizal could do to stop her. Behind her friend's back, she had already spoken to Zarsha and the queen about what she intended to do, getting their reluctant blessing. Jaizal could cry and scream at her and protest to her heart's delight, but she could not stop Leethan from going.

No, the truth was that Leethan did not have the courage to face the pain and distress she was planning to cause her best and oldest friend. It was, perhaps, an act of cowardice. And it was certainly a betrayal. She could only imagine how much greater the pain of her death would be when Jaizal realized that Leethan had brazenly lied to her so that she could leave without having to say goodbye.

"If it's not the dream," Jaizal said, "then what?"

Leethan sighed. "Not *just* the dream, I said. It's also . . . a *feeling*. Something deep inside here." She touched her chest, and while she was not telling the whole truth, she was at least telling part of it. She honestly believed this was what the Mother of All wanted her to do.

Leethan smiled and reached for her friend's hands, giving them both a firm squeeze. "I promise I am not taking the dream literally," she lied. "I believe it means I have a role to play in the battle that is to come, and I cannot imagine how I can play any role at all if I stay here safe in Zinolm Well."

"Have you considered that Nandel might win the battle and march on Zinolm Well?" Jaizal asked, her eyes narrowed. "You don't necessarily have to go to Waldmir; he has every intention of coming to you."

"That may be, but if I can do something to stop him, then I'd far prefer to do it *before* he has all but conquered Rhozinolm. I can't imagine how many people would die before he and his army reached Zinolm Well. Besides, if he's going to come to me anyway, then Zinolm Well is not as 'safe' as you think it is."

Jaizal blinked away tears. "I am old and alone here in a kingdom where I can barely speak the language and know no one but you. If you're going to travel with the army, then I will go with you."

"Someone has to stay and take care of Elwynne," Leethan reminded her.

"Jewel can do that," Jaizal protested. "Or her supposed father could take her."

It was a perfectly reasonable argument, and although Zarsha knew he was not truly the girl's father, he and Ellinsoltah had offered to transfer the girl to the palace now that the secret of her presence in Rhozinolm was known. However, Elwynne was far too wise for her years, and she would ask too many questions—questions no one was yet prepared to answer, and whose answers would leave the poor child confused and adrift. Better to give her some time to acclimate to Rhozinolm culture and learn the language while in surroundings that were becoming familiar, rather than to snatch her away yet again.

"She knows you and trusts you," Leethan said. "She has lost so much already, and I fear my leaving—even temporarily—might make her feel she is being abandoned. Again."

Jaizal's eyes squeezed shut, for she had to hear the truth in Leethan's words. She squared her shoulders and opened her eyes once more, catching Leethan's gaze and holding it.

"Can you look me in the eyes and promise me that you do not intend to kill yourself in some heroic act you think will defeat Waldmir?"

Something inside Leethan shriveled, and she wanted very much to look away, but she couldn't. Not without letting Jaizal see the truth. "I promise," she said, giving Jaizal's hands another squeeze and not allowing herself to blink. She put every drop of strength and conviction and earnestness she could find into her voice, *willing* Jaizal to take her at her word.

Jaizal shivered and lowered her gaze. "I still wish you wouldn't go," she said softly. "Or that you would at least let me go with you. But . . . I'll try to keep my protests to a minimum." She raised her chin once more. "Even so, I reserve the right to try again to change your mind before you leave."

Leethan smiled, while inside the pain and guilt gnawed at her. "I wouldn't expect any less."

CHAPTER THIRTY-EIGHT

Alys stood on the battlements in the rain, shielding her eyes with one hand as she stared out over the water far below. Even on a clear day, she would barely be able to see the ships that formed the final barricade between the attacking fleet and the harbor, but on this foggy morning in the steady rain, she could not even see that much. The only reason anyone inside the city of Aalwell knew the battle had begun was because of the steady communication that reached the palace thanks to the talkers Women's Well had provided for the captains of each ship.

If she truly wanted to know how the battle was going, she'd learn more by staying by Tynthanal's side so that she could listen to the reports he kept receiving, but something inside her had insisted she try to see for herself, even knowing the effort would be futile.

She let her gaze drop to the Harbor District, which from this vantage point appeared to be entirely deserted. She caught no hint of movement anywhere, although she knew there was a company of soldiers at each end, ready to defend the roads that led up the cliffs. Those soldiers were hidden behind the largest

Trapper spells Women's Well could provide, and Alys knew that Delnamal's men wouldn't see them even when they marched into their midst. She'd have taken more comfort from the formidable ambush if Delnamal hadn't fallen victim to such a scheme before, when he'd first sent soldiers to destroy Women's Well and been defeated. There was no doubt in her mind that he was fully prepared for many of his foes to be concealed with Trapper spells, and though she didn't know what he could do to counter them, she knew he had to have something in mind.

Alys shivered as the rain soaked her hair and trickled down the neckline of her gown. The shiver was not entirely born of cold, for she could not deny that she was afraid.

No. "Afraid" was too mild a term for what she felt today.

Somewhere below her in that Harbor District, concealed behind the Trapper spells she feared would be inadequate protection, her little boy was stationed with the rest of the youngest cadets of the Citadel of Aaltah. The lord commander was convinced that the heaviest of Draios and Delnamal's forces would be coming at them overland from Wellshead Beach, and had therefore stationed his most seasoned fighters along the city walls. Boys of Corlin's age were expected to fight in times of war, but they were generally kept in reserve, called upon to enter the fray only as a last resort. Lord Aldnor had therefore decided that they should join the smaller forces guarding the harbor.

Alys's first reaction upon hearing that Corlin would be in the Harbor District had been a panic so intense that she had feared her heart was about to give out and she would perish before the battle even started.

"I *know* Delnamal will be coming to the harbor," she'd insisted tearfully when Tynthanal had finally managed to calm her down enough for coherence. "I *know* it."

"Maybe you're right," her brother had said soothingly, "but in all likelihood, Corlin is going to see action whether he's at the walls or at the harbor. And the harbor is much easier to defend with Trapper spells than the walls are. I believe it is the safer of the two possible assignments."

Tynthanal's argument made sense, and Alys knew that Corlin would very much like to be present when Delnamal arrived. If anyone hated Delnamal as much as Alys did, it was Corlin, and he was probably down there *willing* his uncle to make an appearance. And hoping that somehow, he himself could be responsible for killing him. None of which made Alys feel any better. The terror of knowing her only remaining child might lose his life in battle today overwhelmed Alys's thoughts to the point that she at times feared for her sanity.

With a shuddering breath, she decided that standing outside on the battlements in the cold, drenching rain while she could see nothing of any substance was a sure and certain sign of her weakened mental state, so she hastened back inside.

She'd stood outside so long that she had to stop by her rooms and change into dry clothes before she could return to Tynthanal's office for an update. The moment she stepped inside, she knew the situation was grim. Tynthanal was pacing restlessly, one hand scrubbing at his hair, and the men who huddled around his desk wore expressions of anxiety and stress.

Tynthanal stopped his pacing when Alys stepped in. The lines on his face were deeply drawn, his eyes looking bruised with weariness. She knew beyond a doubt that he wanted to be on the front lines, his lifetime in the military insisting it was wrong for him to stay in his study in safety. He shook his head as he met her gaze.

"They're heading for Wellshead Beach," he told her. "We've lost . . ." His voice broke, and he had to clear his throat to continue. "We've lost so many ships already I've lost count. We're taking some of them with us, but there are just so many of them." He huffed out a deep breath. "They're going to make landfall. It's only a question of when."

She nodded, for of course no one had really believed Aaltah and its allies could prevail in the naval battle. "You're sure they're heading for Wellshead Beach?" she queried, her stomach quivering with such a mix of hope and despair she could not sort through her feelings. She was *certain* Delnamal was going to come to the Well, and that he was going to reach it.

Her certainty was not rational—she knew that. There was nothing about Leethan's prophetic dream that suggested any such thing. But knowing her instincts were irrational did not stop her from feeling them. If the fleet was not heading for the harbor, then the only way Delnamal could possibly get to the Well was if Aaltah was utterly defeated.

"We're sure," Tynthanal said. "They've already sailed past the harbor entrance. The ships that were guarding the harbor are now at their rear and closing in from behind, but . . ." He let his voice trail off.

"There aren't enough of them," one of Tynthanal's advisers said. Alys didn't even know the man's name, but the scars on the old man's face suggested he had seen combat himself in his younger days. "They're sailing into slaughter, cut off from the rest of our fleet."

"Can't you order them to fall back?" Alys asked.

"I did," Tynthanal said with a haunted look in his eyes. "Or at least, I tried to."

"The lead ship was under attack when we heard from them," the adviser explained. "Their talker went dead in the middle of our communication. In all likelihood, it was too late for them to retreat even if they got the message and managed to spread it to the rest of the ships."

"So now the Khalpari fleet has free access to the harbor?" she asked.

"I told you, they're already past it," Tynthanal said irritably.

Alys didn't take his tone personally, and she clamped down on her urge to second-guess him. If the ships guarding the harbor were lost, it was too late to correct the situation now.

Tynthanal sighed heavily and rubbed his eyes. "Sorry. We do

still have lookouts keeping an eye on them, making sure none of their ships veer off to come for the harbor. I'm not sure what we can do about it if they do, but we'll at least have some warning."

She nodded her acceptance of his apology. "And do we know where Delnamal and Draios are?"

Everyone was well aware that if the ship carrying those two men went down, the Khalpari fleet would be decapitated. As inexperienced as Draios might be as a military commander, there was no reason to think he wasn't taking extra precautions to keep his own ship hidden and out of the fray.

"No," Tynthanal said regretfully. "I'm concerned about our informant. We have not heard from him since the fleet launched. It would be difficult for him to reach us from a crowded ship— there isn't a whole lot of privacy to be had—but we still hoped he would help us locate the flagship. I fear his silence is ominous."

One of the talkers arrayed on the desk chirped, and Tynthanal hurried to activate it. Alys slipped away as one of the fleet's captains began his report, not because she was uninterested, but because everything within her continued to insist that she needed to be at the Well to face Delnamal when he arrived.

No matter where his ship was or whether he was planning to come via the harbor or only after Aaltah had fallen entirely, he would not arrive at the Well for a very long time yet. Even so, she gathered the band of honor guards who'd been assigned to join the last defense of the Well and descended to the chamber deep below the palace to wait.

Draios stood leaning against the railing of his fleet's flagship, his breath coming short with excitement as he watched the last of Aaltah's fleet sail out of the harbor in pursuit of the main body of their navy.

Grudgingly, he had to admit that Delnamal's idea of sending Khalpari spies to the mainland to acquire the famous Trapper spells that had been developed in Women's Well had been a sound one. Not only had it allowed the grand magus to research ways in which the spells could be thwarted, but it also allowed their own ship a level of stealth that was heretofore unheard of.

Draios did not like using the stolen Trapper spells to hide his ship, for it made him feel unclean to use the unholy magic of Women's Well. When Delnamal had first suggested the possibility, Draios had physically recoiled from the very thought of it, but a long night of prayer and fasting had finally convinced him that he must do whatever was necessary to ensure a swift and decisive victory. After all, Delnamal himself was hardly a wholesome weapon, and yet the Creator had sent him to Draios, acknowledging that sometimes there were necessary evils in the world.

To get to Aaltah's Well in the manner Draios's lord commander had recommended might well take weeks, even months. Aaltah's walls were formidable, and although Draios's army was likely to arrive in greater numbers than the defenders after the naval battle was won, it would be a long and costly fight to breach those walls and take the city. Sneaking in the back way while the bulk of the army was occupied elsewhere was clearly the best and quickest way to get to the Well, and once Delnamal had performed the sacrifice that would undo the Curse . . . Draios smiled to think of the despair that would fill the hearts of his enemies as the magic they'd come to count on sputtered and died.

As he watched the harbor clear while his own ship stayed behind, unseen, he knew he had made the right decision. It would have been better still if Aaltah had no idea that he was planning to make for the Well—the traitor who'd been communicating with the enemy had served to shore up Delnamal's store of Rhokai before the battle began—but Draios remained optimistic that any forces that had been left behind to guard the approach from the cliffs would be unprepared for the terror they would face when Delnamal and Draios cut through them.

"It's almost time," Delnamal said from behind him, startling him. The murmur of the waves and the patter of the rain had masked the man's footfalls, and even after all this time, Draios could not help but feel superstitious dread whenever Delnamal was at his back.

Draios could not *wait* until this was all over and Delnamal was gone. He thanked the Creator every day for the gift of this weapon, even while praying for forgiveness for his own squeamishness. He was so tired of the way the hairs on the back of his neck prickled when Delnamal approached, of the way his stomach clenched whenever he heard the man's whispery voice.

"Are you ready?" Delnamal asked.

"Of course I'm ready," Draios snapped as he wiped a trickle of rainwater out of his eyes. "I've been ready for months!"

"Then let's do this." Delnamal let his hood slide down, smiling that death's-head smile as he looked upon his erstwhile kingdom. "I am more than ready to go home myself."

Draios nodded, making a hand signal, and the ship began moving toward the harbor. He frowned at the waves that lapped up against the sides of the ship, realizing that if anyone was on the lookout—as surely they would be, even if the traitor *hadn't* tipped Aaltah off to the possibility of an attack from this direction—the ship's wake would be visible, even if the ship itself was not.

"We don't even need the stealth anymore," Delnamal assured him, having guessed his concern. "Their ships will never catch us now." His smile broadened as he looked over his shoulder. "Even presuming they have any ships left by the time anyone sees us coming."

The tail end of the Aaltah fleet was far enough away already that it was hard to see them in the rain-darkened light, but they looked to be surrounded, with one already capsized and one listing heavily. Delnamal was right once again.

Draios nodded briskly, then retreated to his cabin to strap on all his armor and weapons and prepare for the glorious victory that would soon be his.

CHAPTER THIRTY-NINE

Leethan's heart was in her throat as she clutched her cloak tightly around her and slipped through the trees as silently as possible. The moon was full and bright, and though buds were beginning to form on the branches, the mostly bare canopy let in enough light that she did not miss the lantern she had known better than to carry.

There was a light coating of snow on the ground, for the spring was slower to take hold here in the foothills just south of the Nandel border, and she was very much aware that she was leaving a trail anyone could follow. She was likely now past where the most distant of the Rhozinolm sentries patrolled, and her route had been carefully planned and prepared, but of course there was always the danger that she would run into someone who *didn't* know in advance that she had permission from the Queen of Rhozinolm herself to sneak through these woods and cross the border into Nandel.

Under her cloak, Leethan touched the bodice of the modest, high-necked traveling gown she wore. A gown that she herself had designed, and that Prince Zarsha had had made for her. The bodice felt exactly as the bodice of a gown should. A row of large, carved buttons trailed down the center over her sternum, and beneath those buttons, her fingers detected nothing but the expected boning of her stays.

If she were not an old woman, there was no question that the thin dagger that ran behind the row of buttons would be found when she was searched. The success of her mission rested on the typical Nandelite's assumption that as a woman—and an old one at that—she could not possibly be a true threat. Any search they performed would be perfunctory, and the chances of them finding the dagger were slim. And the chances of them detecting the Kai spell contained in that dagger were even smaller, for Queen Ellinsoltah herself had given her the precious concealment spell that had been invented by Princess Alysoon. The concealment spell wasn't perfect—someone who examined her with an open Mindseye and knew what to look for could see past it—but no one would think to search Leethan that thoroughly.

She was stumbling with fatigue by the time she was finally seen by a Nandelite patrol. She promptly fell to her knees and held up her hands in surrender, then closed her eyes and prayed she would not be shot on sight, for men on the brink of war tended to be extraordinarily reactionary. She thanked the Mother of All for the light of the full moon, so that when the men caught sight of her, they immediately saw that she was an old woman rather than a Rhozinolm spy skulking through the woods.

Leethan quickly found herself facedown on the forest floor, the snow melting against her face as one of the men put a knee in her back and bound her hands behind her. When he was finished, he hauled her to her feet, wrenching her shoulders so that she had to stifle a cry of pain. Another of the men put the tip of his sword against her throat, and she held her breath, fearing he'd decided to kill her despite her obvious harmlessness.

"What brings you into these woods at such an unseemly time

of night, madam?" he asked in halting Continental, glaring at her. His blue eyes shone with an ill-concealed lust for blood, and Leethan knew that one wrong word would end her life.

Having been born in Grunir, Leethan did not have the typical Nandel coloring, which was no doubt why the soldier had addressed her in Continental. She resisted a terrified urge to respond in the same language, to try to explain away her impossible presence in the woods at night in this no-man's-land between two armies. But her option to run away from her destiny had passed the moment she had been spotted. She now had no choice but to go through with the terrible plan she had concocted, and that Zarsha and Ellinsoltah had grudgingly—oh so grudgingly!—agreed to.

"My name is Mother Leethan," she said, barely moving her mouth for fear of the sword pressed against her throat.

The soldier's eyes widened, and the other members of the patrol gasped. She noticed that although she had the full attention of the man who held her and the one who held the sword to her throat, the others were all facing outward, vigilant against a trap.

The man with the sword at her throat turned his head to the side and spat. "Traitor!" he snarled. "Give me one good reason I shouldn't run you through right now."

Leethan found she was trembling, her courage hiding somewhere deep inside her chest like a frightened cat cowering under a bed. She had constructed this plan with the sure and certain knowledge that it would lead to her death. That was the whole *point* of the thing. The Mother of All had planned this death for her since she was a young woman and had that very first dream, even if she herself hadn't recognized it for what it was until much more recently.

But somehow it was much harder to face the inevitability of her death with that sword pricking her throat. Stiffening her knees, searching for strength she could wield even when courage failed, she met the soldier's eyes.

"I'll give you two," she said, her voice betraying only the

slightest of quavers. "One is that I am the property of Prince Waldmir, and he does not like others to damage his possessions. The other is that I come bearing information that he will find useful in the battle that is to come."

The soldier scoffed, the point of his sword not wavering from her throat. "You are already under warrant of death. And you wish me to believe that an old woman knows anything about battles and what might sway them?"

"An old woman who has spent the last five months in Zinolm Well as a guest of the queen and the prince consort," she reminded him. "I have been privy to some conversations that Prince Waldmir would very much like to know about."

There was no lessening of the suspicion in the soldier's eyes, but it was now joined by a hint of speculation. "And why have you now turned traitor to these generous benefactors of yours? Or has betrayal simply become a habit you cannot break?" He moved the tip of his sword fractionally so that she could no longer feel the prick at her throat.

Leethan would have sighed in relief, except the danger was far from over. This man was obviously eager for the killing to begin, and he could still decide to start with her. "My reasons are my own," she said, hoping she wasn't making a big mistake. She had an explanation ready, but instinct told her she'd be better served by letting Waldmir draw his own conclusions. "I will tell the prince, but no one else. You might consider that whether to hear me out or not should be *his* decision, not *yours*."

The soldier snarled at her, then lowered his sword, only to backhand her with his other hand. Pain and shock stole her breath, and for a moment her vision swam. He said something to her that she lost beneath the pounding of her pulse in her ears. Then he sheathed his sword and put his hands on her head, fingers digging hard into her hair, driving the pins that held her headdress into her scalp. She managed nothing but a soft mew of protest as tears clouded her vision.

It wasn't until his hands left her hair and began roaming over her bodice that she realized he was searching her for weapons. Which meant he must be intending to let her live and take her into the Nandelite camp.

Leethan didn't think he believed her to be anything resembling a threat, but he searched her with brutal thoroughness anyway, going so far as to shove his hand down the front of her bodice. But even so, he did not recognize the feel of the knife that was hiding in plain sight.

Closing her eyes and gritting her teeth, she tried not to let her surge of triumph show.

Waldmir would see her. She was sure of it. Even after her betrayal, he still loved her. It wouldn't stop him from putting her to death for her crimes—unless he could find a rational reason to spare her. When he had heard she had walked into their camp and surrendered herself, he would feel certain she was bringing him information she believed would save her own life. And because he wanted that so badly to be true, he would be incautious.

When the soldier finally gave up his search, Leethan was still fighting tears. For the first time, she admitted to herself that Waldmir's residual love for her was not unrequited. She had so many reasons to hate him, and yet she had never quite been able to make herself do it.

When the time came, would she truly go through with the plan? In some ways, it was easier to contemplate taking her own life than taking Waldmir's. Everything about this plan was . . . dirty. Despicable, even. Waldmir would admit her to his presence because he loved and trusted her, and she would repay him with murder.

No, not just murder. This was worse than murder. She would use her sacrificial Kai to trigger the spell contained in the dagger and kill . . .

Well, she didn't know how many would die. But the spell would kill anyone in the vicinity of Waldmir's tent. That would almost certainly include any number of other high-ranking Nandelite commanders, many of whom would also be his relatives and heirs.

With one brutal act of betrayal, she would decapitate and disable the entire Nandel army, leaving Rhozinolm's army free to march to Aaltah's aid. No one knew what the chances were a significant number of their forces could arrive before Aalwell fell, but if the battle should turn into a siege . . .

History would not be kind to Leethan, and there was a high likelihood that it would be similarly unkind to Zarsha and Ellinsoltah, if anyone realized that they had been involved. But these were desperate times, and the stakes were too high to allow for squeamishness.

The wait was excruciating. Corlin, along with Rafetyn and the rest of the second-years, crouched on the roadway that led up the cliffs, behind the third set of barricades that had been erected. Although there was no sign of any enemy ships heading toward the Harbor District—the distant signs of battle seemed to have moved past the point where Khalpar's ships ought to have turned if they were heading for the harbor rather than Wellshead Beach—Captain Norlix had ordered that the Trapper spells be kept activated at all times. Each soldier and cadet who guarded the Harbor District was equipped with a counterspell that allowed him to see, but everyone still had to reactivate his spell once as they waited for action that seemed destined never to arrive.

Corlin glanced over his shoulder, once again reminding himself that not everyone at the barricades was a "him." Neither the cadets nor the soldiers had been told exactly what the women who had come from Women's Well were meant to do on the battlefield. Oh, they understood that those women were there to cast some sort of women's Kai spell that it was hoped would nullify Delnamal's reputed powers, but the exact nature of the spell was a mystery.

"I don't know what it's supposed to do, either," Captain Norlix had snapped when Corlin had tried asking him for details. "All I know is that we have been ordered to protect them at all costs while still letting them get close enough to cast their spells."

The captain's scowls had made it clear what he thought of that particular order, and Corlin couldn't say he felt any better about it. There were only two of them—and two more on the opposite end of the harbor—but though they wore armor and swords and claimed to be in training at the Citadel of Women's Well, they looked frail and frightened and very much overmatched. Even Rafetyn cut a more intimidating figure, though Corlin knew much of that was bluster. Rafetyn still looked like a boy in the midst of all these bigger, stronger cadets, and though Corlin had done what he could to help his friend hone his skills, it was clear that Rafetyn would never be even a decent swordsman. Corlin's fear for his friend's safety almost overwhelmed his fear for his own.

"They're clearly not coming this way," one of the other cadets said loudly, only to be shushed by everyone around him. Captain Norlix—along with all the other adult soldiers—was stationed down below at the first barricade, or the cadet never would have dared voice a complaint. Nor would he have ignored the frantic shushing.

"What?" he asked more loudly. "Do you think the enemy can hear me? I could shout as loud as I want and the sound couldn't carry to where the real battle is happening."

"Any louder," Corlin said in a fierce whisper, "and *Captain Norlix* will hear you. That would be worse."

There were a few nervous chuckles at that, but the words must have made an impression, for the cadet fell silent.

"Look," Rafetyn said, pointing out toward the harbor. "What's that?"

Corlin's gaze followed the pointing finger, and at first he could make out nothing through the thick mist and drizzle, for his eyes didn't know what he was supposed to be looking for.

Several other cadets muttered scathing comments, but Rafetyn was used to ignoring them.

"It looks like a ship's wake, only there's no ship," Rafetyn persisted.

Corlin's eyes widened as he spotted it, and a chill traveled down his spine. It would not have been particularly hard for Delnamal to get his hands on a Trapper spell. They were one of Women's Well's most popular exports, and though no one from Women's Well would have sold one to him—or even to Draios—he could easily have used an intermediary.

"Warn Captain Norlix!" Corlin said urgently to Cadet Nandar. At the top of the class of second-years, Nandar had been left in charge of his classmates, and therefore given the only talker their little group possessed.

Nandar looked doubtful, frowning at the wake. "Maybe it's—"

His sense of urgency—and, to be honest, his lack of respect for Nandar—caused Corlin to snatch the talker out of his supposed commander's hand. He then opened his Mindseye and activated the talker while Nandar sputtered in outrage.

Captain Norlix gave Corlin his fiercest glare when he answered. "Where is Cadet Nandar?" he asked in a growl.

If Corlin started defending himself, it would waste precious time, so he decided to leave apologies for later. "Cadet Rafetyn spotted a ship's wake with no ship out in the harbor," he said urgently. "They're coming for us behind a Trapper spell of their own."

He half-expected Norlix to give him a dressing-down even under these circumstances, but apparently he wasn't giving his commanding officer enough credit. Norlix turned to look at the harbor, and Corlin could tell the moment he spotted the wake by the sudden tension in his body.

"Everybody refresh all your spells!" Norlix commanded, then cut the connection without a word to Corlin.

Corlin ignored the filthy look Nandar gave him as he handed back the talker. Everyone swiftly went about refreshing the Trapper spells as well as the spells on their weapons and armor. It was too soon—the wake was approaching fast, but it would still take time for the ship's men to disembark—but there was no reason *not* to do it yet.

Heart pounding, Corlin shared a terrified look with Rafetyn. Many of their classmates had been disappointed to be stationed on the cliff road, thinking they'd be less likely to see action here. Corlin and Rafetyn—who in Corlin's estimation were the only cadets with fully functioning brains—had found the unlikelihood of seeing battle a very good thing.

"Whatever happens," Corlin said under his breath, "stay close to me." Silently, he cursed Captain Norlix—and even Lord Aldnor—for sending Rafetyn into battle in the first place, even though he knew Rafetyn would not have wanted special treatment.

Rafetyn looked at him and shook his head. "You worry about you," he said, looking both frightened and resolute at the same time. He slung his bow off his shoulder. "I need to hang back, and your job is to move forward."

Corlin gritted his teeth to stop himself from arguing. It was true that Rafetyn was better with a bow than a sword and had therefore been assigned to stay behind the barricade for as long as humanly possible. Corlin wished his own skills with the bow had been enough that he could have stayed beside his friend and defended him, but if the battle came to them, his orders were to engage in hand-to-hand combat.

Nerves roiling in his stomach, Corlin watched the ship's wake move ever closer to the shore.

CHAPTER FORTY

The approach into the harbor was not quite as stealthy as Delnamal would have liked. The flagship of the Khalpari navy was powerfully warded and took no damage when it triggered a magic-powered mine concealed in the harbor's waters, but the noise and the sudden gout of water alerted every defender of the danger and gave them precious time to prepare. He could not see any soldiers lurking in the district, waiting for them to arrive, but just because he didn't see them didn't mean they weren't there.

Delnamal used one of the motes of Kai in his aura to set off one of the anti-Trapper spells the grand magus had developed, but unless Aaltah had found some way to counter the counterspell, there seemed to be no defenders awaiting them. Even when the first wave of Khalpari soldiers began disembarking, there was no sign of resistance save for an ineffectual fire spell that no seasoned soldier would fail to look for and disable.

"What is this?" Draios asked incredulously as the ship continued to empty its fighters into the eerie silence of the docks. "What are your people up to?"

Delnamal frowned, feeling unaccountably disturbed by the

lack of resistance. He knew very little about military tactics, but when Khalpar's lord commander had suggested that making landfall would be the most perilous part of their mission, he had fully believed it. He peered over the railing into the deserted district, trying to find any sign of defenders.

The ship had made landfall on the northernmost end of the harbor for the easiest access to one of the roads that wound its way up the cliffs. Although Delnamal still saw no defenders, he now noticed that there was a series of barricades set up along the road, and he understood Tynthanal's strategy.

"Thanks to the traitor," he said, "my half-brother knows we will be coming this way. And he also knows the bulk of our forces will be coming at them over land. He believes he can defend the roads up the cliffs easily with a small force, and so he has concentrated his men there."

Draios looked doubtful. "So he will just . . . let us land?"

Delnamal smiled. "Of course," he said as if this was what he had expected all along. "What harm can we do loose in the Harbor District?" He looked to the top of the cliffs, where the buildings of the main part of the city were barely visible in the gloom and rain. "They don't care if we disembark here. They think they can stop us from climbing."

Already, the harbor front was teeming with the soldiers who had landed, all bristling with weapons and ready to fight.

"Remember to stay close to me," Delnamal said to Draios when it was finally their turn to disembark.

Draios gave him an annoyed scowl. "Yes, yes. Don't treat me like a simpleton."

There was a shout in the distance, then the sound of weapons clashing. A crossbow bolt thunked into the dock disturbingly close to where they were standing. Hastily, Delnamal opened his Mindseye, then used three motes of Kai from his aura to activate the shield spells that had been developed especially for them, as well as Draios's doubling spell.

When he opened his eyes, Draios was surrounded by a veritable army of doubles. The real Draios had a ring of white around his eyes and was suddenly breathing hard as a crossbow bolt passed harmlessly through one of the doubles that stood near him. The boy king was understandably frightened, for he had not the imagination to have truly anticipated the experience of having people try to kill him.

"Keep moving," Delnamal reminded him, for if he alone among his sea of doubles stood still, he would be easily identified.

Draios blinked, then seemed to shake off his fear, striding forward with his sword drawn. Not that there were any defenders within reach. The crossbow bolts were coming from the barricades, far enough away that even spelled bolts could miss their targets.

Draios's troops were pressing forward against the increasing hail of bolts and arrows, and soon the first men were hitting the barricades. They had been thoroughly briefed on what to expect and were prepared to fight enemies they could not see, until Delnamal was close enough to cast another anti-Trapper spell.

"Hurry up!" Draios shouted over his shoulder at Delnamal. "My men are being slaughtered!"

Delnamal rolled his eyes. He doubted Draios cared much more than he did if every man in their mini army died—as long as they served their purpose—but he supposed it was necessary to keep up appearances lest the men lose heart.

His stores of stolen Kai well stocked, Delnamal's legs felt as strong and able as they had before his misadventure at Aaltah's Well. More so, even, as he did not have to carry around all the extra bulk. Stepping off the docks, he hurried toward the fighting. Halfway there, he came upon a soldier who lay with an arrow piercing his shoulder. The man called out to him for help, holding out a hand in supplication. Delnamal opened his Mindseye and neatly plucked the Rhokai from the soldier's chest, ending his suffering and replenishing his own supply of free Kai. In the chaos of the fighting, no one seemed to notice that he had killed one of their wounded—a fortuitous circumstance Delnamal had fully anticipated.

Closing his Mindseye once more, Delnamal continued forward. There were no more bolts or arrows aimed his way, the concentration of the Aaltah defenders now fully focused on those who were trying to force the barricades. Bodies were already piling up before the first of those barricades, the smell of blood and death heavy in the air.

Delnamal managed to snatch the Kai from two more wounded soldiers before he made it near the front line, the Khalpari fighters parting eagerly to let him through. Arrows winged their way toward him now, most bouncing off the powerful shield spell that protected him. But even his powerful, Kai-fueled shield spell was not entirely impenetrable, for a single spell-laden arrow pierced it and slammed into Delnamal's chest.

The force was enough to knock him back several steps, the arrow's spell so powerful it easily pierced the armor and bit into the flesh and bone beneath. Any lesser man would have died instantly, but Delnamal just recovered his balance and reached up to break the arrow's shaft so that one of the Khalpari soldiers could pull the thing through him.

In the midst of all the screams and shouts of battle and the clashing of weapons, Delnamal thought he heard the fearful murmur of the enemy who'd just seen him survive the unsurvivable. No doubt Aaltah had received reports of his powers, but seeing it firsthand was a very different reality. And now they would learn just how inadequate their intelligence was.

Opening his Mindseye once more, Delnamal plucked a mote of Kai from his aura. He didn't bother with knocking down the Trapper spell yet, for the Kai spell that was contained in his belt buckle did not require men to be visible to kill them.

Delnamal activated the spell, then pointed his finger toward the first set of barricades to give it direction. Screams filled the air.

Battlefield Kai spells like the one Delnamal had just cast were meant to be used as a weapon of last resort—or even vengeance. They were mercilessly blunt instruments that made no distinction between friend and foe. There were several Khalpari soldiers who stood between Delnamal and the barricades he had targeted, and those men were screaming and clutching their chests.

Unmoved, Delnamal calmly used another mote of Kai to knock down the Trapper spell that was hiding the defenders. He then closed his Mindseye to see about two dozen soldiers of Aaltah, still busily firing arrows and hacking at the Khalpari soldiers who were already dying. Delnamal was impressed that not a single defender had been affected by the Kai spell. Shield spells designed to protect against Kai were extraordinarily expensive magic, rarely wasted on anyone but the highest-ranking officers. However, it seemed Aaltah had spared no expense to protect even its rank-and-file soldiers.

The unfortunate Khalpari soldiers whom Draios had not seen fit to protect with Kai shield spells suffered briefly as the bones of their rib cages squeezed inward and ultimately snapped, jagged ends puncturing hearts and lungs and dropping them dead in their tracks.

Delnamal felt a pleasant flutter of excitement, despite the hail of bolts and arrows that targeted him, for as well-equipped as the Aaltah defenders might be, they could not possibly be prepared for what they faced.

Once again, Delnamal opened his Mindseye and triggered his Kai spell.

Seasoned soldiers might be accustomed to the risks of Kai spells; however, the successful casting of a Kai spell was *rare*. A man had to be on the brink of death, magically gifted enough to see Kai, rich enough to afford the most expensive of all magics, and clearheaded enough in the face of death to cast it. After which, he died, his threat having ended. And shields designed to counteract Kai spells had to be reactivated after each use.

There was a new tenor to the shouts and cries after Delnamal cast the Kai spell a second time, the music of panic hitting his ears as the defenders died and others—farther up the road and as yet out of range—for the first time fully recognized what they were up against.

"Get that barricade out of the way!" he ordered the soldiers behind him.

None of the men was eager to move in front of him, but there was not a man among them who didn't know how easily he could kill them for disobedience. They rushed toward the barricade, some hacking at it while others hit it with spells that weakened it.

Draios stepped up beside him—one on each side of him, so that Delnamal did not know which was the real man.

"Try to aim your next Kai spell *away* from my men, won't you?" Draios said with a dry edge in his voice, the sound coming from both sides of Delnamal at the same time.

Delnamal resisted the urge to roll his eyes. "Of course, Your Majesty," he said with a slight nod of his head.

There were still bolts and arrows coming at them from farther up the road, as there were likely to be for the duration of their ascent. Many of them passed through Draios's doubles harmlessly. One of them bounced off the real Draios's shield spell, and the boy hurriedly moved, trying to lose himself once more in the sea of doubles.

"Onward!" Draios yelled at his men, and they began the long climb.

Someone brought Delnamal a cheval. The sure-footed magical pseudo-horse might make him an easier target; however, it would allow him to progress with his Mindseye open all the time. It would also give him a somewhat safer angle from which to cast his Kai spells. He did not particularly care if some of Draios's men perished from friendly fire, but he *did* need them to take down the barricades, of which there were sure to be many before they reached the top of the cliffs.

Riding comfortably on the cheval's back, Delnamal took advantage of every opportunity to help himself to the Rhokai of the injured they passed, for it was of vital importance that he not run out of strength—or free Kai motes. Whenever they reached pockets of more spirited resistance, he cast another Kai spell. And however easy the road might ordinarily be to defend, there was no way the enemy could stop a small force bearing an inexhaustible Kai spell to clear the way.

Kailee pressed herself tightly against the wall as she skimmed past the small contingent of honor guards stationed in the Well's antechamber. The Trapper spell kept her hidden from sight, but the guards were moving about restlessly, and she held her breath lest one of them brush against her and discover her presence.

Of course, she was *supposed* to be sheltering with the rest of the women and children. Tynthanal had gently reassured her that she had done more than her fair share to protect her adopted home when she'd spent all those hours at Aaltah's Abbey helping the novice abigails create healing potions. He understood her desire to feel useful—he himself was struggling against his instincts, which insisted his place was on the battlefield—but he could not get over his deeply ingrained belief that it was his duty to protect his wife.

She'd won his permission to keep working on healing potions for as long as possible by promising him she'd rush to the shelter as soon as he told her it was necessary, and at the time she'd made the promise, she'd fully intended to keep it. However, when he had reached out to her via talker and told her what was happening on the battlefield, she'd known almost at once that she had to make a liar of herself.

Tynthanal had described the horror of the enemy's ascent—of Delnamal's continual use of Kai spells, and of Draios's army of doubles—and an idea had immediately sprung into her mind.

One she knew Tynthanal would reject out of hand, so she had kept it to herself and promised him she would drop everything and hurry to the shelter as agreed.

Stopping Delnamal was, of course, of paramount importance. According to Tynthanal's report, it seemed unlikely any of their people had gotten close enough to even *try* Alys's purgative potion yet. But to protect Aaltah, they also had to stop *Draios,* and his defenses had so far proven just as effective, thanks to the spell that made one man become many. Draios was Khalpar's king, and his army would continue to fight for him even if Delnamal was killed.

Unless she was very much mistaken, Draios's doubles were nothing more than illusions, which meant that they would have no aura of Rho surrounding them. Unlike the warriors who relied on their eyesight to move and to fight, Kailee had for her whole life relied entirely on her Mindsight. The army of doubles would be invisible to her Mindsight, and therefore unable to distract her. With this Trapper spell hiding her, she should be able to walk right up to Draios and remove some crucial elements from his spell, thus deactivating it. And making him an easy target.

Of course, it would be possible for *anyone* to try such a tactic, which was why Kailee had almost mentioned the idea to Tynthanal. She had stopped herself at the last moment when she realized that anyone who'd spent their whole life relying on eyesight would find it almost impossibly difficult to pull off such a maneuver. It was considered suicide for a warrior to open his Mindseye in the heat of battle, and even if Tynthanal could have found—and reached—a volunteer who was already in Draios's path, the tactic was unlikely to succeed. Besides which, she knew if she even mentioned the possibility to Tynthanal, he would suspect she might try it herself and would not trust her promise to go hide.

A frisson of fear shivered down her spine as she slipped past the last of the guards and realized that the door to the Well chamber was closed and likely barred. No doubt Alys was concealed by a Trapper spell of her own somewhere behind that door, but even if Kailee could have gotten through the door without the guards noticing, she needed to remain out here so that she might take down Draios's shield spell while there were still men left alive to deal with him.

The thought of experiencing a battle filled her with knee-weakening dread. She did not want to see anyone die, but she could hardly hope to avoid it. Not only that, but she knew she could easily be hurt or killed herself. The corridor was broad, but it was still a corridor, and now that she'd put herself behind the guards, there would be nowhere to run to. In such close quarters, she could be accidentally struck by men from either side. If she believed there were any chance someone else was as likely to succeed at taking down Draios's spell as she, she would have gladly fled the scene.

Trembling slightly with nerves, Kailee fed some more Rho into her Trapper spell to ensure she would remain unseen, then settled in to wait.

CHAPTER FORTY-ONE

"He's heading your way," Tynthanal said, and even in the miniature image projected by the talker, Alys could see the strain—and fear—in his face. "For all our intelligence reports, we never truly understood how devastating Delnamal's powers would be on the battlefield. He has what seems to be an inexhaustible supply of Kai to fuel his spells. And the spells kill too fast and terribly for our men—or your women—to cast the purgative spell. We are throwing everything we can spare at them, but . . ."

Alys nodded, feeling very little surprise. She ought to be afraid of the death that was inching ever closer to her, but there was one concern that blocked out all others.

"Corlin?" she asked in a ghost of a whisper. She had been holding the talker in her hand to speak with Tynthanal, but she quickly moved to one of the benches that lined the outsides of the Well chamber and set it down. She had left the soldiers who were to be her last line of defense in the antechamber outside, and she was now glad for that decision. She could not put on the stoic face required of Sovereign Princess Alysoon at the moment;

she could only be a terrified mother who knew her baby boy was in harm's way.

Tynthanal scrubbed a hand through his hair. "I haven't heard anything, Alys," he said gently. "He was posted at the road on the opposite side of the city, but of course his company has now left its position to join the fight. My scouts from above say there is significant fighting happening to the rear of Delnamal's party, but that is all I know."

Alys nodded mutely, her throat far too tight and thick to allow for words.

"Try to take heart," Tynthanal implored her. "We know he is not in Delnamal's path, and he won't be hit by that horrific Kai spell."

"No," Alys choked out. "He'll only be hacked at with swords or shot at with arrows or crossbows or—" She stopped herself, closing her eyes with a shudder.

Someone she couldn't see said something to Tynthanal, and he nodded. "Alys, I have to go. If I hear any news about Corlin, I swear I will contact you immediately. And please, don't . . ." He let his voice drift off.

She would have liked to try to comfort him, as he had tried to comfort her, but she didn't have it in her to utter the false words. It was her destiny to die here, and Tynthanal would just have to accept the reality.

"Go," she said, making a shooing motion with her hand, for there was so much more at stake than the life of one teenage boy, no matter that she felt her whole world rested in him.

Tynthanal nodded, then his eyes went white. She saw him reaching for the talker, then the image faded away and she was left alone in the vast, empty Well chamber.

The chamber still showed considerable signs of damage, although the rubble had all been cleared ages ago. Several of the benches were cracked, and two were missing entirely. The intricately inlaid floor that surrounded the Well's opening was patched in places with plain gray flagstones, and even the parts that were intact were marked by chips and scratches.

Alys rose on shaky legs, tucking the talker into a pocket of her skirt and walking nearer to the Well itself, trying to take comfort from the low humming sound it emitted along with its gentle vibration. As a little girl, she had often come to the Well chamber to find peace in the midst of the turmoil of her life at court, but there was no peace to be had now. Not when Corlin was out there fighting for his life. Not when Delnamal possessed even more power than they had realized and was heading straight for this precious Well.

Although it was far too soon—even with Delnamal cutting through their forces so easily, he could not possibly reach the Well chamber in less than an hour—Alys drew the knife that would end her life. She caressed the blade lightly, and wondered if she would know Corlin's fate before she died.

It would be a good end, she told herself. A noble one. She would avenge Jinnell, save the land of her birth, and escape the troubles and turmoil of her life. Corlin would be devastated when he found out—she refused to think of it as *if*—and for that she felt yet another surge of guilt. But some wounds were unavoidable, and if her death meant Delnamal's defeat, then Corlin stood a much better chance of surviving this war. She would eagerly trade her life for his, and that knowledge helped her pack that little surge of guilt back down into her core, where it could fester with all the rest of it. Until all of it was gone for good.

Leethan held her chin high as she met Waldmir's fierce gaze and found herself unable to look away.

"Everyone out," he said, and even having known him for decades, she could not interpret the tone of his voice. "Get those chains off her first."

Out of the corner of her eye, she saw the soldier who had hauled her into Waldmir's tent open his mouth to protest, but only a fool would argue with Sovereign Prince Waldmir when he gave an order.

Leethan stood still and passive as the heavy chains and manacles were removed, though she breathed a quiet sigh of relief. The chains had not fully immobilized her, but it would have been somewhere between hard and impossible to withdraw the knife from her bodice with them on. And the weight and awkwardness might have slowed her down so much that she'd be taken down before she managed to make the first cut.

She rubbed her aching wrists while the tent emptied out. It looked like Waldmir and some of his top commanders had been partaking of a cold and hurried meal when she'd been brought in. Plates of meat and cheese and bread were scattered on a large, utilitarian table on which maps were spread.

"Have you eaten?" Waldmir asked with false solicitousness, moving over to the table and putting together a plate.

Leethan urged herself not to speak. Now was the perfect time to perform her sacrifice—while she was alone with him and his attention was divided. She was not so foolish as to think him completely distracted by gathering a plate of food, but he would not expect anything resembling violence from her.

To her embarrassment, Leethan's stomach gave a loud gurgle, causing her to blush and Waldmir to grin. She had been far too nervous to eat anything since breaking her fast this morning.

It was Waldmir's unguarded grin that undid her. In all her time knowing him, she had never seen him unguarded with anyone but her, and a stab of premature grief preemptively pierced her heart. No matter what he'd done, no matter how well she knew that he was not a good man, no matter that she'd convinced herself years ago that any love she'd ever had for him had shriveled and died, she did not want him to die.

"I know you must be frightened," Waldmir said gently, the

grin fading as he approached her and held out the plate, "but you must know that if I can find even the feeblest excuse to spare your life, I will do it. And you would not have delivered yourself into my hands if you did not plan to present me with such an excuse."

The flash of hunger had disappeared as fast as it had come, but Leethan took the plate by reflex. A whiff of the meat—mutton, by the smell of it—made her stomach roll over, and she had to swallow hard to fight the nausea.

Waldmir shook his head, and the expression on his face was unquestionably one of hurt. "Why, Leethan? Why did you steal my daughter from me?"

Leethan let out a shuddering breath. "You sent a five-year-old to the Abbey, and you wonder why I might want to take her away from you?"

Waldmir scoffed and waved his hand as if to dismiss her argument by royal decree. "I had no intention of *leaving* her there, and a visit would have done her no harm." His voice picked up some heat. "Why would you risk your own life and hers by fleeing through the mountains in winter? If she had died in your care, there would have been nothing you could have done to persuade me to spare you."

It was Leethan's turn to scoff. "Don't pretend to be the loving father with me, Waldmir. Your daughters have never been more than disappointments and inconveniences to you. Just as your wives have been." Emboldened by indignation, she strode over to the table and put down her untouched plate.

"That is not true!" he protested with some heat, then had the grace to look abashed. "It is not true of our daughters or of you. My other wives and their daughters were poor substitutes, and I am well aware that I did not give them the love or the kindness they deserved. But that does not mean I would wish harm upon them. I freely admit that I cannot look at Elwynne without remembering the sins of her mother and my nephew, which have now become public knowledge. But she is still my daughter, and I would have grieved had she died. You owe me an explanation."

Leethan shivered and stepped closer to the glowing brazier that warmed the tent, holding out her hands. She should perform the sacrifice now and have done with it. All this talking was merely delaying the inevitable and making things harder for her.

Still and all, she *had* kidnapped and endangered his daughter, and as cold and unloving as he might be, he spoke the truth when he said he deserved an explanation.

You're stalling, an acid voice whispered in her mind, but she shoved it away.

"You won't like or even believe my explanation," she warned, watching him out of the corner of her eye as she warmed her hands by the fire.

"Ah," he said with a nod. "It's one of those vision things."

There was only the faintest hint of disdain in his voice, but she heard it anyway and gritted her teeth.

Waldmir once again scoped out the table of food and maps, popping a hunk of cheese into his mouth before grabbing a wineskin from which he poured two goblets of ruby red wine.

"Yes," she grated. "One of *those vision things.*"

He held out one of the goblets to her, and once again, she took it by reflex.

"What did you see?" he asked, showing no sign that he had noticed her indignation.

Because she saw no harm in it, she told him about her vision of crossing the mountains with Elwynne in tow. He listened attentively, his head cocked to one side.

"I see," he said when she had finished.

She snorted. "I told you you wouldn't believe me."

His eyebrows rose. "Who says I don't believe you? I believed you when you told me I would have no sons, didn't I?"

She didn't know what to say to that and found herself taking a swallow of wine to cover her discomfiture. Her stomach wasn't sure what to make of the sudden intrusion, but after a moment it settled, and she decided to drink more. Perhaps the gentle buzz of alcohol in her veins would make it easier to do what she must.

"So you took her because you believed your goddess wanted you to," Waldmir said. "I can . . . respect that." He sighed. "I can even forgive it, because I've seen enough evidence to put stock in your visions. Perhaps your Mother of All—if She exists—intended me to join forces with Draios and knew Elwynne was the goad that would make it happen."

Leethan's lip curled in disgust. "Is that how you justify selling your daughter to a monster?"

Waldmir blinked at her as if completely baffled by her objection. "If my plans come to fruition, she'll one day be the Queen of Khalpar. What greater future could a man envision for his daughter?"

"And if that marriage is as disastrous as Shelvon's and she gets as little joy from it, that's *her* fault, right?"

"This is pointless," Waldmir said with a dismissive wave. "I have made my bargain with Draios, and I will have many years in which to decide if fulfilling it is advantageous or not. It is *your* future that is in question here, not Elwynne's. I'm sure you're not expecting my royal council to agree to spare you on the strength of your vision, so whatever information you have brought me from Rhozinolm must be something you believe will ensure Nandel's victory in the battle to come." He frowned. "Though I might be just a little offended that you believe we need information from a spy to lead us to victory."

Her hands trembling, Leethan turned her back to Waldmir and put down the wine goblet. She was out of time. If he started pressing her for the information she claimed to be bringing, the situation could deteriorate so fast she would be back in chains before she even thought to draw the knife.

If she was going to do this, it had to be now. No matter how badly she might want to put it off.

Tears stinging her eyes, Leethan drew the dagger.

Kailee's heartbeat was growing increasingly frantic, and she swallowed hard as she pressed herself more tightly into the corner behind the defenders who stood between the enemy and Aaltah's Well. News had trickled in via talker as they all waited for the confrontation they were hoping would not occur. Listening to the reports had very much made Kailee doubt her decision to put herself in the path of the enemy.

Delnamal and Draios had by all accounts sliced through what should have been a nearly impenetrable defense, climbing inexorably up the cliffside road and leaving a devastating trail of bodies behind. Whenever it seemed that the defenders might be gaining a little traction, Delnamal would let loose a Kai spell from his apparently inexhaustible supply, and the hapless soldiers died in droves.

Kailee trembled, her mouth dry with nerves as Alys's retinue gathered in front of the door to the Well chamber, poised and grimly prepared for a battle they did not expect to win. She longed to take down her Trapper spell and let the men know of her presence, for she felt exceedingly vulnerable standing there in the corridor unarmed and unseen. However, she knew without doubt that if the men knew she was there, they would force her to leave.

From the sounds of it, it was already too late for her to flee up the main staircase—there was muffled shouting coming from what sounded like just above—but there was a secret passageway the men could send her through. She eyed the entrance to that passageway—visible to her Mindseye because of the elements in its concealment spell—longingly. Perhaps the men were so focused on the advancing threat that they wouldn't notice her opening that door and slipping through to hide on the other side until the fighting was over.

Kailee shook her head, letting go of the pleasant fantasy of flight. She firmly believed her decision to wait here and take advantage of her unique abilities to sabotage Draios's spell was the right one, no matter how terrified she might be. So she hunkered down, making herself as small as possible, and mouthed the words to a prayer.

The shouting from above cut off abruptly.

The men in the passageway prepared their swords and shields for battle, spreading out as much as possible in the confined space. Kailee saw shield spells being activated, as well as enchantments on swords and knives. A man in the far corner from where Kailee crouched readied a crossbow bolt and aimed it at the opening of the stairwell. She tried to read the spell contained in the bolt, for many of its elements were neuter and within her ability to see, but she was still too inexperienced a spell crafter to guess exactly its purpose. The room fairly bristled with magic, the elements so thick in the armor and weapons that Kailee could see even the smallest details, like concentrations of gems in sword hilts.

Kailee stifled a scream when the crossbow let loose, the bolt flying through the air at an impossible-to-follow speed. All around her, the soldiers in Alys's retinue let loose a battle cry so loud she had to cover her ears. Several men entered through the doorway swinging swords and were met with Alys's retinue, but then something strange happened.

Kailee's mouth dropped open as she watched Alys's soldiers swinging their swords at empty air. She quickly realized that they had to be fighting illusions, that Draios had sent his magical doubles out of the stairway ahead of him.

Into the confusion, she saw more auras of real men—armed

with real, spelled weapons—jump into the fray. The air filled with screams and shouts and the smell of fresh blood.

The screams took on a new, added edge of terror when someone else stepped out of the stairwell.

Kailee could not see the man, of course, but she was instantly aware that there was something very, very wrong with his aura. Most living beings, be they human or animal, were surrounded by a thick aura of Rho that made them look almost like they were glowing. Sometimes, those auras of Rho were interrupted by clusters of other elements—magic items, packed with enough elements to make them visible and noticeable even within the sea of free elements that floated in the air this close to the Well. But the aura she saw now, the one that seemed to strike terror into the hearts of the brave men who'd volunteered to stand between the enemy and Aaltah's most precious jewel, was not like any ordinary aura.

There was a thin, man-shaped aura of Rho, but that Rho reminded Kailee of the moldering, moth-eaten gown she had once discovered in an attic when she'd been exploring as a child. She remembered touching the gown and recognizing the smooth slide of silk, but then finding holes and loose threads, and patches that seemed to slough away at even the most delicate brush of her fingers. And that was how Delnamal's—who else could have an aura that looked so damaged and unwholesome?—aura appeared to Kailee's Mindseye.

The aura was so horrifyingly *wrong* that Kailee wanted very much to look away, but she forced herself not to. She kept staring at it, wondering if those patches and holes were actually made up of the Kai that supposedly clung to him. Kailee had found herself to be fairly gifted at magic, but she was nothing like Alys or Tynthanal, who each had the unique ability to see elements that were not of their gender. If there was Kai surrounding Delnamal, it was *masculine* Kai, and therefore not something she could see.

What she *could* see were the magic items he carried with him. Because she could see only the neuter elements from the spells—and maybe not even all of those—she could not begin to guess their purposes, except that she very much doubted any of them was benevolent.

Delnamal stepped into the room, holding out his hand and just standing there, as if he had no fear whatsoever that he would be hurt. As she watched, a spelled crossbow bolt fired by one of Alys's retinue hit him square in the chest, but he didn't even flinch.

Thanks to her always-open Mindseye, Kailee was the only one in the room who knew when the real Draios entered the antechamber: his was the only aura that entered the room, and then stepped nimbly to the side instead of wading into the fight. Apparently he was content to let his men fight and die for him while he hovered in the back, safe behind his wall of illusions.

Kailee tore her eyes away from Delnamal and scanned Draios's aura, her eyes assessing each spell she could see attached to him. He had something that even with her novice eye she could recognize as a standard—if very powerful—shield spell. She also detected what she suspected was a Kai shield spell. Then there was one other spell that appeared to be contained in some item he wore pinned to his shoulder.

Kailee was certain there were many elements in that particular spell that were masculine and beyond her ability to see. She was also certain that spell was powered by masculine Kai, and that it was the spell that powered his doubles.

Perhaps it wasn't reasonable to feel so certain. After all, she was basing that assessment on one of the few neuter elements she could see in that spell. However, that neuter element was Lix, which she knew was associated with spells of camouflage. In fact, Lix was the element that powered the more traditional—and far less powerful—Trapper spell on which the Women's Well version was based. If she could sneak up to Draios and remove the Lix from his spell, his illusions would vanish.

Shaking with nerves, wishing she could stop her ears so that she did not have to hear the screams and cries of the wounded and dying, she pressed her back to the wall and slid along it toward Draios, skirting past a pair of men hacking at each other with spelled swords.

Just as she moved past, one of the men scored a devastating hit. Something hot and sticky splashed against Kailee's neck and chest, and her feet froze beneath her, her breath suddenly coming in panicked gasps. She closed her eyes and pressed harder against the wall, wishing she could sink through it and escape, wishing she had never come down here in the first place. She had consoled herself that her lack of physical eyesight would inure her to much of the horror of battle, but she'd been terribly wrong.

Raising her hands to her ears, she tried to drown out the screams of men who were wounded and dying and terrified. The blood on her skin felt like it was scalding her, and she shuddered in horror and revulsion as she felt a trickle running down into her cleavage. She clapped a hand over her mouth, afraid she might vomit. A soft whimper escaped her throat, but the sounds of fighting drowned it out.

She was past the fighting now, but only because there were so few men left standing. If she could pull herself together enough to move, she could reach Draios's side in about a dozen steps.

"This is getting tiresome," Delnamal said as Kailee stood plastered to the wall, still unable to leave its false security.

She saw his hand reach up into the aura that surrounded him, disappearing into one of the blank patches where no Rho was visible. Then he fed something into one of his magic items.

"Don't!" Draios shouted suddenly, but he was too late.

Kailee could not see the spell as it flew, but she could both see and hear its devastating effects. The antechamber filled with shrieks of pain, and all the fighting forms went still. Then, the aura of Rho that had surrounded each man dissipated, and she heard the thud of heavily armored men hitting the stone floor.

"You've killed all our own men!" Draios protested, with all the emotion of a whiny child deprived of a toy. If he was horrified by what Delnamal had just done, it didn't show in his voice. Although Kailee couldn't see his illusionary doubles, she could *hear* them, and the chorus of identical voices coming from all through the corridor and echoing off the walls raised the hairs on the back of her neck.

Against the wall, Kailee shook her head, hyperventilating once more as she realized Delnamal had just cast a Kai spell that had killed every soldier in the room. It was sheer luck that she herself had edged past the fighting men and had not been in the path of Delnamal's spell. Oona had spoken of her husband as a man much mistreated and misunderstood, but any man who would do what he had just done was nothing but a monster.

"We don't need them anymore," Delnamal said with such callous indifference that Kailee almost let loose a gasp of indignation.

"Maybe *you* don't," Draios retorted, "but how am I supposed to get out of here when you and all my men are dead?"

"Trust me," Delnamal said. "When I've undone the Curse, there will be so much chaos no one will glance at you twice as you make your way back to the ships. Now let's get on with this, shall we? Stay behind me in case we discover any surprises waiting in the Well chamber."

Kailee willed herself to dash across the short space separating her from Draios and deactivate his doubling spell as she had originally planned, but she couldn't force her shaking limbs to move. She stood there helpless and quivering as Delnamal opened the door to the Well chamber and stepped through, with Draios right on his heels.

She forced out a shuddering breath, realizing deactivating

Draios's spell was no longer of any great importance. Her goal had been to make it easier for one of the soldiers to locate and kill him. But now all the soldiers—including Draios's—were dead. She was *useless* here.

But something still wasn't right with Delnamal's supposed plans. They all knew Delnamal's purpose for coming to the Well was *not* to sacrifice his life. He had consoled Draios over the loss of his soldiers by claiming Draios could escape the palace in the chaos that came when the Blessing was reversed, but clearly that wasn't going to happen. So what, exactly, *was* the plan? Delnamal must have some reason to think he and Draios could escape— even without the aid of the men he had just so recklessly killed.

Perhaps it was a form of hubris for Kailee to think that she might have a chance to stop the plan, whatever it was. Perhaps she was being reckless and foolish for not leaving now when she had the chance. But something about that Well chamber . . . *called* to her. She couldn't explain it, but somehow the thought of turning away felt *wrong* in some fundamental way.

Still shaking and sick, stumbling slightly as if drunk, Kailee stepped forward away from the wall.

CHAPTER FORTY-TWO

Corlin felt a moment of guilty relief when the enemy forces converged on the opposite side of the harbor. Not because he thought it would save him or his fellow cadets from having to fight, but because it would delay the onset of that fighting. Funny how when they were waiting for the attack, he'd decided waiting was the worst part and now he would like nothing better than to have to wait some more.

As soon as it became clear that the attackers were heading to the other side of the harbor, Captain Norlix had given the command to march. At first, they had done so cautiously, concerned that the first attack might be a feint, but it quickly became apparent that it wasn't.

Captain Norlix broke them into squads, ordering each squad to stay together as they ran toward the battle. Suddenly, all the long, agonizing runs they'd been forced to endure during training became something to be thankful for, rather than to curse, for the distance measured in miles. Captain Norlix and his veterans set the pace, keeping it as fast as possible without his men being completely worn out by the time they reached the combat zone.

Even from a distance, Corlin could tell the battle was going badly, for the fighting had already surged past the first barricade before his company had crossed half the distance. He was sure he wasn't the only one suffering from the sinking feeling that they were too late to be of any substantial use. They would fight, and many would die, but they would be like small, yappy dogs nipping at the heels of horses who could easily outpace them.

Corlin wanted to stay near Rafetyn, but Norlix assigned them to different squads. He hoped the archers could hang back from the hand fighting, for he didn't like his friend's chances if he had to draw his sword.

They did not get all the way across the harbor before they encountered the first resistance, for Delnamal and Draios had left men behind to guard their flank. Corlin, near the back of the pack with the rest of the younger cadets, heard the fighting begin long before he was able to see anything. His heart pounding with fear and exertion, he drew his sword as the cacophony of battle reached his ears. Men were shouting and screaming, both with battle-lust and pain, and the clash of swords was deafening. The steady drizzle made everything slippery, and more than once Corlin thought he might drop his sword or that his feet might skid out from under him.

The orderly squads dissolved into chaos as the fighting began in earnest. Corlin gripped his sword more tightly as he found himself standing just behind Cadet Nandar. Nandar let loose a deep-throated roar as he threw himself at a Khalpari soldier, covered in blood, who came into range. The man managed a parry, but he was already wounded and Nandar finished him off with a second strike.

And then there was no more time to think or notice what was happening to his fellows, for a man whose face was hidden behind a grimacing helmet swung a battle-ax at him.

Corlin had never fought with axes before—only swords—so he had no well-ingrained habits to fall back on. Not knowing if even a spelled sword would be strong enough to take a blow from an ax, instinct told him to dodge instead of parry. His heel caught against the leg of a fallen comrade, and he let out a cry of dismay as he fell.

The fall surprised the brute with the ax as much as it did Corlin, and the ax passed harmlessly through the space where his neck used to be. He hit the ground with a loud clang, dropping his sword. The ax-man swung again, and Corlin rolled frantically to the right, where his sword had fallen. The ax missed his neck by a fraction of an inch, but caught his helmet at just the right angle to drag it off his head. His flailing hand found his sword, and when the ax came for him again, the sword bit deeply into his attacker's wrist, right at the join between his armor and his gauntlet.

It was a blow born more of luck than skill, but his instructors always taught that the more skilled you were, the luckier you became.

The brute hollered as his blood splashed bright, and his injured hand loosed its grip on the ax. He tried another swing with his left, but the ax was too heavy to be wielded effectively one-handed, and his aim was off.

Corlin was bringing his sword up under the blow, aiming for another vulnerable joint in the armor, when his attacker suddenly screamed in agony, the point of a sword emerging from the center of his chest in a shower of blood.

Panting and uncomprehending, Corlin watched the ax-man fall dead to the ground. Then he saw Cadet Justal, his eyes alight with battle fury, standing behind the dead man with a bloody sword.

When Justal caught sight of Corlin, he made a sound of disgust. "Damn. I thought I was saving somebody *important*," he sneered, even as he practically strutted with pride. Why he was so proud of having run a man through from behind, Corlin didn't know. Nor could he understand the mindset of someone so stupid he would stand on a battlefield—with men fighting and screaming and dying all around him—and gloat about it.

"Look out!" Corlin yelled, seeing another soldier flying toward them, sword raised high.

Justal hesitated a moment, as if suspecting Corlin of some dirty trick. As if they were still just sparring with wooden swords, hoping to earn the praise of their commander, rather than fighting for their lives. By the time he started turning, it was too late.

The only thing that saved Justal from an instant death blow was the spell on his chest plate, which was apparently stronger than the spell on the sword. The sword bounced off, but the soldier was obviously prepared for the possibility, turning the sword in mid-swing and redirecting it to Justal's massive thigh.

The armor on his thigh was not as strongly spelled, and the sword sank in. Still on the ground, Corlin saw Justal's eyes roll up into the back of his head, and the cadet went down hard, with blood pouring from the wound. The soldier matter-of-factly went for a killing blow, and Corlin got his sword in the way just in time.

With a grunt of what sounded like nothing more urgent than annoyance, the soldier turned away from Justal and concentrated his attack on Corlin.

Corlin knew at once that he was in big trouble. The grace of this man's movements, the effortlessness of his swings, said he was a way more experienced swordsman than Corlin. And Corlin was still on the ground. He tried to get up, but his foot slipped in blood.

The swordsman swung at him, and though Corlin executed a correct—if clumsy—parry, his awkward position meant his sword slowed and changed the swing but didn't stop it. The point of the sword sliced through the left side of his face from cheek to forehead. His left eye went completely dark, and he felt the hot wash of blood that drenched his cheek, even as the pain seemed strangely distant.

Everything seemed to slow down as he watched the soldier jab downward with his sword. He was too slow with pain and shock to block the blow, and he felt the sharp stab of the blade finding the vulnerable spot on his side right above his hip where his chest plate ended.

The next blow might very well have finished him, had not Justal at that moment regained consciousness and grabbed the soldier's leg, setting him off balance. It was just a momentary distraction, for the soldier easily shook him off. Corlin saw his death in the soldier's eyes as the sword swung his way once more. He tried to parry, but his own sword suddenly felt unbearably heavy. The soldier made a sudden gurgling, gasping sound, the sword falling from his hand. Corlin blinked frantically, his vision now so dark and blurry it took him a moment to register the arrow that was sticking out of the soldier's throat. The man fell heavily, landing on Corlin's legs.

Visually following the path of the arrow, he found Rafetyn standing wide-eyed, his face pale. But after a brief nod of acknowledgment, his friend turned away and with shaking hands nocked another arrow.

Weakly, Corlin tried to pull his legs out from under the fallen soldier, but the effort was futile. Turning his head to the side, he saw how his blood was pooling on the ground around him. Neither the wound in his belly nor the one on his face hurt anymore, which was both a relief and a very bad sign. He began to shiver with a chill he feared meant he had lost too much blood to survive.

"I'm sorry, Mama," he whispered hoarsely as the sounds of battle quieted and his vision dimmed. He hoped she would forgive him for insisting on fighting.

His consciousness slipped away.

• • •

Alys's hands trembled as she activated her Trapper spell and placed herself squarely between the Well and the doorway. The reports that had trickled in from the battlefield via her talker had led her to believe the Trapper spell would not hide her for long, but she hoped it would keep her hidden just long enough to perform her sacrifice.

Her eyes welled with tears as she heard the shouts and screams coming from the antechamber. There was no way she could have convinced Tynthanal to let her wait unguarded by the Well, but she wished with all her heart she'd had the persuasive skills to pull it off. If Delnamal and Draios had the kind of magic that would allow them to fight their way through all of the defenders guarding the roads into the palace, then there was no reason to expect a small band of men—even if they were elite members of the king's personal guard—to withstand the assault.

She swiped angrily at a tear that leaked out of her eye. She would have yet more deaths weighing down her conscience, but at least she would not have to bear that burden for long.

Although she had no faith to speak of, Alys found herself mouthing the words of a prayer her stepmother had taught her, asking the Creator for comfort and protection in a time of need. But there was no comfort to be had, not now. Not when men were fighting and dying just outside while she listened, not when she could not know whether her son was alive or dead, not when the only way to prevent Delnamal from defiling the Well was to take her own life and hope the purgative spell she'd created would work as she intended.

Her heart ached, and her limbs felt heavy with dread and despair as she withdrew the knife from its scabbard and pushed back the sleeves of her dress. She *wished* she had faith, for it would be nice to think that she would be rewarded for her noble sacrifice in the afterlife. Nice to think that she was going to see Jinnell again very soon.

But though she believed in Leethan's vision, believed that it was her fate to die here in the Well chamber to save Aaltah, that belief had not opened her up to other forms of faith. If Leethan's dream had been sent by a deity, that deity was not overly interested in the lives of mortals, or it never would have allowed all the atrocities in the world to occur.

A horrifying shriek, joined by many voices, split the air in the Well chamber, the sound echoing off the stone walls, so full of pain and horror that it was all Alys could do not to drop the knife and cover her ears. Her soul shriveled inside her, her heart leaping into her throat and lodging there.

The shriek came to an abrupt end, though the echoes continued for what felt like forever. And then there was silence.

Alys swallowed hard and sank to her knees on the cold stone floor. She didn't know exactly what had just happened out in the antechamber, but she *did* know that a lot of men had died at once. And from the silence that reigned when the echoes faded, Alys knew that there was not a defender left standing.

It was almost time.

Alys put the edge of the knife against her bare wrist, but she dared not cut until Delnamal came into view. If she invoked her Kai too early, and he decided to linger out in that antechamber for some reason . . .

No. Agonizing as it was, she had to wait.

She willed her hands to stop shaking as the door to the Well chamber opened and a black-robed figure stepped through. With the knife already pressed against her exposed flesh, Alys did not need her worldly vision anymore, so she opened her Mindseye—in part to spare herself from the horror of seeing the wound she was about to make.

The moment her Mindseye was open, a gasp of surprise and terror escaped her, the sight of Delnamal's aura shocking her into immobility and incaution.

Thanks to the concerted—and longstanding—breeding program that had produced their mother, both Alys and Tynthanal had some extraordinary abilities. Each of them was capable of seeing some elements of the opposite gender, and for the most part, Alys had been taking her own ability for granted ever since she'd discovered it. But somehow, it had never occurred to her that she might be able to see masculine Kai. It was an element only the most magically gifted men had the power to see, and she had always assumed it beyond her abilities.

And yet, having seen more than her fair share of *women's* Kai, Alys had no difficulty recognizing the huge, dense cloud of multicolored crystals that surrounded her half-brother as he entered the Well chamber.

Perhaps she should have been prepared for the sight. After all, Xanvin had warned in her long-ago letter that Delnamal stole the Kai of those he killed. And she knew that he must have been gorging himself on death on his journey up the cliffs. And yet even so, she found herself staring in openmouthed shock at the glittering cloud of death that surrounded him.

The paralysis lasted only a moment, but that moment cost her dearly.

Alys saw Delnamal's arm move toward her, and she slashed the knife downward on her wrist. But her hand was shaking, and the spell slammed into her and knocked her back onto her heels. She kept hold of the knife—just barely—and made to try again, already doubting she would have time to finish her sacrifice before it was too late. It was her impression that her Kai would not appear immediately, that she would have to bleed enough to make her death a certainty first. But there was nothing left but to try—and thank the Creator she didn't truly believe in that Delnamal hadn't cast his death spell at her.

"Shoot her!" she heard Delnamal yell, and realized that, of course, he had nullified her Trapper spell the moment he'd stepped through the doorway, fully prepared to meet with more resistance inside the Well chamber.

Something slammed into her chest, drawing a cry of pain from her throat and once again knocking her backward. This time, she couldn't keep her grip on the knife. She heard it hit the floor and slide as she collapsed, the pain so intense it whited out her Mindsight. But she didn't have time to wallow in pain. She could *not* give up.

Alys closed her Mindseye. The pain in her chest made every breath hurt, and her bodice was soaked with blood. If the wound was a fatal one, it was marginally possible that because of her bloodline, she might produce and use masculine Kai. But if masculine Kai could have triggered the purgative spell as they had all hoped, there was little doubt it would have worked by now. Her death *needed* to be a willing sacrifice, not a murder.

She had a brief glimpse of Delnamal hovering in the doorway, surrounded by a veritable sea of identical young men, several of whom were pointing crossbows in her direction. Draios, she presumed.

Alys turned over, reaching desperately for the knife and hoping it would take a moment for Draios to load another bolt. Hard to believe it would take long enough for her to get to her knife, slash her wrist, harvest her Kai, and cast the purgative spell, but what choice did she have?

The crossbow bolt that was lodged in her chest hit the floor when she turned over, and she lost precious moments to another wave of pain that stole her will. She groped blindly for the knife, her fingers hitting it—and sending it skittering again. As her vision cleared, she watched in horror and despair as the knife tipped over the edge of the Well and fell in.

She began to shiver as her blood continued to pour from the wound, gathering in a thick pool beneath her, and her vision went dark around the edges. She opened her Mindseye once more, but a wave of dizziness crashed over her. Reflexively, she closed her eyes against it. And found that no matter how urgently she ordered herself to open them, they refused to obey.

CHAPTER FORTY-THREE

K ailee clapped a hand hard over her mouth to trap the cry of dismay that wanted to fly out when she saw Alys go down. The Well chamber was awash with elements pouring from the Well, making it harder for her to pick out the human auras, but she had followed close enough on Draios's heels—stopping to pick up a sword and a healing spell from one of the fallen—to see him fire his crossbow and hear Alys's cry of pain. Then Alys's aura fell to the floor.

The Sovereign Princess of Women's Well—and Aaltah's last hope—was still alive, as Kailee could tell by the aura of Rho that stubbornly clung to her. But she was no longer moving, and the chances that she could successfully perform her sacrifice had died when that crossbow bolt hit her.

With tears in her eyes and terror in her soul, Kailee looked at Draios as the boy king sauntered casually toward the Well, secure in his victory. She clutched the sword she carried more tightly, but though she could clearly distinguish the aura of the real Draios, there seemed little point in trying to murder him now, when all was already lost. She bit down hard on her tongue to stifle a protest when Draios casually kicked Alys's limp body out of his way so he could stand on the lip of the Well and look down.

"That was almost anticlimactic," Draios said. "I expected it to be harder."

Delnamal made a soft snorting sound, then turned away from the Well and strode toward the chamber door. Kailee had to move hastily so that he would not collide with her and discover her presence.

"Where are you going?" Draios asked sharply. "You still have a vow to fulfill!"

"In a moment," Delnamal called over his shoulder. "I just want to close the door. I'm sure there are reinforcements heading our way as we speak."

"It won't matter once you complete your mission!" Draios said impatiently, and though Kailee knew almost nothing about the man, she could hear the faintest edge of uncertainty in his voice.

Thanks to Ellinsoltah's informant, Kailee knew that Delnamal's supposed plan was to somehow undo what he called the Curse by sacrificing himself at the Well. No one in Aaltah actually believed he meant to do any such thing, but Draios could never have raised an army of the size he had without convincing all of Par and Khalpar that they were on a holy mission, and it seemed unlikely he could have pulled that off if he didn't believe it himself.

Perhaps now that the moment of victory was upon them, Draios was finally beginning to contemplate the possibility that he had been duped.

Kailee heard the chamber door close with a heavy thunk. Delnamal remained standing directly in front of it.

"I regret to inform you that one of us is indeed going to sacrifice his life," Delnamal said, "but it will not be me."

Draios went entirely still. "What are you talking about?"

This time, there was no missing the tinge of fear in the young man's voice. Biting her lip, Kailee glanced over at Alys's still form, seeing that the aura of Rho that surrounded her seemed thinner and weaker. But she was still alive, at least for the moment.

Kailee glanced at the healing spell she had almost reflexively grabbed on her way in. It was a masculine battlefield spell, one that was meant to heal wounds far greater than those a women's healing potion could handle, but it still held some of the same elements as did the healing potions she'd taught the abigails of Aaltah to create. She could say for certain that it was a healing spell, but she could not guess how powerful it was or whether it would work to heal Alys's wound.

"I never had any intention of throwing myself into the Well," Delnamal said. "I have never been terribly religious, and if the Creator has any grand schemes for me, I have no intention of fulfilling them."

Ever so carefully, afraid she might make a sound and alert the two men to her presence, Kailee began inching toward Alys.

The crossbow fired again, and Delnamal made a soft grunting sound. However, unlike Alys, he did not fall down. In fact, it looked from his aura as if what he did instead was reach up and casually pluck the bolt from his body with all the difficulty of removing a piece of lint from his doublet. And he laughed.

"Really?" he said, still chuckling. "After all you've seen, you think you can kill me with your little crossbow? How quaint. All you've done is make it easy for me to pick you out from the crowd."

With a yelp, Draios suddenly leapt to the side, his aura staggering about drunkenly. At first, Kailee thought Delnamal had done something to him—although she hadn't seen Delnamal move or reach for a magic item. Then she realized the meaning of Delnamal's words and saw that Draios was trying to lose himself among the doubles again after his shot with the crossbow had revealed his location.

"Yes, yes, very clever," Delnamal said. "But you may have noticed I'm not carrying a crossbow. When I kill you, I'll have to do it up close. So I'll just wait until your spell wears off and there's only one of you. It shouldn't be long now. It's been a good quarter hour since I last refreshed it for you."

As Kailee continued inching closer to Alys, she felt a foolish surge of pity for the young king. Draios was only seventeen years old, and if she was to believe everything she'd heard about him, he had somehow convinced himself—or allowed himself to be convinced—that his attack on Aaltah was not only justified, but righteous. That he was doing what his god commanded of him. What a devastating shock it must be to learn that the hand that had been guiding him had not belonged to his god, after all.

"Why are you doing this?" Draios asked, and she heard a combination of terror and hopelessness and betrayal in his voice. "Why would you want to . . . to kill me, after everything I've . . ."

"After everything you've done for me?" Delnamal supplied helpfully.

Kailee reached Alys's body and sank down to her knees, feeling around gently and carefully to find where the bolt pierced the older woman's chest. She shuddered when she felt the blood that soaked Alys's bodice, and it was all she could do not to snatch her hand away.

"It's nothing personal," Delnamal said. "At first, I merely intended to retake my kingdom, and you seemed my only path to success. But then I decided I didn't really want Aaltah back. Being king was tiresome in the extreme.

"No, what I want to do is punish Aaltah for all its crimes against me. The last time I was here at this Well, my secretary was mortally wounded and fell into it as he was dying. It was clear that the Well reacted poorly to the Kai from the moment Melcor fell.

"My theory is that Melcor's Kai encountered a mote of Rhokai that naturally occurs in the Well. That mote then shattered, releasing yet another mote of Kai and creating a chain reaction. If allowed to continue, the reaction likely would have killed the Well and maybe even collapsed the chamber, taking the palace with it.

"I can't say I know *exactly* what Mairahsol did, but I know she stopped the chain reaction and saved the Well—and Aaltah. But I intend to finish what Melcor's Kai began. And that's where you come in."

Kailee knew she had to get the bolt out of Alys's chest before her healing spell had any chance of working. She hoped Delnamal and Draios were both distracted enough by their confrontation not to notice what was happening.

Swallowing hard against revulsion and dread, Kailee gripped the crossbow bolt with her bloody hand. It was harder than she would have imagined to pull that deeply embedded bolt out of Alys's body, and her hand slipped off the shaft with her first try.

"I don't understand," Draios said. He sounded not like the terrifying enemy king, but like a lost little boy.

Kailee held her breath, not daring to move. The sound her hand had made when it slid off the bolt had seemed terrifyingly loud to her own ears, but neither Draios nor Delnamal had noticed it. She let her breath out in a long, quiet sigh, gripping the bolt once again.

Delnamal chuckled, unmoved by the pain and fear his betrayal was causing. "What is there not to understand? When your spell has worn off and I can easily get to you, I'm going to run you through. Then, as you are dying, I will push you into the Well."

"B-but . . . you said yourself that the chamber might have collapsed if the Kai remained in the Well. Y-you could be killed right along with me!"

"You say that as if you think I care. I would like to survive the catastrophe, of course. The moment I have put you into the Well, I will attempt to make my escape. As you can clearly see, I can take a great deal of damage without actually dying. But even if I am killed, I will have built for myself a legacy the likes of which I never could have dreamed of in my days as king. History may revile me, but it will not be as a coward and a weakling."

Kailee could hardly believe what she was hearing. Certainly it did not jibe with the descriptions Oona had given her of a basically good and decent man who'd been embittered and made cruel by forces beyond his control. Not that Kailee had ever fully believed in Oona's vision of her husband, but she had at least allowed for the possibility that Alys and Tynthanal—and the rest of the Kingdom of Aaltah—were mistaken about his nature.

It was now abundantly clear that it was *Oona* who'd been mistaken. And, Kailee realized, it was also abundantly clear that Delnamal could *not* be allowed to carry out his plan—and there was no one who could stop him except her.

Knowing she didn't have much time, Kailee put both hands on the crossbow bolt, then waited until Draios started talking again to give it a mighty tug.

"Surely there are other, better ways you can build your legacy!" Draios protested, his voice high and shrill with desperation. "With your powers, you are nearly an unstoppable force. You can conquer all of Seven Wells and reign as the king of the world!"

The bolt held fast against the first tug, then came loose so suddenly that Kailee nearly fell. The sound of her faltering was covered by Delnamal's laugh.

"Why would you think I want to be king of the world when I found being king of a kingdom tiresome?" he asked. "You might want to think about what your last words will be. Your spell should run out any minute now. And if you think swinging your sword around is going to deter me, you will be in for a terrible disappointment."

Panting with exertion, Kailee activated the healing spell, laying the brooch in which it was contained on Alys's chest near the wound. She didn't know how long it would take to restore Alys to health—if indeed it was strong enough to heal so grievous a wound—and she hoped Alys would not do anything to draw attention while she healed.

Kailee wanted to take a moment to gather herself, but if Delnamal was right and time was running out, she didn't dare.

She *had* to stop Delnamal from poisoning the Well, as impossible as it seemed.

She could not stop it by killing Delnamal; that much was clear. Unlike Draios, his defenses were not born of spells that she could deactivate.

No, the only way to stop Delnamal was to kill Draios before Delnamal had a chance to throw him into the Well.

Waldmir was far too unguarded to notice when Leethan drew the knife. If she'd been just about anybody else, she doubted he would have allowed her to turn her back on him as she had; certainly he would have found the motion of her hand suspicious as she grabbed the knife's cleverly disguised hilt and withdrew it from the camouflage of the boning of her bodice. In fact, he trusted her so completely that he didn't even notice the first slash at her wrist.

Leethan had imagined performing her sacrifice in noble stoicism, but the pain of the cut drew a soft whimper from her throat.

"What's the matter?" Waldmir asked, the concern in his voice unmistakable. And guilt-inducing.

You have no reason to feel guilty, she admonished herself harshly as she shifted the knife to her other hand, which was already wet with her blood. She was doing what the Mother of All had all but commanded her to do, and although there was no denying that setting off this Kai spell in the midst of an unsuspecting camp was a deeply dishonorable deed, the results would be worth it. She would decapitate the Nandel army, and they would have no choice but to retreat. Whether the army of Rhozinolm could then get to Aaltah in time to render aid was still in doubt, but they would at least have the possibility.

She heard Waldmir's sudden, shocked gasp, and she turned to him, blood now flowing freely from both her wrists as tears also flowed from her eyes. She shook her head.

"I'm so sorry," she choked out, drinking in the sight of him one more time before opening her Mindseye to see that her cuts had run true. A tricolored mote of Kai—just like the ones she had seen in her dream—was shimmering into existence in the air before her.

"What have you done?" Waldmir shouted, an edge of panic in his voice.

His shout roused others, and though she could not see the physical world clearly, Leethan was aware of the clanking of armor and weapons as Waldmir's guards ran to his aid.

"Leethan, no!" Waldmir cried again, and she heard a wealth of emotions in those words.

She reached for the mote of Kai, grabbing it without giving herself time to think or feel any further. She shoved the Kai at the dagger's blade, where the deadly Kai spell was waiting to be triggered . . .

And nothing happened.

Letting out her own cry of shock and dismay, she tried again, but the spell failed to absorb the mote of Kai and failed to activate. Her knees trembled, and she wasn't sure if that trembling was entirely due to the loss of blood. She tried to activate the spell for the third time, and for the third time, she failed.

Again.

The Mother of All had led her here only to watch her throw away her life for nothing? Perhaps this was her punishment for failing to give Waldmir the son he needed.

The shouts from outside the tent grew louder, and she saw a flood of man-shaped Rho auras flow into the tent.

There was some comfort in knowing that she would not live long enough to experience Waldmir's wrath, she thought, shuddering as she closed her Mindseye. Waldmir was staring at her, aghast, with his Mindseye open, and she knew he was trying to prise out the dagger's secrets. Alysoon's concealment spell could not withstand such close scrutiny, and Leethan was sure he now understood exactly what she'd just tried to do.

He closed his Mindseye, his expression one of shock and pain. He started to say something to her, then suddenly whirled on one of the men who had entered the tent at his first cry.

"No!" Waldmir shouted. "Stop!"

Leethan saw the soldier pointing a crossbow at her head. He was close enough that he could not possibly miss even if the bolt wasn't spelled.

Everything seemed to slow down, and she watched in morbid fascination as the soldier's finger tightened on the trigger, a snarl of rage on his face. She had time to see how the blood had drained from Waldmir's face, how his eyes were wide with what looked more like terror than anger as he held out a hand toward the soldier who was about to shoot her.

And then, just as the soldier loosed his bolt, Waldmir threw himself toward her, putting himself directly in the path of the bolt.

His body slammed into her, knocking the breath out of her and taking them both to the floor with a bone-jarring thud. He cried out in what sounded like pain, and the shouting soldiers suddenly went quiet.

"What are you doing?" Leethan asked with what little breath she had left. Her vision was beginning to waver around the edges, but not so much that she couldn't see the crossbow bolt that had lodged itself deep in his back. It must have been spelled after all, for it had pierced his armor.

"Stay back!" Waldmir roared at his men, covering her with his body.

"Help him!" Leethan cried in protest, but her voice was too weak to carry, and no one was going to listen to her anyway. For a moment, she forgot that her whole purpose in coming here had been to assassinate her former husband. And she couldn't quite comprehend that he had put himself in harm's way to save her.

Surely he'd seen and recognized what she had tried to do.

Waldmir's eyes went white, and he touched the cabochon in the brooch that clasped his cloak at his throat. She was instantly aware of the surge of energy that flowed into her blood—the unmistakable rush of powerful healing magic. Her first, horrifying thought was that he'd saved her only so that he might arrange a slower, more creative death to punish her, but he did not immediately get off and order his guards to seize her, and the look in his eyes was one of anguish, not anger.

"You can't save me," she whispered, even as the wounds at her wrists sealed themselves up and her vision began to clear.

As the sovereign prince, Waldmir had an extraordinary amount of power, and he would be free to pardon almost any crime. But this had been a clear and obvious assassination attempt, and though the soldiers hadn't witnessed her failed attempts to trigger her Kai spell, they would find it on her person when the spell hiding it wore off, and they would know exactly what she had hoped to do. The *most* Waldmir could hope for was to commute her sentence to a swift and painless death.

"Why, Leethan?" he whispered back. "What did you see?"

One of his men took a step closer, reaching for him, and Waldmir snarled for everyone to stay back.

Tears clouded Leethan's eyes. *Of course* Waldmir would guess she'd been acting on a vision. He was no fool, and he knew her well. Just as she knew *him* well enough to realize that telling him she'd seen Elwynne ascending to the throne of Nandel would not have the desired effect. A man who would side with the likes of Draios and Delnamal would be appalled at the thought of his throne passing to a woman, even when that woman was his daughter. She hadn't the creativity or the mental reserves to lie to him, so she instead simplified the truth down to something she thought he might find palatable enough to spare her from a traitor's death.

"I saw a way to stop the war of succession that would follow your death." Waldmir's eyes widened, his whole body giving a start, which then made him wince in pain. His cheeks were leached of color, and a fine tremor shook his whole body.

"You need a healer," she said, but when one of his men tried again to approach, Waldmir snarled once more.

"Don't touch me!" he commanded, and the man reluctantly stepped back.

"I'm so sorry," Leethan choked out, and wondered if her own ambivalence had been the reason the spell had failed. No matter how strongly she believed that Waldmir's death was necessary, she had not succeeded in forcing herself to *want* it.

"Don't be," Waldmir said, his voice sounding thin and thready as he stroked the side of her face. "You don't know what a burden it has been upon my soul knowing that I would leave Nandel to tear itself apart. Something inside me died when you told me I would not have a son, and now you have given me hope that my legacy will not be entirely tarnished by my failures as a man and sovereign prince."

"What do you mean?" she asked, frowning as he shivered again. He had lost a lot of blood already. "You *really* need a healer. Now!"

Waldmir shook his head, his eyes going filmy white. He grabbed a mote of what she assumed was Rho and activated a spell in the ring he wore on his thumb. "There will be a lot of fear and confusion," he said, his hand reaching out again and plucking another invisible mote from the air. "Take my cloak and hood, and slip away before order is restored."

"What are you—"

"And if you make it back to Zinolm Well safely, take care of my child. She deserved better from me than what she got."

It wasn't until his hand touched the Kai spell in her knife and an earsplitting roar filled the air that she realized what he meant to do.

CHAPTER FORTY-FOUR

Alys clawed her way up through the pressing darkness of an airless tunnel. When she reached the surface, she drew in a gasping breath that sent pain stabbing through her entire body, and her eyes flew open.

She was in the Well chamber, and there was a pain in her chest so powerful she could hardly breathe around it. In the background, she heard the rumble of male voices, although she could not immediately identify the speakers.

Memory came back to her in a frantic rush.

Delnamal stepping into the Well chamber.

Alys preparing to perform her sacrifice.

Delnamal casting something that deactivated the Trapper spell that had kept her hidden.

The crossbow bolt slamming into her chest, dealing her a mortal wound.

The slide into unconsciousness after her flailing hand had sent her knife skittering into the Well.

She should be dead. A quick glance down at her chest made her wonder if somehow she actually *was* dead, if she was even now awakening to some sort of afterlife as described in the Devotional. There was so much blood soaking her bodice!

She blinked in confusion, then realized two things in quick succession: there was no longer a crossbow bolt sticking out of her chest, and there was a smooth cabochon resting in the space between her breasts, right next to where the bolt had taken her.

Someone had removed the bolt and cast a healing spell on her.

She had not the strength to do more than turn her head to look for her mysterious benefactor, but when she did, she caught sight of Delnamal and Draios. Well, *many* Draioses, all of whom were dancing around in some twisting, turning, complex dance as they moved restlessly around the chamber.

As her wound continued to heal, the pain finally growing less, Alys could see no one else in the Well chamber with her. Her mind clearing more by the second, she began to comprehend the words Delnamal and Draios were tossing at each other, began to see the horror that Delnamal was planning.

How she wished she hadn't dropped the damn knife. She felt along her person as if she might somehow find a weapon she hadn't remembered arming herself with. She didn't know if casting the stolen Rhokai out of Delnamal would stop him from carrying out his plan, but she had to try.

And if they see that you're alive and conscious, she reminded herself, *you might not stay that way.* She did not dare move too much or make any sound to draw their attention.

There were plenty of pins tucked into her gown and her headdress, but none of those would be weapons she could use to perform her sacrifice, and she had nothing else on her person. Turning her head about very slowly and carefully, she sought the crossbow bolt that should have killed her. Eventually, she saw it lying on the cavern floor well out of her reach.

She wanted to lunge for it, but held herself in check. Aside from the danger of drawing attention to herself, there was also the fact that her body was far from fully healed. Just turning her head was an exhausting effort, and she was not sure she had the strength to cross even the short distance that separated her from the bolt. Not to mention that the bolt didn't look particularly sharp. Not like a knife that would slice quickly and cleanly through her wrist. Surely given time, she could create the necessary fatal wound—but once she drew attention to herself, time was not a luxury she would have.

Fighting against a sick feeling of hopelessness and failure, Alys willed the healing spell to finish its job so that she could kill herself.

Kailee was shaking so hard she was half-surprised no one heard her teeth chattering, though she supposed Delnamal and Draios were so focused on each other that it would take a considerably louder noise than that to distract them. It was one thing to decide that she needed to kill Draios before Delnamal had a chance to. It was quite another to actually *do* it. Her chest tightened with panic, and although she urged herself to move closer to Draios, her feet remained rooted to the floor.

"You don't have to do this," Draios was saying, and the quaver in his voice made him sound so young and vulnerable that Kailee's heart bled for him. The sound of his many voices bounced off the walls of the cavern, the echoes and his constant movement ensuring that Delnamal could not pick him out from the camouflage of his doubles. Something that would not be true if Kailee hesitated long enough for the doubling spell to wear off.

"Surely we can come to some sort of mutually beneficial arrangement," Draios continued.

Delnamal snorted softly. "You have nothing that I want. I will attempt to make your death as painless as possible under the circumstances."

Kailee cringed, as she suspected did Draios himself. Delnamal's stated plan was to deliver a fatal wound that would generate

Kai—which by definition did not occur unless the death was a lingering one. Draios would have plenty of time to feel the terror and suffering before he was finally overcome.

Tears snaked down Kailee's cheeks, and she fought against an almost overwhelming desire to flee the cavern. She had come to the Well because she planned to deactivate Draios's doubling spell so that someone could kill him. She knew that in the aftermath, she would have struggled with the guilt of having caused a human being—especially a boy of only seventeen—to die, but she had acknowledged that it was necessary, and there had been comfort in knowing she would only *facilitate* the death, rather than cause it herself. But this . . . this was something entirely different.

She was the one who insisted on seeing the good in people everyone else reviled, who believed that just about anyone was redeemable. How cruel was the fate that had put her in a position where she had to kill someone. She did not want to become a murderer! And yet to give in to her instincts and shy away from what she must do would cause so much more death and destruction.

She glanced desperately over her shoulder, hoping to see that Alys's healing had completed at an impossible speed, hoping against hope that somehow Alys could take this burden from her. But although the princess's aura looked brighter and more wholesome, she was still lying on the floor. Kailee could see that she was moving, if only slightly, but it was impossible to imagine that she could somehow muster the strength to kill Draios—even supposing she knew how important it was for Draios to die.

Still shaking and crying, Kailee finally found the will to force her feet forward. She could not afford to wait any longer. If Delnamal was as invulnerable as he seemed, then Draios would be doomed the moment his doubling spell wore off. How could he fight a man who could not be hurt?

Taking a deep, steadying breath that nonetheless shook and

faltered, she gripped the sword she had picked up in the antechamber with both hands. In order to spoil Delnamal's plans, she
had to kill Draios immediately, for a lingering death would give
Delnamal exactly what he needed. It meant that she couldn't
hesitate, couldn't allow her natural instincts to control her.

Moving carefully—and thankful that Draios's constant movements combined with the echoes masked the sound of her own
footfalls—she approached him, studying the spells that were contained in his armor. One of them was most likely a shield spell,
which she would need to deactivate before she struck.

Kailee had seen enough men wearing shield spells that she was
able to identify it with a fair level of certainty, despite her inability
to see masculine elements. She could see the neuter element
called Cor, which she knew was one of the key elements of shield
spells, and there was a cluster of Cor motes gathered around the
middle finger of his left hand, right where a ring might sit.

She was close enough to him now that if he made a sudden
move in the wrong direction, he might well bump into her. It
took every ounce of her will and self-control to reach out toward
the spell in his ring.

Please hold still, she mentally begged him, for his hands were
moving restlessly as he continued trying to convince Delnamal
not to kill him. If he kept moving like that, the chances of her
plucking the Rho out of the spell to deactivate it without his feeling her touch were distressingly slim.

"Is it my imagination?" Delnamal asked, "or do you have
fewer doubles right now than you did a moment ago? I think
your spell might be starting to wear off."

Kailee shuddered. It was possible Delnamal was just saying
that to torment his frightened victim, but she dared not take that
chance. How much did it really matter if she revealed her presence? Even with his considerable power, it would take a moment
for Delnamal to trigger the spell that had knocked down Alys's
Trapper spell so that he could see her and kill her. And whether

Draios felt her touch or not, it was best she make her strike the moment his shield was deactivated. She had thought about this far too long already.

Swallowing a sob, she reached for the motes of Rho that fueled Draios's shield spell.

She expected to be plucking the motes out of a ring, but it turned out they were contained not by a ring but by a gauntlet that was otherwise invisible to her Mindseye. Her fingertips clanged against the metal, causing Draios to bleat and swat at her blindly.

He hit her arm, but not before she had closed her fingers over the motes of Rho. She lost hold of them when he made contact, but his shield spell was already deactivated.

"What's the matter?" Delnamal asked, the question so absurd that Kailee almost betrayed herself again with a burst of hysterical laughter.

Draios was batting at the air around him as if under attack from a swarm of insects, but Kailee had dodged out of his reach.

Giving herself no time to think, Kailee gripped the heavy sword with both hands, aiming its edge toward Draios's neck, where there should be little to no armor. It took every last scrap of her will to swing that sword, and she knew she had to put all her strength into it. There was some kind of spell still active in the sword, but she didn't know its exact purpose, didn't know if it would lend her the strength she needed to end Draios's life with one swift blow.

A heartbeat later, she learned the spell's nature, for the sword's impact against Draios's neck barely registered in her arms. Having expected a great deal of resistance, Kailee lost both her balance and her grip on the sword when it sliced cleanly and easily through Draios's neck.

CHAPTER FORTY-FIVE

The healing spell was far from finished with its work, but Alys had regained enough strength to roll over onto her side and reach for the crossbow bolt that lay tantalizingly out of reach. The effort left her panting with pain and exhaustion, and she feared herself on the edge of losing consciousness once more.

Holding still and breathing deeply, thankful that neither Delnamal nor Draios had noticed her movement, she continued to watch and wait. As disconcerting as it was to see a score of identical men dodging and weaving and stepping around one another in a dizzying, confusing dance, Alys willed the spell to stay active just a little longer. She *had* to regain more of her strength before she had any chance of stopping Delnamal.

A strange metallic clang echoed through the cavern, followed by a high-pitched yelp of alarm. The sound had risen from the throat of each of the images of Draios that filled the chamber, but she saw one of them suddenly batting wildly at the air around him.

"What's the matter?" Delnamal asked, his voice losing the edge of smugness he'd been carrying since he'd entered the Well chamber.

Alys stared at the image of Draios that was still swinging his arms about wildly, realizing—as surely Delnamal must—that it was the true one. She wanted to yell at the idiot to stop making such an obvious spectacle of himself. She didn't know what was wrong with him, but she *did* know she was rapidly running out of time.

Heedless of the danger, she pushed herself up onto her hands and knees, crawling toward the crossbow bolt that she hoped would allow her to perform her sacrifice, all the while keeping a wary eye on both Delnamal and Draios.

Her fingers had just brushed the bolt when suddenly Draios's head bent sideways at an impossible angle. Blood fountained from his neck, and all his doubles instantly vanished. Alys watched, unable to comprehend at first exactly what she was seeing, as Draios collapsed to the cavern floor.

It was only when his head rolled free of his body that she realized that somehow—impossibly—he had just been killed.

Delnamal roared, the sound so full of unearthly fury that Alys could not help but cringe, even as her eyes remained glued to the boy-king's head. She remained frozen in place, the cavern all but disappearing as her mind flashed back to the terrible, soul-destroying sight of her daughter's head rolling in the dust at her feet. Her chest seized as though her ribs were caving in, her lungs suddenly so tight she could not draw breath. A small, rational part of her screamed that she didn't have time for this, that she should be using this moment of shock and disbelief to grab hold of the bolt and slash her wrists with it. But the horror, the terror, the pain of that memory refused to be shoved back down so easily.

"Who *dares*?" she heard Delnamal howl, and it was followed by a woman's soft sound of distress.

Alys blinked fiercely to clear her vision and was shocked to see Kailee, standing right beside Draios's body with a bloody sword clasped in her hands.

The poor girl was pale and shaking, covered in blood, her mouth hanging open as she stood there as if paralyzed. Delnamal began striding toward her, and Kailee didn't even look up or make any sign that she was preparing to defend herself.

"Kailee!" Alys shouted, no longer caring that she would draw Delnamal's attention, wanting only for her sister-in-law to be safe, or at least to run away from the approaching danger. But Kailee stood immobile, shaking her head.

Delnamal reached out a hand as he walked, and Kailee gasped, the sword falling from her hands and her head dropping backward. Her mouth opened in a silent scream.

Alys didn't know exactly what Delnamal was doing to her, but after all the stories she'd heard about his powers, she had the frightening suspicion that Kailee was about to die.

She shouted Delnamal's name, hoping to distract him, to delay him just a little, but he ignored her as if she didn't exist. She grasped the bolt, tearing her eyes away from Kailee just long enough to determine that the damn thing was not sharp enough for her purposes. By the time Alys had access to her sacrificial Kai and triggered the spell, Kailee would be dead.

Acting on a combination of instinct and desperation, Alys reached for the ring that held her purgative spell. She didn't have access to the sacrificial Kai that she believed was the only way to trigger the spell; however, there was that whole aura of masculine Kai motes hovering around Delnamal. Conventional wisdom held that no one could use a man's Kai but himself, but then none of the Kai that surrounded Delnamal came from *him*.

Kailee's knees gave out, her body going limp, although her eyes were still open and Alys could still hear her rasping, desperate gasps. There was no time to think, no time to plan, no time to doubt.

Using every scrap of strength she could muster from her barely healed body, Alys threw the ring at Delnamal, willing the Kai in his aura to activate the spell.

There was absolutely no precedent to suggest that such a thing could work, and the instant the ring left Alys's hand she was already cursing herself for her knee-jerk decision. She cared for—maybe even loved—her sister-in-law, but no one person's life was important enough to risk letting Delnamal win. The responsible thing for Alys to do was to let Kailee fend for herself while she performed her sacrifice and waited for her own sacrificial Kai to appear. It was what Leethan's dream had led her to expect had to happen for Delnamal to be defeated, and though she had admitted it to no one but herself, she had been more than prepared to leave the troubles and worries and pains of life behind.

The ring sailed through the air—Alys could see it even with her Mindseye open because of the wealth of elements it contained. She watched with regret and hopelessness and terror as it hit the aura of Kai that surrounded her half-brother, and she saw his frantic attempt to throw himself out of the way—just a little too late.

To her shock, when the ring sailed through Delnamal's aura, the motes of Kai it passed through were sucked into it. And then, Delnamal screamed.

When Draios's head mysteriously separated from his body, Delnamal felt a fury so bright and pure it seemed to fill all the hollow places in his soul. He had planned every aspect of this day with careful precision, and had been anticipating with great pleasure the moment he delivered a dying Draios to the Well. It would have been such an unequivocal victory, and he had experienced far too few of those during his life.

Reeling from the intensity of his rage, Delnamal grabbed the mote of Rhokai from the chest of the young woman who had appeared out of nowhere when he'd dispelled her Trapper spell. He didn't know—and didn't care—who she was, but clearly she deserved to die for robbing him as she had.

For the briefest of moments, the rage—the raw *intensity* of it—felt surprisingly good, but acknowledging that pleasure opened the door a crack, letting out all the other emotions that plagued him during his sleep and when he first awoke in the mornings. It all flooded back, and the horror of what he'd almost done staggered him.

On the heels of that flood of anguish came the realization that the plan was not *foiled,* merely postponed. Surely there would be other men sent to this chamber to stop him, and one of them would function for the purpose just as well as Draios. Even the young woman would likely meet his needs, for he knew a mote of Kai would be released if he broke her Rhokai as he'd planned to break Draios's. There was no reason to believe that her Kai would behave any differently than a man's, and even if it did, someone else would surely come along eventually.

Delnamal seized onto the emotions that had escaped their cage, clinging to them no matter how much they hurt, desperate to remain himself long enough to eliminate the threat posed by the malevolence that had taken possession of his body. He had to end this, immediately. He closed his Mindseye, letting go of the mote of Rhokai he'd grabbed and groping for the dagger that was belted at his waist, the dagger he'd intended to use to kill Draios.

But just as his fingers closed around the hilt, the flood of emotions—the *real* Delnamal, who despite everything felt the desperate need to protect Aaltah—ebbed. He managed to draw the blade halfway out, but then he laughed and shook his head at his own weakness. It had been careless of him to allow the craven weakling that resided in his core a glimpse of sunlight, and he shored up his emotional armor to make sure it didn't happen again.

The young woman had not moved when he'd released her, though strangely, her Mindseye was open, and had been from the moment she'd first lost her Trapper spell. Delnamal wondered what she was trying to do, and why there were tear tracks in the blood that spattered her face. But none of that mattered. He opened his Mindseye once more and took hold of her Rhokai to keep her from fleeing.

Even with his Mindseye open, he saw movement out of the corner of his eye. Still holding on to the Rhokai mote to keep his victim from escaping, he turned his head toward the movement. He had thought sure Draios's bolt had killed Alysoon, but the bright moving aura of Rho could belong to no one but her.

Once upon a time, his hatred of his half-sister would have sent him into a fit of rage, and he would have dropped everything to finish her off. But now, he mused instead that she could be useful to him if she survived. Her knowledge of women's magic—especially of the magic of Women's Well—might prove invaluable to him as he tried to re-create whatever it was Mairahsol had done that had allowed him to absorb the Rhokai from Aaltah's Well.

For the time being, he dismissed her from his mind. He was overflowing with strength and free Kai motes from his trip up the cliffs, and she could stab or shoot him a hundred times over and not do him any lasting harm. He would deal with her when he was finished with the little murderess who had tried to thwart his plans. His hand reached for his dagger once more, and he took a step toward his helpless captive.

The Rho-shrouded form on the floor pulled back an arm and flung something in his direction. Something that based on the dense concentration of elements that clung to it was a magic item. Still, he was not alarmed. If a physical weapon couldn't kill him, then he believed a spell couldn't, either.

But as the object neared him, it had to pass through the aura of Kai motes that surrounded him, and something . . . unexpected happened.

Ordinarily, spells were created in an incomplete form and were activated when the caster added the missing elements to complete the spell. But the casting of a spell required an act of will, the purposeful addition of the missing elements—or else spells would be going off all the time when they happened to encounter the missing elements in the air.

And yet when the mysterious magic item passed through Delnamal's aura, several of the Kai motes that were in its path seemed to be drawn into it.

By the time it happened, it was far too late for Delnamal to get out of the way, but that didn't stop him from trying. He let go of the Rhokai mote and threw himself blindly to the side. He didn't feel any impact from whatever Alysoon had thrown, and as he fell, he had the momentary hope that he had somehow succeeded in dodging the magic.

He hit the cavern floor hard, knocking the wind out of himself and sliding along the smooth stone. He slapped his hands down, trying to slow the slide, but something punched him in the chest so hard he could not suppress a scream.

His body bowed in agony, the pain sharper and more overwhelming than anything he had ever experienced. It felt as if a giant had thrust his hand into Delnamal's chest and was even now pulling out his beating heart.

His Mindseye still open, Delnamal saw a tremendous cloud of Rhokai motes fountaining up out of his chest. The black, faceted spheres were tightly packed together, dense and dark as the night sky, though there was an occasional flash of color from somewhere deep within. The cloud gathered above him, its edges bulging and undulating as if there were some living creature in its center, struggling to fight its way free. Then the cloud hurtled toward the Well and plunged downward.

The pain let up suddenly at the same time a flood of emotions—terror, horror, grief, pain—whited out his rational mind. His body jerked as he tried to curl up in a tight protective ball. He was not rational enough to realize that he was teetering on the lip of the Well.

The movement sent him tumbling over the edge.

A stubborn desire to live fought its way past every other emotion, and his hands scrabbled wildly at the edge as he tried to catch himself. But it seemed all the strength of his body had left him with that cloud of Rhokai, and his ruined fingers could not find a grip.

The moment he fell seemed to last a lifetime, and his thoughts and emotions solidified into one.

For the first time in months, his mind was his own and likely to stay that way for more than a handful of seconds. His Mindseye was still open, and he could clearly see that although he had lost the Rhokai that had fueled his unnatural life, the fragments of stolen Kai remained in his aura.

Moments ago, Delnamal had been calmly and coldly planning the destruction of this Well. His entire purpose in *coming* here had been to poison it with a single mote of Kai. And now that he no longer wanted any such thing—now that he was *desperate* to save the Well and the kingdom that he'd been charged to protect when he'd accepted the crown—it was he himself who would destroy it.

Delnamal flailed with his weakened limbs as he fell, trying in vain to find something to grab onto. One arm bumped against the side of the Well, and he dug his fingers into the rock, his nails breaking and tearing down to the quick.

And then he hit something else with his back. He had peered down into the Well many times over the course of his life, and was aware that there were several narrow ledges and small outcroppings that peppered the otherwise smooth sides.

Using every ounce of his remaining strength, he grabbed the ledge he was even now in the process of tipping off of. Thanks to the damage he'd taken long ago, he could not voluntarily bend most of his fingers, but several of them were permanently frozen in a hooklike position and caught on a crack. His lower half went over the edge, but he had just enough of a grip to hold himself while he swung one leg up. He halted there for a moment, panting with exertion and fear, then somehow found another tiny scrap of strength—just enough to get most of his weight supported on the narrow ledge.

His Mindseye now closed, Delnamal could see that his perch was precarious, to say the least, and it was abundantly clear that he could not hold himself up indefinitely. Maybe if he were able-bodied, he'd be able to reach the lip of the Well and pull himself up if he got his feet under him. But he *wasn't* able-bodied, not by a long shot. Much of his strength had left him in that cloud of Rhokai, and he knew that death would soon come for him. There was so little flesh on his bones that he was mildly surprised he hadn't perished the moment the Rhokai had left him.

Guilt and horror threatened to rise up and strangle him, but he had become good at pushing through them. He could not lock them away as he had when the Rhokai had fueled him, could not completely ignore them, but he could *think* through them.

He could not comprehend how he'd let himself for a moment consider the atrocity he'd come here to the Well to commit, and he wondered if the elaborate fiction he'd fed Draios about the power of the Destroyer having entered him might not have a kernel of truth at its core. He had done a great many bad things over the course of his life—he could admit that to himself now—but however badly he had failed at his duties as a man and a husband and a king, he had never wished for harm to befall the Kingdom of Aaltah. Not even in his darkest moments, when he'd happily daydreamed about slaughtering his obstinate royal council, had his malice reached such depths.

Whatever it was that had led him down such a dark and terrible road, it was gone now. Everything he had done since the Rhokai had entered his body—maybe even everything he had done since he'd become king—had been a disgrace, and he shuddered to think how history would revile him. He could not re-write his legacy now, for it was far too late. But he could at least try not to make it any darker than it already was.

Delnamal opened his Mindseye and grabbed one of the free Kai motes remaining in his aura. He used it to activate the Kai spell in his belt buckle. Thrown at men, the spell would crush their chests, turning their insides to jelly. But there were no ene-mies left to defeat save the demons within himself, so he threw the spell at the far side of the Well, where it dissipated harmlessly against the wall, using up the Kai mote.

Grimly, Delnamal reached for another of the motes in his aura.

CHAPTER FORTY-SIX

Alys closed her eyes and breathed deep, then found herself scared to open them again. What if she opened her eyes and found Delnamal still standing there, killing Kailee? Surely that was more likely than that her desperately thrown spell had actually *worked*, and that in doing so it had carried Delnamal into the Well.

Bracing herself, Alys cracked her eyelids open. Delnamal was nowhere to be seen.

Kailee was on her hands and knees, her head down as she gasped and retched. Her gown was splattered with blood, and Alys could hardly believe that the sweet, mild-mannered girl she knew had swung a sword and removed Draios's head from his shoulders.

The healing spell Kailee must have cast on her was still working its magic, as Alys dragged herself to a sitting position. The movement caused a spike of sharp pain in her chest, and she reflexively clapped a hand over the wound, feeling a bout of nausea as she realized once again how much blood had soaked into her gown. A brooch—which was not hers, and which she assumed contained the healing spell—had fallen to her lap, and she quickly grabbed it and pinned it onto her bodice near the wound so that it could continue working.

Still weak and dizzy, Alys forced herself to her feet and staggered toward the Well. Her balance felt uncertain enough that she knew peeking over the rim was unwise, but she could not stop herself. She tried to keep as far back as possible while still leaning her head forward so she could see.

A small, strangled sound escaped her when she saw Delnamal lying on his back on a ledge against the side of the Well. Somehow, impossibly, the bastard was still alive! His eyes were white, and while she watched, he reached for something in the air in front of him.

She knew all too well what he was reaching for, and she hastily retreated from the rim of the Well before he could cast his wretched Kai spell at her.

Delnamal had survived the last time he had desecrated Aaltah's Well, but there was no way Alys could allow him to do so this time!

The sword Kailee had discarded lay only inches from Alys's feet, so she bent and picked it up. She could not get to Delnamal to run him through—much though she might wish to—but surely his perch on that ledge was precarious. Her shoulders heaved with her panting breaths—her body was still far from healed enough for all this exertion—as she neared the edge once again. There was a tiny part of her that said she was taking a foolish risk, that she should wait until whatever reinforcements Tynthanal could afford to send had reached the Well chamber rather than trying to finish off her half-brother herself.

Clearly, the purgative spell she had cast on him had had an effect, and a devastating one at that. But even if it had purged the stolen Rhokai from his body, his white eyes suggested that he might still have free Kai available.

Most likely, he had held on to that Kai mote he had grabbed, waiting to activate his Kai spell the moment she—or anyone else—dared come into view again. But even knowing how foolish and reckless she was being, she could not seem to stop herself.

Reaching the edge of the Well, she looked down again, and once more saw Delnamal pulling something toward him. She hurled the sword down, hoping that it had enough magic in it that he could see it despite having his Mindseye open. She doubted the sword would kill him by dropping on him, but if he instinctively tried to dodge, he might very well fall and finish the job.

At the same moment she threw the sword, Delnamal threw his spell. Alys prepared to die, her mind not registering till a full second later that he had thrown the spell not at her, but at the far wall of the Well.

The sword glanced off the side of the Well, the impact sending it careening harmlessly into the abyss.

"Alys!" Delnamal yelled. "Don't!"

Alys looked about for something else to throw. It occurred to her—irrelevantly—that she could not recall Delnamal ever calling her by anything less than her full name before, even when they were children. Only people who *liked* her called her "Alys," and that was something Delnamal had never done.

She spotted a sword strapped to Draios's side, and bent to retrieve it. Her stomach gave an unhappy lurch when she stepped so close to the headless body, and the memory of Jinnell's head rolling in the dust threatened to rise up and smother her. Gritting her teeth and closing her eyes, she pulled out the sword and turned away.

"I still have a lot of Kai around me," Delnamal's voice called from the depths of the Well, the sound echoing. "You can't let me fall into the Well like this!"

Alys heard the words, but felt as if they had no meaning. No meaning that was important to *her*, at least. She had vowed time and time again that Delnamal would die either by her hand or by her order, and by her hand was the far more satisfying of the two options.

She reached the edge of the Well, once again expecting Delnamal to throw his spell at her, and once again she saw him directing it not at her, but at the wall.

"This Kai cannot fall into the Well!" he shouted at her, then
cast yet again.

"A-Alysoon?" a soft, tentative voice called from behind her.

Alys blinked and turned to see Kailee now on her feet. There
was blood coating the poor girl's hands, and great splashes of it
on her bodice and skirt and even her face. She was visibly shaking
as she held out a hand toward Alys.

"Your purgative worked," Kailee said. "I can already see the
difference in the Well's output."

Alys nodded absently, turning back toward Delnamal. "I know
it worked," she said, for though she had not directly seen any effect, Delnamal would not have fallen if it hadn't. "Though I
don't know why he still seems to have Kai clinging to him."

Alys opened her Mindseye, and she could immediately see
that Kailee was right; the Well was healing. The cloud of elements
flowing from the Well was visibly denser than it had been when
she'd entered the chamber. It wasn't as dense as it had been before the damage Delnamal had done, but she had faith that with
a little time, it would return to normal.

There was still a lot of Kai clinging to Delnamal's aura, however. As she watched, he reached for one of those Kai motes and
put it into a spell contained in a jewel in his belt buckle, then
once again threw that spell at the far wall. She held the sword out
over the lip of the Well once more.

"Alys, please don't," Kailee said. "Mairahsol gave her life to
stop a single mote of Kai from entering the Well. You met her.
You *know* she would not have done that unless the need was desperate. The Kai cannot be allowed to enter the Well."

"I'm using it up as fast as I can," Delnamal called. "I don't
want to destroy the Well!"

"Think about what you're doing!" Kailee cried.

Alys held the sword in both hands over the rim of the Well, determined to take careful aim this time.

"I'm thinking about it," she said with a nod at the floor several feet away, where the ring containing her purgative spell had landed when she'd thrown it. "After I've knocked him in, I'll perform the sacrifice to make sure the Kai doesn't hurt the Well." She frowned. "But perhaps you had better leave. I don't want you to become the new Delnamal."

"I'm dying anyway," Delnamal shouted up at her. "The Rhokai I absorbed from the Well was keeping me alive, and it's gone now. Just wait until I've used up all this other Kai."

Alys laughed, with no hint of mirth. "Oh, now you're the noble martyr who will sacrifice all for the good of Aaltah?"

"Alys, please," Kailee said. "You don't have to do this. He's lost, and you've won. Whether he's truly dying as he says, or whether we will have to execute him, it's over. There's no reason to risk his Kai falling into the Well, and there's no reason you should perform the sacrifice now that the Well is restored."

Alys shuddered and shook her head again.

Everything she'd hoped for was right here in front of her! She could kill Delnamal with her own hands, thus finally avenging Jinnell's death. And then she could sacrifice her own life to set things back to rights. She would never again have to suffer the memory of Jinnell's head falling in the dirt, would never have to wake up to the agonizing knowledge that she would never see her precious daughter again. She would not have to risk learning that Corlin had been killed in the battle of the Harbor District, nor live with the guilt of having failed to protect her children.

She'd told herself before that she didn't want to die, that she had planned to make the sacrifice because it was the right thing to do and only as a last resort. Only now did she realize how massive was the lie she'd told.

"Just wait a little longer," Delnamal pleaded, his voice sounding weaker. He was still steadily reaching for motes in the air and then casting his spell, but his movements were slower and more labored. "They're almost gone."

"Why do you care?" she asked in exasperation. "You launched a war against your own people specifically so you could come here and poison our Well, and now you are trying to save it?"

His movements stopped for a moment, and the white film faded from his eyes as he looked up at her beseechingly. His face was cadaverous, those pleading eyes sunken deep into their sockets, and though he had always hated her, she saw no evidence of that hate in his expression now.

"I have not been myself since I brought Mairahsol to the Well," he said. "I made . . . countless bad decisions in my life, but I would never willingly bring harm to Aaltah. Not when I'm in my right mind. You don't have to understand, or even believe me. Just don't let me fall into the Well before I've used up the last of this Kai."

Alys hadn't noticed she was crying until a tear dripped on the floor by her feet. Her throat felt swollen shut with them, and her chest still ached with the pain of her healing wound, but reason was beginning to force its way back into her consciousness.

There was *no* logical reason to kill Delnamal now. Either he would die on his own, or reinforcements would soon arrive at the cavern and they could haul him out of the Well so he could undergo the trial and execution he so richly deserved. All she would gain was an excuse to end her own life.

"I'm not leaving you," Kailee said. "If you end up having to perform the sacrifice, I will be right here by your side and we can start the cycle all over again."

"Kailee . . ." Alys said in a warning tone.

"No! I'm not going to let you do it, and that's final. If I have to live with—" Her voice cut off for a moment with a choking sound. "If I have to live with what I just did," she said more softly, "then *you* have to live, too."

Delnamal opened his Mindseye again to start casting his Kai

spells. He shifted ever so slightly on the ledge, and they all heard the ominous cracking sound, followed by the skitter of pebbles.

Delnamal froze for a moment, then held one hand up toward her as with the other, he continued to cast Kai spells. She saw that his hand was wretchedly twisted and gnarled, almost clawlike.

"Don't let me fall yet!" he cried, his misshapen fingers straining toward her.

If he were at full strength—and bold enough—he could perhaps have stood up and reached the edge of the Well to pull himself out, but even holding his arm in the air seemed like a massive effort.

More than just about anything else she could name, Alys wanted to let him fall. She wanted to stand here safely on the edge of the Well and watch as the ledge crumbled beneath him and he tumbled to his well-deserved death. And the very *last* thing she wanted to do was to help him in any way.

But if Delnamal fell before the Kai was used up, then Alys would have no choice but to perform her sacrifice, even if Kailee refused to leave. It was one thing to be willing to give up her own life to get her revenge, but quite another to leave Kailee potentially burdened with the same unwholesome power Delnamal had absorbed.

"Help me!" she shouted at Kailee as she dropped to the floor and reached her hand down toward her half-brother, even as the anger she had stored inside her howled in frustration at being thwarted. The wound in her chest protested the motion, but the pain was bearable, the healing spell nearly complete.

She could just barely reach Delnamal's hand, and at first she had not been able to stop herself from jerking away from his loathsome touch. His hand looked even more hideous when seen up close, but it was the thought of touching *him* that made her recoil.

"Hurry!" he urged, flailing for her hand while still continuing to cast his Kai spells.

Alys felt Kailee clamp down hard on her ankles. "I've got you!" Kailee said.

Gritting her teeth, Alys took hold of Delnamal's hand, then brought her other hand around to clasp his wrist. She could feel every bone in his fingers and hand, her own fingers closing easily around the frail wrist. She noted that his fingers could barely bend enough to hold on, although he tried.

The ledge gave way with a loud crack, and all three of them cried out in alarm. Alys tightened her grip till she felt fragile bones grinding against one another.

The weight of any normal full-grown man would have been too much for her to hold. Even as he was—a collection of skin and sinews and bone—Delnamal's weight pulled her farther into the Well, and she thought for a moment they were both going to fall together.

Somehow, Kailee managed to stop their slide, putting her whole body weight on top of Alys's legs.

Amazingly, Alys held on, gritting her teeth with the strain and closing her eyes so that she could not see the depths over which she dangled.

"Stop squirming!" she snapped at Delnamal, for his restless movements made him harder to hold.

"Can't," he said shortly, and she opened her eyes once more.

He was suspended over the abyss now, with no ledge to catch him if he fell. And though she'd thought he'd been scrabbling with his feet for purchase, she saw that his legs were hanging limply down. The jerking movements she'd felt were merely his other hand pulling elements and casting spells at a frantic pace.

Closing her eyes once more, Alys put all of her concentration into holding on, even as her arms and shoulders screamed in protest.

"A little longer," Delnamal gasped out, and Alys suppressed a whimper as the effort of holding him made her hands sweat and she wondered how long Kailee could hold her.

How had it come to this? How was it possible that she was risking her own life—and Kailee's, for if Alys fell it was very possible Kailee would fall with her—to save a man she hated with every fiber of her being? It seemed grossly unfair after everything she'd been through, and she wondered how fools like the late and unlamented King Draios had managed to ascribe a divine plan to their lives. Certainly Alys would never worship any divinity that would put her through this!

"That's the last of it," Delnamal finally breathed, heaving a sigh. "It's safe to let go now. The fall won't break my Rhokai."

Alys's eyes popped open, and she found herself meeting her half-brother's gaze. She could barely recognize the eyes that met hers, and it was not entirely because of the changes in his body. "How do you know?"

"Take my word for it that only deaths by intentional violence break it. Let's not talk about how I know." He swallowed hard, and his voice grew weaker. "I'm sorry about Jinnell. I want you to know that I didn't kill her, but she died because of me just the same."

Tears burned her eyes, and she glared at Delnamal as the familiar hatred flared. "Are you *trying* to make me let go?"

Delnamal's eyelids fluttered, and he shook his head. His breathing was shallow and labored, and his twisted fingers no longer wrapped around hers.

"Just . . . wanted . . . to say that," he whispered, his words so soft she could barely hear him.

She blinked her own tears away and looked at him again, looked at the bones jutting out of his skin, and realized that it was *impossible* for someone to be that cadaverously skinny and still be alive.

There was a clamor of voices from the far side of the Well chamber, and Alys heard Kailee calling for help. The reinforcements had arrived, and they could no doubt pull both Alys and Delnamal out of the Well. But Delnamal would never live long enough to face trial. Not without the Rhokai he had stolen from this Well.

His eyes were closed now, and he hung completely limp from Alys's grip. She couldn't even tell if he was still breathing.

"Let go," he said, his voice even softer and more labored. "Don't . . . don't let Oona see what I've become."

Alys couldn't have said whether it was a conscious choice, or whether her strength finally gave out. But her hands opened, and Delnamal slipped from her grasp.

He made no sound as he fell.

CHAPTER FORTY-SEVEN

Stumbling and nearly blind with tears, Leethan pulled Waldmir's cloak tightly around her, letting her head disappear into the shadow of the hood. She wished she could just pull it down over her eyes so that she did not have to see the devastation that radiated out from the place where she had lain protected by Waldmir's body and the Kai shield spell that had resided in his ring.

The tents and pavilions that had surrounded Waldmir's had all been flattened, and there were dead men everywhere. She had heard stories before about the destructive power of battlefield Kai spells. Of course she had—that's why she'd thought to use one. But somehow it seemed her mind had never fully encompassed the horror.

Shouts and screams came from all directions, each sending a dagger into her conscience, but at least it let her know there were survivors. She picked her way through the bodies and wreckage, expecting at any moment for someone to stop her. But as Waldmir had predicted, what was left of the camp was in chaos, people running here and there, searching for survivors, and trying to figure out what was going on and what to do now. No one paid any heed to her as she walked through the camp, retracing her steps.

A sob escaped her when she passed through the edge of the camp, where most of the tents were still standing. The sentry posts were all abandoned, the tents empty, and she slipped away into the woods like a ghost.

She should be dead. She had not come to the camp *eager* to die, but she had to some extent come to terms with her death. Certainly she had never entertained the notion that she might have to live with what she had just done.

Waldmir was dead, along with countless others. Including most of his potential heirs. The most martial of his nephews—the ones most likely to launch a war to stake their own claims to the throne—would all be in this camp, in the tents reserved for the officers and other elite of Nandel. Which meant they would have been situated near Waldmir's tent, where the worst of the destruction had occurred.

The army was in complete disarray, and although someone would undoubtedly take charge and restore order, there was no question that the survivors would abandon the camp and limp back into Nandel. Rhozinolm would now be free to march to Aaltah's defense, and yet Leethan felt not even the slightest sense of victory.

She had to pause to retch as she remembered the horror of climbing out from under Waldmir's dead body and seeing what the Kai spell had done. Everything within her shriveled, and she wanted nothing more than to curl up into a ball of misery.

But when it came right down to it, it was not *Leethan* who'd cast the Kai spell. It was now abundantly clear that sacrificial Kai did not behave like ordinary Kai. Perhaps something created by a noble, willing sacrifice was simply not meant to be used to kill.

Leethan's mission had been doomed—*should have been* doomed—from the beginning.

There will be a lot of fear and confusion, Waldmir had said. And then he'd told her to take his cloak and escape before order was restored.

He had recognized the spell in her dagger. Known exactly what it would do. And yet he had used his own masculine Kai to trigger it for her.

Leethan spat and wiped her mouth, her stomach roiling. She still struggled against a nearly unbearable urge to just sit down and bury her head in her hands. But she now had the means to keep her promise to Jaizal and return to Zinolm Well safely. Giving up would be an act of cowardice.

When she'd told Waldmir she'd seen a future in which his nephews did not drag Nandel into civil war in an effort to succeed him, she'd meant only to spare herself the slow and painful execution she feared was awaiting her. She hadn't for a moment considered that he might choose to trigger the spell himself, though perhaps she should have. He'd put himself—and his wives—through so much in his desperate quest to secure the succession and not give his nephews cause to start a war. If he believed her when she suggested triggering the spell would prevent that war, then why *wouldn't* he trigger it himself when she failed?

Another sob rose from Leethan's throat, and she clapped a hand over her mouth to try to contain it. Likely there were no patrols roaming the woods, for they would have heard the commotion in the camp and run back, but that was no reason for her to be incautious.

How many men had died from that Kai spell? Leethan couldn't guess, didn't *want* to guess.

The lump of pain in her throat was so large she felt like she was choking on it. The frigid night air and her own despair made her shiver, and she was no longer completely certain she was walking in the right direction to return to Rhozinolm's camp. How ironic would it be if she survived her assassination attempt only to freeze to death in the woods?

Leethan opened her Mindseye to examine Waldmir's cloak.

Nandelites scorned small, comforting things like warming spells, but the cloak might well be armed with one in case of emergency. Using a warming spell for *comfort* would be taken as a sign of weakness, but it was acceptable to use one to keep from freezing to death.

Her Mindseye immediately noticed the warming spell that did, indeed, reside in one of the cloak's fastenings. But when she looked up so that she could grab a mote of Rho to trigger the spell, she gasped in shock.

Hovering by her left shoulder was the red, white, and black mote of Kai that had shimmered to life when she had performed her sacrifice.

"Impossible," she whispered into the night air, no longer feeling the chill.

She was no expert in the principles of magic—neither men's nor women's—but she did know that if a man's Kai appeared and his life was saved by one of the rare spells that could heal a fatal wound, the Kai disappeared.

She swallowed hard and put her hand to her chest, still staring at the impossible tricolored mote. And then, of course, she thought of the dream. The dream wherein she and two other women had performed sacrifices that caused this tricolored Kai to appear.

A gust of wind penetrated the gaps of the cloak, reminding her why she had opened her Mindseye in the first place. Deciding to leave the mystery of the sacrificial Kai until she had reached safety, Leethan activated the cloak's warming spell and closed her Mindseye.

Warmer, but still reeling with emotion and confusion, she grimly set off again in what she hoped was the direction of the Rhozinolm camp.

• • •

Kailee had never felt so cold in all her life. She shivered, her teeth chattering, and all she wanted to do was lie down, curl herself into a ball, and pretend the rest of the world did not exist.

Men were loading Alysoon onto a stretcher—against her objections—and Kailee was vaguely aware of the commotion around her. She was asked several times if she was injured, and though she couldn't quite locate her voice to answer, she shook her head, and so far everyone was taking her at her word. She stood frozen beside the Well, wishing she could scrub the last hour from her memory, knowing it would haunt her till the end of her days. Her arms still remembered the sensation of that spelled blade slicing through Prince Draios's neck, and her brain kept replaying the sound of his body collapsing to the floor.

Everyone was going to reassure her that she had done the right thing, that she was some kind of hero. Those who knew her best would understand her horror, but even they would expect her to get over it with time. But she knew with a certainty she could not explain that she would never be the same.

She had *killed* someone. With her own two hands and with clear and murderous intent. She had come to the Well so that she might help someone else kill Draios, and though she was certain doing so would have left her feeling traumatized, it would not have been like this. She, who insisted on seeing the best in everyone, had killed a frightened seventeen-year-old boy.

Hugging herself almost desperately, she thought about Leethan's prophetic dream, in which three women had sacrificed themselves to defeat the shadowy figures representing Draios and Delnamal and Waldmir. Everyone had believed that Leethan was the woman who would face Waldmir, and that Alysoon was the one who would face Delnamal. But no one had guessed that it would be Kailee who would defeat Draios.

Maybe they should have. From what Kailee had learned of the fateful spell called the Blessing, there was extra power in the female trio of maiden, mother, and crone. Brynna, her daughter, and her granddaughter had played those roles for the casting of the Blessing, and it was not hard at all to see Alysoon as the mother and Leethan as the crone. That had left only the maiden unidentified. Of course, there were few who knew that Kailee was still a maiden despite her marriage.

Kailee stared at the strange mote of Kai that hovered near her chest. Nowhere had she heard a description of sacrificial Kai, but she knew without doubt that the tricolored crystal was exactly that. She had not sacrificed her life to earn it, but she *had* sacrificed her innocence.

Still standing motionless in the midst of all the clamor, she watched as the men lifted Alysoon's stretcher. She wondered if Alysoon had any idea that she had her own mote of sacrificial Kai. It had not been there when she'd lain dying on the Well-chamber floor. Nor had it been there when she'd been trying to knock Delnamal into the Well. No, it had shimmered to life when Alysoon had reached out her hand to keep Delnamal from falling.

A hand gently touched Kailee's shoulder, and she started. Belatedly, she realized that one of the soldiers had been speaking to her.

"Sorry to startle you, Your Highness," he said with an embarrassing amount of pity in his voice. "We need to get you to a medic."

Kailee shook her head. "I am uninjured," she said, although her voice quavered dangerously and she couldn't resist the urge to rub at her chest in remembered pain. She had come very close to dying. Under other circumstances, that horror alone would have staggered her.

"You may not yet be aware of your injuries," the soldier said. "You are covered in blood, and—"

"It's not mine," she assured him. The soldiers, of course, did not know everything that had transpired in this chamber before they arrived. Some of them had undoubtedly seen when Delnamal dropped into the Well, and they could certainly see that Draios's head was not attached to his body. But none of them would guess that it was she who had struck that fatal blow.

"You should see the medic anyway, just to be safe," the soldier persisted, once again putting a hand on her arm. Naturally, he didn't believe her.

Kailee had had a great deal of practice maintaining her patience with those who were overly solicitous, who believed her entirely helpless because of her sex and because of her lack of worldly vision. Always, she'd put up with it and kept her irritation to herself, knowing that most people meant well. Certainly this soldier did.

But just this once, Kailee found she did not have the patience for courtly politeness. She jerked her arm out of his grip.

"I said I'm *fine*," she snarled. "I'm covered in blood because I chopped off a man's head!"

The soldier gasped and took a hasty step back from her, whether because of the heat in her voice or because of her words themselves, she didn't know.

"I do not need a medic," she concluded, forcing her voice back down to a normal volume.

She let out a long, shaky breath. "I suspect I will, however, need some help getting out of here without stumbling over bodies."

She had the sense that the soldier was standing there staring at her, fumbling for what to say. In the end, he settled for saying nothing at all, instead holding out his elbow for her to take.

When she'd heard that Corlin was severely wounded—but alive—Alys's first instinct had been to run directly to his side. He was being treated at the hospital in the Citadel, and the risers had been started again as soon as the Khalpari forces had retreated, so she could have reached his side in little more than half an hour.

It was Tynthanal who had held her back, going so far as to take her by the shoulders and shake her when she'd at first refused to listen. His glare was fearsome, his voice full of command as he leaned into her personal space.

"Don't be an idiot!" he growled at her. "Take a look at yourself!"

"I'm fine!" she snarled back, though that was something of an exaggeration. Kailee's healing spell had done an admirable job of closing the wound in her chest, and the medic she'd been pressured into seeing had wanted to use a second spell to augment the effects of the first. However, there were countless wounded soldiers who would need that spell more desperately than Alys did, so she had refused. Which meant her chest felt as if a boulder had smashed into it, and every breath hurt.

"I said *look*!" Tynthanal shouted. He was not one to lose patience easily, but it was understandable on a day like today.

Blinking, Alys looked down at herself, at her torn and blood-soaked bodice, at the blood that formed spots and splotches on her ragged skirts. She looked like exactly what she was: a woman who had been through a battle and taken a wound that should have been fatal.

"Is this how you want him to see you?" Tynthanal finished. "After everything he's already been through today?"

Alys swallowed hard, ashamed of her selfishness. She had thought only of her need to see her son, and not about the fear she would spark in him the moment he caught sight of her like this. She took a deep, calming breath, and though the need to rush to his side remained fierce, her rational mind returned to duty.

"I will clean up and change first," she assured her brother.

Keeping her promise had taken longer than she'd expected, and it was more than two hours after she'd first learned of his fate when she finally arrived at the Citadel hospital.

The Citadel made a practice of treating all its soldiers as equals, at least in theory. However, either because he was the Crown Prince of Women's Well or because he was the prince regent's nephew, Corlin had been given a private room in which to recuperate.

He was asleep when Alys first entered, lying on his back with his hands clasped over his chest. There was the remnant of a vicious slice wound over the left side of his face, and Alys knew from the healer's report that her boy had been in grave danger of losing his eye. But the worst of the damage was hidden under the blankets, and though Alys knew the wound had been successfully closed and was as well mended as her own, she was just as happy not to have to see it.

Tears dribbled down her cheeks as she carefully sat on the bed beside him, trying not to wake him. She did not want him to feel any unnecessary pain, and could not begrudge him his escape into sleep.

She did not touch him, and as far as she knew, she made no sound, but Corlin's eyes blinked open and he stirred.

"Mama?" he said, his brow furrowing with worry. "Why are you crying? What's happened?" He tried to sit up, but she put a hand on his shoulder to keep him down.

"It's all right," she assured him, even as the tears continued to stream from her eyes, glad that Tynthanal had persuaded her to clean up and change. "I'm just . . . I'm just so glad you're alive." Her voice hiccuped, and she wished she could gather him into her arms and never let go.

He smiled at her, though it turned into a wince as the movement stretched the healing wound on his face. "I'm glad you're alive, too," he said, and she was shocked to see the sheen of tears in his eyes. "When I heard that Delnamal had made it to the Well chamber . . ."

His voice trailed off, and he closed his eyes.

Alys dabbed the tears off her cheeks, realizing that all her plans to protect him had been for naught. "You knew what I was planning to do," she said.

"Not exactly," he said, then opened his eyes once more. "Our assignment was to stop Delnamal from getting up the cliffs, and we were told there was intelligence suggesting he was heading for the Well chamber. I figured you were here because you wanted to confront him, and if you knew he was going to the Well, then that was where you'd be." He frowned at her rather fiercely. "I don't know exactly what happened up there, but I *do* know you could easily have died. You should have told me. I would have hated it, but I would have understood. I'm not a baby."

She took his hand—grateful that he did not snatch it away—and gave it a squeeze. Eventually, she would tell him the whole truth about why she'd been waiting for Delnamal at the Well, but now was most definitely not the time. "I know. And I'm sorry." She swiped away more tears. "I'm not as brave as you are, my darling boy."

Corlin squirmed, and she suspected it was only an effort of will that stopped him from rolling his eyes. "Delnamal is really dead this time, isn't he?"

Alys nodded, remembering the feeling of his hand slipping through hers. He had been a bad king, a bad brother, and an all-around bad man—even before the accident at the Well—but somehow, miraculously, he had done the right thing at the end. The memory of his frantic attempts to rid himself of all that Kai so that his death would not poison the Well would now vie with all her other memories of him to make him into something far more complicated than the villain she had hated with all of her heart.

"He is dead," she affirmed, "and the Well is repaired. And I have it on good authority that you will earn a medal for saving your fellow cadet's life at such great personal risk." It went against custom to award medals to cadets, but then a lot of old customs were changing.

Corlin grimaced. "Why did it have to be Justal?" he muttered, and Alys was surprised into a laugh.

"I take it Cadet Justal is not one of your favorite people?"

"You could say that," Corlin said with a shake of his head. Then his grimace turned into a grin. "But if *I'm* to get a medal for saving Justal, then my friend, Rafetyn, must get a medal for saving *me*." He told her the story of his unlikely friend, whose arrow had saved his life. "The rest of the cadets will positively choke if he and I both get medals."

Unable to stop herself, Alys reached out and stroked Corlin's hair, earning herself an exasperated look. But he didn't pull away, instead tolerating the touch.

"When you're all better," she said, "you can come back to Women's Well. I'm sure Cadet Smithson's family will understand and agree that you have redeemed yourself."

But Corlin shook his head. "Saving Justal does not undo what I did to Smithson," he insisted. "My exile will mean nothing if it is over in less than a year. I will remain in the Citadel of Aaltah at least until the first year is up." He frowned thoughtfully. "Well, likely till my first *two* years are up. You have not met Cadet Rafetyn, but he has had a hard time at the Citadel, and the medal might make things worse rather than better. I owe him my life, and I cannot abandon him to the bullies."

"I would happily offer him a place in Women's Well," Alys said, for there was little she would not do to thank the boy who had saved her son's life.

Corlin smiled. "Convincing his father to let him take it might be a project. Maybe we can talk to Uncle Tynthanal and Lord Aldnor and see if they can persuade him. Then after I've served my year, and if I can bring Rafetyn with me, we can talk about the conditions of my return."

Alys clenched her teeth to keep from remonstrating, for it was clear from the challenging look in his eyes that Corlin was still determined that he would accept the flogging that he would have suffered had he been any other cadet. She had told him in no uncertain terms that she had no intention of allowing that to happen, but her little boy had turned into a stubborn young man. She vowed to have a word with Lord Aldnor before she left for Women's Well. Surely he would agree that Corlin should be spared any further punishment for his past transgressions, and he had a better chance of talking Corlin into forgiving himself than she did.

"I love you so much," she murmured hoarsely, and the tears threatened to return.

"I love you, too, Mama," Corlin said.

And the dam burst. Never before had she allowed herself to lose control in front of her son, but nothing could have stopped these sobs. Not even the lingering pain in her chest.

Corlin held her hand throughout.

CHAPTER FORTY-EIGHT

Kailee felt a flutter of nerves when Tynthanal returned to the royal suite after yet another gruelingly long day dealing with the aftermath of war. The atmosphere throughout the city of Aalwell was one of great hope and excitement, but that did not make the prince regent's job any less demanding. They still had months of economic hardship to overcome, and even the city's joy and relief were tempered with the pain of loss. That the entirety of the fighting had occurred over the course of one long day meant the losses were far, far fewer than they had anticipated, but there were still many grieving friends and family.

"You weren't waiting up for me, were you?" Tynthanal asked. "I'm sure I could have broken away sooner if I'd known."

"I know." She licked her lips nervously, for in truth she'd made her decision three days ago and was just now finding the courage to tell him.

He crossed the room toward her, taking a seat on the sofa beside her. "What is it?" he asked, his concern evident in his voice. Although they did not sleep together, he was well aware of the nightmares that had plagued her since she'd killed Draios. She did not think he fully understood the wound she had put on her own soul when she'd swung that sword, but he was at least aware it existed and was careful not to poke at it.

For half a second, she almost talked herself out of it, but she knew in her heart what she had to do.

"Alysoon is leaving for Women's Well tomorrow," she said, though of course Tynthanal was well aware. "And I will be going with her."

She heard the sharp intake of Tynthanal's breath and wondered if he would argue with her. Even knowing that he would not suddenly fall to his knees and profess his love for her, there was a part of her that *wanted* him to remonstrate. She was going to break her own heart by leaving, and she hoped she would take at least a tiny chip out of his.

She heard him swallow, but his voice came out steady. "May I ask why?"

She squeezed her hands together in her lap and reminded herself that she knew him pretty well by now. He believed in letting her make her own decisions, and he had long felt guilty about all she had lost by coming to Aaltah with him. Even if he desperately wanted her to stay, he was unlikely to say so if he knew she wanted to leave.

"You don't need me anymore," she said simply, and it was at least a portion of the truth. "The Well is repaired and the war is won, with you having led the people of Aaltah to safety. Those who opposed you before might not now love you, but they will be much more kindly disposed toward you and much less likely to voice any dissent they might feel. You can handle the scandal of a divorce."

"Divorce?" he gasped, as if the thought had never occurred to him.

"You can divorce me safely now," she said. "My father might be angry—even if I can convince him it was my own idea, he will likely blame you—but I'm sure Queen Ellinsoltah will not withdraw her support over it." She smiled. "Not that you are much in need of her support anymore."

He shifted uncomfortably. "I . . . I don't want to divorce you."

Again she smiled, sadly this time. "But you don't want to be married to me, either. And I—" Her voice hiccuped to a stop, but she forced herself onward. "I don't want to be married to someone who loves another. I deserve better."

It was only partially a lie. If she felt one iota of hope that he would ever grow to love her, she doubted she would have found the courage to split with him. But he had never once given that hope any soil in which to grow, and if she remained in Aaltah as his wife, she feared she would quickly become embittered and miserable.

"If we divorce," she continued, "and I move on to Women's Well, then I might one day find a husband whom I can make happy and be made happy by in return. And you . . . Well, I suspect your newfound popularity will be such that you might even be able to marry a former abbess without doing any great damage to your political standing."

She could almost feel the hope that surged through Tynthanal's body and was quickly squashed.

"Chanlix has no desire to return to Aaltah," he said. "And I cannot in good conscience ask her to leave her position as lady chancellor to come here and be my scandalous wife." He coughed suddenly and looked away, but Kailee was not offended.

"You won't know for sure unless you ask her," Kailee pointed out.

He shook his head. "I know Chanlix. And I know what living as a respectable woman in Women's Well has done for her. She will not give that up just to be with me."

Kailee opened her mouth to argue, then thought better of it. It was not her job to find him a replacement wife. She suspected

Chanlix loved him more than he realized and that, like Kailee, she would sacrifice a great deal to be with him. But he would have to find that out on his own.

"Will you give me the divorce?" she asked bluntly.

He was silent for a long time before he answered. "If that's what you truly want, then yes."

"Thank you," she said as her heart shattered and she fought not to cry.

It had been a full week since little Princess Elwynne had come to stay at the royal palace, and still Ellin found herself having to stop by the nursery every time she returned to her apartments, as if the little girl might have somehow vanished during the course of the day. She tiptoed to the door and nudged it open, peering into the darkened room.

Elwynne was fast asleep at this late hour, but Ellin was not surprised to find Zarsha sitting in a chair beside the bed. He smiled at her and shrugged, then tucked the covers more snugly under his niece's chin and tiptoed out of the room. It seemed that knowing she was not his daughter had not diminished his love for her even a little bit, and Ellin could clearly see what a good and doting father he would be.

In silence, they walked together down the hall to the parlor that adjoined both of their bedrooms, although Ellin was considering turning Zarsha's bedroom into a bedroom for Elwynne when she got too old to need her governess sleeping in the adjacent room. It wasn't like Zarsha ever slept in it.

One day, she and Zarsha would admit to the child's true parentage, but if they admitted that Waldmir was her father, she would by Nandel law be considered property of the Crown and forced to return. Neither of them could stomach the idea of Elwynne as property, and the only legitimate way to keep her was to maintain the fiction they had created. Zarsha was trying to locate her mother, but that had turned out to be more difficult than expected, for Brontyn had left Grunir and no one seemed to know where she'd gone.

"How is she doing?" she asked Zarsha once they'd closed the parlor door behind them.

Zarsha beamed like a proud papa. "She's got a quick little mind," he told her. "She'll be speaking fluent Continental by the end of the month. And she seems a little more comfortable with the changes in her life each day."

Ellin bit her lip, knowing that it was a lot for anyone to take, much less a five-year-old child. Even at her tender age, Elwynne had already thoroughly learned the lesson that girls were inferior beings, just as she had learned the lesson that any form of comfort or adornment was decadent and wrong. Unlearning those lessons—while also learning a new language and being surrounded by people she barely knew—was understandably hard on her.

"Not so comfortable that she could sleep without her 'papa' sitting by her side," Ellin said, feeling a stir of guilt that she quickly dismissed. There was no question that Elwynne would have a better childhood here, and that would have been true even if there had been no upheaval in Nandel. Most of Waldmir's adult heirs had perished with him. Zarsha had been struck from the succession when he'd married Ellin, but his younger brother, Granzin, had not been among the troops that had marched on Rhozinolm. He was now called the Sovereign Prince of Nandel, but there were several of Waldmir's younger nephews who might dispute the claim when they grew old enough. It would be a long time before Nandel would be truly stable once more, and Ellin knew Zarsha was very worried about what it meant that Leethan had foreseen Elwynne on the throne, for it did not bode well for his brother.

Zarsha poured himself a measure of brandy, holding the decanter up and raising an eyebrow at her.

"No, thank you," she said, though perhaps the brandy might have soothed her nerves. Not that she had any legitimate cause to be nervous. There was no question that Zarsha would be thrilled with her news.

Zarsha took a sip of his brandy. "She did well tonight," he said with a nod. "I think she would have fallen asleep if I'd left, but I didn't have the heart to do it yet. I didn't want to give her the chance to start missing everything and everyone she's lost."

Ellin nodded. Elwynne had taken the news of Prince Waldmir's death hard, for though he had never treated her well, he was the only father she'd ever known, and she'd loved him with a child's devotion. It hadn't helped that Leethan and Jaizal had elected to move to Women's Well, where they could live without the shadow of their decades spent in the Abbey of Nandel haunting them. Elwynne had not known either woman for all that long, but their journey through the Nandel mountains had forged a tight bond that had left all three of them in tears when they parted.

"I dread the day we have to tell her the truth about her governess," Ellin said with a grimace. Elwynne had been told the comforting lie that Laurel had turned back, and though both Ellin and Zarsha hated to perpetuate the lie, they agreed that it was best for now.

Zarsha groaned his agreement, and she could see that the thought had triggered a bout of melancholy. Although they didn't talk about it much, she knew Zarsha was struggling as much as she was with the atrocity they had committed in sending Leethan to Waldmir. Only the two of them and Leethan knew what had actually occurred in that camp—almost everyone else assumed the Kai spell had been triggered by some enemy combatant who had somehow sneaked into the heavily patrolled and guarded camp, although she knew there were rumors in Nandel that the attack had come from within. There were those who looked at Zarsha's brother sitting on the throne and wondered if that had been his plan all along.

Zarsha clucked his tongue at her. "I can see you trying to climb into that rabbit hole," he scolded. "We made the best decision we could under the circumstances, for the good not just of Rhozinolm but for all of Seven Wells."

She shook her head. "And it was all for naught, as the war was over before our army even decamped."

"We couldn't have known that. I won't deny that it . . . weighs on me. But though I am not a man of faith, I am trying my best to believe that we did the bidding of Leethan's Mother of All, and that She has the best interests of Seven Wells at heart."

Ellin sighed softly and refrained from pointing out that Draios had been under the delusion that he was somehow doing the Creator's will by attacking Aaltah and supporting Delnamal. Faith could be comforting to those who possessed it, but it could also be supremely dangerous and could be twisted to justify just about anything. The look on Zarsha's face said he suffered the same doubts.

"Are you climbing into that rabbit hole with me?" she asked with a little smile.

"Where you go, I follow, My Queen," he said, and though there was the customary twinkle in his eye, the spark was not as bright as it used to be.

Fortunately, Ellin knew exactly how to fix it, at least temporarily. Her own smile brightened, and her heart fluttered pleasantly with excitement.

"Then it is my job to lead you to a more pleasant place," she said. "I stopped by the Abbey today, ostensibly to meet with Mother Zarend." She was determined that she would continue her quest to transform the Abbey into a place of refuge rather than a prison, and since she had already overcome the council's initial resistance to her setting foot there, she had taken it upon herself to arrange regular meetings with Mother Zarend. It was early days still, but she thought that because of her visits, there was already a slight lessening of the stigma associated with the Abbey.

Zarsha cocked his head to one side. "Oh? Are you and the abbess concocting some new plan to nudge the Abbey toward greater respectability?"

"I said that was *ostensibly* why I was there. We do already have several ideas to play with, but today I had a different reason altogether for my visit. One that I did not want to tell anyone about until I knew the result." She beamed at him, and Zarsha suddenly sat bolt upright, his mouth dropping open as he stared at her breathlessly.

"Does that mean what I think it means?" he asked.

Ellin put her hand to her belly, hardly daring to believe what the abbess had told her. Only a few short months ago, she'd been convinced that she was not yet ready to have children, and until her suspiciously late monthly, she *still* would have said she was not ready. But the magic of the Blessing acted on the truth in her heart, not the one her conscious mind presented, and when the test had come up positive, she had felt nothing but joy.

"If you think it means you're going to be a father for real this time, then yes."

Zarsha's eyes grew suspiciously shiny, and her smile somehow grew even wider, till she felt it was about to split her face in two.

"And I believe it is time I begin what I'm sure will be a challenging effort to convince my council to change the laws of succession," she added on a fierce swell of determination. "Even if this child is a girl, I fully intend her to succeed me to the throne."

She had more she planned to say, but Zarsha leapt to his feet and lifted her easily into his arms, laughing and squeezing her tight.

CHAPTER FORTY-NINE

Alys welcomed Kailee into her private parlor in the royal palace with a hug. It was clear to anyone who'd known her before that the poor girl was still haunted by the events at the Well of Aaltah. Alys had hoped that returning to Women's Well would lift the weight from Kailee's shoulders—and maybe it still would someday, given time—but so far it had not.

"Am I early?" Kailee asked when Alys reluctantly released her. It seemed she herself was in need of a hug, though she hadn't realized it until she had embraced her soon-to-be-ex sister-in-law. Tynthanal had insisted that the official divorce decree wait until Kailee was safely in Women's Well, out of the reach of Aaltah's Abbey. Although Alys did not believe the people of Aaltah would wish to force Kailee into the Abbey after her heroism, she had agreed there was no point in taking the risk.

"Just a little," Alys said. "Lady Leethan will be joining us soon, I'm sure."

Kailee's shoulders heaved with a sigh, and her lower lip looked like she'd been chewing it raw. By mutual agreement, neither of them had told anyone about the sacrificial Kai that clung to them still after the events at the Well. However, they were both certain that Lady Leethan's choice to come to Women's Well had less to do with a burning desire to live there and much more to do with those Kai motes.

"She *must* have one, too, mustn't she?" Kailee asked anxiously.

Alys arched an eyebrow in surprise. "You mean you haven't managed to catch a glimpse of her yet?" she teased, for ordinarily she could count on Kailee to keep herself extremely well informed, and Leethan's carriage had arrived in Women's Well hours ago.

In the old days, Kailee would have flashed her an impish grin, but this more somber version of her merely shook her head. "By the time I knew her carriage had arrived, she had already contrived to be indoors. I almost decided to pay her a call, but then I realized it would be presumptuous of me."

"No, it wouldn't," Alys protested.

"Of course it would," she answered with some asperity. "If we are to talk about the Kai, then it is only fitting that we three should do it together. If our assumption is correct, that is."

Alys saw little doubt that it was, especially when Leethan had sent a flier ahead and asked for an audience with Alys at her earliest convenience. Leethan's request had not specifically mentioned Kailee, but Alys had included her because *of course* she agreed that the three of them must discuss the issue together.

There was stirring in the antechamber, and soon a royal guard admitted Lady Leethan to the room, announcing her and then bowing as he exited and closed the door behind him.

Alys looked at Lady Leethan and was immediately shocked that this old woman had fled the Abbey of Nandel on foot in the snow and made it through the mountains alive. She had to be at least seventy, her face heavily lined and her curtsy stiff as though her knees did not wish to bend. Then again, she'd had a long journey and was likely still feeling it in her joints.

Out of the corner of her eye, Alys saw Kailee nod, and knew exactly what it meant. As they'd both suspected, there was a mote of sacrificial Kai in Leethan's aura. Alys did not know exactly what role Leethan had played in the defeat of the Nandel army— Ellinsoltah had declined to share any details of the operation, nor had she been willing to confirm or deny any of the rumors about the deadly Kai spell that had killed Prince Waldmir and most of his heirs. But even before Kailee had confirmed the mote of Kai existed, Alys had felt deep down in her bones that Leethan had been involved. Her dream had foretold it, after all.

"It's good to finally meet you," Alys said, gesturing Leethan to the cozy seating area before the fire. "I hope you do not mind, but I asked my sister-in-law, Kailee, to join us, as I believe the purpose of your visit necessitates her presence."

"Pleased to meet you," Kailee said, expertly navigating around the chairs and the coffee table to take a seat on one of the sofas. She had been spending so much time in Alys's apartments lately that Alys had ordered several Aalwood pieces from Aaltah. Women's Well was now growing Aalwood on its own, but they did not yet have enough mature trees with which to make furniture.

Leethan smiled and nodded as she chose a plump armchair. "Yes, it's best that we three put our heads together at once," she agreed.

Alys sat beside Kailee. She could not deny she felt a fair amount of anxiety over the conversation that was to come, so that sitting still was the last thing she wanted to do. She fidgeted with the folds of her layered blue skirts, feeling a brief pang of longing for the simplicity of her mourning attire, which she had set aside as soon as she arrived home in Women's Well. When Honor had dressed her in color for the first time, Alys had broken down in sobs, and she suspected it would be a while yet before she could wholly let go of that distress.

"I will venture a guess," Leethan said, "that you are both aware of the existence of a very special variety of Kai."

"Yes, of course," Kailee answered. "Just as we are aware that all three of us possess one of those special motes." She frowned. "Even though none of us died to earn them."

Leethan shrugged. "I *sort of* did." After swearing them to secrecy, she told Alys and Kailee what had really happened when Prince Waldmir had died.

"He set off that Kai spell himself?" Alys exclaimed. "I don't understand! Why?"

Leethan closed her eyes in what looked like pain. "Because I told him that triggering the Kai spell would prevent a war over the succession after his death—and he believed me." Her voice sounded rough and choked, as if she was about to cry.

Clearly, Leethan considered her claim to have been a lie, which made Alys cock her head. "It seems to me you were right," she said. "There was no resistance to Granzin's succession, from what I have heard."

Leethan shrugged. "Maybe it turned out to be true, but I lied to him all the same. But never mind that. My conscience is my own to wrestle with. What matters is that in his final sacrifice, Waldmir saved me, secured his principality, and put an end to his own sorrow and pain."

Alys's throat tightened with something almost like envy. She knew all too well the lure of a heroic death to someone whose life included too much suffering. Most of the time, she was grateful to have lived through her confrontation with Delnamal—especially when she thought of how abandoned Corlin would have felt if she'd died. Learning that he'd survived his own battle had certainly made her life feel more bearable, but she still suffered the occasional dark thought that living was almost impossibly hard.

"In the end," Kailee said, "we each made a sacrifice, even if it was not the literal sacrifice you saw in your dream."

Leethan turned toward her, and the look of curiosity on her face warned Alys that she was about to ask Kailee about her sacrifice, for unlike Leethan, she had not slit her wrists. Knowing that her sister-in-law was still haunted—and probably always would be—by the memory of killing Draios, Alys hurried to interrupt before Leethan could indulge her curiosity.

"We did, in our own strange ways," she said. "Ways that neither one of us is anxious to discuss."

"Of course," Leethan said smoothly with a bow of her head. "And now we all three are in possession of motes of sacrificial Kai."

"Yes," Kailee said. "And I can plainly see that the edges of our three crystals are such that they could fit together to form one larger crystal."

The words themselves felt portentous, and Alys suppressed a shiver of combined excitement, anticipation, and no small amount of dread. She and Kailee had already seen that their two Kai crystals would fit smoothly with each other, the protrusions on one crystal shaped exactly like the spaces in the other.

"From the description I heard of your dream," Alys said to Leethan, "it ended with the three Kai motes joining together."

"Yes," Leethan confirmed. "Very little of that dream turned out to be literal, although I'm sure we can all see how the events in the dream correspond to what happened in reality."

"But you think that the joining together of the three motes *was* meant to be literal," Alys said, and she felt the rightness of the idea as deeply as she'd felt the conviction that she had to be waiting for Delnamal at the Well of Aaltah. Even after everything that had happened, there was a part of her that remained skeptical that a divine hand was at work, but skepticism was not outright denial.

"I do," Leethan said. "At least I do now that I see we three can make one another's acquaintance without immediately triggering anything. I thought perhaps all we needed to do was meet, but now that Kailee has seen that the motes are meant to fit together . . ."

"Do you have any idea what would happen if we were to join those motes?" Alys asked.

Leethan shook her head. "Before Jaizal and I left Rhozinolm, I triggered a vision in hopes of receiving more guidance." She wrinkled her nose. "For naught. I have no choice but to conclude that whatever happens next is up to us."

Silence descended on the room as they each lost themselves in thought. It was Kailee who eventually broke the silence.

"According to Mairah's notes—at least what we were able to make out from them—the Blessing was cast when a combination of three sacrificial Kai motes was used to trigger a spell. It was clear from Mairah's notes that she had no information on what that spell was, how it was created, what exactly it was designed to do."

"Well, I suppose we know the answer to that now," Alys said.

"Yes. But my point is that the information we've been given suggests the combined Kai should be used to trigger a spell."

"But *what* spell?" Alys asked with a touch of exasperation, still struggling to accept the possibility of divine intervention.

"Maybe . . ." Leethan put in hesitantly, then bit her lip. For a moment, it looked like she had thought better of what she'd been about to suggest. Then her shoulders squared, and she nodded ever so slightly. "Maybe that is for us to decide."

CHAPTER FIFTY

"That's it, then," Alys said as she examined the spell that she, Leethan, and Kailee had been working on for the last three months.

"Looks right to me," Kailee confirmed, and Leethan also agreed.

Alys closed her Mindseye, as did Leethan. They were sitting in Alys's private parlor in the residential wing of the palace. As she had for each of these sessions, Alys had dismissed all the servants and guards so that she and the others might have absolute privacy.

"I guess we can no longer put off making a final decision," Alys said, shaking her head at the golden chalice in which their spell was contained.

Kailee sighed softly, her nose wrinkled with what Alys read as impatience. "I thought we *had* made a final decision. Several times, in fact."

Alys plucked at the folds of her skirt. "Well, sort of. We didn't have the spell ready yet, so it wasn't possible to make a *final* final decision." There were butterflies flittering around in her stomach, and she did not think that the sweat moistening the nape of her neck had anything to do with the desert heat.

"I believe this is what we are destined to do," Leethan said, her face showing no hint of Alys's turmoil or Kailee's impatience.

"Even though your Mother of All refuses to give us any additional guidance?" Alys challenged.

Leethan had tried two more times to gain additional insight into the Mother of All's wishes before she'd given up. Although Alys couldn't claim to be a woman of great faith, she would have felt easier making this momentous decision if Leethan had had a vision of how their spell would affect the world.

Leethan did not rise to Alys's challenge, smiling serenely. Of the three of them, only Leethan had never questioned the wisdom of what they were planning, and Alys envied her the certainty.

"If we were going in the wrong direction," Leethan said, "then I'm certain one of my visions would have warned me of it. The Mother of All knows Her daughters well. She brought us to this moment and has always known exactly what we would do with our Kai."

Alys snorted. "She could have saved us some time by just *telling* us what to do." At least then if the casting of the spell went horribly wrong, Alys could have blamed someone else for the catastrophe. Of all the terrible decisions that had been placed on her shoulders since she had come to Women's Well, this was the most momentous and onerous.

Leethan shrugged. "It is not the Mother's way to demand obedience. She gives us guidance, rather than orders." She held up her hand to forestall Alys's reflexive protest. "And we had enough guidance to bring us to this point, or we wouldn't be here."

"Personally," Kailee interjected, "I'm growing weary of the debate. We didn't spend the last three months working on this spell—and having this argument so many times I feel we could write a script for it—only to decline to cast it when it was ready."

Although Kailee was no more religiously inclined than Alys, she had never seemed to suffer much in the way of doubt, as Alys did. Perhaps that was because of her youth, or perhaps it was a result of the new hardness that had grown inside her since she had killed Draios. She was no longer as haunted and melancholy as she had been in the days and weeks directly afterward, but she was also no longer as warm and cheerful as she had been before. Alys hoped that she would one day make a full recovery—Alys missed Kailee's mischievous smile and easy laugh.

"Do you even remember what it was like when my mother cast the Blessing?" Alys asked, her voice coming out rather more snappish than she would have liked. For all that she was grateful for the results of her mother's spell, the immediate consequences of its casting had been terrible. Alys would never forget the flood-waters that had destroyed the Harbor District, never forget the screams of those who were washed away and the tears of those who were left behind.

"I don't believe this spell will cause the same kind of . . . disruption," Leethan said. "Mother Brynna's spell was far more profound than this one. She changed the very nature of life. We three haven't the power to do anything so drastic as that."

Alys closed her eyes and searched for calm. It seemed to her an act of great hubris for the three of them to make this decision without consulting anyone else. However, unlike Alys's mother, they all expected to survive the casting of this spell, and since there were certainly people out there—mostly men, naturally—who would object to the results, they'd agreed that keeping its origin secret was for the best. There would be some people who might guess they were behind it, but for the most part, the world would remain ignorant of their role.

"I suspect much of the world will consider this very drastic indeed," Alys said, opening her eyes and feeling no calmer.

Kailee shrugged. "The *effect* will seem drastic," she corrected.

"But we aren't changing any elements like your mother did. All we're really doing is changing perceptions. Those elements are always there, even now."

Part of the reason it had taken them three months to craft this spell was that they had originally thought of it as making an actual change to the elements, which they didn't understand how to do. Even consulting Mairahsol's notes hadn't given them any great insight into how Brynna had managed it, for Mairahsol had only learned about the use of sacrificial Kai as a trigger element. The nature of the Blessing itself was still very much a mystery.

It was Kailee who'd realized the flaw in their thinking. As she said, the elements were there already anyway. All the three of them wanted was to make it so that men and women could see the same ones—an ability that already existed in both Alys and Tynthanal, although neither one of them understood how it had happened, except that it had something to do with the manipulation of bloodlines that Brynna and the abbesses before her had set into motion.

"I can guarantee you that men—at least, many men—will see this as a neutering of the elements," Alys said, "and that they will be very, very unhappy about it."

"But they will learn to live with it," Kailee argued. "Just like they've learned to live with the Blessing, at least in much of the world. If we are all agreed that our Kai should be used to further improve the lives of women, then surely this is a positive step."

Alys nodded. It would not make women as large or as strong as men. It would not change the centuries-old power structure that had kept women subjugated, although the Blessing was already chipping away at that. What it *would* do was eliminate the division between women's magic and men's.

"I hate the thought of causing more upheaval," Alys said mournfully.

"It will be worth it," Kailee said, with no hint of uncertainty in her voice. "Now let's stop talking and start doing."

Alys could not say she was as confident as Kailee and Leethan, but she also knew that, despite her doubts, she could not see herself leaving this room without triggering the spell the three of them had crafted. Leethan watched her expectantly, and with one more deep breath for courage, Alys opened her Mindseye.

Hovering in the air before her was the tricolored crystal that had appeared—according to Kailee—the moment she had reached out her hand to Delnamal. Kailee took hold of the shimmering crystal that hovered by her own shoulder, pushing the crystal toward the center of the table, where the chalice—and its spell—awaited.

Alys's hand shook as she took hold of her Kai and pushed it toward Kailee's. She could clearly see the space where her Kai would fit to form a smooth edge, and when her mote was close enough, it seemed to be drawn into the space and snap into place.

Lastly, Leethan fit her mote of Kai into the remaining space, forming a tricolored faceted round gem. Together, they guided the gem into the chalice, willing it to activate the spell they had built.

CHAPTER FIFTY-ONE

Alys couldn't say for sure how the rest of the world was adapting to the new reality of nongendered magic. From her conversations with Tynthanal and Ellinsoltah, she gathered that there were a great many unhappy men in each of their academies—men who felt their status as spell crafters had now been diminished because there were women who could see and manipulate all the same elements as they. But the immediate impact seemed considerably less dramatic than the effects of the Blessing had been. It would take time—who knew how much—before women in the rest of Seven Wells could slough off the stigma of practicing magic enough to change the fabric of daily life. But with Women's Well as an example of the benefits of cooperative magic, Alys was sure that more women would embrace their new talents.

Women's Well had absorbed the change with only a slight hint of anxiety. Some had worried that the unique magic of Women's Well would be diminished once men could see feminine elements, but that worry had quickly been laid to rest. Even with men and women both able to see the unique elements produced by their

Well, Alys's tiny principality could still produce magic seen no-where else in the world. And because the Women's Well Academy had already embraced the concept of men and women working together to craft spells, they were ready to take advantage of the new accessibility of formerly gendered elements.

Alys had been further heartened to discover that the precautions she and Kailee and Leethan had taken when crafting the spell had paid off, and women's Kai was now the only remaining gendered element. What the three of them had done had only complemented the Blessing, not replaced it.

A month after the casting, life was beginning to settle into its new routine, and Alys was . . . well, *"happy"* was perhaps too strong a word, but she could at least claim she had found a level of contentment that had seemed impossible not so very long ago. She had let down her guard so much, in fact, that when Chanlix requested a private audience, Alys suffered no inkling of alarm.

Until Chanlix was shown into her office and Alys got a look at the tension in her lady chancellor's face.

"What is it?" Alys asked in alarm, rising quickly to her feet, her throat constricting with fear. She had allowed herself to grow complacent already, to believe that she would face no more crises in the immediate future.

Chanlix patted the air soothingly and smiled, although that did not entirely erase the tension in her expression.

"Nothing's wrong, Your Royal Highness," Chanlix assured her. "I'm sorry to have alarmed you. I couldn't decide if this conversation was best suited for an official audience or a personal visit, and perhaps I made the wrong decision in the end."

Alys swallowed down the dread and tried to relax, although her pulse was still racing with anxiety. "Surely you realize I've known you long enough to see that all is not well."

Chanlix shook her head. "I assure you, there's nothing wrong. I just . . ." She cleared her throat. "I have to make a difficult decision, and as it pertains to the governance of Women's Well, I decided it was best to consult you before I let myself come to any conclusion."

"Please have a seat," Alys invited, gesturing toward the seating area near the unlit fireplace.

When they were both settled, Chanlix got right to the point. "Tynthanal has proposed. Again."

Alys smiled fondly. Tynthanal's first proposal had come immediately after his official divorce from Kailee, and though Chanlix had not turned him down, she had not said yes, either.

"I suspect he will do so on a regular basis," Alys said. "And I suspect you will eventually say yes."

Chanlix's eyes shone with sudden tears. "Even if it means leaving Women's Well?"

Alys sighed, for she knew just how terrible such a sacrifice would be for Chanlix. Aaltah had not been kind to her, and although with Tynthanal as prince regent, the kingdom would undoubtedly become a freer and more welcoming place for women—even former abigails—Chanlix could never enjoy the level of freedom there that she had found here in Women's Well.

"You love each other," she said quite simply. "Would you have any doubts about marrying him if he returned here?"

"None," Chanlix replied. "But he cannot do that until King Tahrend reaches his majority. We both wish he could, but . . ." Her voice trailed off, and she dabbed at her eyes.

Alys nodded, her heart breaking just a little for her lady chancellor. And for her brother. Chanlix had even more to lose than Kailee by marrying Tynthanal. She would go from being the first lady chancellor in the history of Seven Wells to being nothing but the wife of the prince regent, with no real power. And there was no question that her past as first an abigail and then an abbess would be held against her by the court. She would be shunned and isolated, and it was desperately unfair. Alys knew she herself could never agree to live like that, not even for love. But there was also little Chantynel to think of, who would grow up without a father if Chanlix turned Tynthanal down and remained in Women's Well.

"I hope my brother isn't pressing you too hard for an answer," Alys said, though the fact that he had issued a second proposal so soon suggested that he was, indeed, pressing. "There is no reason to rush into a decision." She shifted ever so slightly in her seat, and Chanlix suddenly grinned at her.

"Are we still talking about Tynthanal's proposal? Or have we moved on to Duke Thanmir's?"

Alys's face heated. "He has not formally proposed," she hedged. She had expected him to tender a proposal the moment he found she was out of mourning, but apparently he had meant it when he'd promised not to put forth an official proposal until she told him she was ready.

Chanlix snorted. "If I'm not mistaken, he and his daughter are due to arrive for a 'visit' later today. How many visits will that be in total?"

In theory, the teasing was better than the melancholy, but Alys didn't allow it to distract her for long. "To answer your previous question, we are still talking about Tynthanal."

To Alys's immense relief, Chanlix allowed herself to be diverted.

"I would not call it *pressure* so much as *persuasion*." She shook her head, her eyes going distant with some remembered conversation. "I don't know how he's done it, but he has somehow persuaded his grand magus—and by extension the royal council—to offer me a position at the Academy of Aaltah as an instructor. To teach those men who are interested—no doubt a handful at most—about what used to be women's magic."

Alys suffered a small pang in her chest, for she realized now that even if Chanlix was not yet ready to voice her acceptance of the proposal, deep down inside she had already been persuaded. Alys had to admire her brother's ingenuity, even as she dreaded losing the company of her closest friend. He had known that

Chanlix could not accept a life of idleness, and he had engineered a way for her to have a purpose in Aaltah in addition to being his wife and Chantynel's mother.

"I suspect that offering you a position at the Academy was a prerequisite for being named grand magus," Alys said ruefully. Draimel Rah-Draimir, the man who had served as grand magus under Alys's father and Delnamal, had perished in the battle defending Aalwell's walls, leaving the position open. Before the victory, Alys doubted Tynthanal would have been able to appoint the grand magus of his choosing without facing considerable resistance from his grudging council. But even though he had been forced to lead from a distance, the defeat of Delnamal and Draios—and the comparatively small loss of life that had resulted from the swiftly ended war—had gone a long way toward winning over those who had once branded him a traitor.

Chanlix smiled fondly. "Yes, I'm sure it was. Just as I suspect he has already planted the idea in the grand magus's mind that someday the Academy might want to consider admitting women as spell crafters."

Yes, Tynthanal had known exactly how to lure Chanlix out of the comfort and security of Women's Well.

"It won't be easy," Alys said, for she imagined there were a great many men in Aaltah who were appalled by the new reality and who would put a lot of time and energy into trying to reestablish their supposed magical superiority.

"Nothing worth doing is," Chanlix replied.

Alys's throat closed as she realized Chanlix had not countered her assumption that the decision was already made. "Words cannot convey how much I will miss you," she said, her voice betraying a faint quaver.

"I haven't said yes yet," Chanlix reassured her, but the shadow in her eyes said it was only a matter of time.

"But you will," Alys said with certainty.

Chanlix seemed about to protest, then stopped herself with a sigh. "Most likely I will," she admitted. "With your permission, of course."

"You know you will have it. As sorry as I will be to lose you, I want you and Tynthanal to be happy, which I don't think you can ever fully manage if you remain apart. You are both too loyal to give your hearts to others, and you should not go through the rest of your lives alone."

Chanlix met her eyes. "And I would say the same to you."

Alys broke eye contact. "That's not the same. I am not in love with Duke Thanmir, nor is he in love with me."

"Maybe not yet," Chanlix conceded. "But to an outside observer such as myself, there seems to be a certain . . . chemistry between the two of you. A certain spark when you are together. Neither one of you is yet prepared to feed that flame, but if you ever do . . ."

Alys rolled her eyes. "You're being a hopeless romantic. You know exactly what Duke Thanmir sees in me." Although she had felt mildly guilty for breaking the confidence, Alys had shared the story of Thanmir's daughters with Chanlix. "And for my part, I am considering our potential marriage as a business arrangement, not a romance."

"I'm not the one who's hopeless," Chanlix replied tartly, but there was a twinkle in her eye that took the sting out of her words. "Explain away the attraction all you like, but I know what I've seen." She reached out and put her hand over Alys's, peering at her earnestly.

"I cannot tell you how happy I am that you've put away your mourning attire," she said. "I hope someday soon you will find the strength and courage to put away the rest of your mourning, as well."

Alys pulled back, affronted, but before she could voice her protest, Chanlix continued.

"You deserve to be happy once more," she said. "And you're *allowed* to be happy, despite your losses."

Alys shook her head, her eyes suddenly swimming. "You don't understand."

"Of course I do. And I am not claiming you can be happy all the time. Nor am I claiming the grief will go away. But we are all better off leaving the past in the past and getting on with our lives. I have every intention of being happy with Tynthanal, and if I can find happiness after the life I've led, then so can you."

Those words pierced Alys's defensive shell and sank deep into her soul. Chanlix had lived most of her life imprisoned in Aaltah's Abbey, forced into prostitution and constant degradation and deprivation. Then she had been raped by Delnamal's men and sent on what was meant to be something of a death march out into the Wasteland. Surely in those long and terrible years, she had believed she would never find happiness again. Surely she had believed herself broken beyond repair. And yet here she was, whole and ready to reach out and seize the life she wanted.

"I don't know that I have your strength," Alys said, tears trickling down her cheeks even as she fought against them.

"*I* know," Chanlix said firmly.

Alys sniffled discreetly and dabbed at her eyes, moved by her friend's confidence.

Could she find happiness with Duke Thanmir?

It was hard even to entertain the possibility without suffering twin pangs of guilt. When Sylnin had died, she'd been certain she would never love again. And when Jinnell had died, it had seemed a betrayal of her dear daughter's memory to set the grief aside for even a moment.

"You are the strongest person I've ever met," Chanlix said, reading her doubts.

Alys scoffed.

"You *are*!" Chanlix insisted. "Don't think that I don't know that you and Kailee and Leethan are responsible for the new magical equality."

Alys grimaced, wishing she could be open and honest with her best friend. But Kailee and Leethan had both insisted that the fewer people who knew the truth, the safer the three of them would be, and the fact that none but the three of them had been able to see the motes of sacrificial Kai had made the secret far easier to keep.

"I haven't the first idea *how* you did it," Chanlix said, "and I doubt I would have guessed if you hadn't told me the whole of Leethan's dream long ago. But I have no doubt that I am right, even if you won't confirm it."

"Even if it were true," Alys argued, "Leethan and Kailee deserve just as much of the credit as I do."

"Leethan and Kailee did not create a new principality where women could live as equal citizens, and they did not make that principality thrive against all odds and at great personal sacrifice. *You* did that. Then you found it in your heart to let go of your hatred for Delnamal when you needed to, and I have no doubt that you will also find it in your heart to let go of the grief."

"I will never truly let go of it. Not completely."

Chanlix made a sound of impatience. "No, of course not. No one does. But you can let go of its constant burden."

Alys took a slow, deep breath. Letting go of the burden sounded like a splendid idea. Even with the threat of war now all but extinguished, being a sovereign princess would always entail more than its fair share of burdens. Especially as Women's Well continued to grow, which she had no doubt it would. Over time, the other kingdoms and principalities of Seven Wells would become more kind and hospitable to women, but until then there would be plenty of women who fled oppression and had nowhere else to go.

The thought of bearing that burden alone was . . . daunting. And even if she chose to marry Thanmir, he was no replacement for Chanlix. Not that Alys was selfish enough to ask Chanlix to stay just to make her feel less lonely.

"Have I mentioned how much I'm going to miss you?" Alys

asked, nearly choking on the tears she was once again holding back.

Chanlix rose from her chair and spread her arms in an unmistakable invitation to a hug. Wordlessly, Alys accepted.

"Remember that it won't be goodbye forever," Chanlix said, although her own voice sounded a little rough. "I will visit regularly, even if Tynthanal cannot get away as often as he would like. And we will have talkers."

Alys nodded mutely even as her heart gently broke.

"You must promise to take care of Kailee," Chanlix continued. "She deserves happiness, too."

"Of course," Alys agreed. "She is young, and she is healing."

Chanlix met her eyes. "We both know that she grew to love Tynthanal, even if she would never admit it. Especially not to me."

"But she chose to leave him anyway," Alys said. "That is a step in the right direction." She smiled faintly as she imagined setting herself the problem of mending Kailee's broken heart. Of course it would not be easy, but it seemed pleasantly achievable after everything else they'd all been through. "When she is ready, I will search high and low for any eligible bachelors I think are worthy of her and invite them to Women's Well for a visit."

"Yes," Chanlix said, frowning thoughtfully. "I think that will be good for both of you."

"Good, but hard," Alys agreed, for she knew the effort was bound to remind her of the days when she'd frantically searched for a husband for Jinnell.

"I have every confidence that the effort will be worth it."

Alys smiled through the prickle of tears. "I'm sure you're right."

EPILOGUE

When Elwynne was directed to a cozy parlor rather than an audience chamber or even Princess Alysoon's office, she instantly wondered whether the sovereign princess had made an unexpected assumption about the purpose of her visit. Crown Prince Corlin was twenty-five now and sure to be looking for a bride. At fifteen, Elwynne was as yet too young to be on the marriage market, but that would not be true much longer. Ostensibly, Elwynne was visiting Women's Well to spend time with Lady Leethan, who was ailing, but it wouldn't be completely unexpected if Princess Alysoon thought Ellinsoltah was in the early stages of planning a marriage for her foster daughter.

Elwynne lowered her head and curtsied, hoping she wasn't blushing at her own line of thought.

"Please do come in and make yourself comfortable," Princess Alysoon invited. She and Prince Corlin sat on the opposite ends of a sofa, and she indicated with a sweep of her hand that Elwynne should sit across from them.

"Thank you, Your Royal Highness," Elwynne said as she took her seat. She couldn't help a quick, surreptitious glance at Prince Corlin. He cut a rather dashing figure in the military-style shirt and trousers he wore despite the fact that he'd officially left the Citadel to concentrate on his education in politics and diplomacy years ago. And he had a nice-looking face, to boot.

Her blush deepened when he raised one eyebrow ever so slightly, showing he was aware of her scrutiny.

"How fares your foster mother? And your sisters?" Alysoon inquired politely.

"Everyone is well, thank you." She smiled. "It isn't public knowledge yet, but the queen gave me permission to share the happy news that she is expecting again."

Alysoon's face lit up. "Happy news indeed!" Her eyes twinkled. "You will never be lonely."

Elwynne held her smile, although she suspected the path she had chosen for herself would be very lonely indeed. "In a way, that's what I wanted to speak with you about."

"Oh?"

"I have another, more private confidence I'm here to share with you," Elwynne said. "One that I am trusting will not leave this room."

Alysoon shared a look with her son at that, and it was Corlin who responded.

"As I'm sure you are aware," he said, "we are unable to promise to keep a confidence if it might somehow be detrimental to our principality."

"I am aware," Elwynne responded with a bow of her head. "But until I am ready to share this confidence with the world, I can promise you that it will have no effect whatsoever on Women's Well."

Another shared look between mother and son.

"Go on," Alysoon prompted.

And so Elwynne admitted—for the first time to anyone—that her foster parents had lied when they'd declared her to be Zarsha's daughter. "Sovereign Prince Waldmir was my true father," she said. "And as such, I plan to claim my rightful place on the throne of Nandel one day."

Elwynne braced herself for any number of unpleasant reactions. Ellinsoltah had proclaimed with great confidence that Alysoon would not laugh at her. But then, Ellinsoltah had not guessed her ward would be forced to share the admission with Prince Corlin, as well. Elwynne had requested a private audience with the sovereign princess, but she could hardly protest the presence of the crown prince. Elwynne didn't know a whole lot about him, but she hoped that as the Crown Prince of Women's Well, he had an enlightened view of the role of women in society.

Alysoon frowned ever so slightly in thought, and Corlin steepled his hands in front of his mouth as he leaned back into the corner of the sofa. Elwynne was gratified to see that neither was laughing.

"How much of Nandel do you remember from your childhood?" Alysoon finally asked.

"Very little," Elwynne was forced to admit. "But rest assured: I know that it will be an uphill battle."

The throne of Nandel had changed hands three times in the past ten years, between two of Waldmir's surviving nephews and one grandnephew. The transitions had all occurred relatively peacefully, but no one who had sat on the throne felt secure in his position, and their principality was a shadow of its former self.

"It is my understanding," said Corlin, "that women are still legally possessions of their fathers or husbands there. That would seem to make your road . . . extremely challenging."

He wasn't wrong. But then he didn't know about Lady Leethan's long-ago vision, which had foretold the day when Elwynne would be Sovereign Princess of Nandel. On Elwynne's thirteenth birthday, Zarsha and Ellinsoltah had sat her down to tell her about the vision Lady Leethan had described to them. Ever since that day, she'd been mulling over—and discussing with her foster parents—how she might make that vision come true. And she had never for a moment doubted that she *wanted* it to come true.

Elwynne loved Rhozinolm. It was, to all intents and purposes, the only home she'd ever known. She remembered little of Nandel except feeling forgotten and lesser and unimportant, so her desire to take that throne had nothing to do with nostalgia for her homeland. Her desire rose from the inspiration of all the extraordinary women whom she'd crossed paths with over her life.

Her foster mother was the Queen of Rhozinolm—the first ever queen to sit on the throne in her own right and not cede it to her husband—and her eldest foster sister was the crown princess. She had spent the last two years quietly studying magic with Kailee Rah-Kailindar, who had formerly been the wife of the Prince Regent of Aaltah. Kailee—who had once seemed destined to a life locked up in the Abbey—had fallen in love with and married a man of Rhozinolm and had been one of the first female spell crafters officially granted a position at the Academy there.

Elwynne was in this room speaking with the first sovereign princess Seven Wells had ever known, a woman who had created her principality from nothing. She'd been rescued from the Abbey of Nandel by two old women whom society had deemed all but worthless. And then there was her half-sister, Shelvon, whom she had yet to meet. Shelvon, who had paved the way for women to join the Citadel of Women's Well, and who was now the first ever female lieutenant commander.

All these women had accomplished the impossible, giving Elwynne reason to believe her own goal was not impossible at all. She smiled at Corlin and Alysoon.

"I believe I am up to the challenge," she said. "Or at least will be one day. There is a real chance that the law granting men ownership of the women in their lives will be struck down in the next year or two. Even in Nandel, it's becoming harder and harder to maintain the fiction that women are somehow inferior beings."

It was a crucial first step—one that had been a long time in coming. But Elwynne knew that Zarsha and Ellinsoltah had been pressing for it, both publicly and in more subversive ways.

"I've been studying magic with Lady Kailee," she said, and saw Alysoon's face brighten at the sound of her former sister-in-law's name. "Unfortunately, I've found I have no great talent for it. However, I believe that I *might* have a talent that the people of Nandel will find more appealing, and I was hoping that perhaps I could hone that talent here."

"Oh?" Alysoon inquired. "What talent is that?"

"Papa . . . *Uncle Zarsha* . . . badgered a former officer of the Rhozinolm Citadel into giving me sword lessons, and I've been told I am promising. But although it is now legal for women to join the Citadel of Rhozinolm, it is not *accepted.* I've spoken to the handful of female cadets who have toughed it out to remain, and their stories are not encouraging. So—with the permission of the queen—I have come to seek permission to train at the Citadel of Women's Well."

Alysoon nodded thoughtfully. "We do have the largest female fighting force in all of Seven Wells," she acknowledged. "I presume you know my stepdaughter, Shalna, is a captain."

"I do. Just as I know my half-sister is a lieutenant commander."

"And does Lady Shelvon *know* that she is your half-sister?"

"Not as of now," Elwynne said. "We have yet to meet. But unless you think it unwise, I think I will tell her."

"I see no reason why you shouldn't," Alysoon said. "I think she will be delighted to know you."

"If you don't mind my asking," Corlin interjected, "why is it a secret that you are Waldmir's daughter? Surely the need for secrecy died when the war ended."

Elwynne shook her head. "Until the legal ownership of women is finally officially outlawed, it is best to maintain the fiction that I am Zarsha's child. *Especially* when I have not yet come of age." She smiled and imagined there was a spark of mischief in her eyes. "If all of Zarsha's various machinations work out the way he plans, then Nandel will not only have granted women their freedom, but also legalized inheritance through the female line by the time I'm twenty—*before* anyone in Nandel has any idea that Waldmir has a daughter who would actually dare to make a claim on the throne."

Alysoon startled her by laughing. "As I suspect you know, my relationship with Prince Waldmir was . . . thorny. I spoke to him very little, but I think . . ." The crinkles at the corners of her eyes deepened. "Well, perhaps it is presumptuous of me to say so, but I think he would have been proud of you. He was a man who respected strength, and I can clearly see that you have a good deal of it."

The words caused a pleasant flutter in Elwynne's chest. She had none but the dimmest memories of her real father, and it was already clear that history would not be kind to him. From everything she had learned about him, the calumny was well earned. And yet even so, it moved her just a little to think that he might have been proud.

"So, do you think it's possible, then? That I might one day be the Sovereign Princess of Nandel?" Even knowing about Leethan's vision, Elwynne sometimes suffered from doubt when she thought about how very far Nandel still had to go before a woman there could be treated as anything resembling an equal, much less a sovereign.

Princess Alysoon's smile was full of warmth and confidence. "Let's just say I wouldn't bet against you."

ACKNOWLEDGMENTS

This series has been the longest, hardest, and most satisfying I have ever written. I had a lot of help along the way—people who helped make the books better and who propped me up when my confidence flagged and the task seemed too daunting. First and foremost is my editor, Anne Groell. I cannot put into words how much I have learned from working with you or how enjoyable you made the always fraught experience of facing revisions. Thanks also to my agent, Miriam Kriss, who's been with me and cheered me ever since my first published novel. Then there's my husband, Dan, who is my first reader and my staunchest supporter. I could not do this without you. The team at Del Rey has taken great care of this series—and given it fantastic cover art—and I'm very grateful for everything they've done. Last but not least are Melissa Marr, Kelley Armstrong, and the rest of the retreat crew. Brainstorming with you—and soaking up the energy we all generated through our retreats—was an integral part of the writing of each book in this series, and I cannot thank you enough.